THE FABULOUS CONCUBINE

Bought this book on return
flight from Hong Kong to Seattle,
November 29, 1989. — 12:30pm

Marlin Dowgsk

The Fabulous Concubine

Chang Hsin-hai

With an Introduction by
H. J. Lethbridge

HONG KONG OXFORD
OXFORD UNIVERSITY PRESS

Oxford University Press

Oxford New York Toronto
Petaling Jaya Singapore Hong Kong Tokyo
Delhi Bombay Calcutta Madras Karachi
Nairobi Dar es Salaam Cape Town
Melbourne Auckland

and associated companies in
Beirut Berlin Ibadan Nicosia

© 1956 by Chang Hsin-hai
renewed © 1984 by Chang Hsin-hai
Introduction © Oxford University Press 1986

First published by Simon and Schuster, Inc. 1956
This edition reprinted with permission and with
the addition of an Introduction
in Oxford Paperbacks 1986

ISBN 0 19 583931 5

Printed in Hong Kong by Ko's Arts Printing Co. Ltd.
Published by Oxford University Press, Warwick House, Hong Kong

INTRODUCTION

'WHEN China awakes, the world will tremble.' Napoleon's prophecy seemed about to be fulfilled in 1900 when the Boxers were wildly attacking the Peking Legations and on the brink of slaughtering the foreigners beleaguered there. In Europe, the phrase *fin de siècle* evokes a movement of decadent poets and aesthetes; in China, the turn of the century was a time of serious, yet quarrelsome, debate about the future of the Middle Kingdom, on which, worried Chinese thought, sunset was darkly falling.

These historical events form the background to *The Fabulous Concubine,* a novel covering the period from the defeat of China by Japan in 1895 to the Russo-Japanese War of 1904, a decade of turmoil, tumult, and uneasy change. Written by a former Chinese diplomatist and scholar, the novel recounts the story of Golden Orchid, the fabulous concubine of the title, set against the crises of early modern China. It is a historical novel with a surprising degree of verisimilitude, an imaginative reconstruction of society and social life at China's turning point.

Historical novels are sometimes irritating to read: the heroic becomes mock-heroic, the dialogue stagy, and the characters stereotypes. Chang Hsin-hai avoids these common pitfalls: Golden Orchid is believable. She is a flesh-and-blood heroine, a woman of obvious intelligence and great charm, a type of woman well known in the literary West, where Dumas' Marguerite Gautier, Zola's Nana, and Proust's Odette de Crécy all adorn literature.

Golden Orchid has then the attributes of a splendid courtesan, but placed of course against a Chinese screen. And the background to her adventures is skilfully delineated in a series of historical tableaux — daily life in Soochow (Suzhou), where China's most beautiful women are reputed to come from, work at the Chinese legation in Berlin, and critical times in Peking (Beijing), where aspiring degree-holders once dreamed of fame and fortune, officials jostled to outdo and outflank their colleagues, and the eunuchs of the Imperial Palace wielded sinister power.

In Europe, a courtesan or mistress had no legal status, no legal rights; but a concubine in China had. Concubinage was an age-old institution. It was a practice that had evolved in a patriarchal society to provide for male offspring. If a man's wife was barren or persisted in bearing only female children, he could — both by custom and by law — take a concubine, and hope that her fecundity would prolong his patrilineal line. This was important in a social system based on ancestor worship. Ideally, concubinage was meant to achieve children. But the motives for taking a concubine — or concubines — were often mixed: the inspiration too often derived simply from infatuation or lust, or the need for pleasing female companionship. The practice, though abused, did serve as a safety-valve in a society where marriages were arranged; for whereas the first wife was chosen by family or kin, the individual chose his own concubine.

Shen Wen-ching, the scholar-official in the novel, was drawn to Golden Orchid by reawakened sexual desire: he fell under the spell of her willowy form and bright eyes behind trellises of fluttering lashes. He was an old man much in love; happily, his love was returned by his affectionate concubine.

There were few respectable careers open to Chinese women in the nineteenth century — only marriage, menial work, and a scatter of low-status or marginal occupations — for the tide of emancipation had hardly reached the country. However, a few intuited that they had a 'fortune between their legs', as Balzac cynically and crudely declared of women in general, and took advantage of this fact. Golden Orchid did, though to a mild degree: she was not a harlot by instinct. But she was raised from childhood to please men, first as a sing-song girl, and then was trained by Lily, the pock-marked go-between, to become a concubine because of her looks.

It was Lily who supervised the binding of her feet. Foot-binding was also an ancient practice but its subsequent disfigurements disgusted Europeans, though surely it differed little from the tight-lacing once common with European women. The Chinese found small feet enticing and highly erotic. They broke into a sweat at the sight of tiny feet in tiny embroidered silk slippers. In Western countries, the wasp waist had the same oddly stimulating effect on males.

One consequence of foot-binding was that it kept a woman almost housebound, so that in public she had to be carried on her amah's back or conveyed by chair, rickshaw, or wheelbarrow. When Golden Orchid arrived in Berlin and wished to explore the grandiose monuments of that parvenu capital city, she found it necessary to loosen the binding-cloths that constricted her feet, to allow her to walk more freely. Her walk, with its little tripping steps, enchanted Berliners. She was young, beautiful, and exotic; and, as anthropologists say, she had 'stranger value'. She became the darling of the staid diplomatic corps, the frock-coated officials of that age.

Golden Orchid was not promiscuous by nature. She had only one night of love with Yung-kai, the son of a Manchu minister, from which she conceived. Yung-kai's subsequent epic ride from Berlin to Peking, on a white charger presented to the Empress Dowager by the Kaiser, is reminiscent of Tschiffely's famous ride in the 1920s from Buenos Aires to Washington, DC, a 10,000-mile odyssey on horseback.

Golden Orchid's lover tried to conceal the fact that he had Manchu blood, though his mother was Chinese, because of the rising tide of anti-Manchu feeling, which had steadily increased as China's decline became visible year by year. Xenophobes, nationalists, intellectuals, students, even the common people, all came to blame the Manchus for China's declension. The Manchus were obvious scapegoats. They were the ruling class at court and in government; they looked different and were alien.

The Ch'ing (Qing) was the last of the imperial dynasties. It was established in 1644 when the Manchus took Peking and overthrew the Ming and ended in 1912 when China became a republic. The Manchus totalled roughly two per cent of the population of China, yet they ruled China for nearly three centuries. They succeeded in overlording the country for so long because they controlled the military forces of the empire and kept a tight grip on the Chinese administration. Their ultimate political power was incarnate in, and exercised by, the Son of Heaven, a Manchu.

After the Manchus seized Peking, they took some years to consolidate their hold and penetrate the South. They established garrisons in various provincial centres, composed of men loyal to the new regime and selected from among the eight banners, the divisions of the Manchu army, each of which sported a flag of a different colour. In a number of key towns, such as Canton (Guangzhou), Manchus and their families occupied special quarters. The men were not pigtailed and their women did not bind their feet. They also differed from Chinese in costume and head-dress and were more adept at horsemanship and archery. Once a nomadic and warrior people, over time they became sinicized and lost their *élan*, isolated as they were among a large and fertile Chinese population. Their martial qualities, like those of the Crusaders and Janizaries before them, weakened with long periods of peace. They quickly caved in — many were massacred — when the revolution came in 1911, to sweep them into history's lumber-room. As a distinct entity, the Manchus are as extinct a race as Etruscans or Carthaginians. They, as it were, are the Red Indians of China's past.

The last Chinese emperor was P'u-i (1906-67), as he is commonly called, the Empress Dowager's grand-nephew — a sad figure indeed — who lost all power after the 1911 Revolution, but was allowed to keep his imperial title, his trappings, and his eunuchs, and continued to reside in the Forbidden City like a shadow until 1924. In 1934, the Japanese made him their puppet emperor of Manchukuo. When the Communists came to power in 1949, they imprisoned him. Released in 1959, he worked contentedly as a gardener in Peking and, ironically, became a member of the National People's Congress (China's Parliament) — an extraordinary destiny for the last of the Manchu Ch'ing dynasty. He had ascended the Dragon Throne as a child, in 1908, and remained half a child all his life.

Why China declined in the nineteenth century has bothered historians and caused debate. Chinese historiographers have explained the flow of history in cyclical terms: the rise, fruition, and decay of dynasties, once they had lost the Mandate of Heaven, the moral right to rule, as evidenced by misrule and its attendant misery. This explanation was inspired by the idea of nature, by the notion of the four seasons: winter always comes (decay) but spring is not far behind (renewal). Western and modern Chinese historians stress more sophisticated factors, such as demography and economics. By imposing peace, unifying the country, and stimulating agriculture and trade, the new dynasty accelerated population increase. In time the pressure on land resources reached its limits. The Malthusian equation was then complete. Conditions again deteriorated, poverty grew, misery spread, banditry surged, and so on.

There is no need to dwell further on these matters, but they do help in understanding the author's observations and the novel's implications. Chang Hsin-hai, for example, refers often to the curse of opium addiction — the pleasures of the seductive poppy — and blames its prevalence on foreign merchants, mostly British, active in the noxious trade. Europeans did exploit China and they took advantage of its military nullity, as the country suffered defeat after defeat from British, French, and Japanese armed forces. But the insatiable demand for opium may be viewed in a different light, as revealing a fundamental malaise in the social fabric. The rise in the consumption of the drug is now recognized as a symptom rather than a cause of China's decay, just as alcoholism in the Soviet Union and heroin addiction in Western countries tell us something about the unfulfilled needs — the underlying stress and strains — of complex societies wedded to technology and modernization.

China was celebrated for its examination system, the selection of officials from among successful candidates, and its centralized administration. Bureaucracy evolved earlier in China than elsewhere, but it was not of the rational-legal kind found in modern Europe. China's bureaucratic structures were always particularistic and highly personal; an official needed to cultivate his superiors and curry favour with them, and to build up a network of personal relationships. Moral rectitude and hard work did sometimes count but were not necessarily rewarded, as poor Shen Wen-ching discovered, caught as he was in a web of intrigue and deceit. In the end, all he wanted to do was to clear his ancestral name and return to Soochow with his beloved concubine.

Gogol ended one of his stories with the words: 'It's a depressing world, gentlemen.' This, one feels, is a sentiment that Shen would have echoed as he lay dying on his journey by boat back to Soochow. Bureaucratic corruption was yet another symptom of decline, an expression of spreading rot. Even senior ministers and court officials were often involved in the grosser forms of bribery and corruption and in peculation, nepotism, and even, at times, in treachery. Yüan Shih-k'ai (1859–1916), a notorious double-dealer who betrayed all he purported to serve, nearly succeeded in having himself made emperor in 1915. Thwarted in his ambition, he died the following year, unlamented by patriotic Chinese. There were many like Yüan at the turn of the century and they are to be found in *The Fabulous Concubine*, notably Hu-mou, the cruel and nasty lecher with the goldfish eyes.

The writing of history — it is a commonplace — owes as much to the imagination, to the creative impulse, as to diligent research. Historians must reconstruct the past in a plausible narrative; but all history is slanted of course, filtered as it is through the mind. The writer of historical fiction proceeds in the same way, though the element of imagination is far larger. Scott's *Waverley* (1814), which established the historical novel as a distinct genre, may be criticized for its abundant romanticism and inaccuracies, but it marvellously succeeds in suggesting to the reader what life was like, what people felt in high and low places, in 1745. In *The Fabulous Concubine*, Chang Hsin-hai combines fact and fiction so nicely that the characters do not appear as mere social types — scholar-official, concubine, lover, villain, missionary wife — but as real people, whose lives become intertwined. In this respect, he may be compared with Alfred Duggan (1903-64) who wrote fine historical novels but was never overwhelmed by history. Like Duggan, Chang Hsin-hai is first and foremost a good story-teller.

Chang Hsin-hai, so far as I can discover, wrote no other novel. In *The Fabulous Concubine*, he drew upon his wide knowledge of official and diplomatic life in Europe and, one assumes, life at the 'court' of Generalissimo Chiang Kai-shek, whose wife — Madame Soong Mei-ling — could be as autocratic as the old Empress Dowager. Nationalist circles were riddled with cliques, intrigues, favouritism, and corruption. Chang wrote his novel with one eye on the China he knew.

H.J. LETHBRIDGE

SELECTED BIBLIOGRAPHY

Ball, J. Dyer, *Things Chinese* (Hong Kong, Oxford University Press, 1982).

Balzac, Honoré de, *Splendeurs et Misères des Courtisanes* (Paris, Houssiaux, 1855).

Fairbank, John K., Reischauer, Edwin O., and Craig, Albert M., *East Asia: The Modern Transformation* (London, George Allen & Unwin, 1965).

Fleming, Peter, *The Siege at Peking* (London, Rupert Hart-Davis, 1959; and reprinted by Oxford University Press, Hong Kong, 1983).

Hummel, A.W., ed., *Eminent Chinese of the Ch'ing Period 1644–1912* (Washington, DC, Government Printing Office, 1943-4).

Johnston, Reginald F., *Twilight in the Forbidden City* (London, Victor Gollancz, 1934; and reprinted by Oxford University Press, Hong Kong, 1985).

Matignon, Dr J.-J., *Superstition, Crime et Misère en Chine* (Paris, Masson, 1902).

Tschiffely, Aimé, *Southern Cross to Pole Star: Tschiffely's Ride* (London, William Heinemann, 1934).

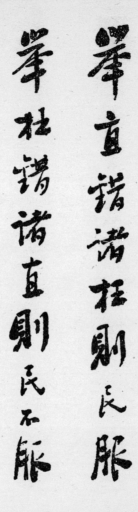

舉直錯諸枉則民服
舉枉錯諸直則民不服

Advance the upright and set aside the crooked, then the people will be with you. Advance the crooked and set aside the upright, then the people will not be with you. CONFUCIUS

The
Fabulous Concubine

a novel by

Chang Hsin-hai

Jonathan Cape

Thirty Bedford Square, London

To

SIANG-MEI

on completing our third ten

PREFACE

THIS is a story about China at the turn of the century, a time of great and stirring events out of which was born the China of today. It deals with people on various levels of Chinese and European society during the period of the Boxer Rebellion, that midsummer madness which began in June 1900 when the Empress Dowager declared war on the foreign powers. The story is set not only in China — principally in the imperial city of Peking, Soochow and the surrounding provinces — but also in Europe, and there principally in Berlin.

Although it is the ordinary people of China — her peasants and farmers and small tradesmen — who promise to be their country's saving force, this is primarily a novel about the governing classes. Its main figures are rulers and diplomats, high bureaucrats, military leaders and scholars, that class whose modes of thought and action have remained a relatively closed book to a Western public accustomed to thinking of China only in terms of its peasantry. In a sense, this is a story about the Chinese official mind. With the exception of a few historical personages, among them the Empress Dowager and some of her ministers, the characters in this novel are fictional.

The heroine of this story and the 'fabulous concubine' of its title is Golden Orchid. A simple girl from the south, she rose, by virtue of her beauty and intelligence, from the position of sing-song girl to that of the concubine of Shen Wen-ching, a leading scholar and Chinese Ambassador to Germany and Russia. These are the two central figures, and a few words about Golden Orchid's profession and background may be of help to the reader.

Sing-song girl was a term coined by foreigners resident in China who did not know how otherwise to describe her. The sing-song girl's main accomplishment was singing, but she also entertained during feasts and banquets where the guests were almost exclusively men. She was not a prostitute in the usual sense of the word. The profession of the sing-song girl was created almost 2,000 years ago by an Emperor of the Han Dynasty; in extending his empire to

Central Asia he saw the need of providing female entertainment and amusement for his war-weary soldiers.

Golden Orchid became the concubine of Wen-ching, and this also requires explanation. Until recently it had been the practice for men in China to take a young woman (and sometimes more than one, depending on the size of the man's purse) as a kind of secondary wife. This was socially sanctioned, and the young woman often became a fully accepted member of the family. The concubine's prestige increased when she gave birth to male heirs if the first legal wife had none. It was not necessary for a man to obtain his wife's consent to his taking a concubine, although in most cases it was asked for and given. The first wife merely accepted the old if hackneyed observation that man is by nature polygamous. As was the case with Golden Orchid, the concubine was often picked from among the sing-song girls. In China, as in any Western country, a pretty girl with a good head can go a long way.

Concubines came into existence in China long before the sing-song girl. Archaeologists tell us that some twenty thousand years ago a proto-Chinese gentleman living in a cave near Peking had a wife who was over forty and a concubine who was about twenty years old. The year 1911 is the terminal date for concubinage in China, for in that year the practice was legally abolished by the republic.

A brief summary of the historical background of this novel may also be helpful. The story of Golden Orchid covers the nine years between the defeat of China by Japan in 1895 and the Russo-Japanese War of 1904. The Taiping Rebellion (1852–1864) had ravaged the rich valleys and fairest provinces of central China, and by the time of the defeat by Japan it was clear that, in order to survive, China would have to undertake drastic reforms. The clamour for radical changes became insistent. There were some who agitated for reform along constitutional lines which would preserve the Manchu monarchy. Others were not satisfied with anything less than a revolution which would establish a republican form of government. This was what actually took place, but not until 1911.

The Emperor Kuang Hsu (1871–1908) was merely a figurehead, for China had long been in the hands of his aunt, the Empress Dowager Tsu Hsi (1835–1908), a powerful, crafty and ruthless woman. In 1898, after the failure of a short-lived reform movement, she became absolute monarch and imprisoned her nephew on an island within Peking's Forbidden City. Commonly known as the Old Buddha, the Empress Dowager did everything she could, in her own way, to regain the prestige of China. Her hatred for the foreigners, whom she believed responsible for all China's woes, culminated in the Boxer Rebellion. From June 17, 1900, when she declared war on the foreign powers, to August 14, the entire foreign population of Peking was in danger of their lives. Relief came when the soldiers of eight foreign powers occupied the city, an occupation which lasted until September 1, 1901, when a treaty was signed.

A few more explanations, and I am done.

The dollar, unless otherwise specified, is the Chinese dollar, then worth about thirty-five cents in American money. The *tael* was equivalent to one and one-third Chinese dollars and was worth about fifty cents.

The story often mentions 'the finger game'. It is played to induce guests at a feast to drink, and this, curiously, is often necessary in China. Two persons throw out a certain number of fingers and each announces his guess with a ceremonial outcry. In most cases neither guesses the right number. If both guess the right number they tie, and they begin the game all over again until one of the contestants guesses correctly. He is the winner, but it is not he who drinks; it is the loser. The point is not to see how much one can drink but to see how often one can win and therefore remain sober. It is not uncommon, however, for the loser to remain steady on his feet in spite of the amount he consumes. 'The finger game' is the equivalent of 'the match game' played by American newspapermen in bars, although the goals and rewards are quite opposite.

In the matter of pronunciation of Chinese words, it is important to remember that there is no way of giving the exact sound of the word through the Roman alphabet. The Chinese language is not constructed on any alphabet but is made up of words or characters each of which has a single sound. The spelling used here only attempts to reproduce that sound as nearly as possible, and the words should be pronounced just as they are spelled.

In Chinese personal names, the family name is always followed by the given name. In the case of the principal male character, Shen Wen-ching, for example, Shen is the family name, while Wen-ching is the given name. While there are millions of Changs, Lees and

Wangs in China (there are theoretically only one hundred original family names for all of China, or an average of one family name for each six million people), given names are rarely duplicated. There is thus as little difficulty in identifying people in China as there is in America.

CHANG HSIN-HAI

CONTENTS

Book One

THE FLOWER-BOAT

THE weather was somewhat cooler than usual this year. According to the lunar calendar, the Festival of the Big Heat had passed, and that meant that the worst of summer would soon be over. The countryside was luxuriant, and Ping-mo noticed that the grass was tall and luscious and the trees, thick with leaves, cast welcome shadows over the narrow paths. It was such a relief, after more than a full day's journey up the river, to be in the big sprawling city of Nanking, then the seat of the Imperial Viceroy.

Ping-mo could not wait to take a stroll among those familiar scenes which had always given him a sense of expansiveness and joy. He turned in the direction of the city's majestic wall, overlooking a beautiful lake which was much overgrown with reeds for lack of care. In the distance Ping-mo was delighted to see again large patches of the divine lotus, with their big, round leaves in all their lovely shades of green. Their pink and white flowers, some in bud and others already full-grown, rising high over the surface of the water on their long stalks, seemed to dance in the gentle summer breeze.

I wish I could go down, he thought, and float in a small boat to lose myself in the fragrance of those heavenly blossoms. How I love to watch the little pearls of water chasing one another on those leaves!

But there were no boats to be had; the lake had been deserted for many years, since the city was devastated by the Taiping Rebellion. Ping-mo did not wish to think of those horrible days of bloodshed. The scene before his eyes was too peaceful for that. He continued to walk aimlessly along the wall. As he did so, he heard the gentle chirping of crickets, which stirred up an old passion within him. From early boyhood he had loved to see these insects fight.

So, pulling up his long gown, he stopped to turn over some of the loose ancient bricks. Out leaped a big black cricket. He tried to catch it with his bare hand — a thing he would not ordinarily have done; at home in Soochow he used a specially prepared net so that the cricket was undamaged when it was caught. But the insect was in any case too quick for him. It hopped away through a crevice and hid in a heap of broken bricks only a foot away.

As he rose to continue his stroll, his face beaming with satisfaction, he ran headlong into Yung-kai, one year older than himself, who had graduated from the same academy a year before.

'I am glad you can still amuse yourself with these childhood pastimes,' said Yung-kai, who had seen from a distance what Ping-mo was trying to do. And then, as if they were not alone, he whispered into his friend's ear: 'The meeting is this evening, as you know. But we must be careful. There are reports that the Viceroy has knowledge of what we are up to. He has posted spies near the temple where we gather.'

Ping-mo was too delighted at meeting Yung-kai to pay much attention to his warning. It was in fact quite unnecessary, for Ping-mo, already a seasoned plotter against the Manchu regime, knew the need for caution.

'You are looking well. And now what are your latest accomplishments in riding? I was so impressed by the way you managed that horse during the graduation exercises. . . . What did you call him?'

'You mean the Black Typhoon?'

'Yes, Black Typhoon, of course.'

'There is not much to tell you, Ping-mo. But I have been thinking lately — thinking how much we young men can really hope to accomplish. We talk glibly about revolution and doing away with the Manchus. But have we ever thought of the consequences? Sometimes I have my doubts.'

Yung-kai paused. Then, looking full in the face of his friend, he continued: 'Don't you realize that you and I are, after all, sons of well-to-do families? Your father is one of the most distinguished scholars in the country. In time he will be a great official.'

'And your father,' Ping-mo added, 'is the President of the Tsung-li Yamen. That I know. Well?'

'It comes to this. If our activities are discovered, we shall involve our families as well as ourselves. I feel we have been too impetuous.'

Ping-mo laughed as though there was no need to be so cautious. He wiped his face with a handkerchief which was much soiled after his journey. The two young men sauntered along, and they had much to talk about. During their period of separation the country, which they both loved so dearly, had been passing from one crisis to another.

'If so mighty a nation can be so easily — and so ignominiously — beaten by so puny a people as these Japanese dwarfs,' Ping-mo said, 'surely there must be something basically wrong. I tell you it is for us of the younger generation to find out what the trouble is — and to remedy it.'

Without knowing it, Ping-mo had thrown a challenge to Yung-kai, but his friend was in no mood for any challenge.

'That is true enough, Ping-mo,' Yung-kai replied. 'I remember you have always said that the entire government is worm-eaten, that it is rotten to the core, and that it must be swept away. I grant you that. I feel as you feel. But frankly I am beginning to doubt how much we can do —'

'What has come over you?' interrupted Ping-mo impulsively. 'Why do you have all these doubts?'

'As I said, you and I belong to the very families upon which you seem to cast such aspersions. To tell you the truth, I would not have taken the trouble to come here now if it were not for the fact that we have been such close friends. I want to see you again and talk to you.'

'Yung-kai, you must continue to have courage.'

'But it is not a question of courage: it is a question of discretion.'

'The die has been cast. After our meeting tonight I am sure your resolve will strengthen. We may be a small group of what you call impetuous young men fighting under tremendous difficulties, but I know the people everywhere are behind us. We are ready for changes. Let us not talk about it any more now. Let's meet our friends tonight.'

The Temple of the Singing Rooster, where the meeting was to take place, was one of the most colourful landmarks in the old and dilapidated city of Nanking, standing where the squalor and charm of its medieval life could still be met at every turn of its crooked streets. The temple was more than usually well lighted this evening, and the fragrance of incense and sandalwood was noticeable as Ping-mo and Yung-kai approached its outer walls. Perched on a promontory from which one had the magnificent panoramic view of the lake at which Ping-mo gazed so longingly during the day, the temple now presented, during the last lingering moments of summer dusk, a haunting and ghost-like appearance. The whole edifice, constructed centuries ago by those master architects who were great lovers of nature, was skilfully spread out so that the lines and contours of the hill upon which it stood could be used to the best advantage. It had now become one massive silhouette, dark and impenetrable against the fading light. From the eaves, gently curving towards the sky, hung two red lanterns which now and then swung in the air and seemed to beckon the two young men into the temple's inner sanctuaries and courtyards.

Ping-mo, becoming more animated as he drew nearer to the temple, was the first to run up the flight of uneven stone steps. He and Yung-kai passed through the outer courtyards and noticed that a ceremony in honour of some departed soul was in progress. A number of people chatting and strolling around were friends or members of the bereaved family, and were dressed in different degrees of mourning. The two strangers passed them and went into the main hall, where some twenty Buddhist monks were chanting the scriptures for the benefit of the soul which had crossed to 'the other shore'.

'There he is,' whispered Ping-mo to his companion, looking in the direction of a monk who appeared stronger and more powerfully built than the rest.

The monk gave them a slight glance of recognition. Ping-mo and his friend went on and, crossing another courtyard, disappeared through a small side door. They now found themselves in a spacious room.

Some fifteen young men had already gathered there and begun their discussion.

'I am sure you all understand,' the chairman was saying, 'why we chose this year to summon you to this city. This was the capital of the great Ming Dynasty. Its founder, you remember, was an acolyte in a monastery not far from this very temple. By assembling here and recalling the memory of this great leader we should strengthen our will for the overthrow of the Manchus. They have ruled over this fair land of ours for too long. It is time we re-established a Chinese regime.'

The young man, who was heavily bespectacled, paused for a moment. He surveyed the audience and noticed that there was satisfaction on everybody's face. He was seconded by another lad who rose and developed the same idea. His speech had a strong Hunan accent.

'To think,' he said, 'that we could be so badly beaten by those monkeys. It is really the greatest disgrace in our history. Look what we have lost. A heavy indemnity, and on the top of that some of our treasured land — the beautiful island of Taiwan [Formosa] and parts of our north-eastern territory! For half a century, ever since 1842, we have been bullied and battered by all the nations of the world. Unless there are drastic reforms, the disasters will be even more serious. We are on our way to extinction. And yet the big, fat officials who are running the government still do nothing but wallow in their luxury and ill-gotten wealth.'

Another member of the audience took exception to the reference to extinction. 'Need we be so pessimistic?' He spoke slowly and with a gentle tone, for he was from Hangchow. 'The aliens may come, but they always disappear in the end. Think of the moon-cakes which we all eat in the middle of the eighth moon. Those cakes used to conceal a secret order to kill all the Mongols. That was how the Yuan Dynasty fell. As for the Manchus, see how degenerate they have become! Who made them so? We, the Chinese. By deliber-ately encouraging them to think that they were a privileged class en-titled to all the pleasures of life without having to work for them, look what we have done to them in the course of two and a half centuries. Have patience, gentlemen, have patience.'

The audience did not approve of this little speech. Everybody thought it lacked seriousness. While the discussion was going on, Yung-kai grew uneasy in his seat. He did not like the attack on the Manchus, for he had some Manchu blood in him, though no one knew it. He kept looking at his good friend Ping-mo and wondered what he was going to say. But Ping-mo seemed to be lost in thought. He was gazing at the ceiling, noticing all the peculiarities of its architecture. It had not dawned upon him at first that the room had no windows. He would have noticed this if the meeting had been held during the day; but it was night, and the room was only faintly lighted by a few candles and by two small kerosene lamps placed on the table in front of the chairman. He looked at the ceiling more closely and discovered a few openings in the corners which were evidently for purposes of ventilation rather than to admit light.

Having established some semblance of order in his stray thoughts, Ping-mo now rose to his feet.

'We have had enough of speech-making,' he began, 'The time

has come for action, for a general uprising. We all realize that the people everywhere have expressed their willingness to give us their support. Our overseas countrymen have left no doubt in our minds as to what they desire. Those in America and in the South Seas are generously giving us their full financial support. Someone here at home will have to make the first move, and then the conflagration will sweep through the country. It is for us to make that move. We cannot shirk this responsibility. We shall have to fire the first shot in some remote city where the official eye is least vigilant. Before the next summer comes round the signal will have to be given, perhaps in Canton. I shall myself go to that city and establish contact with our supporters there, if you so desire. I ask for volunteers to accompany me on this mission.'

So passionate a speech coming from so frail a person had an immediate effect on the audience. Ping-mo belonged to a family of scholars; he had the look of one who has been well protected and carefully nurtured. The long journey of the previous day had left him in some weariness. And yet, when the occasion demanded, he could rise to his feet and show a firm and determined purpose of which his delicate features gave no indication.

As Ping-mo resumed his seat, the monk who had earlier given him a glance of recognition as he passed through the main hall of the temple with Yung-kai also sat down. He had been in the room for some time. He now wore ordinary clothes and chatted freely with those near him. He looked older than the rest. Perhaps the colour of his face made him appear older than he was, for even in the dim light of the candles he looked darker and more weather-beaten: he gave the impression of one who was accustomed to manual labour in the open.

2

WHEN the meeting was over and Ping-mo went to his room, he realized how tired he was. He was just falling asleep when he heard a knock on the door. Who could this be? he wondered. He opened the door and found to his surprise that it was the monk.

'I thought I should come to tell you that it was indiscreet of you to be so outspoken during the meeting,' complained the monk as he sat down on the only wooden bench in the room and made himself comfortable.

Ping-mo sat on the edge of his bed.

'You know, of course,' continued the monk, 'that I am in charge of our secret organization here in this city. I have to be careful, even more than the rest of us. It is not for nothing that I put on the robe of a monk in this temple and have learned to chant the Buddhist hymns. You know the reason. But it seems you don't know that not everybody is to be trusted — no, not even among our own ranks.'

Ping-mo wondered who the monk was referring to.

'The authorities are informed of widespread discontent among the people,' the monk went on to explain. 'They know also that there is organized opposition. They may not be able to fight a foreign foe, but they have enough wits to maintain themselves in power. All they have to do is to seize a few of our leaders, and that will be the end of our movement. I know how devoted you are to our cause, but I cannot say the same for all of us. And I cannot afford to lose you. I would urge that you leave this city at once. I have come to take you to another place where you will pass the night, and early tomorrow morning you must be on your way back to where you came from.'

'Surely the situation is not so bad as all that,' Ping-mo protested.

But he got up to gather together a few of his belongings and was ready to obey. He had met the monk before, but he had not realized until now the strange fascination which he had over him. There was something in his features which showed determination and a set purpose, and something in his eyes which especially captivated Ping-mo.

The two of them began walking through the fields. It was dark, but the sky was bright and clear and the stars were shining, so it was still possible to see the winding paths, scarcely more than a couple of feet wide, which seemed to extend without end through the paddy fields. They must have walked for more than a mile before Ping-mo felt quiet and relaxed. He carried his small bundle of summer clothes and, as he smelled the fragrance of the ripening rice and heard the chirping of numberless crickets, his heart was indeed 'opened up with joy'. He even began humming a few lines of poetry to himself, while his companion walked in front with grim determination, uttering scarcely a word.

Soon they came to a mud hut, where the monk stopped. The two

went in and found a group of coarse-looking people. Judging by
the kind of clothes they wore, Ping-mo concluded that they must
be farmers. He was struck by the presence of two women, each holding a red lantern in her hand; one of them looked quite attractive.
The group was engaged in some mysterious ceremony, with strange
incantations which were unfamiliar to Ping-mo. The people paid
no more than perfunctory attention as the two came in, though
there was enough recognition of the monk to show that he was
known to them. Along the walls were hung a collection of fierce-
looking knives and long spears.

'Who are these people and why have you brought me here?'
queried Ping-mo as the monk led him to the rear of the hut and
showed him a dingy little room where he was to pass the night.

'These people belong to what they call the Order of Righteous
Harmony,' the monk told him. 'They practise boxing, and it is said
that they possess supernatural powers.'

'But how is it that you know them well?' Ping-mo asked.

'Most of them, Ping-mo,' explained the monk, addressing his
friend for the first time by his name, 'are related to me. They are
villagers from the neighbourhood. They, too, desire to do something
radical, as they feel the continuing pressure of the foreigner. But
their faith is not entirely my faith. That is why I am with you. . . .
The evening is getting late.' So saying, the monk went away and
then came back with some soiled farmer's clothing, which he tossed
to Ping-mo.

'I shall not see you off in the morning. But it is best that you start
early and put these clothes on so that you will look like one of the
farmers. Good luck till we meet again.'

Two days later Ping-mo was back in Soochow, which was not the
city of his birth, but one where his father had chosen to live because
of its many historical landmarks and the charm of its surroundings.
He confined himself to his own small study, surrounded by shelves
of the old classics, many of which he knew almost by heart. But it
was too sultry to turn over the pages of books, and he was disturbed
by the experiences of his journey. He had gone away on the pretext
that one of his best friends was ill in Shanghai and that he had to go
there to see him. Both his father and mother had taken it for granted
that Ping-mo had come back from that visit of consolation; and

when they had asked him how his friend was, he merely replied that it was a serious case of dysentery, an illness common at that time of the year, and that it would be some time before his friend was completely recovered.

His thoughts were concentrated on the dangerous work to which he had now committed himself. He reclined on a rattan chair, gently cooling himself with a palm-leaf fan, and in a few minutes, overcome by the humid heat, fell into a deep slumber. He was awakened by the housemaid, a girl of thirteen years, who had been purchased from an orphanage four years previously. As was her usual practice, she brought some tea and a plate of the fresh lotus root which the young master so dearly loved.

The maid blushed as she entered the room, for Ping-mo had taken off his shirt. The upper part of his body was naked, with the fan covering his chest.

'Young master! Young master! I have brought you some tea, and the lotus root is fresh and tender,' she said. 'I am sorry to disturb you, but Tai-tai says that she wants you to go up to her room.'

Ping-mo put on his shirt, bit off a piece of the lotus root, which was indeed delicately fragrant and sweet, and then went slowly up to his mother's chamber.

Madam Wen-ching, a woman of about forty-five or six, was perhaps one of the finest products of China and its ancient culture. There was a quiet dignity about her, and her marvellous poise suggested that she had been submitted to the best of intellectual and spiritual influences from early childhood. She was the mother of three children, one of whom had died when he was barely three. Her daughter had been married to the son of a respectable family, and Ping-mo was the only child who now lived with her. Occasionally her younger brother came to see her. Her relatives were few and her family small compared with other families in China.

When Ping-mo entered her room, Madam Wen-ching was engaged in her daily calligraphy and painting. These were arts she had cultivated since childhood, and now, with her son and daughter grown up, she had ample time to devote to them. She was seated behind a long and spacious table. In the far corner to the left of her was a pot of orchids into which she herself would pour the correct amount of water every day: she would not allow anyone to touch it, even though the maid was always near at hand to perform little tasks for her. The leaves had grown long and graceful, but the flowers were still few and hardly discernible at this time of the year. The petals were yellow-green. There was already some fragrance, noticeable especially when the air was still. For centuries the orchid has appealed to the *élite* in China, for refinement, it is thought, is expressed only by a fragrance that is delicate and subtle, and not by pungency or intensity.

The windows were wide open, and looked out on the distant Tiger Hill. The sight of that hill always reminded Madam Wen-ching of an early period in Chinese history when men were real heroes, even though at times they could be somewhat boisterous. For Soochow was then the principal city in the kingdom of Wu, and deep in the well at the foot of Tiger Hill there still lay an ancient sword, as famous in Chinese history as the Excalibur of King Arthur.

She laid down her brush as Ping-mo entered and, turning to him, said: 'The maid tells me that you were asleep.'

'Yes, Mother. I was so tired with the journey, and the weather is so warm.'

'I hope your friend is rapidly recovering from his illness.'

Ping-mo was conscience-stricken. It was the first time he had uttered a falsehood to his parents, but it was essential that he keep his visit to Nanking secret, not only to spare them anxiety, but also because he was under the orders of the society never to let anyone know of its activities.

Madam Wen-ching's thoughts seemed far away. Her fingers were toying with a pair of jade seals. She was looking at them as if admiring their beautiful carving. It was evident that today she was under some nervous tension, but she had decided to unburden her thoughts to her son, and, having once made up her mind, remained calm; her forehead looked clear and unwrinkled.

'My son, I have long wanted to say something to you,' Madam Wen-ching began.

For a moment Ping-mo thought that his falsehood had been discovered. But his mother went on: 'It has come to my knowledge that your father is doing something which I believe he should not do at his age. He has had a brilliant record as a scholar. He has passed some of the highest examinations, and I believe that he will not have to wait long for another important official appointment. But he has been doing strange things recently. I could excuse him if he were a younger man. But after all he is now forty-eight, and at that age one does not do things which are permissible to a man twenty years younger.'

'Well, Mother, what is it that Father has been doing?' asked Ping-mo anxiously, deeply concerned over his mother's state of un-happiness.

'For the last few months your father has been going out almost every day late in the afternoon and not returning till late in the evening. He tells me that he has been visiting friends from whom he may obtain some information about what is happening at the Court in Peking. Of course, I can understand why he is anxious to have this information, but what I cannot understand is why he must waste his time with these friends in the company of sing-song girls.'

'Sing-song girls?'

'Yes. Your father comes home every night like a man bewitched. And while you were away I had reason to believe things were get-ting worse. I am told that he is actually in love with a girl thirty years younger than he. She is said to be very pretty and very accomplished for her age.'

From the corner of her table she took a few sheets of paper and handed them to her son. 'Look, these are some of the poems which your deeply romantic father has written about this girl, and he tells me that he has been spending his time profitably with his friends!'

Ping-mo glanced rapidly through the poems. He thought they were good. There was one in particular which was full of rich imagery and written with a choice of words such as only his father knew how to use. He began humming the verse to himself:

> Queen of flowers, delicate as thou art,
> I feel thy pulse coursing through my veins.

And as he read on, Ping-mo said to himself, So it has come to such a pass!

'I don't know,' said his mother, 'whether I should tell you this. But I think you are old enough to understand some of my sorrow.'

Ping-mo realized that he had seen little of his father since his re-turn. He felt sad for his mother's sake. But at the same time he was greatly intrigued and wanted to have a glimpse of the girl himself. So she is the queen of flowers—a lovely orchid, he thought to himself.

'Well, Mother,' said Ping-mo as he rose and walked to the

window, 'perhaps it is only a temporary infatuation. When father receives a new appointment he will have to go to Peking, and we shall go with him, and that will be the end of the episode.'

In his anxiety to comfort his mother, Ping-mo forgot that he must stay behind in the south to perform the tasks to which he had committed himself.

'That is what I hope, and I pray that the appointment will come soon.' Madam Wen-ching reached for her brush and resumed her painting. Ping-mo took leave of her and, going back to his own room, put on his thin cotton gown and went out.

Ping-mo knew where his father was to be found. There was no reason why he should go to see his father, except to embarrass him. That, as a good son, he was reluctant to do. But he was, after all, young, and he felt a strong urge, in spite of himself, to see the girl with whom his father had become infatuated. He passed through the streets of the crowded city, which even at so late an hour were still alive with activity. Meats and vegetables were still being sold; the shops were full of good things to eat — nuts, water-melon seeds, 'ox-skin' candy and preserved strawberries, of which Ping-mo was especially fond. The poorer people, stripped to the waist, were carrying pails of water from the city's streams and creeks. The water looked yellow and muddy, but they carried the heavy load home, poured it into large earthen jars, and vigorously stirred alum into it to keep it clean and pure.

The narrow, winding, cobbled streets were slippery with the spilled water, and Ping-mo had to walk cautiously. Soon he passed through one of the gates of the city wall, much less impressive than the magnificent structure he had seen in Nanking only a couple of days before. The city came to an end at the wall. Beyond lay open country traversed by streams. In the distance he saw a number of boats festively decked out.

So these are the flower-boats, he thought. So this is where the fine gentlemen of the country — and the officials — have a grand time with their sing-song girls, while the country sinks to its decay. Wonderful arrangement this is! For a moment Ping-mo tightened his lips, and his face showed hatred for officials as a class, including his own father.

Ping-mo reached the bank of the stream. The first people to greet him were a group of chair-carriers, many of whom were squatting on the ground. Dressed in their coarse, deep-blue tunics, trousers rolled up to the knees, and shod in straw sandals, they were either contentedly smoking their long bamboo pipes or playing cards. They had carried the wealthy officials to their place of amusement, and were now enjoying themselves in their own way, waiting to carry their masters back to their homes when the party on the flower-boats was over.

One of the carriers recognized Ping-mo at once and passed the word to his fellow carriers that the young master of the Shen family had arrived, whereupon there was some consternation and excitement. The men began pointing, and looked at each other, as much as to say that when father and son were found together in these surroundings there was going to be trouble.

'I know one particular spot down the stream,' said the carrier, 'where the lotus is unusually fair and the seeds tender and fragrant. Would the young master want to go there? I can get a small boat for you.' It was his aim to draw Ping-mo's attention away from the flower-boats.

Ping-mo thanked the man and said that he would be glad to have a small boat. But, pointing to where the flower-boats were assembled, he continued: 'For today let me be taken over there.'

A small sampan was placed at his disposal, and he soon found himself on one of the flower-boats moored a few yards from one another.

Ping-mo thought he knew what these boats looked like. But what he saw exceeded all his expectations. At both ends of the boat into which he stepped the boatmen and servants were busy setting the table for what looked like a feast. Many pewter pots of rice wine were being warmed, and food and fruits were being passed to four boats arranged in a circle around the fifth, which served as kitchen. The boat on which Ping-mo found himself was large and spacious. The central portion, which was covered, consisted of two compartments: an outer one where a round table large enough to seat eight people for dinner was placed, and an inner one, curtained off. Along these covered compartments ran two open corridors about a foot and a half wide, so that servants could go from one end of the boat to the other without having to pass through the compartments. In the outer compartment two guests were playing chess, with two others looking on. Ping-mo did not know them well enough to exchange greetings with them. He asked one of the boatmen if Master Shen was anywhere to be found, and was ushered at once into the inner compartment.

Wen-ching was completely taken aback at seeing his son. The flower-boat was the only place where, away from home, he could really enjoy himself and relax, and now his son had invaded it! He did not look pleased, but hastened nevertheless to seem as much at ease as possible, and began introducing his impudent son to every one of his friends. Ping-mo addressed them as uncles, since they were his father's friends. He made each of them a deep and respectful bow, as custom demanded, and, taking a seat near his father, gave the excuse that he had come to talk over some of the plans for his studies and the approaching civil service examination, which was to be held earlier than usual.

Wen-ching said that there was ample time to discuss these plans at home. It was only too obvious to him that Ping-mo had other motives for coming to the flower-boat.

A sickly-looking guest came over to continue the conversation which had been broken off by the coming of the new arrival. Ping-mo sat in silence, trying to make himself as inconspicuous as possible, but all the while his eyes were wandering from one corner of the compartment to another. Where are the sing-song girls? he asked himself.

For the guests were all men, the only girl being a little servant maid who came in and out, bringing tea and handing hot towels to the guests with which to wipe their faces. Ping-mo noticed that the furniture was of the most elegant kind. It was made of the best hard-wood, finished in deep brown verging on black. The tables were covered with marble slabs chosen because the lines or grain gave a suggestion of mountain scenery. The heat in the compartment was oppressive, and there was hardly any breeze, even on the water. But in spite of the heat two of the guests were reclining on a spacious and comfortable divan, playing with little balls of opium which they toasted on the gentle flame of a small lamp, conveyed to their pipes, and then smoked. Ping-mo had heard much about opium-smoking, but it was the first time he had seen the performance at such close quarters. His family was brought up under severe discipline, as be-fitting that of a scholar, and none of its members indulged in that form of debauchery.

Ping-mo observed the operation with the utmost interest. It was casual and leisurely, creating an atmosphere which made it possible to carry on a sustained and friendly conversation. The two men on the divan were now deeply engrossed in their *tête-à-tête*, and Ping-mo overheard one of them say: 'Well, after all, it is good to pass these examinations.'

'Of course; that is what we all work for, isn't it?' replied the other.

'Yes, I know,' casually remarked the first. He recalled how gongs were always struck when an official appointment was made after a successful examination. 'There is nothing that so much inflates one's ego. It's a good feeling,' he commented. Then he turned over his heavy, reclining body and continued: 'Honour, wealth, glory — all the good things of life come together for a successful candidate.'

And these were the very reasons, Ping-mo thought, why he hated sitting for these ordeals. The country was being brought to utter ruin because of this attitude. Territories could be lost, the country could be humiliated, but these so-called scholars must have their official appointment and ill-gotten wealth! His own father was somewhat of an exception, but all the same he wanted Ping-mo to go through the examinations for the identical aims. It was fortunate, Ping-mo thought, that he had reached an age where he could do much as he liked; he had stubbornly refused to do entirely what his father wished.

Ping-mo had been sitting stiffly by himself long enough. He decided that it was time to join the conversation and hear what else they had to say. 'Venerable uncles,' he began, 'may I help you to toast the opium?'

'Why, of course. Sit down near us,' replied Uncle Wang, the more corpulent of the two. 'It is good for a young man to listen to what we have to say. Your father is a great scholar, having passed some of the highest examinations. He has held some important posts. It shouldn't be long now before he is appointed to a greater and even more important post. We hear that you also are an accomplished scholar. Well, like father, like son! Some day you too will become an important person.'

'No, I dare not think so, Uncle Wang,' said Ping-mo modestly.

Uncle Wang smoked his opium and turned to resume his conversation with his companion, a man named Hu-mou, who was as lean as Uncle Wang was fat.

'You were just beginning to tell me how impressed you were by the magnificence of your cousin's residence,' Hu-mou reminded him.

'Oh, yes. As I entered the red gate flanked by two fine-looking stone lions,' Uncle Wang went on, 'there were those two gold characters "joy and happiness" staring into my face. I went through a long corridor, on either side of which was a spacious and lovely courtyard, and the peonies were in full bloom. I was then led into three big halls in which were arranged rows of red-lacquered plaques, with gilt inscriptions describing the official positions he has held. I tell you it was an impressive sight. And do you know how long it took him to attain all that?'

'How long?'

'It all came about in three years. Think of it — three years.'

'But I thought you said that his positions were not very high,' queried Hu-mou.

'That is the point I was going to make. He was only director of a minor financial office. But you should see the number of gifts which he managed to receive every year. As you know, one way to become a successful official is to have a large number of anniversaries. This cousin of mine used to have weddings and funerals remarkably frequently, and the announcement of each of these occasions was a hint to his subordinate officials."

'It is always wise to take the hint, I suppose,' commented Hu-mou.

'You know what happens if the hint is ignored,' said Uncle Wang, chuckling as if he had said something funny. 'Look at the rich collection of antiques he has — bronzes and fine porcelain of priceless value,' he continued. 'He used to mobilize his whole family. He even brought out his parents, who have been dead these many years. But they could still contribute to his wealth. He announced the anniversaries of their birth, of their death, and finally of their marriage, so that there were at least five days in the year on which these dead parents were sure to bring him wealth.' Uncle Wang chuckled until his whole frame quivered and rolled.

But Ping-mo was shocked and dropped the ball of opium which he was toasting. It was an embarrassing moment. Fortunately the servants came in to announce that dinner was being served, and he thought it was time for him to leave the party. But he had come to catch a glimpse of his father's sing-song girl. Not to have seen her was a keen disappointment, though he consoled himself that he had

learned other things on their brief visit. He noticed that his father
was not feeling comfortable at his presence, and so, approaching
Wen-ching, he said that he was going home. His father made no
attempt to detain him, and Ping-mo left in a sampan.

3

WHEN Ping-mo returned to the bank of the stream he noticed that
there was much commotion. The chair-bearers, who when he first
arrived were squatting down smoking their long bamboo pipes, were
now busy removing their chairs and making room for some new
arrivals.

Are there more guests coming? Ping-mo wondered. First three,
and then, after a short while, two more chairs arrived; and from each
of them alighted a girl.

These must be the sing-song girls, Ping-mo thought as he looked
excitedly from one to the other. The first three looked ordinary, but
the last two nearly took his breath away, for they were unusually
beautiful. And as they came down from their chairs and waited to
be conveyed to the pleasure-boats in the middle of the stream, he was
happy that they were introduced to him.

'This is Golden Orchid, young master,' said a chair-bearer as the
last of the girls stepped down. 'And this,' said the same man, turning
to the girl, 'is the young master of the Shen family.'

Ping-mo stood there for a moment without uttering a word, gazing
at the girl with an embarrassed blush. She looked at him with a
most pleasing smile.

'I have been wanting to meet you,' said Golden Orchid. 'Your
distinguished father has spoken about you, and his friends have all
praised you to the skies. I am fortunate to meet you.'

'It is I who am the fortunate one,' Ping-mo stuttered.

'I know how accomplished you are. I know also that you com-
pose elegant poetry, in addition to knowing all the classics by heart.
It is a great honour for an ignorant girl like me to make your
acquaintance.'

'I am afraid all this is an exaggeration,' interrupted Ping-mo. 'I
am not so worthy a person as you believe.'

The sampan was now ready to take the sing-song girls to the boats, and Ping-mo wended his way home through the streets.

I don't blame the old man, he said to himself, for being taken in by so pretty a maid. But, after all, he is nearly fifty. But then again, as they say, 'A man may be old but the heart is young.' He smiled to himself.

Ping-mo knew from his mother that Golden Orchid was a girl of about eighteen. But she was taller than he had expected and well developed for her years. What particularly struck him was her eyes; they were large and black, and the whites had a tinge of clear blue, 'as blue as the sky after rain'. He tried to recollect the wistful look she gave him just before they parted, and almost bumped into a vegetable seller carrying two large bamboo baskets. Happily there was no exchange of angry words, and Ping-mo went on his way with pleasant memories in his mind. He remembered, for instance, that the corners of Golden Orchid's eyes had shadows—those were the phoenix eyes about which he had heard and read so much in poetry, but it was the first time he had actually seen them. They were luminous and moist, and full of feeling. Her hair was combed straight back and was tied into a tight, becoming knot, ornamented with pearls. A neat fringe hung just above her delicate eyebrows, which arched like new moons on either side of her face. He had even noticed that she wore ear rings inlaid with kingfisher feathers, and their deep, almost iridescent, blue contrasted beautifully with the soft and delicate whiteness of her skin.

But, then, the girls in Soochow, Ping-mo thought, are famous for their smooth and lovely complexions.

A dainty and small mouth showing a set of perfectly formed teeth, which he had seen as she gave him that last smile, completed what Ping-mo thought was one of the most divinely beautiful faces he had ever had the good fortune to see. He was happy that he had seen her.

But while he was absorbed in these reveries he was conscious of an inner disturbance, and wondered what it was. He had caused his father some uneasiness. That was bad enough, but he was convinced that it was not the reason for the disturbance. He tried to recall, in his mind's eye, some of his father's friends whom he had met. There was Uncle Wang, who was fat, coarse and vulgar, whose main interest in life seemed to lie in amassing wealth by means which need not be too subtle. And then there was Hu-mou. . . .

Yes, this man Hu-mou was a strange person. He was small and sallow, and his skin was loose. Ping-mo had the impression that if he pinched the face of the man he would find nothing to hold the skin to what little flesh there was beneath. For a man of his size, Hu-mou had an unusually large Adam's apple, sticking out like the wishbone from the breast of an underfed and unfeathered chicken. But it was Hu-mou's eyes which were especially disturbing. They had a way of looking up, again like a chicken dozing off to sleep, and exposing their whites just above the lower eyelids. They were not kind or friendly eyes, but cold and calculating, and Ping-mo felt that they belonged to a man much given to scheming and malicious designs. They were perhaps dangerous and treacherous eyes, he concluded. How different they were from those of the heavenly Golden Orchid!

Thus Ping-mo mused; and as he mused, his steps became careless. He bumped into several other pedestrians, until a child of four fell with a loud yell. The mother shouted angrily:

'You who will die by a thousand knives, why are you not more careful when you walk?'

Ping-mo was deeply embarrassed, though he did not utter a word. He gently picked up the child and went on his way.

When Golden Orchid came to the boat, Wen-ching and his friends had just seated themselves round the table on which were the choicest delicacies. Rice wine which had been warmed in hot water was being poured into small cups, and, although the party had scarcely begun, it was clear there was going to be some heavy drinking during the evening. For it was in the best tradition to drink among congenial friends out in the open on a warm summer night. Poets had done so for centuries, and these men were all scholars in their own right. Big earthen vats, painted with vigorous rustic designs and containing the best wine from Shaoshing, were installed at one end of the boat. The servants were busy emptying their contents into pewter pots.

The guests began with the finger game, followed by the impromptu composition of verses, both of which were intended to encourage drinking. It was an unusual arrangement for drinking, for while with people in the West it is the aim to enjoy drinking as much as possible, the Chinese do precisely the reverse: their object is to drink

B

as little as possible so that they can maintain their pose while attempting to make their opponent lose his balance. It is not so much a contest in the capacity to drink as in the ability to maintain composure and keep a cool head.

The sing-song girls, whose professional duty it is to provide amusement at such parties, confined exclusively to men, were seated between the guests — slightly to the rear. They did not share the food, but helped sometimes to fill the cups, especially of those with whom they had been matched for the evening. Wen-ching's capacity for drinking was known to be limited, and it was interesting to watch Golden Orchid, a young girl of eighteen, exercising her protective instincts over a man thirty years her senior. Singing by these girls was a part of the amusement, and Golden Orchid, as the prettiest of the group, would normally offer only the *pièce de résistance*, and even that would come only after some persuasion by her admirers. But today she was all willingness: somehow she felt that it was better to draw attention to herself than to have it all fixed on Wen-ching. And so, without being asked, she went into the inner compartment and brought out her favourite guitar.

'Yes, by all means let us have some music,' the guests agreed.

'Honourable gentlemen,' replied Golden Orchid, 'if you wish the humble one to sing, I shall be glad to do so. But you will forgive me, as I do not possess a good voice.'

'You don't have to excuse yourself,' said Uncle Wang, who was perhaps as deeply infatuated with Golden Orchid as was Wen-ching. 'We know what a lovely voice you have. Please begin.'

Wen-ching sat in silence. Hu-mou gave no impression of enjoying himself, but now and then cast a glance in the direction of Wen-ching, and as usual rolled his eyes upwards, as though he were concocting something in his mind.

As Golden Orchid began tuning her guitar she was indeed a lovely and adorable sight. Her smooth, jet-black hair and delicately white, oval face contrasted strikingly with her faintly blue and gauze-like garment. It was made of the finest Kiangsi linen, and reached her knees; under it she wore a rose-tinted blouse, perhaps somewhat too loose and large for her body, as the style in those days demanded, but she was more than usually developed for her age, and her full, round bosom looked pleasing to the guests.

When she was ready, she turned to the guests again and said: 'I don't know what to sing, but I shall try what you are all familiar with — the "Lament of Meng Chiang Nu".'

Everybody, of course, did know the song: it was a folk-song describing an event of over two thousand years before, and sung by the people everywhere for quite as long a period. It had four parts, each devoted to a season during which the faithful wife tried to find the remains of her husband who had been exiled to contribute his share to the building of the Great Wall in the arid wastes of the north.

Golden Orchid sang the second verse with deep feeling:

> The lotus trembles in the summer heat,
> The flying insects fill the evening air;
> Let them feed on my limbs,
> Tender and frail as they are,
> Lest they torment my beloved one.

Before she had finished the men burst into vociferous and unqualified applause. They asked for their cups to be refilled and, turning their eyes to Wen-ching, exclaimed: 'Let us drink to our friend, Brother Wen-ching. For here is our proverbial hero and the fair maid. May they live happily ever after.' Wen-ching was pleased; but he was nervous, for how could his friends read his mind?

Golden Orchid had indeed given a wonderful performance. As her dainty white hands moved softly across the guitar, her head slightly drooping, the sweet, melodious, and yet plaintive notes came rolling out of her throat like little pearls; and the last line of the song:

> As I move on my lonely trail
> I hear the call of my love pining by the Great Wall,

which she sang with controlled emotion and yet with such intensity of feeling, increased the effect of the lament and its dirge-like appeal. It recalled to the minds of the guests those early days of their empire when men had to defend it against invading hordes of the northern barbarians; how they had to build the Great Wall with immense human sacrifice. They remembered the love and devotion of the women for men who braved the deserts and crossed the high mountains so that they might be secure in their homes and hearths. What a contrast those days were with the softness and ease in which they now found themselves! But they gave this no more than fleeting thought, surrounded as they were with rich wines and luscious foods. What would Ping-mo have thought if he had been present at the party?

The girls stayed on for some time; one of them played the lute after Golden Orchid had sung. Before they went away it was customary that they make a round of calls on the other boats, which were now arranged, one touching the other, in a semi-circle so that everybody could share the enjoyment. When Golden Orchid stood up to leave, she went quietly up to Wen-ching and whispered in his ear: 'The evening is getting late and the air chilly. I wish that my master would retire early.' He pressed one of her little hands between his own and felt warmth in his blood.

When it was time for the guests to go back to their homes, the servants got busy. Some held paper lanterns to light the way, while other placed wooden boards to the waiting sampans; and when their masters were safe on the bank of the stream, the chair-bearers, who in the meantime had had their own little amusements, perhaps even their own sing-song girls, were ready. Each chair was carried by two men, with a third walking in front holding a lantern.

As Wen-ching sat in his chair and gave himself up to its rhythmic motion, he almost dozed off. He was perfectly happy, having drunk perhaps a little beyond his usual capacity, in spite of every effort on the part of Golden Orchid to persuade him to limit himself. He wondered what his fate would be with this young and lovely little thing who had lodged herself so snugly in his heart. The narrow streets were now quiet and deserted, and his thoughts went on without interruption. There was nothing against his taking her as a concubine: custom and social practice fully allowed him to do so. It was not that consideration which made him hesitate, but rather the thought that for more than twenty-five years he had been married to one of the most refined and cultured ladies of the land.

How would she take it, I wonder? he inwardly asked himself. Besides, as a distinguished scholar of the day who had already gained much official recognition and was now waiting for a bigger and more important appointment, he had to think about his future. Am I not exposing myself to ridicule, and possibly even slander?

But before he came to any conclusion he was at the gate of his house. The little maid who had sat up through the evening waiting to open the door for her master welcomed him, and he found peace and quietness within.

Madam Wen-ching and Ping-mo were sound asleep.

4

WEN-CHING had not known Golden Orchid long. The intense heat of the summer, all the more disagreeable because of its humidity, made it necessary for people of his class to seek relief in their leisure hours among the cool breezes on the water. Wen-ching had only recently taken to visiting these flower-boats, his preference being for the orthodox amusements of the scholar class: writing poetry and playing chess. But he was anxious not to create the impression of being superior by remaining aloof from officials with whom, now more than ever, it was essential that he show a spirit of comradeship. Some concession had to be made in view of his prospective elevation perhaps to the rank of the red button, an honour which no scholar could lightly waive. It was in these circumstances that he became a frequent visitor to the pleasure-boats and made the acquaintance of Golden Orchid. But it was a revelation, to himself no less than to his friends, that his heart was still open to youthful charms — even to those of a sing-song girl. It began as a kind of fatherly interest: she was not only pretty, but she also had intelligence and vivacity. For her part, Golden Orchid was happy to have met a kind and sympathetic elderly gentleman who could take the place of her father. Her mother and grandmother, kind and loving as they were, could not fill the gap.

The death of her father some thirteen years before, when she was barely five, was followed soon afterwards by another experience equally painful, though in a different sense. Her mother and grandmother began looking for an expert to submit her to the tortures of foot-binding, a practice, now happily long discarded, which was then a necessary evil for any young lady of breeding and refinement.

There was one such expert in the person of Lily, who was pockmarked, dark, thick-set and plain. Her voice was deep, and she bellowed like a water buffalo as she talked. But she was popular, for she had personality and could show infinite tact in dealing with people. Her professional services involved many months of very intimate relationship. The entire future of a young lady might well depend upon how comely her feet turned out to be, and that was why Lily had so many favours showered on her. She had, furthermore, inside information about practically all the leading families.

She was discreet, and knew how to use that knowledge to her best advantage when the occasion arose.

Custom required in those days that young ladies, especially of the high social classes, be kept in the house as much as possible, so that access to them by young men was difficult. But there were ways to overcome these difficulties, and this was where our pock-marked lady came into the picture. She was known to have brought many couples together, sometimes for honest matrimonial purposes, but often for clandestine meetings between young men who were pining for love and concubines who were still young in years but cruelly tied down to men who had long passed the prime of their lives. In this Lily was helped by her younger sister, a more attractive woman than herself, who likewise had access to ladies' boudoirs. It was her profession to attend to their coiffure, and calls for her services were so frequent that from early morning to late in the afternoon she might visit as many as twenty families. In the evening she passed all the gossip she had gathered during the day to her elder sister, in whose ability and astuteness she had unquestioning faith. Between the two of them there was not only a good deal of fun, but quite a little profit.

Golden Orchid was then too young for them to work upon. Also her family, though a good one, was too poor to appeal to them. But the two sisters agreed that when the proper time arrived she could become their best quarry. Every circumstance favoured them. There was no doubt about her beauty and intelligence; and, young as she was, they could see that there was a certain charm about her which would make her most attractive to men.

Years passed, and by the age of eighteen Golden Orchid had become a girl of really extraordinary beauty. Whether it is the water or the air, there is something unaccountable in Soochow which has made it famous through the centuries for the charm and beauty of its girls.

Golden Orchid grew up to be tall and stately. There was a quality in the fine texture of her skin which everyone noticed. It was not only smooth and delicate; it also had healthy rosy tints. Her feet had been bound perfectly, though they were somewhat larger than the accepted size and shape, and for that Golden Orchid's mother and grandmother were grateful to Lily, who managed to maintain friendly intercourse with the family through the years. The time had now arrived, she thought, when something could be done to carry out the designs she had conceived long ago. Her visits to the Fu family became more frequent and, as the ladies had few relatives and little contact with the outside world, they looked forward to these visits to hear gossip and learn what was going on in the city. Golden Orchid herself began to go out on little excursions for harmless amusements in the company of Lily, since she was the only woman in whom her grandmother had unfailing confidence.

It was then that she unknowingly fell into the life of a sing-song girl, a professional entertainer. With the collusion of her hairdresser sister Yang Mah, Lily had succeeded in her plans.

5

MORE than four months had passed since the night when Wen-ching went home in the sedan chair, his mind burdened with the thought of what he should do with the maiden who had won his affection. The heat of the summer had subsided, and the days of the flower-boats on the streams outside the city were over.

Autumn arrived early and, where only a short time before there had been noise and festivity, music and singing, there was now the beginning of solitude and desolation. The boats had been anchored under their sheds. The air had become chilly, but it was healthy and bracing. For Wen-ching and his scholar-mandarin friends, whose training in æsthetic appreciation was an integral part of their classical education, the coming of autumn was full of poetry. The long spring, with the slow transformation into life and activity in the fields, is something which everybody can enjoy, but it is only the scholars such as Wen-ching who attach special significance to the advent of autumn. It has a quality which stimulates the mind to sober reflection and somehow chastens the emotions to a depth and purity unknown during the other seasons.

Wen-ching therefore took delight in revisiting the water — often in the company of Golden Orchid. He looked at the lotus: though its stalks were still straight and gaunt, stretching far above the surface of the water, its vitality was gone, and the large round leaves, two or three feet in diameter, were withering and shrinking into a deep yellow far beyond the rim. The patches of reed on the water's edge had become jumbles of irregular and jagged grass projecting like mutilated spears above the water level. Everywhere a note of sadness was creeping in; but there was poetry that could stir Wen-ching to the depths of his soul. Standing on the bank of the stream one day and holding Golden Orchid by the hand, he recited some of the poems of the early classical period. 'Autumn wind rises', he began.

> Autumn wind rises: white clouds fly.
> Grass and trees wither: geese go south.
> Orchids all in bloom: chrysanthemums smell sweet.
> I think of my lovely lady: I never can forget.
> Floating pagoda boat crosses the Fen River.
> Across the mid-stream white waves rise;
> Flute and drum keep time with the rover's song;
> Amidst revel and feasting, sad thoughts come;
> Youth's years how few! Age how sure!

It was a song composed by a great emperor of the Han Dynasty. And as Wen-ching sang, his whole body was tremulous with feeling. Often he punctuated his recitation with a sigh, as the sentiments of the poem seemed to express so exactly his own personal experiences.

'Why do you sigh, my master?' Golden Orchid asked.

'You are too young to understand,' Wen-ching said. 'But look across the water, with its delicate ripples — isn't it much more beautiful now than only a few months ago? There are so few people, we can have all the heaven and earth completely to ourselves. Look at the flowers and the reeds—how they are dying together!'

Wen-ching paused. He was thinking of his own life and that of Madam Wen-ching. There was beauty in the thought that the lives of two people could be so closely identified, but he abhorred the idea of decline and eventual decay. He was still in the prime of his life, yet it was useless to deny that he was no longer young; and with youth standing by his side he seemed to be surer of himself: somehow it gave him new hope and promise. Still holding her by the hand, he turned to Golden Orchid and looked at her with a sense of inner satisfaction.

'It is time that we go back now,' he said.

Upon arriving home, the first thing Wen-ching did was to take down scrolls of painting hung there during the summer, which he started to replace with those that were more appropriate to the season. There was one painting by a great master of the Ming Dynasty of which he was especially fond, depicting almost exactly what he had seen only a short while before on the river. It showed two broken stalks of lotus with withered leaves, and by their side were a few dried-up reeds. The whole painting was done in a few firm strokes, but the effect was impressive, and this he now hung on the main wall of his study.

From the day when Golden Orchid became a sing-song girl, Lily knew that her future was entirely in her hands. She managed to arrange things so that Golden Orchid was always found in the company of Wen-ching. That did not mean that Lily was not afraid of other possibilities upsetting her plan. Golden Orchid's youth and attractiveness had drawn many men to her, and for purely matrimonial purposes there were younger men than Wen-ching who had perhaps a better claim to her hand. But Lily's mind was set on Wen-ching, for he was a *chuang yuan*, one of the highest scholars of the land, with prospects of the most exalted official appointments. If she could only bring them together, if only Golden Orchid could become Wen-ching's concubine, that was all that she aspired to accomplish. It would mean financial success for herself as well as, she thought, glory and honour for Golden Orchid. It was for this reason that she had turned her into a sing-song girl, in spite of vigorous opposition from her grandmother and mother. But she had succeeded; and as a sing-song girl Golden Orchid could only be a concubine. Lily had decided that Wen-ching was to be the man to take her as a concubine.

To that end Lily struck upon a very practicable idea. Unknown to anybody, she found comfortable quarters where, she thought, Wen-ching and Golden Orchid could meet at frequent intervals without being disturbed. In order not to arouse any suspicion, she saw to it that they entered this secret place separately. So, when all was arranged, Lily had a little talk with Golden Orchid one day and told her that, either before or after her professional visits every day, she must try to spend a few hours alone with Wen-ching.

On the day when Wen-ching was reciting poetry on the bank of the stream, Lily took special care to remind Golden Orchid that she was to return to the secret quarters after her usual professional calls, for the first crabs of the season were being sold on the market, and she

was to cook a few for Wen-ching and herself to enjoy together.
Crabs, chrysanthemums, poetry, and then some Shaoshing wine and
a lovely young maiden — the picture was perfect. Lily knew it was
the last word in a scholar's enjoyment of life.

When Golden Orchid arrived, Wen-ching was waiting for her.
Lily was busy in the kitchen preparing the various condiments and
sauces for the crabs. In the middle of the living-room was set a small
table of polished teakwood. In front of the two seats, at an angle to
each other, were placed two pairs of ivory chopsticks, with the usual
soy sauce, vinegar and ginger — all essential for the feast of crabs.
Lily began cooking them as soon as Golden Orchid came in.

'Master Shen, I am sure you will like these crabs,' said Lily.
There was good reason why her pock-marked face should be covered
with smiles.

She then lifted up a string of crabs tied one on top of the other.
'Here are six of them — three male and three female. Look how
large they are. And look how they foam and bubble at the mouth.
That means they are quite alive and in the best of condition.'

As Lily began untying the straw and throwing the crabs into the
boiling water, their greyish-green shells looked almost translucent
and their bodies fat and full.

'You know, Master Shen, this is about the best time of the year to
catch crabs.'

'Why?'

'When the chilly northern winds begin to blow, then the crabs in
the ponds and lakes start to think about storing food for the winter.
That is why they are so fat.'

'Ah, what men do for their selfish enjoyment!' commented Wen-
ching. 'Lily, you should let these crabs alone to pass the winter.
Three male and three female. Think of it!'

Lily smiled and thought that Master Shen was making fun of her.
'I bought these crabs only last night from a peasant who knows my
brother-in-law well. The hunchback, you know.'

'Who is he — this hunchback?'

'Oh, I thought you had met him. He is my sister Yang Mah's
husband.'

'And what does he do for a living?'

'Nothing special. He is a kind-hearted man. . . . The hunchback
told me that the peasant caught one hundred and fifty-six of these

crabs last night. You remember, Master Shen, last night was cold and chilly, and the poor man held the lantern so long that he almost fell into the water and got drowned.'

'In which case we wouldn't be eating these crabs today, would we?'

When the crabs were cooked and brought to the table, they were indeed a pleasant sight. Steaming in the large, jade-like celadon platter, the six carcasses were now transformed into flaming orange-red; and Golden Orchid and Wen-ching took off the round shells as though they were the lids of treasure boxes.

Lily had earlier brought in a pot of warm rice wine, which she had placed in front of Wen-ching's seat, and at the correct moment she quietly and discreetly withdrew from the room, leaving the two lovers completely alone under the most congenial conditions. It was obvious that Wen-ching had never been happier in his life; although at times he had qualms about his conduct, especially when he recalled to his mind the stern Confucian saying that 'never should a gentleman be more careful than when he is alone', he consoled himself by thinking that perhaps even the old sage himself would not be too scrupulous about moral rectitude if he found himself in so charming and seductive an environment.

'Tell me,' said Golden Orchid, 'what does Madam Wen-ching look like?'

'Oh, she is a wonderful woman,' replied Wen-ching. 'She is very accomplished. She is not only widely read in the classics, but she is also a very fine artist. She does the most exquisite water-colours of "mountain and water". And there is a poise and dignity about her which have taken her long years of discipline to develop.'

'But supposing,' continued Golden Orchid, 'she knew that you were spending your time like this with me, what would she say?' For once she had the courage to be coy and coquettish — as a woman to a man — in spite of the disparity in their ages. But she was alone with him and she loved him deeply.

'Now, silly girl, don't ask me such questions. She will not know, and nobody will know.'

So saying, Wen-ching emptied his cup of wine and asked Golden Orchid to refill it. Golden Orchid took a choice lump of meat from her crab, dipped it in vinegar, then in the soy sauce, and held it to Wen-ching's mouth.

He thanked her and, looking straight into her beautiful face as if in deep adoration, he gently stroked her hand and pressed it to his moist and warm face. He felt young and vigorous, and it was pleasant to have such feelings. Unconsciously and in spite of themselves their legs touched under the table; and the touch of the soft yet firm young flesh gave him a thrill of joy which he had not felt for many long years.

Wen-ching now laid down the chopsticks and, holding Golden Orchid's delicate left hand, he gently stroked it again and looked at it admiringly, as if it were the hand of a goddess. It was small, white and soft. The fingers tapered gently to a point. He turned the hand over and looked at the palm, which was pink and moist to the touch.

'You are indeed my goddess, the Goddess Kuan-yin,' said Wen-ching as he gave the hand another tender squeeze and then released it. 'I am waiting,' he continued, 'for some good news from Peking. When this appointment comes, the chances are that I shall have to leave this city, because it is going to be of more than local importance. But how can I leave you behind? I know I shall want to have you with me.'

'Wherever my master goes, if he wants me, I shall go with him,' said Golden Orchid. The words slipped out of their mouths almost in a casual way; they knew that they could no longer live apart from each other.

It took them more than three hours to finish that feast of crabs; and when it was over Wen-ching felt so drowsy that he fell asleep on the couch near by. Golden Orchid gently took off his shoes, covered him with a cotton blanket, and wiped his face as if she were tending a child. She felt happy doing so, and all the time she hummed a little tune to herself.

Before Golden Orchid had time to finish clearing the table, Lily came back and was anxious to know how she had enjoyed herself. The pock-marked woman had planned that the privacy, the crabs and the wine should produce an atmosphere in which the scholar would willingly give himself up to the charms of the young and lovely woman.

As Lily came in and saw Wen-ching fast asleep, she was sure that her scheme had worked out just as she had planned it. Taking Golden Orchid by the arm, she waited anxiously for further details. Her face was radiant with smiles, and she expected confirmation to come at once from the girl's lips. But there was no response; Golden

Orchid looked as matter-of-fact as if nothing had happened, and Lily had to come straight to the point.

'Show me the towel which I placed under the mattress of the couch,' Lily demanded.

'It is still there,' answered Golden Orchid.

'But do you mean to tell me that you never used it, that . . . that it is just as I put it there?'

'No, it was not used,' was the curt reply. 'We were so happy together,' continued Golden Orchid. 'The crabs were delicious, and he drank, and we talked. I am very happy, and I am sure he is happy. He was telling me that he was waiting for information of a new appointment from Peking which will take him away from this city, and we have decided that, when he goes, he will take me along with him. He will, in fact, take me wherever he goes. Now, aren't you glad to hear that?'

But Lily was not easily satisfied. She expected things to happen just as she had planned. She wanted quick results, for every moment of delay might bring complication and change. She had been sure that the crisis would arise, that a knot would be tied which could never again be untied, but it had failed to happen. And keen was her disappointment.

That night when Golden Orchid went home — later than she was supposed to return — neither her grandmother nor her mother said anything. Her grandmother had been reconciled to her grand-daughter's new mode of living, and her mother knew that even though she might express disapproval her words would have no effect.

6

A LARGE crowd had already assembled in the public squares in front of the city temple and the local magistrate's yamen. An announcement had been made that Soochow was given special recognition by the Imperial Court at Peking through a signal honour which had been bestowed on one of its illustrious inhabitants. The magistrate summoned officials to his office and gave them instructions that the news of the imperial honour be conveyed to the recipient in the usual ceremonious manner. One of his representatives, delegated to perform the task, was seated in a green sedan chair conveyed by four bearers, who were preceded and followed by a group of men carrying banners. In front of the impressive procession walked a man striking a gong, and the sharp sound gave a thrill and excitement to the populace which it had not known for a long time. For at least ten years or more such a thing had not happened to the city. Behind the official was a group of men carrying red-lacquered rectangular plaques on long poles, and on these plaques were characters inscribed in gold indicating that the honour was of the highest order.

Upon arrival at the residence of Wen-ching the procession stopped, and the magistrate's delegate, robed in the colourful official costume, entered, followed by a servant who carried a large lacquered box containing the sealed letters of appointment. Wen-ching was already in his formal living-room with Madam Wen-ching and Ping-mo. They were dressed appropriately for the occasion. Wen-ching was in his official regalia, topped with a red button on his hat, from which hung a peacock feather. Madam Wen-ching was in an embroidered red costume, while Ping-mo wore a blue gown over which was a black satin jacket. The ceremony didn't take long, but in the handing over of the letters of appointment, which were in the nature of an imperial command, both Wen-ching and the magistrate's representative had to kowtow as if His Majesty himself were present. The servants brought in tea after the ceremony; but as it was a special occasion, the teacups had lids on them and plates underneath. Upon the retirement of the delegate the magistrate himself arrived to offer the first official congratulations to the recipient of the honour.

All the time the magistrate was inside the house firecrackers were going off outside, and the crowd gathered thick and fast. Fathers and mothers, whether peasants or gentry, came from the far corners of the city, bringing with them their sons, on whom they impressed the importance of being diligent with their studies so that they too might pass the highest examinations and receive such official distinction. The highest offices of the State were open to every class of people; they depended on success in civil service examinations for which anybody with the requisite training and scholarship in the classics could compete. The sons of the gentry obviously had the advantage, by virtue of their wealth and greater opportunities for learning, but the sons of poorer families, from necessity, worked harder and thus often accomplished more satisfactory results.

When the ceremony was over, Wen-ching changed back into his everyday costume; but all through the afternoon he was busy receiving a stream of visitors who came to offer him felicitations. He had not known he had so many friends. People who ordinarily were scarcely acquaintances now claimed that, in some distant way, they were related to him, and many of them went so far as to ask that they be appointed to some minor position in his official entourage. Wen-ching had to be tactful in his replies, for to give any straightforward negative answer would be considered highly offensive. But fortunately for Wen-ching he had less difficulty than he anticipated, inasmuch as it soon became known that his appointment was as an ambassador to Germany and concurrently to Russia, and very few, if any, were willing to undertake such an arduous journey, much less to remain for many years among the 'barbarians' in some strange and far-off land.

Among the guests that afternoon was Hu-mou, who thought that he could have been in Wen-ching's place himself; his literary accomplishments were of no mean order, though he was not as lucky in the examinations. He was most affable when he saw Wen-ching. But in spite of his usually reticent habits, Hu-mou could become eloquent when the occasion demanded.

'Brother Wen-ching,' said Hu-mou, 'today is indeed a day of rejoicing, not only for your own exalted self, but also for your humble friend and for the city of Soochow to which both you and I belong.'

'It is most kind of you to say so.'

'In extending my congratulations to you it is not too much presumption, I hope, to ask that you take care of your less fortunate brothers when you continue to go up the official ladder.'

'On the contrary, Brother Hu-mou,' replied Wen-ching. 'I must ask for your help. You will in time be in Peking yourself — in the government. And as they say, no official abroad can be a success without friends inside the councils of the government itself.'

Hu-mou somehow didn't like the remark. The words seemed to imply persiflage or sarcasm, though neither was meant by Wen-ching's openness and good nature. Wen-ching noticed a faint tinge of uneasiness on his visitor's face and quickly tried to remedy the situation. But the attempt made matters worse.

'I mean, Brother Hu-mou,' continued Wen-ching, 'it is only a question of time before your official rank will be as high as that of any of us.'

'Let me thank you for your good wishes,' replied Hu-mou somewhat coldly. 'And may your career be a long and successful one!' A moment later Hu-mou stood up and, clasping his own hands, bade farewell to Wen-ching.

Wen-ching felt that things were not exactly as they should be, and resolved that he would return the courtesy of a visit as soon as possible.

The first thing Wen-ching did after the guests had left was to call Ping-mo and have a talk with him. The circumstances were similar to those of four months before when Ping-mo's mother summoned him to her study. The same little maid came to his room and said: 'The master asks me to come and call you, young master. He is in Tai-tai's study, where they are talking together.'

Ping-mo's mind went back to that unhappy day when his mother told him the tale of woe.

Has the issue come to a head? So soon after the arrival of such good tidings? Ping-mo wondered. He went upstairs with some feeling of uneasiness. But he found his father and mother in the best of moods, and spread across the teakwood table where his mother was in the habit of painting and doing her calligraphy he found the large yellow folder with whose contents he had already become familiar. But it was a joy nevertheless to pick it up again and read the inscriptions: 'Sacred Imperial Decree: His Benevolent and Ever Merciful Imperial Majesty hereby commands you to be appointed as His Ambassador Plenipotentiary to Germany and Russia, and commands you forthwith to proceed to the Capital to receive the credentials and commands from the Throne. Signed: Lord Yu Kung, President of the Tsungli Yamen.'

'I think, my son, that I cannot tarry too long here in the city,' Wen-ching began. 'I must leave for the north as soon as possible. I shall have to stay in Peking for a couple of months at the least, and then when I come south again I must leave for Europe from Shanghai without delay. But there are many arrangements to make before I leave here. Among these is one very important question which I want to settle. I am thinking of taking you to Europe so that you may see for yourself how these foreigners live in their own countries. What do you think?'

The suddenness of the proposition left Ping-mo almost speechless. He looked at his mother and wondered how she would feel when his father went abroad with that sing-song girl whom he so deeply loved. For Ping-mo was sure that he would marry her as his concubine, although that subject had not yet been brought up. Then he thought of his own interests and activities, of his commitments to carry on revolutionary work. Yet the temptation of going abroad was a strong one. For a long while he stood by the side of the table and did not utter a word.

'Well, why don't you say something, my son?' asked his father.

'I was thinking, Father, that it would be a wonderful thing to visit these foreign lands. But I believe . . . I believe it is best that I stay at home with mother to keep her company. I want to pursue my study of the classics. I must lose no time in sitting for the examinations.'

'That is a worthy thought,' interrupted Madam Wen-ching. 'But I want you to do what is best for you. As for me, I have much to keep me occupied. The appointment is only for three years, and I think that you can learn something from these foreigners.'

'But, Mother,' added Ping-mo, 'what is there really to learn from them? They have come to our land, and what have they done?'

'This is not the time to think about these thing,' interrupted Wen-ching.

'But I can't help it. They have forced opium down the throats of our people; and when we have refused to take it, they have sent their warships and guns to shoot and murder us. They take our land away and ask for indemnities. These foreigners have no moral values, and I hate them for what they have done. I think what we need is radical reforms within our own country, and when we are strong we shall teach them a few lessons, instead of having them teach us.'

'That is why we want you to go,' said his mother. 'You may learn something, and that knowledge can made us strong.'

Wen-ching was surprised that his son had such positive views. He wondered where he got them. Indeed, they were similar to his own, though he did not care to express them at this moment.

'My son,' he said, 'I am glad to know that you have such ideas. But let's not talk about them. You may be right that the ways of the foreigner are those of conquest, of brute force. It may be that they are inferior to us morally, even though their weapons may be sharper

and more powerful. If that is how you feel, I make no insistence
that you accompany me abroad. Perhaps it is better that you
continue in your studies.'

Ping-mo was glad that his father did not press the issue. So the decision was made. Madam Wen-ching secretly rejoiced that her son
was going to stay behind, but she didn't want to say so. She merely
looked blandly into the distance from her large window and saw the
outline of the hills on the horizon clear and distinct. She turned to
her favourite pot of orchids and stopped to inhale some of their
delicate fragrance.

That night, when Wen-ching retired, his mind was harassed by a
multitude of thoughts. He couldn't fall asleep. He was happy that
the appointment had come. It was a distinguished and honourable
appointment: it gave prestige to himself and to his ancestors. But he
had really expected something in the capital itself — some Cabinet
post, perhaps — where he knew he would use his abilities to better
advantage. A diplomatic appointment was the last thing in the
world that he had expected or wanted. He knew no foreign languages and was unfamiliar with the strange manners of the 'ocean
man'. To have to stay away from his own people for three years and
swallow unpalatable food among strange beings who could neither
understand him nor be understood by him — that surely would be a
trial. But the imperial command must be obeyed, and he consoled
himself with the thought that Lord Yu Kung of the Tsungli Yamen,
who was to be his immediate superior, was after all a good and reliable friend, and that if anything should go wrong he would not be
too exacting or censorious.

Then his thoughts wandered to the subject of Golden Orchid. It
was true that he loved her and that he had it in mind to marry her as
a concubine. But there were moments when he doubted whether
such a step would be wise. There were still practical considerations
which restrained him. Now, however, the thought of being alone
among strange people and having to carry on diplomatic life almost
persuaded him. She was, after all, young, intelligent and quick to
learn; and she would probably make a successful diplomatic hostess.
Much as he despised foreign ways, he was prepared to be reconciled
to them so long as he had to live among foreigners.

Tossing on his bed, Wen-ching made up his mind. The next day
he went quietly to the 'little house', where he summoned the schem-

ing Lily. She knew his appointment already and was eager to convey her congratulations to him. The moment she came into his presence she fell on her knees and cried out: 'Master, master, accept congratulations from a humble woman. I knew the great honour would soon come, and now it has come!'

Wen-ching had to help her to rise and tell her that such an attitude was unnecessary. He had asked her to come because he had something to talk over with her. 'I wish,' he went on, 'that you would see Golden Orchid's grandmother and mother on my behalf and convey to them my wish to take her as my concubine.'

Lily's heart jumped when she heard this. So at long last my labours are crowned with success, she thought.

'Her life as a professional sing-song girl is to end at once,' Wen-ching continued. 'But I want to know precisely the conditions under which they would consent to her marriage.'

'I will carry out these instructions this very moment. I am so very happy that my master decides to marry her, because she is such an intelligent girl . . . so beautiful . . . and so virtuous. She will be of great help to my master.'

'In the meantime,' said Wen-ching, 'you can ask Golden Orchid to come to me. Think over the matter carefully and let me know at the earliest opportunity.'

Lily was so overwhelmed with joy that she tripped and fell as she came out of the house. She ran home to tell her sister. They both rejoiced because, as go-betweens in this marriage, they would receive a handsome financial reward from Wen-ching. They were positive that the grandmother could be talked into the bargain, but they were concerned about Golden Orchid's mother. In any case, they thought, the grandmother would always have the last say.

When Golden Orchid arrived a couple of hours later, she was, so Wen-ching thought, the most beautiful girl he had ever seen. Coming into the room from the chilly air outside, her cheeks were radiant with colour. There was a freshness about her that somehow appealed strongly to a man whose life had been mostly that of a scholar and recluse. She was simply dressed and had nothing of that levity which was usually associated with the girls who were professional entertainers.

'Golden Orchid, my treasure,' said Wen-ching, 'it gives me such joy seeing you again. Come near me.'

Left entirely alone with an unprotected girl whose devotion to him was unquestioned from the first days of their contact, Wen-ching could have done anything he wanted with her; but he held himself in check and never went beyond fondling her lovely and delicate hands and looking at her with an affectionate smile. That did not, however, prevent his mind from wandering away into a realm of fancied delight. It would not be long now, he thought, before she would become his very own. Apart from the usual joy, he assured himself, physical intimacy with her would give him increased youth and vitality. For it was a widely accepted belief that immense creative forces were mysteriously released through the harmonization of the male or positive *yang* principle and the female or negative *yin* principle; and treatises had been written, couched not in scientific but in abstruse metaphysical language (with which a widely read scholar like Wen-ching was familiar), dealing with the peculiar subtleties of nature in this process of harmonization. The sign of the circle within which the two halves, divided by an S-shaped line, are locked in an eternal embrace, is a mystical symbol that has sunk deep into the Chinese consciousness, and one of the most potent reasons for Wen-ching's attachment to this girl of eighteen was his implicit faith in the efficacy of this so-called principle of nature.

'Golden Orchid,' continued Wen-ching, 'didn't I tell you that I would be leaving here very soon? It is going to be a long journey. You have no doubt heard about it, and I want you to come with me. I want to take you first to Peking, and then we shall come back and sail in a steamer for forty or fifty days to some far-off, strange land.'

'I shall go wherever my master goes, but what will grandmother and mother say?'

'This is being taken care of. I do not anticipate any trouble. You see, I shall need you very badly in my work. It is out of the question for Madam, my wife, to share all these hardships with me. Besides, it would be a torture to her to be living among strange people with strange manners. But you are young and can learn these foreign ways, and you can get along beautifully.'

Wen-ching had never been happier in his life: the appointment had come as an honour, but it also gave him the best excuse and a justification to do what he had always secretly desired to do.

When Golden Orchid went home that day, she was so overwhelmed by what had happened that she didn't know what to do.

She wanted to tell her mother what Wen-ching had said to her, but she was uneasy, because her mother had never expressed approval of her life as a professional sing-song girl. So she shut herself up in her own little room and, alternating between regret and joy — though most of the time joy triumphed — she imagined to herself all the changes her new life would bring.

She was to be married to a *chuang yuan*, just as the fortune-tellers had said, to a man with the highest literary accomplishments in the country and a high-ranking diplomatic official. She would be only a concubine: but had not Wen-ching told her that Madam Wen-ching would stay in China and that, for all practical purposes, she would go about, see new faces and make new friends, as only the wife of so distinguished a person could? She had heard that she might even be received in audience by Her Imperial Majesty, the Empress Dowager, when she went to Peking. Her head grew dizzy with these thoughts, for she did not forget that she was only a simple, un-schooled girl of a modest family. But Lily was going to talk to her grandmother and mother. What would they decide?

7

'I HAVE helped you before, and I shall stay away this time,' said the hunchback in all firmness, as he ordered another pot of Black Dragon tea in the crowded tea-house.

'But you have spoken to the two ladies before, and we thought that it would be best for you to go with us,' insisted the pock-faced Lily. 'Won't you do us another favour? I promise it will be posi-tively the last one.'

The hunchback's own wife, the hairdresser, and her sister Lily had been pleading for the past half-hour without any result. There was a look of irritation on the hunchback's face, for though he had for many years given himself up to the softening influences of Soochow, he retained the characteristics of a northerner: he was obstinate and unbending. When he was in such a mood, he would speak with the pronounced dialect of his birthplace.

'But, hunchback,' — even his own wife was in the habit of address-ing him by his physical deformity — 'what do you think we should say to the two ladies? Sister has worked so hard all these years for this very day, and she doesn't want to fail.'

Before the hunchback could answer, there broke out a commotion among a group of people some four or five tables down the room. The hunchback asked one of his friends to find out what it was all about. It seemed that, a few days before, some young students who were secretly carrying on revolutionary work within the inviolate confines of the foreign settlements at Shanghai had been apprehended and handed over to the Chinese authorities, who put some of them in prison and executed the rest. The people of Soochow had no interest in any kind of violence; they wanted to be left alone, but this piece of news upset them, for recently there had been recurrent rumours that discontented elements were to be found in many cities along the coast and even in the interior. They began to wonder if they were not harbouring those disturbers of the peace in their own midst. So the people in the tea-house grew nervous, and some of them even began to move away, as it was always safer not to be seen in a crowd.

The hunchback, however, went on talking to his friends and paid no attention, for he knew that not only students had secret organizations, but even among the farmers, both in the north and along the Big River, there were secret societies which wanted to overthrow the government and drive out the foreigners.

'I don't believe,' whispered the hunchback, 'that these youngsters should be so summarily dealt with. They should be left alone. Besides, I have been told that they are real patriots. They want to do something good for all of us.'

Everybody understood it was treason to speak like this, and there was silence when the hunchback finished speaking.

Lily and her sister had no knowledge of the implications of the conversation and insisted on coming back to the subject of Golden Orchid.

'What I feel is this,' said the hunchback's wife. 'I shall accompany my sister to see the two ladies, but you must come with us, because somehow it gives us more prestige to have a man with us.'

'Now you mustn't bother me,' replied the hunchback angrily. 'If you can persuade Master Shen Wen-ching to give a couple of thousand dollars to Golden Orchid's family and also agree to having a ceremony which has some resemblance to a proper marriage, then, I am sure, there will be no difficulties with the two ladies. The point is not to make it too obvious that Golden Orchid is going to be taken as a concubine.'

The two sisters looked at each other with satisfaction. Lily had thought along these lines; but she had not been sure. Now it seemed her views were confirmed by her brother-in-law. Agreed on the correct thing to do, the sisters willingly left the tea-house.

The next day they called upon Golden Orchid's mother and grandmother and found to their surprise that the negotiations presented no difficulty whatever. Golden Orchid's mother was not disposed to speak very much, except to say to her mother-in-law that, after all, her daughter belonged to the Fu family, and whatever an older person decided upon would have to be obeyed. Golden Orchid's mother had been broken-hearted when she first learned that her daughter had become a sing-song girl. From that to being a concubine was no great step, and there was no point in pitting herself against an elder who did not seem much disturbed by moral considerations.

When Lily saw Wen-ching again and reported to him the results of her talks with Golden Orchid's family, he rewarded Lily and her sister generously for their work and instructed them to make preparations for the marriage before he left for the north. He even agreed to sit for a private feast at the same table with Golden Orchid's grandmother and mother to show that they all belonged to the same family. He also saw to it that, in addition to money, some valuable jewellery, including a pearl-and-jade piece mounted in gold, was presented to Golden Orchid with the understanding that she was to leave it all behind on leaving the maternal roof.

But Wen-ching's problems were, of course, only half solved. For whether his plans were to succeed or not depended on Madam Wen-ching. Every other opinion carried little weight compared with that of his wife. Wen-ching knew his position clearly: he assured himself again that there was nothing wrong from the strictly legal point of view and that there would be no social disapprobation (hence no moral stigma), but all the same he wanted to be sure that it would not arouse antagonism from Ping-mo's mother. Nothing must affect their marriage of twenty-five years, a symbolic act consummating the long friendship between two illustrious and scholarly families. For generations the two families had dedicated themselves to the pursuit of learning, and considered the pursuit of wealth and honour beneath them. The marriage of Wen-ching to Quiet Virtue — for this was Madam Wen-ching's name — was arranged when they were still in their early teens.

Since then, Wen-ching had found nothing to regret. His wife was poised and cultivated and had many accomplishments: she was an artist and poet in her own right. And all through her married life her relations with her husband had been peaceful and proper. They respected each other, as the saying goes, 'as if they were guests' to each other. Wen-ching therefore had warm admiration for her; but there was just one little corner of his life which somehow she had been unable to touch. He felt that lacuna without being able to account for it rationally, and sometimes he hated himself for having that feeling. But there it was — a very real fact which he could not ignore. And now, almost in his fiftieth year, in spite of all the weight of his learning and scholarship, he felt that the coming into his life of this young girl of eighteen had mysteriously filled a void in his soul.

But how was he to bring up the subject before his wife? He considered this over and over again, and still he did not see how he could do it without making a fool of himself. He spent days without deciding: at times he would call in Ping-mo and merely ask him whether his mother was in a good mood. To bring up a difficult subject while she was not in the best of spirits would be to invite disaster. But sooner or later a frank and open discussion would have to take place, so one afternoon he casually stepped into Madam Wen-ching's study, where, as usual, she was engaged in her painting. Gradually Wen-ching led to the matter which was closest to his heart.

'I never thought,' Wen-ching began, 'that I should be appointed to such a post. They should know in Peking that diplomacy is not for men of my type. Why don't they choose a younger man who knows the ways of the "ocean man" and understands his language?'

'That may be true,' replied his wife, 'but I have no regrets, even though I shall miss you. Three years pass rapidly enough. And it is always good to be thought of highly, for don't you think that it is a mark of esteem that they give you such an appointment?'

'It all depends,' said Wen-ching. 'By being away in Europe I am likely to lose contact with the important people at the Court, and it is even possible that my personal enemies are trying to get rid of me in this way. But I shall be able to feel out the situation as soon as I arrive at Peking.'

'I really believe you do yourself an injustice by thinking so badly of your appointment.'

'No, I am not pessimistic. But you will agree that there is something in the point which I have raised. We are, after all, scholars, and there is no way in which we can fathom all the secrets in the tortuous minds of these politicians. But let's not talk about these unpleasant aspects. I was thinking that at least you may accompany me to the north and see our friends together again before I leave.'

When Wen-ching said this, he was in earnest. For although he had been thinking of taking Golden Orchid, he could leave her behind for the time being and start with her from Shanghai on the steamer bound for Europe. But Madam Wen-ching was sensitive. She had known all along that the sing-song girl had come into his life, and his remarks seemed almost like a mockery. She therefore came straight to the point.

'Are you sure that you really need me?' she asked.

'What makes you think that I am not sure?'

'Well, I should think that it would be best for you to take the sing-song girl with you from now on. I am not hurt. It is your privilege. Only I hope she will in no way be an obstacle to you.'

'Since you know all about it, Yu,' — the pet name by which Wen-ching was in the habit of addressing his wife — 'I want to talk it over with you —'

'I have planned it for you already,' his wife said quickly, without waiting for him to finish. 'You are no longer a young man, and you will be lonely in those strange lands. Since I am in no position to accompany you, it is acceptable to me that you take this girl.'

'That is very considerate of you, Yu.'

'And, besides,' continued Madam Wen-ching, 'you are going to say that she is young and intelligent enough to learn the ways of the foreigners and will be a help to you in your life as a diplomat.'

'Exactly. You have explained the matter very clearly. So I hope it is agreeable to you that I take her as a concubine.'

'You can do as you please, for other men have married concubines without so much as consulting their wives. But,' continued

Madam Wen-ching, 'there is one condition which I wish you to observe. I do not care to see her, much as I like to see a pretty girl myself. And when she comes back with you after your three-year period is over, then we shall see whether she will live under the same roof with me or not.'

Madam Wen-ching showed no signs of being irritated or upset, although it was only natural that her whole being should be against her husband in such a step. But taking a second woman was part of an institution and a recognized practice, and there was nothing that she could do about it. She was prepared to admit that there were difficulties which could not be solved unless Golden Orchid accompanied her husband.

Although the arrangement was not as perfect as Wen-ching desired, he could proceed with his plans and wait for further developments after he came back from his diplomatic mission.

On the day the ceremony took place, Madam Wen-ching absented herself. Ping-mo was present, though only as an interested observer, and not in any official capacity. Lily and her sister attended to all the details, and the day passed to the immense satisfaction of Golden Orchid and her grandmother. Golden Orchid was conveyed to Wen-ching's house in a green sedan chair, and not in a red one, as would be the case of a woman who was a bride and a real wife. There was no kowtowing before the seats of the ancestors' spirits, so technically Golden Orchid remained outside the Shen family circle. But it was a happy occasion all the same, and friends came from all parts of the city to offer congratulations. Towards evening there was feasting, and, as had previously been agreed upon, there was a private party in the home of Golden Orchid in which even her mother took part. It was customary for a woman on her marriage day to shed a few tears as an expression of sorrow at leaving her parents, and Golden Orchid performed that part of the ceremony with conviction. She was dressed in pink and not in a flaming red costume — another one of those distinctions which had to be observed between a real wife and a concubine.

But everybody admitted that Golden Orchid was a picture of beauty, and large crowds which had gathered to witness the ceremony openly admired her as one of the rarest beauties the city had ever given birth to. Though she had not been in professional life long, a number of her former colleagues were in the crowd, and there was not one of them who did not secretly nurse the hope that, if luck was with her, she would end her career in the same glorious way.

There was only one dissenting voice, and that came from the hunchback. 'I have seen many such marriages, but concubines are not wives, and how many of them have borne fruit? We shall wait and see.'

And when his wife and Lily came back in the evening from the ceremony he said:

'I had to help you when you were in difficulty with Golden Orchid's people. But what happened today was your work. I have always thought that it was not the proper thing to do. How many of these concubines have ended their lives happily? You do wrong to Golden Orchid's mother, who is such a good woman. And you do wrong to Madam Wen-ching.'

8

THE Southern Long Road is a straight and impressive street laid out to run accurately east and west. It is one of Peking's principal thoroughfares and is part of a magnificent plan which was conceived as far back as the thirteenth century. The streets in the other cities of China may be narrow, crooked and incommodious; but Peking was then the capital of the mightiest empire of the world, and the architects wanted to construct a city which was not only the last word in comfort, as comfort was known in those days, but also unequalled in the splendour of its palaces, parks, and avenues.

> So twice five miles of fertile ground
> With walls and towers were girdled round:
> And there were gardens bright with sinuous rills
> Where blossom'd many an incense-bearing tree;
> And here were forests ancient as the hills.
> Enfolding sunny spots of greenery.

Thus did Coleridge describe this unique city purely out of his romantic imagination, not knowing that the realities surpassed anything he could visualize.

For Wen-ching the sights of this metropolis were familiar enough. He was happy to be back after an absence of some three years. But on this previous visit he had been an official of only local importance — only a *taotai* — while now he was the direct personal representative of the throne, and somehow the city produced a different impression upon him. Perhaps his more exalted position was responsible for this difference, or perhaps the fact that he had married such a young beauty. He could not tell, but at all events he was up very early on the third morning of his arrival after a tiring sea voyage. It was to have been a honeymoon trip, but the roughness of the sea and the shabbiness of the accommodations had spoiled things. However, two days rest completely restored him, and he was now ready to pay visits to his official friends.

'Golden Orchid, my treasure, I have a full day ahead of me,' said Wen-ching to his concubine shortly after the breakfast table was cleared. Modern hotels were then not in existence in Peking, and new arrivals went to what were known as *hwei kuan*, or hostels established for fellow provincials. Coming as they did from Soochow, they went to the Soochow *hwei kuan* so that they could meet people from the same city, speak their Soochow dialect, and indulge the habits most familiar to them. Wen-ching could have stayed with one of his friends, if he had been alone or with Madam Wen-ching, but to be accompanied by a concubine made matters different. They were comfortable, all the same; even glad to be left alone. The morning was chilly, and their room was heated with charcoal. When breakfast was over, Wen-ching put on his official robes and stepped into a waiting sedan chair.

There was the usual hustle and noise among the crowds on both sides of Hatamen Street. The sun shone bright and beautiful, and the air was clear and crisp. There were camels with bells round their necks which tinkled with every step they made, and the drivers were still clad in heavy furs, as if they had just arrived from the cold Mongolian steppes. Hawkers selling their wares sang at the tops of their voices, and the knife-and-scissors grinder was blowing his trumpet.

It gave joy and satisfaction to Wen-ching to look at this animated scene from his sedan chair. How different, he said to himself, were these people of the north, but there was the same readiness to laugh and to be amused. Slowly his sedan chair turned out of the Southern Long Road into the Street of Enduring Peace, where there was much less bustle because it was a residential street, and an impressive one. In the distance he saw magnificent arches in all the splendour of their colours, so arranged that they broke the monotony of the long, straight roads, allowing the passer-by to pause and linger over their beauty. The street was flanked on both sides by spreading shade trees. He was approaching the residence of that great personage Lord Yu Kung, who was first on the list of officials to whom he was to pay respect during this visit to the capital. The residence was in a lane, or *hutung*, off the main road. There was hardly anything about it to attract attention, except that the retaining wall, which was of a dull grey colour, was unusually long; and there were two red-lacquered doors with highly polished heavy brass handles, flanked by a pair of solid stone lions.

As Wen-ching was ushered in and passed through numerous corridors and courtyards in which grew century-old cedars and pines, he noticed that the exterior gave no indication of what was within. He was now in the midst of indescribable beauty and elegance. The servant finally conducted him into the spacious main living-room, and even Wen-ching, who had seen so much of the city, admitted that it was a sight never to be forgotten. While he was admiring the exquisite carvings of sandalwood, the rare pieces of porcelain and the priceless paintings and scrolls, His Lordship came in. His features were finely chiselled; he stood straight and gaunt; he was altogether a man of great dignity, and his thick, drooping moustache was most becoming to a man of so exalted a position. The two men stood facing each other for a moment and then paid mutual respect by bowing and holding their clasped hands to their foreheads.

'Brother Wen-ching, I am happy that you are here. It was a long journey from the south, and I hope you were not too uncomfortable.'

'Truly, Your Lordship, it was no pleasure. I kept myself to my cabin almost the entire time.'

'But I hope you were not seasick.'

'I might have done better,' Wen-ching said, smiling. 'Only at rare moments could I have a good look at the sea. It was as black as pitch, and I thought the sea everywhere was blue!'

'Please be seated and make yourself comfortable.'

When a servant had brought in tea and two water-pipes, Lord Yu Kung resumed the conversation.

'There are many problems, Brother Wen-ching, on which I desire your advice and the help of your experience and learning.'

'I dare not be presumptuous, but may I place my humble self

entirely at Your Lordship's disposal? First of all I must express
my deep appreciation and gratitude for the honour which Your
Lordship has conferred upon me.'

'Your own learning and experience, Brother Wen-ching, are freely
acknowledged, and the appointment does not do justice to what you
deserve. His Majesty is fortunate that he can be represented abroad
by so distinguished a scholar.'

'It is most gracious of Your Lordship to say so. Rather, I must
consider myself as being unusually fortunate in having so able and
enlightened a superior who will always guide me in the right
direction.'

'I feel immense responsibility in being placed in charge of the
Tsungli Yamen and having to do with the foreign relations of so
many countries. I would want to discuss with you some of the great
questions with which our country is faced in the presence of some of
my colleagues. You will meet them this evening at the banquet
which I am giving in your honour. Many of them, I am sure, are
your personal friends. But now —'

'Before I meet them,' interrupted Wen-ching, 'I wish to receive
instructions from Your Lordship on many important points.'

'Precisely, Brother Wen-ching,' His Lordship went on: 'It is no
secret to you that the country is going through perhaps one of the
most critical and dangerous periods in its long and glorious history.
You see, since our defeat by those islanders — the Japanese — the
way is now open for all the predatory Western countries to plunder
and destroy us. Before that war they were still under the illusion that
a mighty empire like ours must have some power. That illusion no
longer exists, and they are ready to carve us up.'

Wen-ching gave a deep and painful sigh. 'For centuries,' he said,
'we have devoted our energy to the arts of peace. We have always
believed in promoting refinement and culture. We believe in
government by virtue, in the moral conduct of nations. We have
denounced force and physical power in any shape and form.'

'But unfortunately this means little to countries such as England
or France or Germany. They only talk with their guns and
battleships. Reason is powerless before them.'

'I think they are still barbarians,' said Wen-ching. 'All they know
is the law of the jungle. How different are the pure, exalted and
ethical views of Confucius on the relations of men.'

As a Confucian scholar Wen-ching was always impressed by the teachings of the classics and heartily deprecated the cruel and merciless conduct which he associated with the European powers.

'I know how you feel on the subject,' said Lord Yu Kung, 'and that is the reason His Majesty, with the approval of Her Majesty the Empress Dowager, has seen fit to send you to Europe as his diplomatic envoy to study conditions there. Your reports to my office will be given all the care they deserve, and I shall see to it that they are brought to the attention of His Majesty.'

'Thank you. I shall try to be observant.'

'But there is another thing I wish to speak with you about. You have no doubt noticed that, as a result of the many catastrophes and national disasters, there is a growing wave of discontent in the country. From one point of view this is a healthy sign, because it shows that the national soul is still vibrant with energy; but from another point of view this discontent is embarrassing to the government.'

'I realize,' replied Wen-ching, 'that there is a good deal of irresponsible talk about revolution, about overthrowing the existing government. This must be rigidly suppressed. I have been told that the movement has spread rapidly among the young people, among students who should be devoting their time to the study of the classics.'

'That is quite correct. But there is another movement which you in the south may not have heard much about, for it is largely confined to the northern provinces. Now, you might think that the people here are slow-witted and do not care about what is going on in the country. But even the peasants nurse deep hatred against those foreigners, who have taken away their land and trampled upon them mercilessly. The peasants are especially bitter against our own countrymen who willingly allow themselves to become the tools of these foreigners. They say these people follow the religion of their foreign masters and take advantage of their favoured position.'

'Yes, I know who they are. They are even more mean and despicable than the foreigners,' commented Wen-ching.

'Precisely, and in a way I do not blame those ignorant people for being so incensed against them,' Lord Yu Kung went on. 'But the movement is very widespread. They call themselves the Order of Righteous Harmony.'

'I have occasionally heard about this in the south also. We don't know what the next few years will bring us, but let us pray that the Dynasty will continue to live in peace and quietness.'

'We must, however, learn the secrets of the power of these foreign nations, and I am glad that you have been chosen for this most important mission.'

'I am only sorry that my ability is not equal to the enormous task, but I shall do the best I can, and with Your Lordship's assistance and advice I am sure I shall not fail in my duties.'

'Yes, we have grave responsibilities. These ocean people have treated us with cruelty and savagery. They have forced opium down the throats of our people, they have taken away our wealth, they have taken away our land, they have even tried to control our government. They kick us, despise us and submit us to the worst indignities and humiliations, and now even the Japanese, who derive everything in the way of a civilized life from us, follow the example of those ocean people and wish to dominate us. Has a mighty empire with the most wonderful culture in the world come to such a pass?'

Here Lord Yu Kung paused to calm himself. He secretly sympathized with the members of the Order of Righteous Harmony, popularly known as the Boxers. But, he remarked to himself, these are, after all, simple and ignorant people, and their methods will bring even further disaster.

He turned to Wen-ching again and felt confident, knowing that he was speaking to a friend of long standing, to a patriot and intellectual who must feel as he felt.

'Brother Wen-ching,' he continued, 'we must be patient, and we must learn. It is not enough to be morally superior to these people. They have battleships which we have not: their guns are more deadly and kill more quickly. These we shall have to learn; so the other day I brought before the Cabinet council a measure to send as many of our young men as possible to study abroad.'

Wen-ching was deeply moved by the fierce and impassioned words of his superior, and resolved at that moment that when he returned to Soochow he would persuade his only son to go to Europe with him. When the interview was over, Wen-ching felt more strongly than ever the importance of his approaching mission. The two men rose austerely from their seats, and as a mark of courtesy Lord Yu Kung accompanied his guest to the front gate of the house. Slowly they walked through the corridors and courtyards where the last remnants of the winter plum blossoms were still in bloom and looked at the ancient cedars and pines. As they approached the gate, the servant opened it. Bowing solemnly to His Lordship, Wen-ching stepped into his waiting sedan-chair and went back to the hostel to join Golden Orchid.

He was surprised to find her in the company of another young woman who looked sad and was almost in tears. Wen-ching thought that he recognized her, but he could not recall exactly where he had seen her before. She looked like someone from the south.

'Who is she?' asked Wen-ching.

'Don't you remember her? She was one of the girls who was on the flower-boat with me when I sang the "Lament of Meng Chiang Nu". She lives in this hostel. I was so surprised to learn that she is here in Peking. She was telling me a very sad story about herself. Please go on, Hai-ming. I want my master to hear your story.'

Hai-ming rose to give a deep, respectful bow to Wen-ching and then sat down again. 'I was just saying' — she continued with a slightly bitter smile — 'how my life and that of Golden Orchid have become so different in so short a time. Here she is married to one of the most distinguished men in the land, and I am still a pitiful girl with no future. And only a few months ago there was nothing to distinguish us.'

'Don't talk like that,' said Golden Orchid impatiently. 'Tell my master what you were just going to tell me.'

'I was telling her,' continued Hai-ming, 'that shortly after that day on the flower-boat I decided to come north to join a sing-song house here in Peking. I am older than Golden Orchid, as you can see, and I have been in the entertaining profession for many years without achieving any security for my future. Shortly after I arrived here I unfortunately met a military man who told me that he belonged to a secret society and was getting ready to do some fighting. He had lots of money and wanted to live with me. I didn't like the way he approached me, although I knew that he loved me. I tried to dodge him all the time and gave excuses that I was not well. But I felt that I could not hold out indefinitely and, knowing that my mother needed money in Soochow, I took a thousand dollars he gave me and sent them to my mother.'

'Then the man took her away to Mukden,' added Golden Orchid.

C

'This is the part of the story I want you to hear. It shows what a plucky girl she is.'

'Yes, he took me to Mukden, where he lives,' continued Hai-ming. 'It was a long, long journey. First we went by boat, then we rode in an uncomfortable train. I thought all was over for me. I didn't know where I was going. When we arrived, this man got off the train before me, and I saw him approach a big, fat, ugly woman, probably his wife, and three or four children. In the meantime, his bodyguard, who was instructed to take care of me, took me to an inn just outside the city, where I was kept for over a month. I was frightened, not only by what he did to me, but by what I saw and heard around me. It must have been a robber's den, and I never thought I would come out alive. Sometimes the inn would be full of big, tall, frightful-looking people who spoke with a crooked tongue, but I could understand most of what they said. They had mysterious ceremonies in which they swore eternal loyalty to each other, and they burned incense as if asking the gods to be their witnesses.'

Is it possible that this Order of Righteous Harmony works as far north as that? Wen-ching wondered.

'They said that the country was being devastated and despoiled by the foreign devils and that one day they would rise and take revenge. Nobody seemed to interfere with them. But what frightened me most were the long spears and the big knives which they hid in every corner of the inn. They said also that they had brothers all over the country. One day they went away on a mission, leaving me alone in the care of my guard. By that time they thought that I had almost become one of them; but we are from the south — we are gentle people. How could I ever become accustomed to all that horror? I treated the guard very nicely. But then after a few hot drinks he came into my room and fell asleep on my bed. That gave me an opportunity which I had long been waiting for: I went to the railway station as quickly as my feet could carry me and took the first train that left. I didn't know where it was going, but I knew I was out of danger. So here I am back in Peking after that terrible experience.'

'And now what are you planning to do?' asked Wen-ching. 'Go back to Soochow?'

'Yes, I must go back to my mother. . . . But I have been here long enough. Thank you for your kindness. I think I should leave now.' Hai-ming rose to say goodbye.

'I will see what I can do for you,' said Wen-ching.

'Thank you, and good fortune to both of you.'

After Hai-ming left, Wen-ching sat in his chair wrapped in thought. 'Golden Orchid,' he said at last, 'I am afraid we are in for trouble from now on.'

'But why?'

'I don't mean personal trouble. The country is seething with discontent as a result of the frightful things which the ocean men have brought on us. Some day there is going to be an explosion. Many of the authorities not only refuse to suppress this discontent, they even help it to spread. I had a long talk with Lord Yu Kung today, and I realize more than ever the responsibilities of my diplomatic mission to Europe.'

But Golden Orchid was blissfully ignorant of what was going on. How could she be otherwise? She was the beautiful and lovely concubine of a distinguished person. She was in the capital of an empire that was once a mighty and glorious one, and she had come to see all its wonders and to enjoy herself to the utmost.

9

ONE month in Peking was too short for Golden Orchid. She had hardly any rest. When she was not visiting one of the hundreds of restaurants for lunch or dinner to sample different kinds of cooking from the various provinces which could all be found in this metropolis, she was shopping in the many fairs and bazaars outside the Cheinmen Gate. One day she would pick up a few choice pieces of jade, the next, some silk or rich furs. She wanted all of them. Wen-ching denied her nothing within his means. He thought that, if she was to play the part of a diplomatic hostess abroad, she might as well do it in an adequate manner, befitting the representative of a great empire.

But as he still had many duties to perform before leaving for the south again — friends to call upon, contacts to be made, information to be obtained — he could not afford the time to gratify all the wishes of his concubine.

When Lord Yu Kung gave the dinner in his honour, Wen-ching

left Golden Orchid with the womenfolk of his many friends. They
were only too glad to extend the courtesy. But this was an exception,
for at most of the farewell dinner-parties the two of them appeared
together. Never had Golden Orchid tasted such a variety of rich
foods. She liked the cooking from Shantung best of all. But there
was cooking from Hunan, from Szechuan, from Fukien, from An-
hwei — all of which tasted different; and for light lunches and teas
there was nothing, she thought, to equal the delicacy of food from
her own city of Soochow.

Golden Orchid had been brought up on the cooking of her mother
and grandmother, which was good as far as it went, but the new
gastronomic experiences in Peking gave her such a fresh source of enjoyment that she asked Wen-ching to look for a cook whom they
might take to Europe.

Wen-ching, however, had thought about that long before she had,
not so much for her sake as for his own. Golden Orchid was young
and could perhaps accustom herself to the strange food of strange
lands, but it was impossible for him, he was sure, to swallow from
his plate so gross, so crude and so coarse a thing as a big slab of meat
— sometimes even dripping with blood! As for vegetables, what
could be more tasteless and uninviting, he thought, than plain boiled
potatoes? And fancy eating this food with knives at the table, when
the cutting should have been done in the kitchen! The very thought
of having to eat such meals for three solid years abroad was enough
to make Wen-ching shudder. He had tasted foreign food in Shanghai on more than one occasion, and he thought he knew what he was
talking about. To take a cook was therefore a necessity, and he also
asked his friends to help him find a valet.

Many young men, nephews or cousins of these friends, had been
recommended to him as members of his entourage. The same thing
had happened at Soochow when the appointment came. To accept
all would be impossible; to accept some and reject others would
imply discrimination and would be considered unfriendly. The
matter had been giving him considerable uneasiness. Fortunately
for him, practically all the secretaries and attachés had been appointed directly by the Tsungli Yamen, but there were still one or
two vacancies which had to be filled.

Since his conversation with Lord Yu Kung he realized more than
ever before that he must pay attention to the military organization

of the European powers. He had heard that His Lordship had a son with military inclinations. He was a friend of his own son Ping-mo, and they had graduated from the same academy. Is it possible that His Lordship wants him to go with me? he wondered.

The question bothered him. He tried to recall whether in the course of the interview any hint had been thrown at him which he had foolishly ignored. He thought hard for a long time. Then it suddenly dawned on him that His Lordship had said something about sending young people to study abroad.

Surely that must have been a hint, Wen-ching said to himself. What could be better than to have with him the son of his immediate superior, who was in addition a trusted friend and one of the most powerful officials at the imperial Court?

The next day an unexpected thing happened. As if there had been some mental communication, a young man by the name of Yung-kai came to pay his respects to 'Uncle Shen'.

Wen-ching recognized the name at once, and was pleased to see the young man; the visit confirmed his evaluation of His Lordship's wishes. Surely the son must have called with the knowledge and consent of the father.

'Yung-kai,' welcomed Wen-ching, 'so glad to see you. I understand you know my son Ping-mo well.'

'Yes, Uncle Shen, we are good friends. But he is a scholar, and I am a good-for-nothing.'

'Now, now, Yung-kai, I wouldn't say that. You know we need all kinds of young men. In fact, I am looking for one like you, with all your accomplishments.' Wen-ching noted with approval Yung-kai's fine physique.

'Perhaps you would like to go to Europe with me — to Germany.'

'Thank you, Uncle Shen, for suggesting this. It is an honour, but I don't know if I am qualified.'

When the interview was over, Wen-ching had reason to feel satisfied. Yung-kai, like many other young men, was inspired by deep patriotic feelings to do something for his country. That was why he had appeared in Nanking in the early days of the summer to take part in the meeting of the secret society. But in time he realized that he was unequal to the task, and decided that if he left his comrades he would have to go as far away from them as possible. So he came back to Peking to be near his father and, hearing of Wen-ching's appointment to Europe, thought it was an opportunity not to be missed. Nor was he too scrupulous to make use of paternal influence to enter official life, where, he thought, he really belonged. He called on Wen-ching on his own initiative, without his father's knowledge, and Wen-ching's offer made him supremely happy.

When Yung-kai's appointment was later confirmed, he often went to see Wen-ching and to offer his services. It was thus that he came to make the acquaintance of Golden Orchid.

On one occasion when Yung-kai came to see the ambassador-designate he was told by the house servant that the master was not in. He was on the point of leaving, but on second thoughts asked if the young Tai-tai was in. He had brought a gift, ostensibly from his father Lord Yu Kung; this was a good enough excuse to see the attractive concubine of whom he had already caught a few glimpses.

It was not customary for a man to see the mistress of a house when the master was away, and Yung-kai had enough sense to know this. But the desire to be alone with the famous Golden Orchid, even for a brief moment, was so strong that Yung-kai could not resist it. He had a feeling of guilt in having made the request to see her, and that feeling was heightened by the fact that, as concubine of the ambassador-designate, she was to be his immediate superior. But then, he thought, trying to justify his action, there was nothing wrong in requesting an audience simply as a member of the embassy staff. After all, he was the son of the all-powerful Governor of Chihli and President of the Tsungli Yamen — and Ping-mo's friend to boot. Thus emboldened, he was ushered into the presence of Golden Orchid, who received him courteously.

Yung-kai addressed her as Madam Ambassador. It was the first time so dignified a title had been conferred upon her, and she felt uneasy. Yung-kai looked at her, and she felt the impact of that meaningful gaze.

'I . . . I have brought a small gift with me from my father,' Yung-kai stammered. Whereupon he left a small package on the table when the servant brought in some tea. The gift was not from his father, but from himself. He had had it with him for many days, looking for an occasion to present it to her. Golden Orchid did not open the package, as was the custom, but Yung-kai knew that she would be happy when she saw it. It was a beautiful piece of uniformly green translucent jade carved as a life-size butterfly, which,

Yung-kai thought, would be very effective at state and diplomatic functions. At the ends of the antennae were two little rubies.

'These three years in Europe are going to be an exciting period,' Yung-kai went on. 'My father is very anxious that I accompany you and the ambassador, and I hope that I shall learn much from Germany, where, so they say, military science is well developed. It's a pity that Ping-mo, I understand, is not coming with us. Or do you think that he can still be persuaded to join us?'

'I hope Ping-mo will come, but as yet I don't know him well enough to urge him. We shall see when we go back to the south.'

After exchanging a few more pleasant remarks, Yung-kai took his leave. He was pleased that he had been introduced to Golden Orchid in such favourable circumstances. He might even have made a good impression on her, he thought.

Half an hour later Wen-ching returned to the hostel. Golden Orchid told him that Yung-kai had called to pay his respects and to bring a gift from the President. Wen-ching was embarrassed that this great Court favourite, his immediate superior, should show such friendliness. He did not feel that he could accept the gift, and yet to decline it would be an act of impropriety. He didn't know what to do.

'Golden Orchid, my treasure, I am glad you are enjoying yourself in Peking,' said Wen-ching after a short pause. 'We shall be abroad for three years, but one doesn't know what is going to happen here while we are away. I am a little worried. There seems to be a good deal of nervousness around. For instance, even while I was looking for a cook, I heard all sorts of incredible things.'

'But did you find one?' Golden Orchid was anxious to know.

'Yes, I did. He will be here later in the day to pay his respects to you. He is a big sturdy man from one of the villages in the neighbourhood. He is a northerner, and I thought it unusual that he should be glad to go with us. These people are usually unwilling to go far, let alone cross the ocean. He has been employed by foreigners these many years and knows how to speak a few words of English, which is convenient. I can't make out what kind of work he has been doing, but he tells me that he has been beyond the Great Wall many times, out in the Mongolian desert, with these foreigners.'

'What kind of work can this be, I wonder?' asked Golden Orchid.

'I don't know. The foreigners are such strange people. They are so different from us. He tells me that they went out there to dig in the sand.' Wen-ching could not help laughing as he spoke.

Then he continued: 'Yes, that was what Lao Chuang told me. Just digging, digging in the sand of the desert and carrying away quantities of huge bones and other kinds of rubbish. And that reminds me of another strange thing I heard only the other day. A friend of mine happened to be passing the diplomatic quarter one day and was attracted by the sight of a few foreigners, dressed in very scanty clothing, running up and down and trying to catch a ball. So he came down from his sedan chair, looked with pity on these foolish ocean men, and asked why they should tire themselves for apparently no good reason.* And if they really did want to catch that ball, why couldn't they hire a few coolies to do it for them?' Wen-ching chuckled to himself again.

Golden Orchid was, however, still thinking of the digging. 'Digging for bones!' she exclaimed in horror. Her eyes grew so big that they looked as if they were coming out of their sockets. 'They are really devils then! What else can they be if they look for bones? Why then should we take with us a man who has been employed by these devils?'

Wen-ching had a vague notion that the digging was connected with some kind of knowledge and became more relaxed.

'I suppose there is no harm,' he said after a brief pause. 'It is so difficult to find a man who is willing to go to Europe for three long years. They all believe, for some reason, that they will not be able to come back alive. We should be thankful that Lao Chuang agrees to go with us. He looks like a good and honest enough person. But what I want to say is that the villagers don't like him because he has been with the foreigners. And I don't blame them for that. For many years now, as I told you before, these foreigners have been taking away the land from these peasants. You know what that means. Land which they have inherited for untold generations being ruthlessly grabbed from them! No wonder they are up in arms.'

'But why must the foreigners do this?'

'They say they need land for their churches, and there is nothing to prevent them from getting what they want. The peasants then become angry, and so they appeal to the local magistrates; but these

* The foreign 'devils' were, of course, playing a game of tennis.

officials are afraid and are always on the side of the foreigners. That is why these poor people hate all the foreigners and any Chinese who associate with them, though as a class they are gentle and reasonable enough.'

'But you frighten me,' said Golden Orchid in utter bewilderment. 'Why should we have anything to do with these foreigners? And why should we even go to their countries? How can we live among them? Aren't we looking for trouble ourselves?'

'No, no, my precious,' he explained. 'You don't understand. You need not be frightened. You will learn later. It would take me too long to explain to you now. But I was surprised when Lao Chuang told me that even young women in the country are joining mysterious bands of people to drive out the foreigners. These young women are known as the "red lanterns". They are dressed in red and carry a flaming red kerchief, and it is said that when they throw these kerchiefs they become lanterns, and wherever these lanterns go, there are big fires.'

'That I doubt. I don't believe what this Lao Chuang says,' answered Golden Orchid.

'That, precious, is at least what I heard,' continued Wen-ching. 'And what's more, Lao Chuang tells me that each of these young women carries a sharp knife on her back which flies out of its own accord and can cut off the head of an enemy. She doesn't have to move. Her spirit comes out of her body to direct the operation. Also she is not afraid of any weapons of war. But in order to be really effective, these young women have to be virgins. They must be absolutely without blemish.'

It is difficult to know whether Wen-ching himself believed any of these fantastic stories but he related them with a good deal of amusement to himself. While he was still talking, the servant came in to announce that an old country couple had arrived and asked to see the master and the mistress.

'Why, this is Lao Chuang and his wife,' said Wen-ching, and he commanded that they be shown in.

Lao Chuang was indeed a towering figure, fully more than a head taller than his wife. They wore almost identical cotton-padded blouses. The upper part of Lao Chuang's blouse was a little below his waist, while that of his wife was somewhat below the knees. They both wore trousers, but the man's were tied with ribbons around his

ankles, while those of the woman were free. The man was in black
and the woman in grey.

As the couple came into the room, they both curtsied in the manner of all Peking servants, bending their knees almost as far as the
floor while they swung their right arms across their bodies. They
stood during their interview with their new master and the new
young mistress.

'Lao Chuang tells me, Golden Orchid,' Wen-ching began, 'that
he is an excellent cook.'

'So he is,' snapped back the wife, Chuang Mah, without any modesty. 'He has been cooking for the foreigners these many years and
taking care of them in all kinds of jobs. But I have told him that he
must cook in our way when he comes into your service, Master.
These ocean men eat very coarse food, and their meat is served in
large pieces which are sometimes not even well cooked. They don't
know any better, of course.'

'All right — enough,' growled Lao Chuang, and Chuang Mah at
once stopped talking. 'I know, Master — and Tai-tai,' continued
Lao Chuang, turning now to Golden Orchid, 'that although we are
going far away to the land of these foreigners, I shall cook in our
Shantung style, and for that we shall have to take many kinds of
food which we shall not find in these strange countries.'

So saying, Lao Chuang presented a long list of dried foods he
would need. He even asked whether these foreign lands had fish,
fowl and pork.

Wen-ching could not answer, though the question appeared
absurd, but he knew that the foreigners were beef-eaters and he
could not eat any beef or mutton. But, anyway, Lao Chuang said,
he would need soy sauce, ginger, dried abalone, mushrooms, bamboo
shoots, dried shrimps, lotus seeds and various other condiments, of
which Golden Orchid was busy making mental notes, as enough had
to be procured to last three long years.

But while Lao Chuang was going over the list of things to
be ordered, Chuang Mah for no apparent reason began to sob
bitterly.

'My master and mistress,' she said, 'I almost refused to have my
husband leave me. When he goes, who is going to take care of our
two children and till the fields? Besides, I know that he will never
come back to me alive. But when he dies, will you promise me, my

master and mistress, that his bones will be brought back to be buried in our farm land?'

Having said this, Chuang Mah felt much better; the matter had been in her mind for some time. Wen-ching and Golden Orchid did not know how to reply, as they were not sure about their own return, but they gave full promise that Chuang Mah's request would be observed.

Whereupon Lao Chuang and his wife asked permission to leave. On their way home Chuang Mah was in a state of reasonable happiness and contentment, but not her husband. 'Why must you bring me bad luck?' he growled. 'Why must you talk about my death? We all die soon enough.'

'But who knows what is going to happen to you?' retorted his wife. 'Am I wrong to want to be sure that your old bones will come back to me?'

10

IT was a fine clear day when Wen-ching and Golden Orchid woke up the next morning. Golden Orchid was radiant with joy, her eyes sparkled with brilliance, and Wen-ching began reciting some of the early Tang poems. Clearly they were the happiest couple alive. The cool and comfortable nights of early spring in Peking, the peace and quiet of the courtyard of the rambling Soochow hostel, were the setting for a period of conjugal bliss which Wen-ching had thought was no longer possible at his age. But there they were, as happy as any newly wedded young man and woman. Golden Orchid opened the tall windows to let some fresh air and sunshine into the room. The noise drove some ten or fifteen crows from a willow tree on which they were perched, and they flew away cawing.

'How strange!' said Golden Orchid, turning inside to her lord and husband. 'The crows in the north and south look alike, but what a difference in the noise they make!' Soon a magpie came into view, and Golden Orchid jumped with joy like any child, for that bird is a symbol of happiness. It looked and sang exactly the same as a magpie in Soochow.

'Come, come here and eat,' called Wen-ching as the servant

brought in some steaming *pao-tse* for their breakfast. Wen-ching ate quite a few of these delicious dumplings, with gulps of the strong Black Dragon tea which he loved so much.

'And now, my master,' said Golden Orchid as the table was cleared, 'what are our plans on this lovely day?'

She spoke out of a full and happy heart, out of sheer physical exuberance and vitality. There is no reason, she thought, why my life for a long time to come should not be as full of sunshine as this day. She felt a strong urge to go out and see the city — the magnificent palaces, the spacious parks with their ancient trees, and the temples where she might thank the Goddess of Mercy, Kuan-yin, for the blessings which had been conferred on her.

She wondered if all her happiness was true or whether she was dreaming. Then she heard the distant tinkling of the bells on the camels as they were driven into Peking from the north-west, from Kalgan perhaps or some other parts of Mongolia, laden with furs and other articles which she wanted to see and purchase.

'My precious Orchid,' said Wen-ching, 'we have only a few days to remain in Peking, and then we must be on our way to those foreign parts on the huge ocean liner. I still have duties to attend to, friends to see, instructions to give and receive, and finally there is this dinner given in our honour by the German ambassador this evening.'

'Am I going to this dinner?'

'Yes, you are, my precious. I was told that he took quite an exceptional step in including you among the guests. Acting in conformity with our own customs, the diplomatic people usually invite men only, but this German ambassador has an eye for beautiful women. Somehow he had learned that you are young and attractive and that you are here with me. I don't blame him for wanting to see you. Nor do I mind his feeling like this. And since for the next three years there will be so many of these functions, I thought you should go, so I have accepted the invitation on your behalf. Besides, there is no harm in showing you off, is there?' Wen-ching smiled and tickled her under the chin.

Golden Orchid felt a little hesitant about having to face so many foreigners for the first time in her life. She felt happier when she found out that Yung-kai, the young military attaché — that was his official title — was to be at the dinner also. She would have someone to turn to besides her own husband, who could not, she thought, be of much help to her in such unfamiliar surroundings. It would be fun in any case to see how the foreigners ate and behaved, and she decided to be brave and to learn as much of foreign ways as possible.

Before Wen-ching and Golden Orchid were ready to leave the hostel, the servant came in with a letter which bore the Soochow postmark. It was from Madam Wen-ching; and as he read, Wen-ching's face fell. He raised his head and looked at Golden Orchid. He did not want to spoil her happiness, but he felt that she should know what was going on. It was best not to conceal anything from her.

During the past few days at Peking, while he was going round to the various offices and meeting the high officials of the Court, Wen-ching had noticed a strange uneasiness among them. Lord Yu Kung had not shown quite the affability and warmth he had expected. His Lordship was tense and spoke to him of the gravity of the situation. There were rumours of impending disasters, of secret societies and of agitations among the people. Only the other day, he was told, a leading scholar, Kang Yu-wei by name, had made a petition to the throne asking that he be received in audience so that he could deliver a petition in person to the Emperor urging drastic reforms. That was normally not done. It was considered by every one the height of impudence, especially as the scholar's official position did not qualify him for so high a privilege.

Wen-ching thought, however, that all this agitation for reform on the one hand and for violence on the other was confined, as Lord Yu Kung had told him, largely to the north and to the immediate vicinity of the capital. But he was wrong. The letter which he had just received from Madam Wen-ching showed that the disturbance was much more widespread, and that it had affected the south as much as the north. What was still worse, he now found that even his own household was not entirely immune from it; according to Madam Wen-ching their son Ping-mo was in some strange way involved.

Wen-ching read the letter to Golden Orchid:

Since you left for the north, my life has been, as usual, peaceful and quiet. I find my happiness in my painting. In fact, I have just completed a painting of the Tiger Hill as viewed from my study which is better than any I have done. It may even adorn your office abroad. Our daughter and son-in-law came two days ago to see this new creation of mine. It was an enjoyable occasion, especially as Ping-mo was also at home. But little did I suspect that it would turn out to be an occasion for ruffled feelings and even for some bitterness. Ping-mo and our son-in-law got into some heated argument over the conditions in the country. I don't know what has come over Ping-mo. As you know, he has been a mild and sweet boy, but lately he has been easily excited, and I think he was in the wrong to lose his temper in a heated argument with his brother-in-law. He used some violent words, and he was openly sympathetic towards those who are clamouring for drastic reforms and even for the overthrow of the existing government. These are dangerous utterances, especially for a young man who is the son of a scholarly family on the high road to official honour and favours.

Wen-ching could not read any further. He was upset. How could he avert the calamity which was bound to come if his son persisted in his present mood?

Golden Orchid immediately suggested a sensible course of action. 'Why shouldn't we take him with us to Europe?'

'Yes, I think that is what we shall have to do.'

'Besides, he and Yung-kai are good friends, and they will not be lonely.'

'I know. There is nothing better. But you remember, as I told you, he wants to stay behind for the civil service examinations.'

'That may be just an excuse.'

'In any case, I shall have to write to Madam Wen-ching to find out.'

But Wen-ching gave up the idea of writing, realizing that he and Golden Orchid would be returning to the south in a few days. He would see the family before the letter could reach Soochow.

II

SINCE the previous day, when he had taken the gift to Golden Orchid, Yung-kai had passed an uneasy night. He shut himself up in his own quarters and lay down on his couch surrounded by the richness of his room — the thick carpets in yellows and blues, the priceless porcelains of the Ming and Kang Hsi periods, and the teakwood furniture finished in dark and radiant mahogany. It was an atmosphere of supreme tranquillity, but within him, deep down in his soul, there was a restlessness which he had never known before. His blood seemed to flow warm in his veins, and the image of Golden Orchid floated continuously before his mind's eye. He saw the apparition in a hundred different forms. Sometimes she smiled at him, with a smile so indescribably lovely that it sent spasms of joy through his young heart. At other times he saw her dressed for an official diplomatic function, with the jade butterfly, his own gift to her, comfortably set on her raven-black hair and the ruby tips gently dangling in the air. He saw her surrounded by admirers from different lands struggling to have a word with her, and he even imagined her gracefully dancing with young men from foreign countries.

Yung-kai was now disturbed beyond measure. He tried to reason with himself. But he knew that his emotions had got the better of him and his rational being could lead him to no secure anchor. There was a strong urge to find a flimsy excuse to visit her again, but he restrained himself.

What would the ambassador say? he asked himself.

Yesterday there was still a good enough reason to call on the girl of his heart, but today — today, if he went, would it not arouse the suspicion of his superior?

After all, for three long years our lot is going to be cast together. Would it not be better, even as a matter of policy, to refrain from any rashness? The arguments went back and forth in his dizzy mind.

But clear as his thoughts might be, the temptation was irresistibly strong. He had lived a life of luxury and plenty. He belonged to the family of a rich and powerful official and had tasted the joys of female companionship earlier than most boys of his age. Then, associating with Ping-mo and the other youths had also aroused in him a strong patriotic fervour to which at one time he had decided to dedicate his life. He had now given that up — he thought wisely. But his present life was nevertheless a confession that, in the crossroads of his soul where currents and undercurrents of varying force and strength met and contended for mastery, the battle was won by heredity, by environment, by a life of ease and softness as against the sudden sparks of nobility which shone for a short while and then were no more.

Today Yung-kai knew that if he let himself be carried away by the strong emotions that were churning within him, the consequences would not be happy. How could he face his superior, the ambassador under whom he would have to work for the next three years? What account could he give of himself to his father, who was a friend of long standing of the ambassador's? These were serious warnings, and yet . . . and yet almost automatically he put on his best attire, ordered the servants to have the sedan chair ready, and in a short while was on his way to visit Golden Orchid.

When he stood outside her room, Yung-kai did not know how he would be received. He did not know what to say. He was relieved that Wen-ching immediately put him at ease.

'I am so sorry, Yung-kai,' said Wen-ching, 'that I wasn't at home when you called yesterday.' He stopped for a while to look at the intelligent face of this son of a great official upon whom, Wen-ching thought, he would have to depend so much for a successful career. What a happy coincidence that he was also a friend of Ping-mo's.

'How is your distinguished father?' continued Wen-ching.

'He is very busy, but he is quite all right, thank you, Uncle Shen,' replied Yung-kai.

And then, thinking about their life abroad together, Wen-ching expressed his joy that Yung-kai was to be the military attaché. He thought of his physical prowess, his ability to ride well, his eagerness to learn the foreign ways, his modern outlook. He then thought of his own son Ping-mo. How he wished that he, too, would come.

Golden Orchid did not utter a word. She was absorbed in the conversation, but now and then she cast a glance at the young man. She noticed his thick, fuzzy eyebrows, his finely chiselled features, and she found him handsome.

'Yung-kai,' continued Wen-ching after the formalities were over, 'you have come at the right moment. I have duties to attend to this afternoon, and in the evening we are all going to the dinner of the German ambassador.'

'Yes, Uncle Shen, I am getting ready for the occasion.'

'Knowing the capital as you do so well, how would you like to take Madam —' Wen-ching felt his face grow warm as the word slipped out of his mouth for the first time. Golden Orchid was, after all, his concubine, and the word somehow jarred on the ear. Yet for many years to come her relation to Yung-kai was to be that of the ambassador's 'wife' to a member of his staff. 'How would you like to take her to do some shopping outside the Chienmen Gate?'

Yung-kai was speechless. The unexpected, he thought, had arrived. He was, of course, overjoyed and gladly accepted the offer.

Soon a chair was ordered, and Golden Orchid went into the adjoining room to put on outdoor clothes.

Some modern ways had been introduced in China, but as yet no young man could be seen in the street alone with a young lady. It was understood that a maid would accompany them, and so three chairs left the hostel and began wending their way through the narrow, crooked streets.

But Yung-kai, in his infatuation, had everything planned out to the last detail. His chair was at the front, followed by that of Golden Orchid. The maid was in the last chair. They had been on the way for some twenty minutes when the first sedan chair gave signal for a brief pause. Yung-kai stepped out, walked to the rear and threw a bag of coins to the maid and her chair-bearers. Without a word being uttered, the meaning was clear. Yung-kai and Golden Orchid went on again, finally stopping in the courtyard of a restaurant among the trees just outside the walls of Pai Hai, or the Northern Lake.

When Golden Orchid stepped out of the sedan chair, she realized that the maid was no longer with them. She soon found herself inside an agreeable enclosure, with huge oleanders blooming in each of the corners and a fragrant jasmine climbing a trellis.

'I thought,' said Yung-kai, coming up to her, 'that we should have some lunch before we proceed with our shopping. You must be hungry by now.'

Golden Orchid was indeed hungry, but to have lunch with a young man who was to be a member of her husband's diplomatic mission — and alone with him — was the last thing that she thought could happen. However, before she could straighten matters out in her mind, she had entered the restaurant with Yung-kai. Two rows of waiters curtsied and bowed, and the head waiter, a man in his fifties with a bald head and shining face, led them into an inner compartment.

There was no need for any previous arrangement. Yung-kai had patronized this exclusive restaurant so long that the waiters knew his every whim. It was here that he had brought many of the beauties of Peking for intimate meals. The house knew the kind of food and delicacies that he was in the habit of ordering and the kind of Shaoshing wine which went with the food.

One by one the waiters discreetly withdrew, until Golden Orchid found herself completely alone with Yung-kai in a small and exquisitely decorated room. For a moment there was not a word between them. Golden Orchid sat there placidly and perfectly at ease, while Yung-kai started pouring out the tea which had been brought in.

Then, in all courtesy, Yung-kai said: 'You are the wife of my ambassador, and as such I must address you as madam —'

Before he could finish, Golden Orchid knew what was coming and replied, 'Why so formal? After all, we are not yet abroad. Besides, you are the son of Lord Yu Kung, who is my husband's superior.' And she smiled.

Yung-kai felt supremely happy, noticed once more her dazzling-white, pearly teeth while he was still in the midst of admiring her quick, perceptive intelligence, and said: 'Then may I simply call you Golden Orchid?' He wanted to go on talking, but somehow he felt tongue-tied, and his mind wandered away to the numerous other occasions when he had sat there with other girls with whom he made jokes and had a hilarious time. But today it was altogether different. He was in a serious mood and felt as if he had many confessions to make to a girl he scarcely knew. All his usual flippancy was gone. He closed his eyes, buried his face in his hands and was utterly without words. He was still in that posture when the waiter brought in a dish of fresh-water shrimps and bits of pork cooked with tender baby corn scarcely two inches long. Other food came, and still there was hardly any conversation.

'Why don't you eat, Yung-kai?' said Golden Orchid to break the silence. 'The food is getting cold.'

'I was hungry, but I am hungry no longer. I feel like talking,' said Yung-kai, 'and yet I don't know where to begin.'

Then, as Golden Orchid served the food, Yung-kai started to unravel the story of his life, and his hopes and ambitions.

'Very few people know,' he began, 'that I am half Manchu and half Chinese. My father is a full-blooded Manchu, but he had become so Chinese, even before he married a Chinese lady, my mother, that no one will take him for anything but a Chinese. Most of the

Manchus have become Chinese, anyway. We look alike, we speak alike, we are dressed alike, and there is nothing to tell that I am less Chinese than you are. . . .'

Yung-kai paused to see how Golden Orchid would react to this. She was listening but seemed to be amused at the subject. She even smiled faintly because Yung-kai talked as if he were a foreigner or a stranger.

But Yung-kai continued: 'My mother died when I was quite young, and my father has always been too busy to give me much personal attention. I have enjoyed all the luxury and softness of a protected and pampered life. Nothing has been denied me, and yet I am unhappy. As I grew older I was made to take part in outdoor life, the only thing in which the Manchus still show more indulgence than the Chinese. That was how I learned to ride so well, to enjoy having horses and to develop a strong physique.'

'This is very good,' interrupted Golden Orchid. 'I want to learn how to ride when I am in Europe.'

'But deep in my soul I have yearned for something noble, and the desire is so strong that no amount of easy conquests has ever been able to weaken it. And when I heard about the disasters which have befallen the country, the defeats at the hand of foreign powers and the huge indemnities and concessions, I began to look around and tried to find the reasons, and I said to myself that it is all because the officials and the so-called leaders of our society are so incompetent and corrupt. I know well the kind of life they lead, and that was why I was willing to join the secret societies. Yes, I even wanted to help in overthrowing the present regime. That was how I met Ping-mo.'

Golden Orchid showed great surprise. Now that she knew Ping-mo had been doing something which, she was sure, his parents would not approve or had any knowledge of, the significance of that letter from Madam Wen-ching became clear.

12

LUNCH over, Golden Orchid thought she should proceed with the original purpose of their excursion — shopping. She realized that Yung-kai was in a train of thought which might be interesting to listen to, but all the same she said: 'Don't you think that we should be going?'

Yung-kai had scarcely begun to talk and replied that, since they were near one of the loveliest spots in all Peking, they should look at it. Pai Hai, or the Northern Lake, is a part of the imperial park situated in the heart of the city. It was not then open to the public, being strictly a private preserve for the exclusive enjoyment of the Emperor and those who were very close to the Court. As the son of Lord Yu Kung, Yung-kai was familiar with the extensive lake and its surrounding areas with their ancient cedars, pines and cypresses. On the shores of the lake were pavilions decorated in all the colours of the rainbow and covered with the imperial yellow and cobalt-blue tiles. There were secluded walks whose quietness had not been disturbed for centuries, and Yung-kai thought that not only would Golden Orchid enjoy the beauty of the enclosure, but it would be an ideal spot for him to unburden some of his thoughts and emotions. He suggested that they visit the lake, and to his surprise Golden Orchid agreed. He gave a sign to the head waiter, who went ahead, and after going through what seemed to be rather tortuous ways the man unlocked a door which opened into as lovely a place as Golden Orchid had ever set eyes on.

Yung-kai led the way, and his heart palpitated with joy that he should find himself completely alone, on this hallowed ground, with the girl whom he so deeply and secretly adored. He ran a few yards in front of Golden Orchid, turned and gazed admiringly at her. He then came very close to her and heard her gently complain, in her sweet voice, that he was walking too fast for her. At last the inevitable happened. He held her soft lily-white hand, and walked with her through the lane over which spread the gigantic arms of the ancient pines, and beneath their feet was a carpet of needles which had accumulated for many long years. The path led to the Five Dragon pavilions which looked from a distance as if they were floating on the tranquil water of the lake, they appeared so light and ethereal.

Yung-kai motioned to Golden Orchid to be seated on a stone bench inside one of the pavilions. In the centre was a stone slab with a chess-board. They laid their hands on it, and touched each other. Yung-kai began pouring out his inmost thoughts and feelings.

'I cannot believe,' he began, 'that there is another spot in the entire world where there is so much poetry.' And as he spoke the birds twittered among the branches of the drooping willows, whose branches bent over to kiss the water.

'I hope,' Yung-kai continued, 'that you are as happy as I am.'

'Yes, Yung-kai,' replied Golden Orchid softly. 'I, unlike you, was born a poor child in a poor family, and to think that I am enjoying all the wonders that only the Son of Heaven can enjoy. This is beyond anything I dreamed. And my husband tells me that it is possible that, before I leave for the south again, I may even have an audience with the Emperor or with the Empress Dowager. I am the happiest woman in the world.'

'But, Golden Orchid,' pursued Yung-kai, 'there is something I have been wanting to tell you. It is so sad. I want to be good and to do good and noble things. But I shall always remain alone. I shall never get married.'

'How can you say such things, Yung-kai?' Golden Orchid protested. 'You are young, you are handsome, and you are the son of a rich and high-born family. Surely you can choose a wife from hundreds of lovely young ladies.'

'Yes, that is true. But still I shall remain single.' And as he said those words he firmly grasped both of Golden Orchid's hands and looked at her meaningfully.

Golden Orchid did not know how to take this. She had had a premonition that some such crisis might arise, but now that he had said those words she felt deeply embarrassed. It was useless to console him. She liked him, liked him immensely in fact, and if he had met her before her life was committed to Wen-ching and had asked her to marry him, there would have been no question in her mind. Happier than anyone else, she thought, would have been my grandmother. That old lady — she smiled to herself — would have grabbed Yung-kai faster than the frog catches the fly, though, bless her soul, she is happy enough as it is. But what could be done now? She was Wen-ching's concubine, and she loved him dearly.

'No, no, Yung-kai,' said Golden Orchid after a pause, withdrawing her hands. 'I shall wait to see you married to the most wonderful girl, perhaps to one of the princesses of the Court. In fact, I may even see you married before you leave for Europe. Yes, why not? And then we should all be happy together in those far-off countries.'

But Yung-kai thought she was merely teasing him, that she was not serious. For a long while not a word passed between them. He sat there with his arms resting on the cold stone slab, gazing blankly at the chessboard in front of him. Then Golden Orchid gently placed her hand on his. There was prolonged silence. Only the birds continued to flit about. In the distance, on the other side of the lake, the white Dagoba towered into the sky. And on the water's edge, appearing as if stretching along the base of that Tibetan piece of architecture, was the graceful curve of the white bridge flanked by its marble balustrades. All was peace and silence: for both Golden Orchid and Yung-kai it was a meaningful silence.

Somehow there is a way in which human emotions can be conveyed — sometimes more adequately — without so much as uttering one word. As Golden Orchid again withdrew her hand, she had convinced both Yung-kai and herself that across their hearts there was now a bridge as firm and unyielding as the one before their eyes. Then they stood up.

'It is getting late. We had better go back,' said Golden Orchid.

13

WHEN Golden Orchid was taken back to the hostel by Yung-kai — they did not forget to pick up the maid — they found that Wen-ching had been there for some time. He had spent the afternoon in a last visit to the Tsungli Yamen, receiving stray bits of information on what was going on in the different government offices and in the Court. It was first intimated to him that he could have an audience with the Emperor or with the Empress Dowager, to whom he would have been proud to present Golden Orchid; but the chief eunuch, an ugly monster who enjoyed too much power, relayed word that the audience had been cancelled without making any effort to explain the reason. Wen-ching was not greatly upset by the report, though it would have been a coveted honour to have had the audience. He did, however, wonder why the matter was dropped at the last moment when arrangements had virtually been made.

For people with acute political sensibilities it would have been natural to show some tangible mark of courtesy to the chief eunuch, however reprehensible he might be. Not infrequently gifts of great value were given to him to lubricate the way to the throne itself. But Wen-ching, scholar that he was and thinking that high office had been conferred on him on the strength of his own ability rather than on any aptitude for currying political favours, refused even to make a farewell call on Chief Eunuch Lee. That, he surmised correctly, was the main reason why the audience fell through. The realization, however, came too late, for the mistake — a grievous mistake — had been made.

Wen-ching was therefore not in an especially good mood when Golden Orchid returned, and he told her about the cancelling of the audience.

It was the first time Wen-ching had been unhappy in the company of his beloved concubine. For her part, Golden Orchid was afraid that he might have also learned what had happened between herself and Yung-kai, and her heart beat loud and hard.

But that is a silly thought, she consoled herself. How could he know what happened to me this afternoon?

She said to Wen-ching: 'It is not really so very important to have the audience, is it?'

'Well, no, my precious. But I want to start everything right. To be denied an audience with the throne is in itself not good. But it is the circumstances of the denial that worry me. I have been careless, and from now on we shall have to be cautious.'

Golden Orchid felt relieved that Wen-ching's concern was not over her excursion with Yung-kai but over something entirely different. Then, adjusting herself to the new situation, she said: 'I am not really interested in the audience. Besides, we are hurrying back to the south.'

'All right. We will forget it and get ready for the dinner,' concluded Wen-ching.

While they made elaborate preparations for the occasion, Wen-ching threw out a few remarks that were not entirely intelligible to Golden Orchid. She did, however, hear him say distinctly: 'I am afraid I have offended the chief eunuch, and that is bad.'

By ten o'clock the dinner in honour of His Excellency Shen Wen-ching, the ambassador-designate to the Court of the Kaiser and concurrently to that of the Czar of all Russia, was over.

Yung-kai, dressed in the formal garb of a Manchu soldier, was present in the capacity of a junior military attaché and was seated some distance from the guest of honour and Golden Orchid. His mind kept wandering back to his afternoon idyll with Golden Orchid, and throughout the entire dinner he imagined himself alone with her again. He tried to carry on the conversation around him, but it was all blurred and disjointed. He had enough sense of humour to see that he was playing a ridiculous role. What he should be doing, he thought, was plucking a guitar under a willow tree while gentle breezes blew. But instead of that he was in the midst of a diplomatic function dressed like a soldier.

His sense of the ludicrous was heightened when he saw his superior having trouble with the table utensils. 'These infernal knives and forks!' he could almost hear his ambassador swearing to himself. 'Why can't these foreigners eat in our civilized way and use chopsticks, as we have been doing for thousands of years?' The ambassador was in the habit of referring to China's ancient history, whenever he found himself in a tight corner, as if it had magical power. He was confused as to which hand should do what to cut his food. But this confusion had one important result: Wen-ching had entirely forgotten about the audience and the chief eunuch.

It was still well before midnight when Yung-kai went home, but almost everybody in his father's huge residence was already in bed. Only a few servants were up, to attend to the wishes of the young master. They helped him to doff his military uniform and brought his slippers and night clothes. With the last request for a pot of tea, Yung-kai dismissed them and found himself alone in his room.

As a young man who had lost his mother early in life and whose father had so much to attend to both in his public and domestic life, Yung-kai was accustomed to being alone in his private apartments. He was systematic and orderly in his habits, even inclined to be finicky. But his rooms were furnished in good taste. There were beautiful embroideries and priceless antiques, most of which had come as presents to his father in the course of his official duties. To-night, sitting alone in his rooms, he felt that the experience was something different from anything he had had before. His mind was tormented by a thousand thoughts. For better or for worse, he knew that fate had cast his lot with that of Golden Orchid. There was no doubt that he was in love with her.

But what am I going to do? That was the question which continued to haunt him, and it gave him no peace. He was going to Europe. If either he or Golden Orchid were to stay behind, the problem would be much simpler. But as it is, he thought, we are both going — to the same embassy! For many years our lives will be thrown together, and something is bound to happen. He almost believed that it was the work of destiny.

14

THOUGH mental images have neither form nor substance, they have nevertheless a reality so firm and irresistible as to affect and modify one's mode of living. Into the peaceful and happy life of Golden Orchid had now come an unfamiliar factor which she could neither understand nor properly evaluate. Was it possible that she had found a new source of delight? If she had, she certainly had not sought it out. She had all that a girl of eighteen, with humble origins, could ever hope for. She now had wealth, honour and position, all generously bestowed upon her by the love of a kind and protective husband.

Very often when Wen-ching was away on the rounds of government offices and she was alone, Golden Orchid would throw herself on her bed, her head on her clasped hands, and allow herself to be smothered, as it were, by this altogether unexpected and new-found bliss. Is it all true? she would smilingly say to herself, that this has come to pass? The stars have willed that I be wedded to a *chuang yuan*, the most distinguished scholar of the realm. So I am! In name I am but a concubine, but for all practical purposes I am his fully wedded wife. And as her thoughts ran down the corridors of the future, Golden Orchid would often fall into a deep and comfortable slumber.

But somehow, after that lunch with Yung-kai in the quiet surroundings along the shores of the Northern Lake, things were no longer the same. Into the tranquil and placid water of her life she felt that a pebble had been cast, and disturbing ripples seemed to extend in ever-widening circles. She began to be haunted by the image of Yung-kai, by those dark, brooding eyes, and by the way he looked at her when they held hands across the stone slab. She saw

Yung-kai even in her dreams, and she became frightened by the thought that one day she might betray herself in her sleep and expose the hidden corners of her soul to the full gaze of her unsuspecting husband. What then?

The more frightened she was, the more she wanted to forget herself by finding things to do. But for a young woman in a strange city, far away from home and relatives, there was not much to do. She could not go out to call on friends, for she had practically none in Peking. Nor could she ask her husband to stay with her in the hostel; he was too busy. Now and then she would ask Hai-ming to come to see her, or ask for Lao Chuang and his wife to be brought in, just to reassure them that life abroad would not be as unpleasant as they might think, and that in any case three years would pass soon enough. But Chuang Mah continued to have her doubts, and on one occasion she said that the old turnip, meaning her husband, was in the habit of drinking too much, and then he would forget himself and do funny things.

'He might begin to be troublesome with people,' Chuang Mah confessed with indiscretion. 'It's all very well when I am with him,' she continued, 'but I hate to think what might happen when I am not.'

The little woman looked at her tall husband, who was standing, red in the face, by her side, not uttering a word, though he looked sheepish enough.

'You don't have to worry, Chuang Mah,' Golden Orchid said, trying to pacify her. 'There will be no danger on that score, for he will not be allowed to drink, in the first place. Even if he does without our knowledge, they tell me that these foreign wines have gas and bubbles in them which make people light-hearted and gay, and I want to keep him in a happy mood.'

Most of the time Golden Orchid tried hard to keep her mind away from Yung-kai by calling in a multitude of merchants who had wares and jewels to display and sell. From early morning till late in the afternoon there would be costly silks and porcelains and jades spread before her admiring eyes. Not that she had the means to buy many of them, though the merchants believed she had. Considering what little knowledge she possessed of these objects, it was a marvel that she showed such good taste and had an instinct for the correct things.

Golden Orchid had now been in Peking for nearly two months. She was anxious to leave for the south again to see her mother and grandmother before sailing for Europe, so one day when Wen-ching came back to say that at last he had done all he wanted to do, she was happy, and in a few days they were on their way back to Shanghai and then Soochow.

The sea voyage to Shanghai was on the whole calm, and with Hai-ming to keep her company — for she had asked her to come — Golden Orchid found that time flew quickly enough. As soon as they arrived at Shanghai, they ordered a houseboat to take them back to Soochow. That required an extra day, but it was the most delightful part of the journey, as there was no noise of engines, no nauseating smell of oil and no swarming and jabbering humanity reeking of garlic (which the people in the north are especially fond of). Instead, all was smoothness and calm. Golden Orchid felt soothed by the familiar rivers and creeks of her childhood and by the sound of her own soft-spoken Soochow dialect among the boatmen.

Wasn't it here, she thought, that I first met my *chuang-yuan* husband?

And as the memory of the early days swam back into her mind, she glanced at the people around her and smiled with satisfaction. It had been exciting, during those two months in the north, to meet new people and see new sights. Too exciting perhaps — the image of Yung-kai with his thick eyebrows and his earnest look came back to her. She shook her head as if to chase that image away, although she knew that they would soon see each other again.

For the moment at least she was luxuriating in quiet as she floated down the tranquil water towards her childhood home. She felt snug and comfortable on the soft cushions which Lao Chuang had so carefully arranged for her. She looked at her husband, who was smoking his long bamboo pipe in perfect contentment and reading a book which he held rolled up in his hand. There was Hai-ming occasionally humming to herself, and there was the towering figure of Lao Chuang.

Towards evening, as the boat neared Soochow, Golden Orchid could see a large crowd assembled on the jetty. The local magistrate, as was to be expected, was there with a large retinue. Firecrackers went off as the party landed. But Golden Orchid showed no interest in the official welcome. She stood on tiptoe until she saw Lily, the pock-marked woman, with her sister Yang Mah and the hunchback, and, above all, her own mother, whom she embraced with tears of joy. Madam Wen-ching was not there, and Golden Orchid was glad, for if she had been present Golden Orchid would not have known how to greet her. But Ping-mo was there to meet his father, and she was happy to see him.

Before Wen-ching stepped into one of the waiting sedan chairs, Ping-mo whispered in his ear: 'Mother wants me to let you know that for the time before you leave for Europe, Aunt Golden Orchid will stay with us.'

Wen-ching was pleased, though he had expected as much, and merely nodded.

It had taken Madam Wen-ching a long time to come to the decision. All along she had refused to be compromised on her position, but Ping-mo managed to convince her that, for the peace and quiet of the family and for the good of his father on the eve of a long absence, she should at least accept the fact that Golden Orchid had become his concubine. What had been done could not be undone. There had been long arguments between mother and son, until finally she had said: 'Well, let her come and stay with us till their departure for Europe.'

Ping-mo was happy with the result, though his mother made one condition. 'There is one thing I cannot agree to,' she had said. 'I cannot officially receive her as a concubine, and my relation to her will be as the mistress of the house to a guest and stranger.'

So when Golden Orchid came into the house, the ceremony normally required of a concubine who was being introduced for the first time to the mistress of the house was omitted. But in spite of this arrangement, which pleased neither Wen-ching nor Golden Orchid, she behaved for the next month with tact and propriety. Every morning she presented herself to Madam Wen-ching in her study, took her a cup of green tea, and conveyed a few words of salutation and respect. The relationship was always formally correct, and there was nothing to arouse ill-feeling.

Golden Orchid's relationship with Ping-mo was much less formal. There was natural understanding between the two young people, whose difference in age was a mere two years, and they had many occasions to see and talk to each other openly. So one day, when the opportunity presented itself, Golden Orchid said to Ping-mo: 'Ping-mo, I was thinking that your father will certainly need your services abroad. Has it occurred to you that it would be best for you to go to Europe with us?'

Ping-mo was taken aback by this sudden and straightforward question, but he parried it. 'I know I should go,' he said, 'but the examinations will be coming along, and I should not miss them. I have given the matter very careful consideration, and I had decided to remain where I am. Besides, mother will be so lonely.'

There was a slight pause. Golden Orchid approached the subject from a different angle.

'Has your father spoken to you about it?'

'Yes, he has. Only last night we had a long discussion. I think I have convinced him that it is best for me to stay behind.'

'Then you know your mother is also worried. She wrote to your father when we were in Peking.'

'Let us not talk about it. Mother was simply misinformed. You know I want to go abroad if I can, but if I decide to stay, there must be good reasons.'

Golden Orchid looked at Ping-mo with keen disappointment.

Golden Orchid had been back in Soochow for two weeks. Life had been kinder to her than she had expected. The first day she passed under the roof of Wen-ching's house had been full of fears. In time Golden Orchid got used to her formal relationship with Madam Wen-ching, largely because in Ping-mo's presence she felt at ease, and somehow through his intervention the wide gap between the wife and the concubine, between two women so disparate in age, in background and breeding, became almost non-existent. Having thus established some semblance of harmony and understanding, Golden Orchid asked her husband's permission to spend the remaining few days before the long ocean voyage with her mother and grandmother.

When she arrived, her mother was working as usual at her embroidery. She had been complaining of eyestrain; but she had a contented look, happy in the thought that, though she might have wished a different kind of marriage for her daughter, still she was satisfied, and that was all that counted. 'The wood has been made into a boat' was one of her favourite expressions, and the grandmother had kept on reminding her that, whatever other people might say, they now had a *chuang yuan*, one of the highest scholars in the land, as a member of the family.

The day passed with every member of the Fu family in a joyous mood. The pock-marked Lily arrived, followed by her sister Yang Mah and her hunchback husband. Lily went into the kitchen and talked and laughed hilariously with the grandmother, and the two of them prepared a sumptuous dinner. On that first night of return Golden Orchid shared her mother's bed, and they talked deep into the night. Then, saying good night to her mother, Golden Orchid quietly slipped underneath the pillow the sum of five hundred dollars wrapped in a piece of scarlet paper. Although Mrs Fu was not worldly-minded, she was overwhelmed when she found the money in the morning, for in a lifetime of work with her fingers she could not have accumulated so large an amount.

The next few days passed quickly enough. No relatives called, for there were none, but Golden Orchid went more than once to do some shopping in the company of Lily and Yang Mah, and she noticed that she was widely recognized. Some looked at her with envy, but most of the time the people shared her joy, she thought.

'The people are so good to me and so genuine,' she said to Lily. They all seemed to wish her luck, though perhaps some might have thought it a pity that so good a child had to become a sing-song girl in order to be the concubine of a high and distinguished official.

The day at last arrived when Golden Orchid had to return to her husband for the long voyage. It was a sad parting, particularly for her mother, who had nothing to give to her daughter except her love and prayers — and a small package of plain earth which she scraped up from the yard.

'Keep this, my precious one,' said the mother. 'The water and earth in these strange lands may not agree with you. And when you do not feel well there, place a few particles of this earth from your native Soochow in your food, and you will get well again. This is a belief from time immemorial.'

Book Two

ORDEAL ABROAD

I

THE life of a diplomatic hostess on her first arrival at an embassy is not easy even in the most favourable circumstances. There are visits to be made to the wives of the ambassadors who have preceded her. There are social contacts to establish with the families of the officials of the government to which her mission is accredited. This adjustment to a new life can be very exacting even for one who is experienced. There are niceties of protocol which have to be scrupulously observed. Diplomatic life is a network of rules within rules in which one hopes to achieve results only by cautiously developing a set of conditioned reflexes; and the longer one stays within the game, the surer are one's reflexes. At least that was true at the turn of the century in the capitals of Europe.

Golden Orchid knew nothing of this high and exclusive life. She was now only in her nineteenth year: she knew none of the foreign languages in which her diplomatic life was to be conducted; she came from a country in which the speech, the manners, the dress and the customs, from the European point of view, might as well have been those of one of the inhabitants of Mars; she had not been in diplomatic life before, or for that matter in any kind of public life except that of a sing-song girl going out professionally to entertain the pleasure-seeking officials of a decadent country. Golden Orchid knew she was plunging into the dark, as mysterious and unfathomable as the sea upon which she had been tossed for over six weeks.

But there were a few things which she had in abundance. She had youth, beauty and native intelligence. Her powers of perception and understanding and, above all, her instincts never seemed to fail her. Knowing before she left Shanghai that she was going to enter something completely unfamiliar, she decided to spend her time profitably even during the enforced confinement of the steamer.

There were obstacles to be overcome, the first and most serious being her feet. Lily and her mother and grandmother might be proud of them, but she knew that if she could not walk about freely, modern life would be a closed book to her. She had decided to live a modern life, and so early in the voyage she had brought up the subject before Wen-ching.

'Our new life in Europe,' she said one day, 'will be full of excitement. I was told that foreign men and women embrace each other and dance a good deal. Do you think, Master, that I should do as they do?'

Wen-ching did not know how to reply. He thought over the question, remained silent for a while, and then said: 'Three years is a long time, and I want you to be as happy as possible among these foreigners. So if you think you might want to learn to dance . . .'

Before he could finish his sentence, the image of a tall, blue-eyed, red-haired man with a large nose and perhaps a bushy face putting his arm around the willow waist of his precious concubine came into his mind. It was an unwelcome image. But since he had more or less committed himself, he thought he would please Golden Orchid by finishing the sentence as he had originally intended.

'Yes, my treasure, it you think you might like to dance with these funny-looking foreigners, I suppose there is no harm in learning it,' Wen-ching said.

As to the bindings on her feet, Golden Orchid held her own counsel. She began loosening the bandages and she found that the toes could still stretch out, that her feet even began to resume more or less their natural shape, and that she could walk more freely. Her only explanation for this was that her feet were naturally small, and that when the pock-marked Lily applied the bandages, she cried out at the slightest pain, which softened Lily's heart, so that they were wound much more loosely than they would normally have been. Golden Orchid made no mention to Wen-ching of the gradual transformation; and she thought that it would be safe enough, when the proper time came, to do away with the bandages entirely. This she did before the end of the voyage.

Golden Orchid had had a few lessons in dancing from fellow passengers, and now she even had a smattering of the English language. She became friendly with a missionary family, the Kendricks, and Nancy Kendrick was happy to teach English to Golden Orchid, who one day, she thought, might be helpful to her and her husband John in their mission work after they and their two children returned from their furlough. For seven years they had been stationed in north China, where their work was almost entirely confined to villagers. So they were especially intrigued at meeting a Chinese ambassador who was at the same time a great scholar and his concubine, who had been a sing-song girl.

Nancy told Golden Orchid that their mission was in Tungchow, a town some short distance to the east of Peking, and said that it would give her the greatest pleasure and honour if she and the ambassador would pay them a visit when they returned from their diplomatic mission. As for John, he tried to learn all he could about Chinese history and culture from Wen-ching, who was the first cultivated Chinese gentleman he had met. John was amused, and sometimes felt ashamed, that this had to take place on the high seas rather than in China itself.

When she arrived in Berlin, Golden Orchid was not the shy and frightened girl she thought she would be, but a relatively mature and vivacious woman looking forward to an active role as the mistress of a diplomatic mission. The first thing Golden Orchid took upon herself was to look over the premises of the embassy and make the acquaintance of the staff. These details would ordinarily be attended to by the ambassador himself soon after his arrival, but Golden Orchid knew that they would not interest her scholar-husband.

'Golden Orchid, my treasure,' Wen-ching often warned his concubine, 'you are very good to attend to these details on my behalf, but if I were you I wouldn't be over-enthusiastic. You must go slowly, or you are likely to step on many people's toes, and that would create bad feeling.'

Golden Orchid was sensible enough to heed these remarks, and so for a while she directed her energy to her own improvement. She thought that she should get to know the new environment in which she was to live for the next few years as much as possible. To do so it was necessary to learn the German language, even if this meant giving up English, in which she had made a start. She even thought of going to school, but Wen-ching said it was too drastic a step and did not approve it. Soon, however, this problem was solved.

Through various introductions there came to the embassy one day a man and his wife whom Golden Orchid immediately took to. The man was in his late forties, not tall for a foreigner, and he looked rather handsome with a thick but well-trimmed moustache. His wife Anna was at least five years younger and seemed to be very agreeable and attractive. She said she could cook, though that was

hardly essential, since Lao Chuang was taking care of the cooking.
She could also wash and clean the private rooms and do miscellaneous work. Her plump round features reminded Golden Orchid
of the womenfolk of her native Soochow.

Faustmann knew the English language well and could make himself understood by the new mistress. That was, in fact, one of the
reasons why she decided to engage him. He was a handy man about
the house and could handle all kinds of tools with efficiency. Golden
Orchid's intention was that he should teach her German. So Herr
Faustmann and his wife Anna came to live in the embassy.

Knowing that women could go about in Europe much more freely
than in China, Golden Orchid very soon ordered the embassy phae-
ton and began exploring the city in the company of Faustmann.
Occasionally she would ask Wen-ching to go with her, but most of
the time he chose to remain in the embassy. He was not so curious as
his young concubine, since he believed that no capital in the world
could compare with the majesty and imperial grandeur of Peking.
Also he thought it undignified for him to drive through the streets
with crowds of urchins swarming after him, laughing, shouting and
pointing at his unusual costume or his pigtail.

But Golden Orchid was eager and anxious to see the outside world.
Although spring was fast approaching, April in Berlin could be
raw and chilly, and the wrap she wore made her hardly distinguish-
able from other women, while her pretty round face drew admiring
comments. She could tell from the expressions of the passers-by
that they were friendly.

These drives through the streets of Berlin in a carriage drawn by
two powerful chestnut horses became almost a daily affair, with
Faustmann pointing out the Tiergarten, the Brandenburger Tor,
Unter den Linden, Friedrichstrasse, Wilhelmstrasse, until they became familiar sights. Faustmann would say: ' This is the American
Embassy, *Excellenz*,' pointing to a simple and spacious building near
the German Foreign Office. The British Embassy was one of the
many impressive buildings which had sprung up in the aftermath
of the Franco-Prussian War as a symbol of the new Germany. In
fact, all the embassies looked imposing, including that of Japan, a
country which the Chinese had regarded through the centuries with
scant respect.

Faustmann made no comment and merely satisfied himself with

pointing out the various landmarks, as much as to say: '*Excellenz*, you can draw your own conclusions when you compare these embassies with the hovel consisting of a few rooms which is dignified by the name of Chinese Embassy.' He noticed that such comparisons had begun to take effect, for a look of annoyance was constantly on the face of Golden Orchid.

She was indeed annoyed and kept saying to herself, Ay-ya! Our own embassy has none of the beauty and impressiveness of any of these embassies. One night after dinner she brought up the subject with Wen-ching.

'Master,' said Golden Orchid, 'this Faustmann has taken me to see all the lovely sights of Berlin, and they are truly magnificent — the park with its tall trees, and the patches of lovely flowers as pretty as any I have seen in Soochow or Peking. Now, why do we call these people barbarians, when everything they have is better than our own, or at least as good?'

'No, no, my treasure,' replied Wen-ching. 'It cannot be. There is nothing more beautiful and grand than our own cities. You have been to Peking. Can you honestly say that there is anything here to equal what we have?'

'But I tell you there is. You haven't seen them,' insisted Golden Orchid. 'I admit the palaces and temples in Peking are superb, but you have no idea how truly grand are the streets and buildings in this city — so wide, so clean, so straight and without any of the dust which covers Peking most of the time. And the people all seem to be well-to-do. I haven't seen any poverty. There are no beggars, and men and women all seem to be going about, either walking or driving in carriages, in such orderly fashion. I have not yet seen all the beautiful sights, but I can assure you that I am in love with this place, and shall enjoy living here.'

Wen-ching was glad to hear all this from the lips of one whom he so dearly loved, even though he was certain that it was not true. He smiled at her exuberance and said: 'I am afraid in time I shall lose you. You will become a foreign girl to me.'

As yet Wen-ching did not realize that Golden Orchid was devoting herself seriously to the task of becoming an adequate representative of her country, even more so than himself. His training, background and age had developed in him certain prejudices, but she was fresh, young and eager to learn. Every impression made on her growing and flexible mind was like a seed cast on fertile ground, and it grew in the air and sunshine of the new environment.

Golden Orchid now came straight to the point. 'Master,' she said, 'the imperial Court which you represent is that of a great and proud nation, isn't it? But do you realize that our embassy is the worst and the least impressive of all the embassies in this German capital?'

Wen-ching was surprised. 'I can't believe it,' he said. 'Have you already been visiting the other embassies? We have hardly begun our social contacts with them yet.'

'No, but I have seen them from the outside. Faustmann has pointed them out to me and I can no longer believe that our embassy represents more than the smallest and weakest and poorest country in the world.'

'How can you say such a thing?' Wen-ching cried out, aware that he was now talking to a mature woman in a serious frame of mind, and not merely to a concubine — traditionally regarded as a toy or as one simply to warm a man's bed.

Golden Orchid's development had been phenomenally quick. What she had heard and seen and learned during the six weeks of the voyage, reinforced by the new experiences in Berlin, had brought illumination and meaning to the many talks that she had had with Ping-mo; before she left he had given some indications of his real reasons for remaining behind, and since then she had thought and pondered over many of his remarks. What she saw now of the Chinese Embassy — its physical chaos and disorder, its sickly and inconsequential staff — seemed to confirm the truth of Ping-mo's observations.

Slowly but surely, Golden Orchid thought, she must lead her husband to a correct view of things. She knew he had his limitations, but she knew also that his heart was in the right place and that with adequate knowledge he could be won over to see her point of view.

'Master,' continued Golden Orchid, 'have you noticed that our embassy is flanked by a baker's and a barber's shop? We do not even live in a detached house. We occupy only a few rooms on the top floor of a huge building surrounded by small shops. How can we uphold the dignity of the imperial Court? None of the other embassies are like that. They stand alone, surrounded by beautiful trees and flowers. We have seen the inside of the German Embassy in Peking. It was formerly the palace of one of our princes. So are the other embassies in Peking. Surely we must do something.'

Wen-ching was embarrassed by these remarks. He had not been outside the embassy more than a few times. Secure in the belief that the Middle Kingdom was still the world's leading nation, at least in the arts of peace, he had begun to be engrossed in his studies; and as long as he was given his Chinese food by Lao Chuang and attentive service, he was satisfied. But his concubine had driven him to a point where he must make an investigation, so he timidly went out again, confirmed what Golden Orchid had said, and went so far as to saunter a little in the neighbourhood. But the moment a crowd began to surround him and point to his peculiar garb and appearance, he retired to his apartments upstairs.

'Look, my precious,' Wen-ching said afterwards to Golden Orchid, 'you are quite right. We must find a building all to ourselves, surrounded by a garden. If not for anything else, we must be away from those crowds.'

Wen-ching could not understand how his predecessor could have stood all this irritating curiosity and occasional buffoonery on the part of the populace. The outgoing ambassador had rented the apartments as the Chinese Embassy for a very small rent, something like one-tenth of his representation allowances. It was his aim to save as much of those allowances as possible, together with his own salary, so that he could retire comfortably when he was recalled — perhaps to build a large house or villa in his native village surrounded by the amenities and luxury which he knew in China. Besides, he used to say, when an ambassador had an adequate and impressive establishment, it was not only unappreciated by his colleagues or his government, but often gave rise to rumours that he was making money illegally; otherwise people would ask, how could he manage to maintain it? He would rather be frugal and enlarge his personal fortune than try to keep up a good appearance and be suspected of making illegal revenue on the side. Such an attitude had never aroused criticism, and that was wisdom.

What the ambassador did, the staff members imitated. They vied with each other in renting the smallest room they could find; and there they slept, cooked and amused themselves in their own way, making no contact with the diplomatic corps or the outside world generally. Their amusement was usually gambling or spreading malicious gossip about each other. After a few years in this so-called diplomatic service of His Imperial Majesty, these distinguished officials would return to China with their accumulated personal fortunes.

In time Wen-ching found out all this. It was outrageous, he thought; it was improper. Surely it should not be the duty of the Chinese diplomat to conceal himself abroad. But knowing Chinese officialdom as well as he did, he felt reluctant to do anything drastic against a practice which had been long sanctioned and widely accepted. So he cautioned Golden Orchid that if they tried to effect any change, they would be going into a hornets' nest.

'Golden Orchid, my precious, you are too young. You don't know these things. We must proceed very carefully. You may be perfectly correct in what you say, but didn't you notice yourself that the crows in Peking and those in Soochow are all black? Yes, crows everywhere are black, and if we try to be white, you will soon find out that they will peck us to death. No, no, let's walk as if we were on a thin layer of ice.'

Wen-ching's were words of wisdom. For a moment Golden Orchid was speechless, not knowing what to say. She believed that her husband should be heeded, but she was not happy. 'I may be young and inexperienced, but what I have seen and heard is, as you said, an outrage. We cannot remain indifferent.'

'You see, my precious,' continued Wen-ching, 'if we do not want to be black crows, we should leave the service, but then we accomplish nothing. If we decide to remain where we are, we must be slow and patient and cautious in everything we do.'

'But there is always a limit.'

'I would suggest that you go about your own work and leave matters in the embassy as they are — at least for the time being. But one thing I shall do at once. I shall see to it that we move into more commodious quarters so that the embassy will be regarded with more respect. I don't care what people may say about it. I shall take the risk.'

Golden Orchid felt happier.

The task of finding a new building to house the embassy fell on Faustmann. The Emperor who had come to the German throne some ten years before was an energetic man; he planned to make Berlin the leading city of Europe, if not in beauty, at least in strength. It was to be a symbol of Germany's expanding power. Many new buildings had just been erected, and they looked solid and substantial. Faustmann had no difficulty in finding a new site for the embassy.

It faced Kurfürstendamm; in the rear was a formal garden which led almost directly to the zoological garden which was then the new point of interest for Berliners. Wen-ching took to the house at once, for he loved animals and thought that it would be precisely the place where he could spend his moments of relaxation if he wanted to get away from his books and documents. Faustmann was very happy about it and, finding that everyone was in a cheerful mood, spoke to his mistress in German, '*Excellenz, wir haben jetzt ein schönes Haus.*'

Golden Orchid thought for a while, gave Faustmann a smile of approbation, and then said, '*Ja, sehr schön!*'

2

Months passed. By the autumn Golden Orchid found herself quite at home in her new environment. The diplomatic functions were in full swing again, and there was no question of her ability to cope with them. Her time had not been wasted. She had continually applied herself to the study of German until she could carry on an intelligent conversation. She practised with Anna, who was housemaid, confidante and teacher all rolled into one.

'This is a very funny language, Anna. Such long words — and long sentences. *Ja, schwer, sehr schwer.*'

And Anna, plump, good-natured and always cheerful, giggled when she heard this. Golden Orchid knew she was saying to herself, But, *Excellenz*, surely German cannot be more difficult than your own Chinese language.

'Oh, *nein*, Anna,' said Golden Orchid, without waiting for her to say anything, 'there is nothing simpler than to learn how to speak Chinese. Those missionaries I met on the steamer spoke well enough.' But Anna couldn't believe it.

Golden Orchid had learned to enjoy the company of Anna and gave up other duties in order to be with her teacher of this strange language for half an hour almost every day.

Golden Orchid had furnished the embassy with lovely old Chinese furniture and exquisite pieces of early porcelain which Yung-kai had sent to Berlin only a few months previously at Golden Orchid's request. The young military attaché had arrived in the spring and had been discreet enough to behave as though he hardly knew Golden Orchid. Their relations, so far as the other members of the staff were concerned, were formal and correct.

The only time Yung-kai and Golden Orchid saw each other alone and had a lengthy conversation was when the furniture and porcelain arrived at the embassy.

'The black table shines like a mirror; it is so smooth and looks elegant,' Golden Orchid said when it was being unpacked.

'I thought you would like it. I had it specially made.'

It was a lovely round lacquer table which could seat twelve people. It was heavy, solid and firm. When Golden Orchid gave a few informal luncheons it was an instant success. Diplomatic colleagues praised its unique beauty.

'The workmen in Peking,' Yung-kai had explained to Golden Orchid, 'patiently put on ten layers of the best black lacquer. Each time they put on a new layer it is more beautiful than the last, until it becomes more exquisite than any Coromandel screen of the sort that Europeans love so much.'

'Yes, I said it shines like a mirror, and it is a mirror. Look at the reflections.'

'Of that lovely, lovely face,' Yung-kai commented, looking at Golden Orchid. 'I have also brought some of the best Sung celadons. Nothing but the very best for so distinguished and so charming a hostess. These foreign diplomats, I am sure, have not seen anything so beautiful. They will admire them.'

Indeed they did. The antique wares, tinted in pale green but with no decoration whatever, showed their matchless beauty on the lacquer table. Golden Orchid also bought some Bohemian glass. Eating Lao Chuang's Chinese food in this setting, her guests had the delight of their lives. They spoke of the occasion for days afterwards, and the fame of the young, able and charming Oriental hostess, who only a short while before had known nothing of diplomatic life, spread to every embassy and to the German Government itself.

There was talk that she would be received in audience by the Empress Augusta Victoria in the Schloss Charlottenburg. She had begun to worry about what she should wear for the occasion — whether she should appear in Chinese dress or in the Court dress of a

Manchu princess. In such matters she had Anna as her trusted adviser. She tried on the dresses one after another in front of the full-length mirror in her room, with Anna alone attending her. Now and then Wen-ching slipped in without making a comment, his mind preoccupied with diplomatic affairs or with the scholarly historical work which for many years he had planned to write.

As the months went by, it seemed to Wen-ching that the diplomatic situation was becoming more tense. The daily routine in the office was limited and could be easily disposed of. But there was constant rumour that the German Emperor was doing everything he could to expand his power and influence beyond the seas. That meant that one day his interests would conflict with those of China. The Kaiser was a man in his late thirties, full of vigour and vitality. His image had stood out clearly in Wen-ching's mind from the day when he presented his credentials. He thought that he was a strong person, but he remembered distinctly that the Kaiser's fierce eyes and overbearing military appearance had been too much for him. He wanted to know more about him and his policies, and one day he called Yung-kai into his office.

'What news from your honourable father, His Lordship Yu Kung?' Wen-ching welcomed Yung-kai and asked him to be seated. This was a concession to a subordinate official, and Yung-kai appreciated it.

'Very little, except that I get the impression that he is busy. His letters to me are very short. For some reason there seems to be uneasiness in Peking.'

'Quite right. Yung-kai, I wish to talk with you about the situation. The German Kaiser is an ambitious person, and one day I am afraid he will give us trouble. Have you heard that he is planning to visit Turkey?'

It seemed odd that Turkey should have anything to do with possible trouble in China, but Yung-kai happened to have heard the news and had been wondering what connection there was between the two.

'Yes, I have heard that also, Uncle Shen. What bearing do you think this has on us?'

'You see, Yung-kai, Turkey has been called the sick man of Europe, and I believe that through Turkey the Kaiser will try to exercise influence and pressure on the Suez Canal.'

'I remember passing through that canal. I can see its great strategic importance.'

'Precisely,' said Wen-ching. 'It is a stretch of water which leads to all the countries of the East. We are called the sleeping giant of the East. It's a matter of getting from the sick man to the sleeping giant, as you can see. But I am seriously worried. The Kaiser wants to rival the power of England. It's about time, he thinks, for him to put his foot on the giant — as England has done for so long.'

'Yes, it seems obvious to me now. . . . I have been wondering. In one of his more recent letters to me, father spoke of troubles in Shantung province. It is from there, I presume, that Germany seeks to extend her power to other parts of our country.'

'I believe so. German influence is already strong there. It is our sacred province. That was where, as you know only too well, our two great sages Confucius and Mencius were born.'

Wen-ching was silent for a while. He was angry that foreign powers could not allow even China's great teachers to repose in peace.

'Not long ago the Kaiser made a statement which I think is very significant. He said, "Our future is on the water." To show that he means what he says, he has started to build a strong navy.'

Yung-kai was impressed that his ambassador was so well informed on the international situation. In spite of his knowledge of foreign languages, he himself knew less.

'Yung-kai, the reason I have talked to you is this. I am preparing a memorandum on the matter for the Tsungli Yamen which will, of course, reach the President, your honourable father —' Wen-ching thought for a little while and then continued: 'It will be one of the most important memorandums I have ever submitted. And to make matters quite certain — that is, to be quite sure that it reaches him — I shall be happy if you will be good enough to report to him the gist of our conversation today. Confidentially, much of the information has come to me through the kindness of the British ambassador. You will realize why he is anxious to give it to me.'

Yung-kai thanked the ambassador and rose to leave.

'Before you go, one more word. Please keep this talk entirely to yourself. You understand?'

Wen-ching was satisfied with the talk, and that evening he told Golden Orchid about it. She was glad Yung-kai was singled out for special attention, but Wen-ching was struck by one point she made.

'When the other members of the staff learn of this talk,' Golden Orchid asked, 'won't they say that you are bestowing more than usual favour on Yung-kai? They'll say that because he has a powerful and influential father you have been partial to him. This is just a thought on my part, Wen-ching dear.'

The year of residence in Berlin, with its wide social contacts and knowledge of foreign customs, had so changed Golden Orchid that she began to discard the old way of addressing her husband. The new way, she thought, was much more affectionate and strongly appealed to her. Wen-ching, too, seemed to like it.

'It's a good thought, my treasure,' replied Wen-ching. 'However, they won't know of it. And even if they do, they cannot feel slighted, because I have had such meetings with them before. Frankly, they are an impossible lot. I have no use for them.'

'That may be so, but still they will feel offended.'

'Time and again I have found that they have no interest in international affairs. I have given them every opportunity to improve themselves. Now you have brought up this subject, I might as well let you know that I have subscribed to magazines for them, and newspapers from many countries, and have bought books for them in the hope that they would read them. But they do not even touch them.'

'I suppose they even say that you have insulted them.'

'Exactly. One of them, I was told, commented that this is not a school but an embassy. He said he was not a schoolboy!'

'Of course, he wants to be known as a bureaucrat, even though he may sit like a dummy through these diplomatic functions.'

'And yet, among themselves,' said Wen-ching, 'I understand there is a good deal of activity. Faustmann has often seen them play mah-jongg: that seems to be their great sport, their great passion. And the stakes are very high. Faustmann tells me that feelings sometimes run so high that they fight one another.'

'I don't find this surprising.'

'Yes, my precious, this embassy has become a gambling den. I haven't told you these things before because they are unpleasant, and didn't want to trouble you. But I am afraid worse things will happen with the recent arrival of these two new secretaries.'

'What makes you think so?'

'That is another one of the things I have been concealing from you.'

'But why conceal things from me? I know you do it out of the goodness of your heart, but I'd rather you let me share everything with you.'

'If that is how you feel, let me ask you something. You have seen those two secretaries. One fat, the other small and pale. What do you think of them? I think they look evil. I don't know whether you still remember that fat man Wang who was on the flower-boat when you sang that day, the summer before last?'

'I think I remember him.'

'Why, of course, you must. He also was in love with you. Well, anyway, he was talking a lot that day to Hu-mou. Wang is a good fellow, and he and I still write to each other, as I have told you. He doesn't write often, but he keeps me informed about what goes on in Soochow. Some months ago he wrote to tell me that Hu-mou was preparing to leave Soochow. I wondered where he was going. Then a few days later came another letter to tell me that he was appointed to a high post in the Tsungli Yamen.'

'How did he get that appointment?'

'It seems that the President of the Military Affairs Board is related to him. I vaguely remember him telling me about that. And the President is of course an important man in Peking. But what is interesting is this. Shortly afterwards came the appointment of these two new secretaries. The Tsungli Yamen didn't even ask me whether I needed them. They should know that the embassy is overstaffed as it is. It seems that Lord Yu Kung never referred to this matter in any of his letters to Yung-kai. I have asked the young man about it. And that is upsetting.'

'But I still don't see why you should be upset.'

'I hope I am too sensitive. But I have a feeling that it is a bad omen.'

'We'll just have to keep our eyes and ears open, that's all,' commented Golden Orchid.

'That is the most we can do, I am afraid.'

3

For the next few months Golden Orchid felt worried and uneasy. Christmas came again, her second in Berlin. She lost herself among the crowds and tried to share their holiday cheer. But her heart was persistently heavy, for she was beginning to believe that there was some ground for Wen-ching's fears. Now and then she sought the company of Yung-kai, who was the only person apart from her husband who could occasionally give her some consolation. It was a strange situation, she thought. She was trying to do everything with her husband to enhance the prestige of the Chinese Court in Berlin and promote the interests of their country and she knew she had been doing well, yet she was unhappy. At the back of her mind there always lurked the suspicion that members of the staff were working against her. What could they be up to? she wondered.

Then, shortly after the New Year, Lao Chuang asked to see her. He was not in the habit of making such requests, but he had come into possession of some knowledge which he felt he should confide to his mistress. After some hesitation he went into Golden Orchid's apartments and said: 'Tai-tai, I hope you won't be angry with me, but I have heard things from the secretaries about the master and Tai-tai which I think Tai-tai should know.'

'Let me hear what you have to say.'

'Well,' stammered Lao Chuang, 'one of the secretaries said, though it is best that I don't mention his name, that Tai-tai lives an immoral life by going out so often. They know that Tai-tai is fond of dancing and has even danced with the young Lord Yung-kai.'

Now, it was true that Golden Orchid had danced with Yung-kai — during the holidays. Apart from the fact that she had known Yung-kai in China, he was the only member of the staff who had a sense of self-respect and a desire to improve himself. She had watched him at a safe distance and discovered that he did not easily mingle with the rest. He devoted his time to studying German politics and to being as helpful as possible to his ambassador. She knew that Wen-ching liked him. The staff members were jealous of him, but there was nothing they could do against the son of a man so powerful at Court. Yung-kai had his private fortune in addition to his salary, and he was able to entertain and associate with the diplomatic corps, a thing which the other members refused to do. That was another of their grievances. So far as Golden Orchid was concerned, it was only natural, apart from purely personal reasons, that she should ask him to be with her and with the ambassador at diplomatic functions. It was true that she sometimes sought his company. The staff members must now be making capital out of these facts, Golden Orchid thought.

'But there is even more malicious gossip than what I have said,' continued Lao Chuang. 'It is not for me as a servant, Tai-tai, to tell everything, but these secretaries, I think, are not to be trusted.'

Golden Orchid made no comment. She was satisfied with what she had heard and dismissed Lao Chuang. The servant took a few steps with his gaze fixed on the floor but decided there was more to be said. 'Tai-tai, I should have told you that I went to Secretary Tan's little apartment last night. He was not feeling well and wanted me to prepare some soft rice for him. When I took it to him, I found the small room full of people. Secretary Chow and Secretary Chung were there, and a couple of foreign girls who looked very untidy. I don't know who they were, as I have not seen them before.'

'Well, what were they doing?'

'I could not understand all they were saying. But I thought they were talking about doing some business together, and Mr Chow suggested he might go to Paris. Then the conversation drifted to perfumes and watches and other such things, which, I think, they are going to bring into this country. I have no idea what it is all about, but I thought I should let you know that, even on his sickbed, Secretary Tan is planning to do many things. I suppose this is a part of his duty.'

This was not the first time Golden Orchid had received a report from Lao Chuang about the activities of the embassy staff outside their office. Wen-ching had already been advised that the secretaries were getting involved in many questionable and suspicious transactions. It was one of the little secrets he thought he should keep from Golden Orchid. But no sooner had she heard Lao Chuang's latest news than she hastened to tell Wen-ching. She was genuinely afraid that there would be a major international scandal if the movements of the staff were not kept under control.

'Wen-ching dear,' began Golden Orchid reluctantly, 'I know there is enough trouble for you as it is. News from home is not good, and you have so much to do to establish friendly relations with the

German Government. We have been here well over a year now, and as yet you have not had time to go to St. Petersburg for any length of time. You are, after all, concurrently ambassador to Russia, and you have only stayed there for that short period when you presented your credentials. You would think that these secretaries here would appreciate the difficulties and try to be of some assistance.'

Wen-ching was amused by the long introduction. 'What about these secretaries?' he asked.

'Well, I have my fears about them.'

'What do you mean by fears, my precious?'

Having gone so far, Golden Orchid thought it best to tell everything. She then recounted all that she had heard from Lao Chuang.

There was an unhappy look on Wen-ching's face. He began pacing up and down the room, not knowing what to say. At last he began: 'My precious Orchid, this is a very delicate situation. I have had information of the improper behaviour of these secretaries for some time, and I have as usual kept it from you. But since Lao Chuang has told you these things, I might as well speak frankly. I am utterly powerless to do anything. I can warn these secretaries, but that will have no effect. I can even ask that they be transferred or recalled, but, believe it or not, these secretaries are fully aware that my recommendations to the Tsungli Yamen would not be acted upon. It all goes back to Hu-mou again.'

'How can this be?'

'At the time we left Soochow for Europe, you remember, I took the trouble to pay my respects to Hu-mou. I didn't do that out of love for him, you can be sure. Some day, I felt sure, this man was going to join the Government in Peking. He is a good scholar and he knows a little English, which would qualify him for an appointment to the Tsungli Yamen. The fellow is cunning and wily and difficult to get along with. He has the look of a vicious man. But I tried to cultivate his friendly feelings. I am sure he is now the cause of all my troubles."

Golden Orchid tried to recall Hu-mou. She had vague recollections of the man, of how he looked during that party on the flower-boat. All she remembered was that he hardly uttered a word but seemed intent on absorbing all the conversation around him. And he had the habit of turning his eyes upward, as if weighing the significance of every remark he heard.

'That Hu-mou, if you remember,' Wen-ching went on, 'is a silent man, but his thoughts run deep. He is also an able man. I have known him for some time, though not well. I have even occasionally taken him into my confidence, which is foolish. I realize that now. I am convinced he is doing everything to undermine us. I have yet to find out why. Our interests do not seem to me to conflict. But perhaps Hu-mou sees the picture differently. There are men in this world who are so twisted that they think other people's success is their ruin. That may be how Hu-mou feels. He must have heard of our success here, and he may not like it — I don't know.'

Golden Orchid was speechless with fear and anger. Yet, though the impact of extraordinary circumstances and a wider knowledge of human whims and foibles had matured her, she was still not cynical enough to believe that the human heart could be so depraved as to seek the destruction of others.

Wen-ching poured out some tea and drank it. After a pause, he continued: 'You see, my treasure, I know what these secretaries are up to. As I told you, their ruling passion is money, money, money. It makes no difference what happens to their country as long as they can make money. They don't care where they live or how they live as long as they can save money. They have no sense of personal integrity or dignity, let alone of national prestige. I am sure they have personal instructions from Hu-mou to undermine my authority and create trouble for me. With that power they easily win over the rest of the staff. So what's the good of my confidential reports to the Tsungli Yamen on the conduct of these people?'

'Did you submit reports on them?'

'Yes, indeed. But I don't want you to be distressed by any of the things that are going on in this embassy.'

Wen-ching thought of his work. He read intensively, gathering material for his history. In addition, he had to spend a large part of his time every day thinking about the increasingly complicated and vexatious problems of international relations. His hands were full even if he never set foot outside the embassy. During his moments of relaxation Golden Orchid saw to it that his modest needs were properly provided for. That was all he desired, and his life would have been very happy but for the hidden whirlpools of trouble coming from the embassy staff and now, unexpectedly, from the Tsungli Yamen itself.

He had thought he could take care of the staff simply by ignoring them and hoping that they would ultimately destroy themselves. It was beginning to dawn upon him, naive scholar that he was, that the problem was not to be solved so easily. It was, in fact, getting worse, because he now realized that the staff members and the Tsungli Yamen, through the machinations of Hu-mou, were united against him.

He had thought he could always depend on Lord Yu Kung, but it appeared that His Lordship, though still in charge of the Tsungli Yamen, was progressively paying less attention to the details of his office. His talks with Yung-kai confirmed this impression. While Yu Kung's time and energy were absorbed by the numerous other duties growing out of the tense situation, little Hu-mou had manœuvred himself into a position of almost unchallenged authority in the Tsungli Yamen. Wen-ching's confidential reports went unheeded, and it came as a shock to him when he was told that his friend Lord Yu Kung had never seen or read them. In fact, Lord Yu Kung had complained during a dinner that Wen-ching was not submitting any reports and wondered what he was doing as ambassador in Germany. The reports were being systematically suppressed by Hu-mou and his underlings. It was this knowledge that of late had been giving Wen-ching sleepless nights. He had been justly proud of these reports. Written in the terse and persuasive style of which he alone was capable, they were the result of painstaking and exhaustive study, and conveyed some shrewd observations on China's international situation viewed from Europe. And yet he was informed that these reports never so much as reached the desk of his friend and superior!

'Yes, my treasure,' continued Wen-ching after a long pause, 'I am beginning to find it increasingly difficult to exercise authority in this embassy. I should now be in St. Petersburg — at least for a short stay. Russia is as aggressive as Germany, if not more so. She has her eyes on Manchuria, and she is giving us enough trouble to make it necessary for me to go there again. But I don't see how I can go without first ensuring that the staff here behaves itself. That is why I sent a confidential report to the Tsungli Yamen asking for the recall of the two new secretaries. No action was taken. So I wrote a second report. Still nothing was done. Not only that, the secretaries seem to know every move I make and are secretly laughing at me for being so utterly powerless.'

'But how is it that Lord Yu Kung never knew about these reports?'

'It is easy for Hu-mou to hold them up. It is he who is now attending to the details of the Tsungli Yamen. That is why I sometimes ask Yung-kai to transmit the information. But it is possible that his father pays little attention when he is so busily occupied elsewhere. His Lordship is not the kind of man to be meticulous about such things.'

'Do you think I should persuade Yung-kai to write again to his father?'

'That would not look well. Besides, I am sure Hu-mou, able as he is, must by now have won Lord Yu Kung's confidence completely. No, I would still have you create friendly feelings with the diplomatic and government people here. You don't know how much good you have done, my precious, by being just what you are — by giving these functions and being lively and affable.'

Wen-ching looked dejected and unhappy, and all his learning and philosophy did not seem to help him.

Golden Orchid merely said: 'What then should we do?'

'Sometimes I ask myself if there is something wrong with myself or with the way I treat the world. For it is always wise to seek the cause within oneself if something goes wrong. That is what Madam Wen-ching used to say — and she is right.'

'I think you have treated the staff as well as they have any right to expect from a superior.'

'Yes, to be honest with myself, I don't think I have been ungenerous or unsympathetic or inconsiderate. If I have tried to enforce some discipline and in that way incurred the ill-feeling of the staff, it is entirely because I have the interests of the country at heart. Besides, it is for their own good. No, I think I have tried to be a good man and to do good. And yet, what is the result? Is it possible that the very strength I have is the cause of this trouble?'

Wen-ching paused in his painful attempt to see what was at the bottom of his afflictions.

'If I had the power,' he continued, 'I could straighten out a few things. But I have only responsibilities. And with Hu-mou making himself my secret enemy, it has become an impossible situation.'

'But why, why should he want to make himself our enemy? I still can't understand.'

'Who knows? I have not hurt his feelings, so far as I know. There is one possible explanation. Perhaps he feels that when we return I may be asked to take charge of the Tsungli Yamen. Hu-mou would then be overshadowed. He is terribly jealous and terribly ambitious. So it is perhaps his present purpose to undermine His Lordship's friendship for me and to create the impression that I have failed in my mission. The two new secretaries are his agents, and that is why they can afford to be truculent. In a sense I am helpless. If it goes on much longer, I am afraid I shall have to ask to be re-called. I have a premonition that in time things will become so bad that we shall be ruined.'

This was the unhappiest moment that Golden Orchid had known since she came to Berlin. She was now sure that Wen-ching's analysis was not far from the truth. That night they went to bed sombre and dejected.

4

THE next morning Wen-ching and Golden Orchid awoke to find sunshine and laughter in the air. The despairing thoughts which hung like a dark shadow over them the previous evening appeared to have vanished. The situation had not changed; in fact, nothing had changed, but a good night's rest had given nature a chance to restore their cheerful spirits. When Lao Chuang came in to present his usual greetings with the morning repast he was glad to find his master and mistress in a happy mood. Shortly afterwards Wen-ching went downstairs to his office, where he attended to his daily routine, occasionally calling in one or two secretaries for consultation.

Their visits had become stiff and formal. Wen-ching had been in the habit of encouraging the staff members in their study of the diplomatic situation and, if time allowed, of Chinese classics and history, but that had now been given up. And with relations so strained, interviews were confined to the routine work of the office. This included a few minor questions concerning the Chinese who somehow managed to drift into Germany in small numbers, after an overland trip of thousands of miles, to sell silks and other wares.

These and similar questions of a consular nature were taken care of by Chow, who was in charge of the consular department. He had his own staff, locally recruited.

While Wen-ching was in his office, Anna Faustmann went into the private apartments of Golden Orchid, greeting her pleasantly with a '*Guten Morgen, Excellenz.*'

Golden Orchid replied '*Guten Morgen*, Anna' and, opening a window, looked in the direction of the zoological garden. She was glad to see the tall trees gently swaying in the breeze.

'It is a lovely day, Anna,' continued Golden Orchid. 'I suggest that we take a walk in the park and visit the animals.'

'All right, *Excellenz*. But when we are tired of walking and sit on a bench, we shall have another lesson in German.'

Anna's persistence was a part of her devotion. It could at times be overdone, but Golden Orchid always appreciated it. Thus, in the delightful and carefree atmosphere of the park, the two women spent a pleasant morning. They had their lesson, and they fed the animals.

'That sea elephant,' commented Golden Orchid as they walked back to the embassy, 'may, for all I know, be full of great wisdom. Isn't he ugly, and doesn't he look stupid? One of our great philosophers used to say, "The supremely wise looks stupid." You would think he had that sea elephant in mind when he made that remark.' Golden Orchid laughed girlishly.

'*Excellenz*,' said Anna, 'I am so glad that the German people have a chance to see and meet you like this in the park. They love you dearly.'

'And I love the German people.'

'*Excellenz*, I want to tell you something. My friends are envious of me when they know that I am in your employment. Your beauty and graciousness are all they talk about, and they think that the Chinese must be a wonderful people.'

What an ironic remark, thought Golden Orchid. And then she said to Anna: 'Your own people are so kind and friendly, and living among you has made a new person of me. I would like to see more of the country.'

Anna gladly took up the idea, and for the next months she planned a number of excursions for her mistress. The weather was glorious, and Golden Orchid was willing to be taken anywhere. It served no purpose, she thought, to brood over a situation which was entirely out of her control. As long as Wen-ching was happy in his studies and in his work, not much could be done except to leave matters alone — for a period at least — while she gave herself a holiday. She felt she needed one.

But there were moments when she longed for the companionship of a man during these outings. It would be wonderful if Wen-ching could accompany her; but she knew that was out of the question. He thoughts turned towards Yung-kai. But there were all kinds of difficulties in the way. What would Wen-ching think about it? What would Yung-kai himself think? And, finally, what would the embassy staff think? They were gossiping already. Should she give them an additional weapon against her? She became hesitant and said to herself, No, it will not do.

A few days later there was talk of a visit to Potsdam, which Anna said Golden Orchid must see. It was a lovely town, and they could easily go there and back in a day. And then, as if knowing what was going on in the mind of Golden Orchid, Anna suggested: 'Why don't we ask Herr Yung-kai, the young military attaché, to come with us? He . . . he is a very pleasant young man and so modern in his outlook.'

Golden Orchid looked at Anna as though she had unlocked her thoughts and spread them like an open book. As if agreeing reluctantly, she said: 'Yes, perhaps we might ask Herr Yung-kai to go with us.'

However, one thing must be done, and that was to obtain Wen-ching's consent. As to what other people might think, she would not concern herself, for the moment at least.

For over a year in Berlin Golden Orchid's relationship with Yung-kai had been awkward and distant. They had been drawn to each other by their youth and by a secret understanding of their hearts. Yung-kai had vowed love to her, and she on her part had been attracted to him. But although they were so near to each other, they were separated by a gap as deep and wide as it was unbridgeable. It was impossible for them to be together without causing embarrassment and misunderstanding. Both of them had succeeded in restraining themselves in difficult circumstances, and their relationship was conducted on a strictly correct basis. But a point had now been reached when that restraint was beginning to be irksome; and

Anna, without being consciously responsible, had set the smoulder-
ing cinders aflame again. That same evening Golden Orchid told
Wen-ching of Anna's suggestion, and she was surprised when her
husband agreed to it.

'My precious Orchid,' declared Wen-ching, 'I want you to enjoy
living here in Germany as much as possible. I have said that many
times. Enjoy yourself by all means, and take Yung-kai and Anna
with you.'

Golden Orchid retired to her room and lay down on the sofa,
surprised that so important a step could be taken without any hitch
or searching of the heart. She had long desired to be near Yung-kai,
and there was no doubt in her mind that Yung-kai had the
same desire. It was indeed auspicious that Wen-ching did not
object.

But she turned over and over in her mind what the consequences
might be. Could she conceal this day with Yung-kai from the
knowledge of the embassy staff? What if they learned about it later?
What kind of idle gossip would they start? Would the presence of
Anna make any difference?

She got up and wrote a little note, summoned Anna to her presence, and said: '*Bitte sehr*, Anna, give this to the military attaché.
We will drive to Potsdam early tomorrow morning.'

The next morning Anna's husband ordered a landau drawn by
two white stallions beautifully caparisoned. As one way of preventing the information from leaking to the staff, he was clever enough not
to use the embassy coach. The journey of some sixteen miles to the
south-west of Berlin was one of the most pleasant that any of the
three had ever taken. It was a delightful day, the air was bracing,
and the sunshine poured down. There were short pauses on the way
when all three would descend to stroll in the magnificent pine-woods
through which the road ran. Yung-kai, a lover of horses, talked to
the driver, and remarked on the clean and healthy condition of the
animals. He gently stroked them and whispered a few words in
Chinese in their ears, and the horses nodded as if they understood.
It was more than three hours before they reached Potsdam. The
winding road sometimes brought the carriage to the banks of the
Havel, and Golden Orchid was all excitement when she saw fish in
the river; she felt as if she were back in her own native Soochow.
They stopped for lunch at an inn, and through the window they

could see the magnificent palaces of the Prussian kings — not as grand and magnificent as those in Peking, both Yung-kai and Golden Orchid thought. They looked sombre in their monotonous grey, but all the same they were imposing. For Anna it seemed as if she was treading upon hallowed soil, and she said with pride: 'After lunch I must show you, *Excellenz*, the palace where our Frederick the Great lived, and I must also tell you the story of how that great French writer Voltaire came to live with our Emperor.'

They strolled from one handsome room to another with Anna acting as guide. As they walked, Yung-kai and Golden Orchid held hands for a while, but dropped them as if it were sinful to be so close to each other, and for fear that Anna might see them.

At last Anna said: 'I must show you, *Excellenz*, something which will really interest you. This' — she pointed with pride to Sans Souci — 'is the palace built in the Chinese style. I know you will love to see it.'

'Ah-ya!' exclaimed Golden Orchid. 'I can see Chinese designs and decorations all over the palace.'

'And look at this, Golden Orchid,' added Yung-kai. 'These Chinese porcelains are as lovely as any that father has in Peking. I wonder how and when they were brought here.'

He addressed the question to Anna, and she replied: 'In the eighteenth century, I was told, all over Europe people admired everything Chinese — porcelains, silks, lacquers, wallpapers and even Chinese ideas about politics and social organization. And as you see, these things are still kept here.' She pointed to the walls and corners of the huge rooms, which were filled with beautiful Chinese objects.

Suddenly Anna saw a friend and hailed her. Turning to Golden Orchid she said: 'Excuse me, *Excellenz*. Allow me to say a few words to this friend of mine. I shall be back shortly.'

'You may take your time, Anna,' replied Golden Orchid. 'The military attaché and I will walk in the garden.'

So Yung-kai took Golden Orchid's hand again and led her into the labyrinths of the formal garden. They did not say a word but continued to walk until they found a stone bench among the tall poplars under a boxwood hedge. In front of them was a fountain with a gentle spray of water falling upon the naked bodies of a group of fauns and satyrs dancing along the rim of the pool. So different from and yet how similar to their little escapade in the forbidden palace grounds in Peking!

'Golden Orchid, my precious orchid,' began Yung-kai, 'for almost two years I have waited for this moment.' He squeezed her hand and gazed at her.

'I know, Yung-kai. I know you love me, and I love you. But there is nothing we can do.'

There was silence: there were no words. There was no need for words, for how could words express what was in the hearts of these two young people who so yearned for each other?

And then, as if to regain her balance, Golden Orchid said: 'No, Yung-kai. I am married and I am devoted to Wen-ching, old as he is. I must do everything to help him, and so must you. We mustn't betray him. Don't you think he is a wonderful man, always so kind to those around him, and so generous? He is not modern in his views, but that is no fault of his own. Besides, I am not sure that it is a fault. He understands so much of what is going on, of things that are being done in the embassy and the political situation generally. He means to do good for his country, and he has already done so much.'

Yung-kai could not long remain in his sweet delirium. 'I quite agree with you,' he declared, 'and that is why, I think, my father holds the ambassador in such high esteem. He told me so before I left and in his earlier letters to me. But lately, for some reason, my father does not mention the ambassador so often. It may be that he has so much to do, with the general situation getting worse every day.'

'Tell me, Yung-kai,' continued Golden Orchid, 'what do you think of your colleagues in the embassy? I have noticed that you do not associate with them much.'

'What have I in common with them? They are a wretched lot, if I may say so, and I can't understand how being an official can make one sink so low. What have I not seen and heard within the walls of the embassy! Well, it's no good talking about these things. What can we do? Nothing! So it is best to leave them alone.'

Golden Orchid looked at Yung-kai and thought that possibly she had found a solution to her husband's difficulties. Wen-ching had asked her not to approach Yung-kai, but why not, when he was so deeply in love with her? His father was the only person who, both as Wen-ching's immediate superior in the Tsungli Yamen and as the favourite of the Empress Dowager herself, could effectively intervene.

'Will you do one thing for me, Yung-kai?' Golden Orchid asked.

'Of course. What is it that I will not do for you? You have only to say it.'

'Will you write to your father and tell him all that you know about those secretaries and the trouble they are creating for the ambassador?'

'I have written to tell him already. Yes, without your saying so, for I know what has been going on. But, believe it or not, it seems there is not much that even my father can do — at least for the moment. I can't understand why. But when we go back to Berlin, I shall go over the letters I have recently received from him. There is one long letter in particular which I must show you.'

'Well, was it good or bad?'

'I am not clear, but it seems to contain a good deal of gossip that my father wants me to find out about. You know how it is with these things. But, anyhow, let's not talk about them now.'

But for Golden Orchid this was an important moment. She searched and searched in her soul, remembering the things her husband had done and told her. Surely there was nothing that either she or her husband could be ashamed of. On the contrary, they had done much for the prestige and honour of the Chinese Court, and yet everything seemed to go wrong. There was no peace in the embassy. The secretaries were truculent and behaved atrociously. The friendship of Lord Yu Kung was the only source of security, but was even that friendship beginning to weaken and become uncertain? Yung-kai, she was convinced, was the only man to help her find out.

Golden Orchid did not realize that she had been out in the garden with Yung-kai for some time. Anna, trying to find them, came out of the palace and caught a glimpse of them. But, seeing that they were deeply engrossed and thinking that it must be an affair of the heart which she should not disturb, she went back into the palace, leaving them to look for her.

'Anna, Anna, we have been looking for you,' cried Golden Orchid. 'If you have said goodbye to your friend, I think we should leave.'

On the way back there was not much conversation.

5

GOLDEN ORCHID spend an uneasy night; she tossed by the side of Wen-ching and could not sleep.

In his apartment in the Meineckestrasse, Yung-kai also sat up deep into the night. He recalled to himself that evening at Peking when, after lunching with Golden Orchid at the Northern Lake, he came back and started to keep a diary. He took it out, read what he had written, and smiled to himself somewhat bitterly.

For some curious reason these meetings with Golden Orchid always take place with a royal background, he thought. Last time it was in the imperial park of our emperors, and this time it was in the gardens of the German emperors. Two entirely different worlds with thousands of miles between them. He said wryly to himself, The third meeting — is it going to be another two years hence, with another imperial background?

Yung-kai began to realize that he should have known from the beginning that there was no way in which Golden Orchid could give up her husband and marry him. Even if that could happen, he would become a social outcast. The very idea of a young lord from an honourable and respectable family so close to the Court marrying a woman, however beautiful and charming, as his first legal wife, who had been a professional sing-song girl and someone else's concubine was so impossible that no one would give it more than a fleeting thought.

But Yung-kai did not think of the matter in the light of social conventions or social approval. He loved the girl, and that was all he cared for. That was what made him leave Peking and follow her to another part of the world. But in all the time he had been in Berlin, how often had he even been near her? He had thought about her; he had wanted to hold her in his arms. When he went to bed every night, he imagined that she was lying by his side; he said to himself that one of these nights he would have the things he wanted most of all from her, and dreamed one dream after another. That was why this trip to Potsdam was so sweet and delicious — after nearly two years of restraint. He had thought that his dreams could now become real, but instead, it was made clear to him that they were drifting farther and farther apart. She was devoted to her husband, though she said she loved him, Yung-kai. But what good was that love if there was no tangible expression, if he remained as far away from her as when he first met her?

As he paced up and down his room, Yung-kai's mind became confused, but the urge to possess Golden Orchid physically became so strong and insistent that he vowed to himself that he must get her to his apartment. If he failed, there would be no point in remaining. He would find an excuse to go back to Peking, do something else, and forget he had ever known Golden Orchid.

A couple of days passed, and to his great surprise Golden Orchid came to visit him of her own accord. The poor girl was so distraught, so deeply concerned with what might happen to her husband, that she brushed aside every consideration and sought out Yung-kai. The more she thought about her husband, the more she became convinced that only Yung-kai's father, the powerful Lord Yu Kung, could help him.

'Yung-kai,' she said the moment she entered his apartment, 'I have come to ask you to redeem your promise. You said when we were in Potsdam that you would tell me what your father wrote to you in one of his recent letters.'

So that is what she wants, Yung-kai said to himself. All right, I shall help her to get what she wants, but she is not going away this time until . . .

While Golden Orchid seated herself comfortably in a large easy-chair, Yung-kai brewed some green tea and brought it to her. And then slowly, after some moments of relaxation, he approached her and said: 'Golden Orchid, you know how much I love you. For years I have been pining for you. But you seem to be avoiding me. You seem to be so far away from me.'

'That isn't true, and you know it. I love you as much as you love me. But I am in a difficult situation. I am tortured by a thousand things. Let me talk to you first on what I have come for.'

'Yes, we will talk about that,' answered Yung-kai. 'But if you want me to help you, you must help me.'

'What is it, Yung-kai?'

Without answering her, Yung-kai took a bold step, so bold that he had not known he was capable of it. He went up to her and did what he was told men and women in Europe did in such circumstances. He threw his arms around her and kissed her mouth. It was a long and passionate kiss. It was the first time he had ever kissed a girl. He had shown his affections in other ways — but a kiss was new, as new to him as it was to Golden Orchid. He did not let her go, so sweet and delicious was this new and strange experience. Golden Orchid sat motionless, yielding to the firm grasp of Yung-kai's strong arms and melting in the flames of the powerful emotions surging within her. She offered no resistance, and to Yung-kai's joy and satisfaction she at last responded.

Golden Orchid then pushed Yung-kai away — gently, yet decisively — and he crouched at her feet with his arms on her lap as if he had spent himself. They remained silent, and then, after a while, collecting herself, Golden Orchid turned again to the matter for which she had come.

'Yung-kai, my love,' she began, 'if you really love me, you must do something for me. You know what I mean. I cannot bear to see my husband so dejected and spiritless. He is completely broken. And yet he is such a good man — a kind and honourable man, a scholarly man, with such purity in his heart. He should not have been made an ambassador. They should have kept him in Peking in some other capacity. But instead of that he is being taunted, afflicted and humiliated by these impudent young rascals. The whole thing is degrading, and that is why I must implore you to intercede on his behalf.'

'What do you think we can do?'

'Your father is the only person who can save the situation. For no reason at all — yes, for no reason that I know of — the staff members have consistently created trouble. One would think that my husband was their mortal enemy, and yet what has he done to displease them?'

'This is one of those things which I cannot understand.'

'But it is not so difficult to understand, Yung-kai. The secretaries are being encouraged, aided and abetted by someone in the Tsungli Yamen itself. That is what incenses me.'

'Who is he?'

'Wait, let me tell you something. The ambassador has sent confidential reports on the staff, but they have had no effect whatever. Wen-ching is now a poor cat without teeth or claws. The mice defy him. They pull his whiskers, they bite him, and there is nothing he can do. I am sure these reports never reached your father. Why?'

'That is what I want to know.'

'There is a little snake in the Tsungli Yamen. His name is Hu-mou. He has taken advantage of your father's good nature and his many duties elsewhere. He actually controls all the affairs in the office and does things without the knowledge and consent of your good father. All I ask is that you write to your father and beg him to look into the matter.'

'It is possible that this Hu-mou has gained his ears,' Yung-kai agreed. 'I know for a fact that Hu-mou is a very scheming person, capable of all kinds of meanness.'

'Yung-kai, do you know the man personally?'

'No, but I know a good deal of him. He is ambitious and jealous of the high esteem in which the ambassador is held by many people. But then again there may be other reasons.'

'What do you think they can be?'

'For all I know, you may be correct in thinking that Hu-mou is behind all these troubles in the embassy.' Yung-kai paused, then went on: 'But I have heard a good deal of gossip about the ambassador among the staff, and I am very angry. They say, for instance, that he is niggardly, that he has withheld the salaries of the staff for his own use, that he is trying to make use of his position to increase his revenue in order to satisfy the vanities of a young and extravagant concubine, that one of the staff has even slapped his face.'

Golden Orchid was shocked to hear all this. Although she had a low opinion of the embassy staff, she had never suspected that they could be so cowardly or contemptible.

'Yung-kai,' she said, trying to suppress the fury within her, 'you have been long enough in the embassy. Do you think for a moment that any of these ridiculous charges can have one grain of truth in them? How can anyone utter such nonsense?'

'I am just beginning to learn how rotten our official life really is. There is another rumour about the ambassador which, I hope, won't shock you when I say it.'

'I shall try to be merely amused, Yung-kai. What is it?'

'There is a rumour that the ambassador is making all kinds of profits, even to the extent of selling fruit.'

'Selling fruit?'

'Yes, selling fruit!'

'Why don't they say that the ambassador is selling empty bottles or old rags?'

'And to show you how depraved these people can be, they

circulate all this rubbish among their friends in their letters home. My own father has asked me, in one of his letters, whether any of this can be true.'

'Unbelievable!'

'Of course, I told him it's all nonsense. The fact of the matter is that most of our officials love to hear scandal. They are not interested in whether gossip has any basis of truth or not, whether it makes any sense or not. As long as there is gossip, they love to hear it. And with Hu-mou bent on destroying the ambassador, as you said, and the secretaries in the embassy acting as his agents, why, they purposely spread all kinds of ridiculous stories to create the impression that the ambassador is a miserable failure. That is what they want — to create a false impression.'

'All this is the work of Hu-mou, I am sure. What have we come to, Yung-kai?'

'Now, if you wish, I will write to my father again. But I don't see how things can be clarified until I return to Peking and describe the situation to him in person.'

Golden Orchid was relieved that in Yung-kai at least she had a sympathetic friend: she felt that she could depend on him for active support. But all the same she was horrified by how much she and her husband had been slandered. 'Why, these beasts, they accuse me and my husband of precisely the things they have been trying to do and have failed to accomplish,' she exclaimed. 'Do you know, Yung-kai, that one of the secretaries actually opened a milliner's shop in the name of a local girl with whom he lives, and makes use of diplomatic privileges to import perfumes, free of duty, from Paris? Another secretary has been doing the same thing with wine, and has issued certificates in the name of the consular service to the German Customs so often that one day the Customs official wrote directly to the ambassador to inquire about it. But do you know what happened?'

'What?'

'The ambassador asked the secretary to come into his office, showed him the note he had received from the Customs, and, believe it or not, the secretary snatched the paper from my husband, tore it to pieces and swallowed it to destroy the evidence. You can imagine how stunned my husband was. How can you expect a scholar to deal with such behaviour?'

'Did that really happen?'

'I swear to the accuracy of every word I have said. I had the story from the mouth of the ambassador himself. Am I to say that he is a liar? And do you blame him for being so dejected and thinking that it is impossible to remain here any longer? In fact, he has expressed his desire to resign many times, but each time he was asked to carry on. That might seem encouraging, but I am afraid there is a meaning in that also.

'Let me tell you something else,' continued Golden Orchid. 'One of these same secretaries has been smuggling gold between Switzerland and Germany. It has not come into the open yet. But one day it will, and then the matter will become so serious that it may precipitate an international crisis. It has happened before in our diplomatic service. You remember the case of gold smuggling between Switzerland and France, in another of our embassies, when a secretary was caught with undeclared gold on his person at the French Customs?'

'Yes, I heard about that.'

'I am afraid this is what is going to happen to our secretary. Both Wen-ching and myself are terribly worried, but the ridiculous part of it is that, as ambassador, my husband has no power to prevent it. We are utterly helpless because the staff has the connivance and encouragement of Hu-mou in the Tsungli Yamen. They know they are free to do anything they wish. And then, to add insult to injury, they spread the falsehood that the ambassador himself is doing precisely what they are doing.'

Yung-kai smiled and said: 'As we say in military circles, the best defence is offence. How clever!'

'Now I understand,' continued Golden Orchid, 'why we in Soochow can curse a man by saying that he should die by a thousand stabs. That man Hu-mou deserves every one of those stabs, and one of these days he is going to get them.'

'How despicable! I know the officials of a decadent government think only in terms of their own interests, their own advancement and enrichment. But I did not know that they could stoop so low.'

As Yung-kai said this, his mind flashed back to his association with Ping-mo and those other young men who, after all, he thought, were genuine patriots. He still had the greatest admiration for them.

E

Only a new regime could sweep away all this corruption: of that he was sure.

Yung-kai asked Golden Orchid to remain for dinner, but it was getting late and she was afraid that her husband might be looking for her. Before she left, however, she implored Yung-kai again to give all the help within his power — to write to his father, and let her know what his father replied.

Yung-kai agreed, though he feared he would accomplish little. What he had heard so shocked him that, for the moment, his desire for Golden Orchid had left him.

6

DURING the next few weeks life at the embassy, to all appearances, remained on an even tenor.

Golden Orchid had no qualms about her visit to Yung-kai's apartment. They had, however, arrived at a point in their relationship beyond which she felt she would not consent to go. One more intimate step, and everything would be changed. As things stood now, Golden Orchid had no hesitation in telling Wen-ching practically all that had happened, though she did not tell him of Yung-kai's avowal of love.

'The ambassador wants to see you, Yung-kai,' said Golden Orchid the day after her visit to his apartment. 'He is expecting you in his office.' She was not afraid of what the two might say to each other.

Wen-ching received Yung-kai, as usual, as if he were his own son, and they talked at first in generalities — of how the young man was getting on in his studies, how he liked living in a foreign country and whether he had received recently any news from his honourable father.

'Yes, Uncle Shen,' replied Yung-kai. 'Father seems as busy as ever. Things continue to be rather tense in Peking. He has given me no indication of what they are, but I can read between the lines that he spends most of his time near the Empress Dowager.'

'You are quite right,' said Wen-ching. 'It seems that pressure from foreign countries on the Court is getting stronger every day, and we are powerless to resist. They all seem very aggressive. The situation has become much worse, as you know, since our defeat by Japan over three years ago. If there is any difference between these powers, it is a difference of degree.'

'Father says in one letter that anti-foreign feeling is growing rapidly everywhere.'

"I can understand that. There are no friends in international relations. There is hardly any friendship between individuals, so what can you expect? For example, Russia came out openly to prevent Japan from grabbing our north-eastern provinces. That sounds excellent, but of course she did so entirely for her own interests. She has already taken away all our land north of the Amur River, and now she covets the land south of the river, where our emperors had their origins.'

'I always have the feeling that Russia is a land-grabber.'

'You have probably heard of the secret treaty last year, that was signed on the occasion of the Czar's coronation. In that treaty Russia forced us, among other things, to agree to the construction of a railway trunk line right through our Manchuria. We had no alternative: we signed under duress.'

'If the people get to know of the treaty, there will be resentment against Russia. Isn't that true?'

'Exactly. But the other powers have come to know of it already, and they are unhappy because they are equally self-seeking. The situation is very grave.'

Wen-ching reflected and then continued: 'You see, Yung-kai, I should be in St Petersburg now for a longer residence than last time, but I don't seem able to get away. Perhaps you know why.'

Yung-kai merely said: 'I hope Uncle Shen will go there soon. It is a long and arduous journey. Perhaps it is better to wait until the Spring. Life then will be more pleasant in the Russian capital.'

'During the short period I was in St Petersburg last time, I managed to have many conversations, and I think I know what the Russians are up to. There is, for instance' — at this point Wen-ching seemed to feel that he was speaking too freely to one who, after all, was his subordinate. But at the back of his mind was always the desire that Yung-kai should urge his father to take action against Hu-mou and his minions. He could not say this openly, for he had a sense of personal dignity. He went on, thinking that there was no harm in cultivating the young man's good feelings: 'Let me tell you two very interesting episodes in connection with this Russian treaty which I was talking about. When the Chinese and Russian delegates were assembled to sign the treaty, a very important mistake was discovered in the text. It was made by the copyists — perhaps inadvertently. Instead of saying that Russia would come to the help of China if she was attacked by Japan, the copyists omitted the last two words. That meant that Russia was to come to the help of China whenever she was attacked — which of course made a great difference. It was about lunchtime when the mistake was found out, and the presiding Russian minister very adroitly asked for an immediate adjournment. The text was of course subsequently amended. I always thought this most interesting.'

'I can see that a little carelessness may have serious consequences.'

'Then there was another interesting episode,' Wen-ching continued. 'Oh those Russians — what they would not do to get what they want! You see, Yung-kai, Russia had no steamers of her own to take the Chinese delegates from Peking to St Petersburg. Lord Li was then our chief delegate, and the Russians were afraid that the other powers might influence his Lordship *en route*. They were especially afraid of the British. So they persuaded Lord Li to be a passenger on a French liner. And then, as soon as it stopped at Port Said, the Russian Government took him to one of its own steamers, which headed directly for Odessa. It was almost like kidnapping. In that way the Russians succeeded in preventing Lord Li from having any contact with western Europe. I was told that His Lordship never forgave the Russians: the steamer they sent him was small, dirty and uncomfortable.'

Wen-ching and Yung-kai laughed together at this story, and then Wen-ching commented: 'It just shows how suspicious the Russians are. Well, Yung-kai, what I started to tell you is this: Russia is bringing strong pressure to bear on us. She even has an eye on a warm port in our Shantung province. That's where the Germans have been clamouring for their share. I have been as evasive as I could over this. You can see the extent of our national danger. Now you would think that, in the face of this emergency, our officials would get together and do something for our country. But no, we continue to quarrel and be jealous of one another, and even destroy one another. That is what makes me so angry. I am, of course, only a simple scholar, and the ways of the official world are indeed strange to me.'

Even without the information that Golden Orchid had given him, Yung-kai would have understood quite well what his ambassador was driving at, but he could think of no appropriate comment to make. He gave expressions of sympathy, however, which pleased Wen-ching.

'Yung-kai,' the ambassador continued, 'you are still young, and I hope that you will not have to face the difficulties which men like myself have to face. But let me tell you something more cheerful. The German Foreign Office informed me a few days ago that their Emperor desires to express his friendship to our Emperor and is going to make a suitable gift on the occasion of the anniversary of His Imperial Majesty's accession to the throne. The gift is in the form of a powerful white stallion chosen from the German Emperor's own stables. I have been asked to accept it, and I have.'

Yung-kai was delighted.

'Ah-ya! This is splendid. I love horses myself, and if Uncle Shen so desires, I shall personally see to it that the horse is delivered to His Imperial Majesty.'

Yung-kai had long had a reputation as a young man of singular charm, but he was never so attractive and charming as when the subject of horses was brought up. He was proud of his horsemanship, and the offer of his services was made in a disarmingly spontaneous manner.

'With your permission, Uncle Shen, when the horse arrives I will train it myself for a time,' he suggested. 'In the meantime, I will find out the best route to take and inform my father accordingly.'

Wen-ching had privately considered that this was the proper way in which the imperial gift should be delivered, but he was nevertheless nonplussed by the alacrity with which Yung-kai responded before the request was even made to him.

'Are you sure that you would want to perform such a mission?' asked Wen-ching, as if he were not prepared to agree to the proposition. 'When I accepted the gift, I gave little thought to its delivery, but now you have expressed your willingness to undertake the journey, I feel it is too much — too much for anybody. After all, it is thousands of miles from here to Peking, and although you are a lover of horses and a splendid rider, I don't see how you can do it.'

'Never mind, Uncle Shen, I shall give the matter serious thought. If I feel that it cannot be done, I will let you know, and we can find other means. For the moment I think that I can not only do it but that I shall derive a good deal of profit and pleasure from the journey.'

And so the conversation ended. Wen-ching was happy because through Yung-kai, if he undertook the mission and arrived in Peking, Lord Yu Kung might learn something at first hand of what had been going on in the embassy. But at the same time he felt uneasy. As Wen-ching extended his hand, in the European manner, to thank Yung-kai, it occurred to him that in the veins of the young man there was, after all, still some blood of his Manchu ancestors, bequeathing nomadic instincts which he, as a Chinese scholar, could not fully comprehend.

When the information was conveyed to Golden Orchid, she was frightened. Could it be that her husband had found out what had happened between her and Yung-kai? Could it be that her lover and her husband had had a quarrel over her and that Yung-kai was deliberately being sent away on so dangerous a mission? Surely something serious must have happened. How could Yung-kai ever complete such a long and hazardous journey, alone with his horse for thousands upon thousands of miles, without hurting or even killing himself? And yet Wen-ching calmly told her that he was sending Yung-kai on such an errand!

'What . . . what has happened, Wen-ching dear?' ejaculated Golden Orchid in a state of excitement which Wen-ching could not understand. 'Why are you sending Yung-kai on so dangerous an errand?'

'Nothing has happened, my treasure,' replied Wen-ching, remaining as calm as ever. 'It is only that the German Emperor professes the warmest regard to our Emperor, and in order to further friendly relations he has seen fit to present to His Imperial Majesty a beautiful white horse, which I have accepted.'

'Yes, but —'

'With the Russians casting a covetous eye on our Shantung province, it is to our advantage that the German Government should show some interest in that part of our land. "To fight poison with poison," as we say, or as the venerable Lord Li has well said, "Use the barbarian to defeat the barbarian." It's a good principle to see German power marshalled against Russian power. That is why I would not think of declining this gift, and I am glad that Yung-kai has volunteered to deliver it in person to His Imperial Majesty.'

'But how can Yung-kai do it?'

'You need not worry. No doubt he knows exactly what he is doing. Besides, I didn't ask him; he made the offer himself.'

'But even so, you shouldn't allow him, Wen-ching dear.'

'I have heard from Ping-mo that Yung-kai was trained from very early days to be an excellent horseman. He has the blood of his ancestors in his veins. No, no, there is no reason to be afraid of anything.'

Golden Orchid's anxieties were set at rest. From her husband's manner, it did not seem that there was any ill feeling between him and Yung-kai. That was the principal thing. If he had no knowledge of what had happened in Yung-kai's apartment the previous day, there was no cause for worry.

'If Yung-kai feels he cannot deliver the horse, I can always have it transported on a steamer like the one we came on. So don't worry. Only wait and see what this horse looks like. It will be brought to us in a few days, and we shall have quite a little ceremony.'

7

Two weeks later Wen-ching was officially notified that the gift would be made at Easter. There began then in the Chinese Embassy a commotion such as it had never known before. A representative of the Kaiser himself was to ride the horse to the embassy, accompanied by his adjutants and by members of the German Foreign Office, and a stable in the neighbourhood was assigned to the animal. In the meantime, Yung-kai expressed his firm belief that he could manage the journey alone without, as he said, any 'mortifying' consequences.

'Let me tell you, Uncle Shen, how I shall do it.' Yung-kai spread a map in front of the ambassador. 'From Berlin to Moscow, which is a distance slightly under a thousand miles, I believe I can ride with ease. From Moscow I shall take the horse by train to Omsk to give it a good long rest. Then I take a steamer up the Irtysh River, through Semipalatinsk, and thence to Lake Zaisan until I reach the Chinese border. From Chuguchak, which is the first Chinese town, I will be in my own country, and although there are mountains and deserts to cross, I believe that the fifteen hundred or so miles to

Peking, as the crow flies, can be covered without disaster either to myself or to the imperial gift, if the magistrates of the towns on the way are given ample notice beforehand.'

The plan was accordingly communicated to the German Foreign Office, and it was said there that so audacious and so grandiose a project had never been heard of before. The impression made on the German Government and the imperial household was such that it immensely increased the prestige of the Chinese people not only in Germany but all over Europe. Imagine a nation, which was supposed to be at the nadir of degeneracy, with the best of its manhood debilitated by opium-smoking, suddenly proclaiming that a mere military attaché was to undertake such a gigantic and spectacular adventure. On being apprised of this news the German Government decided that the delivery of the gift should be made an occasion of even greater pomp and ceremony than originally planned. It was even suggested that the young military attaché should be received in audience by the German Emperor and be given his blessing.

When the day arrived, the streets of Berlin were filled with immense crowds, for the event was widely publicized in all the papers, and Kurfürstendamm, where the Chinese Embassy was situated, was the scene of the wildest demonstrations of curiosity and well-wishing. Imperial carriages led the procession, followed by an impressive military band; then came foot-soldiers and finally the imperial gift itself. On the back of the horse was a tall straight figure, a handsome general in his middle forties, with his drawn sabre dazzling in the sun. Behind him were more carriages filled with high-ranking officials representing the Government.

The reception-rooms of the embassy were gaily decorated for the occasion. At ordinary times they were large enough to hold three or four hundred guests easily. Today they were unable to accommodate the crowd that came surging in. The ambassador was in his official robe as a mandarin of the first order, flanked on his right by his lovely young concubine and on his left by the military attaché Yung-kai, the hero of the hour, in full military regalia.

Wen-ching looked serene and dignified: it was one of the proudest moments of his life. Facing them were members of the German delegation. Then at the appropriate time a message was read in German on behalf of the Kaiser offering congratulations to the Chinese Emperor on the twenty-third anniversary of his accession to the Dragon

Throne and extending everlasting friendship to the Chinese nation. The sentiments were fully reciprocated by Wen-ching, who as usual spoke in Chinese, which was then translated into German.

Champagne was served. Wen-ching held up his glass and drank to the health of the German Emperor. The German delegation likewise held up their glasses and drank to the health and happiness of His Imperial Majesty Emperor Kuang Hsu. In a short while the ceremony was over. Then followed a long period of revelry in which wine flowed freely, and servants were busy passing Chinese foods and delicacies to the guests.

Yung-kai was seen most of the time talking to the dashing general who had ridden the gift horse, von Scheidermann, a member of the inner circle in the palace of the Emperor and one of his trusted confidants. Yung-kai introduced him to Wen-ching and Golden Orchid, with whom von Scheidermann seemed to carry on a very lively conversation.

Yung-kai intended to leave as soon as the preparations were completed. He had obtained some information about his route from Lao Chuang, who was as deeply interested in the journey as Yung-kai himself. It was Lao Chuang's pleasure to pay constant visits to the stable to see that the horse was being taken care of properly.

'Young lord,' said Lao Chuang one day when they were together at the stable, 'why don't you take me with you? I can serve you well. I have lived in the wilds of Mongolia and know how to take care of you.'

'Thank you, Lao Chuang,' replied Yung-kai. 'I thought of that, and I am sure you could give me valuable help, but I'd rather you stayed where you are, to serve Tai-tai and the ambassador.'

Lao Chuang was a faithful servant and realized that, if he asked for long leave — a euphemism for resignation — it would cause great inconvenience to his master and mistress, so he did not insist. On the other hand, he was becoming increasingly disgusted with the way in which the members of the staff had been behaving and wanted to see no more of them. He despised the secretaries. He was convinced that he could be of great service to Yung-kai, though it was quite correct, he thought to himself, that, as the young lord had said, he should remain where he was to serve Tai-tai.

Yung-kai sought the company of Golden Orchid during his last few days in Berlin. On the eve of his departure he had a last long meeting with Golden Orchid in his apartment. She came without the slightest hesitation. They vowed eternal love and devotion to each other. There were long silences, as though without speech their souls could commune with each other more freely and intimately. The few words that were spoken were carved indelibly on their hearts. First there were tears in Golden Orchid's eyes, then in Yung-kai's. They held hands; they kissed, until finally they cast away all their inhibitions. In a passionate embrace they rapturously merged into each other — and became one.

'Remember, my dearest, dearest Yung-kai,' said Golden Orchid as she at last tore herself away, 'that you will take the greatest care of yourself. We shall meet again in Peking, and that will not be long.'

'Yes, my sweetest sister, my own heart and liver,' said Yung-kai with a sigh, 'I shall wait for you there. Even if we are not man and wife in this world, we shall be united in the next. I shall wait for you — always.'

The next day, when Yung-kai left, Golden Orchid stayed in her room. All she wanted was to be left alone. She even sent away Anna, who was anxious to see the scene of departure.

Yung-kai was dressed in the blue silk gown of the military officer, split at the front and back from the waist down; the two flaps covered his legs as he mounted the horse. From the waist up the dress was richly embroidered with spherical designs and finished with a narrow collar of the finest sable. The cuffs were also of sable, horse-shoe shaped. The hat bore a sable band some four inches wide and on the crown sat a coral button the size of a large pigeon's egg, to which was attached a tassel made of stiff bristles over a foot long.

As soon as Yung-kai mounted the horse there was an outburst of wild cheering from the curious and admiring crowd in front of the embassy. He rode eastwards out of the city.

8

'GOLDEN ORCHID, my treasure,' said Wen-ching one day after the excitement over Yung-kai had subsided. 'This morning I received an unusual cable from Peking, but I don't know what to make of it. Believe it or not, the Tsungli Yamen has appointed me concurrently ambassador to Austria-Hungary. I can't believe it. This is too good to be true.'

'What do you think it can mean?'

'I don't know. But I do know this: we must not take this news at its face value. There is a hidden meaning somewhere. How would you interpret it?'

'Well, is it possible that Lord Yu Kung has now learned the truth about our difficulties, and this additional appointment is a reaffirmation of his confidence in you? After all, the appointment was made by him and must have received his agreement.'

'That is a good surmise, but I want to reserve my judgement. I would accept your interpretation if things were normal. But, as we know only too well, they are not.'

'What else can it mean, then?'

'It might be a smoke-screen behind which some new malicious scheme is being concocted against me. I may be over-suspicious, but I am not inclined to be optimistic as long as Hu-mou is still so powerful in the Tsungli Yamen.'

Wen-ching paced up and down the room deeply wrapped in thought.

'Perhaps you may be right, Wen-ching dear. But there are good people as well as bad ones. And the good people can triumph sometimes.'

'I am afraid not in this case, my precious. The appointment reminds me too much of our classic formula to destroy a man. You shower favours on him and then, when he is off his guard, stab him. There are so many examples of this kind of thing in our history.'

That evening, there came another cable conferring one of the highest decorations — the Order of the Brilliant Jade — on Wen-ching. The two cables had been dispatched from Peking simultaneously and reached Berlin within a few hours of each other.

'I am more perplexed than ever,' declared Wen-ching. 'Why should Peking shower honours on me? I hope you are correct, my precious, in thinking that good ultimately triumphs over evil. I like to think so myself. But there are forces to pull me away from that belief. This second cable has made me more sceptical than ever.'

'I like to think that Yung-kai's father is beginning to straighten things out for you.'

'If these honours had come to us later, after Yung-kai's arrival in Peking, I might be inclined to believe that, too. But I have a suspicion that before Yung-kai reaches Peking some very unpleasant things are going to happen, and there is no way I can prevent them.'

'So you think that behind this is still the wickedness of Hu-mou?'

'Am I to believe that Hu-mou has become friendly all of a sudden? He has every reason to want to destroy me, and has long had the opportunity of undermining Lord Yu Kung's friendship for me.'

'Has there been any fresh indication recently?'

'Not exactly, but Wang has been writing to tell me a few more things about Hu-mou. I asked him to let me know all about him.'

'And what did he say?'

'He said that Hu-mou wants the people of Soochow to have the impression that he is the most important man the city has produced. Up to now, I happen to have had this honour, and he hates it.'

'What are you going to do?'

'We must wait and see. However, I must arrange to go to Vienna as soon as possible to present my credentials. Vienna is near; it is not like going to St Petersburg.'

The man who was in charge of the Chinese Embassy in Vienna held the rank of first secretary. As such he was chargé d'affaires in the absence of an ambassador. Wen-ching had known him for many years, though not well. In the next few days he thought he would send a wire to this man Lin Liang and ask him to come to Berlin and make arrangements for his trip to Vienna.

Lin Liang came as instructed, and then something occurred which confirmed Wen-ching's fears. When Lin Liang arrived in Berlin, he paid official calls on all the staff members of the embassy before asking for an appointment with his new superior, Ambassador Shen Wen-ching. That was an uncommon procedure. However, Wen-ching gave him the usual exchange of courtesies when they met, and in order to make Lin Liang feel quite at home, purposely recalled their many previous meetings, not as officials but as scholars, so that they could talk on a footing of equality and without being embarrassed by the difference in their diplomatic ranks. The interview started pleasantly enough, and then Wen-ching naturally brought up the subject of his impending visit to Vienna.

'Brother Lin Liang,' Wen-ching addressed him, 'I have heard of your manifold accomplishments in Austria-Hungary. You are sincerely to be congratulated, and I am sure that the Court will give you tangible expression of their appreciation of these services.'

'Thank you, Mr Ambassador, for making such friendly remarks,' replied Lin Liang. 'I have been in Vienna for many years. I have no great accomplishments to speak of, but I think I have performed some valuable services. For example, a group of our officials in Peking are purchasing large amounts of ammunition from the European countries, and I have been dealing with this matter in Austria-Hungary. I understand the same is being done in Sweden and Belgium.'

'Yes, yes, Brother Lin Liang; in these troublous times I can well understand that our Government should stock up with as many modern weapons of war as possible. It is ridiculous that we should try to defend ourselves with our antiquated weapons against the tremendous fire-power of the foreigners. We must have their weapons to defeat them.'

There was a short pause, and then Wen-ching continued: 'The Court in Peking really has no need to give me the burden of another appointment. You should continue in your work, and I think in time you should be appointed ambassador yourself. I am already in charge of two embassies, but I can't even cope with one. And this Vienna appointment has come so suddenly.'

'But, Mr Ambassador,' replied Lin Liang, 'your wide scholarship and ability are matters of common knowledge, and this new appointment is to be expected.'

'However that may be, the appointment has been made, even though I feel unequal to the task. And now, if you will be kind enough, Brother Lin Liang, you will please, upon your return to Vienna, arrange a time for me to present my credentials to the Austro-Hungarian Government. There is ample time, as it will take many days before the papers arrive from Peking.'

'Well, of course. . . . But about this matter,' stammered Lin Liang, 'I wish . . . I wish the ambassador could stay here —' Lin Liang hesitated. 'I will do what I can, but I have been told that the Government in Vienna is extremely busy, and there may be some delay.'

'As I said,' rejoined Wen-ching, 'there is no hurry. The credentials will not be here for some time.'

Lin Liang looked disturbed and struggled to say something.

Finally he said: 'Mr Ambassador, I wish that you would remain here and not go to Vienna.'

Wen-ching was stunned. He didn't know what to say. He thought to himself, This is the most unusual thing I have ever heard. Here I am, appointed by the Court to be concurrently ambassador in Vienna, and this charge d'affaires has the effrontery to ask me not even to present my credentials. What kind of a trap is this?

Thoughts of Hu-mou, the embassy staff and the recent new honours tumbled about in his mind — I thought so — just as I suspected. This is part of some new trickery.

Lin Liang sat in his chair with his eyes riveted to the floor. Controlling himself, Wen-ching answered: 'Brother Lin Liang, as you know only too well, I cannot go against the instructions of our Government. None of us can. I will have to present my credentials as soon as they arrive.'

Lin Liang said: 'If the ambassador remains here and postpones the trip to Vienna — indefinitely — I . . . I shall see to it that he receives the sum of eight hundred American dollars, or even a thousand dollars, every month.'

This was too much for Wen-ching. His face became red with anger. Scholar though he was, he struck his desk with his fist, and said, in the angriest tone he had ever used in his life: 'How can you say such a thing? How can you suggest such a thing? What do you take me to be? I had a much higher estimation of you. So that is what you are!'

And without further ado he left his office, went upstairs to his room and lay down on his couch, panting for breath. He had heard much about corruption among officials: in fact, there was much evidence of it in his own embassy, but this was the first time he had been confronted with it in so daring and brazen a manner. Long devoted to the study of Confucian principles and imbued with the ideals of personal honour and integrity, he was amazed by Lin Liang's offer. It upset his mental and moral equilibrium, particularly as he had not even the small merit of being subtle, perhaps because Lin Liang was from Kwangtung, where the people are not known for their delicacy.

There was nothing for Lin Liang to do except depart without saying goodbye to his ambassador.

When Golden Orchid came into the room, Wen-ching told her what had happened. 'My precious one, my suspicions are not groundless. The crisis is rapidly coming to a head. Those honours which were conferred on me are, as I said, meant to delude me and divert my attention. It is now quite clear. That Order of the Brilliant Jade — why, I am sure I shall never live to see it. And as for the additional ambassadorship to Vienna — I'll tell you what has happened.' And Wen-ching recounted Lin Liang's interview with him.

'You can see, my precious one, that they expected me to agree to Lin Liang's proposition, in which case I would have fallen straight into their net. Oh, how malicious can human beings be! The arrangement with Lin Liang was all made beforehand by Hu-mou — before the appointment was even made. . . . But I shall proceed as if nothing has happened. I shall go to Vienna as soon as the credentials arrive. If I don't present them, the fault will be mine.'

Golden Orchid did all she could to pacify and comfort him. That night they retired early, but for Wen-ching sleep was out of the question. He kept turning over and over in his mind the implications of this strange incident.

Quietly he slipped out of bed and went to his study. Surrounded by all the wisdom of Confucian lore, he felt more mystified than ever by the problem of evil. 'Repay evil with goodness,' so said one of the ancient sages. And Wen-ching said to himself, What else have I done but try to be good to all those in the path of my life? And yet . . . what is the result? I have worked hard and studied hard. In fact, my whole life has been that of a scholar, and I owe what I am to my scholarly attainments. Must I then be punished in such a cruel manner?

He folded his arms, placed them on the edge of his desk, and rested his head on them. . . . Now I remember, he thought, why one of my friends, Mr Fu-nien, used to say to me that a book bearing the title *How to become an Official* should have been compiled and be my *vade mecum*. I thought he was joking, but I realize now — alas too late! — that he knew exactly what he was talking about. Look at Hu-mou. His personal morals are reputed to be very low, especially in matters concerning women. He has had affairs with the daughters of his friends and even with pretty servant maids. He has accepted bribes galore. And yet, in spite of all this, he seems to sail on this official sea without any tempest, without so much as a ripple. Here is a secret I long to know. As for the members of the staff here, why, I have done everything for their welfare, but they show no appreciation. They insist upon doing improper and even illegal things — going about with street-girls and entering into petty business relations with them in order to make money. They don't seem to be any the worse for these deeds. Now I understand why the fortunes of the country have fallen so low. That is why Mencius used to say, 'No nation can be attacked unless it is first attacked from within.' How can we have the strength to resist aggression when we are so worm-eaten within ourselves? You cannot have corrupt officials without ultimately feeling their effect on the Government and on the country as a whole. In time I may be sacrificed, as I think I will, but what I worry about is the country. One day it will totter to its ruin. . . . For Lin Liang and for others of his ilk, to offer bribes and accept them is, I presume, the normal thing. It is something taken for granted, and probably he didn't understand why I was so angry. But to me it is an outrage! An outrage!

Wen-ching continued to meditate, but to no avail. Downcast and gloomy, he went back to bed. It was almost dawn. He fell asleep, and soon afterwards Golden Orchid woke up. She quietly got out of bed and gently pulled the blanket over Wen-ching. She looked at him and saw a face shadowed with cares and worries. It was a sad face, with the temples rapidly greying.

In her spacious dressing-room, which was for her the most intimate part of the house, she lighted some incense in front of the figure of Kuan-yin and prayed. She asked for divine blessing. She asked the Goddess of Mercy to intervene and help solve her husband's troubles. When she raised her head again, she saw the pictures of her mother and grandmother in the corner, and tears rolled down her cheeks.

9

AFTER a week's riding, Yung-kai had reached the territory which had previously been part of Poland. The cobbled streets of many of the German towns were sometimes slippery for the horse, but otherwise Yung-kai had so far encountered little difficulty. Soon after leaving Berlin he had changed his sumptuous uniform for one less conspicuous, and so, on his journey, little attention was paid to him save for the fact that he was of a different race.

Yung-kai noticed that, as he proceeded eastward, the cities were less opulent, the stretches of countryside between them larger, and even the physical characteristics of the people were different. The faces became less heavy, the build smaller and the women prettier, with softer and more delicate features. He tried to talk with them in German, which was understood, but the people chose to speak among themselves in their own tongue, which had no resemblance whatever to German. The wayside inns and taverns in which he spent the nights were very hospitable but more and more shabby.

Yung-kai saw many scenes which reminded him of northern China — little girls, often barefooted and with colourful kerchiefs over their heads, driving small groups of geese along muddy and uneven country lanes, or fairs to which were herded here a head of cattle, there a hog, to be sold or exchanged for cloth and other commodities for daily use. He also saw men, evidently of a different race, wearing black beards, with skull-caps and garments which reached to the knees, who seemed to be acting as middlemen in the transactions of the fair. Yung-kai was intensely interested in all these fresh experiences.

After passing a large city called Posen he arrived at a village which the native people called Wrzesnia. It was no different from any of the other villages he had passed, but the inn was larger and its courtyards more spacious, and he thought he would spend a comfortable night. He was not deceived. The host was unusually genial. He came out and gave Yung-kai a hearty and almost royal welcome, groomed the horse himself, gave it some fodder, and then tethered it in a large stable.

When Yung-kai said that he was on his way to China with the white horse, the man's eyes almost popped out of their sockets, and he began to show Yung-kai such respect that it became almost embarrassing. He brought out his best wines, and, in front of a huge log fire, served a sumptuous dinner such as Yung-kai had not tasted even during those elaborate diplomatic functions in Berlin.

'But surely you are not going back to Russia,' said the innkeeper as he raised the glass to drink to the health of his distinguished guest.

'I am Chinese, as you can see. What makes you think that I am going back to Russia?'

'Well, everybody passing through here is either going to Russia or has left Russia. This is the first time that someone has come who is going all the way to China through Russia.'

So saying, the innkeeper raised his glass once more and added heartily: 'And you are so cheerful and gay a young man. You see, people going to Russia are usually cheerful and gay. They are as free and full of mirth as you are. That's why I thought you were going there. But those coming back from Russia are not so cheerful. In fact, they look sullen and unhappy. But I am talking too much. It is an honour to have you here, sir, and may you enjoy yourself while you are here.'

When he went to bed that night Yung-kai did not feel well. He had a chill and something of a fever. It was then that he became uneasy, and, thinking of the long and arduous journey still ahead of him, he began to wonder whether it was not, after all, wiser to have someone to take care of him in case something should happen. During these moments of weakness his thoughts naturally flew like arrows to Golden Orchid. He wondered whether he should send a wire to ask that Lao Chuang be released from the embassy to become his valet and travelling companion. He realized what an inconvenience it would be to Wen-ching and Golden Orchid to be without the services of their devoted and faithful Lao Chuang; but the wire was sent, and arrived as Wen-ching and Golden Orchid were having breakfast.

Without even reading the contents, both Wen-ching and Golden Orchid were shocked; they surmised that the wire came from Yung-kai, as it bore the stamp of some strange and unknown city. 'Please let Lao Chuang come at once if possible to accompany me.' So read the wire.

Golden Orchid was the first to speak — almost hysterically, without even consulting Wen-ching. Lao Chuang happened to be in the room. 'Lao Chuang,' she said, 'the young lord asks that you go to him at once. I think something has happened. It may be that he is ill, that he wants you to take care of him during the rest of the journey. You had better go at once.'

Important as she knew the practical considerations of the mission were, the fact that she and Yung-kai had spent a night of love on the eve of his departure influenced her even more. She thought more of his well-being than of anything else.

She continued: 'Use your best judgement, Lao Chuang. If you find that the young lord is really ill, tell him that I want him to come back to Berlin and give up the journey. After all, we can find some other means of delivering the imperial gift.'

Wen-ching gave his approval, and Lao Chuang left. A week later another wire came from Yung-kai saying that the servant had arrived safely and that they were now on their way to Moscow, where they would take the train for a full eighteen hundred miles to Omsk. They would then be fully rested for the overland journey through Mongolia to Peking. The message, thought Golden Orchid, was reassuring, though she wished Yung-kai had turned back. She had no knowledge of the difficult country ahead of Yung-kai. If she had, she would certainly have insisted that he return. But at least she had the consolation that Yung-kai was not now travelling alone, that Lao Chuang would take good care of him.

For the next few months life became strangely vacant for Golden Orchid, even though events came crowding on her. There were the usual teas and dinners to attend, yet time seemed to hang heavily on her hands. Now that Yung-kai and Lao Chuang had left the embassy, she found it increasingly necessary to depend on Anna. She studied German with more than usual application and made rapid progress in the difficult language, so that she began to feel at home in Berlin and to enjoy many of the diplomatic functions.

It was during this period that she was received in audience by the German Empress, whom she found to be very charming and attractive. Von Scheidermann was commissioned to accompany her to the Schloss Charlottenburg. And there in the spacious and luxurious rooms were assembled not only the wives of the diplomatic corps but also many of the Court ladies, all elegantly dressed, their colourful gowns trailing behind them. The wife of the Japanese ambassador was present, but although she was as pretty as a butterfly in her kimono, she felt she was being overshadowed.

Golden Orchid was dressed for the occasion like a Manchu princess, with a long lemon-yellow gown reaching to her ankles. Her shoes were of black satin, raised on pattens. She walked slowly and gave an impression of great elegance and stateliness. Covering the upper half of her body was a small blue sleeveless jacket trimmed with embroidery. But the most impressive part of her attire was the huge head-dress, like an elongated hexagon, ornamented with jewellery. In the most prominent position was the jade butterfly which Yung-kai had given her. Flanking the butterfly were a large peony studded with stones of different colours and a phoenix made of kingfisher feathers and alive with dazzling blues and greens.

When Golden Orchid entered the audience hall accompanied by von Scheidermann in his resplendent uniform, she was easily the most strangely beautiful woman in the palace. Soon there was a crowd around her. Many of them were her colleagues; she smiled and exchanged a few words of greeting with each.

The Empress was seated at one end of the hall. Von Scheidermann returned at the appropriate moment and, offering his arm to Golden Orchid, conducted her towards the Empress. Some ten paces away from her he stopped and released his arm from that of Golden Orchid. Golden Orchid advanced four more steps, then stood still and genuflected slightly, in the manner of the Manchus. The Empress sketched the gesture of rising from her seat, waved her hand in the direction of the empty chair on her right, and asked her guest to be seated. Golden Orchid did as she was requested, and then said a few words in German which she had practised earlier with Anna. 'May Your Majesty reign with His Majesty the Emperor for ten thousand years!' she said.

It was the usual Chinese salutation, which the Empress well understood. She replied: 'Please convey the same sentiment and our best wishes to His Imperial Majesty the Emperor of China.'

The Empress then deliberately introduced a note of informality and continued: 'How beautifully you speak our language. How long have you studied it?'

'This is the third year of my residence in your wonderful country, Your Majesty,' replied Golden Orchid. 'I could not fail to try to learn your language. It is a beautiful language. Besides, I have always believed that speaking one another's language is the best way to promote friendly relations between nations.'

'You are quite correct,' replied the Empress, and they both smiled.

Golden Orchid then looked at von Scheidermann. Soon she stood up, showed the courtesy of going backwards for three steps while still facing the Empress, and was then escorted back to the other guests.

The function was unique and semi-official, but it was impressive. There was satisfaction among those present. No similar event had been seen in other European capitals.

But as fate would have it, Golden Orchid came back to the embassy to find bad news awaiting her. Wen-ching had received a cable from Peking which confirmed some of his worst fears. It was not the kind of news which he could withhold from Golden Orchid. He decided to break it slowly and, if possible, tactfully.

So, when she had come back and changed, Wen-ching brought her a bowl of lotus seeds which he himself had cooked over a small, slow fire. Every one of the seeds looked whole and complete, the liquid was as clear as water, and with the seeds were cooked three or four of the dry red dates which they had brought from China.

'Eat this, my precious,' said Wen-ching. 'I would have you know that I prepared it myself.'

'It is delicious,' replied Golden Orchid. As she put the seeds into her mouth, they crumbled and melted, so thoroughly were they cooked. But as she ate, Golden Orchid could see that there was a cloud over her husband's face though he continued to perform little acts of kindness and affection.

So she said: 'I have been meeting all the distinguished ladies in the palace. And the Empress is most charming. . . . But is everything all right in the embassy?'

'Yes, just as usual. But a cable from Peking came during your absence.'

'What is it about?'

'Nothing serious. It is one of those things I fully expected, and I don't want you to be upset by it.'

'But tell me, Wen-ching dear, what is it?'

'Well, didn't I say that it was too good to be true that I should be appointed as ambassador to Austria-Hungary? I didn't want it in the first place, and now the Tsungli Yamen has seen fit to relieve me of this extra duty.'

Wen-ching knew the significance of the cable only too well. To have asked him to take up this extra duty and then to relieve him of it, after what had happened between him and Lin Liang, was much worse than not to have asked him at all, but he wanted to soften the blow as much as possible for Golden Orchid. However, she realized at once that a serious thing had happened and that her husband's influence at the Court of Peking was now at an end. The cable, she thought, indicated some even worse catastrophe. In spite of every effort on Wen-ching's part to belittle its significance it was a shock to Golden Orchid. They could hope that with Yung-kai's arrival at Peking the danger would be over.

'How long, Wen-ching dear, do you think we shall have to wait before Yung-kai reaches Peking?'

Wen-ching was surprised at what seemed to him rather an irrelevant question, but he replied: 'Why, another four or five months, perhaps. But why do you ask?'

'It is clear that only Lord Yu Kung can help us in this ugly situation, and he must know what has been taking place. Yung-kai is the only person who will be able to give him a true picture.'

Weeks passed and nothing happened, but over the embassy hung a heavy air of gloom and uneasiness. Wen-ching seemingly found refuge in his classics and historical writings, but there was nothing to relieve the anxiety of Golden Orchid. She waited for more news from Yung-kai, but nothing came. Where is he now? Is he in any danger? Is Lao Chuang serving him well? Does he sleep well? Does he eat well? These and many other questions passed through Golden Orchid's mind.

Miles and miles of desert, of waste space, with wild people, bandits, high mountains — all these, she had now learned, Yung-kai must pass through before he could be safe in his own country. She confined herself to the embassy, declining to attend any of the social functions to which she was so often invited, especially after her successful audience with the Empress. She became irritable and was in a state of high nervous tension. Even Anna, upon whom she normally depended for some comfort and solace, could no longer distract her. Anna would sometimes come to her room and give her little bits of miscellaneous information — to please her or let her know of little happenings in the embassy. But Golden Orchid only wanted to be left alone — with Wen-ching.

In the meantime, the members of the embassy seemed to be busy. They were asking for leave, some to visit other parts of Germany, others to go to Vienna, though for what reasons neither Wen-ching nor Golden Orchid could make out. Any news of these movements angered her. She would not have the names of any of the embassy staff mentioned in her presence, for in her mind they were the epitome of evil — men who were absolutely dishonest, immoral, wicked, among whom she had the misfortune to be cast. She hardly knew them, and yet they were in the embassy to plot and scheme for her ruin and the ruin of her husband. Golden Orchid remembered many things which her grandmother and mother had taught her when she was a child. Both were devout Buddhists, believing in the chain of births and rebirths, and they used to say that sometimes one had to find the explanation of what happened in this life in some previous existence.

Is it possible, Golden Orchid said to herself, that these people who are causing me and my husband such unhappiness were our bitterest enemies in our previous life?

Days dragged on, and Golden Orchid looked pale and wan and listless. She no longer had any zest for life, for life was fast ebbing away from her.

Since the night when she had gone to Yung-kai's apartment and given him all that he demanded and she could give, out of an unusual combination of love and expediency, she had noticed that a change had come over her body. Whether Yung-kai or Wen-ching was responsible for the new life within her, not even she could tell. In due course Wen-ching was told and he was very happy. A new bond to tie him to the young woman whom he loved so deeply — there could not have been a more welcome event in his life.

But the thoughts coursing through Golden Orchid's mind were of a different nature. She was confused, not knowing what to wish for. Here was a great event in her life, and yet who had brought it to her? One day she thought the fatherhood belonged to Yung-kai, another day to Wen-ching, depending on her mood or her predilection at the moment. But whoever gave her this seed of new life — secretly she had little doubt that it was Yung-kai — there was an inward satisfaction which she could not communicate to the outside world.

But suddenly all was changed. The cares, the worries, the uncertainties and the dejection she had had to go through all these months had been too much for her. She had a miscarriage, a 'small birth', and all was over! She was taken to hospital, and Anna attended her. It was fortunately a matter of only a few days, but they were bitter days.

For Wen-ching the blow was still more unendurable. The good news of another child, the first to be borne him by Golden Orchid, had more than counterbalanced the sorrows which had been afflicting him. Indeed, he became so elated that, alone in his study, he was heard chanting some of his favourite poems — among others, those by Tao Chien, a poet who lived in the fourth century, also a period of utter chaos and confusion, who gave up his worldly ambitions to live the life of a recluse on a small plot of land in the country, refusing, as he said, to 'bend his knee' in search of an emolument at the hands of those he despised. Wen-ching had long admired the character and integrity of this gentleman of the 'five willows', as he was called. His was an example to be followed when he returned to China after all the sordidness of official life was over.

But the moment he turned his thoughts in that direction, his mind filled with obstinate questionings. Must the world of practical realities, of which official life is a part, be devoid of moral values? Is the life of a recluse, amid streams and mountains and away from the hubbub of human activity, the only way in which one can maintain personal honour and integrity? Is the moral life a negative life? Is it ever possible for a man to plunge into the maelstrom of human affairs and still manage to keep his head above the eddying currents? This last question was exactly the one he had tried to answer by his own life, but Wen-ching knew that he had not succeeded.

And yet he was not reconciled. For the entire fabric of Confucian thought rested on the belief that the moral imperative must be implied in all human action, no matter where it may find expression. Surely, Wen-ching thought, there must have been periods in the history of his race when the world of realities was fully informed with the life of the spirit, when theory and practice, the real and the ideal, succeeded in creating a genuine harmony.

But there was no evidence of this now. Times have changed, Wen-ching said to himself. There were periods when the Empire was in the hands of men of absolute purity and integrity. They were giants. But now — now sneaking rats like Hu-mou hold the power. No wonder the Empire is disintegrating. He thought of Tao Chien again and chanted one of his poems:

Swiftly the years, beyond recall,
Solemn the stillness of this fair morning.

I will clothe myself in spring clothing
And visit the slopes of the Eastern Hill.
By the mountain stream a mist hovers,
Hovers a moment, then scatters,
There comes a wind blowing from the south
That brushes the fields of new corn.

Alas, for Wen-ching there was unfortunately neither to be any new corn nor any wind blowing from the south to dispel the mist. The mist had, in fact, gathered so thick and fast that nothing could scatter it.

Yung-kai was still on his way — where, how and in what condition, there was no way of finding out. Actually he had by now crossed the Russian border into China and was on perhaps the most difficult stage of his journey. It was to be some time before he would see the gates of Peking. Things might very possibly turn out differently for Wen-ching and Golden Orchid if Lord Yu Kung met his son in time. But before that could happen, Hu-mou and his accomplices knew they must strike; and with such force and telling effect that there would be no way in which Wen-ching and his young concubine could avoid the blow, even if they knew every move in the plot.

Lin Liang, as chargé d'affaires in Vienna, was involved in extensive munition deals. Once Wen-ching had refused his bribe, cables and letters began to fly between Peking and Vienna, between Peking and the embassy staff in Berlin, and between the staff and Vienna — all under Hu-mou's instructions. It took a few months before Hu-mou's designs matured, but in time he was sure that the plan could not fail either at the Vienna end or with the staff in Berlin, who had long been under his control. If things went well and according to plan, he would reward them for their services with diplomatic promotions which were well within his power to recommend. This idea was easily conveyed to Berlin and Vienna.

The only person Hu-mou had reason to worry about was Lord Yu Kung, whom everyone knew to be a close friend of Wen-ching's. From the day Hu-mou went into the service of the Tsungli Yamen he began a careful study of his chief. He found that as an official so near to the throne itself, Lord Yu Kung had duties connected with many government offices, of which the Tsungli Yamen was only one.

Lord Yu Kung was a member of the Grand Council, which was the highest policy-making body of the Court. Hu-mou devoted himself to his work and succeeded in persuading His Lordship to concern himself only with policy, give up the administrative duties of the Tsungli Yamen and entrust them to his care. In this way it soon became apparent to everyone that the real power in the yamen resided in Hu-mou's hands. His word became law, and His Lordship's concurrence a mere matter of formality. All appointments were henceforth made by Hu-mou, and from that moment he was so flooded with gifts from those in office as well as from those seeking appointments that he became almost at once a wealthy person.

There was practically nothing in his household which had not been given to him — from the food at the banquets with which he entertained high officials to Madam Hu-mou's shoes and even her toilet-paper. He saw to it also that Lord Yu Kung received his share of the presents — gold watches and jewels sent by ambassadors from abroad for which His Lordship had an especial liking.

Every morning, before His Lordship was even out of bed, Hu-mou made a personal report. It was part of his plan to be friendly even with His Lordship's gatekeeper, to whom now and then he gave gratuities so that he would always be informed as to His Lordship's movements and the names of his daily visitors.

One morning, as Hu-mou made his customary call, His Lordship was in a bad mood. He had not heard from Yung-kai for some time, and he was worried.

'Brother Hu-mou,' he said, 'do you remember how it came about that I gave the consent to my son to ride back with the horse?'

'I think Ambassador Shen had reason to be proud of the gift from the German Emperor and thought that perhaps it was good for brother Yung-kai's career to present it to our Emperor in person.'

'Do you remember the wording of the ambassador's original cable?'

'Not the exact wording, Your Lordship, but I remember it was very impressive.'

'That must have been the reason I agreed, I suppose.'

'I think so, Your Lordship.'

'As I see it now, the journey doesn't make sense.'

'Perhaps the ambassador has some very important message to convey to Your Lordship through Brother Yung-kai.'

'Well, couldn't he have asked my son to take the horse by some other way?'

'It would seem so, Your Lordship.'

His Lordship was never informed that it was Yung-kai's own wish to come back to Peking in the way he had chosen. Nor did he realize that it was Hu-mou who, in his subtle way, induced His Lordship to give his consent. For Hu-mou was quite sure that something would happen to make His Lordship anxious and unhappy. That would be the time to undermine most effectively the friendship between His Lordship and Wen-ching.

Hu-mou had uncanny prescience of how events would turn out. He knew what every step and every word would lead to, and accordingly he was in a position to direct the emotional responses of his superior. The matter of Wen-ching's political reports was among the simplest. All Hu-mou found it necessary to do was to suppress them, and His Lordship reacted precisely in the way that Hu-mou had predicted. The episode with Lin Liang was presented in such a manner that His Lordship thought Wen-ching was being unreasonable, and so he decided that there was no need for Wen-ching to continue as ambassador to Austria-Hungary. In these as in many other things Hu-mou could direct His Lordship in almost any way he wished.

10

THUS the stage was set for the *coup de grâce*. Quietly, patiently, relentlessly, with infinite resourcefulness and a minute attention to details, the mind of little Hu-mou in Peking worked for the destruction of Wen-ching. His office, where he spent most of his waking moments, alone and in a continual monologue with himself, was filled with cigarette smoke most of the time, for cigarettes had just been introduced, and in that haze the eyes of Hu-mou saw his victim trying futilely to extricate himself from the tangled web that Hu-mou had woven.

Had not Wen-ching gathered all the honour and adulation of the people of Soochow which should rightfully have been his? Hu-mou was just as much a native of that city as Wen-ching. Then why should he not add glory to his ancestors and make his own family the one and only illustrious family of the city? So long as Wen-ching was recognized as the great scholar of the land and a successful diplomat to boot, with an attractive young concubine who had become the rage of Berlin, so long would Hu-mou's official and diplomatic life be retarded and handicapped, and therefore Wen-ching had to be sacrificed on the altar of his ambition. If he lacked power, it would be a different proposition. But now that he had this power in his hands, he would be the greatest fool in the world if he didn't exploit it to his best advantage.

The web of destruction had now been woven. It remained only for the victim to fall into it and be strangled. One afternoon, when Golden Orchid had scarcely regained her health, a cable came from Peking, which Wen-ching decoded. As he turned the pages of the codebook, his face showed signs of anxiety, then froze. He slumped in his chair and exclaimed, 'Now at last it has come!'

'What is it, Wen-ching dear?' asked Golden Orchid, sharing all his grief and trepidation.

It was no good trying to conceal it. Wen-ching read the cable to his beloved concubine, and this was what it said: 'The Tsungli Yamen has been informed that the embassy in Berlin has issued an illegal document to an Austrian merchant authorizing him to buy ammunition from Germany and Austria-Hungary. Please report at once.'

'How fantastic!' exclaimed Wen-ching. 'How is that possible? Even a child knows that no embassy is permitted to issue any such document without instructions from the Board of Military Affairs. Besides, how can an embassy document be of any value without the embassy seal, which I have under lock and key? Can it be that it was stolen by a member of the staff? Why was the document issued for Austria-Hungary also, after the chargé had offered me a bribe and I had spurned him? This is a most unusual thing!'

Solemnly Wen-ching went to the safe where he had been keeping the seal, carefully examined it, and found no signs that it had been tampered with.

'But,' said Golden Orchid, 'it is possible that the Consular Service has used its seal. That is in the custody of Secretary Chow. He is responsible for it and uses it for his consular work every day. The seal is in his care, and he doesn't have to ask you for instructions every time he uses it, does he? He is the man to question.'

'Yes, yes, you are quite right, my precious one. I see now,' said Wen-ching. 'They make the Consul issue the document and then blame it on me.'

'That is obvious.'

'When I come to think of it, I remember some Austrian did come to me and talk about ammunition. I became angry with him and told him that only the Board of Military Affairs at Peking could issue a certificate for the purchase of munitions. So now he has got hold of the Consul!'

There was nothing else Wen-ching could do except call the Consul in. He laid the cable before Secretary Chow and asked him whether he knew anything about it. Chow, looking like a man possessed, muttered something unintelligible. Not only were his words incoherent, but his movements also became unco-ordinated. He was normally a cautious man and at least outwardly courteous and respectful; but now, confronted with the revelation of an act which he knew was criminal, he completely forgot that he was speaking to his superior. Wen-ching tried to calm him and asked him how on earth he could have issued a document which he knew to be worthless.

After a long pause, Chow admitted to Wen-ching that he had issued such a document and that he had been deceived.

'It . . . it was entirely the work of my German secretary, Mr Ambassador; she . . . she . . . well, never mind! The only course now open to me is to commit suicide. Yes, how can I continue to live?' Chow began sobbing like a child.

'Well,' said Wen-ching, who felt in a sense quite relieved, since the facts were now established and the responsibility determined, 'it needn't be so serious as all that. The principal thing is to reply to this cable from the Tsungli Yamen.'

Whereupon Chow asked for a sheet of paper and drafted, in the presence and in the name of his ambassador, a reply reporting exactly what had happened. This is what he wrote: 'The German employee in the Consular Service declares that she has been in close touch with Austrian merchants, and since there are difficulties in obtaining munitions, she made use of the name of China. Chow Su-ying, not understanding the meaning of the language of the certificate, carelessly signed it and sealed it with the Consular Seal.'

Wen-ching considered the episode closed for the time being and assured the Consul that the reply would be dispatched at once and they would await further action on the part of the Tsungli Yamen. He then returned to Golden Orchid's room and discussed the episode with her.

'Now that Mr Chow has admitted what he has done, surely we have nothing to worry about,' said Golden Orchid. 'Mr Chow will have to face the law and I am sorry for him, but if he is so foolish he deserves it.'

'I have always said that that German woman would let Chow down. For two years they have been living as man and wife. The man is completely befuddled, mesmerized, and the woman is only making use of him and of her position in the consulate to further her own ends. But I am afraid there is another angle to this matter. It is not as simple as we are making it look.'

'Really? What makes you think so?' Golden Orchid asked.

'Knowing as we do Hu-mou's mind, the recalcitrance of the embassy staff and the whole atmosphere of conspiracy against me, how can you doubt that the episode has been created to destroy me — not the Consul? You wait and see.'

Days passed. The Tsungli Yamen sent no further cable to Wen-ching. Wen-ching's reply, as drafted by the Consul, had reached Hu-mou's desk; as usual Hu-mou looked vacantly into his smoke-filled room and smiled a faint smile. No one in the Tsungli Yamen dared to make any comment or pass any judgement. Hu-mou continued to add the last finishing touches to his web. He was waiting for the opportune moment to have a word with Lord Yu Kung, who now hardly put in an appearance in the yamen.

'The embassy in Berlin has replied, Your Lordship, to this munitions document,' said Hu-mou. 'I think in all fairness we should conduct an investigation.'

This sounded reasonable, and so, with the vermilion brush, Lord Yu Kung wrote his approval on the petition which Hu-mou had prepared and submitted in person.

After a week of anxious waiting a cable from the Tsungli Yamen came to Wen-ching. It said: 'In order to find out the facts of the case and determine the responsibility the Tsungli Yamen has decided to conduct an investigation.'

Wen-ching showed the cable to Golden Orchid. 'I don't want to frighten you, my precious Orchid, but we shall have to be prepared for the worst. If the Tsungli Yamen — or, rather, Hu-mou — had been satisfied with my earlier reply and accepted the fact that Chow is the culprit, the present cable would not have been sent or be worded as it is. You will see that, step by step, he will place the responsibility on me. I don't mind an investigation —'

'Why, yes,' interrupted Golden Orchid, 'let them have the investigation. It will establish just what Chow has admitted.'

'You are too naive, my child. The investigation will be made merely to create an impression of fairness. It is but a smoke-screen. It will not be impartial. Hu-mou has already made up his mind how it will be carried out.'

'What makes you think so?'

'If he has set his heart upon destroying me, how can the investigation be impartial? I must answer the cable, of course, and say that I welcome the investigation. What else can I say? But I shall suggest that the Tsungli Yamen appoint an ambassador of equal rank — our ambassador in London or Paris, for instance — to come here and find out the facts of the case. But don't be surprised if the suggestion is rejected and Hu-mou dispatches someone over whom he has absolute control, one who will carry out his intentions. My guess is that he will send out some minor official. He will pretend that he is conducting an impartial investigation. ... . No minor official can investigate anything in which a superior official is involved: that has been the accepted practice. But Hu-mou is going to ignore that practice.'

The reply was accordingly sent by Wen-ching with the recommendation that some near-by ambassador be sent at once to collect all the evidence on the spot and meet all the witnesses before other things should intervene. Since the matter was of the utmost importance, the reply went on to say, it should not be allowed to drag on.

When the cable was delivered at the Tsungli Yamen, Hu-mou was closeted with a minor official who had been recalled not long before and was anxious to be given another appointment abroad. This man, Tung-chen, had come back to Peking with many costly presents, which he distributed to all the senior officials at the Tsungli

Yamen. Knowing that Hu-mou had become the most powerful person and that his words carried more weight than those of Lord Yu Kung himself, he paid a call on Hu-mou at his home shortly after he returned to Peking and left with him a beautiful piece of Italian sculpture — a nude female figure which he knew would appeal strongly to Hu-mou. For Madam Hu-mou he left a valuable Swiss watch studded with rubies and sapphires. Those presents immediately established a special relationship between Tung-chen and Hu-mou; and when Wen-ching's reply came, Hu-mou had already decided that Tung-chen was the man to be sent to Berlin. Regardless of the time and expense involved, Tung-chen was to conduct a 'fair and impartial' investigation.

Wen-ching received the expected cable. It said: 'Please be informed that the Tsungli Yamen is dispatching Mr Tung-chen to investigate the case and that he is proceeding to Berlin at once.'

The two long months before Tung-chen appeared in Berlin were a nightmare. The embassy seemed like a morgue. Golden Orchid, who once looked so young, so fresh, so vivacious and so full of charm, now looked wan and sallow. She would not eat, and she lay on her bed tossing as if she was being dragged to the very gates of hell.

There was no one for her to talk to except the good and faithful Anna, who would know nothing of the labyrinths of the Chinese mind — the Chinese official mind. Golden Orchid now knew how to express herself in German, but it was still beyond her power to convey to Anna the cynical, crooked and wicked ways of Chinese officialdom. As for Wen-ching, his mental perspicacity added torment to the tragedy. He saw clearly the steps which were being taken to destroy him, and yet there was nothing he could do to prevent them.

But Faustmann managed to ferret out all the relevant information from his wife Anna and was anxious to help. He suggested that he might be able to obtain valuable information from some of the munitions works in Berlin. He remembered the ambassador being very angry with an Austrian visitor who said that he wanted to have something to do with munitions. He might be able to track this visitor down.

After careful consideration, Wen-ching decided that there was no harm in letting Faustmann go about finding out more facts, although the facts were already beyond dispute. The ultimate decision was in the mind of Hu-mou and not in the facts. If that mind had been made up — and it was evident to Wen-ching that it *was* made up — no further facts were going to alter the situation. But at least, Wen-ching thought, they could do no harm.

Faustmann went about his new task with doggedness and thoroughness. After more than two years of service both he and Anna had become so attached to Wen-ching and Golden Orchid that nothing they might do, they felt, could quite repay the many kindnesses they had received. Faustmann lacked the social standing to see many people who might have been of help to him, but slowly and patiently and with infinite faith in the righteousness of the cause, he was able to move the hearts of many strangers. Finally he wormed his way into a conference with the director of a munitions firm, who consented to issue a document on what he knew of the case. Faustmann was overjoyed and hurried back to Wen-ching to show him the statement:

June 20, 1898

As Director of a semi-official organization established to deal with all questions in connection with the sale of munitions, the undersigned hereby certifies that some time ago an Austrian merchant, Mr Schwartz, approached the Society with the proposition that we deliver to him a consignment of munitions to be sent to China.

In reply to his proposition we demanded that he deliver to us a properly certified document from the Chinese Embassy at Berlin. In order to fulfil our request, Mr Schwartz approached the Chinese Ambassador at Berlin, who, according to Mr Schwartz's own information to us, refused to issue such a document in view of the fact that the purchase of munitions must be authorized by a certificate, or *huchao*, which is issued only by the Board of Military Affairs in China.

Some time later, Mr Schwartz obtained a certificate signed by the Chinese Consul at Berlin and stamped with the seal of the Consular Service, which was issued to him, according to information confidentially provided to us, without the knowledge of the Chinese Ambassador at Berlin. Since such a document did not fully satisfy

F

our wishes, we hesitated to accept it and finally decided not to honour it for the supply of any munitions. We have the honour to be,

DIRECTOR OF WEDEPAK
*Organization for the Exportation
of German Munitions of War*

'There now, Excellency, what do you think of this document?' said Faustmann with just pride. 'In order to show that every word is authentic and that the document is issued by a responsible official, you will see, Excellency, that the letter paper is that of the organization itself and properly signed.'

'Thank you, Faustmann, for this act of kindness,' replied Wen-ching. 'I fully appreciate it.'

As he said this, Wen-ching was deeply moved by the devotion and loyalty of an employee who was a man of a different race. 'What an ironic situation!' he muttered to himself. 'My own people whom I have tried to treat decently are like a pack of wolves wanting to tear me to pieces.'

'I think, Excellency,' continued Faustmann, 'that if you send this statement at once to Peking, everything will be clarified. It establishes beyond any doubt that Mr Chow was negligent in his duties and that he alone is responsible.'

Faustmann realized that he was going beyond his duties, but the situation was unusual, and his sincerity made amends.

'I have always thought,' he continued, 'that the girl in Herr Chow's office would do no one any good. I should have told you long ago, Excellency, that ever since she came in, Herr Chow has been acting like a man bewitched. What he sees in her I don't know. With a large, bulbous nose, skin like an orange peel and a fat body,' —Faustmann stretched his arms sideways as he said this — 'I hardly think she is a beauty. And yet they go about like man and wife.'

Wen-ching pretended that the information was new and thanked Faustmann again for all the assistance he was giving to him.

11

On the eve of Tung-chen's departure for 'the tour of investigation' Hu-mou gave a dinner in his honour. Held at Hu-mou's deliberately simple house in Peking, it was no elaborate and ostentatious dinner with innumerable courses, for Hu-mou did not believe in making a show of things. He was successful in giving the impression that he lived in frugal and modest circumstances befitting his modest salary. He did not come from an affluent family, and there was nothing beyond his limited means to justify a grand style of living.

The guests departed early. Tung-chen stayed behind, as he knew that Hu-mou still had a few last words of instruction to give. 'I think, Mr Director, that you should have a full report only a few days after my arrival at Berlin,' said Tung-chen. 'The procedure is quite clear, and the case can be settled easily.'

'I know,' replied Hu-mou, 'that I am trusting the matter to one of the ablest men in the service. Mr Chow, the consular official, must have received some money from the Austrian merchant. It is clear that otherwise he would not have issued the document. It may be possible that his German employee — or shall we say his very intimate friend — has taken the bribe, whatever the amount might be.'

'That I can find out.'

'But in any case you will use your best judgement. And if you can make Consul Chow say that he received concurrence from Ambassador Wen-ching in issuing the certificate and that the ambassador even shared the bribe, that is all that is necessary. What is there to prevent the consul from saying so? After all, it is to his advantage.'

So saying, Hu-mou rolled his eyes more vigorously than ever, and there was just a faint smile of smug satisfaction on his face. So that should be the end of Wen-ching, he said to himself, and he turned to look at Tung-chen again.

'I understand, Mr Director,' said Tung-chen.

'And now,' added Hu-mou, 'let me know where you desire to be posted after the investigation is over. I will see what I can do.'

Tung-chen's official position was not high, but Hu-mou had confidence in his unquestioned loyalty and personal devotion. He was prepared to reward him well — once he had performed the mission. Tung-chen, for his part, knew where he stood and was not going to allow the opportunity to go by without making the most of it. He did not care for being *en poste* in Europe. There were other, more profitable, plums which he thought of picking. Seeing Hu-mou well disposed, he said: 'On my way to Berlin, I shall visit Singapore. I shall see what the place looks like. Since I have always found warm places congenial to my health, I think I should like, if I may, to be appointed to a post there.'

What Tung-chen really envisioned was a fabulous fortune waiting for him from the Chinese residents in Malaya. The number of Chinese emigrants in that area, then as now, was enormous. Some were exceedingly rich, many poor. But rich and poor alike were devoted to the mother country, perhaps simply because they were away from it, and the Chinese Consul-General had always been regarded by the Chinese colony as a 'father' to be honoured, respected, fêted and showered with gifts. There were many ways in which this 'father' could make a fortune of his own. Passports and visas alone were a steady source of income, but others were even more profitable.

Tung-chen knew to the minutest detail what these were; he estimated that with this consular appointment he could comfortably retire for the rest of his life. He was determined that the Berlin mission should be carried out without a hitch; he would do everything to implement the wishes of Director Hu-mou.

Now that the crisis had come and there was still no news of Yung-kai's arrival in Peking, Golden Orchid became doubly worried. What has happened to him, she kept asking herself, among those strange peoples who might do anything from kidnapping him and keeping him in permanent captivity to murdering him for his possessions. The fact that Lao Chuang was accompanying him gave a certain measure of comfort, but what could Lao Chuang do, alone, in the midst of the inhospitable wastes? With her husband in so sad a predicament, the thought that Yung-kai might also be lost was almost too much for Golden Orchid.

The news of the arrival of Tung-chen came at last. Wen-ching had to be at the railway station to give him an official welcome, bitter as the experience was. In any case it was best to forestall any possible contact between Tung-chen and the embassy staff or the consul himself. When Tung-chen, accompanied by his nephew, stepped from the train, he was wreathed in smiles and was the most affable person in the world. He had never met Wen-ching before, but greeted the ambassador as though he were a long-lost brother. He was disarmingly cordial, his back was curved as if in deep humility and reverence in the presence of a senior official.

Wen-ching immediately saw through Tung-chen's pretended humility. His face was lean and haggard-looking, and one of his eyes was hidden under a patch. As if conscious that everybody knew he had come on a dark and sinister mission, he admitted to Wen-ching that he was most unfortunate in being asked to perform so thankless a task.

After Tung-chen had had a rest and, with his nephew, lunch with Wen-ching, Wen-ching decided it was time to start. The three retired to the office, and Wen-ching asked that the consul, Mr Chow, be called in.

'Please be seated,' said Wen-ching when Mr Chow had been introduced. Without further ado he plunged into the subject. 'As you know, Mr Tung-chen has taken the trouble to come from the Tsungli Yamen at Peking to find out the facts about the munitions certificate which you issued some time ago. It is true that we have reported them by cable. But we should be thankful that the Tsungli Yamen has gone to the extent of sending an investigator. Will you please tell Mr Tung-chen all you know about the matter?'

Mr Chow was perplexed. He looked at Wen-ching, his face pallid with fear and grief. Then he looked at Tung-chen. He had the appearance of one who was being sentenced, and was about to plead for clemency, for forgiveness. A moment later he was actually on his knees before Tung-chen. Incoherently, he said: 'Forgive me, please forgive me. I didn't know what I was doing.'

Both Wen-ching and Tung-chen had to help him back to his chair. Tung-chen said: 'Mr Chow, there is nothing serious. Please do not get so excited. We will straighten everything out. Only tell me what you know.'

Mr Chow became more quiet. Tung-chen's voice, he thought, was reassuring, and Mr Chow appeared to understand what Tung-chen wished to convey. Then he continued: 'Mr Investigator, I have always had such faith and confidence in my secretary. She is a German lady. She seems such an able woman, but how was I to know what sort of company she was keeping when she left the office every day? So when she came to me with the certificate in question which she had prepared all by herself, I thought it was one of those routine documents which I was in the habit of signing and attaching my consular seal to every day. It was written in a language which I understand but imperfectly.'

While Mr Chow was making the confession, neither Wen-ching nor Tung-chen uttered a word. Wen-ching was inwardly happy that Chow's version was identical to that in the draft of the cable sent to the Tsungli Yamen when the case was first known. Wen-ching almost began to blame himself secretly for being so suspicious of the investigation and of the evil designs of Hu-mou and Tung-chen. Now that Chow had made the confession — for the second time — all that was needed was for Tung-chen to render a report, and the whole matter should become a closed issue so far as Wen-ching was concerned.

But during the next few days, while Anna, Faustmann, and the other servants were listless, uneasy and cheerless, there were quiet entrances and exits of fast-moving feet as though secret encounters and clandestine meetings were going on. All talking was done in whispers; nothing was audible except the patter, patter of innumerable feet proceeding from no one knew where and dying softly away among their own echoes.

Four days later the mask of the inquisitor, the willing tool before whom dangled the glittering gold and honours of his new, exalted position as China's consul-general at Singapore, appeared once again, one eye still under a heavy bandage. Had not Hu-mou promised him the new appointment if he dutifully obeyed and carried out what he wanted? Who was Wen-ching to deny him these riches? Why should he care what happened to Wen-ching? Tung-chen nursed an inward satisfaction as he came knocking at the door of Wen-ching's office.

'Mr Ambassador,' said Tung-chen as he came in wearing the familiar look of servility and modesty. 'I am sorry that I have not come to pay my respects to you during the last few days. I hope Your Excellency is well. And how is Madam? I heard she was not well. What a pity! But I hope she is getting better.'

Hypocrite that he was, Tung-chen knew that honeyed words cost him nothing and that he could be generous with them. Having seated himself and spun out much unnecessary verbiage, Tung-chen then slowly and as if reluctantly unsheathed the waiting knife by saying: 'Mr Ambassador, it is so difficult these days to trust anybody. I know how well Your Excellency has treated the staff here. Known as a renowned scholar and as a good man of such outstanding virtues, you could not have done otherwise. . . .'

Tung-chen went on with his introductory speech, and Wen-ching looked at him and did not say a word, but he knew that quite soon the knife was going to fall on his neck.

'Mr Ambassador,' Tung-chen continued, and smiled as if he could not believe it, 'do you know that this vicious Mr Chow, this man who all along has admitted that he alone was responsible for the munitions certificate, has now given me some new facts? The ungrateful beast! He said that you — you, Excellency — gave him permission to issue it and that you, Excellency, also shared in the bribe. I can't believe it, but that was what he said, and what am I to do except report to the Tsungli Yamen this additional information?'

Even though he knew perfectly well that Tung-chen had come to say these words, Wen-ching was shocked beyond belief when he heard them. These lies were all concocted by the malicious minds of his conspirators, and they had merely made the consul say them. And why shouldn't the consul do as they wished? If the Tsungli Yamen, through Hu-mou and the inquisitor Tung-chen, gave him the cue to reduce his own guilt and to make the ambassador share it, it was a god-sent opportunity he would not miss. The ambassador would even be assigned a larger share of the blame because of his higher position.

It was understandable that the consul should have been in such mortal fear when he first saw Tung-chen, and fallen on his knees begging for mercy. He had frankly and openly admitted his guilt. He was not unaware that Tung-chen could, if he wished, keep him in the embassy, and later, through the usual extra-territorial privileges, have him sent back to China to be given the severest punishment his crime deserved.

But four days calmed his fears. During that time Tung-chen had sent for him and talked to him — perhaps alone, perhaps in the presence of his nephew. Those little intimate talks had made the situation crystal clear. While he was not going to be completely absolved from blame he now learned that the main target of attack was not himself but his ambassador. Instead of regarding him as the persecutor, the consul now worshipped Tung-chen as a saviour.

Stupid man, the consul said to himself, how could he have been so foolhardy as to issue that document! He realized now that it couldn't have gone very far. How could it be valid for Austria-Hungary, with which his official post had nothing to do? How could it be valid anywhere? Could it be that this infatuation for his secretary had blinded him? She was a plain woman, and yet . . . and yet. All kinds of questions occurred to his no longer feverish mind. But it was no use pursuing them any further. He had done a foolish thing, and the consequences of this foolish act were to be suffered equally by his ambassador. Whatever Tung-chen's motives might be, he had granted to Mr Chow a new lease of life, and seemed to him the greatest of benefactors.

But for Wen-ching and Golden Orchid how different was the story!

12

THE prolonged strain kept Golden Orchid in bed. The doctors advised her to leave Berlin for a change of air, but to go away was out of the question, not only because of the expense, which Wen-ching could ill afford, but because it meant leaving her husband while he was in the midst of his troubles.

She no longer had any taste for food. If Lao Chuang had still been there, he could at least have prepared rice soup and little titbits and condiments to soothe her. Anna did all she could to take the place of Lao Chuang. Fortunately, what she could not do in the way of cooking was more than compensated for by her care, devotion, and loyalty; and Golden Orchid was able, now and then, to sit up and look at herself in a hand mirror, tidy her hair and apply some powder and rouge to her wan and sallow cheeks. Wen-ching, deeply concerned over her health, refrained from conveying to her the last words which the inquisitor Tung-chen had spoken.

'You are looking much better today, my treasure,' Wen-ching continued to tell her with the coming of every fresh day. He was not speaking the truth, and he knew it. But he saw to it that no further upsetting news was brought to her ears.

'That man Tung-chen, what new lies is he inventing, Wen-ching dear?'

'Let's not talk about him, my precious one.'

'Anna is remarkable. She has even learned to prepare the food more or less in the way I want it. She said Lao Chuang taught her.'

'And her husband too is remarkable,' he said. 'I never expected that this German couple would turn out to be such wonderful people.'

'They have proved to be our best friends in these years in Berlin.'

'Yes, my treasure, that is a solid satisfaction, isn't it? . . . But you should rest, my sweet.' Tucking in her blanket, Wen-ching went to his study.

Now that Tung-chen had told him what purported to be new facts in the case, a cable from the Tsungli Yamen to decide his fate was a matter of course. He, Wen-ching, the finest flower of Chinese classical scholarship, a *chuang yuan* of whom all Soochow — in fact, all China — was justly proud, was to be brought low by a few petty officials! Yet he still refused to believe that he would not be vindicated eventually and perhaps have new honours conferred upon him. He would go back to Peking, tell his friends and the Court what had happened, the miseries he had endured as an ambassador in spite of the valuable contributions that he and Golden Orchid had made to China, and the whole affair would be clarified. Wen-ching was not by nature an optimist; but his spirit was kept alive by a deep conviction that moral values must in the end win recognition, that good must triumph over evil, or else human society would be impossible.

In the meantime the staff, knowing that their ambassador had no power over them, made themselves the self-appointed censors of his letters and telegrams. There was hardly a letter that did not show it had been opened by them before it was delivered. Every move he tried to make was thus known to them, and they knew who his friends were.

The coming of Tung-chen had convinced them that the days of the ambassador were numbered, and so they gave parties, drank and shouted with girls they picked up on the streets, sang and played on the rickety old piano until the strings were ready to snap, as if to say,

'Drive us out, Mr Ambassador, if you can! We are now the masters, not you and your concubine.' This is what is known as beating a dead tiger, or stoning a man while he is struggling in the water, and the embassy members seemed to find immense satisfaction in the sport.

Wen-ching and Golden Orchid had to stand it as best they could. Only Faustmann and Anna dared, now and then, to express astonishment and to say to each other: 'Why, this is unbelievable among a group of so-called well-brought-up Chinese gentlemen, or for that matter among any group of decent human beings. This kind of conduct does not exist among the lowest of human outcasts.'

Faustmann had the courage once to step into the reception-room while a rowdy party was going on. He received a box on the ear from one of the secretaries for what was considered unwarranted presumption, but his harangue in German produced an effect on the girls who were taking part.

'Do you know,' he shouted, 'that the ambassador is occupying this embassy and that his lady is sick upstairs?' Whereupon the girls, lowly born as they were, hid their faces in shame and soon left the place.

But the ambassador and his lady were not destined to remain long in this embassy near the zoological gardens. Well might the embassy have merged with the zoo; its inmates were no better than the wolves, hyenas and jackals only a stone's throw away.

The cable from Peking in response to Tung-chen's report of the new 'revelations' arrived early one morning. Wen-ching opened it, decoded it himself, and there, staring him in the face, were these words: 'Ambassador Shen Wen-ching and Consul Chow Su-ying, having been found responsible for the issuance of the illegal certificate for munitions, are hereby relieved of their posts. They are forthwith to return to the capital and answer the charges. Tsungli Yamen.'

Tsungli Yamen indeed! This was the *coup de grâce*, successfully administered by Hu-mou to eliminate the most serious obstacle to his political ambition. How smoothly and neatly the whole operation had been carried out! One step led to another until the propitious moment arrived when, with Tung-chen's report, Hu-mou drafted the cable and approached Lord Yu Kung for his official sanction.

It was during a meeting of the Grand Council when all the senior officials were present. The discussion centred on the critical situation facing China. Russia was showing aggressive designs not only in Manchuria but also in Mongolia, in Ili. The President of the Board of Military Affairs asked: 'What has our ambassador Shen Wen-ching been doing all these years in St Petersburg?' Another requested: 'Show us some of his reports. Why were we not informed of Russian intentions earlier?' Still another said: 'We are supposed to checkmate Russian designs through the good offices of the German Emperor. Have we any reports on the matter from our ambassador in Berlin?'

The discussion was heated, and Lord Yu Kung had nothing to satisfy the wishes of the council members. When the meeting came to an end, his mood was sullen and he could not feel friendly towards Wen-ching, however well disposed he might have been at the time when Wen-ching was appointed to the high diplomatic posts. It was at this moment that Hu-mou very cleverly produced Tung-chen's report of his 'investigation'. Lord Yu Kung shook his head, the lines on his face became drawn, and then Hu-mou commented: 'Your Lordship, the council is in an ugly mood. We should at least ask Ambassador Wen-ching and the consul to come back and defend themselves. It will be for their own good.'

He then produced his draft of the cable. Lord Yu Kung read it, his face as grim as ever, and without a moment's hesitation gave his approval. The victory for Hu-mou was complete.

13

THE departure of Wen-ching and Golden Orchid from Berlin was a diplomatic event. They had been strange and unfamiliar figures when they first arrived slightly less than three years before. They had come from a distant country with strange customs and manners, different from anything that the diplomatic corps or the German Court and Government had known before. It was thought impossible that anything like understanding or friendly intercourse could result from a mission representing so huge an unknown quantity. Wen-ching was more an object of curiosity, sometimes even of ridicule, a museum figure, than the diplomatic representative of a proud and venerable nation.

In less than three years he and his charming concubine, through tact and good sense which transcended racial and cultural differences, made themselves almost indispensable in all important diplomatic functions. Wen-ching held faithfully to the Confucian doctrine that the only real difference between human beings was one of education and culture; all others were of little consequence. Differences in appearance, dress, customs, manners and in historical and cultural background were real enough; but they were accidents of nature and environment and, as such, superficial. At the bottom of their hearts all civilized peoples, Wen-ching believed with Confucius, were animated by the same desires and motivated by the same ideals of conduct, the same recognition to be good and to do good, to shun evil and to refrain from evil deeds. The similarities between human beings, he was convinced, were much deeper and more impressive than their differences.

Acting on this theory, he found that he and Golden Orchid were successful in their mission to an unusual degree. But now, on the eve of departure, he could not avoid a bitter smile. His very success was one of the reasons of his failure — and it was a dismal failure, an ignominious failure, to be virtually dismissed from office.

When the news of his recall spread through the city, the German Government and the diplomatic corps, in an informal way, expressed their regret that he and Golden Orchid were leaving them and made it clear that their absence would be keenly felt for a long time. Faustmann came into the office with cuttings from the morning newspapers, which, without exception, spoke of Wen-ching and Golden Orchid in the most glowing terms. The *Illustrated Berlin News*, the most widely circulated daily in the city and an official organ of the German Government, was very frank in its comment. It had conducted its own little inquiry into the unusual case, and this is what it said:

> In connection with the impending departure of the Chinese ambassador we have received some interesting information about the case, which is creating a great stir among the diplomatic circles in Berlin.
> The Chinese ambassador is the victim of an intrigue in which the secretary of the embassy, who is at the same time the con-

sular official, gave with his own signature and with his consular seal an illegal document for buying ammunition not only in Germany but, curiously enough, also in Austria-Hungary. He gave his certificate secretly without the knowledge of the ambassador and of course without his authorization. The ambassador is now obliged to leave because he is responsible for every act of his embassy staff although he has nothing to do with the whole affair. Many people who know the inside story and who are directly connected with it have issued documents which prove beyond any doubt that the ambassador had no knowledge that such a certificate existed. The whole affair is obviously a personal intrigue, but the political significance of this incident and its details are not yet entirely known.

Faustmann's face was red with fury when he read this account to the ambassador. It was not simply because of his devotion to Wen-ching; he was indignant that so widely respected an ambassador should be treated so shabbily by his own Government. Faustmann had other cuttings: he insisted that Wen-ching should know them all and know also that public opinion in Germany was behind him. He read an extract from another paper, the Berlin *Courier*:

The Chinese ambassador is retiring from Berlin, after a stay of about three years, as the result of an illegal performance on the part of the consular official of the Chinese Embassy who signed a document with the seal of the Chinese Consular Service without authorization.

With the retirement of His Excellency Shen Wen-ching the Berlin diplomatic corps loses one of its most popular and capable diplomats. He is a noted scholar and a great savant of his own country's history and literature. He is a *chuang yuan*, which means that he is recognized as one of the most distinguished scholars of his land and is exceedingly popular with all circles in Germany with which he came into contact. With the departure of the wife of the retiring Chinese ambassador, Berlin also loses a person of great culture and singular personal charm. She is young, beautiful, and represents the very best of Oriental womanhood.

'By comments like these, Mr Ambassador,' said Faustmann, 'you have already been vindicated. The *Daily Courier* and the Berlin *Post* brought out the same points. Always the misconduct of the consul in using the seal of the Consular Service without authorization and without the knowledge of the ambassador. Please keep these comments, *Excellenz*.' Faustmann handed the newspapers to Wen-ching.

'Here you have, Mr Ambassador, the opinion of all the papers in Berlin,' he continued. 'There is every reason to believe that they know exactly what happened. They must have their channels of information. It cannot be a matter of coincidence that they give substantially the same version. It is . . . it is, if I may say so, a shame that the Chinese Government is treating you and Madam so badly and unjustly. I shall continue to do everything within my power, limited as it is.'

'Thank you, Faustmann, for letting me know what has been written in the papers. You have done enough for me. You have been very kind indeed and I appreciate it. Both you and Anna have given us much comfort.'

Wen-ching could not say anything else to Faustmann. Grateful as he was for what his German employee had done, he knew it was all to no purpose. The key was not to be found in the truths and falsehoods of the case, but in the heart of Hu-mou and his henchmen. Faustmann stood for only fairness and justice: that was his ideal of human conduct. The approach was also a legal one. He could not understand the complexities and undercurrents of Chinese officialdom.

Wen-ching was now entirely resigned to the situation. He felt sad and deeply hurt, but he had philosophical calm. His only concern was that Golden Orchid should completely regain her health. He looked forward to the return journey. To be on the high seas for over six weeks, away from all irritation and familiar sights and people, would give her a good chance to regain her normal self.

In less than ten days the British liner *Hesperides* was leaving Genoa for Hong Kong and Shanghai. Wen-ching booked a spacious stateroom: he and Golden Orchid would travel in the style of respectable diplomats, though it might be for the last time.

For the next few days the embassy was again a beehive of activity, with a stream of people coming to say goodbye and express their last word of sympathy. The onerous part of the move was the disposal of all the elaborate furniture and possessions once bought to enhance the prestige of Chinese representation in the German capital.

Wen-ching looked at the pile of furniture and sighed. 'Other envoys,' he said to Golden Orchid, who was now out of her sickbed and felt happy at the prospect of an early homeward journey, 'come here with a couple of suitcases to represent China. They save every penny and go home with enough to retire on for the rest of their lives. They succeed. But look at us, foolish people that we are!'

'But all these articles were bought with our own money and I want them in China,' retorted Golden Orchid.

Porcelains, bronzes, rugs, tables, chairs, taken singly, were not especially valuable, but together they formed a priceless collection. Golden Orchid particularly wanted to save the delicately polished black-lacquered table on which she had served so many successful diplomatic meals, but Wen-ching found that the packing and transportation would cost more than he could now afford, the Tsungli Yamen had paid him an amount which barely covered the return passage for the two of them. Besides, there were uncertainties awaiting him upon his return.

'It's no use,' Wen-ching said, throwing up his hands, 'we have lost everything already, and in my present mood I am not going to waste time and energy trying to salvage a few material possessions. We shall take only those things which we can pack ourselves. The rest I shall distribute to our many friends here who have given us such comfort during our hour of distress. For Faustmann and Anna we will leave substantial souvenirs.'

Golden Orchid, about to raise some objection, gave in as soon as her husband mentioned the German couple.

'I have been a poor scholar all my life,' Wen-ching said, 'and I shall become one again upon our return. All these years I have taken from my salary, every month, varying amounts to defray the expenses of the embassy. The expenses allowed were not adequate to maintain this embassy with all its entertainment.'

'It was perhaps all my fault. I loved entertaining.'

'There was nothing wrong in that. What I was going to say is that I have drawn freely from my personal resources and I still have receipts which I will show to the Tsungli Yamen. But I know what the answer will be. "Serves you right if you want to spend your own money for the good of the embassy." So I shall not get back a single penny.'

'We are so inexperienced,' said Golden Orchid. 'We should have done as other Chinese envoys do, and then there would have been no trouble at all. They save their salary and pocket what remains of their diplomatic allowances by not entertaining.'

'Exactly. What's more, sometimes the staff demand their share. The division of the spoils has frequently given rise to ill feeling, though they usually manage to patch up their differences in the end. You can see why staff members prefer such chiefs to an ambassador like me. They must have thought I was foolish to use my own salary for the embassy. And they had no chance of a share of the allowance when I used it all up. That is another one of the reasons they are bitter against me.'

Wen-ching paused, and then continued: 'Do you know, my treasure, these secretaries are so cynical that they believe, on the basis of what they know of the conduct of other ambassadors, that we have made lots of money and have refused to give them a share. They feel that we have grown fabulously rich while they have got nothing. It pays to live in a hovel even when one is making money.'

'I see. Others make money from their position and appear poor. We are poor and make a show of being rich.'

'There you have it in a nutshell. But there is a difference — a world of difference. Others think only of themselves, while we unfortunately happen to think of our country. Oh, my precious Orchid, what a sordid world this is, where honour and integrity, even when they exist, are not believed in. We are not fit for this kind of life, but it is tragic that we have to pay so dearly in order to learn all this.'

Somehow, after this explanation by Wen-ching, Golden Orchid felt quite composed. It had been a costly lesson, but at least she had become enlightened. She was young, but she was prepared for the long, hard battle still ahead of her.

'Never mind,' continued her husband, 'Madam Wen-ching still has some money which she inherited from her family, and somehow we shall manage to live a happy life when we return. Perhaps that is what I should have done in the first place — followed my own inclinations and lived in accordance with my training and background. When has official life ever been clean — in any age? But I confess I didn't know that it was so evil. A plain and simple life, surrounded by the things we love — birds, flowers, poetry, a little wine, and some congenial friends of like disposition — that is all we want, and that is what we shall have in Soochow.'

Golden Orchid was sure of one thing: for her to live on the inheritance of Madam Wen-ching was impossible!

That, however, was not something to think over now, and she called Anna to her. 'Anna,' she said, 'you and your husband have served the ambassador and myself well. Both of you have made us happy during these years in Berlin.'

'Thank you, thank you for saying so, *Excellenz*. It has been an honour to us.'

'We shall soon leave. Before we go back, however, the ambassador and I wish to present you with a few things — just for dear memory's sake.'

'How can we thank you enough for your kindness, *Excellenz*?'

'You know there is one piece of furniture I love more than anything else. It's the black-lacquered table. I want you to keep that as a souvenir.'

Anna was so pleased that she didn't know what to say. She thought it was the most beautiful table she had ever seen.

'And there is something else, Anna. The ambassador and I have been very much touched by your devotion and loyalty. And so please accept this from us.'

Anna was overwhelmed. It was a round white jade plaque about six inches in diameter, resting on a teakwood stand, which Golden Orchid had always kept in her bedroom. On it was delicately carved a mountain scene with two Taoist figures seeking the elixir of life. Anna had long admired it.

'Jade in China,' explained Golden Orchid, 'has always meant purity and virtue. May this plaque keep your soul always pure and virtuous.'

The train left in the morning. Long before the hour of departure a throng of people came to bid farewell to the most widely loved ambassador and ambassadress that China had ever had. Ambassadors from many countries came with their wives, as did German friends in different walks of life. Even the Japanese ambassador was there with his wife. Many of them brought flowers, and as the train began to move, there was a lump in Golden Orchid's throat.

There were friendly men and women whom Wen-ching and Golden Orchid had been taught to regard as barbarians; but it was among their own people that there were implacable enemies determined to destroy them! Golden Orchid sobbed, and tears flowed freely down her cheeks. Wen-ching gave a last respectful bow to the crowd, his hands clasped in front of him, as the train began to move.

'What is going to become of them?' everyone asked. They looked at one another and wondered.

Book Three

VINDICATION

In the lower reaches of the majestic Yangtze River and all along the coast to the south, stretching for hundreds of miles, people were now enjoying a life of peace and plenty. They had almost forgotten the ravages of the Taiping Rebellion. The cities had prospered, and the looms of Soochow were busy turning out fabulously beautiful silks which found their way into the interior of the country and into the markets of foreign lands. The kilns of Kiangsi, Chekiang and Fukien were again making those lovely porcelains which had won the admiration of the world for two centuries.

Golden Orchid's mother, even though her daughter had become the concubine of a high official and could afford to take life with ease, continued to be diligent with her embroidery. Her delicate work was much in demand for weddings, to decorate the bridal chamber, anniversaries, birthdays and even for funerals. She was happy living with her mother-in-law; and Lily, the pock-marked woman, and her sister Yang Mah now and then came to ask for news of Golden Orchid.

Old Mrs Fu could still recall those days when the 'long-hair' rebels, during the Taiping Rebellion, drove the family from one city to another, when she lost her children and settled down almost penniless in Soochow. Suddenly, without any apparent reason, it seemed to her that she was on the threshold of another period of uncertainty and disorder.

Wild rumours began to fly that the farmers were angry and refused to work in the fields. There was talk of secret societies and organized revolt, of dissatisfaction with the local magistrates, of driving the foreigners away. Though they did not fully understand what these rumours were about, the two Fu ladies were much disturbed. Soochow itself, thank heaven, seemed to be peaceful enough. But how long could it remain peaceful when other cities like Shanghai, Nanking and Hangchow, all so near to Soochow, seemed already to have been thrown into confusion?

One day, as Grandmother Fu and her daughter-in-law were having dinner with Yang Mah and Lily, Yang Mah's hunchback husband rushed in and told the two sisters to return at once. On arrival at their modest cottage, just inside Soochow's city wall, they found their nephew, a strapping lad of twenty-three, in a deplorable state. His head was bandaged with a piece of dirty cloth, and he was still shivering from some unexplained fright.

All these years this nephew had been a hard-working peasant on a farm in Shanghai which was his patrimony. He was married, and had a certain amount of education. Since the journey from Shanghai to Soochow took some hours even by train, it was not his habit to visit his aunts except during the New Year holiday. Now, without any warning, he was in Soochow, wounded. Surely something very unusual had happened.

'What is it? Tell me what happened, Ah Zung? Why have you come — in this manner?' inquired the pock-faced aunt.

Yang Mah brought in a hot towel with which Ah Zung wiped his face. He drank some tea and began to feel better.

'It looks as if you have been in a fight of some sort,' remarked the hunchback.

'Yes, Uncle,' replied the young man. 'But it's a long story. My land which father left for me and on which he is buried has been in the family for so many, many generations, but it is now in danger of being lost.'

'How is that possible?' asked Lily. 'We always understood that you were working well on it and the crops were plentiful.'

'You see, Aunt, since the foreigners came to Shanghai, things have been getting worse for us every day. They get hold of the local riff-raff, who create all kinds of trouble for us. They form gangs to force us to part with our land. First they come to us and offer various sums of money to buy our land. Many of my neighbours sold theirs. They needed the money. They are plain good-for-nothings: they always need money to gamble and smoke opium, and spend on women. The riff-raff know they are weak characters and help to drag them deeper and deeper so that they will sell all they have to the ruffians, who in turn convey the title-deeds to the foreigners. But they can't do this to me.'

'What did they try to do?' Yang Mah asked.

'They made matters very plain to me. They told me that these foreigners must have a race-course. They must have thousands of acres of land so that they can play games and ride horses. They have already succeeded in driving away hundreds of farmers from their land. I have seen with my own eyes how their houses, built by their ancestors many generations back, were levelled to the ground. But I told them that, however hard they may try, they will not succeed in making me give up my land.'

'Well done,' said the hunchback uncle quietly.

'What would my father think of me if he were alive? I went to his grave every day and prayed that he would give me strength to resist these rascals' — Ah Zung stopped for a moment and took a deep breath. 'That went on for months,' he continued. 'Every time these rascals came to me, I said no. But they were insistent. The foreigners were getting impatient and encouraged them to press me. I knew I was in danger but still I continued to plough the land and sow the seeds. At last the foreigners themselves came —'

'Ah-ya! I would have been frightened,' exclaimed Yang Mah.

'They rode their horses over my land and trampled on all my crops. They came in groups of three or five, jumped over the little creeks which separate my land from that of my neighbours, and now all you see on my land is waste and utter chaos.'

Ah Zung broke into tears as he remembered how all his labour and efforts had been reduced to nothing by these 'foreign devils'. He was not, however, so angry with them as with the rascals who were willing to do anything under orders from these foreigners. He went on: 'When my fields were devastated, the evil men came back and tried to convince me that I would get nowhere by being obstinate. They said it would be much wiser for me to sell my land as the others had done. One day, when we were in the midst of some argument, I lost my temper. With a few of my fellow villagers I drove them away. We used everything we could lay our hands on, stones, bamboo sticks, hoes and scythes. We thought we had succeeded in giving them a lesson, but they shouted that they had the full backing of the foreigners and that we would pay dearly for our foolish act.'

'What a dangerous situation you were in!' commented Lily.

'It was dangerous, Aunt Lily. The struggle continued for a long time until finally one of the rascals used a gun. One villager was shot dead, and I got a bullet in the leg and a knife-wound in the head. When it was all over, I knew I couldn't remain in the house, so I took the first boat from Shanghai, and that is why I am here.'

Once more Ah Zung broke into tears and said almost inaudibly that he was sure his land had now been taken by the foreigners and his house razed to the ground.

'Nobody can help me,' continued Ah Zung, 'but I want my aunts and my uncle to know the horrible things that have happened to me.'

Lily, Yang Mah and her hunchback husband were shocked beyond words. What could three low-born people do in the face of the overwhelming power of the foreigners at Shanghai?

The hunchback asked Ah Zung: 'Why didn't you bring the matter before the local magistrate?'

Ah Zung said: 'After tremendous difficulties and spending lots of money I succeeded in seeing one of the minor officials in the *taotai*'s official residence.'

'And did he try to help you?' the hunchback asked.

'All he did was to show me sympathy — as if that was good for anything. I couldn't see the high-and-mighty *taotai* himself. They told me it was impossible, however much money I might spend. This minor official was frank enough to tell me that he had hundreds of similar cases and that he was completely helpless. He told me there was no way to find any redress for these wrongs. And he gave me to understand that the *taotai* was mortally afraid of these foreigners. If he tried to do anything for the farmers, the chances were that he would lose his job. He has learned to keep his mouth shut.'

That afternoon, after assuring Ah Zung that he could stay with them in Soochow indefinitely, the hunchback left for Nanking, where he had been summoned to attend one of the periodic meetings of the White Lotus Society, which of late had become more and more active in the whole Yangtze valley. Its headquarters were in Nanking, and the man who was directing its activities was the old monk. In the last three years he had grown into a powerful leader. He was often to be seen in the Temple of the Singing Rooster, where many of his secret meetings were held and where Ping-mo had first met him. As the temple was one of the few interesting landmarks in Nanking, overlooking a lovely lake, it was frequently visited by sight-seers, among whom were high official dignitaries: and as long as he could keep himself secret, the old monk relished seeing the multitude of people parading before his eyes every day. He was avidly interested in the information which he collected through his agents, whom he scattered in the local organizations. The branch in Soochow was under the direction of the hunchback, who had proved himself, in the course of the years, to be a highly competent agent.

When the hunchback left Soochow for Nanking, he travelled by houseboat. It was a cheap mode of travelling which enabled him to maintain close contact with the people. There was no indication that he was on an important mission. He smoked a long bamboo pipe like any other farmer. His clothes were dirty and greasy like those of any small tradesman. He spat and swore like any villager. In fact, he was one of them. But he had his ears wide open and he knew the pulse of the people. He knew, for instance, that there was a wave of discontent against the Court at Peking, against the local magistrates, against all officials, and against the foreigners, who were becoming more and more truculent and intolerable.

The people were angry with the local officials because all that those officials knew was how to trample upon the poor, humiliate them, lord it over them and then get their money and property without any compensation.

They were angry with the high officials in Peking, although they never saw them, because the rumour was going around that China was losing land and paying huge indemnities for wars in which she was always defeated. They had a feeling that those officials in Peking must be just as bad and incompetent as the local officials with whom they had the misfortune to deal.

And they were angry with the foreigners simply because they had been told that they were the root of all trouble.

The peasants and the common people had not been able to visualize how wicked the foreigners were, but lately posters had appeared in the villages which made matters quite clear to them. One of these posters showed a man with yellow hair and a long nose slicing a water-melon marked 'The Middle Kingdom' surrounded by others of the same appearance each waiting for his share. Everyone knew from the poster that the territory of China was being carved up. A second poster showed a picture of a mulberry leaf, representing China, and a silkworm chewing assiduously from its edge and working its way inward. That silkworm was marked 'Russia'.

Ignorant as these peasants were, they knew what was going on, since everything that happened was quietly but rapidly spread from one village to another along the banks of the mighty Yangtze River. The people had an uncanny intelligence service. Reports from Shanghai came in oftener than from other cities, and these showed that the people were especially angry with two classes of Chinese who seemed much worse than the foreigners themselves and who were getting more numerous each day: those who worked for the foreigners and those known as 'rice Christians'.

The story of Ah Zung was typical. What the foreigners did was, of course, hateful. But that at least was something to be expected. They went about the streets in Shanghai pushing and beating up the people as much as they wanted. They had taken over the city and established their own administration. They had imported hundreds of dark-faced and hairy men from India whom they had converted into policemen, and these, too, maltreated the people. But the worst were those two classes of Chinese.

'They are our own people,' Ah Zung said to his hunchback uncle before he left for Nanking, 'but what scoundrels they are! I was told there were no such people before. They receive rewards from the foreigners. They obey the foreigners. They are the servile dogs of the foreigners. And just because they have the support of the foreigners, they feel that they are better than their own people! That is what makes me most angry. They go about with their heads in the air —'

'Don't worry,' commented the uncle. 'They'll be having their tails between their legs soon enough.'

'Oh, how I hate them!' said Ah Zung. 'But they tell me there is still another class of people who are even worse. As if that is possible! I haven't met many of them.'

'That is true, my nephew,' explained the hunchback, 'I know these people only too well. They are everywhere.'

'And they are called "rice Christians", aren't they?' asked Ah Zung.

'Yes, my nephew, and what a wretched lot they are. They are worse than those rascals from Shanghai. But, listen, you mustn't mix with these people, understand? We call them the "second hairy ones", just as we call the real foreigners the "first hairy ones". And one of these days we are going to deal with them.'

'But, Uncle, they are not any more hairy than you or I,' protested Ah Zung.

'Who knows? They may have it all inside. Anyway, that is what we call them.'

'But what is it that makes them so hateful?'

'I'll explain to you, though it is a long story. After the foreigners come to our country, many of our ignorant people took to smoking opium. Now, that is a very bad thing. It weakens the people, and every year we lose large sums of money by consuming that poisonous drug. You know how many people in your village have acquired this vicious habit.'

'Yes, I do. I know many of them. They look pale and sickly. They also become lazy and don't do any work.'

'That's it — that's exactly what the foreigners want. But what I wish to tell you is that these foreigners want to force their religion upon us, as well as opium. I don't know much about their strange religion, but, anyway, it teaches us not to worship and respect our ancestors. Now, think of that — these foreigners want us to worship instead some invisible god whom they call Jesus. There is also a virgin whom they call Mary. It is said she never married, and yet she gave birth to this god. It is about the funniest thing I have ever heard.' And the hunchback laughed so heartily that the hump on his back heaved up and down.

Then he said, 'Don't worry, Ah Zung. One day we shall get even with all these men. Now you stay where you are and be a good boy. Take care of your aunts.' And so the hunchback left the house.

All along the way from Soochow to Nanking the hunchback was given wide recognition. He inspected the weapons that were stored away in the out-of-the-way villages. None of them were modern: they consisted of long knives, spears, axes and a miscellaneous assortment of metal tools ordinarily used for farming. The only modern 'weapon' they had was paraffin oil, which had come in with foreign trade and could be found in the remotest parts of the country. Large quantities of this oil were stored away in rectangular cans for incendiary purposes, which were to play an important part in the uprising being planned.

When the hunchback arrived in Nanking he at once went to visit the old monk, who was waiting for him in the Temple of the Singing Rooster. In the small room near which the students held their meetings, the old monk told the hunchback that in north China, where the people were usually slower to move and act, movements for popular discontent were also spreading like wildfire — more so even than in the south.

'The most interesting news that has come to us,' continued the old monk, 'is that the literary men are joining the movement — not students such as we have down here in the south, but mature men who have great literary accomplishments and have passed the civil-service examinations. I have been told that the Empress Dowager and the young Emperor are on the worst possible terms.'

'Their temperaments are quite different, I understand.'

'Not only that, but the Emperor is progressive, and his aunt, the Empress Dowager, is hopelessly conservative and wants none of the reforms which the Emperor is trying to introduce. The young Emperor listens a good deal to a literary genius from Kwangtung. His name is Kang Yu-wei. I am not clear about the entire development, but the news came to me from that young man Ping-mo.'

'Yes, I have heard a good deal about Ping-mo. He is a fine young man, and both my wife and my sister-in-law often see the family of the girl who has become the concubine of Ping-mo's father. In fact, it was they who arranged the match. Ping-mo's father,' continued the hunchback, 'is now the ambassador, as you know, in Europe.'

'Well, it is good that you know Ping-mo, for tomorrow the students are having another meeting, and you and I shall attend.'

'I have not actually met Ping-mo. It is best perhaps that he doesn't know who I am.'

'Very well. But this you should know: our society and the students' organization keep close to each other. They need us, and we need them. After all, we are struggling for the same ends. When the moment comes, we shall be very strong. No one can resist us.'

2

THE meeting was held, as usual, in the dead of the night. It was attended by some eighty or ninety young men, and Ping-mo was in the chair. He was giving a report of what had been taking place in Peking.

'Things are coming to a head,' said Ping-mo. 'We shall avoid violence and bloodshed if we can, but the Empress Dowager is a wicked, sadistic and stupid woman. She is completely ignorant of the needs of the people, but she continues to be the dominating influence. The Emperor is better informed and knows that the country must go through many reforms before it has a chance to survive. He has intelligent people around him, though he is a weak man himself. He has the help of a remarkably learned and well-informed man called Kang Yu-wei. I should like to ask one of our friends here, a fellow provincial of Kang's, to tell us something about this man.'

Ping-mo then called upon a nearsighted young man, small for his age, who wore a pair of thick glasses.

The young man spoke the national language — curiously and meaninglessly known as mandarin — with a strong Cantonese accent, but he was understood by everyone.

'This Mr Kang is a genius,' he began. 'He has great knowledge, both ancient and modern, Chinese and foreign. He is an amazing person. He has not been abroad, yet he knows what's going on in foreign lands. He knows their history. He is a Confucianist. He does not believe that any country can surpass us in moral ideals. He presses hard for reforms, but he does not believe in giving up Confucianism.'

The last remark received wide approval. 'That's the kind of leader we want,' many cried out.

But the remark also stimulated heated discussion. One young man said that it was impossible to be modern and progressive and yet believe in Confucian ideas. His arguments were persuasive, and Ping-mo had difficulty in restoring order. Eventually the speaker, whose name was Seeto, was able to go on. 'Gentlemen,' he said, 'let me tell you what happened to Mr Kang during a dinner with some foreign friends. One of these friends made the remark that while Confucius was all very well for China over two thousand years ago, his teachings were useless in this modern age.'

'That was a good comment,' the modernist faction exclaimed. 'And what did Mr Kang have to say?'

'Well, for a little while Mr Kang simply looked at the foreign friend. But finally he said, "Your Jesus Christ came only five hundred years later than Confucius. Is he also useless to you in this modern age?"'

'Wonderful! Wonderful answer!' yelled the more moderate reformers.

'But Mr Kang went further. He said, "Confucius teaches people to behave, rather as a mathematician teaches us to add, subtract, multiply and divide. If three times three made nine two thousand years ago, they still make nine today. Three times three do not now make eight".'

There was renewed applause among the moderate elements.

'It so happened,' continued Seeto, 'that another Chinese friend was at the dinner, and he challenged Mr Kang's accuracy. "Learned as you are, Mr Kang, you really should know that mathematics have indeed advanced with the times. When we in China ask for a foreign loan, three times three invariably make seven. When we return the loan, three times three make eleven!" '

The modernist youths now began to cheer and laugh, but then they suddenly discovered they were laughing at themselves. The meeting settled down in a more friendly mood. But Ping-mo decided that this was hardly in keeping with the gravity and seriousness of the occasion. Ping-mo believed that, as the self-appointed saviours of the nation, they should be in dead earnest. He said: 'This Mr Kang is such a champion of reform and modernization that in four months he wrote some sixty-three petitions to the Emperor. If those petitions had been acted upon, I can assure you there would be no need for any revolution. But the unfortunate thing is that these petitions have all been rejected by the Empress Dowager, and Mr Kang had to run for his life.

'He got on board a British man-of-war, which brought him to the south, where he is now in hiding with a price on his head. To give you some idea of the wide scope of his reforms, Mr Kang advocated, for instance, the abolition of the antiquated civil-service examination and the establishment of military academies where young people would learn how to use modern weapons of war. He asked for the creation of modern schools and colleges. He urged that modern Japanese books be translated into Chinese, and new industries established. To show that he remains basically Chinese, he asked that Confucianism be made a State religion. And to show that an antiquated monarchy is out of place in modern life, he wanted to introduce constitutionalism so that the people might have a part to play in the Government. In all these new ideas Mr Kang had the support of the Emperor.'

The audience clapped their hands in approval.

Ping-mo then went on: 'Now, gentlemen, you can see for your-selves that this Mr Kang is a man of great vision and foresight. But there was one thing he lacks. Alas, he has no worldly wisdom. Mr Kang was betrayed by the treacherous Yuan Shih-kai. Both the Emperor and Mr Kang were poor judges of human character. That Yuan Shih-kai was a blackguard and a traitor. He was a man of unusual ambition. If Mr Kang had understood human character, he could have done something. As it was, he had to flee for his life, and everything fell to the ground. And we, the younger generation, must now carry on where he left off. We are called upon to do what he failed to do.

'We are a nation,' Ping-mo continued, 'which prides itself on having developed a high moral sense, but why is it that we have the untrustworthiness and treachery of a Yuan Shih-kai? We believe in Confucianism, but how is it that at critical moments in our history we have always had acts of betrayal on the part of those we have trusted? It is all very well to say that the foreigners are our enemies. They are. I do not deny it. But we must first eliminate the enemy from our own midst. My own father — well, it is best not to talk about him now. . . . As students and young men, we must try to look into our own hearts.'

There was warm applause. But then Ping-mo developed a line of thought which was not popular.

'Gentlemen,' he said, 'we have, of course, a just grievance against our foreign enemies, but I must emphasize that our worst enemies are among ourselves. It is true that the foreigners have brought one humiliation after another upon us, but have we ever thought that at least some of them are trying to help us?'

There was immediately a shuffling of feet. The hunchback and the old monk didn't like the question at all. They knew too much of the cruelties of the foreigner to appreciate such a sentiment. The audience became restless, and Ping-mo noticed it, but he went on as if a challenge had been thrown at him: 'I know for a fact that some of these foreigners are trying to do just what Mr Kang tried to do. They wish to help us to become a modern nation, and they are establishing schools and colleges so that all this modern knowledge may be introduced to us.'

Ping-mo had gone much further than was wise. Even some of his friends began to show a little nervousness, and the old monk thought it was time to intervene; everyone knew that he was in charge of the whole White Lotus organization in the area and had the right to speak.

When he stood up, he looked impressive. He had a large head and a bronze skin. There was fire in his eyes, and he looked stern. He was slow in his words, but what he said was pointed and had a note of finality.

'I have heard some interesting remarks today,' he began, 'and I think we have had a long enough session. It is time to adjourn. You are young men of learning and I admire your enthusiasm. But the poor people, the peasants, the unknown masses in the villages, have suffered through all these years, and the reasons for these sufferings are easy to find out. We shall eliminate them. First there are our own officials. They are intolerably effete, self-seeking individuals, cowardly and spineless. That includes everybody in the Government and the Court. There are Yuan Shih-kais everywhere — smaller than he but equally despicable. This is agreed by all of us. Then there are the foreigners. You don't know how hateful and cruel they are. But we do, we the poor people. We have suffered too much at their hands to see any good in them. They, too, must go. There is no compromise. Both are equally our enemies, and the people are getting ready to exterminate both our corrupt officials and these foreigners. On with our revolution!'

The old monk sat down; there was dead silence and the meeting automatically came to an end.

Shortly after midnight, when the sprawling city of Nanking was perfectly quiet, Ping-mo, who was staying in a small farmhouse, was awakened by a gentle knock at the crude door. He got out of bed, groped his way in the darkness to the door, unlatched the wooden bar, and saw to his amazement two peasants, each holding a small lantern and a big sharp knife. They summoned him to go with them at once.

'What is this?' exclaimed Ping-mo in horror.

'The Old Teacher' — that was how the old monk was referred to by his underlings — 'has asked us to take you to his presence. Don't be frightened, but put on your clothes and come.'

Ping-mo recollected that three years before he had had an almost identical experience. Then the old monk himself had accompanied him to a place of retreat, a mud hut where he saw some of the strangest things he had ever set eyes on. Much had happened since then. Ping-mo had himself become a seasoned revolutionary. He had travelled as far as Canton to establish liaison with students and young men who were fired by the same zeal as himself to introduce a new order. He had even taken part in some abortive attempts to wrest power from the local magistrates.

But three years had also seen radical changes in the organization of the peasant societies. Their numbers had increased by leaps and bounds. The new recruits were men and women in the villages who in one way or another had been maltreated by the 'second hairy ones' under the growing influence of the foreigners. Many of them had had their land and property taken from them, as Ah Zung had, and some of them even believed that little children had been kid-napped and abducted, and their bodies made into foreign medicine.

Mothers were careful not to lose sight of their children, as there were wild stories — in which they implicitly believed — that for-eigners were sending agents about the countryside to lure them away. One story was that an agent had only to tap an unwary child on the head, and from that moment all the poor child saw was a tiger on one side and a river on the other, and so had no alternative but to follow the agent.

The peasants willingly enrolled in the secret societies which promised them ultimate redress. With the increase in numbers the old monk grew in power and began to enforce stricter discipline. He ruled with an iron hand, and any infraction of the rules meant severe punishment.

Ping-mo did not realize that he was in for just such punishment, but as he walked through the fields with his two escorts, instead of reciting poetry to himself as he remembered having done three years earlier, he was full of fear. He entered the same mud hut as before, and on the walls was the same array of long spears and knives. He was pushed into a reasonably large room where he saw a number of people in all kinds of strange costumes, but none whom he knew. There were no women this time. He stood there for some time until the two escorts, who had disappeared into an adjoining room, came back and began stripping him. They then tied him to a bench in the middle of the room. The old monk appeared from the adjoining room, went to a table bearing two thick, burning candles, some

G

lighted incense and a fierce-looking idol: the figure of a great patriot of the Sung Dynasty, Yueh Fei. While the monk muttered strange incantations, the rest of the people in the room fell down on their knees and kowtowed. This lasted only two or three minutes, but it seemed longer to Ping-mo, who was shivering in cold sweat.

When the ceremony was over, the old monk stood up, followed by the others, and, turning to face Ping-mo, said: 'Ping-mo, for what you said tonight during the meeting you should be punished severely. But in view of your deep devotion to our cause, which we all recognize, I have decided to reduce this punishment to fifty strokes with the bamboo.'

So saying he left the room, and the two escorts carried out the punishment. He was later carried to a bed, where he passed the remainder of the night in pain and mortification, having learned that he must never again say anything good about foreigners.

3

A FORTNIGHT later Ping-mo was back in Soochow. He had learned a valuable lesson. But he still couldn't believe that he, so ardent and devout a champion of radical reforms, should have been rudely humiliated by an old monk who, both in scholarship and in social position, was his inferior.

And yet Ping-mo felt sure this old monk was no common person. His appearance, dark and tanned though it might be, had some indefinable quality which commanded respect. His eyes shone with a mysterious light, and people were reverent in his presence. Also he had more knowledge than was usual among the peasants. Ping-mo recalled that the old monk had once said that he was not in sympathy with the crude and coarse manners of the peasant rebels. Was it possible then that he was descended from as good a family as his own or perhaps even nobler?

But whatever he might be, he was an unmistakable leader of men whose commands were obeyed in more than one city in this Yangtze area. His words had a note of decisiveness in them, and his movements, slowly and deliberately taken, were quiet and dignified.

Surely such a person was worthy of some inquiry, and Ping-mo decided that he would find out something about him.

Meanwhile Wen-ching, the former ambassador to the Court of the Kaiser and of the Czar, together with his beautiful and talented concubine, had returned to the house where he had spent the longest and happiest period of his life as a scholar and savant. It was here that he had brought up his family. One boy died when he was scarcely three years old. But there was Ping-mo, who had grown into fine young manhood, though Wen-ching had not yet found out what he planned to be. And there was a daughter who was happily married into a good and solid family.

Wen-ching looked about him and saw the familiar faces of those of his own blood. He saw familiar objects, scrolls, paintings, book-shelves, chairs and tables. Life was now peaceful and quiet, and his spirits revived a little. He had become a forgotten man, or, if not forgotten, he lived in the memory of his fellow city-dwellers with a stigma on his name. He loved this quieter life, and yet it was im-possible for him not to feel mortification. He was just over fifty — not yet an old man but also no longer young. He began thinking about the remainder of his life, but knew it was no time to plan for the future.

The case planned to victimize him was pending, and he must hurry to Peking to fight it out as best he could. If he stayed in Soo-chow it would be thought that he was afraid to face the issue, that he was guilty. Yet if the invisible enemy had sufficient power to cripple him, surely he must also have enough reserve power to defeat him if he fought.

Wen-ching knew that the battle was uneven. But there was no alternative. He could not remain silent. He was constantly over-whelmed by a feeling of deep humiliation, of a terrible wrong having been done to him, and sorrow lay so heavily on his soul that at times he fell into a state of utter futility and helplessness. What was the use of fighting in the dark against invisible forces arrayed behind the impersonal facade of the Tsungli Yamen? It was in the name of that office that he had been recalled and dismissed from his post, and the Tsungli Yamen was the Government itself! Who ever heard of an individual in all the history of China fighting against the Govern-ment? It was sheer stupidity. The very idea seemed absurd, and any person entertaining such an idea must be either a fool or a lunatic.

Wen-ching's mind tossed on a sea of uncertainty. Fortunately for him Madam Wen-ching was a woman of supreme intelligence and breadth of mind. The return of Golden Orchid to the house could, with a lesser woman, have precipitated a crisis. Three years ago Madam Wen-ching had not recognized her officially as her husband's concubine. She had merely tolerated Golden Orchid to spend a few days under the same roof on the eve of her husband's departure for Europe.

If he had returned in normal circumstances, Madam Wen-ching would have insisted that her husband have another house where he would live with his concubine. But with a crisis facing him it was only natural that Wen-ching should constantly seek solace and advice from a maturer woman, his own wife. Golden Orchid might have developed within the last three years; but even so, Wen-ching felt he must rely more on his wife than on a woman thirty years younger than himself, however much he might love her.

Madam Wen-ching's mind was perfectly clear as to what her husband was thinking. She could not, intelligent woman that she was, raise at that particular moment what at best was a petty personal question. With her usual generosity she simply invited Golden Orchid to stay with her as if that was the most natural thing to do. Golden Orchid appreciated this, and felt that she was dealing with a superior woman with whom things could always be discussed in a rational way, without rancour or personal bitterness. There would be many issues in the future, she thought, which they would have to face together, and she was thankful that Madam Wen-ching was a woman she could respect and admire. Apart from occasional visits to her mother and grandmother, Golden Orchid now spent all her time with Wen-ching, Madam Wen-ching and Ping-mo. The little maid, grown into young womanhood, attended her.

Wen-ching told his wife of the three years of his ambassadorship. There was nothing to regret. He had done what was humanly possible. He had accomplished more than expected of him. He had improved China's relations with Germany, and German aggressiveness towards China had considerably lessened. He gave credit to the role which Golden Orchid had played.

'I believe all that you have told me,' Madam Wen-ching said. 'I am confident that your ability has enabled you to accomplish many things. I also believe that your young concubine was a great help to you. But there is always a reason for everything, and there is a reason for your downfall.'

Wen-ching remained silent. His wife went on:

'I don't know about life in Europe, but with us in China ability does not ensure success. There must be something in which you have failed. Have you asked yourself the question "In what have I failed?" '

Wen-ching felt uncomfortable at what his wife had said. Did she imply that there was some defect in his character which was responsible for his downfall? But he admitted calmly: 'Perhaps you are right. Perhaps there are shortcomings which I have not thought about sufficiently.'

'It is usual for human beings to attribute any failure to external causes,' continued Madam Wen-ching. 'But when one goes deeply enough, one often finds the seeds of failure within oneself. It is one of the most difficult things in life to know yourself; but unless you do, you cannot be master of yourself. Unfortunately there is no mirror for your mind, as there is for your face. You must keep on rubbing and polishing it before that mental mirror can shine and show clearly the image of your soul, and that is a bitter labour indeed. I am afraid you have not used sufficient effort in that direction.'

Wen-ching felt that there was nothing so defective in his soul as to justify what had happened to him. None of us is perfect, he thought to himself. I am far from being perfect myself. But I can call on the Almighty and ask Him if there is anything in me so immoral as to justify the deep humiliation which I am suffering. But again he remained silent and allowed his wife to finish her lecture.

'You remember what Confucius said,' continued Madam Wen-ching, 'about daily examining one's personal conduct on three points. First, in carrying out the duties entrusted to you by others, have you failed in conscientiousness? I have confidence that you have not. But he mentioned two other points — whether, in your intercourse with friends, you have failed in sincerity and trustworthiness; and, lastly, whether you have failed to practise what you profess in your teaching. It is on these two scores, Wen-ching, that you must examine yourself. You have told me that Hu-mou is a despicable person. That I can quite believe. There are people who take delight in hurting others. But do you seriously think that the wickedness of a single person is sufficient to destroy you?'

'If anything, I have been too sincere, and I don't think that I have not practised what I profess. As for Hu-mou, I don't know him well. We have seldom met. I have done all I can to please him — that is, as much as does not hurt my dignity. He is a native of Soochow, and although I do not count myself as such, I have lived here long enough, and I had hoped that he and I would be friends.'

'If I were you, I wouldn't concentrate entirely on Hu-mou.'

'But I am positive he is the cause of all my trouble.'

'We all know that life is a constant and unremitting struggle against the malice of men. This is especially so among officials in China. Not that I have had any experience of my own.'

'No, but I admit you were born in a family which for generations had known official life.'

'The positions of honour are few,' continued Madam Wen-ching, 'and the number of men aspiring to them are many. It is a question of the relative number of pegs and holes. When the holes are few and the pegs many, a good fraction of the pegs is bound to be eliminated. And you can be sure that recourse will be had to all kinds of tricks — sometimes very dishonourable tricks — to eliminate them. The problem is how to avoid being eliminated. You have not succeeded.'

'It is true that if I had played the game according to its own terms, if I had left behind all moral considerations, this unfortunate thing wouldn't have happened. But that is precisely what I refused to do. I am the square peg that does not fit into the round hole. I wanted to raise the level of official life. In that I failed. My immediate concern is how to wash away all the mud and make myself clean again. I don't think I shall ever be able to regain my lost position, and I don't mind.'

'I am not worried about that either,' rejoined Madam Wen-ching. 'We are not rich, but we have enough to live a simple and dignified life — you as a scholar and I as an artist and poet. But it is essential that you fight to win back your reputation.'

There was silence. Wen-ching wondered to himself how a problem like the one he was facing would be solved among Europeans. He did not pretend to know much about European habits and ways of thinking, but it seemed him to that there was an important difference in the Chinese way of doing things.

He said: 'In Europe people are always talking about laws. In a sense there is an advantage in that. Laws are legal prescriptions. They are something definite and determinate. It is in relation to these laws that conflicts and disputes are considered and finally judged. That is why, when my troubles started, my German employee Faustmann — a fine and devoted man — was not worried. He was sure that the evidence presented to any court of law would immediately exonerate me and that I would be completely vindicated and even compensated. I couldn't convince him that unfortunately things do not operate in that way in China. Even when I took the trouble to explain it, he could not understand.'

'I am afraid the most you can expect to do is to prove to your friends that you are honourable and have been the victim of a plot. Having accomplished that, you will have to retire. That is my hope.'

But Wen-ching couldn't get over this interesting difference between the European and the Chinese approach to legal problems. There were courts of law in China, to be sure, but they were not taken seriously. No one in his proper senses would think of bringing a dispute before a court, because the settlement of any dispute was through mediation. Some sort of compromise was effected through the intervention of friends; when the sharp edges were polished off and some harmony or understanding established, the dispute was somehow resolved.

But Wen-ching refused to see any ground for mediation in his case — either he was guilty or he was innocent. And, besides, mediation was out of the question for him. Mediation between him and an impersonal Tsungli Yamen? Impossible! The root of the trouble, Hu-mou, had cleverly become an invisible factor. It was not a case of Hu-mou against Wen-ching, but of the Government itself against Wen-ching, even though, behind the Government, was the sinister hand of Hu-mou.

In matters affecting the human heart Madam Wen-ching could often show more wisdom and shrewdness than Wen-ching. She was not against the case being placed before a court of law, especially as she knew that the law courts were undergoing some radical changes along modern lines. Still she was not unmindful of the old adage that 'to untie the bell you must find the hand that tied it'.

'I believe,' said Madam Wen-ching, 'some contact should still be made with Hu-mou, however bitter the experience may prove to be.'

'I thought so too,' replied Wen-ching. 'But now, as I consider the matter again, I think any contact with Hu-mou is useless. He has done the damage. It is part of his strategy to place the matter out of his control, so that there would be nothing he could do even if he wanted to. And he does not want to — that is sure.'

In this mood of uncertainty, Wen-ching decided to wait for further developments before going to Peking. But a few days afterwards came the news that Yung-kai was now within the Great Wall with the imperial gift and that it would not be long before he would be in Peking itself. This convinced Wen-ching that he must leave for the north at once, whatever the consequences might be. Golden Orchid, of course, agreed promptly.

Yung-kai had been almost eight months on the journey. Even though Yung-kai himself had volunteered to undertake the mission, Wen-ching felt that the young man left Berlin with his authorization and blessing and that it was his duty to return him to his father, Lord Yu Kung, in a state of health and good spirits. His own sorrows and misfortunes began to fade into the background. Accordingly he informed Quiet Virtue that he was leaving for Peking with his concubine on the first available steamer.

'I feel I should go with you this time,' said Madam Wen-ching, 'but I am such a bad traveller, and I know I shall be terribly seasick, even though it is a matter of only five or six days.'

The real reason which restrained her was that if she went she would acknowledge Golden Orchid to the world as the recognized concubine, and that she was not prepared to do. Besides, she had discussed with her husband all the aspects of the issue and the line which he should pursue. She did not believe that Wen-ching would receive justice. The utmost that he could hope for was to have his name cleared, and then she expected him to retire to a scholar's life in Soochow.

So, before her husband left for the north, she again said: 'Remember, Wen-ching, I shall not be at all unhappy if you spend the rest of your life in literary pursuits. That is what you are made for. That is where you are going to make your name and your lasting contribution. But go to Peking and clear up the mess. We must all die; but there are three things which can make us immortal — establishing our virtue, accomplishing worthy deeds, and leaving behind words that are true. That is all one can expect to be remembered by in future generations. That is what we mean when we say that our soul is immortal. I do not believe that the soul itself continues to exist in the next life, as this new religion from the foreigners tries to make us believe. As regards the body, it disintegrates the moment we cease to breathe. I believe that when you come back to pursue the scholar's life, you can accomplish these three things. I am not at all sorry that you are giving up official life.'

Madam Wen-ching continued to spend most of her time in her study attending to her painting and the delicate breeding of her orchids. She maintained her poise and mental equilibrium. She was unruffled within, her face was free from wrinkles, and her skin was as smooth as a young woman's. The arrangements in the study remained substantially the same, the only difference being that she now had a canary in a bamboo cage. And when Wen-ching left for Peking, she opened her windows and looked into the distance at the Tiger Hill. There was a clear and beautiful view of early autumn. The fields looked mellow and were full of grain waiting to be harvested. The canary sang as the fresh air came wafting into the room, and Madam gazed towards the horizon where the outlines of the gently undulating hills looked firm and distinct. She was always happy with distant views.

Before Wen-ching left Soochow for the north he spoke to Ping-mo. 'My son,' he said, 'take care of your mother during my absence. I have done her great wrong. For that I am deeply sorry.'

Before Wen-ching could go any further, Ping-mo's eyes were wet with tears. 'Father, please don't say that. I know what it is all about. Perhaps if I had gone to Germany with you, I could have been of some help.'

'That may be true, my son. But if Hu-mou was bent upon hurting me, your presence or absence would have made no difference.'

'I am torn between going with you to Peking and staying behind with Mother. I know she is deeply upset, even if she doesn't show it. She would be very lonely if I went.'

'Yes, stay where you are and give her all the comfort you can.'

'Father, I know you are contending against tremendous odds. Oh, how I wish I had the power to fight against all the evils of the official world! But I shall pray for you. I shall constantly visit the tombs of our ancestors. I am sure my prayers will be answered, for I cannot believe that evil can permanently triumph over goodness.'

'It is good of you to say this, my son. You have given me strength. Let's wait patiently and see what the result will be.'

4

YUNG-KAI was almost at the end of his stupendous journey. He had not only come well within the Great Wall, but he had passed Lanchow and Kansu province, passed even Paotow, and had reached Tatung in Shansi province. In a few more days it was possible that he might enter the gates of Peking itself.

He decided to rest a little in order to prepare himself for the warm welcome which he knew would be waiting for him. Lao Chuang was tired, and so was the poor horse. There was no need to hurry now that the journey was virtually at an end. All they had to do was to look their best, and Tatung was a logical choice as a stopping place before they made the grand entry into Peking. The local magistrate provided them with food and new clothing.

There was one spot near Tatung which Yung-kai had heard much about. In fact, Lao Chuang had been there once before when he was in the service of those foreigners on their archaeological expeditions. He said the place was well worth seeing, and Yung-kai decided that now was the time to visit this grotto long famed for its beautiful Buddhist sculptures, done some fifteen hundred years before at a time of chaos and confusion, when religious faith was the only thing which kept life going. Figures of Buddhas and saints, of bodhisattvas and apsaras, and of angels flying on luminous wings filled the caves which lined the cliffs.

That night Yung-kai could not sleep. He was restless, and there were pains in his head, in his back and in his limbs. Occasionally he shivered feverishly. He called Lao Chuang, who asked the innkeeper for hot water in which he dissolved a special tea to encourage perspiration, and thought that by the morning his young master would be well again. Yung-kai covered himself with heavy bedding, but still he felt chilled. Lao Chuang lay on a couch beside him, and noticed that the young master passed a very fitful night. Now and then he fell asleep, but he tossed and muttered unintelligibly. Lao Chuang quietly went to the bed to see that the covers were on Yung-kai's body. Then he gently placed his hand on his forehead and to his horror found it burning hot. The young master must have a very high fever, he thought, and while he prayed that he would be better in the morning, he wondered what he should do if the fever continued.

Morning came and Yung-kai was only slightly better. He did not feel well enough to get up. He saw Lao Chuang and gave him a faint smile.

'Young master, how do you feel?'

'Better . . . except that I feel so weak, and my mouth is dry and bitter.'

Lao Chuang hurried to get some water with which Yung-kai might gargle and brought a hot towel to wipe his face. The fever was still there, though not as high as it had been during the night. Lao Chuang did not wish to encourage too much talk and said that it would be best for the young master to lie in bed for another day, and then all would be well.

In the meantime, Lao Chuang asked the house to recommend a doctor and went to the local yamen to inform the magistrate that the young lord had been taken ill. A wire was sent to Yung-kai's father at once. All Tatung was now in a state of excitement — which was understandable, as Lord Yu Kung was one of the great officials of the land — and the best doctors in the town came to visit the patient. They looked at his tongue and found it to be thickly coated. They felt his pulse, first with two fingers, then with three. But however they felt it, they found that it ran very rapidly. They consulted books on astrology and were not encouraged. They found that there was a conflict somewhere in the elements — either between fire and metal or between earth and water, they couldn't decide which. They drew up prescriptions of herbs which in the main agreed with one another, but they couldn't very well have a composite prescription, and so they decided that the one given by the oldest and most experienced of them should be tried first. It produced the desired effect in reducing Yung-kai's temperature. But when night came, Yung-kai relapsed into the same feverish state and mumbled deliriously. All Lao Chuang could make out were frequent references to Golden Orchid, whom he called his loved one, his 'heart and liver'. The next day the doctors came once again and gave some more herb medicine, but it was apparent to them that the patient was not improving. Yung-kai was red and flushed and his head appeared to have become swollen.

It was not till the fourth day that his father, Lord Yu Kung, arrived in Tatung in the company of a doctor from the German hospital which had recently been opened in Peking. Herr Geheimrat Doktor Edelstein proceeded forthwith, to the horror and amazement of the Chinese herb doctors, to unbutton Yung-kai's clothes and found, as he expected, rose-coloured spots all over his body. It was a clear case of typhus, he declared; and he proceeded to explain to his Lordship that it was a highly infectious disease carried by rat-lice, fleas or bedbugs, and that Yung-kai was in very critical condition. The Chinese herb doctors listened attentively, looked at one another, and left in disgust, saying: 'These foreigners are strange people. They accuse us of being superstitious, but is there greater superstition than to believe that human beings fall ill because of rats and bedbugs? These things are everywhere, and yet people are no more ill than we are!'

But Dr Edelstein continued to explain to Lord Yu Kung that Yung-kai must have slept in all sorts of unclean places on his journey, and it would be the easiest thing in the world for the disease germs to get to him. As for Lao Chuang, he had been exposed to the same danger, but might have acquired immunity in his earlier trips to Mongolia when the germs attacked him. Not all people necessarily became ill when they were exposed to any given disease.

It was difficult for the German doctor to give an explanation that would be satisfactory, but even as he proceeded to give the patient some solution of acetate of ammonia and citrate of potash, he found that the lungs were becoming congested and breathing was difficult. The doctor gave orders that the windows be opened and unnecessary furniture, curtains, etc., removed, all of which again struck the Chinese doctors as most unreasonable; their immediate response to illness was to have everything closed so that the patient would not catch a cold.

Dr Edelstein tried to relieve Yung-kai's difficulty in breathing by giving him a few drops of ipecacuanha wine and a little brandy which he had brought with him. But in spite of all his efforts for three days to save Yung-kai, Dr Edelstein admitted that the patient was beyond cure. On the night before the young man died, the doctor found that his temperature at times shot up to 106 degrees. He continued to mumble unintelligibly, but the father noticed, as Lao Chuang had a few days previously, that the words 'Golden Orchid' were constantly on his parched lips. As he gasped for his last breath, his arms moved frantically as if trying to drive something away. The monks had already been summoned into the room and were reciting the Buddhist scriptures. These they thought might exorcise the spirits which by now must be clinging to the body of the dying man and trying to pull him into the other world. Exactly what Yung-kai was attempting to do no one could tell, but it occurred to those who knew that he had visited the sculptured grottoes that his mind must be tormented by the thought that idols, saints and angels were beckoning him to the 'other shore'.

Lord Yu Kung's grief knew no bounds. His immediate reaction was that the journey had been wholly unnecessary and that Wen-ching had contributed to the death of his son. But there was nothing that His Lordship could do now except gather together his son's belongings and hurry back to Peking to give him a fitting burial. There he would talk to Wen-ching and Golden Orchid, who were expected from Soochow.

There were few personal belongings which Lord Yu Kung could assemble. But lying underneath the hard straw pillow was Yung-kai's diary. It looked like a full record of the journey. This His Lordship put away among his own belongings to be read carefully on his way back to Peking. He summoned Lao Chuang, gave him money and instructed him to take the imperial gift to Peking alone as soon as arrangements were completed for the young lord's remains which could leave Tatung a few days later.

On his way back to Peking, laden with sorrow, Lord Yu Kung began to read Yung-kai's diary.

After describing his departure from Berlin in the middle of April with the glorious display of popular admiration and enthusiasm, Yung-kai wrote that he continued to make good time until he felt rather indisposed at Wrzesnia. When Lao Chuang arrived and they went on to Moscow together, he felt much better now that he was attended by a servant. He did not seem much attracted by what he saw on the way, as his mind went back constantly to the last days in Berlin, and the diary showed deep concern for Wen-ching and

Golden Orchid. The account threw a flood of light on his son's relationship with the ambassador and his concubine, and this was precisely what Lord Yu Kung wanted to know. He did not have to proceed very far to find out that his son was deeply in love with Golden Orchid, and he now understood why before he died Yung-kai was constantly mumbling her name.

When I return to Peking [Yung-kai had written in his diary] I shall wait for your return, my own sweet nightingale. Oh, Orchid, my Orchid, now I know I can never, never live without you. But fate has been cruel to us, has it not? Why did we meet in such unhappy circumstances? If only we had met so that you and I could become man and wife, a source of eternal and everlasting joy and happiness to ourselves! You a maid of nineteen and I only three years older — what an ideal combination! What is there to prevent us from being eternally happy when our hearts yearn for each other? You know I have always yearned for you, and even if you sometimes protest, I know from your smiles and from your large limpid eyes, so full of love and warmth, that you too yearn for me. And yet there is everything in the world to prevent us from locking our souls together. We are much worse off than the cowherd and the weaving maid up in the Milky Way. At least they can, once a year, cross the great barrier and merge into each other. But where are we? And what can we do? There are so many barriers which neither you nor I can overcome.

You are now the concubine of my ambassador when you should be my wife. Nothing in the world can ever change you from one to the other. And even if it could, the fact that you have been a concubine makes it impossible for me, scion of a noble family, to take you as my wife. Not only will my father not allow it, but the whole of the social tradition is against it. We discussed this together, you remember, my dearest one, when you were in my apartment that night, and we agreed there is no solution. . . .

'So Golden Orchid has been in his private apartment. Such freedom is most unbecoming,' commented Lord Yu Kung. He read on —

But, oh, the last time we were together, it was adorable, it was heavenly. How shall I ever forget the divine ecstasy that you gave me! For almost three years I waited for that moment, and when it came at last we overcame all obstacles, and our bodies and souls became one and indivisible. Oh, how I trea-

sure that precious memory. When there is true love as there is
between you and me, nothing, not even Heaven itself, can prevent us from belonging to each other. We defied everything.
O brave girl! how nobly you brushed away all considerations!
You completely forgot that you were someone's concubine, and
I . . . I scattered all social considerations and the disapproval
of my father to the winds, and so completely did we merge and
melt into each other that we really became one. Nothing now
can ever separate us. Once we have become one, we shall
remain permanently one.

At the end of this entry Yung-kai had drawn a symbol thus:

— one of the oldest symbols of Chinese mythology, a symbol of deep
cosmological and mystical significance. Within that circle of
rounded perfection, of complete harmony and unity, are at work the
two basic principles of life and the universe — the principle of *yin* and
yang, the female and the male principles, the two polar entities,
which act and interact and thereby generate all the creative forces
which are responsible for the self-perpetuation of the cosmic order
and of all forms of life. It is a symbol of complete synthesis, of
ultimate reality.

As he read this part of the diary, Lord Yu Kung, despite his grief,
felt like breaking into a smile but could not. He merely closed his
eyes, shook his head and then said to himself, If only he had lived!

Yung-kai had not behaved as he should. What if his conduct with
Golden Orchid should become known? The diary, or at least that
part of it which described the intimacies with Golden Orchid, must
remain secret. Yung-kai could not have behaved like this if he remained at home in Peking. It would have been an intolerable
scandal. But young men who come under the deleterious influences
of foreign ideas are apt to do all kinds of impossible things and bring
shame and disorder to their families.

Lord Yu Kung read on, and it seemed that during all that part of
the journey when Yung-kai boarded the train with Lao Chuang
from Moscow to Omsk, and then took the boat from Omsk to the
Irtysh River, his thoughts were mostly with Golden Orchid and the
affairs of the embassy. He referred constantly to the possibility of
Golden Orchid's bearing him a child. What if there was a child?

What complications would ensue from such an event? He, Lord Yu Kung, grandfather to a child born not from wedded love, but with a woman who was a concubine to a friend whom he had recalled from his diplomatic post! The very thought of such a thing filled him with dismay. But who was there to know all this except Yung-kai himself and Golden Orchid, and Yung-kai was now dead. Not even Wen-ching would know it, since he would naturally consider the child his own, if Golden Orchid kept a discreet silence — which, he was sure, she would.

Learning these new facts made Lord Yu Kung feel he had established a new relationship with Wen-ching. He turned to the next few pages, and there before his eyes was a clear account of what had happened at the embassy in Berlin.

It was a revelation so complete that he felt as if he were a blind man seeing the light of day for the first time. Yung-kai spoke of the meanness and pettiness of his colleagues at the embassy, of their vulgar pleasures, of their niggardliness, of the thousand ways in which they made money illegally, of their brazen abuse of diplomatic privileges, including smuggling, and of his certainty that they must receive the protection of the Tsungli Yamen itself for all these evil deeds!

'Have I really been asleep all this time?' His Lordship exclaimed. 'Has all this been happening under my nose? Incredible!'

'I have the deepest sympathy for the ambassador whom the staff seeks to destroy,' said the diary. 'My father not only has no knowledge, but I have reason to believe that he even thinks that the ambassador is to blame. That is why I must explain things to him the moment I arrive in Peking.'

Here Lord Yu Kung paused. What grounds are there for my son to say such things? he asked himself. He tried to recollect comments made about Wen-ching by his colleagues in the Tsungli Yamen. He had become somewhat hazy about them, but he did remember that there was a feeling of antagonism towards Wen-ching. For what reason he did not know. Whether that atmosphere was purposely created and who was behind it all, he had no means of finding out.

Another entry read:

It is perhaps a mistake that the ambassador maintains such scholarly aloofness. He does not deal with his subordinates on their level or tactfully enough. That is his weakness, and the

gap between him and them seems to become wider every day. I
know that other ambassadors play mah-jongg with their staffs,
and I was told that they even share in the profits of illegal transactions. In that way there is harmony — of a bad sort, to be sure,
but if harmony is all one wants, there is the formula. If only
Wen-ching knew or was willing to act on such a formula. But
he confines himself to his study and hardly ever meets his staff
except on official business. It doesn't work, and they loathe him
for it. I know that the ambassador does the correct thing, but
it can be effective only if my father backs him up. I have the
impression that father is being constantly fooled by someone in
his own yamen. I shall have to find out for him. I know he is
exceedingly busy with many important affairs of state, but that
is no excuse for him not to look carefully into the wiles and
tricks of his subordinates in the Tsungli Yamen.

Lord Yu Kung was disturbed. He might not be especially resolute
or forceful as a person, but could he relish what amounted almost to
an indictment of his character by his own son? Could it be, he asked
himself, that he had done injustice to a man in whom his confidence
had been shaken and undermined by some sinister force? Did it
need a dead son to arouse him from complacency?

Lord Yu Kung, it must be frankly admitted, was a good man, but
his goodness was not the product of his own strong will or conviction.
He had not climbed to his present eminent position either by virtue
of his mental perspicacity or by his determination to overcome
obstacles. His honours were given to him largely because of the
closeness of his relationship to the Court, and on many occasions he
had failed to give a good account of himself largely because he was
lacking in firmness, in judgement or in strength of character. His
face showed refinement and dignity. The features were delicately
chiselled, but his chin had a tendency to recede, and his mouth, like
a door with ill-adjusted hinges, was always slightly ajar.

Lord Yu Kung lacked the necessary qualifications to distinguish
himself even if he had confined himself to the Tsungli Yamen alone
at this time of national crisis. The additional duties in the other
offices and in the Grand Council, which were heaped upon him because of his blood relationship to the Court, dissipated so much of his
limited ability and energy that there were chinks all over his official
armour. And well did his unscrupulous underlings know how to exploit and penetrate them. He was inwardly ashamed that his son

saw his weakness as clearly as anybody, and whatever he might resolve to do now, there was little that he could do to remedy the situation. The whole apparatus of the Government had moved against
Wen-ching, and it would require infinite resourcefulness for a man
with even greater ability than Lord Yu Kung to undo the wrong
which had already been done.

Besides, Lord Yu Kung was not even clear how Wen-ching's recall
had come about. He was totally in the dark about Hu-mou's painstaking efforts, about the meticulous care with which everything had
been planned. All that he recalled was that an 'impartial' investigator recommended by Director Hu-mou had found Wen-ching and
his consul equally responsible for the illegal document, and without
taking any further trouble to inquire into the matter, he gave his
approval to their recall.

With new light being shed on the whole affair, Lord Yu Kung
didn't want to think about it — not at least for the moment. He
knew it was going to be upsetting, and he didn't care to be upset at a
time of deep sorrow.

He read on in the diary to a point where Yung-kai was entering
the most exciting phase of his journey. There was a short description
of Moscow before he took the train for Omsk. The city seemed to
have produced a deep, unfavourable impression on Yung-kai's mind.

Berlin is bad enough [so Lord Yu Kung continued to read].
The streets may be wide and clean and orderly, but the city
itself is overbearing, arrogant and militant. But Moscow is
worse — much worse. The heart of the city is the Kremlin, and
that seems to me to be the very embodiment of wanton cruelty
and tyranny. How different it is from our own Forbidden City,
which is almost its counterpart. The Forbidden City is also an
exclusive preserve or enclave for our reigning emperors, but it
is tranquil and kind; there is even an atmosphere of gaiety and
cheerfulness about it, with its colourful roofs reflected in the
radiant blue of the sunlit sky. And yet it is awe-inspiring and
in keeping with its imperial dignity and grandeur.

But in Moscow I felt none of these things. The crenellated
walls of the Kremlin look formidable and forbidding. They are
cold and they strike a chill in the heart. In the streets of Moscow there seemed to be a perpetual look of fright on the faces of
the people — that was what struck me most of all. Their
features were frozen and appeared as if nothing in the world
could thaw them out — not even the coming of Spring. We are

both monarchies, and yet what a difference! We have had a culture of our own for thousands of years in which, in spite of our weaknesses, we have tried to cultivate and develop the basic human qualities. The Russian people, on the other hand, have no roots of their own, or if they have any, they are deep in the primeval forests from which they have barely emerged. No, no, I would rather explore the wide expanses of the desert than remain here.

'The young man seems to have been very observant,' commented His Lordship. 'It was promising that he made such comparisons. It shows that he was using his mind. If only he had lived!'

From Moscow Yung-kai took the train for Omsk and thence for Semipalatinsk, where he took a steamer and sailed for four days up the pleasant Irtysh River. He and Lao Chuang then crossed Lake Zaisan, which was remarkable only for its size. There was nothing very interesting to see, and the water was grey. The steamer stopped at Topliefmus, and that was the beginning of the overland journey. Upon entering Chuguchak after leaving the Russian border, Yung-kai knew that he was within the domain of his own country.

At this point in the diary Lord Yu Kung found a poem, written very obviously for Golden Orchid:

> In the sky, floating clouds,
> On the earth, a gentle breeze,
> The cool air blowing through my hair;
> How can I not think of her?
> The moon in love with the sea;
> The sea in love with the moon,
> Ah, on this sweet, silvery night,
> How can I not think of her?
> Blossoms drifting on the water;
> Fishes sporting in the stream.
> Swallow, what is that you are saying?
> How can I not think of her?
> Bare trees shivering in the wind;
> Wild fires aflame in the evening glow;
> The sun still colouring the western sky;
> How can I not think of her?

Lord Yu Kung smiled faintly at the immaturity of the verse, though it was full of feeling. And then he suddenly closed his lips and thought that his son was at least happy. 'Would that he were still alive!' he said again. And he buried his head in his hands and closed the diary for a moment. The mule-cart which was taking him back to Peking rocked His Lordship to sleep.

The moment he awoke, he began turning over the pages of the diary again. It was for him a way of escape, for otherwise he would have had to spend his time thinking over the wrongs he might have done Wen-ching.

> The garrison commander at Tacheng, [he read on] came out to welcome me. Russian big-noses everywhere . . . whole town came out to see me and the horse. . . . I was surprised to find a number of sea-gulls, since we were hundreds of miles away from any sea. I was told that they follow the course of the Irtysh River and come all the way from the Arctic north. That is why the town is often called the Town of Sea Gulls.

Then came the account of the trip to Urumchi, seven hundred miles away:

> The country is rich in all kinds of vegetables and fruits. The grapes and apples are particularly luscious. I don't remember having eaten such fruit anywhere. There is also wheat, maize and even rice which I thought was grown only in south China. Most of the people whom we passed are Moslems, and the relations between them and the Chinese have at times been very bitter. Lao Chuang was attracted to the women of this area. They all look well fed and plump, especially those in the neighbourhood of Manas, where we had a long rest. How he got to know so much in so short a time I will never find out. He came back to the inn and told me that the Moslem men here are very free with the women, who live only for their pleasure, and they can discard them whenever they wish. I thought it was very bold of him to tell me such things. Besides, he was asking for trouble, for if ever his wife Chuang Mah got to know that he was being so free things would not go well for him. When morning came — it was a glorious morning — and I told Lao Chuang to be ready to move, he seemed to be reluctant.
>
> It took us three months to reach Urumchi, and if all the territory to Peking is like what we have just covered, we should encounter little difficulty.

The account of Urumchi itself interested Lord Yu Kung:

> I had an opportunity to see something of the city, and I was struck with the fact that there is any amount of water — and

good water too — in a vast surrounding desert! There is a river just outside the city, but the streets are dirty. They are littered with the skins of melons, and the flies must number millions! The melons, I must say, are delicious. This is a strange city inhabited by people of all races. The most noticeable of these races are the Kazaks, broad-shouldered men who spend most of their time on horseback. They wear tall leather boots and pointed caps with flaps on both sides which reach to their shoulders. Even when they shop, they do not get down from their horses or camels, and I am told that they bargain in an unusual manner. They stretch their hands into one another's sleeves and decide on the price merely through the pressure of their fingers on the arms — secrecy in the desert.

There are other peoples who crowd the streets of this City of the Red Temple — Mongols, Tibetans, Tungans, Kalmucks and Kirghizes. They are all excellent horsemen. The women here look formidable to me, with their black quilted coats and white cotton headdresses. I am afraid even Lao Chuang is no match for any of them, and he is no weakling.

All in all, this short rest in Urumchi was a pleasant one. I wish it could be longer, but we have to be on our way to Kucheng, the next big town, which we expect to reach in a week. . . .

Kucheng — meaning the ancient city — is a large town and is the terminus of the camel trail coming from the east across the Gobi Desert. There is a large number of Turkish inhabitants, and I thought that their national dish — *pilau* — which is made of chopped mutton, onions, spice, carrots, sometimes rice and roast fowl, was very palatable indeed. With that we ate large flat cakes of bread fully over a foot in diameter. The only unpleasant experience was that the inns were full of bedbugs, which were quite a nuisance. I had some very bad bites. The local people don't seem to mind them at all. I asked Lao Chuang how he stood the attack: they did not seem to bother him either!

With the mention of bugs and bites, for the first time in the diary, Lord Yu Kung almost jumped up, as if he had found the key of understanding. And so it was: a confirmation of Dr Edelstein's opinion. Dirty inns and bedbugs — why, that was the cause of his son's death! He shook his head and read on:

. . . Lao Chuang was in especially good spirits. He had lots of time to himself. He was very free and talkative with the local people. He had all sorts of stories to tell them about the life he knew in Germany, and with his open and frank manner and his readiness to laugh and crack jokes he made friends very easily. He told me that he was going to look for more fun in Hami. . . .

We passed through a number of oases — Head Waters, Three Mouth Spring, Big Rock, Seven-Cornered Fountain, etc. — and were warned that the region was infested with horse thieves. I instructed Lao Chuang to be very careful, as the knowledge of the prize steed in our charge had by now spread to all parts of this area. It so happened, as I learned afterwards, that no one dared to touch the horse when it was known that it was a gift for the Emperor. Any harm done to it would, of course, result in the severest form of punishment. So we had no trouble whatever, it turned out. On the way, however, we did see, at Liaotung I believe, just before we came into Hami, a poor man who had his left hand cut off. He was pointed out to me as having stolen a horse, and the amputation was his reward! The idea was revolting, and I felt very unhappy. I thought the punishment was horrible, but that is the kind of rough justice that one gets out in these desert parts.

Hami by all accounts is a handsome city set in a fertile oasis. The first thing I did upon arrival, after going through a fine avenue of trees, was to present myself to the Moslem Khan, who must be about forty years of age. He is a fine-looking man, with aquiline nose and prominent features, and he welcomed me in the most cordial manner. I must say that my whole trip is being made easier by the fact that I am the son of a great official so near to the Court and that I am taking an imperial gift to His Majesty.

Lord Yu Kung was glad that his position had contributed to the pleasure of his son's journey.

All the officials on the way have been notified of my impending arrival. There have been no formalities to go through, and wherever I go there is a warm and friendly reception. Well, this Khan belongs to a dynasty which has made Hami its capital ever since the reign of Emperor Kang Hsi. That means two and a half centuries. There is a large Turkish population in these areas, and they have their own Moslem bazaars and their own city. There is also a large Chinese population, who likewise have their own shops and their own town. And then there are two different sets of morgues and temples for two different habits of living and dying. But they seem to reside together in a harmonious manner. And why shouldn't they?

The Khan is the titular head, with the actual power in the hands of the Chinese. He lives in an impressive palace built in the Chinese style, and there is a high mud wall around it. It has a citadel in which he keeps his sentries. As soon as I went into his reception-room, he had a huge melon ready for me. His official entourage paid their respects to me, and when they left the room, he and I were alone for some time and fed on that luscious melon.

In his jovial and hearty manner he said to me: 'You have heard, of course, my young lord (it was very courteous of him to address me in this way), that Turfan is famous for its grapes, Kuldja for its horses, Kucha for its women and Hami for its melons. I know you didn't go through Turfan, but you must have tasted its grapes in Urumchi. As for horses, you have the finest one in the world, I understand. I want to see it later on. It remains for you to enjoy our melons and our women. Here is the melon, and we reserve the women till the last.' With that he laughed a hearty laugh, and we had a most delightful time together. He wanted to learn all he could from me about the life and manners of people in Europe, and he was so delighted that he assured me he would go there as soon as there was an opportunity.

Towards evening he assembled his official entourage again and gave me a wonderful dinner, even more elaborate than the one I had at Urumchi. We had shark's fins, bamboo shoots, bird's-nest soup and all the delicacies I have not have for three years. The company was hilarious, and the wines added gaiety to the occasion. I don't remember how much I drank, but with the finger game going on all the time — in which I proved to be a constant loser — I must have drunk more than was good for me. All I remember is that I was carried to a spacious room beautifully decorated in the Moslem style, and there I was put to sleep on a huge *kang* which was warmly heated underneath. What happened afterwards I cannot describe in detail because I don't know precisely. But I do know that, in the middle of the night, when the effects of the wine had more or less subsided, I woke up to find myself sleeping between the naked bodies of two lovely young women. I was the most embarrassed person in the world. There was nothing I could do. I recalled what the Khan had said earlier: 'We reserve the women till the last.' So that was the trick! I know I gave a frightened look, and as the room was lighted, my female companions noticed the state of anguish I was in, and they soon put me at ease. I swear I was not responsible for what happened afterwards. The Khan was indeed the biggest rogue in the entire world. The women were very gentle to me. They were very well developed and their skin was delicately smooth and white. They were Turkish girls, and one of them had a thick line of joined eyebrows, as many young women here have. They both had large black eyes — and oh, how bushy they were, much more so than Chinese girls. Well, it is best that I keep in my mind what happened rather than have it recorded in this diary. But, anyway, when dawn came and I was fast asleep again, the two of them must have left me. There was no one to disturb me, and so I slept far beyond the usual hours. When I woke up I did not find any trace of the girls. Could it be that is was all a dream? I wish it was, and yet, I confess, I wish it was not.

When I got outside the palace I looked for Lao Chuang, but he was nowhere to be found. I strolled about a bit in the town, and I must say that most of the women I met on the streets and in the bazaars were beautiful. They are not veiled and wear flowing white drapery which, with the utmost freedom of their bodies, makes them exceedingly coquettish and desirable. The bazaars are full of fruit and vegetables of all varieties, and the city is covered with parks, sparkling streams, and flowers. . . .

Since water-melons are a speciality in Hami, I was taken to an orchard where I saw each melon resting on a bone-dry, sand-baked patch absorbing the intense heat of the sun. The grower takes care of each one individually, turning it over and over again so that it receives a uniform amount of sunshine on all sides. Each melon is marked when it is still young and tender. . . .

. . . The Khan was waiting to show me how to hunt with falcons. After a light repast I went out to see some of these ferocious-looking birds. They stood perched on the hands and arms of the Kirghiz trainers. They had thick paddings of leather thongs just above the talons and also wore a small hood strapped underneath the beak, evidently to prevent them from tearing their quarry. In the same way fishermen in south China have something around the necks of the cormorants when they release them to catch fish. The way falcons are caught is interesting. Usually in the autumn nets are stretched out in the desert under which are placed chickens and pigeons as snares. When the falcons swoop down on them, their feet get entangled in the nets and they are then easily caught. It does not require more than two weeks to tame these wild birds, and then they are ready to go out and hunt hares and foxes. That usually takes place in the winter, and the birds, after their service is over, regain their freedom early in the summer.

The time I was there was not the regular hunting season, but I thought it was not bad that, as a demonstration, the hunters bagged two hares.

Before I left Hami the Chinese postal commissioner came to see me. He told me this whole area became a part of the Chinese Empire in the Han Dynasty as early as two thousand years ago. He knew that the Russians here now are trying to tell these different races that they should be independent, that they should be on their own, that they should eventually free themselves from Chinese rule because they are not a part of China. 'The more I live here,' he said, 'the more I appreciate the remark of Commissioner Lin's that the greatest menace to China will not be Britain or Germany or Japan, but Russia. Russia is our greatest danger.'

The postal commissioner also told me that the importance of these regions has never been overlooked by the Chinese emperors, and he took me to see a temple which was erected in honour of a very recent general, Tso Tsung-tang. Of course I had heard ever since I was a child that this general was the one who quelled the Moslem rebellion. A walk through the gateways, the red-lacquered pillars, the courtyards and the curved roofs, and finally to the temple itself was therefore a thrilling experience. In the centre of the hall was a raised platform, and there inside a beautifully carved enclosure was a portrait of the great General, dressed in his yellow robes and a mandarin's cap. He wore a moustache and looked very stern.

Our next large city on leaving Hami is Ansi and then, beyond that, Yumen, the Jade Gate, which is the entrance to the real China.

5

LORD YU KUNG spent the night at the house of a local magistrate. He was comfortable, but it was a long time before he fell asleep. He thought about his children and silently shed a few tears over Yung-kai's death.

Yung-kai was not his only son, but His Lordship's other numerous sons and daughters had not turned out as well as they might have done. His daughters were all married into respectable families, of sufficiently high social standing, but there was nothing in them to make him particularly happy. From his sons he did expect something, but they all proved to be disappointing.

The oldest son was addicted to the company of actors and actresses, but life on the stage was unfortunately never considered a respectable occupation. His great passion was to be able to sing the traditional Chinese operas and play the part of Chu-ko Liang, a great prime minister of a bygone age. This he did well — so well, in fact, that he once gave a command performance for the Empress Dowager in the Summer Palace just outside Peking. Lord Yu Kung could never forget that evening. He did not know whether he should rejoice or feel ashamed that his own son appeared before the Old Buddha in the capacity of an actor. He was happy that the performance pleased Her Majesty, but he wished that his son pleased her in some other role.

His Lordship had been afraid that Yung-kai would not turn out to be much better. He was too fond of horses and he spent much of his time out in the open. It was also thought that he was unstable, and there were few indications that he was devoted to scholarship or to things of the mind. He did not know what to do with this young son, and his decision to allow him to accompany Wen-ching to Germany was made in the hope that Yung-kai would get away from what Yu Kung thought was developing into a life of profligacy and recklessness. It made him happy to read the diary, because among other things it flattered him and made him feel that his decisions, when he made them at all, were usually correct.

The diary showed that in the three years Yung-kai had spent in Berlin he was developing into a responsible and promising young man. The liberties which he seemed to have taken with Golden Orchid were not exactly something to make a father proud, but they were perhaps allowable for a young man who was unmarried and lived in a foreign environment where, he had been told, relations between men and women were relatively lax. That he had undertaken so arduous a mission showed ambition and courage: it was a feat that any father might well be proud of, and His Lordship was convinced that if Yung-kai had survived and succeeded in delivering the imperial gift in person, the Emperor would have conferred upon him a high official post.

The more Lord Yu Kung thought about the death of his son, the more sorrowful he became. The next morning, when he resumed his journey to Peking, he could not resist continuing his reading of the diary:

Leaving Hami to go in the direction of Ansi is an unforgettable experience. We are now in what is known as the Black Gobi, an enormous plain so windswept that the sandy surface has all but disappeared. We are constantly in the midst of storms, and grey grit mixed with tiny black pebbles blows in our faces and is extremely annoying. It has been hard on the imperial horse, and more than once we almost lost our way. But luckily the telegraph poles which were erected only a few years ago have served as our guide. I can't tell what would have happened to us if these poles had not been there. But all the same our hearts have been heavy with the scenes of desolation which surround us everywhere. Now and then we have come across the carcasses of abandoned animals. On the third day Lao Chuang and I counted the skeletons of three mules, one horse, and two camels. Today the sun is blazingly hot, which is a welcome change. . . .

We at once pitched our tents. Lao Chuang has had so much experience in pitching tents that they stand firm and unmovable in spite of the terrific gusts. It seems uncanny, but the imperial gift looks as if it responds every moment to the care and consideration which the two of us have showered upon it. At night it lies on the ground in a completely relaxed state, its eyes so kind and soft, as much as to say, 'I have nothing to be afraid of as long as I am under the protection of these two men.'

This morning the horse was in the best of spirits. It frisked and gambolled with Lao Chuang's pony, which we picked up before we left Hami. But hardly had we proceeded for an hour or so when we saw a dead mule being torn to pieces and devoured by a pack of wild dogs and crows. The crows kept on circling above us and over the carcass. We did not linger and knew that by the next day all that remained would be the skeleton, for we were told that usually the bones are picked clean within forty-eight hours.

All along we have had cold nights, even though the days were blazingly hot. When we came to the Ravine of Gorillas, however, the cold became really insufferable. It was towards dusk that we approached the ravine cut between massive rocks. It looked dark and sombre. It is believed to be a dried-up and abandoned river-bed where, as the story goes, man-eating gorillas used to come down from the surrounding mountains to drink. But it turned out to be one of the most magnificent scenes I have ever beheld in my life.

As the sun was setting, the whole surrounding area was transformed by the most gorgeous colours. The granite walls of the ravine remained grey and forbidding. But above and beyond, hanging over the bare and rugged hills and precipices, what delicate blues, mauves and purples, seeming to be all alive and changing their subtle hues with the passing of every moment! In the distance, fragments of quartz glittered in the declining sun and around them long stretches of green turned into grey, or grey turned into green. And such silence! A silence that works its way down into the inmost recesses of one's soul and makes one feel as if one were merging and dissolving into the universe. I hardly dared to breathe, so quiet was the surrounding atmosphere. Now and then the silence was disturbed by the movements of those little lizards which have accompanied us during all these days.

Protected by the huge rocks of the ravine, I thought that we would pass a pleasant night, but it turned out to be so cold that sleep became quite impossible. And yet I was not fully awake either. It was a very queer and unusual feeling, and the night seemed to be interminably long, stretching almost into eternity. The whole atmosphere produced the utmost discomfort, and yet I could not tell where that discomfort lay.

As I closed my eyes, I felt as if my consciousness was slowly and vaguely sinking and disappearing far into the distance until it finally came to a mere speck. But it did not vanish entirely. I was almost on the borderland of sleep, and yet the intense cold prevented me from going into that blessed state. The numb ache of my extremities continued to be a reality in my consciousness, which had by then so well withdrawn from the outside world and which would perhaps have become completely quiescent if the remote parts of the body failed to stimulate it and keep it alive.

I lay utterly still, and my mind began to wander away until, curiously enough, I no longer felt the discomforts of the cold. It had gone beyond what one might call the 'point of saturation' and lost its oppressive urgency. I was then at the bottom of my consciousness, and the mind had become a sort of vague grey sea in which fanciful thoughts kept whirling and whirling nebulously around. Or, as I recall one persons's describing it, 'Little hard islands of fact would keep appearing in this grey ocean, though it was essential not to land on them, for they were always painful. With practice the swimmer could change direction whenever an island loomed up and push himself off into the deep sea again. Some of the islands, however, were unavoidable, and all you could say for the sea itself was that it was slightly less painful than reality; it was somewhere else but nowhere very desirable.' What a beautiful and apt description; that was exactly what I felt all through that extraordinary night. . . .

The more I travel with this Lao Chuang, the more I admire him and the men of his class. He is truly an exceptional person, but I have reason to believe that he is also typical of his class. He is completely uneducated and therefore he is not burdened by any accumulated 'wisdom' which we of the so-called higher social classes are taught it is profitable to have. I cannot help always having in my mind the comparison between this simple product of the village — healthy, robust, brimful of cheer and bubbling with fun — and the embassy staff whom I left in Berlin — I hope for ever. What a difference! Those are supposed to be descendants of good families, young men who have gone through a course of classical training — but none of them has the sense of freedom, the spaciousness and the love of life which Lao Chuang seems to possess in abundance.

Their outlook is narrow, their world is small and restricted, they never dare to look people honestly and squarely in the face. It seems as if they are permanently obsessed by petty desires, insane jealousies and the desire to take advantage of the other fellow — all for a minor and inconsequential gain of a few dollars or a possible slight elevation in their social or official position. Can life mean no more than the attainment of these trivial ends? And then I turn round and see the ruddy and weather-beaten face of this sturdy Lao Chuang, self-schooled, self-disciplined into a character, without benefit of formal education. . . .

There were times when this consuming journey left me breathless. A still, small voice within me tells me that I cannot finish it. It is too much for my flesh as well as for my spirit. Ever since we came within the boundary of our own empire, at Chuguchak, it has been a long and unrelieved monotony of wind, cold, heat, desolation, loneliness, against a background of unending wastes and desert land. My mind was able to cope with the situation in the early weeks; but as the journey dragged on, it became more and more dreary. Were it not for the prospect that in another fortnight or so we should see the terminus of the Great Wall and, beyond that, a more tolerable and hospitable life, my soul would very likely have been smothered by the surrounding sand and I would have given in.

But Lao Chuang, this uncouth product of the soil, is as intrepid as ever. I keep on wondering to myself what it is that seems to give to him this inexhaustible supply of vitality and strength to resist the infinite cruelties of nature. He has not been ill for a moment since he joined me. He must have an iron constitution. His feet are always sprightly and his face constantly breaks out into flashes of smiles which are truly disarming. He eats the same food as I do. Where then does all his energy come from? I confess I don't know.

We have now passed the Jade Gate — Yumen is what we call it. It will not be long now before we come to Kiayukwan, from which the Great Wall begins to wind its grandiose way, over mountains and deserts, for fifteen hundred miles before it reaches the sea. It is a short stretch from the Jade Gate to the Great Wall — perhaps not more than fifty or sixty miles — but the desolation is beyond words. We saw any number of remains of what at one time must have been pleasant towns and villages. Could it be that the desert is alive and gradually extending its domain towards the south? . . .

My eyes caught sight today of a couple of verses inscribed on the walls just outside Kiayukwan. The words have become quite blurred, but I think I made them out. 'When I leave thy gates, O Kiayukwan, my tears never cease to run.' And well may they flow until the last drop that remains in the body is dried up in the desert. There was no way in which the poor banished fellows could ever go back to see their kith and kin. This exile from the Middle Kingdom was a form of living death inflicted on all and sundry for having incurred the wrath of the Imperial Throne.

. . . Today I also discovered something quite unusual on the wall just outside the gate. One patch of it was pocked with a myriad of marks, and at the foot of the wall was a large heap of pebbles which have lain there for generations or even centuries. I wondered what they were, and Lao Chuang examined the wall and the heap of pebbles as if he were a trained archaeo-logist. I eagerly waited for the verdict. He scratched his head, burst into a smile, and then gave me this colourful explanation: 'That is the work of the ghosts of the departed souls. The body was dead, perhaps torn and eaten by wolves and mad dogs, like the carcasses of those mules and camels which we saw, but the soul came wandering back to find its way into the gate again for peace and consolation. Finding the gates closed during the night, the soul decided to scale the wall, and that is how the little pieces broke off to form this tremendous heap of the ages.' An interesting explanation, which he no doubt fully expected me to believe. But I found out later that every one of those lost people leaving the gate has been known to throw a small rock or pebble. If it rebounded, it meant that he would return; if it simply dropped into the heap, he went away with a heavy heart, for he knew that his fate was sealed.

If we expected that life would be easier after entering Kia-yukwan, we were soon disappointed. For there were still long stretches of sand to cross. But on the whole the space between the inhabited spots was much shorter. . . .

The city of Kanchow had a delightfully built wall, though only some three miles long. The local magistrate, as usual, treated me to a sumptuous feast, and I fully expected that I would be toasted with wine made from the local grapes, which were so good and plentiful. But no, I was told that the wine came all the way from central and southern China, and of course it was the usual rice or millet wine. This is one of the mysteries which I have not been able to solve. All the wines which I tasted in Europe were made from grapes, and yet in Kanchow, where there is any amount of good grapes, wines are not made from them. Why should this be?

On the streets I found many people who didn't look Chinese at all. They looked European, and yet they were dressed in Chinese clothes and spoke our language. I talked to one of these strange persons, and he told me that his people had been there for a thousand years! They were Nestorians.

As strange people preaching a strange religion, these Nestorians might have been driven out or persecuted. But, instead, the Chinese Emperor of the Tang Dynasty, who was then the mightiest monarch of the known world, issued a proclamation to welcome them. What a supreme example of toleration! We like to feel that China is a mighty ocean into which everything can empty itself. This was how the proclamation was worded: 'The truth does not always appear under the same name, nor is divine inspiration always embodied in the same form. Religions differ in various lands, but the underlying principle of all is the salvation of mankind.' So the Emperor allowed Nestorianism to circulate wherever in the world we hold sway.

Now, isn't this an unusual document? It was issued in 638. Its large and magnanimous spirit showed that the Emperor was sure of the solidity and soundness of the moral and spiritual foundations of his great empire. It's that sort of thing which makes me proud of being Chinese. Compared with this spirit, how puny are the present-day Chinese, not to speak of those members of the embassy at Berlin!

The diary then went on to describe the trip from Kanchow to Liangchow and finally to Lanchow:

On arrival at Lanchow my spirit was again lifted by the warm welcome of the magistrate of the yamen, and we felt much better. We crossed the Yellow River before coming into Lanchow. The water was truly yellow and muddy. There was hardly any vegetation around. There were no trees, and the banks were cut into rows of cliffs, into that same loess, that deposit of loam, of loose but fertile soil which covers large areas of northern China.

The whole area was grey, sad and depressing. The currents ran very swiftly, and we were told that if we wanted to cover the distance to Peking quickly, we could do it by taking one of those rafts which float down the river. That would take us about a month. The offer was tempting, but we decided that we would continue with the slower overland journey — slower but also much safer. I looked into one of those rafts, which were no more than inflated goat or bullock skins carefully roped together and then allowed to slide down the river. It is a popular mode of travelling, but it requires skill, though if I were alone with Lao Chuang, without the imperial charge, I would have tried it. Supposing through some accident we fell into the water, Lao Chuang and I could perhaps still save ourselves, but not a beast of such size and weight, and that is the last thing in the world we would want to see happen.

6

Lord Yu Kung carefully placed his son's diary among his own personal documents on arrival at his palatial residence in Peking.

He had been alone since the death of his lady some ten years before. During that time his loyalty and devotion to the Empress Dowager and his fondness for his youngest son Yung-kai had grown. The sudden and unexpected death of the latter just at a time when father and son were about to be reunited and when Yung-kai was on the threshold of what promised to be a distinguished career of his own virtually made His Lordship an emotional cripple. He had staked all his hopes on the boy.

Yung-kai's return, he had thought, would soon be followed by a suitable match with a desirable girl, from a desirable family. That would have meant the blossoming of the family tree. But now that was all over. More than that, the reading of Yung-kai's diary had given him access to new information about his son's relationship to Wen-ching and more particularly to the concubine Golden Orchid. He would soon be coming face to face with Wen-ching — but in the most strained circumstances.

'Only the Almighty knows!' exclaimed Lord Yu Kung as he sat down on the divan in his well-appointed study. 'Less than three years, but how things have changed!'

He was restless. No sooner had he sat down than he stood up again, walked up and down the thickly carpeted floor, and then summoned old Lao Lee, the servant who used to wait on Yung-kai.

'Lao Lee, bring me some tea,' said Lord Yu Kung, without so much as looking at the servant when he came in.

'Ay, master,' replied Lao Lee. Through his long association with the family the servant knew every mood of the master, but now he did not know whether he should say something to console his grief or keep a discreet silence, as servants should. It would have to depend, he thought, upon what the moment offered when he brought in the tea.

Lao Lee wore a small moustache hanging like two miniature new moons from his upper lip. His shoulders drooped and his back curved slightly, bespeaking years of submission and gentleness. A few minutes later he returned and, laying down the covered cup, said: 'This is some green tea from the Dragon Well in Hangchow. I thought my master would like it.'

His Lordship seemed still engrossed in deep thought. Receiving no response, Lao Lee turned to leave the study. But before he got to the door he looked back and volunteered a remark.

'Master, I heard that Master Shen, the ambassador to Germany, has returned to Peking and is anxious to have an audience with my master.'

These words struck a responsive note. Lord Yu Kung immediately raised his head, looked in the direction of the servant, and said: 'I have had news that he is coming, but how do you know that he has already arrived?'

'I heard it from the servant of the President of the Board of Rites. He came to see me yesterday. The ambassador arrived a few days after my master left for Tatung. May the soul of the young master rest in peace! *O-mi-to-fu!*' And then Lao Lee was bold enough to stammer: 'I heard . . . I heard that Master Shen is in some sort of trouble. He is such a fine gentleman and scholar.'

'You servants must never gossip about these things,' Lord Yu Kung warned in a severe and peremptory tone. 'But what else did you hear, now that you have mentioned Master Shen?'

H

'I was told also that Master Shen has come with his concubine and that Madam Shen remains in Soochow.'

'Tell me, Lao Lee, did you have occasion to see this Master Shen's concubine while she was here some three years ago? What sort of lady is she?'

'No, Master, I never saw her. But the young master spoke about her once or twice. I have an impression that they knew each other well and that the young master liked her.'

Lord Yu Kung was quite taken aback by this fund of new information coming as it did from this unlikely source. So they knew each other even before they went abroad, and I sent my son to Germany to complete what was begun here — right under my nose! he thought.

Lord Yu Kung again paced his spacious study, and for a while he even blamed himself for being, in a manner, responsible for his son's death.

Meanwhile Lao Lee was standing near the door, not knowing whether he was doing the correct thing in being so communicative. But he felt that his loyalty to the family imposed a duty on him to tell all he knew and that his knowledge might set in proper perspective the problems which he knew were bothering his master upon the death of his youngest son.

'As they say,' Lao Lee broke out — and he smiled as he spoke — taking advantage again of his long service with His Lordship, 'you can conceal things from the masters and mistresses of a household, but you cannot conceal them from the servants.'

'Then what else are you withholding from me?' Lord Yu Kung wanted to know.

'No, Master, there is not much more that I know. But the young master used to confine himself in his study. Thinking that he might call me, I always stayed just outside his door. One night I remember falling asleep, and the young master took pity on me, fearing that the dampness and cold might get into my old bones. That night found the young master in alternate moods of dejection and great joy. He wrote a lot, though I don't know what he was writing. But at times he would stand up and walk about, humming to himself the little ditties which he had learned in the south. Yes, I heard him sing these unfamiliar tunes to himself, and I rejoiced at his happiness. I also heard him mention the name of Master Shen's concubine.'

Lord Yu Kung did not utter a word, and after a long pause he dismissed the servant.

During the next few days Lord Yu Kung kept himself in the house. His visit to Tatung had taken more than ten days of his time, but as President of the Tsungli Yamen and as a member of the Grand Council it was necessary that he attend to his numerous duties. Yet he felt like confining himself to the house; the only visit he made was to the Empress Dowager, to whom he was in the habit of paying his respects every once in a while. Though he did not feel like seeing the other officials, they came to see him. From morning till night there was a long stream of carriages and sedan chairs in front of his residence. Most of the visitors came to convey their condolences, some to report to him the worsening situation.

They told him of a foreign church being burned somewhere in Shansi, where there were wild rumours of children continuing to disappear and of their eyes being gouged out to make foreign medicines. There was another report of some missionaries and their Chinese collaborators being molested somewhere in Shantung, possibly for the same reason. Lord Yu Kung did not know whether he should welcome such news or feel sad. His loyalty was to the Empress Dowager, and what he thought about these matters would have to depend on Her Majesty's attitude. Generally he knew that attitude, but still it was best to wait and see exactly what her present stand was.

Among the visitors who came most often and stayed the longest with him was his immediate subordinate, Director Hu-mou of the Tsungli Yamen. This was only natural, and the conversations covered all the details of the work in the office, though most of all they talked about Wen-ching's case, which had stirred not only the Tsungli Yamen but the entire Government.

'Tell me, Brother Hu-mou,' said Lord Yu Kung, 'has Ambassador Wen-ching reported himself to the yamen? I heard he has arrived here in Peking.'

'Not yet, Your Lordship. I too have heard that the ambassador is here, but so far he has not appeared in the Tsungli Yamen.'

Lord Yu Kung merely uttered a grunt and said nothing.

'It is really a pity,' continued Hu-mou, 'that the ambassador was so careless. We have indeed lost one of our most distinguished diplomats. And such an accomplished scholar!'

'Yes, it is a very rare combination. We need men like him during this critical period. Wen-ching's experience abroad would have been very valuable. He must have known men and events which few of us have. As a matter of fact, I was thinking that upon his return, after his period of service in Berlin and St Petersburg, I should recommend him to Her Majesty to take over my work at the Tsungli Yamen so that I could devote my time to the Grand Council.'

Lord Yu Kung made these remarks with a vague purpose. He wanted to sound out Hu-mou. The reading of his son's diary had given him a new picture. The added information about the Embassy staff and their relation to Wen-ching had provided him with a new point of view.

Hu-mou made no comment. Indeed he was shocked to hear what His Lordship had just said. He began reflecting; and as he reflected, his eyes as usual automatically rolled upwards, exposing the white below the iris more than they normally should. He thought to himself, If that is what he, Lord Yu Kung, had in mind — asking Wen-ching eventually to take over the duties of the Tsungli Yamen — then what I have done was done none too soon.

Hu-mou took up the thread of the conversation. 'On the completion of his years of service,' he said, 'Ambassador Wen-ching would have been a useful and important diplomat in any capacity. Therefore it is all the more strange that he did what he did.'

'Frankly, Brother Hu-mou,' replied Lord Yu Kung, 'do you personally think that Ambassador Wen-ching, with all the prospects of new and more important assignments, would be so foolhardy as to be involved in this munitions case? How much was he supposed to have taken? Only a paltry couple of thousand dollars, isn't it? Do you think seriously that even a fool would risk his career for so small an amount of money?'

Hu-mou was decidedly uncomfortable on hearing those words and hurriedly added a few remarks quite different from the earlier assumed sympathy.

'Yes, it was a small sum,' he said. 'But who knows? It may be that his concubine was spending more money than she should. After all, she was a sing-song girl. The Tsungli Yamen had other reports to show that the ambassador was dealing in all sorts of things — even in selling fruit by using diplomatic immunity.'

'Now, now, Brother Hu-mou, we must be reasonable. An ambassador, one of the most distinguished in the country, with an enviable career before him, and a scholar and gentleman to boot — do you seriously think that he would be so much out of his mind as to stoop so low?'

Hu-mou realized that he had gone too far. But he could not easily retract. 'No, I don't think so either. But the reports were all submitted confidentially by the members of the embassy. I have not taken the trouble to show them to Your Lordship because I too believe they are incredible. But when this munitions case developed and the investigator Tung-chen confirmed Wen-ching's involvement, then I thought it was my duty to let Your Lordship know.'

'Thank you, Brother Hu-mou. It was most considerate of you.'

At this point Lao Lee came in to announce that the President of the Board of Rites had arrived to pay his respects to His Lordship. Hu-mou asked for permission to leave.

Hu-mou was uneasy that night. Everything had worked out as he had planned, and there was no reason to suspect that any part of the plan was going awry. And yet the conversation with Lord Yu Kung was not what he had expected. But the most disturbing development was the return of Wen-ching himself to Peking, which he had not expected.

Hu-mou thought over the steps he had taken one after another. He was satisfied that the plan had unfolded itself smoothly, without a hitch. He was proud that he was a supreme plotter. And how ably, he thought, he had produced the impression of being a neutral observer, even willing to be helpful to Wen-ching, but with his hands tied because the case was too notorious for him to minimize or suppress it.

As for Wen-ching himself, Hu-mou thought that he would be so frightened by the consequences of the frame-up that he would not dare show his face again. Had not this happened with Consul Chow Su-ying, who was recalled at the same time as Ambassador Shen Wen-ching? Chow was so terrified by what the Government might do to him that, on his way back to China, he left the steamer in Japan, and was not seen or heard of again. Hu-mou had expected much the same of Wen-ching, who, he thought, would at least hide himself in shame in some unknown village somewhere in south China and allow himself to be forgotten by the world. Perhaps he might even cut off his hair and don the Buddhist garb to escape from the common gaze. But instead of that, here was Wen-ching brazenly making his appearance in Peking itself! That was unbelievable! What could it mean?

The more Hu-mou thought about it, the more nervous he became. His conversation with Lord Yu Kung certainly did not allay his anxiety. Hu-mou sat deep into the night and smoked furiously as he poured more and more tea down his parched throat. Cigarette-smoking was then a newly acquired habit, but Hu-mou had become addicted to it to such a degree that people could well believe that he had been at it for the better part of thirty years. He was quite shocked himself to see in front of him a large tray of ashes and dis-carded stubs mixed with the dregs from his teacups. The smell was foul and sickening, but still he allowed the dirty mess to stare at him while he paced the floor of his little room.

At every corner he turned he saw the gifts of his numerous diplo-matic protégés either hanging on the walls or lying on the tables and cupboards. He was fond of luscious naked ladies in white marble; at least three such statuettes had been sent to him from Italy. There were also clocks from Switzerland and France, one of which gave out soft and melodious chimes on the hour. It struck again not long after Hu-mou began pacing.

One o'clock in the morning, Hu-mou said to himself. He went to his bedroom. Madam Hu-mou was asleep, with a dim light from a paraffin lamp placed at a safe distance from the bed. As Hu-mou came in, he turned up the lamp and awakened his wife.

Madam Hu-mou's goggle eyes, resembling those of a goldfish, were famous and constituted a very distinctive part of her physical personality. They were now wide open and, staring at her husband as he slipped into bed, she said in her deep voice: 'Haven't you any sense? What time is it? You should have been in bed long ago in-stead of smoking those infernal cigarettes and bringing all that foulness into the bed.'

'Will you stop talking? What do you know? You have a pig's head anyway, and you don't understand,' retorted Hu-mou.

At that, Madam Hu-mou's eyes became even more globular, and she sharply replied: 'What do you mean? What is it that I don't understand?'

Hu-mou and his wife were known not to be on the best of terms.

They had been married for over twenty years and had three children. The two daughters had been married into nondescript families. The youngest, a son in the middle teens, had been showing signs of some neurotic ailment. He was, to say the least, a subnormal child. He had developed the habit of going straight up to any guest and speaking to him at a safe distance of some six inches! This mannerism had caused embarrassment on numerous occasions and certainly made no contribution to the conjugal happiness of his father and mother.

However, the child was sound asleep in the next room and gave no immediate cause for any friction between Hu-mou and his wife. But Madam Hu-mou had spoken as if she had both taken and thrown back a challenge.

'What's the use?' growled Hu-mou. 'Can't you see that Wen-ching is now back in Peking?'

'Well, is that any reason why you should be so unpleasant? You have done everything to cripple him in his diplomatic life. You have ruined him. You have succeeded in doing what you wanted.'

'Not so loud, woman.'

'No, I will not be quiet. If Wen-ching chose to come back to Peking, what is that to do with us? He is only looking for further trouble for himself, isn't he?'

'That is what you think. That is why I say you have no understanding. Do you think that things are as simple as they appear to you? Can't I make your wooden head see that in daring to come up to Peking, Wen-ching might possibly have something up his sleeve or the advice of some friend to fight the case? I don't know that he has but it is something to think and worry about. As for you, you would never see the matter in this light, would you?'

Madam Hu-mou gave no response but merely turned away from her husband and grumbled: 'You are always thinking, thinking, thinking yourself into all kinds of unlikely situations.'

7

Wen-ching and Golden Orchid had been in Peking for over a fortnight. The news of Yung-kai's death had been conveyed to them, and Lao Chuang had given a full and complete account of the trip to Golden Orchid. Both Wen-ching and his concubine tried hard to control their emotions, especially since they had a crisis of their own to contend with.

Their temporary quarters were in the Soochow *hwei-kuan*, the hostel where they had lived on the eve of their departure for Europe. They had now two spacious rooms as against the three they had had before. That was a small difference. But the real difference was so big and solid that they felt it every moment they breathed the air in those rooms.

Before, there were constant calls on Wen-ching to receive the felicitations of his fellow officials, great and small, high and low. Now, he was always alone with Golden Orchid. Before, everyone struggled to say that he knew Wen-ching personally, that he counted the ambassador-designate among his best friends. Now, everyone grew silent when Wen-ching's name was mentioned. Even among his old colleagues, as soon as they heard Wen-ching's name, there were some who would pretend not to know him, saying: 'Who is this Wen-ching?' and the answer would invariably be: 'Oh, that ambassador who was involved in the munitions case and was recalled.' At best one would hear: 'What a pity! He was known to be a scholar, and yet what a stupid thing he did!' For it was taken for granted that the accusations against Wen-ching were true. But with all these difficulties he was thankful that he could still count on a few, a very few, friends who were staunchly loyal to him and who believed in his integrity. And then of course he had the love, devotion and affection of Golden Orchid.

'That is all one has a right to expect from the world,' said Wen-ching to Golden Orchid, with whom he now spent every moment of his life. 'This great misfortune has become the criterion for genuine friendship. After this I know who are my friends and who are not. Do you know, my beloved treasure, that this servant of ours, Lao Chuang, is a man of sterling qualities? Have you seen him waver for one brief moment? He is as loyal and devoted to us as he ever was. In fair weather and foul he remains the same Lao Chuang.'

For some reason these remarks of her husband's about Lao Chuang stirred Golden Orchid deeply, and tears began flowing down her cheeks.

'How silly of me!' she said, as she looked at her husband and smiled faintly.

Golden Orchid felt something that she could not express in words, but she knew that the old world had disappeared with the death of her beloved Yung-kai, and that she was now standing in a new and unfamiliar world where the human heart had been revealed for what it really was — selfish, unsympathetic, cruel. How the officials delight in the misfortunes of others! she said to herself.

Lao Chuang came in to see if he could be of any service to his lonely master and mistress. Wen-ching thought that this was a good opportunity to say things he had wanted to say for some days.

'Lao Chuang, you have been with us for three years and I hope that you have been happy in our service. It was wonderful of you to accompany the young lord Yung-kai all the way from Berlin. It is, of course, deeply sad that he died before he arrived at Peking.'

'It was Heaven's wish, Master,' Lao Chuang commented.

'Yes, I suppose it was. . . . Lao Chuang, you know the state I am in now, but I want to say something to you. I want to see to it that you are amply rewarded for what you have done —'

'But, Master,' said Lao Chuang before Wen-ching could go on, 'I have been richly rewarded already.'

'No, no, Lao Chuang. Besides, I want to tell you that I shall not stay long in Peking this time. Perhaps a couple of months, and then the young Tai-tai and I are going back to the south to live — for good. I wish we could take you with us, but you belong to the north where you have your family, and that is where you should remain.'

So saying Wen-ching got up, took something from the table beside his bed and handed it to Lao Chuang. 'Here is a hundred taels of silver, and with that I want you to buy some five *mou* of land for your family.'

Lao Chuang was overwhelmed.

'Yes, take it, Lao Chuang!' pressed Golden Orchid. 'Both your Lao-yeh and I have always said that you have been a faithful and loyal servant, and we want you to remember us with the land which you will buy with this money.'

Lao Chuang did not feel that he should accept the gift. But he did not wish to decline it and gave profuse thanks to Wen-ching and Golden Orchid. 'May the good Buddha confer upon my master and mistress all the blessings you deserve!' With these words Lao Chuang took his leave and said that he would go back to his family the next day if he was permitted.

The village of Ming-ho is some twelve miles to the north of Peking. And so early next morning, after a full breakfast of meat dumplings and a huge pancake which he washed down with a pot of hot tea, Lao Chuang got on a donkey and set out on his journey. By four o'clock in the afternoon he was home, and the villagers joined Chuang Mah and their two sons in giving Lao Chuang a warm welcome. The little grey courtyard in front of the adobe cottage, where during the day the harvested wheat had been thrashed, was gaily decorated with huge paper lanterns, and Chuang Mah, a woman of sense and some wisdom, also saw to it that a modest feast was provided for the relatives and the villagers. When the party was over and the last guest had departed, Lao Chuang and his wife repaired to their simple inner apartment. Somehow Lao Chuang had a feeling that his wife was not entirely happy.

'What's the matter with you, old woman? Aren't you glad that I am back to help around the house?'

'You don't understand, you stupid melon,' retorted Chuang Mah. 'Of course I am glad. What do you think? Don't you think that you have stayed away long enough and that I need you to be with me? For three years you have been away in a foreign land. What worries have I not known? I fully expected that only your bones would be brought back. Of course I am glad that you have returned as healthy and strong as you are.'

'Well, then, why don't you show any signs of happiness? What's more, we are rich, with all the money you have been receiving regularly as my wages. And look what there is in this bag!'

'Not so loud! I don't want even the children to know that we have all this money. There is something I want to talk over with you — very badly. The village people have a feeling that we have grown rich, and some of them, even among our relatives, are jealous of it. Only the other day they were saying: "Oh, Lao Chuang has become rich by serving those foreign devils." But I told them you were not serving any foreign devils now. Before, yes; but not now. I explained to them that you were away in a foreign land, but your master was one of our own people.'

'That is true enough, and didn't they understand?'

'They did, I am sure, but they purposely say: "What is the difference?" What I am afraid of is that if we are not careful we may be in for trouble. With all this hatred against everything foreign and against the Chinese who work for the foreigners, it is possible they will call you "the second hairy one", and then life may really be dangerous for us. Now you understand, you big turnip.'

'All the more reason why I should stay here and meet these villagers and convince them that I am just the same as any one of them,' commented Lao Chuang.

But Chuang Mah wouldn't think of buying any more land with the money that had been given them. She suggested instead that it should be buried under the house as soon as possible.

'Why do you think I gave this little feast today?' continued Chuang Mah. 'All these years I have been worshipping our ancestors and praying that they would protect you while you were far away in a foreign land. I have also been giving little gifts to the village people so that I might continue to have their friendship. Even so I know there are unfriendly people about. And so, after a few days of rest at home, I want you to go away and find work in Peking so that I can say Lao Chuang is just as poor as ever and needs to work to keep the family going.'

'All right, if that is how you feel about it, old woman, I shall do just as you want.'

Lao Chuang had always had faith in the judgement of his wife, and so after a few days of rest and work in the field with his two sons, who were now big and strong enough to stand on their own feet, he made preparations to leave for Peking again. In fact, he did not leave a day too soon, for on the very morning of his departure he learned that some three miles away a young man who was working at a Catholic mission there was terribly mauled and almost killed by a group of angry villagers, many of whom had turned into 'boxers' and were openly shouting for the murder of all foreigners and of those Chinese who were in their employ.

On his return to Peking, Lao Chuang's first thought was to approach the Tsungli Yamen. There he might learn of a newly appointed diplomat in need of a servant who had been abroad. At the Tsungli Yamen he might also hear about some foreign diplomat in Peking looking for a servant. But on second thoughts he decided that working for foreigners at this time was dangerous.

His weary feet carried him into a teashop, where he rested and thought the matter out a little more clearly. There were a few people whom he recognized, even though he had not seen them for many years. He exchanged greetings with them and was surprised that they were not very friendly. He found that none of the visitors at the teahouse were gossiping or talking as much as they used to. He wondered why, and then he saw on the walls and pillars large notices which read, 'No discussion of national affairs.' They were not Government orders but had been posted there by the management of the house in order to avoid trouble with the local authorities.

'I'll go to the Tsungli Yamen later,' Lao Chuang finally decided. 'Let me go and pay my respects first to my former master and mistress.'

Once the resolution was made, he felt less tired, and in less than an hour he was at the doorstep of the Soochow hostel, where he saw Mistress Hai-ming leaving. He remembered that she was a good friend of his young mistress.

'Tai-tai,' saluted Lao Chuang, 'may you be in the best of health. I have not seen Tai-tai these many years, and I am happy that you look more prosperous than ever. I am the humble one who was in the service of Master Shen.'

'Oh, yes, of course. You are Lao Chuang, aren't you? Why, only a few moments ago your mistress was telling me all about you and saying what a good servant you were to them.'

'You see, Tai-tai, my former master and mistress are so good to me, and I hate to leave them. But you know what happened, and they will leave for the south very soon. I have come to pay my respects to them, and perhaps they can help me to find some work in another family.'

'If that is what you want, it's very simple. How would you like to come and work for me? Of course, you will not get as good pay as you did from Master Shen, but there are only two of us and there is very little work. Here, let me give you my address — 31 East Silla Hutung. Come and see me tomorrow morning.'

When Mistress Hai-ming mounted the carriage and went her way Lao Chuang congratulated himself on finding work so easily. In this happy mood he went in to pay the visit he had intended. He was warmly received by Golden Orchid, who expressed regret that Wen-ching was not there to welcome him back also.

Hai-ming had remained in Peking for a long time in rather pitiful conditions. With Golden Orchid in Germany, there was no one to whom Hai-ming could turn for comfort and consolation. There was only one profession open to her, and that was to go back to be an entertainer in a sing-song house. She got on well enough in that familiar *milieu*, but a time came when all such professional entertainers must exchange their exciting though uncertain life for security and anchorage.

That was what Golden Orchid had accomplished at the very beginning of her career. But Golden Orchid, Hai-ming thought, was born under a lucky star, and not one in a million could be as fortunate. She herself would be happy with only one tenth of what Golden Orchid had. She had no beauty to speak of, but she was not devoid of talents, and in fact she had been reasonably successful as an entertainer very largely because of her quick wit and ready repartee with the scholars and officials of Peking.

Among these officials was Hu-mou, who had lately become fond of sing-song houses, where he sought relaxation after his work at the Tsungli Yamen rather than going home to his goggle-eyed wife and his abnormal son. Hai-ming, with her usual astuteness, found out that Hu-mou was no minor official in the Tsungli Yamen. After three months of undivided attention, during which she managed to draw him out and give him every satisfaction, he asked her to live with him in a separate house some distance away from his home.

The 'small house' at 31 East Silla Hutung was precisely what they both wanted. It was clean, and the courtyard had some fine old trees. The main section consisted of three spacious rooms. The living-room had foreign furniture and was decorated with foreign pictures given to Hu-mou by his diplomatic subordinates. At one end was the study, which served also as a dining-room. As the clandestine establishment was only a love-nest, there was no entertainment, and a separate dining-room was not needed. At the other end was the bedroom, which Hai-ming furnished with soft cushions and richly embroidered silks to satisfy the desires of her fastidious paramour. The other sections of the small house were given over to the kitchen and the servants' quarters.

An old woman, Kang Mah, was employed from the very beginning to serve as a cook and to do miscellaneous chores. Hu-mou insisted that one servant was all that was needed in order to save expense; but now that he had lived happily with Hai-ming for a year, he was ready to give in to some of Hai-ming's wishes. So when she insisted that there should be an additional manservant, Hu-mou made no strenuous opposition. In fact, when he saw Lao Chuang on the first day, he rather liked him. Hai-ming on her part thought it was best not to remind Hu-mou that the new servant had been in the employ of Golden Orchid and Ambassador Wen-ching. The suggestion, in fact, had come from Lao Chuang himself. For when he found out who this new master was, he expressed the wish that Hu-mou should not know his past. Hai-ming understood and agreed with him.

The arrangement was about as good as Hai-ming could expect. She was lonely, though she was not entirely unhappy. But deep down in her heart she knew that her instincts as a woman were not fully satisfied. What she really wanted was to become, like Golden Orchid, Hu-mou's concubine. She would then have status, low as it might be. But there was no indication that Hu-mou desired her to become a concubine. Whether it was because he was afraid of Madam Hu-mou or because he wanted to avoid additional financial responsibility — for he was a niggardly person — she had no way of knowing. All she knew was that, though a small man, Hu-mou had an enormous sexual appetite, and there was little doubt that he was keeping her only for his gratification. He came to her regularly after work at the Tsungli Yamen was over, and all he wanted was to have a good dinner and then go to bed with her. Late at night he would return home to Madam Hu-mou.

Slow and stupid as Kang Mah was, she understood the situation and would occasionally stutter a few words of compassion to Hai-ming, whom she insisted upon addressing as Tai-tai, which is an honorific bestowed by servants only on the mistress of a household. One day Kang Mah complained that Hu-mou was not giving her enough money to buy food with. 'The master eats well, but how does he expect me to provide him with good dinners for the single dollar that he gives me every day? Why don't you run the house, Tai-tai?'

At the mention of money Hai-ming became furious. 'Don't ever talk to me about money. Why don't I take over? Do you suppose that is at all possible? And how much do you think I get from the master?'

This was only too sadly true. After a full year Hai-ming counted that all she had managed to save was less than two hundred dollars, and half of that amount was taken from Hu-mou's wallet after he had fallen sound asleep.

'I have never met a man more niggardly than he is. Why, I could have made as much in two months in the sing-song house. What am I living for anyway?'

And again Hai-ming wailed that hers was an unhappy lot compared with that of Golden Orchid. It was faith and hope that kept her life going, but now it seemed that the prospects of accomplishing anything were fading away.

8

It was many days after Lord Yu Kung returned from Tatung before Wen-ching managed to make an appointment with him. Wen-ching had kept himself entirely within his apartments in the hostel. The sole purpose of his return to Peking was to see Lord Yu Kung and to fight his case, and yet curiously enough he felt reluctant to meet His Lordship in person. On Lord Yu Kung's side there was the same feeling. For what were they going to say to each other under conditions which had become so strained, when for many long years they had been the best of friends?

But the step had to be taken, and so one morning Wen-ching consulted Golden Orchid and decided to write a letter to His Lordship asking for the appointment.

My Dear Lordship: Please accept once more my profound sympathy for the death of your worthy son. That he was Your Lordship's favourite son has made the loss doubly heavy. Ever since the time when you showed me the honour of asking me to take care of him in the embassy in Berlin, I have in all respects considered him as if he were my own son. That was the only way to regard him. The long friendship between Your Lordship and my humble self, the same deep friendship between Yung-kai and my own son Ping-mo, who chose to stay behind in Soochow at the time I left for Europe, and above all the high qualities of your worthy son's own personality and character — these have drawn him very close to my heart and to my concubine's.

In the three years that Your Lordship's son was in our care, I was most happy to see him develop into a fine young man, ever serious in the discharge of his duties and anxious always to be helpful to others. His untimely death was a severe blow to Your Lordship as well as to my humble self. There is no way in which I can offer consolation to a revered and respected friend except to say that Yung-kai gave his life in the glorious service of His Majesty and of Her Majesty the Empress Dowager.

I am now back in Peking under circumstances which are too painful to relate. But I can assure Your Lordship that there is much more in the unfortunate event which has required my recall than meets the eye. It is said that there is no justice in official life, but my long association with Your Lordship, which I dearly treasure, has convinced me that Your Lordship is eminently a man of justice and will not allow things to stand as they are without a very thorough, painstaking and impartial investigation. I humbly request, therefore, both in the capacity of Your Lordship's subordinate official and as a friend of long standing, that you reopen the case in the light of all the pertinent documents and evidence so as to establish the responsibility and give justice where it is due. I have the honour to be Your Lordship's humble servant,

SHEN WEN-CHING

The letter was dispatched by a special messenger to Lord Yu Kung's private residence rather than to the Tsungli Yamen, where cables and letters and reports were tampered with.

Lord Yu Kung read the petition carefully — very carefully. He admired the classical beauty of the language. He folded it, put it back in the envelope and then started pacing up and down his study, striking the letter on his left palm as he walked. He made no decision. But he finally sat down at his desk and wrote a reply acknowledging receipt of the petition and asking Wen-ching to come to lunch with him the next day.

When Wen-ching arrived, almost too punctually for Chinese

official appointments, Lord Yu Kung was already in his large living-room. The servant ushered Wen-ching all the way from the ver-milion gate into the presence of the master. The moment Wen-ching stepped into the drawing-room, his eyes met those of Lord Yu Kung for the first time in three years, and for a bare second they looked at each other in a manner unfamiliar to either of them in the long years of their association. But the stiffness soon softened into cordiality, and they bowed to each other, seemingly glad to meet again, as if nothing had ever come between them.

It was not until lunch was over that the two men went back to the drawing-room. The servant had left after bringing in tea, and then the two plunged into the subject about which, all during lunch, not a word had been spoken.

It was Lord Yu Kung who began. 'Brother Wen-ching,' he said, 'the case against you in Berlin is over as far as I am concerned. I wish you would remain in Peking, as I am thinking of recommending you to the Empress Dowager for some other assignment either in the capital or in the provinces.'

'Thank you for the kindness, Your Lordship,' replied Wen-ching, 'but these years in Berlin have given me an uneasy time, and I am planning to leave official life entirely so that I may devote my time and energy to the pursuit of my studies.'

'Please don't talk of retirement yet.'

'However, even if you are kind enough to consider me for another assignment, I wish this case, which has damaged me beyond repair, to be thoroughly investigated first. Many things may be unearthed about which the world as yet knows nothing.'

'I was thinking that since we are passing through a very difficult period internationally — and domestically too — we might as well put aside all our personal problems for the time being and concen-trate on our national affairs. If I get you an appointment to an-other post, Brother Wen-ching, wouldn't that in itself be a kind of vindication for you?'

'I thank you again for the suggestion. But as you know, Your Lordship, my life has been that of a scholar, and as Confucius used to say, "A scholar may be killed, but he cannot be humiliated." I feel very strongly that I have been humiliated for no reason at all.'

'Let's not talk about humiliation where there was none intended. Besides, a new appointment will take care of that.'

'I have tried to be honourable and to maintain the integrity of our diplomatic service,' Wen-ching said. 'I have also tried to build up an unblemished tradition worthy of our official life and to raise our international standing. I am conscious of my limitations. But that has been my purpose, and Your Lordship will agree with me that I should not be rewarded with disgrace for trying to carry out that purpose.'

'What then do you think we should do, Brother Wen-ching?'

'I propose to do something very simple. Apart from any personal interest, if all the facts of the case are known and the responsibility is established, may it not serve as an example so that such injustices may not occur in the future?'

Lord Yu Kung said nothing but thought to himself that Wen-ching was both an impossible idealist and an obstinate man. He was sure that no good would come of the investigation when all the evidence, as he knew it, pointed to his being implicated in the unfortunate incident.

But His Lordship wondered, can it be that he indeed has evidence to support himself? The question would not have entered his mind if he had not read his son's diary.

'Aside from the merits of the case, which we shall not discuss for the moment,' continued Wen-ching, 'I would like to tell Your Lordship about some of the strange happenings in the Berlin Embassy in the years when I was there. I tried to be tolerant and lenient. I knew soon after I took over my duties what was going on among the staff. As I was deeply interested in the policy of the foreign powers towards our country, I wanted to spend my time in studying it, and so I drafted and sent lengthy reports on what I learned and observed —'

'But,' interrupted Lord Yu Kung, 'that is precisely the complaint of the Tsungli Yamen against you from the very beginning. I have not read, as president of that office, more than one or two very sketchy reports on your observations. We were anxiously waiting for them as we needed the information to help us to decide what to do.'

Wen-ching was really stunned when he heard this. For a long time he sat there speechless.

'I remember one occasion,' continued Lord Yu Kung, 'when the members of the Grand Council were very angry that we had received no reports from you.'

These words were more than Wen-ching could bear to hear. 'Why, those reports,' he said, 'were something of which I could be proud. The number of words I wrote and sent to the Tsungli Yamen must be counted in millions. Does Your Lordship mean to say that you have not seen more than one or two sketchy reports from me? Why, that is impossible. This is precisely one of the things Your Lordship would do well to look into. I am sure the reports have all been suppressed so that Your Lordship would have the impression that I was negligent in my duties.'

It was now Lord Yu Kung's turn to be stunned. 'If that is the case,' he said at last, 'then I shall indeed look into it. That does sound serious. Please go on, and let me know some of the other things you have on your mind.'

Encouraged by Lord Yu Kung's fresh interest, Wen-ching gave him a lengthy and detailed account of his troubles in Berlin. He told him of the embassy staff, how they resented all attempts at improvement, how they engaged in smuggling and other illegal activities, how their insubordination seemed to be sanctioned by some higher authority. Nowhere in his account did he mention Hu-mou by name, but the implication was clear that it was someone of authority in the Tsungli Yamen who was behind all the trouble.

Wen-ching told of Lin Liang's attempt to bribe him, and he gave a full account of the crucial and implicating munitions document. 'I am not wise in the ways of the world,' he said, 'but how could I be so foolhardy and stupid as to be a party to an illegal document which must find its way to my political enemy in order that he might incriminate me? The document was to be valid in Austria-Hungary at a time when I had been already relieved of my concurrent duties there. It was to be delivered to a man who had tried to bribe me and whom I had spurned. To issue such a document would be like handing him a dagger so that he might stab me. Would I do that? I am giving Your Lordship all this information — unbelievable information — as a background to this unusual case in which I am supposed to be involved. All this is news, I am sure, to Your Lordship.'

When this incredible tale was told, the two men sat in silence. Lord Yu Kung wore a look of deep worry and uneasiness. Was it possible that he had been acting merely as a figurehead in the Tsungli Yamen all these years? It might well be, for he had other important duties to attend to, and he thought that he could rely on his immediate subordinate Hu-mou, who was entrusted to take charge of all the administrative details of the office. If all that Wen-ching had told him was true, who then was the arch-conspirator? Before he read his son's diary or had the opportunity of hearing all this from Wen-ching, he frankly had misgivings about his friend's competence and integrity. All the information he received about Wen-ching seemed to put him in the worst light possible. But now the picture had changed. What was he to do about it? As if he had not troubles enough! His youngest son dead, and on top of this the increasing difficulties of both the domestic and international situation.

'It is not that I am obstinate, Your Lordship,' said Wen-ching after the tenseness had subsided somewhat. 'I have told Your Lordship these few things, and perhaps you are beginning to see new light. But the country — the country as a whole still believes me to be at fault.'

'Yes, something must be done, and done quickly.'

'My reputation has been damaged beyond repair. How could I live as a gentleman and scholar? I can give up my official life. In fact, as I said, I am planning to retire among my books in Soochow. This is the arrangement I have made with my wife, and I shall join her in pursuing a life devoted to art and literature. But I cannot do it without, first of all, clarifying the entire situation and letting the country know where the blame really belongs. I have to redeem my good name. Having done that, I can give up everything. That is why I implore you, Your Lordship, to call a meeting of the Grand Council to which I may present my case, with all the pertinent documents, and then if it is still found that I am in the wrong, I am prepared to suffer any punishment required by the gravity of the case.'

Wen-ching was happy that he had had this session with the president of the Tsungli Yamen. He felt that he had perhaps revived the confidence of his friend in him. Lord Yu Kung still sat there without saying a word, and then at long last he made one further remark: 'I'll think it over. I feel you are entitled to a hearing if that is what you wish.'

9

IT took a long time before the machinery of the Government was put into motion. Wen-ching's case was not an ordinary one, nor was Wen-ching himself an ordinary person. The usual Courts would have attended to the matter if it were merely 'another' case, but in this instance the Grand Council decided to summon all the presidents of the six boards, together with other officials who were intimately connected with the Court. The Chief Secretary of the Council personally found out the time that would be convenient to all for the special session.

It was on a cold December morning that Wen-ching received the formal notification from the Chief Secretary of the Grand Council. The huge red envelope bearing the vermilion square seal of the Council was addressed to him in his former capacity as Imperial Ambassador to Germany and Russia. The simple message inside asked him to be present at the special session to be convened at noon on the fifteenth of the month. The message had been expected, but Wen-ching held it in his hands nervously. Golden Orchid did not utter a word, but leaned against him sobbing and shedding tears.

'Now, now, my precious one,' Wen-ching consoled his concubine, 'I know how you feel. Calm yourself, for this is what we have asked for, and we have nothing to be afraid of.'

'But supposing, Wen-ching dear, that something should happen to you,' said Golden Orchid, and wept again.

'How can anything happen to me when I know perfectly well that I am in the right? I have implicit confidence that, even though evil may triumph for a moment, ultimately the goodness of the human heart must prevail. Justice must prevail, or the teachings of the sages would have no meaning and would be useless.'

'I may be a child,' commented Golden Orchid, 'but these years have taught me much, so very much, and one of the lessons which has cut deep into my soul is that in this world of wickedness there is no right and wrong. If there were, we would not be where we are.'

The fifteenth of December was one of the worst days in Peking in the memory of Wen-ching. Early in the morning, even before daybreak, the winds howled from the north. The sky was thickly covered with a blanket of fine yellow sand coming from the Gobi

Desert. Even though the windows were all tightly closed, Wen-ching and Golden Orchid could hear the rustling of the fallen leaves, and the room looked sombre and grey. The smell of the delicately falling particles of sand invaded their nostrils as they settled on the tables and chairs. Golden Orchid lay in bed with the curtains down, too upset even to say 'May heaven and your ancestors protect you on this day' to her husband as he left in his sedan chair for the Grand Council chamber a mile or so away.

Wen-ching was among the first to arrive. Quietly and in a formal manner he bowed to the Chief Secretary, who had been there half an hour before him to attend to the details of the proceedings. He was conducted to a seat at one end of a long table placed in the middle of the room. Alone he sat in dead silence, occasionally looking at the ornate decorations around the walls and on the ceiling. There were dragons and clouds painted on the beams in all the colours of the rainbow. But his mind was too occupied to notice details.

In about twenty minutes the special session of the Grand Council was to start its deliberations. The President of the Board of Rites took the chair at the opposite end of the long table. To his right sat Lord Yu Kung as President of the Tsungli Yamen. To his left was the Chief Secretary, and then along the sides were seated the Presidents of the Board of Ceremony, the Board of Punishment, the Board of Works, the Board of Military Affairs, the Board of Finances and four other high-ranking officials of the Court. All twelve members of the Council around the table were in their official garb indicating their office and rank. All of them wore a red button as large as a pigeon's egg on the top of the hat to show that the wearers were of the highest rank.

The presiding official gave a few brief remarks by way of introduction.

'During this period of tension both in our domestic and international affairs,' he began, 'it is unfortunate that we have assembled here to pass our judgement on one of the most extraordinary cases that has been presented to us. The defendant is our respected former ambassador Shen Wen-ching, who for three years has represented His Imperial Majesty in Germany and Russia. The Tsungli Yamen has received reports sent by the chargé d'affaires in Austria-Hungary, Lin Liang, that the ambassador was involved in the sale of munitions for which he issued a document to the Austrian merchant Emil

Schwartz to enable him to purchase munitions both in Germany and in Austria-Hungary, and for which he received the sum of two thousand dollars. The case is a serious one, and I now call upon the President of the Tsungli Yamen to give us the details.'

Lord Yu Kung preferred to stand up. He was an impressive-looking figure and asked, before he proceeded, that an important correction be made in what the President had just said. 'The document in question,' he explained, 'was actually issued by the consul in Berlin, Chow Su-ying, in his own name and in the name of the Consular Service under his charge.'

Lord Yu Kung then proceeded: 'Upon receipt of this information, which was cabled by the chargé d'affaires Lin Liang in Vienna, the capital of Austria-Hungary, the Tsungli Yamen dispatched a special investigator in the person of Tung-chen to conduct an inquiry into the matter. His first cabled report was that the consul admitted the responsibility of having issued the document on his own initiative which was in substantial agreement with the report of the ambassador himself when the existence of the illegal document was first brought to his knowledge. Four days later Tung-chen sent another cable in which he said that the consul had made a new confession indicating that the document in question was issued with the full knowledge of the ambassador, to whom he paid a portion of the money he had received, whereupon the Tsungli Yamen concluded that both the ambassador and the consul were implicated, and an order was issued whereby they both were relieved of their duties and recalled.'

The President of the Board of Military Affairs then made a short speech in which he said: 'Since the facts have been established, I do not see any reason why we should continue with this session. I would like to ask the Chief Secretary merely to find out what the punishment is for both these officials and then the Grand Council can act accordingly. The President of the Board of Punishment is here with us and he will, I am sure, give us the desired information. But where is the consul? Shouldn't he appear in this session also?'

All eyes were now directed to the President of the Board of Punishment, but he was noncommittal and showed no desire to express himself.

The chairman then continued: 'This is one of the points I was going to bring up. The consul Chow Su-ying is now, from what I know, in hiding in Japan and has refused to come back to the country. Is it possible he is conscious that he alone is guilty and has chosen to end his life in Japan?'

The President of the Board of Ceremony then requested that the Council hear from the witness himself.

'Gentlemen of the Grand Council,' began Wen-ching as he stood up, 'honourable and respected Councillors of the Throne, humbly do I ask you for your forgiveness in having you assemble to consider a case in which my humble self is supposed to be involved. I wish to declare at the very outset that the document was issued on the sole responsibility of the consul Chow Su-ying without any prior knowledge or agreement on my part. Please consider the unusual circumstances of the document. It was issued to an Austrian merchant to purchase munitions in Germany and in Austria-Hungary, in which latter country, at the time the document was issued, I was no longer ambassador. Let me relate briefly the circumstances of my appointment to that office and my subsequent recall therefrom.

'When the appointment was made — now over a year ago — I asked the chargé d'affaires to make arrangements for me to present my credentials from the Throne to the Emperor of Austria-Hungary. It was then that a most unusual and to me unheard-of thing happened. Lin Liang had the audacity, in his conversation with me, to ask that I stay away from Vienna and that, upon following his advice, I would receive from him the sum of eight hundred dollars every month. Gentlemen, on hearing this, I did what all of you would have done under the circumstances. I lost my temper, grew angry, and dismissed Lin Liang from my presence. I have not seen him since. I immediately reported what happened to the Tsungli Yamen, but I was told that my report never reached the desk of Lord Yu Kung.'

'Is that a fact?' asked the President of the Board of Ceremony, who began to show some interest in the case.

'That is a fact,' replied Lord Yu Kung. 'I never saw the cable. What's more, I have a growing feeling that many documents for the Tsungli Yamen sent by Ambassador Shen have been suppressed from my view. This of course is my responsibility. I am taking a serious view of the matter and have been conducting an inquiry.'

'Now, gentlemen,' continued Wen-ching, 'you can see that this episode could not have made me a friend of Lin Liang's. I reported him as being worthy of the severest disciplinary measures. But instead of any action being taken against him, I was asked to relinquish my concurrent post in Vienna. Something must have happened at Peking: someone must have stepped in to help Lin Liang. What it was and who it was I have no way of knowing.

'Anyhow, at the time this munitions certificate was issued, I was no longer ambassador in Austria-Hungary. This certificate gave permission to purchase munitions in a country where our chargé had become my avowed political enemy. Now, I am not a wise man. That I admit, but can you believe that I was so much out of my mind as to make myself a party to an illegal document which, as anybody knows, would fall into the hands of that enemy? Please give me the benefit of the doubt, and don't think that I was quite such a lunatic.'

'Mr President,' commented the President of the Board of Military Affairs, 'these remarks by the ambassador are entirely irrelevant. We cannot deal with events which are only imaginary. There is nothing to substantiate these statements of the ambassador. What we want are positive facts which are borne out by documents.'

'Thank you for saying so,' continued Wen-ching. 'Let me then show to our respected President of the Board of Military Affairs and to the other members of the Council a few documents which I have.'

While Wen-ching looked through his papers in the briefcase which he had brought with him, there was quite a little stir among the members. They whispered to one another, nodding their heads as if in anticipation of something sensational, and the long feathers projecting from their hats danced in the air as they moved their heads up and down. The President of the Board of Military Affairs, however, remained apart from the rest, looking somewhat sombre and morose.

'Here is one document, gentlemen,' resumed Wen-ching, 'which may prove something. I have in my hands this sheet which I shall pass around. It is the confession, in his own handwriting, made by the consul Chow Su-ying when I first asked him about the munitions certificate on receiving information from the Tsungli Yamen.'

'This sounds most interesting,' commented the President of the Board of Military Affairs rather sarcastically.

'I hope that it is more than merely interesting. I hope it may be accepted as conclusive evidence,' continued Wen-ching. 'May I read it and then pass it around?'

'Yes, do, please,' said the President.

'It reads as follows:

The German employee in the Consular Service declares that she has been in close touch with Austrian merchants, and since there are difficulties in obtaining munitions, she made use of the name of China. Chow Su-ying, not understanding the meaning of the language of the certificate, carelessly signed it and sealed it with the Consular seal.

That, gentlemen, was written and drafted by the consul himself in my presence as a cable reply to the Tsungli Yamen when it first inquired about the document.'

'Did you receive this cable, Lord Yu Kung?' asked the President of the Board of Works.

'Yes, this is on file at the Tsungli Yamen.'

'Is there any way,' asked the President of the Board of Works, 'to prove that this draft which the ambassador has just read and is now being passed around was actually written by the consul? The consul is not present at this meeting, and he can neither affirm nor deny that it is his writing.'

'That is an excellent question,' said the President of the Board of Military Affairs somewhat loudly and triumphantly. 'Yes, who is there to tell that this may not be a forged document?'

He sat down, and then immediately stood up again and added: 'A person who is involved in such a criminal case is capable of anything.'

These were strong words, and the session became tense at so blunt a statement from the President of the Board of Military Affairs. Even the attendants who lined the walls far away from the conference table heard the remarks and began looking at one another in wonder and amazement.

After the excitement had subsided somewhat, Wen-ching stood up and explained with quiet dignity and effective control over his emotions: 'I don't think there is any doubt that it is Consul Chow Su-ying's own handwriting. Allow me to pass around also a number of other documents which he wrote and drafted in the course of his official duties and which bear his official signature. I think a comparison of these documents with the cable draft will establish conclusively that it is the handwriting of the same person.'

Again there were looks of wonder and approving nods of admiration for the care with which Wen-ching had prepared his defence.

But the President of the Board of Military Affairs without so much as taking the trouble to compare the specimens of Chow Su-ying's handwriting burst out: 'Even if the consul's draft confessing that he alone was responsible for the issuance of the document was written by him, is it not possible that he made the confession at the time under force and pressure by the ambassador?'

At this the presiding official, the President of the Board of Rites, gave a faint smile and asked Wen-ching: 'Ambassador Shen, were you, at any time in your life and career, a military man? And did you carry a gun and threaten to kill the consul if he did not make the confession, as he did, in his own handwriting?'

The tension of the session was much relieved by the peals of laughter which followed these remarks. Then the chair asked if the ambassador had other documents to show.

'Yes, Mr President,' answered Wen-ching. 'While we are on the subject of documents, I might as well put forward what I have.' He then passed round the original letter, with a Chinese translation, issued by the director of Wedepak, which was the organization for the export of German munitions of war. It was addressed to the Tsungli Yamen and dated June 20, 1898.

'A copy of this document,' explained Wen-ching, 'is on the official file at the Tsungli Yamen. In view of the constant disappearance of important documents in that office I have kept the original which is now being passed round. I may further explain that this organization Wedepak is the central organization in Germany dealing with the sale of munitions and is informed on everything concerning matters which take place in that country. The director assumed the responsibility of saying in his letter that the consular document was issued "without the knowledge of the Chinese ambassador at Berlin" and that this information was "confidentially provided" to him.'

'Yes, but did you not also threaten the director of Wedepak, at the point of the gun, to issue this letter to the Tsungli Yamen?' inquired the President of the Board of Ceremony.

With this there was renewed laughter, but the President of the Board of Military Affairs still looked glum and unpleasant.

'But perhaps,' the President of the Board of Ceremony wanted to know further, 'you gave a handsome bribe to the director in the same way that Lin Liang tried to bribe you?'

'I am sorry,' replied Wen-ching, 'that I have not yet learned the gentle art of bribing, least of all with the "ocean man", whose languages I am still ignorant of. And now I have a further document to offer you.'

With this remark Wen-ching produced the original letter written by no less a person than the Austrian merchant himself, Emil Schwartz. It was also accompanied by a Chinese translation.

'A copy of this document,' explained Wen-ching, 'is also filed at the Tsungli Yamen. It was given by me in person to Lord Yu Kung. This document was obtained by the same Faustmann who obtained the document from Wedepak. Let me explain. Shortly after the arrival of Mr. Tung-chen to "investigate" the case, things happened in the embassy at Berlin which this Faustmann thought were queer and unusual. He was a faithful and loyal assistant, and in spite of my persuasions to the contrary he said that he would do everything to find out the details of what he was sure was a plot against me. He told me that his sense of justice was outraged, and so he began contacting the merchant himself. On August 2, 1898, late in the evening, he brought me this letter now before you.'

The Chief Secretary was then called upon by the presiding official to read the letter.

Hotel Eisenach, Berlin
July 29, 1898

To the Tsungli Yamen, Peking

Sirs: I take the liberty of making the following statement:

As a merchant dealing in arms for many years I have not had any difficulties with any country. The certificate issued by the Consular Service of your embassy at Berlin has given me such difficulty for the first time in my career. Through my agents I first approached your ambassador at Berlin, who categorically refused to issue a certificate for the importation of arms to China. After a few days my agents informed me that the Consular Service at Berlin could issue the necessary certificate upon payment of ten thousand dollars. I accepted the offer and received that certificate, which you now know.

Since then I have had nothing but troubles and difficulties. After my arrival at Vienna, where I was told that the certificate is not proper, I began to understand things, and since your ambassador at Berlin had categorically refused to issue it, the said certificate was of course delivered to me by the Consular Service without the knowledge of your ambassador. Then Mr. Tung-chen, the Chinese investigator, came to Berlin to make investigations and made me sign a short declaration which he dictated to me himself. As I look at the matter now, it still remains absolutely incomprehensible. I have learned, however, that your ambassador at Berlin is being blamed, which is curious, because he knew nothing about my certificate. It is clear to me that there is in the matter a personal vengeance as there are also special reasons even to create an international scandal, of which I am the first victim from the financial point of view, for the merchandise which was purchased could not be delivered to me. Since the certificate issued by your Consular Service is irregular, it is natural that the money which I paid through my agents should be returned to me. I have the honour to be, Sirs,

EMIL SCHWARTZ

There was unusual silence after the Chief Secretary had finished reading. Though not a word was spoken for some time, it was clear that the cumulative evidence to establish the complete innocence of Wen-ching was beginning to take effect.

At the start of the session there were indications that the President of the Board of Military Affairs was determined to hold Wen-ching responsible. In that he was supported by the President of the Board of Works. The presiding official and the President of the Board of Ceremony were inclined to be sympathetic towards Wen-ching. Lord Yu Kung, as the immediate superior of Wen-ching, had to remain more or less neutral. The rest did not commit themselves one way or the other. But the documents which had been passed round not only began to rally support for Wen-ching, but also the 'personal vengeance' referred to by the Schwartz document gave many members of the session a new perspective.

The President of the Board of Military Affairs broke the silence at last. 'Are we really to believe,' he said, 'that any or all the documents circulated among us are authentic? The ambassador has a wonderful ability to produce documents, and I am sure he has many others which he also wishes us to believe.'

'I have other documents,' replied Wen-ching, 'but I think those I have produced are enough for the moment. I hope you gentlemen do not pay me the compliment of thinking that I possess any unusual ability to influence other people and make them write out documents to establish my innocence in this unfortunate case. It the President will permit me, I would like to pass round cuttings from many of the Berlin newspapers when the news spread that I was being recalled. When you read these, I hope no one will ask "Is it possible that the ambassador has bribed the editors of these papers or compelled them at gun point to write these articles on his behalf?" Here are cuttings taken from the leading newspapers published on the same day, July 28, 1898, the day after I was recalled. The papers are the *Illustrated Berlin News*, the Berlin *Courier*, the Berlin *Post* and the *Daily Courier*.'

Wen-ching passed the cuttings to the Chief Secretary, who, upon the instructions of the chairman, circulated them to all the members of the Council.

Everyone studied the cuttings and their translations with great care. The President of the Council was deeply impressed by them and called on the Chief Secretary to give a brief report.

'Gentlemen,' said the Chief Secretary, 'you have all read these cuttings. I have no comment to make except to say that this is, to the best of my knowledge, the first time such warm tributes have been paid by foreign newspapers to one of our own ambassadors and his hostess — and this ambassador happens to be one whom we have chosen to disgrace by a summary recall.'

The session had now been going on for over three hours, and everyone was beginning to be restless. It could, however, be fairly presumed that the members had a good picture of the case and understood what it was all about. The storm which had raged outside had now subsided; and with their hunger growing the officials of the Grand Council were all anxious to go home. The chairman sensed this feeling and started to wind up the meeting. But before he did so, he called on Wen-ching for the last time and asked if he had anything more to say or to show.

Wen-ching hesitated for a moment and then said: 'I feel that we have been here long enough. But with your permission I will show only one more thing in my possession. I knew for some time that the consul Chow Su-ying and his German secretary were in love. We all know, also, that the consul is now in Japan. There is no question but that he has no intention of coming back to Peking. That was clear even at the time he left Berlin. He left behind a number of envelopes on which he wrote in his own hand his address in Japan with the corresponding foreign script written by his German secretary-lover. These envelopes are meant to be used by her in sending letters to him. Now one of these envelopes happened to be picked up by one of the embassy servants. Here is also a picture showing the two lovers together.'

The envelope and the picture were passed around to the great amusement of all the officials. Some even forgot they were hungry or had been anxious only a short while before to hurry home. Never in the lives of any one of them had they known a case of a Chinese official taking an 'ocean woman' as a temporary wife. The envelope did not excite as much interest as it should, but everyone tried to grab the picture and freely made comments on the German girl. Some had never seen an 'ocean woman' in their lives, and great was their curiosity. She wore a large hat, which most of the officials thought was ugly and must be most uncomfortable.

'How could she walk without that heavy hat falling down all the time?' one official was heard to say.

She wore long skirts which reached the floor so that her feet and shoes were completely invisible. 'I would like to know if the feet of these "ocean women" are as small as those of our women,' commented another.

For that he drew a quick reply from many. 'How can you be so ill-informed! The feet of these women are as large and ugly as our carp. It is best that they are not shown in the picture.'

But everyone agreed that the face, shaped like a goose egg, was rather pretty and pleasant looking, considering that it was marred by two deep-set eyes like those of a monkey, and some of them thought that, like the monkey, her body must be covered with hair, for they had seen thick layers of it on the arms and bodies of some foreign men. The thought of a hairy female body produced some strange grimaces on the faces of the officials.

For some time the picture continued to grip their attention. And then from loud and facetious comments unworthy of their exalted positions the officials relapsed into faint whispers, and the discussion moved from the head to the feet then to the bulky middle portion of the body.

'Look how immodest she is,' whispered the President of the Board of Ceremony. 'She wears no collar, and are we to believe that she goes about with a bosom half exposed to public view? We had better introduce some of our etiquette and decorum to these barbarians.'

But no one listened, as they were all interested in knowing what those two huge sacks were on either side of the half-exposed bosom. And they laughed as they examined the picture, which was the closest view most of them had ever had of an 'ocean woman'.

But the chairman was anxious to wind up the business of the day and called the session once more to order. Wen-ching asked for permission to make one final remark.

'In the documents and in the newspaper cuttings which have been submitted,' Wen-ching said, 'you have seen references made to "personal vengeance", to "intrigue", or to a possible plot against me. I don't know how true this is, but there is one part of the case which has excited my curiosity as it must excite yours. When the munitions certificate was discovered, I was of course as keenly interested in its investigation as the Tsungli Yamen. The yamen thought that I was myself involved, which was understandable. But there is a generally accepted principle that an official who has become the subject of investigation can be investigated only by one who is higher in rank or who is at least his equal.

'Also, the case needed to be studied as soon as possible, for delay meant the disappearance of vital evidence.

'For these two reasons I cabled to the Tsungli Yamen, as I had a right to do, asking that our ambassador in England be dispatched at once to conduct the investigation. Any impartial person would deem such a suggestion eminently reasonable and therefore acceptable. But my request was ignored and refused. Instead, the Tsungli Yamen appointed Tung-chen, who is a minor official many grades below that of an ambassador, and it took him more than two months to arrive on the scene of investigation. Are we to believe that no one among the many diplomats in Europe was qualified to conduct the investigation? Besides, who was responsible for the appointment of Tung-chen? That Tung-chen was both spiritually and physically blind. He came into the embassy with a cotton patch on one eye, and the other one could see only with difficulty. He had, I must say, a wonderful sense of humour, for he told me one day: "I shall be blind doing this thing." How true his words were, for since then, I have been told, he has indeed become completely blind. I was thinking that, small as these details are, they are not insignificant, and they should be brought to the attention of this distinguished body. And is it possible that the extraordinary steps which were taken indicate that there might be some intrigue or plot after all, and that it came from the Tsungli Yamen itself?'

The last remark by Wen-ching was interpreted by everyone as an attack on Lord Yu Kung. But His Lordship knew, from the previous conversation he had had with Wen-ching, that it was not meant for him. The chairman, however, turned to Lord Yu Kung and asked him if the accusation had any validity.

'As you all know,' explained Lord Yu Kung, 'my duties have been heavy. I am President of the Tsungli Yamen, but owing to the tenseness of the present situation, my time and effort have been largely spent with you gentlemen of the Grand Council for the determination of our national policy. I have to wait in audience, as you also know, with the Empress Dowager. And so the details of administrative work at the Tsungli Yamen have for some time past been entrusted to an able director, Mr Hu-mou, who did exactly as the ambassador has told you. When I come to think of it now, there are things I cannot understand. The ambassador, in one of his private letters to me, asked to be relieved of his duties. Rather than doing as he wished, I thought I should wait until the three-year period was over. But my staff at the Tsungli Yamen, especially the director Mr Hu-mou, also made the recommendation to keep the ambassador in Berlin. This munitions case occurred just as the three-year period was about to expire.'

The chairman made no comment and stood up, for the first time during the entire session, to close it.

'Gentlemen,' he said, 'you have today heard all the facts and the evidence in connection with this unusual case of a munitions certificate issued by the consul Chow Su-ying at Berlin, reportedly with the knowledge of the ambassador Shen Wen-ching. I hope you will all study the case carefully so that we may render a just and impartial judgement. The meeting is hereby adjourned.'

I

After adjournment the President of the Board of Ceremony, who had not made more than one or two remarks during the session, asked for a few words privately with the President of the Council.

'Brother Pan-king, I studied the case before I came, and I have a very strong feeling that someone in the Tsungli Yamen, as Wen-ching himself intimated, has a deep grudge against him. This is indeed a case of personal vengeance.'

'But you don't mean his Lordship Yu Kung himself?'

'No, of course not. But I wanted to be impartial, and so I didn't say much during the proceedings. I think Wen-ching made a wonderful defence of himself. He presented the evidence in a skilful manner. But the whole issue, as I see it, can be reduced to a very simple matter. Please read this.'

The President of the Council took the sheet of paper and read:

> ... when a staff member has serious doubt as to the compatibility of an instruction he has received with administrative regulations and rules, it is his duty to place his point of view clearly before his supervisor and, if it is not accepted, he should ask for written instructions. Once such instructions have been received, they must be carried out.

'Brother Pan-king, doesn't this make Wen-ching's case crystal clear?'

'But who gave you this?'

'A senior official in my own yamen, a man of great learning who spent six years of his life in European universities. I asked him to study the case, and he had no hesitation in saying that it should be thrown out and dismissed. It has nothing to stand upon. Then he gave me the quotation from a learned book which, he said, is the recognized stand in the civil service of any civilized country.'

'In other words, if Consul Chow was asked by Wen-ching to perform something irregular, he should have asked for *written* instructions. And there were none.'

'Any responsible official in the Tsungli Yamen should know that, in the circumstances, Wen-ching should not be in the least affected. He must continue to be ambassador in Berlin. Where will you or I be if any one of our subordinate officials does an improper thing without our knowledge? It's the same in Wen-ching's case. But he was recalled, as well as the real culprit, Consul Chow Su-ying.

You can draw your own conclusions. If it is not some personal vengeance, what is it?'

'Hm! I'll look into the matter. Thank you,' replied the President of the Grand Council.

10

WEN-CHING hurried back to the Soochow hostel without a moment's delay. His sedan chair had been waiting for him during all the hours of the meeting. Now that the storm had subsided, there was even a little sunshine glinting through the lattice of the sedan-chair. As he relaxed in his seat while the four coolies carried him, he had a sense of satisfaction and even forgot his hunger. He believed he had made a good case for himself and that he had generally created a good impression on the members of the Council. In ten days he would probably learn the Council's decision. During that time, he knew, there would be some manœuvring. Hu-mou would surely have a report of the hearing. There was no question that he would be busy trying to influence the opinion of the councillors, while he, poor Wen-ching, would have no one to go to, except perhaps to see Lord Yu Kung again. But that he could do only when he had some new and important information to give, or when he was asked

On arrival at the hostel, he found Golden Orchid out of bed. Her face was pale, her hair dishevelled and there were marks on her face to show that she had again been in tears. She was not alone, and Wen-ching was surprised to find Hai-ming in her company, for he had not seen her for many years.

'How are you? How are you?' saluted Wen-ching. 'I haven't seen you for such a long time, Miss Hai-ming. I hope you have been well and prosperous these many years.'

'Thank you, Shen Lao-yeh,' replied Hai-ming. 'I could be worse, but at least I am warmly clad and not hungry.'

In the meantime, Golden Orchid asked for some light food and tea to be brought in, for she was sure that her husband must be famished after a long meeting, about which she had not said a word to Hai-ming, though there was no harm in doing so. After tea Hai-ming excused herself, saying that is was getting late.

'What do you think Hai-ming is now?' said Golden Orchid to her husband after Hai-ming had left the room. 'Believe it or not, she is now the mistress of our much-hated Hu-mou.'

'Then why do you keep her here? How long has she been with you?' inquired Wen-ching nervously.

'But don't get excited, Wen-ching dear. She has been telling me everything. It seems that she hates Hu-mou as much as we do, though for different reasons.'

'What do you mean? I hope you are not naive enough to confide in her. For all I know, she may be laying a trap for you to get important information from you. Always these traps! One can never be too careful.'

'Please don't think that I am such a child. Leave it to me. There is one other thing I want to tell you. The last time Hai-ming was here with me, you didn't meet her. On leaving the hostel she met Lao Chuang at the gate, and he is now her servant. The other day Lao Chuang came to confirm the bad relations between her and Hu-mou.'

'All this sounds suspicious. Lao Chuang is another who knows everything about us. I am coming to distrust everybody, but how can I help it when we have gone through so much? Hai-ming and Lao Chuang can be a most damaging combination against us if they work for Hu-mou. Lao Chuang was a servant in whom we reposed implicit confidence. Anyway, it's strange that they should both be with our arch-enemy now. All I warn you is to be very careful. However, go on.'

'I think Hai-ming is absolutely loyal to us, and I am going to prove it to you later on. As for Lao Chuang, I have no doubt at all about his faithfulness. I have not said a word about today's meeting of the Grand Council. She did ask me where you had gone, and I thought it was best not to let her know. Well, from the accounts she has given me, it seems that she had to become Hu-mou's mistress.'

'What do you mean?'

'You remember how she was kidnapped and taken to Manchuria by the military man and how she escaped? She came back to Peking and then resumed her professional work as a sing-song girl. She was getting old, she said, and she wanted security. So when she met Hu-mou and when he finally asked her to live with him, she readily consented. She did so because she thought that by living with him she might one day become his concubine. She always pointed to me as an example to be followed.'

'If she only knew what you have gone through!' Wen-ching commented.

'Well, anyway, Hu-mou has been keeping her, but the prospect of becoming his concubine is getting farther and farther away. Madam Hu-mou is a real tigress, and Hu-mou keeps Hai-ming only for his pleasure — without the knowledge of his wife.'

'All this sounds interesting, but —'

'If Hu-mou treated her well, she might perhaps remain contented, but she tells me that they always quarrel, and Lao Chuang has confirmed to me how once Hu-mou beat her up and tore her hair. The devil is very tight with his money, and Hai-ming says that what she gets from him is less, much less, than what she would get from the sing-song house. She says she cannot support her mother, who lives in the south.'

'All this is very interesting, as I said,' commented Wen-ching, 'but still I want you to be exceedingly careful and to confide nothing in her.'

'But wait. Hai-ming tells me that sometimes the devil talks about us. He doesn't know that Hai-ming and I have known each other for some time, that she is really devoted to me.'

'But are you sure of that?'

'Nor does the devil know that Lao Chuang, now in his service in his "small house", was in Berlin with us. Hu-mou simply believes that Hai-ming is an ignorant sing-song girl and Lao Chuang another servant. Hai-ming tells me that he is a maniac and a brute, and the things he has done to her, especially in bed, are utterly indescribable. I would blush even to tell you. There are moments when he seems to be normal, and then he tells her the thoughts preying on his mind. He talks about us and about how much he hates us. Hai-ming pretends of course that she doesn't know us and warns him to be gentle and kind to all people, because acts of kindness are always rewarded in the next life. "Kind to Shen Wen-ching or to any of his people?" Hu-mou shouted back one day. "I should say not. Besides, I don't believe in the next life. I shall rejoice to see him and all his people suffer. He thinks he is a great scholar, an able diplomat. He even aspires to sit on my head. I'll show him who does the sitting — he or I. We come from the same city, and my people have suffered enough at the hands of the Shen family. He does not even know that my people have been spurned by the Shen people just because we happened to be poor and ordinary." '

'Did he really say that to Hai-ming? He must be insane. I have no knowledge that my family had anything to do with Hu-mou's family. In fact, I barely know Hu-mou himself.'

'But, anyway, Hu-mou hates us so deeply that he wants to destroy all of us. Hai-ming says that she can't stand him. She has been so badly treated by him that one of these days she will leave him. But she swore to me that she would not leave him until she has inflicted some harm on him which he richly deserves. Hu-mou boasts to her that he is now very rich, that he even has gold hidden away, but still he is so niggardly with her that she does not feel there is any sense in continuing to live with him. Well, to prove that my judgement is correct all along and that you need cherish no suspicions, here is something I want to show to you.'

So saying, Golden Orchid handed Wen-ching some papers.

'What are they?' Wen-ching wanted to know.

'Read them for yourself, and you will be very happy that they have come into my hands.'

Wen-ching turned over the sheets one by one. His face became taut, it showed signs of profound emotional disturbance, and then he gave a loud cry of joy.

'Orchid, my precious treasure,' Wen-ching exclaimed as he firmly grasped one of his concubine's hands. 'Why, these . . . these are the most valuable documents I could ever have. Did Hai-ming give them to you? Did she, really?'

'Yes, she did, and they were taken with the help of Lao Chuang. Now have you any suspicions about Hai-ming and Lao Chuang? But read them first.'

Wen-ching turned back to the first sheet, held it in his quivering hands and read:

May 24, 24th Year of Kuang Hsu (1898)

MY RESPECTED AND HONOURED DIRECTOR HU-MOU: I have today followed your instructions in giving to the Austrian merchant Schwartz a handsome sum of money with which he is to proceed to Berlin at once and try to obtain from Consul Chow Su-ying a certificate to enable him to purchase munitions in Austria-Hungary.

When he succeeds in his mission and returns to Vienna with the document I shall further inform you. Your obedient servant,

LIN LIANG

The second sheet read:

May 31, 24th Year of Kuang Hsu (1898)

MY RESPECTED AND HONOURED DIRECTOR HU-MOU: I have great pleasure in reporting to you that Schwartz is back with the document we need. He did the work quietly and quickly. He told me that he approached the German girl secretary with whom Chow seems to be deeply in love, and the document was in his hands within two hours. Shen Wen-ching has no way of knowing and no way of finding out that the consul has issued the document. The document is now safely under lock and key. You can do as you think best. Awaiting your instructions. Your obedient servant,

LIN LIANG

Wen-ching turned to the third sheet and found that it was in Hu-mou's own handwriting, evidently a draft containing the instructions he gave to Tung-chen on the eve of his so-called mission of investigation. The sheet was creased and crumpled: parts of it were even slightly torn, but there was no damage to the writing itself. It said:

1. Proceed to Vienna before you go to Berlin. Consult Lin Liang, who has the document in his possession.

2. The consul has confessed that he alone was responsible for the document. Don't contradict him. But tell him quietly and secretly that he can put the responsibility on his ambassador and assure him that, by doing so, he reduces his own guilt, and that in any case he will be protected. If, in incriminating the ambassador, we find it necessary to sacrifice the consul, we shall have to do it.

3. When the consul has been won over, call for another meeting and make him say, in the presence of yourself and the ambassador, that he issued the document with the previous knowledge of the ambassador, who also shared in the bribe.

4. The reward of your labour will be as we have agreed upon.

Finally Wen-ching read a short cable sent to Hu-mou by Tung-chen in which the 'investigator' said simply: 'Everything carried out according to instructions.' It was sent from Berlin.

Wen-ching was wild with excitement and looked happily at Golden Orchid, who sat there quietly with her eyes riveted on the face of her husband as if scoring a great victory over him. With hands still trembling with joy he folded the sheets and with some difficulty replaced them within the large envelope.

'Now tell me about the meeting of the Grand Council today,' said Golden Orchid anxiously. 'I want to know everything about it. You have not spoken a word so far.'

'I know, my heart and liver, my precious treasure. It is all because I am so excited about these documents. . . . The meeting was all right. I made a good case for myself — I think. But before I tell you anything, you will have to tell me how Hai-ming got hold of these papers.'

'But do you think they are authentic?' asked Golden Orchid, showing that she, too, could be cautious.

'I think so. Of course I cannot recognize Lin Liang's handwriting, but the list of instructions to Tung-chen is in Hu-mou's handwriting and the last sheet of paper was from the telegraph office. I have no doubt they are all genuine.'

'Well, Wen-ching dear, isn't Lao Chuang a wonderfully faithful servant? I'll tell you how he got those papers. He cleans Hu-mou's study every day, and he was sure that sooner or later he would find something important to us. He opened the drawers of the desk one morning and found one of the documents now in the envelope — I don't know which —'

'Incredible!' commented Wen-ching.

'But, anyway, he thought there might be more and, sensing that Hu-mou and Hai-ming were on bad terms, he decided to persuade Hai-ming to become his accomplice. He waited for a few days, and sure enough two nights ago Hu-mou came back quite drunk and became very violent with Hai-ming. That same evening Hai-ming almost decided to run away, as she couldn't stand him any longer, and after Hu-mou fell asleep she ransacked his wallet for money. During the daytime that wallet, like your own, is always tied round his belly. There inside the wallet she found the rest of the papers now in the envelope. She couldn't understand all that was written and asked Lao Chuang what they were about. It was then that Lao Chuang persuaded her to come to see me.'

'Heaven protect us, my sweet Orchid! The evil ones will always have a bad end — that I know. And so will Hu-mou. The meeting today did not openly lay any blame on Hu-mou, but I think the Grand Council now has deep suspicion that Hu-mou is the arch-conspirator behind my case. At least I think some of the councillors have. Lord Yu Kung was most helpful. I had a feeling that I had lost his friendship, but he certainly gave no such impression today. I shall go to see him again tomorrow morning with these papers, and they should establish beyond the shadow of a doubt that the whole case is a plot conceived by Hu-mou and aided and abetted by Lin Liang and Tung-chen.'

When Wen-ching and Golden Orchid went to bed that night, it was the most comfortable, the most enjoyable night they had spent together for many a long, long month.

The next morning Wen-ching called for a sedan chair again and asked to be conveyed to the residence of Lord Yu Kung. The weather was chilly, and there was even a suggestion that it might snow. Instead of the long wait which he fully expected, as he had not written for an appointment, Wen-ching found that Lord Yu Kung was in fact anxious to see him again after the meeting of the Grand Council the previous day. But Lord Yu Kung looked worried and took Wen-ching straight into his study.

'I am sorry to have to tell you, my dear friend and brother Wen-ching,' began Lord Yu Kung, 'that your case has turned for the worse. I received the report only this morning shortly after I got out of bed.'

Wen-ching's face fell and he wondered what it was that had taken place.

'What occurred was this,' resumed Lord Yu Kung. 'You must have noticed that the President of the Board of Military Affairs yesterday was not at all friendly to you.'

'Yes, I noticed that. But what has he done?'

'Immediately after the meeting he got on his horse and rode to see the Empress Dowager at the Summer Palace. He can see Her Imperial Majesty whenever he wants to, owing to the present tense military situation. He also had the assistance of the Chief Eunuch.

He gave a full report of the meeting and twisted everything that was said. For instance, he told the Empress Dowager that everyone at the meeting was against you, that the documents fully established your guilt, and that you even tried to contradict the documents by producing false evidence. He worked up a terribly angry mood in the Empress Dowager and then calmly suggested that you should be given the supreme penalty.'

With those words Wen-ching's face became deadly pale. He was stunned and sat in stony silence. He realized, as Lord Yu Kung also did, that once the Empress Dowager had made up her mind, nothing could change her. An appeal to the Emperor would even make matters worse, for the Emperor had become, as everyone knew, a mere figure-head, and the Empress Dowager was the real ruler.

Wen-ching thought that his cause was now lost. He began wondering what the connections were between Hu-mou and the President of the Board of Military Affairs. But it served no purpose to speculate at this late hour. Quietly he pulled out of his sleeve the envelope in which were hidden what to him were the most precious documents in the world. He did not dare believe that these could save the situation, but just the same he handed them to Lord Yu Kung.

His Lordship read slowly every word that was written on the documents, and without losing a single moment asked that his carriage be made ready at once. Then gently he said to Wen-ching: 'Leave everything to me and go back to your hostel.'

'But where are you going, Your Lordship?'

'I must hurry to see the Empress Dowager myself with the additional evidence you have now given me. You will hear from me. In the meantime, remain quietly at your hostel.'

Lord Yu Kung was almost on the point of resigning himself to the inevitable. The President of the Military Board had made a clever and desperate move, and he wondered whether it was in his power to counteract it. He also thought of the Chief Eunuch, who had previously cancelled Wen-ching's audience with the Empress Dowager because he had not given him a gift. With the combination of two such powerful people, what chances were there for the ambassador with four meagre documents? But fortunately for him Lord Yu Kung was on more than speaking terms with the Chief Eunuch.

11

Two days passed, and not a word. Those were the two most harrowing days that Wen-ching and Golden Orchid ever passed — worse even than all the previous agonizing experiences. The prospects were dark indeed; and there was absolutely nothing they could do. Patiently they waited for the momentous decision of the Grand Council. But how could anyone be patient when so vital a decision was being made and when they knew that, whatever they might think or do, it would exercise no influence — positively no influence — on its final outcome? So astute had been the move on the part of the President of the Board of Military Affairs!

For long hours Wen-ching and Golden Orchid sat together, often without saying a word to each other. Wen-ching tried to maintain some semblance of calm, though within he was as tormented as Golden Orchid. He had sat through the meeting of the Grand Council, and though he had no assurance that he would be vindicated, he had the feeling, difficult as it was to convey to Golden Orchid, that the justice of his cause and the friendly sympathy of some of the participants of the session might very well help him out of the desperate situation. But now there was this sudden turn for the worse. The only spiritual comfort he could find was again in the great poems of the Tang Dynasty and in the wisdom of the ancient classics. It was then that he began to feel a sense of calm, even though it was the calm of stoicism.

'I have done all that is humanly possible,' he said to his concubine. 'The result must depend on the will of heaven,'

Golden Orchid was thinking along the same lines, but she decided to find out herself, if possible, what the will of heaven was going to be.

So after lunch on the second day she persuaded Wen-ching to take a nap and went out to consult the renowned fortune-teller Blind Man Wang, who lived half a mile away. She thought at first of asking Hai-ming to accompany her, but on second thoughts she went alone, as she did not wish anyone to share with her the knowledge of so important a matter.

There were only two or three others ahead of her and she did not have to wait long for an audience with the blind fortune-teller. When it was her turn, she gave Wen-ching's eight characters signifying the year, the month, the day, and the hour of his birth. She sat quietly without so much as moving from her seat and eagerly watched the fortune-teller mumble to himself and count on his fingers.

At long last the blind man straightened his body and said: 'I wish you had come to see me early in the morning, when my mind is clearer and therefore works better.'

'I am sorry, sir,' replied Golden Orchid, 'but I simply did not have the time.'

'Well, never mind,' replied the fortune-teller. 'There are not many visitors now and I shall instruct my assistant to close the doors for the day, as I want to talk to you at some length.'

He did so and resumed: 'I may tell you that in all the years I have been a fortune-teller, only once before have I come across such great characters. They are very unusual and they belong to a very important person. I presume they are those of a man?'

'Yes,' was the reply.

'And he is now in the fifty-first year of his life. Last year, his fiftieth year, was a very significant one, with a difficult pass. If he had gone over that pass smoothly, all would have been well. But he did not, and the troubles have come to a climax during the current year. However, don't become worried, young lady.' He knew from her voice that the person in front of him was a young woman.

The blind man became silent again and once more mumbled and counted on his fingers.

'This man who, I presume, is your husband,' continued the blind man, 'is a man of extraordinary ability. He is the greatest scholar of the land and has passed the highest examinations. His characters are those of no less a man than a *chuang yuan.*'

'Yes, sir, he is a *chuang yuan.*'

'He has an unusual combination of the five elements. He lacks metal and water. It is the deficiency in these two elements that has made him such an extraordinary person, but it is the same deficiency that in other respects has given him a handicap. He is frank and honest, and his mind is able to grasp easily the essentials of a situation. But his frank and straightforward nature can often create misunderstanding. He is always anxious to help others, and yet this desire to help is sometimes misconstrued. He is apt to arouse jealousy in others, and little people often bite him like insects and hurt him behind his back.'

'How true — how very true!' commented Golden Orchid.

'This trouble he is in now which was created by these little people to hurt him will be overcome, but it will leave an ugly scar on his soul. It will be necessary for him to lie low when the storm is over. Even so, he will have to be careful, and then, when the sky is all clear and the crisis over, he will soar into the heavens again and re-establish his honour, his reputation, and his great name for posterity.'

'But, sir, will he have many children?'

Blind Man Wang began counting on his fingers again. And then he said: 'All I can find from his characters is a son and a half. You know what that means, of course. A son and a daughter. Both of them are from the first legal wife. It is not likely that the concubine will bear him any children. You are, I take it, that concubine?'

'Yes, sir, I am,' replied Golden Orchid with a note of sadness. 'Is there any way in which I may overcome this difficulty?'

'That may be possible, but it is not within my power to predict. I would advise you to do one thing on your way back. I suggest that you visit the Temple of the White Horse, which is not far from here. And, praying earnestly to Kuan-yin, the Goddess of Mercy, you may receive a special blessing from her.'

Golden Orchid paid the blind man generously for his services and did as he suggested, though the hour was getting late and Wen-ching might be looking for her. But she decided to finish what she had set out to do. At the temple, she paid for a pair of red candles, which she lighted and placed in front of the gilt image of the Goddess of Mercy. Between the candles she lighted a bunch of incense which she stuck in a burner. Then, grasping a bamboo receptacle in which there were perhaps a hundred bamboo sticks, she reverently knelt down and began shaking it. She took the first stick that came out and dropped on the floor, and on it she saw the inscription 'high'. She read the number, and with it she approached the slip of yellow paper giving a detailed description of that number.

The language was not simple, but Golden Orchid managed to understand the meaning. At least she thought she did. It said:

> The blue dragon and the white tiger
> In a mortal combat they struggled.
> The tiger pined for his last breath,
> High into the heavens the dragon soared!

Noble and glorious was the flight.
But alas! heavy the load, the load of slime
It carried, and its many wounds brought it down,
And now it rests on a swampy marsh.

The more Golden Orchid read this, the more mystified she became. There was no clue at all as to whether she was going to have any children by Wen-ching, which was the main purpose of her prayer. But instead there was this blue dragon which was obviously her husband. For was he not born in the year of the dragon? All seemed well with the dragon. There was this triumphal flight into the heavens, but why all of a sudden did it go down to the swampy land? The message was a good one, and yet it left behind a note of deep dissatisfaction. Golden Orchid decided to speak only of the good things if Wen-ching should want to know where she went during his nap.

When Golden Orchid returned to the hostel Wen-ching was having tea and cakes by himself.

'Where did you go?' he asked.

'Well, I thought that, for the fun of it, I should consult Blind Man Wang, and so I was with him all the afternoon.'

'What did he say?'

'He gave me great encouragement and said that the trouble will all be over.'

Wen-ching normally did not attach much importance to the predictions of fortune-tellers, but he was not averse to hearing what Golden Orchid had to say now when he was in such a desperate situation.

That night, at any rate, they spent more comfortably, and when the third day of waiting came, they were very glad, soon after breakfast was over, to see the card of Lord Yu Kung brought in by the servant of the hostel. Out of courtesy, Wen-ching went to the main drawing-room of the hostel himself and accompanied His Lordship to his apartments, as he knew that the final hour had come to hear the decision of the Grand Council. Golden Orchid was ready, and as Lord Yu Kung appeared, she was at the door to give him a warm and cordial welcome. It was the first time that she met the great man. She gave a gracious and reverent bow to His Lordship, who sat down on the seat of honour while she went to bring in some tea herself.

'I hope you are comfortable in these apartments,' Lord Yu Kung said.

'There are only the two of us, and our life is simple,' said Wen-ching.

'Madam Wen-ching chooses to remain in the south, doesn't she? It was many years ago that I met her, and I still recall the gracious manners and the classic beauty of her features. There are not many ladies these days who combine beauty with such refinement and culture of the ancient world. She is well, I hope?'

'Thank you, she is. She still continues with her painting and her calligraphy, and I hope that it will not be long before we can join her in a life of quietness and calm.'

Golden Orchid brought in the tea and took her seat by her husband, slightly to the rear.

Lord Yu Kung looked at her and was much taken by her youth and charm. Her eyes, he thought, were unusually vivacious. He thought of his son Yung-kai and all that he had written in the diary. 'I hope you enjoyed living in Germany,' he said to Golden Orchid.

'Yes, thank you, Your Lordship,' replied Golden Orchid. 'I hope one of these days Your Lordship will have a chance to visit those foreign lands. They are quite wonderful.'

'I presume they must be.' There was a short pause, and then Lord Yu Kung took from his sleeve an envelope which he handed to Wen-ching.

'Brother Wen-ching, you must have been anxiously waiting for this, and it is my supreme happiness to deliver it to you. Let me explain. This is only a draft of the decision of the Grand Council. The formal document is being drawn up and it will be a few days before it is done. But yesterday I was with the chairman and the Chief Secretary of the Grand Council, and the draft now in the envelope agrees with the general sentiment of the Council members and is in consonance with the wishes of the Empress Dowager.'

'So Her Majesty has expressed her sacred wishes on the matter in which my humble self is involved?'

'I have told you what happened immediately after the Grand Council ended its session. Fortunately I got wind of the visit to the Summer Palace, as I told you also, of the President of the Board of

Military Affairs, but fortunately also you gave me those documents. When I saw Her Majesty she happened to be in a good mood. I lost no time in delving right into the subject, and she repeated to me all that she had heard from the President of the Board of Military Affairs. I showed her all the documents I had brought, and within one short hour I managed to straighten out everything. She showed keen interest in the four extra documents, but what really moved her was the self-confession written by the consul himself and the cuttings from the newspapers. Her Imperial Majesty has now completely exonerated you and instructed me to conclude the matter as I see fit in the name of the Tsungli Yamen. The Chief Secretary is now attending to the details.'

Lord Yu Kung got up and was ready to leave. 'I shall see you in a few days, Brother Wen-ching.'

He glanced at Golden Orchid, who was sobbing, so overcome was she with intense joy at the news. All the bitterness, all the pent-up unhappiness of these many months, the feeling of having been terribly and deeply wronged, and the triumph of vindication — it was a medley of confused emotions pulling her now one way, now another, until she exploded in a flood of tears and went to her bedroom. There was no time even to thank Lord Yu Kung for the good tidings and for all that he had done for them.

Wen-ching once again accompanied Lord Yu Kung all the way to the main gate of the hostel. He was himself almost in tears, and as they bowed goodbye to each other, he said to Lord Yu Kung: 'I am indeed bounden to you for life.'

It was quite some time before Wen-ching and Golden Orchid could quieten their nerves. The excitement was too intense. Finally Wen-ching pulled out the draft document and slowly read it — read every word of it while Golden Orchid listened:

The Grand Council in a special session convened in its chambers at the Palace of the Tranquil Heart on the Third Day of the Eleventh Moon in the Twenty-Fourth year of the Glorious Reign of His Imperial Majesty Kuang Hsu hereby makes known its decision to dismiss the case under its adjudication, to wit,

Defendant: Former Ambassador Shen Wen-ching, who, having been found to be innocent, is hereby cleared of all the charges made against him, for the following reasons:

That during the period of Shen Wen-ching's ambassadorship in Germany the consular official Chow Su-ying, who served at the same time as one of the secretaries of the embassy, did, in collusion with his secretary, of German national origin, issue a certificate for the purchase of munitions which he signed and sealed with the consular seal under his charge. The said certificate was issued and delivered to the Austrian merchant Emil Schwartz enabling him to purchase munitions of war in Germany as well as in Austria-Hungary, in consideration for which the said merchant paid the sum of ten thousand dollars as bribe to be divided between Consul Chow and his German secretary.

In the course of his negotiations the said merchant Emil Schwartz brought the certificate to Austria-Hungary and it came to the knowledge of the Chinese Embassy at Vienna, whereupon the embassy cabled to the Tsungli Yamen for investigation of the document.

Consul Chow Su-ying, in the course of the investigation, openly admitted that the said certificate was signed and delivered by him to the Austrian merchant in his name as consul, but subsequently he cleverly gave the information that the certificate was issued with the agreement of the ambassador, to whom he paid the sum of two thousand dollars. Whereupon the Tsungli Yamen, in consideration of the assumption that both the ambassador and the consul were involved in the case, brought the matter before our special session.

The Grand Council has carefully examined all the relevant papers and documents bearing on the case and is firmly convinced that the accusations made against the ambassador are not supported by adequate evidence and are therefore groundless.

The Grand Council is of the opinion that whether or not ambassador Shen Wen-ching is guilty depends entirely upon whether or not he gave prior agreement to Consul Chow Su-ying, who signed and sealed the document, and upon whether or not he received any portion of the bribe.

The consul affirms that he did consult the ambassador on many occasions, that he obtained his agreement, and that further he gave him a portion of the money.

The ambassador, however, denies that he had any knowledge whatever that such a certificate had been issued by the consul in collusion with his secretary and that, further, he received no portion of the money.

There was no third party present to corroborate the statements of the consul, nor are there any written documents to substantiate his position. For this reason the Grand Council does not deem that the mere assertions on the part of the consul can be in agreement with the actual facts, nor does it consider that these assertions can establish the guilt of the ambassador.

Further, the Grand Council is firmly of the opinion that in the normal procedure in the issuance of such a certificate, it is the ambassador who should sign and seal it. Such a procedure has been confirmed by the Tsungli Yamen. Since the consul Chow Su-ying affirmed that the ambassador had given his consent for the issuance of the certificate, he should have left it to be signed and sealed by his superior. Why then did he proceed to sign and seal it himself and assume the responsibility which is not his so as to bear the blame for himself alone? Chow Su-ying has been in the service long enough to know that one does not issue a document, ignore his superior if the superior agreed to it, and voluntarily carry the burden of guilt entirely on his own shoulders. This is entirely against common sense, and that is why the Grand Council deems it improper to impose any faith or trust on the mere assertions by the consul without other evidence.

Further, in the early days when the case was discovered, the consul Chow Su-ying, in his own handwriting, drafted a cable which was sent to the Tsungli Yamen admitting that due to a lack of understanding of the language of the document he negligently signed and sealed it. When later the investigator arrived on the scene, the consul changed his stand and said to the investigator that he signed the document under the instructions of the ambassador. On this point the Grand Council desires to make it clear that Chow Su-ying is after all not a country yokel but a diplomatic official; that if he had knowledge of the ambassador as his superior official embarking on any illegal undertaking, it was his bounden duty to report the matter at once to the Tsungli Yamen; and that even if he did not wish to report, he certainly should have described subsequently to the Tsungli Yamen the actual conditions under which the certificate was issued and given. Instead of that he admitted, without any hesitation and in his own handwriting, that 'Chow Su-ying, not understanding the meaning of the language of the certificate carelessly signed it and sealed it with the consular seal'. How can he then, after the arrival of the investigator, deny the responsibility which was clearly his and try to make the ambassador share it with him?

It is true that the German woman secretary also testified that the ambassador had prior knowledge of the certificate. Such testimony is, however, of no value whatever because the entire case grew out of the collusion between her and the consul, and a study of all the documents has established a strong suspicion that the two are in love with each other, which makes her testimony all the more valueless.

The Grand Council affirms that there is nothing in fact to establish even any suspicion that the ambassador was guilty of any misconduct and that it cannot incriminate him merely on the strength of unsubstantiated and unsupported statements on the part of the consul and his secretary. The consul is hereby ordered to appear in the local court for further judgement. The charges against the ambassador Shen Wen-ching are deemed groundless and are hereby dismissed.

LEE PAN-KING
President of the Board of Rites
Chairman of the Grand Council

When Wen-ching had finished reading the lengthy decision of the Grand Council, he sat motionless and sighed deeply. His eyes were closed, his lips held tightly together. The occasion called for rejoicing, for wild rejoicing, and yet there was silence, dead silence, until Golden Orchid went up to her husband and said, as if timidly: 'Wen-ching, my dear, why don't you say something?'

'This is incredible! Unbelievable! I never thought that the Grand Council would go to that extent and be so thorough. How meticulously was that judgement prepared! I knew that I would be exonerated from any blame, but certainly not in that manner. A few perfunctory remarks perhaps, to say that I am innocent — that would be all. But I didn't think that the Council would take the trouble to arrange the arguments in such a systematic and orderly manner, sustained with such logic and clarity. I am impressed. It is a masterly document, and it has restored all my faith in the essential goodness of the human heart.'

'Oh, I am so happy, so very happy to hear you say this,' remarked Golden Orchid. And she held both his hands.

'But the development of the entire case is so very strange. The ups and downs, the sudden turns — now for the better and now for the worse — seemed to be determined by a number of little incidents, the fortuitous circumstances which sometimes have nothing to do with the case itself.'

'I have long come to believe now that, in Chinese official life, there is no such thing as right or wrong,' commented Golden Orchid, still holding her husband's hands.

'But let me go on. The fact that Hai-ming is a good friend of yours, that she is the mistress of Hu-mou, that Lao Chuang becomes their servant, that the President of the Board of Military Affairs enjoys the privilege of seeing the Empress Dowager at any time he desires, that he and Hu-mou have some special relationship, that Lord Yu Kung for some reason re-establishes his faith and confidence in me — all these things have no basic relation at all to the case itself. Have they?'

'No, apparently not.'

'And yet they have all contributed somehow to the decision of the Grand Council. I cannot get over the strange and mysterious ways in which human destiny is determined. One thing the more, one thing the less, and our fate would have been completely different. Well, well . . .'

'We were ruined, we were on the verge of complete and irrevocable destruction,' said Golden Orchid.

'But now, my precious child, we can calmly look forward to a new lease of life. And whom are we to be thankful to? Some Supreme Being, I suppose, who arranges the pattern for the lives of all of us — with kindness and justice.'

Wen-ching again closed his eyes and for a brief moment was wrapped in grateful meditation.

'That is why,' said Golden Orchid, 'in my heart I have worshipped heaven ever since this great misfortune has fallen on us. I prayed day and night, and my prayers have now been answered.'

She thought for a while. Then suddenly she said, 'But how can we say that our faith has been completely restored when we have still lost everything — position, honour, riches? Not until we have regained all these can we say that our life is normal again. Think of the pain, the agony, the suffering, the anxieties, the sleepless nights which you and I have gone through all these years — and all for what?'

'What has come over you, my precious one? We have won the victory. This is just the beginning, and everything from now on will be all right — will turn out as you wish.'

It was indeed an unusual situation. As long as the case was hanging in the balance and Wen-ching's fate unknown, Golden Orchid was afflicted with fears of what might descend on them. If the wickedness in the heart of a few people could bring them to where they were, surely that wickedness could land them in further misery and suffering, or even worse, when they decided to fight it out in the open. That was why friends counselled delay in proceeding to Peking when they returned from abroad. Through all the days of travail Golden Orchid was full of evil foreboding. But now with victory in her lap she was not satisfied with the decision of the Grand Council.

For Wen-ching it was enough that he had been vindicated. But for Golden Orchid it was something more important: it was to be the beginning of another long fight, and this time she was going to take the initiative, not only to recover what they had lost, but to pay back those who had hurt them so terribly.

12

Two days later the formal decision of the Grand Council was published in the *Metropolitan Gazette*, and all Peking knew that the case against Wen-ching had been dismissed. The news spread rapidly and was discussed in the offices and corridors of the different yamen, and at the dinners and social gatherings of official Peking. Almost without exception every discussion of the case began with the question 'Who is supporting Wen-ching?' And when it came to be known that it was Lord Yu Kung who had been instrumental in saving him, the officials asked themselves: 'Is it possible that Lord Yu Kung was actually bribed by Wen-ching? Or can it be that Wen-ching's concubine has used her seductive charms to get the support of His Lordship?'

No one rejoiced that justice had been done. 'Justice? How naive! Only children talk about justice, or perhaps bookworms. In the world of realities there is no right and no wrong. It is all a question of power, strength, influence. If you have these, even though you may be wrong, you are right. If you do not have these, even though you are right, you are still wrong!' Those were the prevailing principles in the last days of the Manchu Dynasty.

It was a time of impending national calamity, but few people in power really cared. What could the Boxers with their incantations do? And even if a few 'ocean men' and their Chinese associates were murdered and their churches burned, what had such things to do with their lives? Feasts, pleasures, concubines, mistresses, sing-song girls, flower-boats, riches, honour, position, wealth — these were the things that mattered; and China's self-styled aristocrats and their next-door neighbours, the bureaucrats, had grown cynical enough not to inquire how they got them.

Wen-ching, unfortunately, belonged to a type that was rapidly dying. His mental and spiritual sustenance came from the classics, and until recently he firmly held the belief that the real world should be guided by the ideal world. Even if there was a gap between them, he thought, it should never be a wide one. But deeply disillusioned as he had become, he was encouraged that he had won a victory over the forces of evil. Beyond that, however, he was not interested in going: he did not wish to be a martyr or a missionary. Not so Golden Orchid! She was willing to repay evil with evil, if need be.

Among the first men who visited Wen-ching to offer him congratulations was Hu-mou himself — Hu-mou, who had been sure he would see Wen-ching slaughtered, who had waited to hear Wen-ching beg for mercy. This same Hu-mou graciously offered felicitations to Wen-ching, now that his plot had miscarried. How perfectly had it been conceived, how smoothly it had worked, and yet, and yet . . .

'How are you, my dear Ambassador?' Hu-mou came rushing into Wen-ching's apartments the morning after the news appeared in the *Metropolitan Gazette*. 'Please accept my sincere congratulations on the great news we have just received. I always knew you would come out well.'

Wen-ching tried to look sardonically pleasant. 'Quite well, thank you,' he replied. But he looked stiff as he spoke, and he added: 'I must really thank you for all that you did.'

There was a pause. And Hu-mou's eyes rolled upwards, not

knowing how to take Wen-ching's last remark. He feigned ignorance, and how well he did it. 'It's a wonder to me,' he said, 'how you stood the impertinence of your staff all those years. I was just trying to improve the situation for you when the impossible happened. As a first step I thought of recalling those two secretaries. I don't know what took place before Lord Yu Kung issued the order of recall for you. Thank heaven, it is now all over.'

So it was His Lordship's responsibility! Wen-ching said nothing. It was an awkward silence. And then Hu-mou stammered: 'You are staying here for some time, I hope, my dear Ambassador?'

Wen-ching knew what was coming and tried to forestall it. 'I shall be here only a few days more,' he said, 'settling some private affairs, and then I am going back to Soochow.'

'Why, of course, but surely as fellow townspeople, you and Madam are coming to have dinner with us before you leave.'

Having failed to forestall the invitation, Wen-ching answered: 'Thank you, Mr. Hu-mou, thank you. As I said, I shall be here only a very few days, and there are so many private things to attend to. Besides, we are not feeling too well. Thank you, we dare not trouble you and Madam Hu-mou.'

'Why, no trouble at all. In fact, I was thinking of inviting you soon after your arrival here to "wash the dust from your feet", but my duties at the yamen have been heavy recently. Just at present, however, I have some free evenings. Shall we say then two nights from today?'

'No, no, really, thank you. You are a very busy man, as we all know. I dare not disturb you. Thank you.'

It now came to a point when the conversation could not be prolonged. Wen-ching had again done something that no one long in Chinese officialdom would have done. Any other person in his place would have grinned and chatted with Hu-mou as if they were still friends, at least as if there was nothing between them, and he would certainly have accepted the dinner invitation. But Wen-ching did none of these things. He made it clear that they were not exactly on speaking terms.

Hu-mou excused himself, and even as he left, he said: 'Both Madam Hu-mou and your humble brother will still be counting on you to dine with us. Do let me know later when you will be free.'

But Wen-ching broke no rules of courtesy when he accompanied Hu-mou, though in utter silence, to the main gate of the hostel.

When he came back to the apartments, Golden Orchid said furiously: 'The impertinence of that arch-devil to come to see you!'

'No, no, my precious one, you mustn't speak like that,' Wen-ching replied softly. 'You and I will have to call on Lord Yu Kung to thank him for all that he has done.'

'I am glad you say so, because that is exactly what I have been thinking.'

'Very well. I shall have to send a special messenger to deliver a note to him to see if he is free to receive us the day after tomorrow.'

Lord Yu Kung invited them both for lunch. Decking herself out with all the finery and jewels she possessed, Golden Orchid appeared with Wen-ching in Lord Yu Kung's drawing-room. She had acquired the foreign habit of wearing fur on outer clothes, instead of as a lining, and that day she wore a most becoming sable cape. As the room was only slightly heated, she wore it throughout the meal. Lord Yu Kung was charmed by the young face whose whiteness was set off by the dark fur. He noticed also that Golden Orchid had delicate hands, well padded and yet not fat, the soft, rounded fingers tapering to a fine finish with faintly rose-coloured nails. In her hair Golden Orchid wore the jade butterfly with ruby antennae given to her by Yung-kai three years previously. She thought that His Lordship might recognize it, which indeed he did, for it had once been owned by Her Ladyship, who had given it to her son on her deathbed.

'How beautifully it sits on her hair!' Lord Yu Kung said to himself.

For some reason unknown to himself his heart seemed to beat quicker. The memory of the two dearest people in his life — his wife and his son — and of their curious link with the young woman now sitting at the same table with him produced a medley of feelings which he could not describe. There was that jade butterfly, and there were those years of obvious intimacy between Yung-kai and Golden Orchid far away in a foreign land which the diary had disclosed. They drank a few small cups of Shaoshing wine, and the blood ran even warmer in His Lordship's veins.

Wen-ching raised his cup again and proposed a toast thanking Lord Yu Kung for his timely assistance.

'The fault was really mine,' replied Lord Yu Kung in all humility. 'If I had spent more time at the Tsungli Yamen, if I had not been so ready to trust Hu-mou, and above all if I had only taken heed of what my son used to tell me in his letters from Berlin, the case could not have arisen.'

'It is good of you to say so, Your Lordship. But I am now more conscious than ever of my own weaknesses, and that is why I want to tell you that I am returning to Soochow to live quietly. I joined official life with the hope of accomplishing something. I have failed — and I would have been destroyed if it had not been for Your Lordship. I am giving up official life for good: I am not cut out for it.'

Golden Orchid was uneasy while Wen-ching spoke. In her young mind she was thinking that since she had already been thrown into diplomatic life, she was not going to give it up easily. She knew now that it was all a matter of playing the game, and she was going to play it! Lord Yu Kung's reference to Yung-kai gave her, she thought, a good opportunity to take part in the conversation.

'Your Lordship,' she said, 'allow me to express my very deep sympathy for your loss of Yung-kai. He was growing into a really fine young man, and we feel that his untimely death has given us as much unhappiness as it has Your Lordship.' As she spoke, she was on the verge of tears, and she looked at the pair of ivory chopsticks in front of her rather than at the two men.

And then she continued: 'My husband has been talking about going back to the south. Before we leave, we are going to Yung-kai's tomb to pay our last respects.'

The suggestion took Wen-ching by surprise, and yet there was nothing he could do but agree to it. Lord Yu Kung was deeply touched. He looked at Wen-ching and said that he would give instructions to prepare for their visit if they desired it.

Having received agreement from the two men, Golden Orchid at once turned back to the thoughts uppermost in her mind. It might be a long time before she had another opportunity to speak to the President of the Tsungli Yamen, and she decided to make full use of the present chance.

For here was her husband, who had been falsely accused, the near victim of a vicious plot. The plot had not succeeded, but was she to be satisfied with that? Why shouldn't the conspirator himself now be brought to justice? Was he to go scot-free because he had failed in his plans? Why couldn't her husband claim some compensation? And couldn't he also be reinstated in the diplomatic service? Unless those things were done, the case, so far as Golden Orchid was concerned, was not closed. She had lived abroad long enough to understand that those were the steps which must be taken as soon as the case was cleared. In fact, some of her diplomatic friends suggested no less when she left Berlin for Peking. Hadn't the Turkish ambassador said: 'We shall hope to see you back in Berlin as China's ambassador'?

But when Wen-ching said that he had made up his mind to spend his remaining years with his books, he did it for more than one reason. He felt he was more at home with his books; more than that, he knew also that political life in China was different from that of the 'ocean' countries. There was no firm stand for law and justice: it was a matter of political influence, and the knowledge that Hu-mou was in alliance with the President of the Board of Military Affairs and perhaps with others as well convinced him that it would lead him nowhere if he insisted upon absolute redress. There was no such thing as impersonal justice when everything depended on the personal equation.

Lord Yu Kung directed the conversation back to pleasant generalities and asked if it had been really uncomfortable living in a strange country.

'It was at first,' commented Golden Orchid. 'But I got accustomed to it, especially when I learned to speak some German.'

'But even so, aren't they so very different from us in every respect?'

'That also, Your Lordship, one gets used to. I got to know some of the Germans so well that I even liked them — I liked them for their straightforwardness and frankness. They are so refreshing after all the deviousness of our own Chinese mind.'

Wen-ching was embarrassed and hastened to give an explanation, which was not much of an improvement. 'What Golden Orchid means is that one knows where one stands in dealing with the "ocean people".'

'That's interesting,' said Lord Yu Kung. 'I believe myself, after having had contacts with these people, that this is generally true. Well, I suppose we are too old a country, and often things are not the same as they appear. Age breeds cynicism, and we are a cynical people'.

His Lordship smiled as he said this. Wen-ching was relieved that Golden Orchid's blunt remark had produced no ill effect.

'I would not mind, Your Lordship,' suggested Golden Orchid, 'if I had to spend another three years in some other country.'

Another blunt statement. This time Wen-ching looked worried. He wished that she had not said it.

But Lord Yu Kung was kind and generous. He wiped his thick, drooping moustache and said: 'The opportunity will yet come. For the time being I hope that Brother Wen-ching will stay in Peking. We shall see what we can do.'

Lord Yu Kung was sincere in wanting to be helpful, but he knew that he had to feel his way for some time before he could give any suggestions for a new appointment to the Empress Dowager. It was a big step he had taken in saving Wen-ching: the next step should not follow so closely upon the heels of the first.

13

YUNG-KAI was buried in Lord Yu Kung's family graveyard among the Western Hills outside Peking. The journey was long and un-comfortable, especially for Wen-ching. But he thought that it was good to be away from Peking for a few days before starting on his journey home to Soochow. The men who had kicked him into a pit and then stoned him were now eager to call on him, professing they had known he was innocent. Some persisted in inviting him and Golden Orchid to dinner. But the very thought of these loathsome people nauseated him, and more than ever he welcomed the idea of spending a few days among the hills. He sent a wire to Madam Wen-ching to tell her that the case had been concluded in his favour, and that if Ping-mo was available, he should come to Peking at once to accompany his father back to Soochow.

The weather was cold when he and Golden Orchid boarded mule-carts two days later. But the sun shone bright; there was no wind, and the air was clear and crisp. With them went two servants sent by Lord Yu Kung to wait on them. The separate carts were laden with food, bedding and cooking utensils. The distance be-tween the Soochow hostel and the north-western gate of Peking was easily covered. From there the wide road leading to the Summer Palace and beyond to the Temple of the Purple Clouds and the Jade

Fountain, where they were to stay, was laid out with long slabs of granite, and the springless carts rumbled along noisily and uncomfortably. The drivers often veered to the path by the side, which was much softer, and with thick cotton padded rugs on which Wen-ching and Golden Orchid could alternately sit and lie down, they arrived at their destination five hours later without overtiring themselves.

During all that time Golden Orchid could not help comparing the outing to a similar one she had had with the very young man whose tomb she was now visiting — with her husband. What irony! No two worlds could be more different. Then she was riding to Potsdam in an impressive horse-drawn carriage, beautifully dressed as the 'wife' of the Chinese ambassador and the cynosure of Berlin's admiring crowd. By her side was the young, handsome military attaché whose heart melted in adoration of her youth, her beauty and her intelligence. Today she had come to pay her last respects to him, in a slow-moving cart, some ten thousand miles away from where they had been together less than a year before.

On her arrival Golden Orchid lay down on an enormous, warmly heated *kang*, one of those contraptions with which Yung-kai had grown familiar in his travels across the deserts of Mongolia. She slept and felt better when the time came for dinner.

It was one of the happiest, most intimate little dinners that Wen-ching and Golden Orchid had ever had. After the fever and turbulence of three years, which reached the height of their intensity during the days of the Grand Council meeting, their minds were now completely at rest. They were also away from the city, away from the undercurrents which beset the official life of an ancient metropolis. Here in the memorial hall of Lord Yu Kung's family burial-ground, almost within a stone's throw of a venerable temple in whose numerous courtyards were massive trees planted in the Tang Dynasty over a thousand years before, there was the utmost peace and tranquillity. Not a sound could be heard except the music of the pines and the occasional clear notes of the temple bell. The very air they breathed, so still and clean, produced a mood of serenity which Wen-ching found to be purifying.

This is what I have always longed for, and this is what I shall have in Soochow, he said to himself, with immense satisfaction.

Golden Orchid prepared for bed, while Wen-ching talked.

'While you were sleeping,' he said, 'I went to the temple and met the abbot.'

'What sort of person is he?'

'You will see him tomorrow. Quite an ascetic, I think, and so different from the usual run of abbots. His face has deep spiritual qualities. I am sure you will like him.'

'I hope the first thing we shall do tomorrow is to visit the tomb of Yung-kai,' said Golden Orchid.

'We shall, my precious. But, oh! this life in the neighbourhood of an old temple is so wonderful. How I'd love to have it for the rest of my life. It isn't the same as the churches in Europe.'

'But you must admit they are beautiful in their own way.'

'Of course they are. All the same, the Christian churches and Buddhist temples start from such different premises. Their churches are planted in the market-place, while our temples retreat into the bosom of the mountains. Their church has evolved its elaborate rituals and ceremonies and all its delicate yet sublime architecture as if anxious to attract people within its portals. But the moment they leave, they are back to where they were — in the market-place and the values which it stands for. Not so the Buddhist temples. Rather than going to the people, they leave it to the people to come to them. And people rarely make such an effort unless they really yearn for the sustenance which the temples can give. The temples need not have recourse to any ritual to draw the people within their walls. All they offer is peace and quiet surroundings.'

Wen-ching moved to another subject.

'You know, I was thinking,' he continued, 'the only problem now — when we go back to Soochow, that is — is how to adjust the relationship between you and Quiet Virtue. We shall all have to live together. I presume there will not be much difficulty, will there?'

'No, I don't think so. She has treated me well, and I don't see why she shouldn't continue to do so. But then, of course, we have so far spent so little time under the same roof.'

'She is, after all, a mature woman — so full of understanding. She has her own interests and preoccupations, and I know that you on your part have tact and intelligence.'

'You know, Wen-ching dear, I have great admiration for Madam Wen-ching. But may I say something about her?'

'Of course.'

'But promise that you won't scold me, even if I am too frank. Although she treats me well, I don't feel that I can approach her — that is, emotionally. I can admire her, but I don't feel that I can be warm towards her. Are you going to scold me for saying this?'

'Why should I?' And Wen-ching smiled. 'But let's talk about something else. In that lunch with Lord Yu Kung you brought up the subject of another period of ambassadorship abroad. You shouldn't have done that, my treasure. Frankly I was a little nervous.'

'I noticed it. But why? Why should you be nervous about it? After all, the Government has done you an injustice. True it has now been corrected, but the only way the Government can truly clear your name is to reinstate you in the diplomatic service.'

'I didn't know that three years of residence abroad had so completely westernized your mind.'

'But this is a simple case of common sense, isn't it? The Grand Council has now declared you to be completely innocent. Isn't it fair then to say that the Government admits it is in the wrong and that, therefore, it should make good what it has taken from you — your name, your reputation, and your position? Is that "western"?'

'Yes, but —'

'Do you mean to imply that we call ourselves a nation with a culture and civilization of four thousand years and yet do not possess the most elementary feelings of justice and ordinary decency?'

Golden Orchid was quite agitated about the matter, and that placed Wen-ching in an uneasy situation. Although he had not been in official life long, he knew its pulse; but Golden Orchid wouldn't understand it because it was not something that he could explain or make clear on purely rational grounds. What she said might be correct, but he knew that the Government would not think of doing what she was convinced it should do.

'I tell you, my precious one, matters are not as simple as you think.' This remark, which was no explanation, irritated Golden Orchid more than ever.

But Wen-ching continued: 'The fact that the plot has failed is in itself a great moral triumph for me. I am satisfied. If we are given another diplomatic post, there are likely to be more troubles and more plots, and at my age I do not consider it worth while to invite further troubles if I can avoid them and live a peaceful life among my books and do the things that I want.'

Golden Orchid made no comment. Wen-ching continued: 'If our official life were run on rational lines, as you think it should be, all I can say is that we would not be where we are today. This official life is like an uncharted sea full of reefs and shoals, and it takes a sailor of infinite skill and patience to avoid hitting any of them. I should know my destiny by now, and I must confess that I do not possess the skill. I should know now where my strength is and where my weakness. No, no, I lack the ability to be a skilful sailor. So why not avoid that rough sea altogether and sail in a stretch of water where I know all is calm and tranquil?'

'I am not convinced.'

'No, precious one, I have decided to give up those so-called honours, high position and all worldly aspirations. Let others have them if they can. I am content to follow the advice of that old philosopher Lao-tse.'

'But I thought you were a follower of Confucius,' Golden Orchid retorted.

Wen-ching smiled because he felt that in a sense he was caught. 'But, you see, I can be both at the same time. Don't be misguided by the foreign idea that if you are one thing, you cannot be another; that if you are a Protestant, you cannot be a Catholic, or vice versa. We are much more flexible.'

'Flexible! What do you mean? Yes, too flexible!'

'But, anyway, I was going to tell you what Lao-tse once said: "Conduct your triumph as a funeral." This is precisely what I am going to do. He also said: "The way to do is to be." "The more he yields, the more they yield to him." Don't you think these are very wise sayings?'

'I don't understand them.'

'Lao-tse also said: "I am satisfied there is nothing to be done but to make the best of what cannot be helped, to act with reason oneself and with a good conscience." I think these are all full of wisdom, and I mean to follow them.'

'I think you are giving in too easily.'

'Confucius would give me the same advice, for didn't he say: "When a country is ruled by reason and justice, you can become an official. When it is not so ruled, the only thing is to retire"?'

Wen-ching felt that the talk was becoming too abstract for Golden Orchid and he recited to himself softly some of his favourite passages from the classics.

'What is it that you are reciting to yourself?' Golden Orchid wanted to know.

Wen-ching smiled again, and then said, 'Why, from the Confucian classics, of course. You are too young, my treasure, to know the meaning of all this. But since you have asked, I'll tell you. Now, listen to this: "One must learn how to limit oneself. With limitation comes equanimity. With equanimity comes serenity. With serenity comes peace of soul. With peace of soul the mind is able to deliberate. With deliberation comes accomplishment and fulfilment." All this is from Confucius. Is it any wonder we say that these sages of antiquity are infinitely wise? They seem to know every page of the book of life.'

'But I'll wager they don't know the scoundrels of this modern age.'

'They do, my precious. They understand the human heart so thoroughly and so well. There is really no short cut to spiritual fulfillment. It implies rigid discipline, and that in turn involves a series of mental conditionings. One thing leads to another until you reach genuine enlightenment. And the beginning is a very modest one — know how to limit oneself, not how to expand! Tomorrow we shall see the temple and its surroundings. But you are tired, my precious one, and we should be in bed.'

It was on the spacious *kang* that they slept, hard and almost unfriendly, but the warmth deep within it, the warmth of the cotton-padded blankets, and above all the warmth of Golden Orchid's young flesh, surrounded though they were by the still and chilly air of the wintry hills, melted them into one pulse of supreme joy and delight.

14

THE next morning found Wen-ching in a wonderfully happy mood. For a long time he had not had such restful and joyous sleep. The wisdom of Lao-tse and Confucius, of Confucius and Lao-tse, merged and twirled in his mind until, scholar though he was, he could not tell which was which.

'If one never assumes importance, one never loses it.' The sound of these words still rang in his ears in the morning. But how true! How true! Why then seek importance when, having it, one runs the risk of losing it and then becomes unhappy?

Wen-ching sought the company of the abbot while Golden Orchid got up, washed her face and then returned to the *kang* for a few moments longer. She was radiantly beautiful. It was remarkable to see how, after her cares and worries had been dissolved and washed away, she quickly rallied to her earlier vigour and recaptured the delicate beauty which had always been hers. After all, she was only twenty-one. And this morning, after a good night's rest, her skin had a peculiarly translucent quality. Its texture was fine and delicate; its firmness such that one could almost see her youthful vitality surging under the surface, and that surface, so smooth and white and satin-like, was moist with a thin layer of dew which made the face look soft and gentle.

When Wen-ching came back with the abbot, Golden Orchid was ready to visit Yung-kai's tomb. It had only recently been completed, and it looked new and fresh. As yet it had no tombstone describing the brief career of the young man. Some hundred yards away from the memorial hall where they spent the night, the tomb was one among many belonging to Lord Yu Kung's family, and near to that of Yung-kai's mother. The tombs were all on the slope of a knoll which was covered with a canopy of magnificent trees, mostly cedars and white pines. The whole concave arrangement faced the south so that it was always bathed in a flood of sunshine.

Golden Orchid stood on the knoll and could see vast stretches of farmland for miles around. It was obvious that this was no haphazard or accidental arrangement. It was, in fact, planned by a master mind with a profound knowledge of *feng-shui*, of 'wind and water'. The art of *feng-shui*, now a victim, like many other ancient practices, of modern science, sounds like pure superstition; but behind it there was an effort to maintain a balance with the forces of nature — an effort to be in unison with its vital energy so that human creations, be they tombs, houses or residences, could be in harmony with their surroundings or in keeping with their inner rhythm, and thus ensure the welfare and prosperity of the

K

generations to come. The belief was that absence of this harmony could well mean disaster and misfortune for members of the family.

The two servants who accompanied Wen-ching and Golden Orchid had by now lighted two white candles (white being the colour of mourning in China) and the incense in front of Yung-kai's tomb. Behind these they had placed a bowl of rice, four bowls of other food, and some fruit. The abbot began chanting some of the Buddhist sutras — on mercy, compassion, salvation and deliverance — one of which was familiar even to Golden Orchid and plainly audible:

> Calmly triumphed o'er the pain of death
> Even as a bright flame dies away;
> So was his last deliverance.

For a brief moment Wen-ching and Golden Orchid knelt in front of the grave, each with a different train of thought in mind. When they got up, Golden Orchid lowered her head, took out her handkerchief and wiped away the tears. The ceremony was simple and it was over in a few brief moments.

Upon retiring to their own private room, Wen-ching asked Golden Orchid to stroll with him in the spacious grounds of the temple, but she preferred to remain behind — alone.

'Tomorrow we shall be going back to Peking,' said Wen-ching, trying to persuade her, 'and I should like you to see the glorious cedars and pines and the stately ginkgos with their golden leaves for which this temple is famous.'

'I am a little tired,' replied Golden Orchid. 'I'd rather that you leave me behind so that I may have some rest before we leave tomorrow.'

'You may have your way, but there are beautiful things to see which are better than anything you have seen in Europe. There is poetry and romance in these carefully arranged gardens which cannot be seen in any other temple. There are moon gates, gourd-shaped gates and others of varying shapes and forms through which one is always presented with a new and fresh view of beauty. There are little semi-circular bridges with white marble balustrades over little streams of water in which are stocked fishes of all sizes and colours. Are you sure that none of these things appeals to you?'

'Well, if that is what you wish. But I am tired and feel like resting before that hard, bumpy and uneven journey back to the city.'

What Wen-ching had in mind was that when they returned to Soochow their time would be increasingly spent among the surroundings of nature, and going over the temple grounds would be an effective introduction, he thought, to a life of quiet meditation and peace. Little did he know that his beloved concubine was far more deeply touched by the little ceremony at the tomb than he could ever be and sharing the delight of seeing the temple with Wen-ching was not among her present thoughts.

So Wen-ching withdrew his persuasion and, thinking that the air outside was a little chilly, he felt it was best after all to leave Golden Orchid alone. He put on a thickly padded cotton gown and joined the abbot outside.

Golden Orchid lay quietly on the *kang*, but her mind was busy with memories of Yung-kai — of his little flirtations with her in Peking before she went abroad, of his ride with her to Potsdam and Sans Souci and of all the happy and passionate experiences with him in Berlin. She got up and, as if in a trance, she slowly walked back to the tomb she had visited only a short time ago. The candles were out, the incense was reduced to ashes and the food was covered with dust. She was alone, and she knelt again within the curvature of the knoll just behind Yung-kai's tomb and wept as she communed with the spirit of her departed lover. How long she stayed there she did not know, but when she stood up, her feet were numb. She limped back to her room before Wen-ching and the abbot returned.

Early the next morning they were on their way back to Peking. Three days later Ping-mo arrived. The joy of reunion between father and son for the first time after the thick cloud had been lifted was deep and intense.

Wen-ching felt a lump in his throat, as his austere Confucian training did not allow him to express his joy openly — even to his son. 'How is your mother?' was all that he could say.

'She is very happy, Father,' replied Ping-mo, 'and she is very anxious to have you back as soon as possible. I need not tell you that she has been to the tombs of our ancestors to tell them the good news.'

'Yes, they have indeed given us protection, and I, too, must hasten back to give them my thanks and to ask them always to shower their blessings on us. The world is full of wickedness and malice — I mean at least the official world — but even so we must tread the path of correctness, and then there is nothing we need be afraid of.'

Ping-mo made no comment. He merely looked at the face of his father. It was a good and kindly face. But there were signs of weariness. It almost looked as if it had been seared; but given a prolonged rest and care there was no reason, Ping-mo thought, why his father should not be his normal self again. All the same, he felt deeply hurt that his father had been so very much abused. He thought over Wen-ching's last remark. It was all very well to talk about being correct or to repay evil with good, but in hard, practical life, young as he was, he firmly believed that evil must sometimes be uprooted with violence. He had dedicated his life to revolutionary work, and the bitter experiences of his father's official career made him even more eager and determined to continue that work.

'Father,' said Ping-mo as he sipped a little of the tea which Golden Orchid had brought in, 'I was thinking that in going back to Soochow it would be more restful for you if we hire a houseboat to go through the Grand Canal than to travel on one of the foreign steamers.'

'Won't the voyage in that case be much longer than is necessary?' objected Wen-ching. 'What do you think, my precious?' he asked Golden Orchid.

'I, too, prefer being on the steamer,' replied Golden Orchid. 'But I suppose Ping-mo must have good reasons for making his suggestion.'

'Well, I was thinking that we could keep together on a houseboat without being disturbed by others, and then also at this time of the year the sea can be rough, which would not be agreeable. It was rough when I came. As Father said, the way I propose will take much longer. But it is certainly much more comfortable.'

The suggestion suddenly sounded sensible to Wen-ching. Ping-mo's motive was a purely patriotic one. The steamers plying along the Chinese coast were all foreign, which to Ping-mo was an infringement of his country's sovereign rights, and he didn't think that any self-respecting Chinese should travel in them. But there was something even worse which he openly expressed to Golden Orchid when they were alone.

'Look, Auntie,' said Ping-mo, for that was the way he was supposed to address his father's concubine, ridiculous as it might sound, as he was actually two years older, 'how can you ever think of travelling under such humiliating conditions on a foreign steamer?'

'What do you mean by humiliating?' Golden Orchid wanted to know.

'Well, don't you see that the foreigners treat us Chinese even in our own country no better than animals?'

Golden Orchid was bewildered. She had been abroad for three years while Ping-mo had never left Chinese soil, and in all those years she had been admired wherever she went, dined with the most distinguished foreigners, and been given the most complimentary attention. What could Ping-mo possibly mean?

'Look, Auntie,' he continued, 'I know more than you think. Do you remember coming up to Peking on one of those steamers before you left for Europe?'

'Yes, but what was so bad about it?'

'Bad! Can you imagine anything worse? You travelled in what is known as the mandarin class. What an ironic description! Do you remember how uncomfortable, how dirty your stateroom was?'

'It was the best we could get.'

'Exactly. But there is another class reserved exclusively for the foreign passengers — clean, comfortable, with large staterooms and a lot of service. No Chinese of whatever class, even though he is willing to pay for it, is ever given that accommodation.'

'I don't believe a word of what you say. We had that kind of accommodation on the steamer all the way from Europe to Shanghai.'

'But not on any of those steamers sailing in China's own waters! If you don't believe me, try to find out. You don't even know that the parks in Shanghai and the race course, made out of land which was robbed from our poor peasants, do no allow any Chinese to go in — except the servants who are employed to keep them clean.'

'That cannot be,' maintained Golden Orchid, rather stunned by all this fresh information. So she concluded, 'All right, if you insist, then let us do as you suggest and return by houseboat.'

At this Ping-mo was happy and his face broadened in a smile. 'Well, then, we shall start in two or three days. We shall take the train to Tientsin, and from there we shall be in a spacious and comfortable houseboat which I shall set about hiring at once. You will never regret it — of that I can assure you.'

Golden Orchid gladly gave in. She thought she knew her mind and what she wanted, and yet, without knowing why, she yielded to Ping-mo, for all his prejudices and irrational ideas. She tried to recall the first time she met him, perhaps some three and a half years ago, when she was being carried in a sedan chair on her way to the flower-boats where Wen-ching was relaxing and enjoying the cool breezes of the lake with his friends. He was then a shy young man. She had seen something of him again before going to Europe. Then came a long separation. What happened to him during those intervening years when she was away in Berlin? All she heard was that he was studying, studying hard for the civil-service examinations. Then, upon her return from abroad, they lived under the same roof; but that was only for a short time, and the burden of the anxieties resulting from Wen-ching's misfortunes was so heavy that she scarcely had any chance of knowing Ping-mo. Now for the first time it dawned upon her that she was dealing with a young man who seemed to have very definite views on everything. That intrigued her. She was glad that the journey would allow her to know him better.

Wen-ching called on Lord Yu Kung and said goodbye to him, the only person in fact whom he felt it his duty to see. He was surprised to find that there were actually many people waiting to bid him farewell as the train pulled out from the station. No less a person than Hu-mou himself was among the crowd.

What a cunning little fellow, Wen-ching said to himself. Can I ever get rid of him? And then he hastened to beckon his son Ping-mo to catch a glimpse of the little man who had been the source of all his woes and sorrows. For a brief moment Ping-mo's eyes met those of Hu-mou. It was a cold and frigid encounter. Ping-mo remained silent, but the image of Hu-mou's vicious face stayed in his mind long after the train started moving.

15

THE houseboat was as comfortable as one could imagine. There was nothing that either Wen-ching or Golden Orchid could find fault with. It was almost brand-new, and Ping-mo had obtained it with no difficulty at all. He merely let fellow members of his secret society know that he was in need of such a conveyance. It was relayed to Tientsin, where he found the boat ready for his use. News was also sent to all the towns and villages along the canal so that they might give some help when it was needed. The boat was provided with servants, and Wen-ching enjoyed the meals with a relish, among peaceful surroundings impossible in a foreign steamer. There was no noise of the engines, no nauseating smell of the smoke, which was a sure stimulus to sea-sickness.

Smoothly and quietly the boat glided on from one village to another. Wen-ching was perfectly happy, the only drawback being, he thought, the slowness, as he was anxious to be back home.

The boat was about thirty-five feet long. Its greatest width was about twelve feet. The middle portion constituted a unit by itself undisturbed by the boatmen, who occupied the extremities which were connected by two gangways over a foot wide running the entire length of the boat on either side. The middle portion was divided into three compartments, with two bedrooms at each end and a spacious room in between where meals were served and where the three members of the Shen family could relax after the table was cleared. The chairs and couches were a bit stiff, but still they were comfortable. Though they were no more than mats, the beds were so well padded with layers of cotton that it was a delight to lie on them. These mats proved to be more comfortable than the bed which Wen-ching and Golden Orchid had had at the Soochow hostel.

As they slowly proceeded towards the south, the weather became increasingly warm, and both Golden Orchid and Ping-mo were glad that Wen-ching was getting all the rest he needed. Father and son had much to talk about — conditions at home during the three long years while Wen-ching was abroad and Wen-ching's own hectic experiences as a diplomat. The reminiscences were, of course, very unhappy, but even so, Wen-ching had a sense of well-being on the houseboat which was most satisfying. His worries had been left behind, and his time was now being spent, hourly, in the company of two people dear to him. With what he had gone through in Berlin and the devotion of Faustmann and Anna, it was inevitable that Wen-ching had good words to say about the foreigners — the 'ocean people' — and that was perplexing to his son.

'Why is it, Father,' asked Ping-mo one day, 'that these people are as good as you say and yet behave so atrociously when they are in China? They are cruel and aggressive. If only they would realize that they are the guests and we the hosts, all would be well. But they don't behave like guests. They bully us, they kick the poor people around, and they make us feel as if we, not they, were the intruders.'

Wen-ching had heard such things before, but, as was the case with Golden Orchid, they were unreal to him because he had not personally experienced them. They were, anyhow, unpleasant subjects, and Wen-ching would allow nothing unpleasant to disturb him on so pleasant a voyage. Occasionally, therefore, he talked about his own plans, about what he would do in the years ahead, but he often restrained himself, thinking that those matters had better be discussed with Quiet Virtue. Although the weather was getting warmer every day, it could be chilly during the night when the boat was tied to the shore. Wen-ching's principal amusement was playing chess between long period of reading, reclining on a mat with pillows piled high behind his back.

The circumstances were ideal for Golden Orchid and Ping-mo also. They could really come to know and understand each other. After all, from now on they would be living under the same roof for no one knew how long, and each was anxious to know the temperament, the likes and dislikes of the other. While the meals throughout the voyage were provided by the boatmen, Golden Orchid often volunteered to do a little cooking herself. When she went ashore to buy fresh food, it was both necessary and pleasant that Ping-mo accompany her. These little outings became increasingly frequent as the days wore on, and there grew up in time an intimacy between them which both heartily welcomed.

It was all very well to maintain the 'auntie' and 'young master' relationship during the early days of the voyage, but in time there was a strong urge in their hearts to overcome that barrier which was as artificial as it was irksome. One day, during the usual shopping, it unconsciously dissolved.

'Did you hear what those villagers said?' remarked Ping-mo.

'No. What did they say?'

'They were all saying how pretty you look. I don't blame them for saying so; it is true.'

Golden Orchid was silent, but she looked at Ping-mo with her large eyes, the right corner of her dainty little mouth curling slightly, and continued her shopping.

A moment later Ping-mo again remarked: 'Do you know, Golden Orchid, it is becoming quite embarrassing?' It was indeed embarrassing, for the words had unknowingly slipped out of his mouth. Till now she had been to him always 'auntie', but all of a sudden this wide social gap had been bridged.

Ping-mo looked wistfully into Golden Orchid's eyes and said: 'What have I done? You will forgive me, won't you?'

'What is there to forgive, Ping-mo?' Golden Orchid stressed his name clearly and firmly, as much as to say: 'You should have so addressed me long ago, and I am glad that you have done it at last.'

A long silence ensued, during which they held each other's hands. Then Ping-mo picked up the thread of what he had started to say. 'I was going to say that it is becoming embarrassing because I have heard a number of remarks among these villagers.'

'I, too, have heard them,' Golden Orchid said, smiling.

'Have you noticed how they keep looking at us?'

'What if they do? We are strangers here, and perhaps they are just curious.'

'Yes . . . but there are other reasons. I just heard one woman say, "Ay, isn't she a fine-looking young wife?" Your beauty, your dress, your carriage and the softness of your speech have all impressed these country people and they regard you as superior to any woman they have ever seen. But there is another remark I heard which I shall keep to myself.'

'What is it, Ping-mo? Tell me.'

'You won't be angry if I tell you?'

'Why should I? You will only be telling me what you have heard.'

'Well, one man remarked that I am a fortunate young husband to have so beautiful a woman for a wife.'

'Blind talk! I don't believe it. You made it up yourself.' And she looked at him as if reproachfully. 'How can you say such a thing?' she continued, when down in her heart she was glad that Ping-mo had said it.

From that moment onward their relationship was no longer the same. Ping-mo had to be careful, of course, of what he did or said in the presence of Wen-ching, but he knew that a new attachment had grown within him for Golden Orchid.

He began to reappraise the situation. If they had returned on the foreign steamer, this new situation would not have arisen. But it was his own choosing to travel slowly on the canal. He was glad that he had his way, but he realized also that these new developments were disturbing and uncomfortable. There might even be complications. And so he decided that from then on he must keep a safe distance from Golden Orchid and try to talk strictly about impersonal affairs, about things that had nothing to do with their own lives. But supposing she wants to be personal, what then? Ping-mo asked himself.

The next evening Golden Orchid did not feel she wanted to confine herself to Wen-ching and found her way across the middle compartment to seek out Ping-mo. She wanted to talk — just talk — and so the two of them sat out in the open behind Ping-mo's compartment as the moon, still in the shape of a delicate curve, rose slowly from the east.

'Tell me, tell me, Ping-mo,' Golden Orchid began, 'what have you been doing these years while your father and I were away in Europe?'

Ping-mo tried to be formal and stiff. 'Well, nothing. I have been studying, as everyone knows, and preparing for the civil-service examination.'

'But what else?'

'What makes you think there is something else?'

'Well, I feel that you are quite a different person from the one I first knew.'

'But, naturally. I have added more than three years to my life.'

'That is understood.'

'Anybody can change in even less time than that.'

'No, I don't mean that,' replied Golden Orchid. 'You seem to have become so positive, so sure of yourself, and that does not come from being immersed in books. I feel that you have acquired experience. That does not come from books either, but from having come into contact with people, from doing things instead of merely acquiring book knowledge. I may be young, but I think I know more than you believe. You can't fool me, and I am awfully curious.'

What Golden Orchid was trying to do was to make Ping-mo confess, among other things, his experiences with girls. A young man of twenty-three from a distinguished family — why, it was time he got married, and a number of matches must have been proposed.

'To tell you the truth,' replied Ping-mo, 'Mother wanted me to get married last year, but I was not interested. There is something more important on my mind than marriage.'

'Ah, that sounds interesting. Tell me what it is.'

'Oh, I have been doing some travelling, here and there.'

'Why were you travelling?'

The persistence with which Golden Orchid asked these questions was so devastating that at last Ping-mo began to give way. So finally he said: 'If I tell you, will you swear that you will keep it entirely to yourself, that you will not let Father know?'

'I'll swear to anything you wish.'

'Well, you see, Golden Orchid, what I said about not travelling on a foreign steamer should give you some indication of what goes on in my mind — Oh, it's no use. You won't understand.'

'Why do you think I won't understand?'

'Can't you see that our country is terribly weak, and if we are not careful it may completely disappear.'

'Disappear? What do you mean?'

'I thought you wouldn't understand. I don't mean that the country can actually vanish. But the country can be cut up by the foreign devils as they have been trying to do all these years. They can divide us up and control us separately as they have done in Africa, and then China will disappear as a country. Now do you understand? It is our duty to prevent that from happening. The Government is powerless. It is full of incompetent officials who care only for their own selfish interests and are not the least worried about what goes on in the country.'

'But what can you do about it? I think you are right. Your father's own case bears out your statement.'

'Now, if you promise to keep silent, I'll tell you what is being done.'

'I give you my word. I have given it already, haven't I?'

'There is a society in the country consisting of young men like myself who feel that the present Government should be overthrown, and then we shall set up a new Government which will consist of modern, enlightened and patriotic people who will know exactly what to do with these foreign devils.'

'But isn't that a very dangerous thing to do? When the Government finds out, won't all your heads be chopped off?'

'You are right. That is why we must be very careful. The secret society has many members all over the country, and we have been doing very well indeed.'

'Do you mean to say that you are a member?'

'Yes, Golden Orchid, but do not let drop a word of it in front of anybody. There is something else I want to tell you. There is a separate organization called the Boxers who are bent upon driving out the foreigners. To a certain extent our aims are similar, but there is a vast difference between us. These Boxers are, after all, ignorant people, and no one is sure what they may do. All they have is burning patriotism and a deep hatred of the foreigner. They feel that the foreigner has cruelly maltreated them. What we try to do is to keep an eye on them so that their patriotism will not be misdirected.'

'You have my full sympathy if what you tell me is all true. But still I feel you are doing something very dangerous.'

'But, Golden Orchid, it is getting late. You'd better go back to your own compartment. Besides, I have already said too much. But you will keep everything to yourself? Tomorrow I shall begin to show you a few things in the villages to explain what I've been telling you.'

Ping-mo was glad that at any rate they had talked about something not strictly personal, something to interpose between himself and Golden Orchid. But he wondered if it had been wise to reveal so much of his work to her.

16

THE voyage on the Grand Canal had now taken the party into the heart of Shantung, the most sacred province of all China. It is the province which has given birth to some of the greatest thinkers and sages in Chinese history, including Confucius and Mencius. It is the part of China which the Kaiser had coveted. To travel through it slowly, as Wen-ching was now doing, was therefore a deep emotional experience. But fate decreed that in the early part of 1899 the wisest province of China was to become its most stupid province. It had become a centre of passion, violence and utter ignorance. For the good peasants had been led to believe in the Boxer movement.

Ping-mo and Golden Orchid now found themselves in the midst of these Shantung peasants. They felt as if they were strangers from a foreign land. They were from the south, whither they were returning, where nature is much kinder and life has more to offer in the matter of food, clothing and shelter. The people are gentle in their manners, unlike the Shantung people, who are much more sturdily built and appear also more combative. But the secret society to which Ping-mo belonged had members from the north and the south alike, and in spite of the many local differences, he felt that he understood the problems of the Shantung people as if they were his own. So the next day, when his father was having his usual nap after lunch, he persuaded the boatmen to stop at a near-by village and took Golden Orchid ashore on another of their shopping expeditions.

'I promised yesterday to tell you some of the things I am doing,' began Ping-mo. 'I shall keep my promise and show you something you have not seen before.'

So saying, Ping-mo took Golden Orchid by the hand and went through the crooked streets of the village. They were dirty and uneven. The weather being cold, the villagers were clothed in their cotton-padded garments. The dialect was unfamiliar to Golden Orchid, but by listening carefully she could make out most of it. She had, after all, lived in Peking, though not for long, and she found that there was great similarity between the Shantung dialect and that spoken in Peking.

Ping-mo stopped at last in front of a mud hut and took Golden Orchid inside.

The smell which invaded her nostrils was thick and stifling beyond measure. It was not an unfamiliar smell, but it was unusually concentrated. Ping-mo opened another door, and Golden Orchid saw the most shocking and pitiable sight that she had ever set eyes on. In two small rooms were assembled some twenty men and women engaged in opium-smoking. The rooms reeked with the thick smoke. It was a nauseating smell, and Golden Orchid was surprised to find that, in spite of the cold weather, most of the inmates wore very little. Some were in reclining positions, with one leg resting on the other; others lay on the bare earth; but they were all busy with their opium pipes, furiously smoking and completely oblivious or unmindful of what was going on around them. No one bothered to look at either Ping-mo or Golden Orchid. The few who were not smoking were playing dice.

'Look, Golden Orchid, look at these people, how degraded they are. Once they all belonged to good and perhaps well-to-do families, but now they have become outcasts.'

'But how . . . how did they become like this?'

'Their families don't want them any more. Some might go back if they got rid of this evil habit, but how can they once they have contracted it?'

'I have heard that there are places where one can get rid of it.'

'That is not true, Golden Orchid. For a time one may get rid of it. But after a while one feels uncomfortable all over the body, and sooner or later goes back to it. The habit kills everything. First a person loses his ambition, then his will power, and finally his sense of shame. He refuses to do any work. He doesn't care about anything, about how he looks or what he does. He is no longer a moral being. Father, mother, wife, children — they no longer mean anything to him. He hankers after the black stuff and converts anything he can lay his hands on into money so that he may buy it and continue to smoke.'

'Well, I know all this. But why do you want to show me so ugly a sight?'

'You may know some of it, but I am sure you don't know the whole story. You don't know, for instance, that this curse has invaded the entire country. I want you to stay a little longer, for there is something else you don't know. Look at that pile of tickets by the side of the man in that thin dirty rag of a shirt. Do you know what they are?'

'Of course I do. They look like pawn tickets.'

'Precisely. That man has sold all the worldly goods he ever possessed until he has nothing more to sell, and now he sells those tickets. Look at these people! Every one is a living corpse. Soon they will be placed in six thin slabs of wood and buried in the neighbourhood. Not even the dogs would go near them, for there is nothing on their skimpy bodies that the dogs can feed upon — and the dogs don't like the smell of opium either.'

'Ping-mo,' protested Golden Orchid, 'I still don't see why you should show me this disgusting sight, even if I don't know all the evils of opium smoking. I thought you were going to show me something pleasant. Let me leave this place.'

Golden Orchid was angry — angry at the strange and unusual way in which Ping-mo was behaving. She liked him and had looked forward to this long voyage not only for rest and relaxation but also for the chance of a deeper intimacy with him. But he struck her as being something of an eccentric. On their way back to the boat, Golden Orchid was depressed and silent.

'I know you are angry, Golden Orchid,' said Ping-mo, 'but there are reasons for what I have done. Didn't you ask me yesterday what I have been doing all these years? Well, just that!'

'What do you mean? You have a wry sense of humour.'

'No, I am serious. I am not trying to be humorous at all. I am in earnest, and I want you to share that earnestness with me.'

'Can't you explain it to me then? And must you show me all this dirt and squalor and human depravity as if it was necessary for me to see it? Look at my shoes and my dress — going through all these crooked, uneven, dust-laden alleys and streets.'

'I am sorry. But let's find a village teashop where we can rest for a short while before we buy the food and go back to the boat. Or perhaps it's best that we buy what we want first and then have some tea.'

Ping-mo was quick and certain of what he wanted. He bought some pork, a live fish and some vegetables in addition to the usual soy sauce, bean oil and ginger. He then sat down with Golden Orchid at a teashop and started to unburden himself of what he had long wanted to say to her.

'Do you think I was silly in showing you that den of opium addicts? I have my reasons, Golden Orchid, if you will forgive me. What you have seen is true not only of that village but of the entire province and of the entire country. Millions and millions of our country people have contracted that deadly habit.'

'So much the worse for them. Couldn't they have avoided it? They have only themselves to blame.'

'That is where you are wrong. The opium habit has been forced upon the poor people.'

'Am I to believe what you say? Why is it not forced upon me or you or other people?'

'Do you really wish to know who forced opium upon the people?'

'Who?'

'Again you will not believe me, but I am telling you the truth all the same. Yes, the foreigners. It is these foreigners who want to weaken and wreck our people and get our riches.'

'You take me for a child.'

'Unbelievable, isn't it? But that is the honest truth.'

To Golden Orchid these words were indeed unbelievable. 'I knew you would tell me that, but, as you said, I don't believe you. I know better. I have lived among the foreigners, and I think they are fine people. In fact, in many respects they are better than our own people.'

'Never speak like that to anybody here. This province is full of Boxers, and they will kill you the moment they know that you care for the foreign devils. This province of Shantung is under the rule of Governor Yu, and he has decided to drive every foreign devil out of China. I don't agree with his method, but I do say that the foreigners have done us a great wrong.'

'I can't believe that you are right. After all the troubles your father has gone through and the sympathy and assistance we obtained from a man like Faustmann and his wife Anna, it is difficult to make me hate the foreigner.'

'But you don't understand. The foreigners in their own lands may be good people, but for some reason they all become bad when they come to our country. How I wish I could make you understand! I have been told that the moment they reach the Suez Canal they leave behind all their moral considerations. Exactly! In one hand the foreigner holds the Bible, and in the other opium. That is what he has been doing all along. He talks about salvation at the same time as he destroys our bodies and souls with this vicious drug. How can the gospel of the love of God come from any land which sends us opium? You must believe me. The foreigners treat us like savages when actually our ethical standards are higher than they could ever hope to reach. They *talk* about morality; we *practise* it.'

'Would you say then that the attempt to ruin your father is the way we practise morality? If you think you know what you are talking about, certainly you can't say that I don't — after having suffered so much with your father.'

'You are right in this. We have the problem of a corrupt and rotten Government which we must deal with. But I am speaking of a different issue. I have with me a statement from our own *tao-tai*, our own mayor of Soochow, and I shall read it to you.'

Golden Orchid did not want to listen, but Ping-mo insisted and took from his pocket a wrinkled sheet of paper which he began to read: ' "From ancient times to the present day there has never been such a stream of evil and misery as has come upon China with the curse of opium. From the time opium was first introduced until now, a period of over one hundred years, the number of deaths caused by it must amount to millions. Now, there are enlightened people in China who blame the Chinese for using opium, but they are equally clear in their minds that the real cause of the trouble is the avarice of the foreigners, their desire to make money out of the poor people, and we therefore look upon them with hatred." There you have in a nutshell the curse that has been visited upon us.'

'I am going back to the boat,' said Golden Orchid, walking away.

Ping-mo followed, but he continued to talk. 'Are you now convinced, Golden Orchid? That is why we hate the foreigners. They say that we, the Chinese, are by nature anti-foreign. What nonsense! Are we to love them and adore them, as you, Golden Orchid, seem to do, when they are doing everything to destroy our people, drain away our wealth and then send their guns and warships to take away our land?'

'All this may be true, but still I believe that we ourselves are to blame,' replied Golden Orchid.

'Why?'

'Why don't we establish a strong government, a government of upright, honest officials who would put a stop to this trade in opium? I tell you again that after what your father has gone through, I have learned a good many things.'

'There I agree with you, Golden Orchid, but I think you are stubborn about these foreigners. Supposing we were to go to them preaching all the good things that Confucius has taught us, and at the same time weaken their governments and spread poison among their peoples. Would we have a right to expect them to be friendly to us? We would be devils in their eyes. Isn't that true? Use a little imagination, Golden Orchid, and you will see my point of view.'

'What's the good of talking about these things? I am tired. I still have cooking to do. And in the meantime your father must be wondering what has become of us.'

'But now you do understand, I hope, what I have been doing all these years you have been away. I mean to continue my work.'

'All I can say is that you are looking for trouble not only for yourself but also for your father and for all of us.'

By the time Golden Orchid and Ping-mo got back to the houseboat, it was quite late. Wen-ching was awake. For the first time during the journey he looked old and worn out. The weather was chilly but not exactly cold, and Wen-ching was bundled up in thick clothing, playing Chinese solitaire with thirty-two cards and anxiously waiting for the return of the two young people.

'Where have you been, the two of you?'

'I am sorry, Father,' replied Ping-mo. 'It was all my fault. I thought that since we are sailing through the great province of Confucius, we should see something of it.'

'The boatmen are anxious to move on, as I am. We have been on the canal for twenty days, and we haven't gone very far. From now on I am going to ask the boatmen to get the things we need after dark when we stop, so that the two of you can stay with me and not go away shopping or sight-seeing.' As Wen-ching spoke, he seemed short of breath and did not look well.

'Are you all right?' Golden Orchid anxiously inquired.

'I think I am. But I do feel rather tired today. And yet I had a long sleep.'

Golden Orchid placed the palm of her soft little hand on his forehead and said: 'You seem to have a slight temperature. I'll see that you go to bed early today and tomorrow. I'll ask the boatmen to cover as much distance as possible every day so that in another twenty days we should be home in Soochow.' Golden Orchid gave Ping-mo a significant and somewhat reproachful look.

Never again did Golden Orchid and Ping-mo go ashore. But that night, as Golden Orchid slept under the same blanket with Wen-ching, it struck her all of a sudden that she was sleeping with a feverish old man. His temperature had gone up, he was warm all over his body and he complained of aching arms and legs. His sleep was sporadic, and through the night he groaned faintly as if he were on the verge of some real illness. Golden Orchid wiped away his perspiration and kept him well covered with the thick blankets. For her to sleep was out of the question, and, lying awake, she kept seeing the horrible sights which she had seen during the day and hearing the unpleasant remarks which Ping-mo had made.

When the day broke Wen-ching was much better. The fever seemed to have subsided, but he was still not his normal self. The next twenty days were a period of unbroken devotion and selfless service on the part of Golden Orchid, relieved now and then by what Ping-mo could offer. Ping-mo was also extremely worried. Fortunately the days were cheerful and full of sunshine, and as they continued towards the south, the very landscapes, with their smiling fields, gave joy to Wen-ching's heart.

But even so Wen-ching was a changed man, and his face showed signs of rapidly declining health. He looked pale, and yet at times his cheeks felt hot and flushed. He complained of general lassitude, but Golden Orchid took care of him as if she was a practised nurse. Later on there were indications of internal hæmorrhage, which frightened both Golden Orchid and Ping-mo. They decided not to let Wen-ching know about it.

'I shall be all right as soon as I am home again,' Wen-ching said to Golden Orchid.

She hoped and prayed that he would be well again — soon, completely — but deep in her heart she was weighed down by a heavy stone of sorrow. Occasionally she consulted Ping-mo, who tried to assure her that there was nothing to worry about. He spoke, of course, only to console her. He said he knew the best physician in Soochow, and that he would ask him to attend his father the moment they were home. He was sure that his father would be restored to health.

'There is then no point in consulting any physician on the way?' asked Golden Orchid. 'We could stop sailing if necessary.'

'I think it is better not to stop,' replied Ping-mo. 'The important thing is to cover as much distance as possible every day.'

Madam Wen-ching, her younger brother, her daughter-in-law and the little maid were all at the pier when Wen-ching and his party arrived. He was carried to a waiting sedan chair at once and put to bed. But then he was already very ill, though neither he nor Golden Orchid nor Ping-mo fully realized it.

But Wen-ching was happy, supremely happy that he was at long last at home with his wife. He started to tell her at once what had

happened at Peking, but Madam Wen-ching knew better and told
him that he had ample time to tell the story. He must now remain
quiet and rest.

'Now that you are home, Wen-ching,' she said, 'you must rest
and forget everything that has happened. Our friend, Mr King, the
physician, will come to see you.'

Ping-mo had gone to see the physician without anybody's knowing
it. Wen-ching in the meantime felt much better and insisted upon
talking to his wife.

'I would not have fought,' he said, 'as hard as I did if it had not
been for what you said, Yu. You are a wonderful wife. I owe you so
much.'

'You are kind, Wen-ching, but this is no time to speak of these
things.' Wen-ching took his wife's hand, and his tears began to
flow.

When the physician arrived, he felt Wen-ching's pulse, looked at
his tongue, and shook his head slightly. 'I am afraid it is a bad case
of typhoid. If the intestine is ruptured, there is danger. Let us hope
that it is not.' He advised that there should be complete rest.

Golden Orchid had a few words with the physician and described
the conditions of the patient during the voyage.

'I shall do the best I can.' Then the physician turned to Madam
Wen-ching and said: 'I am afraid it is too far gone.'

There was continual hæmorrhage for the next three days, and on
the morning of the fourth Wen-ching joined his ancestors in the other
world. He died at the age of fifty-one, broken in spirit but rejoicing
in the knowledge that he had completely regained his good name.
He had not lived as a man worldly-wise, but as a man of honour and
integrity. He died as one.

Book Four

MIDSUMMER MADNESS

IT was fourteen months later. The forsythias, known as the 'welcome spring' flowers, were just beginning to bloom. Golden Orchid had gone to stay with her mother soon after the death of her husband. Her grandmother had died before Golden Orchid returned from Europe. Her mother, busy as ever with her embroidery, had found living alone somewhat trying, even though the pock-marked Lily and her sister Yang Mah frequently visited her. Sometimes they brought their nephew Ah Zung, who continued to live with them, as he was afraid to go back to Shanghai. But now for over a year her daughter had been with her. It was a matter of necessity for Golden Orchid.

Seven days after Wen-ching died, Madam Wen-ching called Golden Orchid for a short talk. It was something which she too had fully wanted — and expected. For how could she and Madam Wen-ching live together under the same roof when the only bond between them — Wen-ching — was gone?

'Golden Orchid,' Madam Wen-ching said, 'it is sad that so soon after my husband's death I must ask for an understanding with you. But the seven days of our deepest mourning have passed. Golden Orchid, you are still a very young woman and you have a full life ahead of you. I wonder if I may hear what your plans are for the future.'

Golden Orchid was relieved that Madam Wen-ching came straight to the point, in so open, frank and rational a manner. It increased her admiration for her. But instead of making her own wishes known she thought that it would be a mark of courtesy to hear what Madam had to say.

'Tai-tai,' Golden Orchid said, although it would have been no breach of etiquette if she had addressed her as 'elder sister', 'Tai-tai, I will do whatever you think I should do.'

'I was thinking,' Madam Wen-ching continued, 'that I myself will be spending increasingly more time in the future on my painting and poetry. I still have a son to take care of until he gets married. As for you, don't you think it is best that you do whatever you like? I want to make a proposition which I hope you will agree to.'

'Yes, I am sure it will be a good one, and I shall be prepared to accept whatever you propose.'

'Wen-ching had you as a concubine all the years he was abroad. He was happy with you, but there is nothing now to bind you to the Shen family.'

'That I understand.'

'Then would you like to be on your own again? If you feel that my suggestion is difficult to carry out, you may stay with me as long as you wish. Only you may find life here irksome.'

The conversation had been conducted by Madam Wen-ching with diplomatic finesse — and consideration. Yet it was made quite clear to Golden Orchid that they should from now on live separately from each other.

'Tai-tai,' Golden Orchid replied, 'if you feel that it is right for me to go back to my mother, who needs my care, I shall go back to her after five of the seven-day periods * have passed. I shall continue to be in mourning for Wen-ching after I leave this house, and I shall take nothing away from here except what belongs to me personally.'

'That is well said, Golden Orchid,' Madam Wen-ching said, 'but I shall see to it that you are properly provided for even after you leave me, until . . . until perhaps you find another husband or become otherwise independent.'

'Thank you, thank you for being so considerate,' Golden Orchid replied.

'It is my intention to give you the sum of twenty thousand dollars.† We are not rich, as I am sure you realize by now, but I think that this amount I offer you will tide you over for a number of years. There is only one thing I request of you in return for this parting gift, and that is that whatever you do in the future to earn a living, you will use discretion and good judgement. Do nothing that will cast a shadow over the good name of Wen-ching. There is nothing which we treasure so much as a good name. You have treasured it yourself.'

What Madam Wen-ching hinted at was that Golden Orchid should not, at least for a year, go to the north, and that, on the pay-

---

* Each period of mourning consists of seven days, the first five such periods being of deep mourning.

† One U.S. dollar was then worth something like two and a half Chinese dollars.

ment of the separation money, she should not resume her life as a
sing-song girl. The two women parted as good friends. It was agreed
that the money was to be given to Golden Orchid by Madam Wen-
ching's brother as soon as matters in the Shen family had become
more settled. But months passed, and still the money was not delivered. Whether Madam Wen-ching actually gave the money to
her brother or whether the brother had used the money for his own
purposes without Madam Wen-ching's knowing it, there was no way
of telling. Fourteen months had now passed, and still there was no
money. Fortunately Golden Orchid did not feel any immediate
pressure, as she had some savings of her own. In any case she and
her mother could live, in a humble way, on the income from her
mother's embroidery.

But all the same, encouraged partly by her mother and partly by
her own desires, Golden Orchid felt she should call on Madam
Wen-ching to find out what had actually happened to the money.
Ping-mo came to see her often, and sometimes she felt she should
bring the matter up before him. But it was possible that Ping-mo
had no knowledge of what his mother had proposed. Out of pride
and personal honour she allowed the matter to drift while she made
her own plans.

'Mother,' Golden Orchid said one day, 'what would you think if
I went back to the north again? There is nothing to keep you here
either, and I want you to go to Peking with me — or perhaps to
Tientsin.'

'What do you want to do up there that you cannot do here, my
child?'

'I like Peking and I know people there. I am getting restless after
staying at home for so long. Frankly I was thinking of setting up a
sing-song house of my own. After all, I've got to make a living. That
money which Madam Wen-ching promised I shall never see. Hai-
ming is still up there. She is an able girl, and I think she can be very
helpful to me.'

The mother was not especially taken by the idea, for she thought
that in time another man might marry Golden Orchid as a concubine. In fact, she had discussed it with Lily and Yang Mah every
time the two sisters came to see her. But Golden Orchid seemed to
have made up her mind. She wanted to leave Soochow for another
reason. Ping-mo came to see her often. Much as she liked him, she

thought it would be improper if his frequent visits led to gossip which might very well spread to Madam Wen-ching's ears. It was best, therefore, to leave Soochow altogether.

Her mind made up, there was nothing to prevent Golden Orchid from leaving for the north. Her mother finally gave in, and they took with them Yang Mah.

But the real incentive which drove Golden Orchid to take the step was one which she kept to herself. She was anxious to get married again, but she did not feel that she still had to depend upon anyone as a go-between. She had an objective clearly before her mind, and she was determined to explore all its possibilities. For was it not true that Lord Yu Kung had been alone these many years? If only . . . if only her plans worked out, she thought, what could she not accomplish! Her arrival in the north was fortified by this well-defined vision, and her desire to have a sing-song house of her own was only a means to its realization.

Hai-ming came down to Tientsin from Peking soon after she learned that Golden Orchid had returned to the north. She had severed her relations with Hu-mou, but Lao Chuang was still in her service and accompanied her. It had been her intention to work out some arrangement with Hu-mou, even though he had not consented to have her as his concubine. But during the past year it had become all too evident that such an arrangement could not be made. Hu-mou continued to be mean and niggardly to Hai-ming, and one day, on a slight pretext, he struck her. As she thought she had suffered enough she struck back. This led to a terrific scuffle in which she proved to be quite the equal of Hu-mou. But she was badly mauled and bitten on the arm, and the same night she left the 'small house' at 31 East Silla Hutung with Lao Chuang and went straight to Tientsin. There she was welcomed by Golden Orchid.

It did not take long for the two young women to set up a sing-song house. Before they had time to settle down, they were already on the way to success. They rented an impressive two-storey house, facing south so that there was a constant flood of sunshine. Extra space at the rear they converted into private quarters for themselves, for Golden Orchid's mother, and for Lao Chuang and Yang Mah.

The news that the former concubine of a distinguished scholar and ambassador had opened a sing-song house spread like wild-fire. Out of sheer curiosity everybody was anxious to see and meet her. Before long large numbers of officials of the Government at Peking began flocking regularly to Golden Orchid's establishment, though the train journey between the two cities was an expensive one and took more than five hours. Indeed, it came to a point where nothing of importance either of a personal or of public nature among these officials could be consummated without first being christened with a feast held at the House of Willow-under-the-Moon, the name by which Golden Orchid's new house came to be known.

At all times of the day and night carriages and sedan-chairs filled the narrow street in front of the house. In addition to Hai-ming, Golden Orchid had the assistance of six attractive young girls, all from the south, whom she chose herself. No sing-song house in the memory of Tientsin had ever had so much to offer in the way of entertainment, delicious food, solid physical comfort, to say nothing of the soft and beguiling charms of female companionship.

It was part of the unwritten code of the sing-song houses of this high class that none of the girls was allowed to keep a guest overnight, nor was a guest supposed to pay for the entertainment and feast soon after they were over. Payment was to be made to the mistress, in this case to Golden Orchid's mother, only on the occasion of a major festival. There were four such festivals in the year.

For two solid months the merchants and officials vied with one another in the splendour and luxury of their entertainment. When the Dragon Boat Festival arrived, everybody in the house, from Golden Orchid herself to Yang Mah and the servant girls, became so rich that they didn't know what to do. No one had believed that the patrons could be so lavish or had so much money to spend, and with so little restraint.

But uppermost in Golden Orchid's mind was one thought: When would Lord Yu Kung do her the honour of patronizing her house? Or would he never come, even as a guest? Hai-ming's thoughts were on Hu-mou, who, she was afraid, might appear out of a clear blue sky.

Two days after the Dragon Boat Festival a party was given at the house by one whose name seemed familiar to Golden Orchid. He was Lee Pan-king, President of the Board of Rites, who as chairman of the Grand Council had issued the order which established Wenching's innocence. His Excellency was on a brief visit to Tientsin. Very largely out of a sense of curiosity, he, like the other officials, desired to have a glimpse of Golden Orchid, the famous beauty, diplomatic hostess and erstwhile concubine of the man whose honour he had saved. Golden Orchid wondered for a long time who Lee Pan-king might be: she could not place him. All she knew was that he must be an official of very high rank. As a matter of policy, she felt that she should herself extend a welcome to the party.

Golden Orchid knew none of the guests, though there was one who looked familiar. This was Mr Wu who, years before in Soochow, she remembered, persuaded his wife to protest to her mother and grandmother for allowing her to become a sing-song girl under the misguided protection of the pock-faced Lily. Golden Orchid was both happy and embarrassed to meet an old friend who must, she thought, have become an official of some consequence, important enough at any rate to be a guest of His Excellency Lee Pan-king.

'My respectable and charming hostess.' Mr Wu stood up with wine in hand as Golden Orchid entered the room. 'May I drink this cup in your honour?' So saying he emptied it and said *kan pei*, which means 'Your health'.

Golden Orchid became red in the face and replied, 'I dare not accept the honour. It is for me, rather, the humble one, to raise my cup in appreciation and gratitude for the presence of so distinguished a gathering.'

With that Golden Orchid emptied her cup to Mr Wu as a mark of courtesy; another to the host of the party who in the meantime had been introduced to her as His Excellency Lee, a great friend and admirer of her deceased husband; and still another to all those present.

'She has the capacity of the sea. How lovely, how admirable!' commented Mr Wu.

Suddenly it dawned upon Golden Orchid that His Excellency was the President of the Grand Council. She had never been so nervous. She apologized profusely for the lack of attention on the part of the house, and for a brief moment she went in to give instructions to the girls to sing, dance and entertain the guests in a manner befitting the importance of the occasion.

When Golden Orchid reappeared, Mr Wu introduced another guest who, like himself, had been present on the flower-boat where she had first made her appearance as a sing-song girl.

'And this gentleman here, you remember, Golden Orchid,' said Mr Wu, 'is Uncle Wang.'

'Why, of course, Uncle Wang. Just as I thought,' replied Golden Orchid. The memory of what the man had done for Wen-ching in Berlin came back to her. If she remembered correctly, Uncle Wang supplied much information about the devil Hu-mou in his letters to her husband.

'. . . Of course, Uncle Wang, I beg your pardon. Why, you have put even more prosperity on your honourable body since I last saw you. That was why for a moment I didn't recognize you. A cup of wine, Uncle Wang, for old time's sake.'

Thus Golden Orchid emptied another cup of the mellow Shaoshing wine, which made Uncle Wang very happy. The party was now in full progress, brimful of laughter and gaiety, with everyone making jokes and indulging in the familiar finger game. Even Mr Wu's twelve-year-old son, whom he had brought with him, was thoroughly enjoying himself.

Uncle Wang, as common and vulgar as ever, was louder and more boisterous than the rest. He was fond of teasing children. And so, turning to Mr Wu's son, he said: 'Master Wu, I was told that you are a very clever boy. But do you know, a person who is clever when young may be foolish when he is old?' And he laughed and laughed, thinking that he had put the child in a tight corner.

Without a moment's hesitation and with a face like an autumn lake without a ripple, Master Wu struck back: 'Then, Sir, you must have been very clever when you were young!'

The father was annoyed and embarrassed, but the whole table roared with laughter, and finally Uncle Wang was gracious enough to raise his cup to Mr Wu for having sired a truly clever son. But at heart he was hurt.

It was nearly midnight. Three large urns of wine had been consumed. It was time the party came to a delightful end. But somehow there was no disposition on the part of the guests to leave. Instead there was more gaiety and still more drinking. Words began to flow with less and less restraint. Then Mr Wu said something which caused awkwardness.

'That Golden Orchid,' he stammered as he stood somewhat precariously on his feet, 'isn't she a beautiful girl? But she is not a virtuous girl — I tried to save her many years ago.'

It was evident that Mr Wu had passed the boundaries of discretion. The host quickly summoned the servants to help him to lie down on the couch inside. But Mr Wu wanted none of that.

'She wanted to be a sing-song girl,' he continued, 'and so she became the concubine of our great scholar, Brother Wen-ching. Yes, it's the concubines who rule over all of us nowadays. . . . Let's drink to the concubines.' With that Mr Wu emptied another cup of wine while everybody else looked embarrassed and displeased.

Golden Orchid was listening nervously in the next room. How she prayed that someone would soon stop Mr Wu from uttering this insulting nonsense!

Uncle Wang, too, had had his share of the wine. He didn't like what Mr Wu had said, and in his forthright manner asked him to be quiet. 'Why don't you mind your own business, you fool?' he shouted.

Mr Wu retorted, 'Your fat head cannot stop me from saying what I want to say. Do you know that Golden Orchid, out of respect for her deceased husband, agreed that she would not take up this profession again, not at least in the north?'

That was more than Golden Orchid could tolerate. She came out to face Mr Wu and said that what he had just uttered was false.

'How dare you say that I do not speak the truth?' challenged Mr Wu. 'Didn't you agree to two conditions after Wen-ching's death? And haven't you broken your promise by being what you are? Madam Wen-ching has treated you nobly, and how have you treated her?'

So it was Madam Wen-ching whom Mr Wu really wanted to defend! During the time when she was alone as a widow in Soochow, she had become an intimate friend of Madam Wu, and Mr Wu could not bear to see Golden Orchid being, as he thought, unfaithful and disloyal to her.

By this time Uncle Wang's curiosity was excited. 'Let's hear, let's hear what those two conditions were.'

'Well, if you want to know, though it is none of your business,' said Mr Wu, 'the first condition was that she would not appear in the north in the capacity of a sing-song girl —'

'That is not true,' said Golden Orchid with some vehemence. 'What we agreed was that for one year I would not go to Peking. The year has passed, and I am now here in Tientsin, and Tientsin is not Peking. Now let us know what the second condition was.'

'You are a clever girl, but did you not receive the sum of twenty thousand dollars, upon acceptance of which you agreed not to go back to the profession out of respect for your husband? Isn't that true? Let me hear what you have to say to this.'

Golden Orchid had been anxious all along to save the face of Madam Wen-ching, who had behaved so well to her, and so she had not mentioned the matter of that money even to Ping-mo. But now she was challenged, and in self-defence she had to make the matter clear.

'That money,' she said quietly, 'was unfortunately never given to me. I was supposed to receive it from Madam Wen-ching's brother. But whether he is still keeping it or whether he has used it for his own good, I have no way of telling. All I know is that I have not to this day received anything from him. Since you brought up the matter, Mr Wu, you are entitled to know all the facts.'

Mr Wu was completely taken by surprise, but even so he stuttered 'That is impossible!'

'Yes, Mr Wu,' continued Golden Orchid. 'What I have said is the truth. You can find out. I would appreciate it if you would find out for me what has become of that money. I need it as a young girl with no one to rely upon. I also have a mother to support. You, Mr Wu, are among the high officials. You have many kinds of income. Are you to deny me what I am legitimately entitled to?'

'Well said, Golden Orchid!' shouted Uncle Wang. 'What able officials we have! I thought they were showing their ability on the great national issues of the day. They are now showing equal ability in interfering with the private life of a young and helpless girl. How wonderful!'

Words now began to fly about with scant consideration for personal feelings, and if Lao Chuang had not come in at this moment the party might have ended in a most unhappy manner.

'Tai-tai, Tai-tai,' Lao Chuang shouted. He was almost incoherent. He panted for breath and his forehead was wet with perspiration. 'What shall we do? The town is on fire!'

'What do you mean, the town is on fire?' shouted Uncle Wang.

'They are burning the Catholic churches. I saw it with my own eyes. And what is worse, there is looting and robbery going on at this very moment. They may even come here before we know it.'

What had happened was that the long-smouldering hatred

against what the foreigners had done for more than three generations had come to a head. The secret societies working quietly among the millions of the common people, the Boxers who had mesmerized the ignorant masses into the absurd belief that they could become impervious to any weapons of war, and the young revolutionaries of Ping-mo's type had all come to the conclusion that the foreigner was indeed at the root of China's woes. It was the Boxers who now had the upper hand. They had become restive and impatient for action; and it was common knowledge that, with the connivance of some of the country's leading personalities, including the Empress Dowager herself, an explosion of real violence on an immense scale would soon break out. The only question had been when and in what manner.

There was now utter chaos in Golden Orchid's house. Without bidding farewell to one another the guests left to return to their homes. The host, Lee Pan-king, had fallen asleep while his guests and friends were indulging in the luxury of an altercation; he thought that to see nothing, hear nothing, and feel nothing, was the best way to remain neutral. Now he was rudely awakened and noticed that everyone was hurrying away without so much as saying goodbye to him or thanking him; he surmised that something terrible must have happened within the house. As he left the room, he tripped and fell, hurting his right leg. Golden Orchid asked Lao Chuang to carry His Excellency to her own apartment.

'What is going on?' inquired His Excellency.

Golden Orchid had made up her mind to be kind and friendly to anyone who had helped Wen-ching during his ordeal. This was her first meeting with the President of the Grand Council, and she called Yang Mah and the other female servants to attend to the needs of the great official, while she herself talked over with her mother and Hai-ming what they should do, in view of the chaos and disorder spreading over the city. She dispatched Lao Chuang to bring in the latest information.

'Mother dear, I am afraid that something terrible is happening to all of us. There were rumours even when we first came here. But I was then told that the situation was well in hand, and the Boxers were being driven into the interior. There was general belief that, in any case, Tientsin, Peking and the big cities would be perfectly safe. That has turned out to be wrong.'

While Golden Orchid was speaking they could hear a distant rumbling which they well understood. From the window they could see the sky painted red by the many fires in the city.

'Look, Mother, we must gather together all the jewellery we have,' said Golden Orchid excitedly. 'If things really become worse, we shall have to leave this place at once.'

She turned to Hai-ming. 'What are we going to do, Sister Hai-ming? We put all our money into this house. Fortunately in these two months we have had it back and much more. But if conditions really get out of hand, where can we turn? Where can we go?'

'The only place we can still go is back to Peking. I've been thinking about it. There in Peking you and I still have friends.'

'But what's the good of friends when they have to look after their own affairs?'

'The Government will be there, and the Government will see to it that peace is maintained in the capital even if there is disorder elsewhere. I am sure of that.'

'I think you are right. We can at least depend upon the train to take us out of Tientsin quickly.'

But before Golden Orchid could decide what to do, whether to discharge the servants or ask the sing-song girls to go back to their families, she had to wait for more definite information, and for that she depended upon Lao Chuang.

2

IT was fully two hours later when Lao Chuang came back. His hoarse voice and distraught appearance indicated that all was not well. 'No good, no good, all heaven is crashing down on us,' he said. 'We must get ready to leave at once. What I saw and heard is beyond description.'

Curiously enough, when everyone seemed to have lost his head, Golden Orchid began to acquire unusual composure. 'Nevertheless, Lao Chuang, you must tell us what you saw and heard,' she said calmly.

'We must pack and go to the train as soon as possible. There is not a moment to lose. Already people are leaving by the thousands.

L

I am afraid the trains are going to be crowded. If we delay, it is possible that we shall never be able to leave.'

'But be steady, Lao Chuang. Are you sure we must leave for Peking?'

'Where else can we go, Tai-tai? All other ways of leaving Tientsin are slow and dangerous.'

Lao Chuang very naturally thought also of his own little family in the village just to the north of Peking, but it was true that the route to Peking was the only route open to them.

'But tell us what you saw,' Golden Orchid requested.

'The streets are full of people running in all directions. One man told me that the Boxers began by wanting to kill all the foreigners, but they are now killing and robbing our own people. It's the women and children who are suffering the most. I saw a huge crowd of people attending some kind of a ceremony. There were flags and banners, and on many of these I saw eight big characters: "Help the Throne, eliminate the foreigners. Heavenly soldiers and their Heavenly Generals!" I went closer. As I happen to be taller than most people, I saw everything very clearly.'

'Well, go on, Lao Chuang,' Golden Orchid urged.

'In the middle of the circle was a platform on which the Boxers burned candles and incense. All round the circle they planted long knives and spears and tridents. And then two of the Boxers came into the circle and shouted to the crowd: "Anyone who wants to join the Heavenly army, let him step up." They had a piece of red cloth around their heads and their waists. The upper part of their bodies was completely naked. One held a trident and another a long knife. At the first call for recruits nothing happened. After some beating of drums mingled with more yells for recruits, I saw five young men who looked like peasants stepping into the circle. They were made to stand in a line, bow three times to the southeast and shut their eyes. And as the beating of the drums became louder and louder, the two Boxers went up to the recruits and whispered in their ears for a long time.'

'And did you find out what was whispered?' Hai-ming inquired.

'I did,' continued Lao Chuang, 'but it took me some time. The Boxers invoked the spirit of the Sacred Monkey, the Holy Pig, the Teacher of the Long Staff, the Teacher of the Short Staff, all characters from an old story-book. They were supposed to come from space and take possession of the bodies of these recruits. You should have seen the faces of those peasants. They were both happy and afraid. And then, with their mouths tightly shut, they were commanded to fall on the ground and remain there quite motionless for some time. When they stood up again, there was foam around their mouths. That was a sure indication to the gazing crowd that the spirits had actually arrived and entered the bodies of the recruits. They were then given long knives and staffs, which they brandished fiercely in the air. From that moment the recruits were supposed to be impervious to all weapons of war.'

While Lao Chuang talked, Golden Orchid decided that it was best to assume as little responsibility as possible for the lives of those under her care. Her mother and Hai-ming agreed.

As Golden Orchid was about to let the girls and servants know that they must go back to their homes, in came another messenger to announce that a house only two or three hundred yards down the street had been set on fire. This messenger, a maidservant, had also taken upon herself to find out a few things and confirmed everything Lao Chuang had said. She had seen the Boxers carry cases of paraffin to the house, and then deliberately and in cold blood set it on fire. 'This is the home of a "second hairy one," ' they proclaimed to the people. That meant the home of a native Chinese on friendly terms with the foreigners. The Boxers also assured the people that no other house would be affected: there was no need to move anything out.

'I couldn't believe it,' the maidservant said, 'and I stood there waiting to see what would happen. I saw the flames coming through the roof, and then a few minutes later it began to spread to the neighbouring houses like any other fire. I knew then the Boxers were lying. But I was shivering and dared not say a word. They would have killed me if I had. Other people began to doubt also. The Boxers noticed it and got very angry with the crowd. They said that their lack of faith could not be tolerated, and they started to be rough with the people. I don't know what happened afterwards, for I ran home as quickly as I could. . . . No, no, Tai-tai, we must all go away and leave this place if we do not want to get into trouble. If you will excuse me, I must go at once to see my mother and children.'

This dramatic announcement gave them no alternative, and everyone was willing to leave the house. To each of the girls Golden

Orchid gave a handsome sum in cash, while she instructed Yang Mah and Lao Chuang to pack up all that was valuable and be ready to leave at a moment's notice. She then took her mother by the hand and went into her own room in the rear. Doffing their outer garments, they each put on a spacious cloth pouch of the type used by men and stuffed into them all the gold and jewels in their possession. Then they changed into old clothes and went to Hai-ming's room to persuade her to do likewise. Leaving her mother with Hai-ming, Golden Orchid dispatched Lao Chuang to hire a mule-cart.

'Lao Chuang,' she said, 'pay the man generously and say that we are leaving at once. Tell him also to harness one of his fat mules. A lean, sickly beast won't do. Understand?'

In a short while the house which only a few hours before was the scene of lavish entertainment, with beautiful young girls singing to the accompaniment of the guitar and the lute, was littered with discarded clothing and upturned chairs and other pieces of furniture. His Excellency Lee Pan-king had been awakened by Golden Orchid. His leg was not badly hurt, and the after-effects of the wine had all but disappeared. Lao Chuang obtained a carriage which would take him to the Viceroy's yamen. Golden Orchid was quite sure that nothing would happen to so high an official. She saw him to the carriage herself, and as he said goodbye he calmly invited her to call on him when she came to Peking.

When Golden Orchid left for the waiting cart she gave instructions to Yang Mah to padlock the door of the house. The streets were now glutted with fleeing people, and the cart made little headway. Fortunately Lao Chuang knew the city well, and by winding through narrow streets where there were fewer people than on the main ones, they at last reached the railway station. But the sight there horrified everyone. The station was already full of people. Most of them had unrolled their bedding and were lying on the bare floor waiting for the next train. It was almost impossible to walk through. The station-master happened to be a young man who had once visited Golden Orchid's sing-song house, and she implored him to give her all the help he could.

'How many are you?' asked the station-master.

'Five of us — my mother and I and Hai-ming. You know Hai-ming of course? And then we have two servants — a man and a woman.'

'I can't promise you anything. Everyone in that crowd will try to get on the next train. But I will do everything I can for you. The train should leave in an hour. For the moment relax and make yourselves comfortable.' So saying, the young man took Golden Orchid and her company to his own office and gave them some tea.

When the time approached for the train to depart and the iron gates were opened, the crowd which rushed in to occupy every available seat was large and unmanageable, but Golden Orchid's group had been escorted earlier to a compartment and locked in so that no one else could get in. They felt secure, but the noise and cries which they heard along the corridor in the train and outside on the platform were heart-rending and pathetic. Women with bound feet who could hobble along only with the greatest difficulty were pushed about and trampled upon. Children lost their parents and were even crushed to death. And when at last the train drew out, almost an hour later than its scheduled time, there were people, with their bundles and all the earthly possessions they could carry, inside the engine itself, as well as on the roofs of the carriages.

It was four o'clock in the morning; the compartment was dark, and Mrs Fu and Hai-ming managed to doze for a while. But Golden Orchid could not sleep, tired as she was.

Why must we leave like this? Why didn't I ask His Excellency Lee to take us under the protection of the Viceroy? Well, what's done is done. But how long will even Peking be safe? Golden Orchid asked herself. What could they do there? Who could offer them asylum?

Her thoughts went to Lord Yu Kung, and they gave her consolation. But she wanted to meet him again under better circumstances. Then she grew practical. After all, she thought, the immediate thing is to get away from all this disturbance. Peking is the home of the Empress Dowager, the Emperor, and all the great officials of the land. Surely Peking will be safe. Surely also Lord Yu Kung will give me, the unfortunate concubine of his friend Wen-ching, the protection I need so badly.

The train slowly jostled along. Golden Orchid called Yang Mah and there was no answer. She had fallen asleep, but Lao Chuang was wide awake and answered: 'Is there anything I can do for you, Tai-tai?'

'Nothing,' replied Golden Orchid. 'I thought you might be asleep also.' And then after a pause she said: 'From our life in Berlin to this — what a change, Lao Chuang.'

Lao Chuang sighed. 'This is what Heaven has ordained. What can one do?'

'I wonder what the conditions are in the train. Everything has become quiet now.'

'I would like to go out if you will allow me. Perhaps I may pick up some important information.'

Lao Chuang left the compartment for half an hour. When he came back he had talked with an old man who had once been a minor official in Peking and obtained news which was by no means reassuring.

'Tai-tai,' he said, 'a man told me that the Empress Dowager has now thrown herself in with the Boxers. This is very bad news. It means that the Government is not suppressing the Boxers but encouraging them. And when we get to Peking, conditions there may be just as bad as in Tientsin. The same looting, arson, killing of Chinese and foreigners alike, perhaps. I am terribly upset by the news. I don't know whether I shall ever see my family again.'

The information that Lao Chuang had picked up was only too true. The Boxers had now come out into the open in Peking.

Within the ranks immediately surrounding the throne there were at first two opposing camps. One camp asked for the suppression of the Boxers, while the other encouraged them. That was when the views of the Empress Dowager were still unknown. The Emperor was already a virtual prisoner and had no influence whatever on national policy. It was the Empress Dowager surrounded by her eunuchs and sycophants whose every word had become the supreme law of the land. She was a forceful personality, wilful, bigoted, domineering and totally ignorant of even the most elementary facts of international life. She felt, with reason, that she had been humiliated too long by the foreigners, and she thought childishly that by making use of the Boxers to kill and eliminate them, she could regain her prestige and the respect of the world. She had already begun to imprison and decapitate those who dared to say anything against the riff-raff from whom the Boxers were recruited.

The train had now been running for over two hours, and there was already a streak of light from the east. It was dawn, but it was a dawn of uncertainty. Two hours more or at most three, and Golden

Orchid would be in Peking. That was as far as her mind could look.

The train gave a jolt and pulled to a sudden stop. It had done that before, and there was no reason for apprehension. But half an hour elapsed, then an hour, and still there were no signs that the train would resume its journey. Cries of anxiety began to be audible. Dawn in the meantime had become clear, open daylight, and it promised to be a warm and sultry day.

Golden Orchid as usual dispatched Lao Chuang to find out what the delay was all about. 'If you find any food, Lao Chuang,' she also said, 'be sure to buy some. Perhaps a few boiled eggs and some tea.'

Little did Golden Orchid realize the conditions of the world outside her compartment as she issued these orders to Lao Chuang. In every carriage men, women and children were packed like sardines, with expressions of despair and agony written clearly and unmistakably on their dirty, frightened faces! They were all hungry, and the children whined and moaned. Lao Chuang walked along the train looking into every compartment. All were the same — horrible steaming smells and anguished faces. He then met two scouts who were just coming back from their exploration to report their findings to the driver.

The rails in front had all been torn up by the Boxers, not for stretches of a few yards, but for miles, and the scouts said that it was hopeless to try to repair them. The train had to be abandoned. Even if it could proceed, it would perhaps run into frenzied mobs all along the way. Half the distance to Peking had been covered, but there were still some forty miles to go. At least there was no town of any size near where the train had stopped; and that meant that, if they chose to and if they were fortunate, the poor refugees might still be able to lose themselves among the peasants and avoid being detected by the Boxers.

Lao Chuang was worried, terribly worried. The prospect of rejoining his family was growing more and more remote. Anything might happen to his wife and two sons, he thought. And that drove him frantic. Perhaps the money which he and his wife had carefully buried under the ground in their hut had already been taken. His wife might even have been raped or his sons killed. His imagination ran wild, and he became black with despair. Slowly he walked back to the compartment and told the sad story to his mistress.

'Tai-tai,' he said, 'you asked me to buy some food. Not only is there no food to be had anywhere, but the train is not going any farther. The rails have been torn up by the Boxers, and everybody in the train will have to find his own way. What shall we do?'

Mrs Fu, Hai-ming and Yang Mah looked at one another in horrified bewilderment and helplessness. Then Golden Orchid asked to be taken to see for herself what was going on. Her decision was quick.

'Lao Chuang,' she said, 'the situation is indeed desperate, but we've got to do something. As you can see, most of the passengers are poor people, and they are still hoping that somehow the train will take them to Peking. The railway people are afraid to break the bad news. They are afraid that the crowd may become desperate and get out of control. What I want you to do is to go quickly to the nearest village and get some food for these poor people. Here is some money.'

So saying, Golden Orchid took a handful of silver coins from the inner pocket around her waist.

'Now listen to me carefully,' she continued. 'The village must have some food. Get some bread — anything. I was told the nearest village is about a mile from here. Put all this food on a cart. I am sure the village must have several carts. Order any extra carts to be ready to take us to Peking. The crowd here will need them. And tell the villagers they will be well paid.'

When Lao Chuang had gone, Golden Orchid went along the train and offered what consolation she could. She was like an angel of mercy to the people. Though as yet she had nothing to give to them she assured them that there was nothing to be afraid of, that they were out of danger as long as they were no longer in Tientsin, and that all would be well. She told them also that those who could should walk to the nearest village and get some food. She knew that the food which Lao Chuang had been asked to purchase would be enough for only a small fraction of the crowd, and she meant that fraction to be women and children. Her soothing message had an immediate effect in pacifying the people.

She then walked to the engine, where she found the few remaining train officials in conference trying to decide what they should do. Golden Orchid persuaded them at least to send someone to the last station to procure some food, for otherwise there might be danger of a panic driven by hunger. The men did not care for this advice. One of them said: 'But, young lady, you don't know what the situation really is. The Boxers have now broken out everywhere. It is lucky for us that they don't know there is a trainload of people marooned here. If they knew and came here we should all be lost. Surely we don't want to invite trouble by letting people at the last station know that we are helpless here. Besides, the rails may still be repaired, and then we shall proceed to Peking. Perhaps the destruction is not so bad as we first thought.'

'Thank you, thank you for the encouraging information,' replied Golden Orchid. Actually she was not encouraged. Upon her return to her own compartment she found her three women anxiously waiting for her, and she told them what she had done. Then she said: 'I am afraid it is hopeless to wait. It may be a long, long time yet before the train moves — if ever. But I hate to leave these poor people. We are all desperate, and I shouldn't abandon them.'

Hai-ming looked at Mrs Fu and did not seem to approve. 'I'll tell you what we should do, Sister,' said Hai-ming. 'If Lao Chuang comes back with the carts we have ordered, we should go our way. What do you say? All that remains is some forty miles, and we should be able to cover that distance in two days.'

'All right, if that is how you feel.'

'You have done all you can, Sister, to take care of the crowd. My guess is that the train will not, as you said, go any farther. We shall be much safer with the carts and shall get to Peking much quicker.'

Lao Chuang came back within two hours and reported that the food in the village was almost gone as many people from the train had been there already. But he had procured two carts, which were ready to leave. Golden Orchid got Yang Mah to help her unpack the clothing and made everyone dress like a servant or peasant in tunics of coarse blue cloth. They climbed on to the carts and were on their way to Peking.

3

TRAVELLING was difficult. For two solid months there had been no rain in the area, and the narrow roads in the countryside had been cut into deep ruts. The dust was so heavy that even a slow pace was a strain on the mules. Golden Orchid and the four others with her managed to cover some five miles before it became dark. They were thankful that they had done as well. They put up at an inn for the night as comfortably as they could and resumed the journey the next morning.

It was then that trouble began. One of the drivers refused to go on. 'I am not going any farther,' he said. 'I don't want this business any more.'

Lao Chuang, who was asked to negotiate with the man, became very angry, but Golden Orchid told him to control himself; conditions were trying enough. She asked him to give the driver more money.

But even that failed to change the driver's mind. He was stubborn and glum. He would not speak. After a long while, he said: 'I have heard that the hairy soldiers have arrived and that they are fighting with our big brothers. I don't want to run into the thick of it.'

At this point the other driver joined in and said: 'We are all Chinese. The big brothers are helping the Son of Heaven to drive out the foreigners. They will protect us, and so what have we to be afraid of? Let's go on.'

Lao Chuang in the meantime had become temperate in his tone and added: 'We need not go all the way to Peking. As soon as there is a train, we shall get on it.'

At that the first driver laughed and said: 'You are dreaming. The rails have been torn up not only at the spot we left yesterday. I know for a fact that our big brothers have melted them all the way to Peking with their heavenly powers. I must go back.' Whereupon he turned his cart and drove away.

'If he wants to go back, let him,' said the second driver, 'I shall still take you.' This came as a very encouraging surprise. Then he continued: 'Only, there are five of you. My cart is large enough to accommodate you, I think. There is, however, only one animal. It isn't strong enough to pull you.'

Lao Chuang volunteered to walk with the driver to lighten the burden. Golden Orchid suggested that as soon as they found another cart on the way they would hire it. In the meantime she offered to pay for the extra load. That was agreeable to the driver, and so the company resumed their journey. Towards noon, after they had gone another four miles and rested at a wayside inn, Lao Chuang and the driver came in with the welcome news that another cart had been found, so they could split up as they had done the day before.

Lao Chuang reported that while he was sitting on a bench eating his food with two strangers, they told him that hundreds of foreign troops had been landed at the port of Taku east of Tientsin, and that they were fighting with the Boxers all along the way towards the big city. From Tientsin — after they had captured it — there was no question but that the foreign troops would continue to fight their way to Peking.

Golden Orchid knew that the future was uncertain. But for the present the important thing was to get into Peking before the disorder became worse. So she ordered the two carts to continue the journey at once. They managed to keep fairly close to each other, but toward dusk something happened which upset her plans. Coming in the opposite direction was a crowd of people, some running, some also driving carts, but they all seemed to be in a panic. As the roads were narrow and the dust kicked up by the hundreds of running feet of both human beings and animals obscured any clear view of what was happening, the mule pulling the cart in which Golden Orchid and her mother were riding got out of control. The noise and crowd were too much of a shock to the animal, and, as if possessed by an evil spirit, it began to gallop so fast that the cart almost overturned. The driver later discovered it had been going in the direction of Tungchow instead of Peking.

Hai-ming, Yang Mah and Lao Chuang had failed to follow and they were completely lost. The distance between Tungchow and Peking is a matter of perhaps thirteen miles, and there was little cause for worry. But the fact that the two women were now alone with the driver when it was rapidly growing dark was a source of great anxiety. Mrs Fu was already a sick woman, having been so terribly jolted that she lay on her bedding without uttering a word. But Golden Orchid ordered the driver to go on. 'Let's go to Tungchow then; the sooner we get there the better.'

Then, turning to her mother, she said: 'Mother dear, have courage a little longer. We shall be all right. As long as we keep moving, nothing will happen to us.'

The fact that the driver had been well paid, and that all day he had been in a happy mood, was one reason why he willingly obeyed every instruction that Golden Orchid gave him. More than once he suggested that they stop for a short rest, to which Golden Orchid gently replied: 'When we come to the next village, but not now.'

When they came to the next village, it was so quiet that it appeared deserted. The villagers had thought it wise to lock their doors and stay inside their houses. The arrival of Golden Orchid and her mother startled them, but when they found it was only two harmless women, one of whom was young and attractive, even though her face was now covered with a thick layer of yellow dust, they flocked round the cart. Some remarked that they must be rich ladies on their flight; others wanted to know how conditions were where they came from; still others wanted to know where they were going. Their curiosity soon became so annoying that it looked as if they would be in more danger with the villagers than with the driver. Another hour, Golden Orchid found out, and they would be in Tungchow. Without hesitation she gave instructions to the driver to proceed so that they could pass the night in that city.

4

GOLDEN ORCHID's mother spent a fretful night in Tungchow. She had many things to worry about. She and her daughter had on their persons all their worldly possessions. Even though Tungchow itself might be peaceful, the trip to Peking was likely to be attended by numerous hazards. When she went to bed on the *kang* she had a fever. As a southerner, she was accustomed to the comforts of life, which were denied to her in the north, and the fright caused by the mule's bolting made sleep impossible. She was still hoping against hope that Hai-ming, Yang Mah, and Lao Chuang would be able to find them so that they could travel to Peking together.

When Lao Chuang's cart became separated from Golden Orchid and her mother, he tried desperately to rejoin them. He was under the impression that they were still going in the direction of Peking, and he asked everyone he passed whether they had seen the ladies. His description of them was clear enough to identify them. Every now and then when there was a small crowd, Lao Chuang would mingle with them and ask: 'Did you by any chance pass a cart with a mother and daughter in it?' And then he would add: 'The mother is middle-aged and the daughter is in her early twenties and very attractive. They are from the south.' And the people, even though they were fleeing from trouble, would respond: 'We did not have the good fortune to meet them.'

But in one village Lao Chuang came across a young man who, he was sure, was a southerner. 'Young sir,' Lao Chuang said, 'I have been trying to find two ladies in another cart who have become separated from us. They are a mother and daughter from Soochow.'

'From Soochow?' the young man exclaimed. 'What are their names?'

'The mother is Fu Tai-tai and the daughter is Madam Golden Orchid.'

'Golden Orchid!' the young man shouted in utter consternation. 'Where did they go? And where is your cart?'

Lao Chuang took the young man to the cart where Hai-ming and Yang Mah were waiting for him, and of course Yang Mah recognized the young man at once.

'Ah-ya! Young master! Oh, how happy I am to find you here, young master!' She grabbed his hands with great joy. And then she said: 'But how is it that you too are in this foul-smelling and dirty village?' Then, turning to Mistress Hai-ming, she said: 'This is our young master Ping-mo.'

Now, Hai-ming had not seen Ping-mo before, nor had Lao Chuang, but to know that the son of Master Wen-ching was with them was a source of such overwhelming joy that they forgot all their troubles and misfortunes.

'Master Ping-mo,' said Hai-ming, 'we always thought that you were in Soochow. What brings you here?'

'No matter,' replied Ping-mo. 'The story is a long one. But where are Golden Orchid and her mother? We must find them.'

'They must be in front of us,' said Hai-ming, 'for the mule which pulled their cart was suddenly frightened by some noise and bolted. It's possible that they have gone in another direction. Even if we don't find them on the way, I am sure we shall find them in the

Soochow hostel, for we were talking about going to that familiar place before doing anything else on arrival at Peking.'

'Good, that is at least some consolation,' said Ping-mo. 'In that case we need not hurry. It is getting late, and the cart can't carry four of us anyway.'

That night they put up at a wayside inn and decided to make for Peking the next day.

Yang Mah insisted on knowing how it came about that Ping-mo was so far away from home.

'Young master,' said Yang Mah, 'now that you're here, can't you take all of us home? Let's find Tai-tai and Fu Tai-tai, and then we'll all go back to Soochow. I am sick and tired of being in this uncouth place. I am so frightened by what is going on. I have seen those wild men with red cloth around their heads and their waists. They are so murderous-looking with their long knives and spears.'

'Yang Mah,' warned Ping-mo, 'promise me that you will never speak like that again. They will kill you if they hear you. We have no way of going back. The wild men are everywhere, and we can't get through them. But everything will be all right — someone will control these wild people.'

Ping-mo was in no position to explain everything to Yang Mah, but the secret society to which he belonged had long been afraid that the Boxers might be unruly, and so it sent to the north a number of its young men to establish contact with them and to explain to them that everything had to be done in an orderly and systematic manner. Ping-mo was one of these young men. The Boxers were inclined to follow the advice of these better disciplined and educated youths until the Empress Dowager stepped in and wanted to make use of the Boxers for her own purposes. The moment they knew that they had the support of the Empress Dowager herself, they began repudiating all that they previously accepted. They became truculent, and no one could control them any longer.

Ping-mo had thus found himself unable to carry out his mission. He had to give up the duties for which he had been sent to the north. He decided, therefore, to look for Golden Orchid and give her as much protection as possible from the dangers and uncertainties to which she was now exposed. For he had information that the Boxers meant to create extensive chaos and disorder so as to derive personal profit thereby.

When the troubles arose in Tientsin, Ping-mo went to that city and found his way to Golden Orchid's sing-song house, only to learn that she had left on the previous day for Peking. He decided to follow her. He also learned that trains had stopped running, which meant that the only mode of travelling left for Golden Orchid was the mule cart. So he obtained a mule himself from one of the secret societies and trotted out towards the north, in the direction of Peking, convinced that by going through the string of villages he would not have much difficulty in finding her. It was thus that Lao Chuang met him, and Ping-mo was happy that he was now on the right track. It was only a matter of a day or so, he thought, before he would find Golden Orchid and her mother.

In Tungchow there was the same burning of churches, the same brutality and cruelty inflicted upon foreigners and the Chinese who associated with them. But Golden Orchid believed that as long as she remained in the garb of a poor peasant woman, she would not run into danger. Then suddenly a thought came into her mind: Why, Tungchow is the home of the Kendricks! The memory of that missionary family was vivid — especially her memory of Mrs Kendrick, with whom she had struck up such a friendship on the voyage to Europe. That was many years ago. But although the association was of short duration, she recalled the beauty of Mrs Kendrick's face, so soft, benign and gentle. And she had taken such trouble to teach her the English language.

Golden Orchid recalled that she had had two lovely children travelling with her. And didn't she ask me to see them upon my return? She thought, What's happened to them now that there is such trouble? Is it possible that they are still in Tungchow? If they are not, where have they gone?

These thoughts were disturbing. Here she was in Tungchow itself where their mission was. Not to try to see them and to offer them what little help she could would be unpardonable. And yet how was she to do it when she herself was in such an uncertain predicament? To try to find them now would be to expose herself to unnecessary danger, for would she not be taken by the Boxers as a friend and associate of the foreigner? For a long time Golden Orchid did not know what to do. She thought of talking the matter over with her mother, but she was certain that her mother would not understand. Also, the news in the city was not at all encouraging; she was told by the innkeeper that troubles had already broken out everywhere. No one could be sure that there would be no riot endangering the security of everybody in Tungchow.

Golden Orchid thought for a long time, and then she approached the innkeeper and asked him what he would do if anything should happen.

'Ah-ya!' said the innkeeper. 'I am but an old man. I am not afraid of anything, and I don't believe that anything will happen either to me or to anyone under the roof of this modest inn.' With these remarks he smiled and began stroking his sparse beard.

'What makes you think so?' Golden Orchid asked.

'Let me tell you something, young lady,' he continued. 'Whether one dies or not at any given time is all written in the book of the Prince of Hades. I could have died two months ago, and yet, as you can see, I am still very much alive and kicking. I was then terribly ill, and so I bought for myself a coffin and had the clothes made, ready to slip into them and be carried into the wooden box when the hour came, but the hour did not come. My number was not called.'

Pointing to a lamp, he said: 'When the oil is consumed, the light goes out. That is how I thought about myself. I thought my oil was burned to the last drop. But it seems that I still have some oil within me. I don't worry over what is going on in the city.' The innkeeper smiled again with a sense of complete composure and unconcern, and then he left her.

Golden Orchid reflected. There were advantages and dis-advantages in taking the Kendricks with her, she thought.

But Golden Orchid had always felt at home with foreigners: the thought of Faustmann and Anna and of all they had gone through for her and Wen-ching was a strong stimulus, and she decided to see the Kendricks again. She had been drawn to the American mission-ary family. She had such pleasant memories of them. But most of all, Golden Orchid had never hesitated to help those who needed help. So she called in the innkeeper again and, asking him to watch over her mother for the time being, she set out in search of the Kendricks.

She went from one narrow street to another disguised in her shabby clothing and did not look much different from any country wench. But that walk through the dusty, winding streets of the city revealed to her the extent of the damage which had already been done. Some of the burned houses did not look as if they had any-thing to do with the foreign missionaries. They were within the area usually inhabited by the townspeople. Once or twice facetious re-marks were thrown at her. But that, she thought, was natural for any young woman walking alone, even in normal times. She was not afraid, though she carried on her body a large portion of her jewels and gold cut into ten-ounce bars. But it was safer, she thought, to walk on the wider streets, where there were crowds of people, than on the narrow ones. And then all of a sudden she saw the steeple of a church rising high into the sky some distance from her.

Soon she found herself outside a walled enclosure. The gates were locked. She looked in and saw that the 'compound' was littered with stones and bricks. A portion of the church had been demolished and showed traces of fire. She walked round the wall and found large sections of it torn down. She gathered enough courage to go in. But before she did so, she looked around to see if there was any-one watching. There was no one. Close by were the servants' quarters, and peering through the window where the paper was badly torn, she saw an old couple busy over some hemp which they were working into rope. For fear of frightening them Golden Orchid knocked gently on the window, smiled to them and asked them to open the door.

'Come in, come in,' stammered the old man rather nervously. 'We thought at first that you were one of those Boxer girls, what they call the "red-lantern" girls. But you seem to be well-born.'

Golden Orchid was surprised to learn that, in spite of her coarse peasant dress, she could not completely conceal herself.

'Have you come to us to find somebody?' inquired the old woman.

'Yes,' replied Golden Orchid. 'I have come to find out where the minister of this church is and his family.'

'But they are not here any more,' was the immediate reply of the old woman. 'They went away long ago.'

'Where have they gone? But, first of all, is the minister's name Kendrick?'

'Yes. Mr Ken-de-li. But they left before the trouble started.'

'But tell me, young lady,' said the old woman. 'You don't seem to belong to these parts here. Your accent shows that you come from the south.'

'Yes, I am from the south, and I know the Kendricks well. I met them on a steamer many years ago. And where are their children, Peter and Margaret? They are still small. Peter must be eight or nine. And Margaret, I remember, is two years younger. Tell me where they are.'

With that Golden Orchid took out a silver piece and gave it to the old woman.

The old couple looked at each other for some time and did not know what to do.

'No, no, we cannot take any money from you, thank you. But tell me, do you really know the Kendricks well? You are one of their friends?'

'Yes, you can believe me. It is over four years since I travelled with them — on a large steamer going to a far and distant country. Mrs Kendrick taught me to speak English. Now are you satisfied?'

The old couple began to talk to each other away from Golden Orchid. It was nearly five years ago, they recalled, that the little Kendrick girl had had an attack of measles, and then a few months later the whole family had gone to Shanghai and from there they returned to America, the country of the flowery flag. Yes, there was no mistake about it.

Presently the old man came back to Golden Orchid, his face wrinkled with smiles. He said: 'Young lady, please stay with my old woman for a while.'

He then left his hut and went through the ruins of the church. A quarter of an hour later he came back, his face still beaming with smiles, and said to Golden Orchid: 'Please follow me.' Holding a kettle of hot water, the old man led her through fallen debris, through rooms which had been badly burned and finally to a dingy corner where there was an inconspicuous trapdoor. This he slowly opened, and they walked down a flight of stone steps to a short subterranean tunnel.

At the end of the tunnel stood Mr Kendrick, still tall and straight; and although his face was not clearly visible, it was evident that he had aged considerably. But Golden Orchid recognized him at once, even though he was dressed in Chinese clothing. The joy of this sudden and wholly unexpected meeting was indeed unbounded.

John Kendrick extended his arms and held both of Golden Orchid's hands in his own. 'But why have you come?' he asked.

'We are, of course, exceedingly happy to see you, but are you not exposing yourself to unnecessary danger? Let me take you to Mrs Kendrick and the children.'

'So you are all together, after all. That's wonderful.'

Mrs Kendrick was lying on a mattress on the floor with Peter and Margaret on small stools beside her. She jumped up the moment Golden Orchid came in and hugged and kissed her as if she were the angel of salvation.

'Oh, my Golden Orchid, I knew we were going to see you again.' And, with tears in her eyes, Nancy Kendrick hugged and kissed her again. 'We looked forward to seeing you and your husband at our home, but look at this — this is our home now, and we don't know what is going to happen next.'

Golden Orchid kissed Peter and then Margaret. Both looked like poor little waifs, for their faces were so sorrowful.

'But look, Mrs Kendrick —' began Golden Orchid.

'Just call me Nancy and my husband John.'

'Well, Nancy, I have come to take you away from this place. I am here with my mother. My husband died over a year ago. Anyway, you can't stay here like this indefinitely.'

'Tell us what happened to your husband.'

'It's a long story. I'll tell you later. For the present, let's talk about your leaving here.'

'But where can we go?' asked John. 'If we can only find our way to the coast, we may board a steamer and leave north China. But there is no way of getting to the coast. The route to Tientsin and Taku is cut.'

'Why not come to Peking?' rejoined Golden Orchid. 'That is where I am going with my mother. The distance is only a bare thirteen miles. The Government is there, and it won't permit all this disorder to go on. Besides, there are other Americans whom you can join, and your embassy will offer you protection.'

'We have been thinking about that also, Golden Orchid,' said Nancy. 'Out here, where we are almost alone, life can be dangerous. You should have seen the mob that surrounded our church two days ago. If it had not been for that faithful old couple you have met, we would have been killed. But I know we cannot hide like this indefinitely.'

'There is, however, one thing about Peking. It may be just as bad as anywhere else or even worse,' commented John Kendrick. 'What did you hear outside? A few days ago I received this document, which clearly shows that the Empress Dowager is now behind the Boxers, and that was the reason the people here in Tungchow started to become disorderly and even wanted to kill us. I don't know what has happened to many of our Chinese friends who are called the "second hairy ones".'

John gave Golden Orchid a crumpled sheet of paper which bore the frightening message issued by the Empress Dowager herself:

> Ever since the foundation of the Dynasty, foreigners coming to China have been kindly treated. In the reign of Tao Kuang and Hsien Feng they were allowed to trade and to propagate their religion. At first they were amenable to Chinese control, but for the past thirty years they have taken advantage of our forbearance to encroach upon the Chinese people and to absorb the wealth of the Empire. Every concession made seems to increase their insolence. They oppress our peaceful subjects and insult our gods and sages, exciting burning indignation among our people. Hence the burning of chapels and the slaughter of converts by the patriotic braves. The Throne was desirous of avoiding war and issued edicts enjoining protection of the embassies and pity towards converts, declaring Boxers and converts to be equally the children of the state. With tears have we announced in our ancestral shrines the outbreak of war. Better it is to do our utmost and carry on the struggle than to seek self-preservation involving eternal disgrace. All our officials, high and low, are of our mind. They have also assembled, without official summons, several thousand soldiers. Even children carry spears in the defence of their country.

'It is clear,' said John, 'that this is a declaration of war by the Boxers on all foreigners.'

'I knew it was coming,' said Nancy, 'sooner or later. I do not at all condone the action of any of the foreign powers in China. We have treated her badly, and I am ashamed of it. Now we must pay the penalty.'

'Please, Nancy,' cried Golden Orchid, 'let us keep calm. Let's see how we can get away from here. That is what I have come for.'

'You are a very sweet girl,' said Nancy as she took Golden Orchid's hand and gently patted it. 'But, no, you shouldn't have come. In good time, John and I will take the children away from the surrounding terror. I opened the Bible this morning, and at once these lines from Joshua met my eyes: "It shall come to pass that when they come out against us we will flee from them!" Yes, we will flee. Only John and I were wondering where to, and now you have come to help us. What an angel you are!'

'Do you know, Nancy dear,' John added gently, 'that what I read this morning in Samuel is almost the same as you read in Joshua? In verse fourteen it says: "And David said unto all his servants that were with him at Jerusalem, Arise, and let us flee; for we shall not else escape from Absalom: make speed to depart." So this is the Lord's word to us, and there is nothing for us to do but to obey.'

Margaret became hungry and clung to her mother whining and wanting to be fed. Peter stood like a little man, as if he knew what it was all about. Presently they heard footsteps through the dark corridor. It was the old man returning to report that there might be fresh outbreaks of trouble during the day and that, if they decided to leave, it would be best to go as soon as possible.

'Young lady,' the old man said to Golden Orchid, 'perhaps you can explain to the Kendricks better than I can. I have seen lots of things which are not good, but I have not said anything to them. Early this morning, just before you came, there was a crowd of people in the neighbourhood going through a ceremony of inducting both men and women Boxers. Surely you have seen that before, haven't you, young lady?'

'No, not exactly, but I have heard about it.'

'Well, if you haven't, better not see it, for it is a horrible sight.'

'All right, old sir,' said Golden Orchid hastily, 'I am going away this very instant, and if you can get hold of a cart and be ready in two hours, I will come back with my mother, and together we will make for Peking.' Then, turning to Nancy and John, she asked them to get ready at once, and left to fetch her mother.

'What do you think, John?' asked Nancy. 'Is it a wise decision we are making?'

'Yes, darling. I cannot say that Peking will be safe, but the distance is short and we may reach there without mishap. Golden Orchid should be a great help on the way. But there is another thing which I haven't mentioned so far. The troops from the powers have landed at Taku. They may even now be at Tientsin, and by the time we reach Peking, they may be there also. We shall then be safe.'

5

It was about two o'clock in the afternoon. The day was hot, intensely hot. In fact, for thirty years north China had not known so hot a summer. For months not a drop of rain had fallen, and the uneven, dust-laden roads wound through long stretches of solitude and desolation, amid surroundings in which hostility might manifest itself without warning. Sometimes the carts had to climb rocky steeps and make their way along river-beds. They pitched and stumbled, producing a feeling more uncomfortable than being seasick. The only way in which the poor animals could keep their feet was to find holes between the rocks, for the rocks themselves were slippery, having been worn and polished by centuries of traffic. Very often the mules tripped and fell. Once everybody pitched forward, and little Margaret bumped her head against the side of the cart. The journey was becoming unbearable for Golden Orchid's mother. Her face was covered with sweat, and she looked pale. Golden Orchid thought that since they had been on the road for two hours without, thank heaven, any serious mishap, it would be advisable to stop for a short while. So she jumped down from her cart and went to see the Kendricks.

'What do you think, Nancy? Shall we stop for a rest? It must be hard on the children. There is no way of reaching Peking today anyhow. We shall have to pass the night on the road. As we are at a village now, some hot water or food, if we can get it, will do all of us good.'

The carts stopped in front of an inn. Golden Orchid entered to talk to the innkeeper, and, in order to escape notice, she took a quiet room at the back facing a spacious yard. But even before the visitors had time to settle down the yard became filled with people. Where they came from and how they got wind there were foreigners there, no one knew. But here they were — a crowd of people, most of them with unpleasant looks, the men stripped to the waist, with their pig-tails wound round their heads as if ready for action.

There were women in the crowd also, though they were not the 'red lanterns', and even children, who had joined the crowd purely out of curiosity. The children were the first to approach the paper windows of the room, which had to be closed, even though it was stiflingly hot. They poked their fingers through the paper and peered at the frightened inmates. John Kendrick made his children face the wall and eat as much as possible of the steamed bread which the innkeeper had brought in. But the noise outside was becoming unbearable, and there were unfriendly knocks at the door with sticks and stones.

This was the first time Golden Orchid had learned of the hostility of the country people towards foreigners, and she became very nervous.

'John,' she said to Kendrick, 'I must go outside and face the crowd. I know they are against you and not me. I shall be perfectly safe.'

'No, Golden Orchid, they will hurt you also,' replied John. 'You know what they will take you to be. Just stay inside and remain quiet. The crowd will disperse.'

John had had an experience only a few days before. He had learned that it was wiser to avoid the crowd than to face it.

But the crowd did not disperse. In fact, it was getting noisier, and a gong was struck, as if calling all the villagers to gather in the yard. Then Golden Orchid took matters into her own hand. She opened the door and went out, closing it behind her, and faced the people in a frank, open, and confident manner.

'Friends!' she shouted. With that first word she was surprised that the people became quieter, as if eager to hear what she had to say. Golden Orchid noticed that the crowd was much smaller than she had thought and became more confident.

'My good people, I want to say something to you,' she continued. 'I know why you are here. These "ocean people" have done us wrong, great wrong. That we all know. I am Chinese like the rest of you, and I know it also.'

'Then why do you still help them?' cried a big, powerful man in the rear.

'I will tell you why,' replied Golden Orchid with great presence of mind. 'Those people inside that room,' she continued, her hand pointing to the room while she still faced the crowd, 'a man and his wife and their two small children — they are different. They are my friends and they are your friends.'

'No, no,' continued the big man, 'all *tien-chu-chiao* [Catholics] are our enemies. They have taken away our land. They have oppressed us. They are bad people, and you, you who try to protect them, you too are bad.'

The situation became tense. There were even cries of *Ta! Ta!* (strike! strike!), and though the crowd was small, it looked menacing, and the noise became louder and wilder.

'You are wrong, my good people,' Golden Orchid shouted back. 'I have papers here to show you that those inside the room have nothing to do with *tien-chu-chiao*. In fact, they hate the Catholics as much as you do. They are believers in *yieh-su-chiao* [Protestants].'

Golden Orchid spread out the sheet of red paper which was a kind of *laissez-passer* issued by the local magistrate at Tungchow for the protection of the Kendrick family.

The sight of the document produced an immediate change in the crowd, for the official word could still hold the people with its magical spell. Golden Orchid seized the opportunity to pursue the point she had made.

'I said that these "ocean people" inside the room are your friends as well as my friends. Mr Kendrick is a doctor, and last year he vaccinated hundreds of children in his hospital in Tungchow, so that we do not hear of smallpox any more in the neighbourhood. Surely you who live so near Tungchow must know about this. Perhaps some of the children here in our midst have been saved by the good doctor.'

Golden Orchid stopped, waiting for a comment. There was none, but she noticed that the people began to speak among themselves. The previous harshness rapidly melted into something soft and gentle and finally into something positively friendly. It was the women who took the initiative, for they were the beneficiaries of the doctor's work. The new friendly atmosphere quickly spread to all the other members of the crowd.

It might perhaps have been difficult to quieten the crowd had it been larger. But Golden Orchid proceeded cautiously and continued to appeal to reason. Before she had finished there were actually requests, among the women, that they be allowed to thank the good doctor and his wife. John Kendrick then stepped out, stood by the side of Golden Orchid in his Chinese dress and stiffly gave the traditional three bows to the crowd. The people were so delighted that what promised to be an unpleasant and even ugly scene turned out to be a warm send-off, with gifts of food and tea for the journey ahead. When Golden Orchid and the Kendricks went back to the two carts, it seemed as if they were the leaders of a triumphal march.

But the experience was deceptive. The Boxers had just begun to make trouble, and they were still unevenly received by the people in different districts. The fact that the Kendricks got away safely this time did not mean that the rest of the journey to Peking was going to be equally fortunate.

The carts went slowly on, traversing the same dusty roads and the same uneven cobblestones. As they drew nearer and nearer to Peking, Golden Orchid and the Kendricks felt more and more anxious. The children had been brave; but they were not only dirty, they were also tired with the heat and discomfort of the journey. Food they had had aplenty, though it was not the kind they had been brought up on, and there was danger that the whole family might be exposed to dysentery, malaria, typhoid or, worse, cholera. And besides, they might still be seized by an angry mob.

The more Nancy Kendrick thought of these things, the more frightened she became. She hugged the children to her body and put her head on John's shoulder while she said, 'Father, save me from this hour. Father, glory be Thy name,' and both she and John felt peace within them as she said, 'I know Whom I have believed and am persuaded that He is able to keep that which I have committed unto Him.'

Golden Orchid, in the other cart, talked to her mother. 'No one can call me a "second hairy one". It's the ignorant who accept this foreign religion. I can always out-talk the people and make them believe that I am one of their supporters.'

The mother felt better when her daughter spoke to her like this, but she had never suffered such hardship in her life, and she was worried lest something worse had befallen Hai-ming, Yang Mah and Lao Chuang.

'Daughter dear,' she asked Golden Orchid, 'do you think that those three are now safe in Peking? And how soon do you think we shall see them?' She looked worried as she spoke. She felt better when she began to count the beads of her sandalwood rosary, which she always carried wherever she went.

'O-mi-to-fu! O-mi-to-fu!' she muttered to herself. And in her mind's eye was the image of the smiling bodhisattva showering blessings on all who happened to be in trouble.

And so the two carts went slowly and heavily on. Golden Orchid's cart was in front. The driver walked alongside the mule helping the animal whenever there was a difficult stretch of road. At such times Golden Orchid would often walk herself. But most of the time she sat in the front and had an unimpeded view of the hot and steaming countryside, now overgrown with millet fully six feet high.

Suddenly the two carts drew near what was known as a rain procession. Golden Orchid called the driver to halt, as she had previously heard that the people in such a procession were likely to be in the worst of moods.

'Stop, driver, stop,' cried Golden Orchid. 'Let's not go any farther. Let's leave the road and hide ourselves in the millet field until we find out what this is about.'

There was no doubt that it was a rain procession. The driver came back to report that there were several hundred people in it, led by the magistrate of the village himself, decked in his official robes.

'They are on their way to the temple,' the driver said. 'You should have seen the magistrate, his face covered with perspiration. There has not been a drop of rain for three months, and you can see for yourself that even the millet, which does not need much moisture, is beginning to wilt. Let's keep quiet here and not move.'

'But you look a little frightened,' said Golden Orchid. 'What's wrong, driver?'

'Don't let your foreign friends hear this. But as I stood there watching the procession go by, I heard people cursing the *yang-kuei-tse*. It is the foreign devils, they say, who have brought on this drought. The people have prayed and prayed, and still there is no rain. They blame it on the foreigners because they have undermined the faith of the people in their own gods by preaching all this nonsense about *yieh-su* [Jesus Christ]. I tell you' —the driver whispered in Golden Orchid's ears — 'if these people find out that there are foreigners about, they will stone them and beat them to death. Let's all be very quiet.'

And so they all lay hidden in the tall millet some distance from the procession. Now and then there was a breath of fresh air, and the children, Nancy thought, behaved extraordinarily well. They played with the little grasshoppers and the crickets, which were still young and tender at this time of the year, for their wings do not grow to their full size till about the end of summer and the beginning of autumn when they begin to chirp.

Golden Orchid tried to look calm, but she was in fact much perturbed by the news. She wondered to herself whether it was proper to let the Kendricks know about it, for it seemed to her that it would be some time before they could move on. Even after the procession had passed, the discovery of these foreigners might start an unpleasant episode.

'The situation, I gather, is this,' Golden Orchid said to John and Nancy. 'The people are terribly angry with the foreign religions — with both the Catholics and Protestants. I can understand why. You must excuse me for saying so. They have worshipped Buddha as my mother does. They have their own gods and deities. Then along came your foreign religions to denounce these gods and say they are false. You have gone into their temples and desecrated their gods; you have even knocked them down, and by doing so you outrage both heaven and earth —'

'But we don't do that,' protested Nancy.

'No, not you. You and John don't go so far. That I believe. But you preach a new religion which undermines the people's old faith, and because of this they believe the rain gods do not send any more rain to them. Therefore they conclude the whole land must be swept clean of the foreigners. Now, all this is silly superstition, you may say, but there is also good sound common sense in it as the villagers see it. I can understand them.'

Golden Orchid realized, however, that this was no time to discuss the basic issues of belief, and they all remained silent till the procession had long passed. Exhausted with the heat and hunger of the journey, the children fell asleep on their mother's lap. When darkness had fallen they emerged from their hide-out and started to look for a place to spend the night.

Golden Orchid was afraid that to visit an inn in the company of her foreign friends would not be wise. As they resumed the journey she asked her mother to sit with Nancy and the children in one cart while she sat with John in the other.

'I was thinking, John, that we should be now quite near Peking, and I want nothing to happen between now and our arrival.'

'What have you to suggest?'

'We must first find an inn. I would suggest that my mother and I see the innkeeper, and then after we have secured the room, you and Nancy and the children can come in without being noticed. What do you think?'

'Just as you suggest.'

'I am only afraid that the innkeeper may be in sympathy with the people or may even be one of the Boxers. I think it is a necessary precaution.'

The arrangement worked well, for Golden Orchid saw to it that the innkeeper was adequately paid. Then early in the morning the two carts started on the remainder of the journey. At four-thirty in the morning, when it was barely daybreak, they started rolling along, with the two children still sound asleep in the laps of their parents, and two and a half hours later they saw the silhouette of Peking's towering eastern gate in the distance. Thus came to an end this strange and nerve-racking odyssey.

From the gate to the Diplomatic Quarter, where all the foreigners were congregated — diplomats, missionaries and merchants — was but a short distance. The travellers were anxious for news, but it was not encouraging. The big city was seething with the wildest rumours of impending disaster. However, the Kendricks felt that, if they had to suffer, they would at least be among their own people, as well as nationals of ten other countries numbering almost one thousand.

'Golden Orchid,' said John as soon as the carts drove into the American mission compound, 'we cannot thank you enough for all that you have done for us. You will have to stay with us here — yes, you and your mother. Not that this area is necessarily safer than the city itself, but Nancy and I feel that we should provide you from now on with as much comfort and protection as this area will allow.'

'Thank you, John,' replied Golden Orchid. 'I am happy that we have completed the journey as well as we have. But mother and I have other things to do. As I told you before, we left Tientsin with some other people whom we have lost. It was the stampede which brought us into Tungchow. I must thank the stupid, frightened mule for enabling me to meet you again. Good-bye, then. I shall now try to find those people. And I think I know where to find them.'

'It makes me so sad that you must leave,' Nancy said, shaking her head.

'But we shall see each other again — now that we have met. I shall be staying at the Soochow hostel.'

Nancy and Golden Orchid hugged each other and there were tears in their eyes. 'Cheer up, Nancy. All will be well,' said Golden Orchid, and she disappeared with her mother among the milling crowd of the sprawling metropolis.

'Take good care of yourself,' shouted Nancy. To her husband she said, 'What a remarkable girl!'

6

It was now the third week in June. On the day when Golden Orchid and the Kendrick family left Tungchow for Peking, the Tsungli Yamen, now with a rabid hater of the foreigners as its President, had informed the foreign diplomatic missions that a state of war existed. Lord Yu Kung had resigned, but had been asked to remain as one of the immediate Court attendants. The Taku forts, which served only as a symbol for the protection of Peking, had been captured by the foreign admirals. The Government was shocked by the action, and the Empress Dowager had summoned all the high-ranking ministers for an immediate audience with her. Her mind had actually long been made up, but the seizure of the forts gave her the excuse she needed to exterminate the foreigners. Seated on her dragon throne and with her ministers, in their resplendent official garb, all on their knees, she made the solemn announcement that the capture of the forts was a deliberate act of war on the part of the foreign powers and that therefore all the diplomatic missions must leave within twenty-four hours.

'Know ye,' she said in her concluding remarks, 'that instructions have been issued to all military officers to mobilize their forces in order to carry out our divine will.' The audience came to an end in complete and absolute silence! It was in this way that the anti-foreign movement became a matter of public policy.

When Golden Orchid left the diplomatic quarter to find her way to the Soochow hostel, she did not realize that there was already disorder and confusion created by large-scale burning, looting and massacre everywhere. Peking had proved to be no exception.

Tientsin was by now much worse than when she had left it. Even Tungchow, which she had left only two days previously, was going through terrible agonies.

'Mother dear, this is awful. But don't be frightened,' Golden Orchid said. 'Soon we shall find our way to the Soochow hostel. It is a large and peaceful place, and then you will have some rest.'

'But I don't see how we can reach this hostel,' commented her mother. 'I have never seen so many people going about in such haste.' For the first time in her life she saw a camel, with a few small patches of fur still remaining on its huge dirty body. She thought it an ugly beast, but it was a new sight, and for a while she almost forgot the bustle around her.

From the crowded main thoroughfares Golden Orchid instructed the driver to go into the *hutung*, but there the congestion was still worse. For the contents of the houses of rich and poor alike were being poured into these narrow winding streets, often making passage quite impossible. Chairs, tables, boxes of food and clothing were being dumped on carts and carriages as if everyone was moving out of the city.

'The people are in a panic,' explained Golden Orchid to her mother. 'Even so I think no place is safer than Peking. The thing to do is to remain as calm as possible.'

This, however, was no encouragement for her mother, who, like Yang Mah, wished every moment that she were back in Soochow. But she had learned to have confidence in her daughter, and to see her unperturbed was some consolation.

At long last the driver of the cart brought the two ladies to their destination. There was the Soochow hostel where twice before Golden Orchid had stayed with her scholar-husband. While other houses and residences had been burned or looted, the hostel was intact. But it was nearly deserted. On previous occasions Golden Orchid had counted as many as sixty or seventy guests, but now there were not more than ten, so the manager told her. He was hale and robust as ever and gave Golden Orchid a warm welcome. He was a fat man and, in spite of the large, round, palm-leaf fan with which he kept cooling himself, his body, naked to the waist, was covered with streams of perspiration.

'This is my mother, Fu Tai-tai,' said Golden Orchid. 'But tell me,' she asked the manager, 'hasn't anyone been here recently to ask for me?'

'Not that I know of, Madam. But I'll soon find out. Let me first show you to your room. You may choose whichever one you want, but perhaps you wish to stay in the room you and the ambassador had over a year ago? It happens to be vacant.'

'That will do very well.'

Golden Orchid and her mother soon made themselves comfortable, and memories of her previous visits came crowding into Golden Orchid's mind. But she was too worried over the whereabouts of Hai-ming, Yang Mah and Lao Chuang to be concerned with anything else.

'I am positive,' she said to her mother, 'that they would be here in this hostel if they reached Peking. What could have happened to them? They should have been here before us.'

The manager himself brought tea to the two ladies and said that his inquiries so far had been fruitless. 'However, don't worry. They will be here soon enough.'

'Do you remember Mistress Hai-ming?'

'Of course I do. That lady who used to stay here also?'

'Yes. We left Tientsin together when that city was in great turmoil. On our way to Peking there was a stampede, and in the ensuing chaos our cart took us to Tungchow. That is where we have come from. But they didn't make any detour and should have been here long ago.'

'Oh, they have probably met somebody, or perhaps something else might have happened. Madam, anything is possible these days. But we shall be on the look-out for them.'

Early next morning Ping-mo, Hai-ming, Yang Mah and Lao Chuang came into the hostel in as strange a group as one could find. Yang Mah rushed in to see Golden Orchid. Her face beamed with joy as she announced that the young master was with them.

'What? Did you say that Master Ping-mo is here with you?'

'Yes, Tai-tai. Look at him. Here he comes.'

But before Ping-mo and Golden Orchid could greet each other, Yang Mah broke into a flood of tears. 'If it had not been for Lao Chuang, we would have been here earlier. Oh, I wish the young master would now take us all back to the south. I was so frightened.'

'What happened, Lao Chuang?' Golden Orchid inquired.

'After we got separated,' said Lao Chuang, 'I became desperate, of course. I tried to find you everywhere. And then in a small village —'

'I was also trying to find you.' Ping-mo finished the sentence for Lao Chuang and looked happily at Golden Orchid. 'I knew I was going to find you.'

'On arrival at Peking,' Lao Chuang continued, 'we at once made our way to the hostel. Then in an empty space just outside the western *pai-lou* we found ourselves in a large crowd. I was curious and stopped to look.'

'Lao Chuang is always curious,' Yang Mah complained.

'Anyhow, I saw many things. There was a platform draped in red, with candles and incense. The Boxers were in the midst of praying for the spirits to descend and enter the bodies of the new recruits. The usual things, you know. Now, I don't happen to believe in all this nonsense, and I couldn't help laughing.'

'That was a very costly laugh for all of us,' added Hai-ming. 'For the crowd at once went for poor Lao Chuang and started to beat him.'

'They did — wicked people. I looked for young Master Ping-mo, but instead I saw Mistress Hai-ming and Yang Mah. They saved me.'

'But where were you then?' Golden Orchid asked Ping-mo.

'I was there, but I suppose I was lost in the crowd. Let Lao Chuang continue.'

'Luckily the young master did come to me, or they would have killed me. Well, a Boxer soon approached us and took all of us to an unknown hut where we were confined and interrogated. The young master tried to tell him who he was —'

'I don't blame him for not knowing me,' Ping-mo broke in. 'How could he?'

'Yes, but they did find out who you were, though,' rejoined Lao Chuang.

'Not until we had all suffered,' added Hai-ming. 'I had to take out all the money I had on me, just to show that we were sympathetic to the Boxers. And Yang Mah was terribly frightened.'

'Anybody would have been frightened, Tai-tai,' Yang Mah explained. 'Imagine seeing some ten people in a small room all stripped to the waist. On their naked bosoms was pasted a piece of yellow paper with an awful-looking figure. It had a head, the hands had sharp, pointed fingers, but there were no feet. It had large eyes. On one side was a green dragon, on the other a white tiger. We all bowed reverently to these people.'

'We had to,' added Ping-mo. 'That was how we left without further trouble. But its all over now.'

Golden Orchid took Ping-mo by the hand and led him into her room. 'Ping-mo, you don't know how happy I am that you are back with me,' she started. 'There are decisions to make — important decisions — and I cannot make them without you.'

'Why do you think I have come all this distance from the south?' replied Ping-mo earnestly. 'I knew from the very start that we — that is, our party of young intellectuals — could not control these Boxers once they turned into a huge mob, and they have! The government has given them every encouragement. I must be near you from now on. Tell me what you have in mind.'

'Ping-mo, you know I could have taken Mother and gone back to Soochow. To be away from all the troubles that I knew were coming. But I cannot do that. I am driven by a strong impulse to stay in Peking, come what may.'

Ping-mo, impressed by the note of deep seriousness in Golden Orchid's words, was prepared to hear whatever she had to say.

'Ping-mo,' continued Golden Orchid, 'Peking has dear memories for me, perhaps more than it has for you. Your father and I were here on two occasions, and I am here now to discharge a debt to myself and to your father. You know what I mean.' Golden Orchid buried her head in her hands as she spoke.

She looked up, after a brief pause, and was satisfied that Ping-mo understood what she meant. Then she continued: 'There is no reason why I should have lost a husband and you a father.'

'I have been thinking about it also,' Ping-mo said at last, 'but perhaps not exactly along the same lines.'

'Your father went through agonies of pain just because of the wickedness of that little devil Hu-mou. I saw him suffer. I went through those painful days with him. Ping-mo, to those I love I am prepared to give everything. But those I hate, those who have damaged and hurt me, I seek only to destroy. There is no middle ground. And I hate that Hu-mou more than any mortal in the world. You don't know, you can't know even a fraction of the misery, the sadness which that devil gave to me and to your father. Call it revenge if you choose. But there is something more than just personal revenge. That Hu-mou is the incarnation of the devil, and the world would be happier without him.'

Ping-mo gave her a long and penetrating look and then he said: 'And you think we now have the opportunity?'

'Yes, and, what's more, I shall not let it go by. There is no such thing as allowing wickedness to go unpunished. The wicked will have to go to hell, and that is where I shall send that devil. I cannot understand that Christian sentiment of turning the other cheek. Only saints can do that, and I am no saint. I am all too human.'

'But why,' asked Ping-mo with surprise, 'why mention the Christian religion? What's come over you? You don't mean to tell me that you have been associating with Christians!'

'I forgot to tell you, Ping-mo.' She explained her meeting with the Kendricks, and how she had helped to bring them to Peking.

'That was a very unwise thing to do,' reprimanded Ping-mo. 'It was very dangerous.' Angrily he lectured her again on the misdeeds of the foreigners and their Christian missionaries in China.

Golden Orchid listened to his fiery discourse and regretted having brought up this subject. She should have known that Ping-mo would argue with her, as he had on the houseboat. There was no point in talking about it, anyhow, when they were discussing something much more important.

But Ping-mo went on: 'This Boxer movement is the logical outcome of what we have received from the foreigners in a hundred years of utter ruthlessness. The movement is unfortunately in the hands of ignorant people, and it will fail. That is the tragedy of it. But, even so, we have to go on, if only to show to the world that we can be angry when we are abused. It is a very costly anger. But strangely enough the world will respect us because we are angry. Otherwise we shall die a slow and ignoble death. Even in death we shall be despised and trampled upon.'

'All right, Ping-mo, let's not talk about this unpleasant subject,' said Golden Orchid.

'You brought it up yourself, Golden Orchid. I don't want to talk about it. However, remember this: foreigners want to teach us to be humble and meek with their religion, but humility and meekness are the very things they despise. What they respect is courage, courage to fight back. They teach us to show the left cheek when the right one has been struck. Actually there is nothing they despise more. What they respect is to strike back on both cheeks when any one of your cheeks is struck. These foreigners are such insincere people. They preach one thing and do exactly the opposite. When they see others do what they preach, they despise and bully them.'

'Ping-mo, I am surprised you are so bitter against the foreigners.'

'Not any more bitter than you and I are against Hu-mou, and for the same reasons. That little devil has done my father wrong, and you and I are going to settle the account with him. That is exactly what China is doing to the foreigners. The only difference is you and I will not fail, while I am positive that we as a nation are going to fail miserably.'

'Let's talk about Hu-mou then.'

'Leave the matter to me. I think I have the means to deal with him.'

'You really mean it? You have the means? Tell me what they are.'

'What can be more simple than for me to contact a Boxer organization through one of our branch societies and say to them that there is a man rabidly hostile to them in the Tsungli Yamen? We can then leave it to the organization to take such action as it deems fit.'

'You think the plan will work? It sounds excellent. It does seem to be easier to carry out such plans when there is so much confusion.'

Golden Orchid was overjoyed, but she thought it over again and again. She held Ping-mo's hand and looked at him admiringly for having offered so simple and clean-cut a solution. Then she continued: 'Ping-mo, your plan is good, very good. But I have one also. If that should fail, we can always come back to yours. You know Hai-ming?'

'What about her?'

'Well, you may be interested in knowing that for some time she was Hu-mou's mistress, and she hates the little devil as much as anybody I know, and I am sure she would be glad to take revenge on him.'

'But are you sure of Hai-ming? And of her feelings towards Hu-mou?'

Golden Orchid smiled.

'Why do you smile?' Ping-mo asked.

'Oh, nothing. I was thinking your father once asked me the same questions in this very hostel.'

7

On a hot summer day Peking can give an appearance of utter calm and tranquillity. The tiles of the palace roofs — golden yellow, jade green and cobalt blue — reflect the blazing sun, while the palaces themselves stand noble and majestic, lined with row upon row of white marble balustrades carved in the sinuous forms of dragons; in the parks the cedars, white pines and cypresses stand ageless and erect in the motionless air. But now peace was no longer there. Within its towering walls and in the hearts of its million people there was hate mingled with fear such as they had not known for a thousand years. For many days the warm air had been laden with sickening smells of burning houses and rotting and decaying flesh. Now that the Boxers had been let loose, with death and destruction staring everyone in the face, the inhabitants of Peking were interested only in packing, hiding, fleeing, escaping, though no one knew where.

But Golden Orchid seemed as composed as ever. She felt cool in her room, which faced a spacious courtyard covered by a high canopy of reed matting to shut off the rays of the sun. She looked at herself in the mirror and felt satisfied. On her jet-black hair was her jade butterfly. She put on a little more powder, touched her lips with a little more rouge and then gave herself a last full look in the mirror. Her straight, lissome body was dressed in a thin and gauze-like silk garment with a faint suggestion of azure green. But what pleased her most were the full, round breasts which she had learned, in Europe, not to bind as Chinese ladies were then in the habit of doing.

Golden Orchid took leave of her mother and entered a waiting sedan chair, then difficult to procure, and was carried away for an important visit. Stepping down before the vermilion gate of the residence of his Lordship Yu Kung, she saw the old manservant, who at once recognized her and announced her arrival. His Lordship was not expecting her, but gave instructions that she be conducted into the elegant and spacious drawing-room.

In a few minutes Lord Yu Kung appeared, tall, straight and gaunt as always. They exchanged courtesies; Lord Yu Kung expressed his sorrow at the death of Wen-ching and asked the cause of it.

'He had been so depressed since those Berlin days, and on our way back to Soochow he contracted typhoid fever and passed away soon after our arrival.'

'That is sad indeed. I heard that you have since been in Tientsin.'

'I went there more than a year later — to eke out a living. I was hoping that Your Lordship might come and patronize my house.'

'I had hoped so myself. But I have not had time to go to Tientsin at all. I have, as you probably know, resigned from the Presidency of the Tsungli Yamen, but my duties with Her Majesty the Empress Dowager are even heavier on account of the present disturbance.'

'I can understand that. But your director Hu-mou is still at the yamen, isn't he?'

'Yes, he is an able man and knows well how to serve under any superior. The new president is Prince Tuan, and as a strong and implacable enemy of the foreigners, he is very much in favour with Her Majesty now.'

'And Director Hu-mou of course does what Prince Tuan wants him to do.'

'Exactly. That is the way to get on in the official world.' His Lordship smiled a wistful smile, with a faint suggestion of disapproval.

'I suppose Director Hu-mou, as in the days we used to know him, is still a very useful and influential man.'

'Oh, yes, that man is uncanny in removing all the obstacles in the way of his advancement. That was what he did to Brother Wen-ching, as you know well, and he almost used his trick on me. Fortunately the Court is still behind me.'

Golden Orchid moved to another subject. 'If things should become any worse — that is, if foreign troops should come here into the capital by the thousands with their powerful guns — what are we going to do?'

'I hope such a calamity will not happen.'

'I think that living abroad has made some difference in me. I feel, Your Lordship, that you have the power to do something to delay the crisis. Surely we don't want it to happen if we can help it.'

Lord Yu Kung in fact had been deeply anxious. He wished he had the power. But he was in a difficult and delicate position. He was close to the Empress Dowager, but he could not freely express his views when he knew that she was bitterly angry with the foreigners. The strongly anti-foreign elements had now got the upper hand. Men like Prince Tuan were wielding enormous influence, and it was wise that Lord Yu Kung and those who were not in sympathy with him should maintain a discreet silence. His Lordship pondered over the words of Golden Orchid, and it occurred to him that it might be useful if he could arrange to have her received in audience by the Empress Dowager.

'The first time you were here in Peking, on the eve of your departure for Europe, the Empress Dowager wanted to give you an audience. It did not take place. If I arrange one for you now, would you like it?'

'Thank you, thank you, Your Lordship,' replied Golden Orchid. 'But Wen-ching was then the ambassador-designate. Today I am nobody, a mere mistress of a sing-song house.'

Golden Orchid was right in having doubts. But Lord Yu Kung thought that if even one more person would express views similar to his own, it would mean a certain amount of gain. Perhaps Her Majesty would be glad to receive a woman who had been abroad in an important diplomatic capacity.

Two days after this interview a green sedan chair from the palace arrived for Golden Orchid. The hostel leaped into a state of the greatest excitement. Golden Orchid had been summoned for an audience with the Old Buddha! What glory! What supreme honour! But surely there must be a reason for this unusual event. The mistress of a sing-song house to be received in audience with the mightiest person in the land, when the capital, in fact all north China, was seething and boiling with the crowning discontent of the century! What was the reason? Everybody was anxious to find out.

An audience of this nature would ordinarily be attended by a good deal of fuss and fanfare, but it was given by the Old Buddha

for an important and urgent reason: it was no mere matter of ceremony. She dismissed all the eunuchs and attendants and commanded that Golden Orchid be conducted into the Phoenix Palace,
where Lord Yu Kung waited. Golden Orchid was so excited that
she felt as if her heart were jumping out of her body.

At last the Empress Dowager appeared, attended only by two
young maids-in-waiting, who immediately retired. She was a delicate woman, calm, sedate and unruffled both in her movements and
manner of walking. Both Lord Yu Kung and Golden Orchid
prostrated themselves in front of the august presence, but the Old
Buddha slowly and with great dignity stepped forward to help them
to their feet again. She looked tired, and her eyes, with loose pouches
under them, were those of one in deep concern. Then softly she
spoke: 'We have commanded you to come for a very special reason.
Please be seated.'

This was a very unusual gesture, never in living memory given to
any of her subjects.

The two maids-in-waiting brought tea, which was again unknown.
In this friendly atmosphere of relaxed tension and strict privacy the
Empress continued: 'We have heard that you stayed in Berlin, in
the country of Great Virtue [two Chinese characters standing for
Germany], with our ambassador Shen Wen-ching. You were very
popular and you were a great success. That has given us deep satisfaction, but we regret that the ambassador could not be here with
you today. We would like you to tell us something about these
"virtuous" people among whom you lived and the other peoples
you have seen.'

'Your Majesty, the humble one, with your Imperial blessing, was
in Europe for three years and knows Germany better than the other
countries. The German people are an energetic race. They are a
powerful nation. They are rich and the people seem to be well fed,
and I was told that their soldiers are the best in the world. How I
hope that one of these days Your Majesty will have the leisure to
travel there and give them some of Your Majesty's wisdom. I am
sure they will feel highly honoured and show Your Majesty their
deep respect.'

'This is well said, but why is it that these countries continue to be
unfriendly to us when we have done everything to be friendly to
them?'

'Yes, Your Majesty,' Golden Orchid answered, 'they have been most unappreciative of Your Majesty's gracious solicitude.'

'Nations, like human beings, should behave reasonably towards one another. They should respond to the commands of the moral law which rules all humanity. But look what these foreign powers have done to us. We've not had a day of peace since the reign of our glorious ancestor Chia Ching. They say they want trade, and they force it down our throats even when we do not desire it. Haven't we already opened up Canton and the other areas to accommodate them? We have done everything to please them, but they have done everything to hurt us. That is what I cannot understand. They behave as if they were the masters of the house. It is not without reason that we call them barbarians. They want our wealth, our riches. That is all they desire, and they have no scruples about resorting to any measure to obtain them.'

The Empress Dowager sipped a little of her tea and commanded the guests to do likewise. Having refreshed herself, she gave a long list of China's grievances brought on by the aggressive policy of the foreign powers, and concluded: 'There has been nothing like this in the entire five thousand years of our history.' With this last statement the Old Buddha clenched her fist and struck hard at the arm-rest of the dragon throne.

The silence which followed was deep and tense. Golden Orchid shivered within her and dared not speak a word. But she told herself, This is exactly what Ping-mo has been saying. One would think that he had been Her Majesty's high adviser all these years.

Lord Yu Kung had not spoken a word during the entire audience and would not risk any views now, though he knew he enjoyed the Empress Dowager's favour.

In a tone of sarcasm, the Old Buddha continued: 'The foreigners do anything they want with us, but have we not at least the right to show our righteous wrath and our anger? And then they say we are anti-foreign! Is there anything more ridiculous? Yes, we *are* anti-foreign *now*, but only because they have been deliberately anti-Chinese for at least a hundred years. What else can we be? That is why the Boxers have now risen to drive them away — yes, even exterminate them.' Even as she said this, her mind went back to the heap of ruins to which her Yuan Ming Yuan, more beautiful and magnificent than Versailles or any palace in the world, had been reduced by the joint British–French forces of 1860. From that day on her bitterness and hatred against the foreigners became the guiding principle of her life.

At this point Lord Yu Kung had the courage to say: 'What Your Majesty has said is the absolute truth. The only thing to think over is that these foreign nations have great fighting power. Supposing we fail —'

'That is what worries me,' snapped the Old Buddha. 'That is why I have summoned you, you who have lived among these foreigners. Perhaps you have a way out of this difficulty.'

The Old Buddha was now in a more sober and receptive mood, but, even so, who dared offer any suggestion? There was silence for a long time. And then the Empress Dowager went on — this time very quietly, as if speaking to herself: 'Yes, we have tried to be friendly, but all to no avail.' The tone of her voice was almost pathetic.

Turning to Lord Yu Kung, she said: 'Do you remember what took place two years ago? Do you remember bringing the Prussian Prince to our audience? Yes, Prince Henry.'

'I too remember Prince Henry, Your Majesty,' said Golden Orchid. 'He came to our embassy to see Wen-ching before he came here. We even had a farewell banquet for him.'

'Well, my child,' said the Old Buddha, 'during the audience, when we were freely exchanging remarks, he made the petition that we receive the ladies of the foreign diplomatic missions. We were glad that he made the petition because we were prepared to show our friendliness. We gave a sumptuous reception at the palace to which all the foreign ladies were invited.'

'Yes, I remember it was a grand occasion,' commented Lord Yu Kung. He adored the Empress Dowager for her intelligence and knew also that there was one side of her nature which was eminently rational. He suggested: 'Perhaps if Your Majesty continues to show friendliness to these foreign powers a day may come when they will appreciate it and abandon their aggressive policy. Even wild animals, so the saying goes, sometimes listen to reason.'

And Golden Orchid timidly suggested: 'Yes, His Lordship may be right. Let them be given one more chance to know that this Boxer movement can be suppressed if from now on the foreign powers will behave properly.'

'Very well,' assented the Old Buddha, 'if the two of you think so. We shall be glad to give a further expression of our friendliness. What would you suggest?'

'The foreigners have most to do with the Tsungli Yamen,' continued Lord Yu Kung, 'and that is now in the hands of men like Prince Tuan and his followers, who are known to be anti-foreign. If Your Majesty will remove them and appoint them to some other posts —'

'We shall not hesitate to have some of them shot to please these foreigners — if that does any good. Prince Tuan belongs to the Imperial Household and we still have use of him. But who is immediately under him? We will begin by shooting him first. That should be sufficient indication of our continued friendliness.'

Golden Orchid thought the crucial moment had arrived. Lord Yu Kung had Hu-mou's name on his lips; he hesitated to mention it, but he remembered how towards the end of his presidency Hu-mou had been cruel to him, as cruel as he had been to Wen-ching. If he mentioned his name, he was sure Golden Orchid would be more than happy. And there was no reason why he should not please Golden Orchid.

'Well, then, tell us,' the Old Buddha commanded.

'There is one man who does all the planning for Prince Tuan. The foreigners know his attitude well, and his elimination would be highly gratifying to them.'

'Then let us know the man this very instant.'

'Director Hu-mou,' was Lord Yu Kung's laconic answer.

Golden Orchid sat taut in her chair, her eyes closed and not a muscle moved, so intent was she to know how Her Majesty would react to those fatal words 'Director Hu-mou'.

The response came quickly. 'All right, send him to the executioner. Yuan Shih-kai will be commanded to carry out our Imperial wishes.'

The audience was over. Lord Yu Kung and Golden Orchid prostrated themselves again before the Old Buddha and retired. It was a long walk through the palace courtyard to where the green sedan chair was waiting to take Golden Orchid back to the Soochow hostel. Lord Yu Kung accompanied her, but there was not one word of conversation between them. The sun shone brilliantly over the golden roofs and dazzled their eyes. Golden Orchid walked slowly, pensively, but with great restraint and dignity. Her thoughts were incoherent. At times her mind flashed back to Yung-kai when he left the embassy on his white horse on that long overland journey to Peking. At other times she thought of the intimate hours she had spent in his apartment. But one thought especially eddied round her mind: Has the hour really struck for Hu-mou? And then, as she was approaching the gate where his Lordship was to say goodbye to her, she looked up into the clear, blue sky, where clusters of white clouds were sailing peacefully towards the west, and she gave a long, deep sigh and merely said: 'Thank heaven!'

As Golden Orchid stepped into the waiting sedan chair, she turned and, facing Lord Yu Kung, she stretched out both her hands in a manner which she had learned in Europe, and said, smiling: 'Your Lordship, I shall never be able to repay you for what you have done.'

Lord Yu Kung took the small, dainty and perfectly groomed hands in his own, felt their cool, soft, smooth skin and merely smiled back.

8

GOLDEN ORCHID could now afford to take her mind away from her immediate problems. With the solution of the greatest of all problems, in the shape of Hu-mou's impending execution, she thought that all others were minor and subsidiary.

Some time during her sojourn in Berlin she had seen a performance on the stage of the story of Salome. She could not understand what it meant, but the gruesome scene of a head on a platter had haunted her ever since. It now came back vividly in her mind, and she could not wait to see on the platter the head of her most hated enemy.

But for the present she wanted relaxation. She wanted to go out and see the sights of Peking — with Ping-mo — yes, Peking, even now when the city was beginning to writhe in its agonizing travail and torment. And yet who knew? All this might well be over and seem like a bad dream if the Old Buddha decided to put a stop to it. Ping-mo was the only person to whom Golden Orchid gave any information about the imperial audience.

They went out to the Northern Lake, behind the palace, to that same restaurant where four years previously she had had lunch with Yung-kai. It was the same wonderful view she saw — the dagoba towering into the blue sky, the white marble balustrades, and the graceful camel-back bridge forming a perfect circle with its own shadow in the water. The lotus with its huge pink-and-white blossoms covered every part of the lake. The walks were still carpeted with needles from the ageless pines. And that stone table where she and Yung-kai had sat opposite each other holding hands — that too was still there. She gave one furtive look at it and then directed her eyes elsewhere.

When Golden Orchid and Ping-mo came back to the restaurant, they sat down for some tea and cakes and a plate of the freshly cut lotus roots Ping-mo was so fond of. Golden Orchid brought up the subject of the Emperor, who was known to be somewhere in the neighbourhood of the Northern Lake. He was reputed to be a great lover, and it was her desire to meet him if she could.

The restaurant was practically deserted, and the owner had time to sit down and chat with his two guests. 'This is a sad, sad story,' he commented. 'No one is allowed to see the Emperor now. He lives alone on the Ocean Terrace.' And he pointed to a small island in the distance.

Ping-mo knew the story; his sympathy had been with the Emperor and with his ill-fated attempts at reform, to make China a modern nation, a strong and progressive nation, along those principles which his secret society knew so well. But he pretended ignorance and waited to hear what the innkeeper had to say.

'The Emperor, as you perhaps know,' continued the innkeeper, 'has been in virtual imprisonment since those hundred days of reform. The Empress Dowager was angry with him and so she placed him on that small island in the South Lake —' He stopped, fearing that he had spoken too much in front of people whom, after all, he did not know well.

'Please go on,' said Golden Orchid. 'What has been happening to him? I promise you that we shall not utter a word after we leave here. We see where you stand and we are on your side.'

'Well, if you promise not to repeat it, I will tell you something which I think is worth hearing. You see, when the Emperor was confined to this island all by himself, he made one request. He asked that the Pearl Concubine stay with him. He really loves her. But a group of eunuchs stepped in, and you know what eunuch politics is — this country is being ruined by the eunuch mentality. Officials, scholars, everybody admires and emulates and flatters the powerful eunuchs. But they have no sense of right or wrong, justice or injustice. All they are interested in is the advancement of their own selfish desires, and they do this by always being on the side that has the most power.'

'But, my dear man,' interrupted Golden Orchid, 'aren't you getting away from the story you set out to tell us?'

'Pardon me. Where was I? I was going to say that the eunuchs, in order to please the Empress Dowager, said: "All right, the Emperor can have the Pearl Concubine, but she must stay on another island near by." Hence the present arrangement. She is so near the Emperor, and yet so far away.'

'What do you mean?' asked Ping-mo.

'Well, she is behind bars on that other island, at this very moment. Poor woman, she is ill-fed and ill-clothed. She pines for her imperial lover. You can imagine how the Emperor feels about his beloved concubine being in such distressing conditions. Now, to make a long story short, all that love, all that devotion, between these two people has melted the hearts of some of the attendants, even though they are under instructions to carry out the wishes of the eunuchs.'

'What do they do?'

'Well, miss, some of these attendants are risking their lives to help these two imprisoned people. They have cut away the lotus between the two islands, which are some three hundred feet apart, and in the dead of the night a small boat appears at the Emperor's island so that he can be ferried across to his beloved one. No crossing on moonlight nights, of course. In this way the Emperor manages to see the Pearl Concubine, but between them there is still the iron railing. No one dares to take that down. Perhaps in time someone will. The man who has the key to the iron door stays with the palace guard. But the important thing is that the Emperor does meet his beloved concubine. What goes on when they meet — with the iron railing in between — no one has seen and no one will ever know. . . .' And the innkeeper looked wistfully at the two young people.

Early next morning news spread among restricted official circles that the Empress Dowager had taken a stand against the Boxers. It was said that some of them were even to be executed outside the Chienmen Gate, and this was correctly reported as the last step to be taken to show friendliness to the foreigners. It was also rumoured that Yuan Shih-kai had been commissioned to carry out the imperial orders. Before he did so, Yuan sent his agents to the diplomatic quarter to explain the purpose of the move. But he was as wily as he was unscrupulous. He had to obey the orders of the Empress Dowager, but by so doing he was making himself an enemy of the Boxers, and the time had not yet come for him to take sides.

So he gave a banquet, to which he invited some of the Boxer leaders. They took him for their new patron. He treated them well and said that the time was rapidly approaching when they would be called upon to prove their usefulness to the country. Without hesitation they all said that they were ready. They affirmed that they had completed the necessary training and were now immune to any gun or knife. If he so desired, they said, they were willing to undergo a test.

That was precisely what the wily Yuan wanted. He would then be obeying the orders of the throne without, at the same time, incurring the displeasure of the Boxers. So he at once put a group of these fanatics — at their own request — before the firing squad. He gave instructions, in accordance with the wishes of the Empress Dowager, that Hu-mou be included among them. When the soldiers fired, everyone of course was killed. But those who were still at the banquet actually believed that the dead deserved the punishment, for they obviously had not received proper discipline, or perhaps there had been some blemish in their character.

Yuan then chose a second group to face the firing squad — with, naturally, the identical result. When the banquet was over, those who managed to leave did so without a murmur and with no hatred towards Yuan, thinking only that they were themselves to blame for the lack of adequate training! To the very last they naively but firmly believed that they would be absolutely immune from physical destruction if they had the proper discipline.

Golden Orchid and Ping-mo waited anxiously to hear the news that their worst enemy was dead. Lao Chuang was asked to be near the execution ground and see Hu-mou's family come to claim the dead body. In fact, he went over the dead bodies himself, but he was surprised that he could neither find Hu-mou's body nor see any member of his family claiming it.

Lao Chuang hurried back to the hostel and dejectedly reported to Golden Orchid and Ping-mo that Hu-mou's body was nowhere to be found.

'What can have happened?' Ping-mo asked, looking at Golden Orchid in utter bewilderment. 'Is it again one of those tricks of Yuan Shih-kai's? He is one of the foxiest men alive.'

'There is no question,' Golden Orchid said, 'that Yuan reported to the Empress Dowager that her orders had been faithfully carried out. If Hu-mou is still alive, some powerful man must have brought pressure to bear upon Yuan. Of that I am sure. You and I are then in danger of our lives.'

The situation was critical for Golden Orchid and Ping-mo. How were they going to find out what had happened? Ping-mo suggested that Golden Orchid visit Lord Yu Kung again, but she preferred to think the matter over carefully.

'Why not take Hai-ming into our confidence? She may throw some light on the matter, for she hates Hu-mou quite as much as we do.'

But Hai-ming was nowhere to be found. Worse than that, Golden Orchid's mother told them that Hai-ming had not slept in the hostel for many successive nights. Golden Orchid and Ping-mo became hysterically worried and wondered whether they had been betrayed by Hai-ming after all. She was once Hu-mou's mistress. Was it possible that they had now become reconciled? In that case, there was no doubt that everything that had happened, including the audience with the Empress Dowager, had become known to Hu-mou.

It was the most terrifying night Golden Orchid and Ping-mo had ever passed. They were in two separate but adjoining rooms, and, casting all considerations to the wind and unmindful of any gossip that might ensue, they visited each other and talked and planned what to do.

They were together until the small hours of the morning. Then, just before daybreak, a loud knock came at the door. They were mortally frightened. Golden Orchid tried to be as calm as possible. She went slowly to the door and opened it. It was Hai-ming! She almost collapsed on the floor in front of Golden Orchid.

'Why, Hai-ming,' exclaimed Golden Orchid, 'what has happened?'

Golden Orchid helped her to her feet and led her to her bed. Hai-ming was shivering; her hands were cold. Her hair was dishevelled and her clothes seemed to have been torn.

'Where have you been, Hai-ming?' asked Golden Orchid.

For a long time Hai-ming did not utter a word. Ping-mo brought a hot towel with which Golden Orchid wiped her face. And then, with fiery and bloodshot eyes, Hai-ming grasped her hand and exclaimed: 'I have killed Hu-mou! Yes, I have killed him. At long last he is dead.'

Golden Orchid and Ping-mo looked at each other and couldn't believe what they had heard.

'Do you mean,' said Ping-mo, 'do you mean to say that you yourself have killed Hu-mou — with your own hands?'

'Yes. That is exactly what I have done.'

Now that Hai-ming had done what she had long wanted to do and said what she had wanted to say, she grew calmer. She continued: 'I will tell you what happened. But let me have some tea first.'

Ping-mo brought the tea, and then she resumed: 'I have been going back to the house where he kept me as his mistress. I found out that he still went there. I told him that I had repented and would be glad to live with him again if he, on his part, would treat me decently. He was still haughty, but at last he gave in. Then one night he came into the house in a state of great excitement and told me he was thankful he had that extra house, that there was someone to whom he could come. I asked him what had happened. At first he hesitated to tell me, but afterwards he gave me to understand that the Empress Dowager, for some unknown reason, had issued instructions to have him shot, that Yuan Shih-kai was the man to carry out the orders.'

Hai-ming drank some more tea, and went on: 'So I asked Hu-mou how he had managed to escape from the trap. He said: "I am fortunate in having the President of the Board of Military Affairs as my friend and confederate. He intervened and foiled the scheme. We went to see Yuan, who agreed to have a Boxer captured instead of me. That Boxer died in my place".'

'So that was what happened,' said Golden Orchid with great relief. 'Now things are becoming clear, Ping-mo.'

'He slipped into bed with me and I showered assumed sympathy on him and did everything to please him and make him happy. He was overwhelmed with joy. I gave him wine, and then, after having his pleasure with me, he sank into a deep and profound sleep. My opportunity had come. I swore to myself that I must take revenge — for myself, for you, for Ping-mo's father, and even for the Boxer who died in his place. Quietly I slipped out of bed and picked up the knife which I have carried with me ever since the day the military officer kidnapped me and took me to Manchuria. It was his knife. I took it and plunged it into Hu-mou's naked body. I aimed at the heart. He cried out. It was not even a loud cry — and then it was all over.'

Golden Orchid and Ping-mo were spellbound and speechless. Golden Orchid was sitting on the side of the bed, while Ping-mo leaned against the bedpost. Neither uttered a word.

Hai-ming pointed to a small package she had brought with her. 'The knife is still inside that package if you wish to see it.'

By now it was daylight. Ping-mo clenched his teeth and began untying the knot of the cloth package. It was wet. He took it to the window. In front of his horrified eyes was the blood-stained knife some six inches long, its steel still glistening in the light of the early dawn. By the side of the knife were two bloody lumps of tissue. Ping-mo recoiled and said as if automatically: 'But what are these?'

'Those?' commented Hai-ming. 'Those were his eyes, his wicked eyes. They will not roll up any more as they did when his vicious mind was engrossed in wicked schemes to hurt other people.'

Golden Orchid did not want to look at the package. But somehow she felt irresistibly attracted, in spite of herself, to that direction. She almost fainted.

Hai-ming was now her normal self again. She sat on the side of her bed and drank tea as if she were really enjoying it. Looking at Ping-mo and Golden Orchid, she said: 'The disturbance in the city has made my job so much simpler. Normally I should at least try to hide his body. Now I need not. I left it where I stabbed him with a list of ten crimes on it, for any one of which he deserved to be killed. I have also branded him as an anti-Boxer because I am sure it will be the Boxers who will break into the house first.'

Ping-mo looked at Hai-ming and felt strangely fascinated by her. It was incredible that so frail a woman's body could be so compact with hatred, of a kind so venomous that it went straight for its object without the slightest hesitation. However, justice was done — that was the principal thing. And Ping-mo recalled the famous lines of Lao-tse: 'Heaven's net is very vast. Though it is wide-meshed, it loses nothing.'

Ping-mo said aloud: 'No wickedness can escape the wrath of Heaven!'

9

'My distinguished colleagues,' said the ambassador from Spain, 'I leave the matter to your consideration. If you desire to ask instructions from your governments, you have a right to do so, and we will assemble again in a few days to discuss any new developments.'

'There is no need,' objected the Russian ambassador. 'The situation is clear enough. It is for us to make up our minds and report the decision to our governments. As far as my government is concerned, we have decided what we shall do. If need be, we shall proceed independently, irrespective of what the diplomatic corps as a whole may agree upon.'

At this point the American ambassador became uneasy and spoke out: 'After all, my distinguished colleagues realize that my government has more at stake in the situation than other countries. Many missionaries are Americans, and they are suffering all over north China. If I were to tell you some of the stories I have heard from those who have been fortunate enough to come to Peking and join us here in the diplomatic quarter, it would make your blood boil. Why, only the other day the Kendrick family arrived from Tung-chow, and they told me some appalling things. But I can assure you that not every Chinese is Boxer-minded. The Kendricks were saved through the courage and devotion of a young Chinese woman and her mother. If we can establish peace with the Chinese Government, I am all for it. The Empress Dowager has given us an olive branch, and I think we should accept it.'

This made some impression. For a time the assembled dignitaries whispered to one another and made no comment.

The occasion was an unusual one. The diplomats were all seated in the reception room of the Spanish Embassy in shirt sleeves. Peking was the only capital in the world in which foreign diplomatic missions lived and talked business together in a specially allocated area. Whenever there was an issue affecting their common interests, they had a meeting called by their doyen to discuss and decide upon common measures to be presented to the Chinese government. Union meant strength; that was the first lesson they had learned in dealing with the 'wily' Oriental — and the Chinese were the most Oriental of Orientals. Now that the missions were confronted by the common danger of the Boxers, there was no question that the bond should be made even firmer. Every afternoon they assembled by turn in the different 'compounds', with their wives and children and the families of their staff, to exchange information and ideas on the events of the day.

The Spanish ambassador, the senior member by virtue of his long residence in Peking, had received, on the previous day, information that the Empress Dowager had taken a new and important step of conciliation. As the matter called for serious and earnest consideration, he invited the heads of the missions to his drawing-room. Eleven other countries were represented — France, Germany, Austria-Hungary, Belgium, the United States, Britain, Russia, Italy, Japan, Portugal and Holland.

The American ambassador waited for other opinions. The British ambassador was inclined to agree with him, but he was still inclined to view the situation with concern.

The French ambassador, twisting his neatly trimmed moustache now with his right hand, now with his left, said: 'I am sorry that I cannot entirely agree with my distinguished American colleague. But the Protestant missionaries are from his country and from England. How about the Catholic missionaries? They are mostly French, are they not? And the French Catholics are suffering very much, more so than the Protestants. Here in Peking, only a few miles from the diplomatic quarter, the Catholic mission at Peitang is already under siege. We all know it. I would be the first to welcome any conciliation, but what proof is there that the Chinese Government truly desires it?'

The Spanish ambassador, as chairman, then called attention to the fact that the Empress Dowager had executed one high official, from the Tsungli Yamen itself, who was known to be a Boxer sympathizer.

'That was meant,' he concluded, 'to show the diplomatic missions that the Chinese Government wanted to live in friendly relations with the rest of the world.'

The German ambassador could no longer keep silent. The Geheimrat knew all along that the Chinese Government was disposed to take, as far as possible, a conciliatory attitude towards the whole tragic development of events in China. But he was the ambassador extraordinary and plenipotentiary of the German Reich. He was under instructions to stand for his rights. The young and vigorous Kaiser was not to be trifled with. He had launched the policy of *Drang Nach Osten*. He had always thought that Germany was entitled to a sizeable morsel of that juicy steak known as the Chinese Empire.

For a time, while Wen-ching was ambassador in Berlin, the Kaiser was persuaded that he must go slow with his policy. It was for that reason that he allowed the Kaiserin to give a reception to Golden Orchid at the Schloss Charlottenburg. It was for that reason that he made the gift of a white steed on the anniversary of the Chinese Emperor's accession to the throne. But with Wen-ching's recall and disgrace it became all too clear to him that the Chinese Government was a hotbed of intrigue, of petty jealousy, of murderous rivalry, dominated by grasping and corrupt officials who looked after their own personal interests more than those of their Empire.

From then on he pursued his policy with firmness, and for the price of the lives of two German missionaries he succeeded in carving out for himself a large slice of the rich and fertile territory in China's sacred province of Shantung. It had everything he desired — a beautiful harbour, with a magnificent coast-line in close proximity to all the strategic areas, wonderfully salubrious climate, rich and productive soil, and millions of sturdy and trustworthy people who could be depended upon to build up for him a powerful empire in the East. He had given instructions to his diplomatic envoy at Peking to be on the alert for any fresh opportunity. And what could be better than the present turmoil of the Boxers, whose certain defeat would immeasurably increase his sphere of influence and power in China? How could the envoy therefore regard with any sympathy the American policy of conciliation?

'Don't let ourselves be misled,' exclaimed the German envoy, 'by what we have heard about the Empress Dowager. Has anyone here actually seen the body of this high official of the Tsungli Yamen who was supposed to have been shot under her instructions?'

He paused for an answer. There was none. Then he continued: 'This man Hu-mou is known as the one who has been responsible for the anti-foreign policy of the Tsungli Yamen. When I heard that he was going to be shot, I sent my agents to the scene of execution. They have reported to me. They told me that a Boxer, a peasant, who had some resemblance to Hu-mou was shot in his place. Don't you see, my distinguished colleagues, that it was all a trick on the part of the Chinese Government to fool us again?'

The suggestion that Hu-mou had escaped being executed, even if there was no proof, came as a great shock and caused a furore among the diplomatic dignitaries. What had actually happened no one, of course, was in a position to know. The agents of the German Embassy had not found out the truth of Hu-mou's death. The fact that his body had not been seen and identified on the execution ground was a strong argument to support the German ambassador's position, which was immediately supported by the Russian diplomat.

'It is too late,' he argued, 'to speak about conciliation. Even if the Empress Dowager has expressed her willingness to be at peace with us, it should have been done many months ago. Now, it is too late. She should have suppressed the Boxers before they grew strong. All our relief forces are now on their way. When they meet and join hands here in Peking, they will be so formidable that nothing in China will be able to resist them. What then have we to be afraid of? The soldiers of the Imperial Russian Army are at this moment, as I speak, in Tsitsihar enforcing law and order among the Chinese population, and that is what we intend to do wherever we go.'

Not everyone regarded this Russian stand sympathetically. The American diplomat as usual took strong exception to it. 'The task of our distinguished Russian colleague,' he said, 'is simple, of course. That we all see. There are all the riches of Manchuria at his back door. Besides, there are practically no Russian nationals to protect as against the hundreds and the thousands whose lives we, along with some other countries, must protect and save.'

The Russian diplomat felt the sting of those words. His British colleague deftly tried to mollify passions all round. But the Japanese ambassador, who until then had looked glum and unprepossessing, asked to say a few words. Little did anyone expect that he would add fuel to the fire.

'Our distinguished Russian colleague,' the Japanese commented, 'was quite right in saying that Russian soldiers are now enforcing law and order. I have just received a report, and I am sure we shall all be glad to know how this law and order is being enforced. He spoke about Tsitsihar, and my report came from that city. The Russian Cossacks rounded up a community of some three thousand Chinese merchants in that city whom they forced to give up all their possessions. The entire body was then compelled to cross the Nonni River. When they arrived at the bank, there was not a single boat to take them across. Then the Cossacks began to enforce law and order, if you please. They lined themselves behind the three thousand Chinese with fixed bayonets and compelled them, men and women, young and old, to jump into the water. The cries and moans of that huge crowd of unfortunate people, so the report tells me, shook the heavens until they were drowned by the angry water of the mighty river. There was then complete peace, complete law and order.' The Japanese ambassador quietly sat down.

The face of everyone in the audience turned pallid. Everyone looked in the direction of the Russian diplomat, expecting an explosion. But nothing happened; the Russian diplomat simply directed the attention of the gathering to something else.

'What can we expect when we are virtually at war already?' he commented. 'What has any of us to be afraid of? There are some four hundred and fifty guards in this exclusive diplomatic quarter to protect the lives of all of us. These guards will soon be reinforced by the troops now on the way. Besides, we already have outside Taku eighteen men-of-war, forty-one transports and two medical ships, which are ample to take care of our needs. What have we to be afraid of? We all know these to be facts.'

But while everyone else chose to remain quiet the American ambassador was vociferously angry. 'Of course we are not afraid,' he exploded. 'Whoever made the faintest suggestion that we are afraid? It is not fear that we are concerned with but decency.'

A protest on so high a moral plane was unusual in diplomacy. But as the American diplomat was making these remarks, he was not unmindful of the safety of the large American community for which he was responsible. Four hundred and fifty guards! What could they do to prevent an avalanche of Boxers if they decided to rush into the unprotected area? He continued: 'Now that our distinguished Japanese colleague has told us what has happened in Manchuria, let me tell you something that happened on the high seas. Our Russian colleague —' the American was so angry that he dropped the usual preface 'distinguished' — 'our Russian colleague had no comment to make on the gigantic swimming gala of the three thousand Chinese in the Nonni River. Perhaps he may have some comments to make on the following story. One of our destroyers had the misfortune not long ago to strike a reef outside Peitaiho —'

'I protest,' exclaimed the Muscovite. 'This is a diplomatic conference. This is not a story-telling contest.'

But he was over-ruled, as everyone was interested in hearing what the American ambassador had to say.

'It so happened,' the American diplomat continued, 'that a small Chinese cruiser was near by. The captain of that cruiser asked the American skipper if he needed any help. At that moment a Russian man-of-war came by, and its captain reprimanded the American skipper for being on friendly terms with the Chinese captain. "The Chinese are our enemies," said the Russian. "You should have captured the captain and sunk his cruiser." Whereupon the skipper replied: "How in decency could I do any such thing when the Chinese captain came to me with an offer of help? And, besides, we are not in any official state of war." The Russian captain turned a deaf ear and was about to carry out what he thought should have been done. Then quietly but firmly the American skipper faced the Russian and said, "Though my destroyer is in difficulty, I have enough guns available to deal with you," and he directed his guns towards the Russian craft. The Russian captain left the scene in disgust. This incident occurred only about a month ago. Yes, gentlemen, I don't care what you think of my country, but I believe that we should all have a sense of decency and fair play — even in international relations. I personally happen to have great admiration for Chinese civilization, and we do wrong in renouncing our Christian principles in our dealings with China.'

Before the American diplomat could finish his speech people began to cough and there were noisy whisperings among them as if they were wondering whether he was in his proper senses.

'Imagine talking about Christian principles in dealing with China!' exploded the German ambassador, loud enough to be heard by the others, and then he chuckled to himself as if he had made an unusual observation.

'*Mein Gott!*' he said as he stood up. 'It is time to call off the meeting. It's a waste of time — and in such hot weather. Fancy talking about Christian principles to these swine! If only we would all do what I have done, there would be no such problem as we are facing today.'

What the brave German diplomat had done everyone knew. For it was only the previous day that he had done it, and the incident was fresh in the mind of everybody. The French ambassador thought that his German colleague might as well carry away all the laurels while he was at it. He therefore said: 'The political situation is indeed very grave. And what, pray, did you do?'

'I am glad you ask,' came the prompt reply from the German. 'Imagine, here in the privileged sanctuary of the diplomatic quarter the Boxers have been allowed to roam about without hindrance. That has been going on for many days now —'

'Yes, the Boxers. Always those Boxers!'

'If our distinguished French colleague will not interrupt me, I will tell you what happened yesterday. I came out for my morning constitutional — one needs it badly these days — and, right in front of my eyes, what did I see? Sitting with the driver in one of those hooded carts was a full-blooded Boxer with a piece of red cloth round his head and a red sash around his waist. And what do you think he was doing? Nonchalantly sharpening his big knife on the sole of his slipper! Can you imagine such insolence? And what do you think I did? Invoke Jesus Christ and talk Christian principles to the murderer?'

'Had he then already murdered someone?' inquired the American diplomat.

'That is irrelevant. If he was not then a murderer, there is no question that he had murderous intentions. Well, anyway, I resorted to the use of my walking-stick, and before he could escape I had given him a sound lesson. He ran into a neighbouring alley —'

'And of course there was no time for the Sermon on the Mount,' interrupted the French diplomat.

'No, indeed! I went after him. Before I could catch him, someone, no doubt full of the milk of human kindness and Christian mercy, intervened, and the rascal disappeared. I never saw him again, which is a great pity.'

The Spanish ambassador was about to end the session when the American diplomat suddenly asked for another word.

'One moment, please, my distinguished colleagues. I have some information which I have just received,' he said. He raised his voice above the noise of the dispersing gathering. 'The man who has been giving ideas to Prince Tuan in his anti-foreign policy is actually dead. The report is absolutely reliable. He was the same man whom the Empress Dowager wanted to have shot. It is true that he escaped. But it is true also that he is now dead — murdered by the hand of his mistress.'

The gathering roared with laughter and left the room amidst such comments as 'How credulous these Americans are!' 'Another example of your Christian principles!'

When the American diplomat returned to his quarters, he found his wife in the drawing-room with two other ladies having tea. One of them he recognized. It was Mrs Kendrick of Tungchow. The other was a Chinese lady whom he had not seen before. She was young, attractive, and at first he thought she might be one of the converts.

Mrs Kendrick hastened to introduce them. 'Mr Ambassador,' she said, 'I wish to introduce you to Madam Golden Orchid, the wife of the former Chinese ambassador in Berlin.'

'Pleased to meet you, Madam!' replied the ambassador in a very friendly manner.

Mrs Kendrick immediately turned to the purpose of Golden Orchid's visit. 'It was Madam Golden Orchid who was kind enough to bring me the important message which was placed in your hands. What did the other foreign diplomats say about it?'

'Do you, Madam,' asked the American diplomat, turning to Golden Orchid, 'have it on reliable authority that this director of the Tsungli Yamen is dead? It is very important that I know the absolute truth.'

'What I have told you is the truth,' replied Golden Orchid. 'I know the girl who killed him. What's more, the girl is staying with me and my mother. It was the wish of the Empress Dowager that he should die, and he is dead. And you know of course why the Empress Dowager wanted him to die, Your Excellency.'

'Yes, yes, I know — But what are we going to do about it?' The American diplomat looked deeply perplexed and began pacing the floor, muttering to himself: 'It all seems to be too late now — too late. And the situation is very grave!'

'You must do something, Mr Ambassador' said Golden Orchid in desperation. 'The Empress Dowager does not wish for trouble, and the death of this director is an expression of her wish to live at peace with the rest of the world. You know that, while there are die-hards who insist on wiping out the foreign population, there are others who want a policy of peace. If this last peaceful measure of the Empress Dowager is repudiated by the foreign diplomats, then the diehards will gain the upper hand, and the consequences will indeed be very grave. Time is running out rapidly. We must do something.'

'I know it! I know it! But I must think it over,' exclaimed the American diplomat, his face showing signs of deep irritation. Without so much as saying goodbye to Golden Orchid, he retired to his office and summoned two of his closest advisers for consultation.

'If it was only a matter concerning the United States alone, I think we know what we would do. But there are eleven other foreign diplomats, each with his own particular national interests to look after.'

'I am afraid,' said one of the advisers, 'that many of the powers are trying to fish in muddy waters. The worse the situation becomes, the better it is for them to expand their interests at the expense of China.'

'That's exactly it,' replied the ambassador. 'But as a matter of record, I think we should let Washington know that the Empress Dowager did give further expression of her desire to live in peace by having one of her high officials executed.'

'I'll see what I can do. The wires, I understand, have already been cut, and there will be difficulty in sending out any message.'

While this discussion was going on, Golden Orchid was speaking to Nancy Kendrick. 'I know you are with me, Nancy,' she said, 'and therefore I cannot insist too strongly that you and your husband do all you can to make your ambassador persuade the other foreign diplomats to pursue a policy of peace. We must stop this senseless slaughter. If we fail, the floodgates will be thrown wide open for the worst bloodshed in all history.'

With this warning Golden Orchid took her leave and was again lost among the milling crowds outside the diplomatic quarter.

10

EVERYWHERE there were divided counsels. The opposing forces on both sides now pulled one way, now another. There was hesitation and uncertainty. At the Chinese Court, Prince Tuan was angry that the foreign diplomats had intervened in China's domestic affairs and prevented his son from ascending the throne. The very idea! Was there any limit to the impertinence of these foreigners? He was therefore against all conciliation with the hated foreigner. But then even the most faithful and devoted followers of the Empress Dowager — among them Lord Yu Kung — saw in the enlarged disturbances the end of the entire regime and insisted on caution and on the suppression of the Boxers. There was even less unity of purpose among the foreign diplomats, though it was disunity of a different kind. The time for cutting up this succulent melon China had arrived, and nothing, not even the execution of ten more high-ranking officials, was going to prevent it. But who was to be given the juiciest and largest slice? That was the insoluble question, and the quarrel promised to be a long and bitter one.

Days went by and still no indication was conveyed to the Empress Dowager that her friendly attitude would be reciprocated. In audience after audience the followers of Prince Tuan seized the opportunity to urge that only drastic steps could save the situation. Sedan chairs lined up outside the gates of the Forbidden City in the small hours of the morning, waiting for them to be thrown open so that the officials could rush in and gain the ear of the Old Buddha. But it was the same tune, from the first to the last. 'Let the Boxers do as they please, and soon the foreign menace will be over!'

The weather was insufferably hot. A portentous storm of fine sand particles hung like a pall over the city of Peking. As if hiding itself in shame, the sun was no longer visible, but the oppressive heat was felt everywhere. Sand particles stuck to the wet and ever-perspiring skin; penetrated the roots of the hair; even made food gritty to the teeth. Everybody's nerves became hopelessly frayed.

Lord Yu Kung was now in a most uncomfortable position. He was in no personal danger, for he had discreetly refrained from making his private views known to anybody except Golden Orchid. His position as a close confidant of the Empress Dowager would be in no way affected, as far as he knew. But he was concerned for the safety of Golden Orchid. It was necessary that he take an unusual step.

Lord Yu Kung hastened to the Soochow hostel and visited Golden Orchid. It was three in the afternoon. Though His Lordship was dressed in a thin linen gown and carried with him a beautiful goose-feather fan, he kept mopping his face with a handkerchief. He went straight into the courtyard and found it cool. There was a giant oleander in bloom in each corner; everything was peaceful and quiet. There was not a person in sight. His Lordship looked through the open windows. On a bed asleep he saw a middle-aged woman who, he was sure, was Golden Orchid's mother. Between the window and the bed was the reclining figure of Golden Orchid herself. It was a lovely sight.

She was resting after lunch. Lying on a spacious rattan couch with a rattan pillow under her head, she wore a beautifully embroidered pair of slippers. But it was the beautiful body, so placid, so supple and so completely at rest, that caused the heart of the middle-aged widower to beat more rapidly than usual.

Lao Chuang had gone out; he had made plans to go back to his wife and his two sons in the village. Ping-mo, too, was away. No one knew where Hai-ming was, and Yang Mah was having a siesta of her own in the servants' quarters.

Lord Yu Kung stood for a while and felt he should leave the courtyard and ask the keeper of the hostel to announce his arrival. But the urge to linger was irresistible, and he succumbed to it. Here in front of him, only a few feet away, was the apparition of a divinely sweet face under the cover of a thin layer of perspiration. He thought he could smell her fragrance, though it could well have come from the oleanders. Golden Orchid wore on the upper part of her body a thin, gauze-like, short-sleeved shirt, unbuttoned at the throat — and such a delicate and white throat! But more than that, the gentle curves and contour of her youthful body — that was something which he had never thought it would be his good fortune to set eyes upon. The whole train of thought about his son Yung-kai and his intimate relations with her came rapidly to his mind. But propriety demanded that he see the keeper of the hostel, and so His Lordship tore himself away from the courtyard. He had not taken more than ten steps when he met Yang Mah. 'Will you tell your mistress that she has a guest?' he said to her.

For a while he waited, and then he was ushered in.

'Golden Orchid,' began Lord Yu Kung, 'forgive me for coming to you so suddenly. But I have important news for you.'

Golden Orchid was not so much interested in the news as in the fact that His Lordship had done her the honour of visiting her and her mother. She had been worried that she would not have time to make herself look her best. However, His Lordship soon set her at ease, and in a serious, fatherly tone gave her to understand that Peking was on the brink of the worst catastrophe in history; there was going to be a reign of terror, with bloodshed and massacre on a horrible scale; the city would be sacked and, as a matter of practical wisdom, it was best for her to seek immediate protection.

'I am not exaggerating,' continued Lord Yu Kung. 'I have intimate knowledge of the mood of the Court. I know the attitude of those who surround the Empress Dowager.'

'But where can we go? There is even worse trouble outside Peking. When the worst comes to the worst, all I can do is to move to a very small house and live there as a poor peasant girl. In that way I believe I may avoid trouble.'

'That is why I have come today. You can choose one of two things. No one, I believe, will touch me or my property. Why not, then, move into my house? It has many rooms. Or, if you prefer, you can move into the small house which used to be occupied by my gardener. It is next door to my own house. I can take care of you and your mother.'

'But I have other people to take care of. There is Yang Mah, for instance. Lao Chuang is going back to his village very soon, but there is also Hai-ming and Wen-ching's son Ping-mo.'

'I didn't know that Wen-ching's son was here. But they can all live with you under the same roof. How would you like to move this very day? The matter is pressing.'

Lord Yu Kung's proposition was accepted, as it turned out, none too early. For the next day, when Golden Orchid had scarcely settled down in her new quarters — she had decided to occupy the gardener's cottage — Ping-mo came back with news of the worst thing that had taken place in Peking up to that time. The German ambassador, the Kaiser's envoy, the man who was in the habit of taking his daily constitutional even during these hectic times, had been shot and killed by the Boxers! The situation had thus been so much aggravated that the Boxers thought it best, under the circumstances, to enlarge the troubles so as to direct the attention away from the murder of so prominent a person.

'The entire diplomatic quarter,' reported Ping-mo, 'is now under siege, and no one knows what is going to happen. It is possible that all foreigners in the area may be massacred. My agents told me that the foreign diplomats are now in a terrible state of fear. Their troops are on their way to Peking. But they will have to fight every inch of the ninety miles. If they succeed in arriving quickly they may still be able to save the people. But who knows if they will ever arrive? Or if they do, they may find their countrymen already slaughtered.'

Ping-mo showed signs of deep anxiety. He was all for the extermination of foreign influence, but not in the manner proposed by the Boxers. His main interest was to see the downfall of his own effete and corrupt Government which had made it possible for the hated foreigner to become so powerful.

Once the Boxers had gained ascendancy, he knew matters would be out of control. With every passing day he was convinced that events were developing precisely in the direction he feared most. He could not see how his work as a revolutionary leader could be continued. As he was deciding upon a course of action, he received orders to live with the other members of his secret society and hold himself ready for any emergency. He did not want to leave Golden Orchid, but the orders had to be obeyed. In any case he felt that since she and her mother were being properly taken care of, it was just as well that he was free to do anything the situation might call for.

'Golden Orchid,' said Ping-mo, 'I have decided to leave here — perhaps for some time.'

'But where can you go when the whole city is in such a state of confusion?'

'You know you need not worry about me.'

'But I do worry.'

'I have so many connections. I shall come to see you from time to time. So goodbye, and take good care of yourself.'

'One moment, Ping-mo. Aren't you going to say goodbye to Lord Yu Kung?'

'No, it is better not. You convey my regards to him for me.'

And so Ping-mo went away to join the other members of his society and to see if they couldn't still exercise some measure of control over the forces of disorder which had now been let loose on Peking. Even as he left, the skies were flaming. Huge fires were razing to the ground thousands of houses in the busy commercial sections just outside Peking's main gate. In a matter of a few days the city had been completely flooded with Boxers. The platforms which they erected could previously be counted on the fingers. But now they were everywhere. They had grown like mushrooms. Every *hutung*, every alley in Peking had now half a dozen or more of those platforms on which stood savage and ignorant men exhorting and warning the curious crowds to join them, on pain of being treated as traitors if they did not. The least that every family was expected to do was to make cash contributions, and there were many who made them willingly and generously.

II

On the 26th of June, Yang Mah came rushing in to report to Golden Orchid that some eight thousand homes were being burned that afternoon outside Chienmen. The next day over one thousand houses were burned in the eastern part of the city, followed by three thousand more near a church. In every case, Yang Mah heard people say, the Boxers wanted to burn only one house. But the fire spread; and when it did, no one was allowed to move anything. The Boxers explained that the people must have done something to rouse the ire of the gods, and therefore everything must be left untouched in order to pacify them. Those who did not believe in this nonsense and tried to save something from the fire were mercilessly hacked down, so that not only were large areas left in ruins, but mingled with the ashes were mutilated human bodies charred beyond all recognition. Dogs by the hundred came from no one knew where to feed on these dead bodies, and what remained decayed and decomposed in the blazing sun. For miles around the nauseating smell of carrion, the most difficult of all smells to endure, became the most noticeable fact in the big city.

It was a strange life Golden Orchid was living. She saw little of Lord Yu Kung. He was often summoned to the Summer Palace a few miles to the north-west of Peking where the Empress Dowager now held daily audiences to direct the emergency. So he posted guards round his residence as well as round the gardener's cottage where Golden Orchid was staying; and he was sure that no one, not even the Boxers, would have the effrontery to disturb the tranquillity of those premises. Lord Yu Kung was right. For Golden Orchid enjoyed the peace and quiet almost of the countryside, though the knowledge that there was so much death and destruction immediately outside distressed her.

In the meantime, conditions within the diplomatic quarter, now under siege, which she had visited only a few days before, were getting desperate. She thought of the Kendricks. And when Lord Yu Kung was at home on a rare occasion, she asked him if she could somehow send a messenger into the besieged area and find out how her friends were faring.

'I don't think that it is either possible or practical,' replied Lord Yu Kung. 'The people are now utterly mad, and in this frenzy anything can happen. Your messenger would never be able to pass the lines. When he is found out, he will be torn to pieces before he can even open his mouth to explain himself. I would advise you to keep to yourself as much as possible.'

'But I am worried about those friends of mine.'

'If the mob ever learns that you are in touch with the doomed area of the diplomatic quarter, there will be trouble. This quiet place, with the protection I can offer, might be transformed into a mortuary. No, no, I wouldn't risk it.'

'But is there really no way left, Your Lordship, whereby all this bloodshed can be averted?'

'I don't know, but I must keep you here and prevent you from having any contact with the outside world. The sentiments you have just expressed are praiseworthy. It's well that you should express them to me, but take care they are not known outside.'

'Very well.'

'Don't suppose I am not thinking hard how the lives of those innocent foreigners may be spared. This whole outburst may have good reasons, but all the same it is a wild and stupid way of trying to get what we want. We shall regret it — and, speaking confidentially, the Empress Dowager herself will live to regret it.'

For days on end Golden Orchid felt a frenzied agitation. Lord Yu Kung's palatial residence, to which Golden Orchid had easy access, was a small universe by itself, complete and self-contained, so that she could live as if in a world apart. All the summer blossoms were at their best. The oleanders and the lotus were especially beautiful. And Golden Orchid tried to amuse herself by watching the play of the goldfish bred by Lord Yu Kung himself and kept in huge vessels all over his garden.

But it was impossible to remain calm. Lao Chuang had gone back to his village. Ping-mo had left her, and now even Hai-ming disappeared for many days at a stretch. There was Yang Mah, always a devoted and loyal servant. And of course her mother, blissfully ignorant of what was going on outside, found consolation in the Buddhist scriptures. She continued to burn incense before an exquisite porcelain figure of Kuan-yin, the Goddess of Mercy, and to count her rosary. It seemed that nothing could disturb her tranquillity, and it was as well that she was engrossed in religious piety. Now and then Yang Mah brought Golden Orchid stray bits of news of what was happening. Golden Orchid sometimes felt the urge to go out with the maidservant and find out a few things herself, but she had been warned that it was now exceedingly dangerous for a young and pretty girl to appear among the crowds. However she might disguise herself, it was not a risk worth taking. And so life went on, its monotony occasionally broken by the brief visits of Lord Yu Kung.

Then one morning something happened. It was a small thing by itself, but it opened up a new world of realities for Golden Orchid. Lord Yu Kung's old servant, Lao Lee, brought in a small bamboo stick about ten inches long. There was nothing about it to excite curiosity. She thought that perhaps the old servant had caught some crickets to amuse her. But when she was told that the stick had been brought in by a small peasant boy in the early hours of the morning, to be delivered to Mistress Golden Orchid in person, she

N

took a good look at it and found both ends were stuffed with rags. She pulled them out and found a piece of paper securely lodged inside. It was a message from the Kendricks. She read it hastily and learned for the first time the frightful conditions prevailing in the besieged diplomatic quarter.

The message read:

Our dear, dear Golden Orchid! We don't know whether you will ever receive this message, but we hope that God is protecting you. We have now been under siege for six long weeks, and we are desperate. It is through the intervention of the Almighty that we have not all been massacred already. There are nearly a thousand of us, of all nationalities. There are also two thousand Chinese converts with us — men, women, and children. Some five hundred guards are defending the area against the fury and hatred of thousands upon thousands of Boxers and the murderous soldiers from Kansu. But we can't go on like this indefinitely — unless the allied forces reach us in time to save us.

We understand they are on their way from Tientsin. But, oh! when can they reach Peking? We are all praying they will be here soon. In the meantime, our food supply is getting short. We have begun feeding on horses and mules, and even stray dogs are not spared. Our diplomats have even been on stealing expeditions, and they are such experts! They have stolen eggs and vegetables from the peasants. The other day the Empress Dowager had the wickedness to taunt us with a gift of watermelons. At first everyone was happy because they looked so luscious, but then it dawned upon us that they were sent by our enemy. Could they be poisoned? And no one dared to touch those melons.

Typhoid, dysentery, and many other diseases have taken a heavy toll of the people. Children are dying right and left, and we are most thankful to the Lord that our two children are still with us. But they have become so thin and undernourished that you will not recognize them when you see them again.

Golden Orchid, wherever you are, you must try to do something. We know how you feel. We know also that you have powerful friends at Court. Can't you in some way persuade them to see the folly of all this and lift the siege? We have the assurance of all the diplomats that when peace is re-established, they will do everything to rectify past errors. Do save us from this appalling situation. May God help you!

JOHN AND NANCY

Poor Golden Orchid! A mere helpless observer of this huge drama of domestic and international intrigue — what could she do to direct it one way or the other? And yet, impossible as it all seemed, she brooded heavily over the message as if it were within her power to do something. That night she had horrible dreams and nightmares. And every time she woke up, her mind hovered over one enormous and significant fact. It tormented and perplexed her.

Six long weeks of siege with only five hundred guards manning an area difficult to defend, and yet the defence had not collapsed. How . . . how was this possible? Surely there must be a reason for it. If the Boxers, now joined by the Kansu soldiers, were really unified in their determination to overwhelm the diplomatic quarter, what was there to stop them? That small quarter was no impregnable fortress. There was not even a wall to protect it. Why then was the area intact? Could it be the result of divided counsels among the highest officials of the Court?

Given now to a life of solitude, Golden Orchid had developed the habit of having long monologues with herself. She very often thought aloud. Her mother wouldn't understand; it was no use talking with her.

There are certain things in this strange situation, she said to herself, which I cannot understand. The Boxers and the anti-foreign officials, with the backing of the Empress Dowager, are now bent on the destruction of the foreign population. Why then haven't they succeeded. What is preventing them from carrying out their plans? They have the numbers and the equipment. A few well-directed artillery shots from the guns erected on the high walls overlooking the diplomatic quarter, and all would be over. And yet, and yet, nothing like this has happened. There must be a good reason for it. What can we do, then, to prevent this from ever being carried out?

Golden Orchid was correct in suspecting that not only was there discord among the high officials, but that the discord was so deep as to make action hesitant and indecisive. She waited until she had the opportunity to talk it over with Lord Yu Kung.

When he came Golden Orchid at once placed the Kendrick

message in his hands. His Lordship was amazed and asked her how the message came to her.

'They had it sent to me, Your Lordship,' replied Golden Orchid.

'How?'

'Well, never mind. I'll tell you later. But, anyway, what can we do? We must still try to stop this madness.'

For a long time Lord Yu Kung did not speak. He merely looked at Golden Orchid with wonderment. Then, taking a deep breath, he said: 'I don't blame you for taking such a deep interest in the matter.'

'Young as I am, I have seen something of the world, and I am convinced that we are experimenting with something hopelessly dangerous. It is sheer ignorance.'

'You are right. But things have gone so far now that I don't see how we can call off the whole matter without danger either to the foreign diplomats or to ourselves.'

'I think that if we do not harm the foreigners, they will not harm us.'

'Unfortunately it is not so simple. This is the question that bothers me: their relief forces are on the way. If we do not harm them, what guarantee is there that these forces, when they eventually reach Peking, as they certainly will, will not harm us? You said they will not. I am not so sure.'

'We can at least try to get that guarantee. If we place the Boxers under proper control and lift the siege, I will try to get the Kendricks to approach their ambassador and, through him, the diplomats of all the other foreign powers, to withdraw their relief forces. We must try to stop our own insane action in the first place. It is childishness to believe that the foreign threat can be suppressed merely by killing a small number of defenceless people in the diplomatic quarter. We make the situation ten times worse.'

'All right, Golden Orchid, do your best to obtain that guarantee. Now, let me tell you a few things, but you must be discreet. The attack on the embassies was not originally part of any plan.'

'Oh, really?'

'What happened was this. Since the dethronment and virtual imprisonment of the Emperor by the Empress Dowager two years ago, Prince Tuan has wanted his own son to be placed on the throne. His ambition is to be the father of the next emperor. Understandable, isn't it?'

'Yes.'

'The Empress Dowager concurred. Now, I and others do not think this is right. But the scheme was ultimately abandoned, not because of internal opposition, but because some foreign diplomat intervened on behalf of the present Emperor. That infuriated the Empress Dowager no less than Prince Tuan. The power of the foreign diplomat had become too real to be comfortable. Hence the deep and irrational hatred of him.'

'This is most interesting.'

'So when the Taku forts were captured, it was at once taken as an excuse for open belligerence. It was seized upon as an act of war to justify Prince Tuan's desire to annihilate the foreign embassies. The whole thing was an expression of anger; it was not rationally thought out. Now that we are on the back of the tiger, as the saying goes, it is difficult to get down again. But I know for a fact that many of the highest officials are not sympathetic towards the siege. There are divided counsels.'

It occurred to Golden Orchid that the military commanders detailed to attack the embassies were themselves half-hearted about the whole thing. It was an idea worth toying with, and so she boldly suggested to Lord Yu Kung: 'Can we somehow convey to the commanders that if the embassies are destroyed, the relief forces will bring them to justice? Can we let them know that, as a matter of practical wisdom and for their own sake, it is better to leave the diplomatic quarter unharmed?'

Lord Yu Kung looked at Golden Orchid again in bewilderment. This girl, he thought, is uncanny, absolutely uncanny; he had been nursing that idea himself for some time. How was it possible that she knew it? It was a good idea, but there was one obvious difficulty. How could those commanders escape the wrath of Prince Tuan or even of the Empress Dowager herself for not carrying out their orders? He mentioned this to Golden Orchid. But she was ready with a prompt answer.

'Why should not the commanders raise their guns so that the shells will go over the diplomatic area and still give satisfaction to Prince Tuan that they are being fired, that his orders are being obeyed?'

Lord Yu Kung stood up. Unbelievable! The girl knew too much! The commanders had been instructed to do precisely what Golden Orchid suggested. But Lord Yu Kung was still worried over one thing — how to prevent the relief forces, when they came into Peking, from seeking vengeance and, like the Boxers themselves, getting out of control? Golden Orchid on her part promised to convey this fear to the diplomatic body through the Kendricks. She would do her utmost.

12

FOR the next week or so the ten-inch bamboo stick was busy, playing a part out of all proportion to its intrinsic worth. Messages quietly shuttled back and forth which might well affect the lives of thousands of people and the relationship between China and the rest of the world.

Those were anxious days, and Lord Yu Kung's face was lined with anxiety. All official contacts had been cut. Technically China was at war with the powers — after sending the ultimatum which followed closely upon the seizure of the Taku forts by the allied admirals. From that time on, any contact had to be made through private sources. And His Lordship realized how important it was — for both sides — to maintain that contact. He absented himself from the audiences of the Empress Dowager and stayed at home.

He knew that he had succeeded in saving the diplomatic quarter, with all its inmates, from destruction; but he wanted to know that he could do the same for the entire city of Peking, with its million inhabitants, when the allied relief forces arrived. He worried so much that almost overnight his hair, which had been raven black, turned grey. What he had done could well be considered treason. If Prince Tuan or any of his political enemies got wind of it, he could be decapitated, irrespective of how close he might be to the Empress Dowager.

In this moment of desperation he tried to seek some solace and relaxation. He also wanted enlightenment from someone wiser than himself. So he turned to an old and trusted friend for advice. Mr Kan Ming was in the seventy-fifth year of his eventful life, and for thirty years had been friend, counsellor and mentor to His Lordship. Mr Kan was a widely travelled man, having received a part of his adult education at the University of Edinburgh. He knew the

Chinese classics as well as anybody. But he also knew what perhaps nobody in China then knew. He was a brilliant scholar of the European classics and could quote Virgil, Dante, Goethe and Voltaire in their original languages, and knew Shakespeare from beginning to end.

That was an accomplishment for anyone in any country. In China, then, he was unique. But he had had a turbulent youth, and even known moments of flippancy. Once upon a time he had lost his pigtail; he cut and delivered it to a fair young lady in Scotland as an earnest of his love and devotion. He had now been known for years as the sage of Peking. Not that he was appreciated by his own people, who in fact had no use for him, but foreigners flocked to him for his deep understanding of both the East and the West.

Lord Yu Kung, however, had taken to him strongly; and in these uneasy days, when he was so uncertain of everything, his mind constantly went back to Mr Kan Ming. And so one evening, when the sun had gone down behind the western hills, though it was still warm and sultry and the crickets were beginning to chirp lustily underneath the flower-pots in his garden, a small table was set in the spacious patio. It had taken some time to trace Ping-mo, for he had been busy with the work of his secret society, but he was present when the old gentleman arrived. The disturbances in the city had practically put an end to all social amenities, but Lord Yu Kung wanted very much to entertain his old friend, disturbances notwithstanding. He also wanted young people to listen to him.

'My venerable Brother Kan,' said Lord Yu Kung after the table was cleared, 'what do you, with all your learning, think of the situation? You are a man both wise and experienced, and you know we all respect you.'

'Thank you for saying so. But I am neither wise nor experienced. You see, I have a prejudiced view of things. All I have learned from life seems to be the acceptance of what fate has to offer. I look now only to the moment, to the present. For instance, you offered me this dinner. I enjoyed it, in spite of all that is going on.'

'I am glad that you enjoyed it.'

'But that is not the point. Do you remember the Tang poet Tu Fu, who said: "Each creature is merry its brief little hour, so let us enjoy the moment while we may." Tu Fu lived in one of the most glorious periods of our history, the Tang Dynasty, and yet all he cared for was to enjoy what a brief moment might have to offer. "Alas! I see another spring has died. When will it come — the day of my return?" Deep nostalgia! Infinite regret! It was not without reason that he felt like that. It it because the realities of life are so bitter and cruel. Through the ages I have noticed one recurrent theme — there again I may be prejudiced — that the human heart is most of the time given to viciousness and the destruction of other people. That is why many of us feel so frustrated.'

'But why is the human heart, as you feel, so vile?'

'I think I know the answer. You see, the human instinct is basically creative. Now, it is not the setting up of the goal and our exertion to achieve it that are difficult. But every inch of the way towards accomplishment, towards fulfilment, we meet obstacles, barriers erected by our fellow mortals to defeat us. So much of our energy is dissipated in the attempt to overcome these barriers — if we ever succeed in overcoming them — that there is hardly anything left for what we originally set out to accomplish. The vicious, the makers of trouble, sit astride the barriers they have created, and they laugh and scoff at us. It is they who triumph: it is they who enjoy all the worldly riches and honours. But the wicked ones cannot remain on a pedestal for ever. Someone with a deep and strong passion comes along and overthrows them. That explains most of the violence in the chequered life of our country.'

Lord Yu Kung asked if the same thread did not run through the history of European nations.

'Yes, there are vicious people everywhere,' replied Mr Kan Ming. 'But excuse me for being quite frank. When a Chinese is vicious, he can be very vicious indeed, more vicious than anyone. I am not speaking of the common peasant. He is simple, frank and honest, and his heart is often in the right place. But I am speaking of the Chinese official or of those close to official life. Remember what Chang Hsien-tsung of the Ming Dynasty used to say? "The Almighty," he said, "created everything for the good of man, but man has not done one thing to repay Him." And so when he came to power, there was only one word that he recognized — the word "kill," which he wrote seven times! Such hatred did he have for the wickedness of the men whom he superseded.'

'But surely not all officials are like that,' protested Lord Yu Kung, breaking at the same time into a faint smile, as if his protest was not meant as an earnest expression of disagreement.

'Of course not. There are exceptions — like yourself,' Mr Kan Ming hastened to add. 'But exceptions prove the rule. The vicious European hurts you like a nail; the vicious Chinese like a screw. When the nail strikes a hard layer and cannot go any further, it gives up. It gets bent itself. But the screw keeps on boring from all sides until it goes straight in and gets what it wants.'

Golden Orchid and Ping-mo looked at each other, surprised that so learned a man could converse in such simple language. But they thought that he had made a good point.

'But it's a fact,' continued the septuagenarian, 'that among the Europeans there is at least a sort of unwritten code which everybody accepts. If there is enmity, it is at least open and above-board. There is a good fight, but there is, as they say, no hitting below the belt. With us there is no such code of conduct. We hit everywhere, up, down and from the sides. We have recourse to all kinds of wiles and meanness. We strike the enemy when he least expects it. We use honeyed words when we hide a dagger in our stomach, as we say. What other people, for instance, have taken the trouble to waste their mental energy in thinking out the thirty-six or the hundred and eight underhand tricks to defeat one's enemy? There is the "bitter flesh" trick, or the "golden cicada shedding its shell" trick, and God knows what else. . . . Well, well, this sounds like blasphemy to my own people. Isn't it true that we have a special phrase to describe joy over other people's misfortune? There is such a word, I admit, in the German language — *schadenfreude*. But none of the other European languages has such a word, and words are often expressive of a people's psychology.'

'Yes, I remember that word *schadenfreude*,' Golden Orchid quickly added. 'I heard it often among the staff when Wen-ching was in trouble in Berlin. I didn't know what it meant at first, but it was so often on people's lips in those days that I wanted to find out. But, Kan Lao Pei-pei, isn't it true that in Europe they also speak about the sense of fair play, about sportsmanship?'

'I am glad that you know these things, Golden Orchid,' replied Mr Kan Ming. 'You have been very observant. Yes, they cultivate that spirit of sportsmanship while they are young, and the idea behind it seems to be that it is nobler to accept defeat with honour than to have victory with dishonour. Good, good, I am glad that you brought up the subject.'

Mr Kan Ming was happy because he knew that he was speaking to a truly appreciative audience.

'But you know, Golden Orchid,' pursued Mr Kan Ming, 'the same ideal existed in China in ancient times. There are many references in the game of archery to the fact that those who were defeated frankly and openly went up to the victors to congratulate them. The spirit has died out with us as have so many other good things. Today it is the most difficult thing in the world to make a Chinese acknowledge defeat, much less to accept it. He nurses a deep grudge against the victor. He is bitter against those who are abler than he, against those who are more accomplished in any way, and he tries every means to defeat them — honourably if he can, but dishonourably if he cannot. Most of the time, of course, it's dishonourably. As a race, we do not believe in sympathy, for sympathy and *schadenfreude* are the opposite of each other. We consider it foolish to stand for the underdog. That is considered meddlesome. We rejoice, as the saying goes, in stamping on the tiger once it is dead. The old Egyptians have a similar saying: "When the cow is down, the knives are many and sharp".'

Ping-mo, as a young patriot, took strong exception to some of Mr Kan's observations. But he did not want to be openly disrespectful, and so he quietly commented: 'It seems that this is true of the European also, doesn't it? They have found out now that China is only a paper tiger, and see how quickly they all come in to tear it to pieces. And recently I've heard a lot of talk about carving up the luscious melon that is China.'

Mr Kan knew that Ping-mo had made a good point. But he pretended not to have heard it and pursued his own line of thought. 'I am sorry,' he continued, 'that I am speaking with such bitterness. But at my age I am no longer afraid of saying what I believe to be right. The sad thing is that this is true, not only now when our moral life has sunk so low, but apparently even in the best of times, during the Tang Dynasty, for instance. Remember what Li Po used to say? "My whitening hair would make a long, long rope, yet would not fathom all the depth of my woe".'

There was a slight pause before Mr Kan Ming went on: 'Look at myself now. It was good of you, Brother Yu Kung, to say that I am wise and experienced, but I am a burden to myself and to society. The more I seem to have in me, the greater the intrigue against me. My life has been one long history of unwarranted bitterness and spite against me. And so today I limp around in Peking with this cane. Read what is inscribed there.'

Ping-mo took the cane. Inscribed on it were eight characters, meaning 'I depend and yet do not depend. I do not depend and yet I depend'.

'What do they mean, Brother Kan?' asked Lord Yu Kung.

'They mean just what they say. My own people, because I have some learning in the Chinese and European classics and may possibly be of some use in the present development of Chinese society, have no use for me. They dishonour me, and the result is that today I have to depend upon some of my foreign friends to keep me alive. Of course I am still proud of being Chinese, proud of being an inheritor of a truly great and noble culture which it is our duty to carry on and develop. But there is nothing that we see and hear in our everyday life, in the things that we do today, that is at all worthy of that pride. I am called upon to be guardian of what was but no longer is. Isn't this sad?'

It was pathetic, thought Ping-mo. He did not agree with the old gentleman on everything, but he was glad that Mr Kan, with all that he had experienced in life, fully confirmed what he had always felt — that the ruling classes in China were the most wicked, the most vicious people, the more so because they had such a charming and beguiling façade. He was glad that he had dedicated himself to revolutionary work, to the creation of a healthier order of society. But alas, what difficulties! With the ignorant Boxers in power, encouraged by an equally ignorant Empress Dowager and her cohorts, he did not see how this youthful dream of an orderly and more rational society, where men would be employed according to their ability and character, could ever be realized.

Mr Kan noticed the effect of his remarks on Ping-mo. He liked the young man, especially when he was told that he was the son of the much-respected Wen-ching. He had known Wen-ching, though not well; and he thought the example of that distinguished scholar himself was as good as any to bring home his point.

'Yes, take the example of our dear friend Wen-ching, the father of this young man,' Mr Kan continued. 'Though I did not have the privilege of knowing him well, I have always considered him as one of our best products. Learned, upright, a man of real dignity and integrity, a man who, I believe, was never capable of harbouring an evil thought, let alone doing anything evil — why, he was a man whom we badly needed in these critical times. And yet he must have died of a broken heart, a victim of that viciousness and maliciousness which cover our present society like a thick layer of offal. We are where we are — disorganized, defeated, lost — for very good reasons, and these are to be found in the decay of our own soul.'

It was a dark and grim picture that Mr Kan painted. There were moments when Golden Orchid was on the verge of tears; Wen-ching's life had been wasted and brought to a premature end just as Mr Kan had said — through the wickedness of the human heart.

'But what are we to do, Kan Lao Pei-pei?' she asked.

'There is not much, I am afraid, that men of my age can do. We have done what we could, and we have failed. I have failed, and Ping-mo's father has failed. And yet there is no such thing as an absolute failure. When I was a student in Scotland, they used to tell me about the Irish, that they went forth to battle though they always fell. That is the spirit. Even though we fail, we must not cease fighting. It is for the young to continue the fight until it is finally won. Some have committed suicide when they have seen good continually conquered by evil, as in the case of the great prime minister Chu Yuan more than two thousand years ago. Others have died of a broken heart, as in the case of Wen-ching. Still others at long last give up the fight in disgust and try to get as much joy out of what remains of life as they can. Like myself.' Mr Kan Ming smiled a rather bitter smile and continued: 'Even as we do all these things, we know we are wrong. We still like to see the fight con-tinued. The work of the conquest of evil is an ever-recurrent and ever-continuing task. The younger generation must take up the cudgels. Always keep your eye on those who enjoy power, for power is the source of all evil. The ordinary, common people are relatively free from it. Once they get into power themselves, however, they may become as evil and corrupt as the present ruling classes. But that is another problem, to be solved by those who come after you. Well, Ping-mo, and you also, Golden Orchid, both of you are now in the best position, by virtue of your youth and energy, to do the most good. Keep on doing what your conscience tells you is good. Even if you fail, you sow seeds which will flourish later. I see unlimited chaos and disorder ahead of us — for a time, at least. This great city of Peking will know many tragedies, and there is nothing to prevent them. But it will survive as it has survived before.'

Lord Yu Kung pricked up his ears like a dog when he heard those words. 'Do you really think there will be great suffering for all of us?' he asked Mr Kan. 'As bad as the cities in the south during the Taiping Rebellion?'

'And worse than the occupation of Peking itself in 1860 by the British and French forces, when the old Summer Palace outside Peking was burned down. Its fountains, its rococo façades, its mirrors, its chandeliers, built and imported to please the fastidious taste of Emperor Chien Lung, were all demolished. Remember those strings of priceless black pearls which for hundreds of years were the greatest treasure of the Empire? Those were stolen and later presented to Empress Eugénie. Only this time it is going to be worse — much worse. The foreign troops now in Tientsin will surely occupy the capital — and soon. There are not two countries this time, but eight, and some of those have but recently emerged from the wilderness. The prospects are grim.'

Mr Kan raised his cup of wine to thank his host for the evening. 'When will such an evening come again?' he asked sadly. He took his cane and slowly walked away.

Lord Yu Kung accompanied his guest to the gate as the usual mark of respect and courtesy. In the distance they heard the booming of the guns. And then, the next moment, from the courtyard of a neighbour's house came the soft notes of the lute gently caressing the stillness of the night like the translucent wings of the dragonfly humming on the quiet surface of a summer lake.

Mr Kan Ming disappeared into the great unknown, much as Lao-tse did on the back of a buffalo through the gate of Kiayukwan.

Book Five

THE CICADA

YES, the booming of the guns! Those were the same guns that were first heard in Tientsin. Through ninety miles in a frenzied sea of red sashes, of knives six feet long, of tall and glistening spears, of naked, sweating torsos smeared with dirt, the soldiers of the allied forces — wild Cossacks, dark Gurkhas and Sikhs, ebony-toothed Annamese under French commanders, Europeans, Japanese and Americans — pushed slowly and relentlessly until they came under the very shadow of the towering eastern gate of Peking. The same gate through which Golden Orchid and her mother had led the Kendricks to their own people, in the diplomatic quarter, barely two months before. The capital then still had a semblance of authority. But now that authority had vanished. The Empress Dowager, knowing the inevitable, had gathered her immediate entourage and was now on her way to the western provinces. The dragon was in flight! She dressed in peasant's clothing and hurriedly climbed into a cart no better than that in which Golden Orchid had ridden from Tungchow.

But before she started on her long and uncertain journey, she did not forget some things which had to be done. For one thing, there was no longer any need for the Emperor to be confined to the Ocean Terrace. So the eunuchs put him, the Son of Heaven himself, on another cart following his imperial aunt. The Pearl Concubine was dead. In front of the palace which the Empress Dowager was leaving was a well in which the water had rapidly receded as a result of continued sultry weather. Nothing would be more appropriate, so thought the Old Buddha, than that it should become the imperial concubine's sepulchre, to pour her tears in.

One word of command, one look from her cold and incisive eyes, was enough. The Chief Eunuch hurriedly sent for the already wan and emaciated Pearl Concubine, and in a short while all was over. The Chief Eunuch simply announced to the Emperor that his imperial lover was now dead. Pale as a figure cut in alabaster — and equally lifeless — the Emperor, having doffed his imperial robes and dressed himself like any common peasant, made his way over the Western Hills and into the province of Shansi.

Meanwhile the imperial city, with its numberless palaces and ancient temples in which were hidden art treasures dating from time immemorial — sacrificial vessels, bronzes with their delicate patina, porcelains in all their subtle and sophisticated colours, rich and gorgeous silks, sculptures and carvings of jade, with sables and other furs, and rare books by the hundreds of thousands from an age when the Vandals, Visigoths, Lombards and their kin were still roving the cold earth of Europe — lay at the mercy of the invading troops. Its million people, nurtured in the refinements of the Confucian lore, with their soft and gentle manners, now found themselves completely helpless in the presence of these foreign soldiers, who for three solid days, immediately after the occupation of Peking, were given absolute freedom to indulge in the wildest orgies.

Lord Yu Kung, helpless, followed Her Imperial Ladyship into the wilderness. He could no longer give protection to Golden Orchid and her mother. He was summoned, and he had to leave abruptly.

The poor women did the best they could to protect themselves. The mother furiously counted her rosary, asking the Goddess of Mercy to protect her and her daughter. But it was of no avail. Her lips quivered with the names of the gods and bodhisattvas of the Buddhist hierarchy as her entire body shook with fright; and two days later, even as Peking was being subjected to the deepest humiliation and in spite of all the care that Golden Orchid could bestow on her, her life ebbed out and she peacefully died. Poor Golden Orchid sobbed on the bosom of Yang Mah, now the only person in the world to share with her the uncertain days ahead. Ping-mo was busy with his secret society and could not be found, nor was there a trace of Hai-ming.

Yang Mah always wished that she had never come to Peking. Now that she had been caught in the midst of it all, there was only one thing she could do — see to it that no harm was done to herself or her mistress.

'Tai-tai,' Yang Mah urged, 'we cannot stay here by ourselves. Suppose some of these wild foreign soldiers find us? I am terribly afraid. We must look for another place which is safer.'

'No, Yang Mah,' replied Golden Orchid, 'there is no safe place anywhere. But you are right, we shall have to join the crowd. By doing so we shall be less conspicuous and may suffer less.'

'Of course, as long as we are not discovered, we shall be all right.

But we are too near His Lordship's big house, and someday it is going to be looted by those foreign soldiers. They will then find us, and anything can happen to us.' Yang Mah was shivering all over as she spoke. 'I don't want to frighten you, Tai-tai,' she continued, 'but when I went out this morning trying to buy some food, what I heard and saw was truly horrible. The foreign soldiers have been in the city only two days, and what have they not done?'

'I know. The old servant in the big house has told me all about it. He tells me that he is going to stay where he is, no matter what happens. He says that he has been in the service of His Lordship's family since he was a mere boy, and he is going to protect his master's property even if he dies doing so. And I am worrying because I feel quite sure that His Lordship's house will be looted.'

'What shall we do?'

'That's what I have been thinking about all this morning. I hate to leave the old servant alone. And yet what could I, a mere woman, do when the soldiers come in to look for treasures? Lao Lee knows much more than I thought. He even thinks he knows how many foreign troops have come into Peking. The largest number are the Japanese, he told me, and there are thousands of Russian, British, French, American and German troops. Altogether there may be thirty thousand of them.'

'Thirty thousand!' cried Yang Mah. 'Is it really true? Thirty thousand of them! And they tell me many of them are as black as coal. I have not yet seen any "foreign devils" that are black.'

'Yang Mah, these "foreign devils" may not have black faces, but they can be quite black in their hearts. I have done all I can to protect them. It remains now to see what they are going to do for me and for the people in Peking. Oh, yes, Yang Mah, there are dark-faced "foreign devils" also. They come from the same country as the policemen in Shanghai.'

And so Golden Orchid and Yang Mah talked on in Lord Yu Kung's garden cottage. They had premonitions of hard and difficult days ahead, but as yet all they knew was hearsay. Lao Lee came to them. He looked haggard and pale. His little walrus moustache had become straggly. His mouth was open as if he were wondering what he should do. But he went straight to Golden Orchid, curtsied as usual — for he could never forget his manners even in this period of turmoil — and said that news was very bad, very bad indeed.

'Tai-tai,' Lao Lee said, 'the soldiers from the foreign lands are already burning and plundering houses in many parts of the city. We are fortunate in being in the eastern part of the city, for the Japanese soldiers on the whole have been behaving well. But the southern and western parts of the city are awful — simply awful.'

'Well, that is to be expected, Lao Lee,' said Golden Orchid calmly. 'From now on we must try to be cool and courageous. I have been thinking, however, that we should all leave the big house. Life after all is more important, and you, Lao Lee, must come with us.'

Lao Lee hesitated for some time, looked at Golden Orchid, and then, biting his lips as if to show his resolution, he said slowly: 'Tai-tai, you are right, we must try to be cool and courageous. I shall remain here even if that means death. I cannot leave my master's house. But you, Tai-tai, you must go away at once — with Yang Mah.'

There was still something on Lao Lee's lips that he wanted to say. At last he said: 'A woman's honour — that is something precious, more precious than life itself.'

He paused for a moment, and then he continued: 'I don't know whether I should tell you. But His Lordship's best friend and his entire family are all dead.'

'Who is that?' asked Golden Orchid.

'You wouldn't know him, Tai-tai. He was the President of the Board of Rites, Master Lee Pan-king.'

'Master Lee! Why, of course, I knew him.' And then, turning to Yang Mah, Golden Orchid explained that this was the same master who was chairman of the Grand Council and dismissed the case against Wen-ching, the same master who fell asleep in Tientsin on her bed before they left for the train to Peking.

'Yes, I remember,' said Yang Mah. 'Such a fine man, and dead with all his family! What happened?'

'Late last night,' said Lao Lee, 'Master Lee Pan-king knew that the end had come. He had returned from Tientsin only a few days before. He called Madam Lee, their two daughters, their son and his wife, and said to them: "I have received imperial favours all these years and I have done all that can be expected of me. Now that the capital has fallen and the Empress Dowager and the Emperor have left, we must all go back to our ancestors." So saying, he calmly gave each member of his family a cord, and together they hanged themselves on the beams of their spacious living-room. Their servant discovered the bodies this morning.'

Lao Lee continued after a pause: 'What Master Lee was most afraid of was that his womenfolk might be defiled. There is ground for this fear, because there are reports that the women have been suffering terribly at the hands of these foreign troops. The wells are full of corpses — of women. So are the moats around the city wall. There are already so many corpses, of rich and poor alike, that the water refuses to flow.'

Yang Mah was terribly frightened, and she was sure of one thing: she was not going to remain with a pretty mistress in the house by themselves. She was anxious to leave as soon as possible. All these days the coffin of Golden Orchid's mother had been unburied. In spite of large quantities of lime and the ancient methods of embalming, the smell was insufferably strong because of the hot weather. Golden Orchid had still hoped that, as a last act of filial devotion, she would see her mother properly buried. But Yang Mah thought there was no time to lose and, finding a suitable spot under the weeping willow scarcely ten yards from the bedroom they had been sharing, they buried the coffin with Lao Lee's help. Golden Orchid knelt before her mother as the coffin was lowered into the earth.

'And now, Lao Lee,' said Yang Mah, 'let's get ready to join the crowd and lose ourselves among them. There is no way to escape from suffering, but at least in this way there is a better chance to escape from something much worse.'

Lao Lee repeated that he intended to remain where he was, but knowing that the two women would be better protected among the poorer people, he suggested that he take them to a nearby hut where his own relatives and the families of the other servants had taken refuge. Having done that, he came back to his master's residence and resigned himself to whatever might happen.

2

FOR more than a month Golden Orchid and Yang Mah lived like any two beggar women among a crowd of some two hundred people in a hut surrounded by an open space of about an acre, about half a mile from the Soochow hostel, All kinds of wild stories were being circulated during these days of confinement. Practically all the temples in the city and in the vicinity had been burned or damaged, because it was believed that the Boxers still lingered in them. Looting of the houses of the rich officials and the palaces had been going on every day, and news of it no longer made an impression on Golden Orchid. But there was one thing that could still shock her every time she heard it. Large numbers of women, both old and young, had been raped, and in most cases the victims had either committed suicide or were mercilessly killed by the soldiers.

'Yang Mah, Yang Mah,' Golden Orchid kept saying, 'I don't mind if we lose all our worldly possessions, but I shall take my own life if some of the soldiers come to this spot and begin to molest the women.'

'I know it, Tai-tai,' replied Yang Mah. 'But I think we are quite safe here.'

'I know what you are going to say. We are fortunate that there is a Japanese flag on the gate of this refuge to show that we are merely a group of poor innocent people.'

'And the Japanese will protect us.* Do you know, Tai-tai, what someone told me yesterday? Of all the soldiers from many countries the ones who behave the best are the Japanese.'

'I have heard that also. I couldn't believe it. Next to the Japanese are the American soldiers. I have done what I could to save the lives of Americans in the diplomatic area. The English soldiers seem to be all right also. The French behave badly, but the worst of all, as everyone knows, are the Russians, the Cossacks, who are really wild men. Their faces are covered with hair.'

Suddenly came the voice of a young man who seemed to be in his early twenties. He was the very picture of a beggar boy, and yet on close examination his features were refined and bore signs of good breeding. Golden Orchid at once thought of Ping-mo and wondered if he, too, could possibly be near.

'You mustn't speak so loud,' warned the young man. And then, looking at Golden Orchid, he continued: 'I can see that you too are from a good family. You need not speak so well of the Japanese. They can behave as badly as any of those "ocean soldiers". After

---

* Quite a contrast to the large-scale and systematic atrocities later committed by Japanese soldiers, especially in Nanking in 1937.

all, they are all monkeys, except that those from over the ocean are worse. They are the monkey ghosts.'

The young man smiled to himself as he made those last inconsequential remarks, and Golden Orchid was rather annoyed. She remained silent and, looking at Yang Mah, she pointed to her head, meaning that perhaps the young man was a bit queer.

But the young man edged towards Golden Orchid and whispered more nonsense in her ear: 'Talking about monkey ghosts, do you want to hear a story? It's true. My uncle used to have a farm out in the Western Hills. Every night a pack of monkeys came and picked the farm clean. My uncle got desperate, and then he hit upon what he thought to be an excellent idea. He managed to catch two or three of these monkeys and, knowing how we were all frightened by foreign devils, he painted these monkeys white and let them loose the next night. The pack came as usual, but when they saw those white monkeys they were so scared that they ran for their lives. They never came again.'

The story was funny enough, though Golden Orchid didn't know how to take it. She thanked the young man and turned to Yang Mah again.

'Of course, Yang Mah, one can never be too sure of anything. But the main thing is to make ourselves look as dirty and as beggarly as possible so that none of the foreign soldiers will ever think of coming near us.'

Yang Mah gave her mistress some hot water to drink out of a rusty tin, thrown away by the soldiers, which she had salvaged. She also took out from a filthy bag a cold and hard ball of steamed bread which was to be Golden Orchid's breakfast.

Out of the same instinct for self-preservation all the inmates of the camp looked as dishevelled and unkempt as Golden Orchid and Yang Mah. The weather was hot, and on their bodies were all kinds of soiled rags. A steaming, pungent and indescribable smell filled the air far away from the camp. But it produced the desired effect: no one went near the camp except the Japanese guards on duty, who, having learned modern sanitation, wore masks over their mouths and noses. The black hair of the refugees was long and uncombed. Laden with a thick layer of Peking dust, it covered unwashed faces, fell on shoulders and backs in ugly knots, and in time became the breeding ground of insects and lice. One morning Yang

Mah looked at what had once been the sweet and pretty face of her young mistress, and she was overcome with grief. 'Yes, this is a hard life,' she muttered. 'How can she endure it? It is only a few weeks since we came here, and yet there are already streaks of grey hair on her head.'

She went to Golden Orchid and tried to say a few soft words to console her. Her mistress was happy to see her. 'Oh, Yang Mah, I am glad you are here. What am I to do? My head must be covered with lice.'

Yang Mah looked closely at Golden Orchid's hair and gave a cry. 'Ah-ya! I am so much relieved. I thought, Tai-tai, that this hard life had turned your hair grey, and I felt so sorry for you. But now I see it is only the lice. Let me take them off for you.'

Yang Mah was so proficient with a small comb that in ten minutes the grey hair was black again, and the two women laughed over it together.

3

No one knew where Hai-ming was. Any one of a hundred things might have happened to her. But there was no need to worry about her, for she was a plucky girl, often resourceful, and she could meet any situation with a sure confidence born of bitter experience. Golden Orchid was not deeply concerned about her, knowing that she could take care of herself. But she was not so sure about Ping-mo. He was too impulsive. His patriotism often got the better of him. One assertion of such feeling, at the wrong time and place, and he would be killed. If only, Golden Orchid wished, Ping-mo could be like that young man who spoke to her a few minutes previously. Such a queer person and yet so wise!

Ping-mo was in fact not far away. When he left Golden Orchid he tried to find out all he could about the worsening situation. But he had difficulty in returning while the people of the city struggled to escape from the foreign invaders. He dodged and hid himself; and when, a few days later, he succeeded in making his way to the gardener's cottage where he had left Golden Orchid and Yang Mah, they were nowhere to be found.

He tried to find Lao Lee. Lord Yu Kung's residence looked the same as ever from the outside, but inside he found disorder. The patio which used to have the choicest plants and flowers, and which not long before had been the scene of the dinner with Mr Kan Ming, was littered with silks and furs from Lord Yu Kung's wardrobe. The delicate woodwork on the massive beams which partitioned the huge living-room had fallen to the floor and been trampled into a thousand pieces. On his way to the study he found an imperial jacket, once the pride of His Lordship, lying among the debris. The lining was made of the fur of the golden-haired monkey found only in the high mountains in Szechuan on the Tibetan border. In the distance Ping-mo thought that the fur was the hair of some marauding soldiers who had fallen fighting among themselves over the loot. But as he stepped into the study, he was horrified to see the decaying body of Lao Lee slumped in a position of prayer in front of a porcelain figure of the Goddess of Mercy. But the head of the goddess was missing.

Ping-mo left the house as quickly as his feet could carry him; he was afraid that it might be only a matter of time before he himself would suffer the same fate. There was nowhere he could go, and as he was trying to cross the familiar Street of Enduring Peace, there came past a group of German soldiers, all stripped to the waist, each riding a horse and holding the reins of three or four more horses.

It was an unusual sight for Ping-mo. He was frightened. There was hardly anyone on the street, and he tried to lie down and hide himself under battered tables left behind by street merchants. But his curiosity got the better of him, and now and again he looked to see what the soldiers were doing. They wore no uniforms because the sun was unbearably hot, but they had impressive-looking helmets with steel spikes. They all had fierce-looking moustaches. It was apparent that they were not having an easy time; there were more horses than they could take care of. Ping-mo saw a few Chinese boys leading some horses as they walked behind the soldiers. He became more interested, and as he lifted his head to have a better view of these boys, a soldier caught sight of him, got down from his horse, and ran straight towards him, whip in hand.

Without asking any questions the soldier gave Ping-mo a terrific lash and yelled, '*Heraus! Schwein!*'

Ping-mo didn't know why the soldier struck him, but, smarting under the pain, all he could say was 'No Boxer, no Boxer,' as he shook his head from left to right and from right to left.

It so happened that the two little English words, which were about all that Ping-mo could utter, saved his life, for the German soldier not only understood them, but also, realizing that the young man spoke some English, decided that indeed he could not be a Boxer. He looked Ping-mo over carefully, as if, for a moment, he had doubts about his decision. He thought there was something in Ping-mo's manner which indicated that he was not from the common crowd of Peking.

From that moment the German soldier, in spite of his ferocious appearance, became quite gentle. He took Ping-mo by the hand, dragged him into the cavalcade, gave him the reins of a couple of horses, and simply ordered him to follow the soldiers. Whither the procession was heading neither Ping-mo nor any of the three other boys similarly dragooned into the service of the Imperial German Army had any way of finding out. All they knew was that they were marching towards the northern part of the city; and when finally they stopped, it was within the spacious grounds of one of the few remaining temples. It happened to be a Taoist temple, where the German soldiers pitched their tents and made themselves at home.

The four young men were left alone to do what they wanted, but before the soldiers retired, they gave them to understand that they would be well treated as long as they worked loyally, but that any attempt to escape would be followed by severe punishment. Ping-mo looked about him and came to the conclusion that it was neither possible nor advisable to try to escape, as a soldier stood guard at the gate of the temple with fixed bayonet. Besides, even if he did succeed in fleeing, where could he go? He decided that it was the better part of wisdom, for the moment at any rate, to do as he was told.

After a short rest the young men began to talk. One, called Cheng, told Ping-mo that the soldiers were really officers.

'I have been with these German officers for three days,' explained Cheng.

'How do they treat you?'

'Not badly. They have any amount of what you would consider very strange food, as you will see later.'

'But are you going to remain with these foreign troops?' Ping-mo asked.

'That is no longer a practical question,' broke in another young man, Li-san. 'You speak as if there were a choice.'

Cheng added: 'These German troops won't let you go. They'll shoot us if we try to escape. The need our services.'

'You might like to know,' commented Li-san wryly, 'that these horses we have been taking care of are some of the eighteen hundred just arrived from San Francisco. And do you know where that is? Yes, they come all the way from the country of the Flowery Flag. I have a feeling that the foreign invaders are going to be here for a long, long time.'

Ping-mo felt very sad when he heard this, but they all agreed that there was nothing they could do. China was a defeated country. Peking was in a state of utter chaos. They must stay quiet and watch and wait for developments. That night they were given straw, which they spread out at the base of the two stone lions by the side of the temple. They lay down and tried to sleep, but this was difficult, as the officers sang and drank barrels of beer which were installed in the main hall of the temple.

Ping-mo passed a restless night and had strange dreams. At one time he saw his father weeping. With him was his mother, writing brush in hand, going to his father to wipe his tears. At another time he dreamed he saw Golden Orchid; all of a sudden, some foreign troops came riding through the woods and took her away to a mountain retreat. He called out, trying to protect her. When he awoke, it was already the early hours of the morning, and the young men got up to attend to their work of grooming and feeding the horses again.

Ping-mo talked to the fourth of his companions, who turned out to be a Manchu and who had spent some years in Germany as a student. He knew German and could speak it fluently. And that was the reason, Ping-mo found out, why all four of them were being treated so well.

'My name is Ting-lo,' the young man said, 'and I came back from Berlin only two years ago. I have been working as a junior official in the Tsungli Yamen.'

Ping-mo hesitated whether he should reveal his identity, for he thought that the young man would certainly have known his father when he was ambassador in Germany. He finally decided that there was no harm in doing so. Ting-lo took his hands and said:

'Why, of course, I met your honourable father. He was always very kind to us students, and we thought very highly of him.'

Ping-mo and Ting-lo became friends and swore that, during the difficult days ahead, they would do all they could to help each other. Ting-lo told his friend that, as long as Peking was under occupation by eight different countries, they should make use of the protection of the German troops and do everything to please them.

'But certainly I have not joined a revolutionary society to become a virtual slave of the German army,' Ping-mo objected.

'When it comes to patriotism,' Ting-lo said, 'I hope I am second to none. I can see your point of view, but we must remain cool and use our heads. We are better off than if we try to leave here. With these people I can at least talk in their own language, and as you will see, that makes a world of difference. Supposing I do succeed in escaping, how can I be sure that some other foreign troops will not take me for a Boxer and blow my brains out? And that is true of you also. As long as we keep together, you, too, will be all right. You will be safe. I have been with these officers two weeks already, and I should know.'

'But look,' added Ping-mo, 'I have another problem. I must find out where my father's concubine is. Perhaps you know her —'

'You mean Golden Orchid?'

'Yes, Golden Orchid.'

'Why, I never thought that she was in Peking. Of course I know her. I knew her when she was in Berlin. She was the rage of the city. I don't mean that I was actually acquainted with her, but I used to see her, like the other students, and we admired her beauty and intelligence. But tell me, how is it that she is here?'

Ping-mo was embarrassed. He did not want to tell Ting-lo that Golden Orchid had gone back to the profession from which she was taken to be his father's concubine. All he cared to say was that, after his father's death, she wanted to come back to Peking with her mother to live.

'How unfortunate that she should be caught in the midst of all this trouble! She should have remained in Soochow. That's where she comes from, isn't it?' asked Ting-lo.

'Yes. We must try to find her and give her protection. I was looking for her when the Germans pressed me into service.'

Before the four young men could finish their conversation the bugle sounded, and the officers assembled in the front courtyard for their morning inspection. There must have been some hundred and fifty of them. They were junior officers. They were all smartly dressed in white uniforms, with black boots almost reaching the knees. The impressive-looking helmets were no longer to be seen. In their place were white topees, commonly worn by foreigners in China during the summer.

Then the young men heard a sudden clicking of heels, and a high officer, obviously a general, stepped in front of the assembled men and made a long speech. He was tall, bedecked with rows of military decorations, and his thick moustache looked awe-inspiring.

'Let none of us forget,' exhorted the General, 'the words which our great and beloved Kaiser uttered when you left the fatherland. "You are about to meet," he said, "a crafty, well-armed, cruel foe; meet him and beat him! Give no quarter! Take no prisoners! Kill him when he falls into your hands! Even as a thousand years ago the Huns under their king Attila made such a name as still resounds in terror in legend and fables, so make the name of Germany resound through Chinese history a thousand years from now." Those, you remember, were His Imperial Majesty's words, and you must do as you are commanded. "The German flag," he also said, "has been insulted and the German Empire defiled. This calls for condign punishment and revenge. So I send you out to avenge the wrong, and I will never rest till the German flag, together with those of her allies, floats victoriously above the walls of Peking, and I have dictated peace to the Chinese Government."

'Remember then these words from His Majesty. We are proud that our own General von Scheidermann is now the commander-in-chief of all the allied forces, and we have no doubt that he will dictate the kind of peace which the Chinese deserve.'

As Ting-lo slowly interpreted the General's words to Ping-mo, the son of China's former ambassador in Berlin leaned against the pillar of the stable completely stupefied. Why is the German Kaiser so bitter against my country? he wondered. What have we done to him to deserve this? Father used to tell me that he did everything he could to improve relations between our two countries.

Ping-mo saw no solution to the riddle. The subject of Germany's expansionist policy was one on which he was not adequately informed, and in this state of doubt and confusion his mind went back to Golden Orchid. She alone would be able to tell me something. If only I knew where to find her! Ping-mo muttered to himself. How I hope she is not suffering. . . . She still has Tang Mah by her side, I hope, and also Hai-ming. But they are all women, and women are in great danger. If I had only known, I would have kept Lao Chuang.

The more Ping-mo worried, the more incoherent became his thoughts. In a fit of desperation he turned to Ting-lo and said: 'Ting-lo, you must help me — you must help me to find Golden Orchid, for I have a feeling that she may be in danger.'

'All right, my friend,' Ting-lo replied. 'I'll do everything within my power. But we must be patient. We must look for opportunity. Everything must be carefully thought out and planned. Any impulsive action may lead us to ruin.'

4

THREE days later Ting-lo thought that he could say a few comforting words to Ping-mo. His knowledge of German made him an especially useful person. He was often asked to run important errands, not only between the different German camps, but also between the Germans and the other allied powers. In this way Ting-lo got to know conditions in Peking better than anyone. He was given a pass written in German, French, and English, so that he could visit virtually every part of the city.

One day he came in contact with a curio dealer outside Peking's main gate, half of which had now been burned down. By sheer coincidence this dealer helped to increase Ting-lo's prestige among the German officers enormously. In his collection was the highest decoration ever given by the German government to a foreign dignitary. The Supreme Order of the Black Eagle, studded with precious stones and jewels, had been given by the Kaiser to the Emperor Kuang Hsu when he was in the friendly mood which yielded the gift of the white steed. In the looting the decoration was stolen from the palace, with other valuable objects, by a Cossack and sold in Tientsin for the paltry sum of ten dollars. It then found its way back to Peking and into the hands of the curio dealer.

When Ting-lo called on him, during an interval between errands, the curio dealer, knowing that Ting-lo was in some manner connected with those in the foreign forces of occupation, showed him the German decoration. Ting-lo recognized it at once. He persuaded the dealer to part with it and assured him that he would be amply rewarded. Ting-lo took it to the Phoenix Palace, the Empress Dowager's former quarters, now occupied by General von Scheidermann. The curio dealer was rewarded with a sum fifty times what he had paid, and Ting-lo's prestige rose perceptibly.

Ting-lo told Ping-mo about this and took from his pocket a pass identical with his own, written in the same three languages.

'You and I can now go wherever we want,' explained Ting-lo. 'I told the German officers that there is much work to be done and I need your assistance. They issued this pass for you without any hesitation. We may now be able to find Golden Orchid.'

Early next morning, after saying goodbye to Cheng and Li-san and assuring them that they would be back by evening, the two young men left the Taoist temple and walked south. It was the first time Ping-mo had had the opportunity of seeing the city, with any feeling of security, since it had been torn asunder by the forces of destruction, and he found it difficult to believe what he saw.

Ten short minutes after they left the temple, they came to the foot of the city wall, and Ping-mo saw a pile of corpses. 'Look!' he said to Ting-lo. 'These must be the bodies of the last defenders of the city shot and then thrown from the wall. What pain on their faces!'

Even as Ping-mo said this, he shivered within himself, and then he saw a number of crows and dogs descending upon what remained of the human feast. All the intestines and viscera had been devoured and also the flesh on the arms and legs, but the dogs continued to gnaw the bones, still red with blood and entangled with garments, which had been torn into shreds. The crows fought, pulling the hair from the skin and exposing the skulls.

Nauseated, the two young men left the wall, entered the narrow lanes, or *hutung*, and came to a few of the larger houses where they thought they might have some respite, but the same horrible sight was repeated in a hundred different ways. It was as if they were going through hell itself. They had seen pictures of purgatory painted with the lurid imagination of the Buddhist mythology, but these pictures were as nothing compared with the realities in front of their eyes.

They finally sought refuge in a house which must have been the home of a high official. The furniture had been knocked over and broken, littering the floor. A thick, lovely carpet with a beige background, decorated with blue floral designs, was cut into small pieces. But there was complete calm. The two young men stepped into the patio, and under the eaves of the house they saw a large Ming bowl, with bold floral designs, full of goldfish still quietly swimming under a thin layer of water plants. They sat down on the steps, mopping the sweat from their faces.

'Tell me, Ting-lo,' Ping-mo broke out. 'I feel as if I have known you for a long time. You said you knew my father and also his concubine. Tell me how they were in Berlin — I mean, were they doing good for our country?'

'Well, Ping-mo, as students we didn't know much. But we knew that Golden Orchid was very successful. She performed her functions with dignity.'

'I am so glad to hear that.'

'Now, if you want my frank opinion, many of us did believe that your distinguished father should have declined the offer of being ambassador. This is not spoken in any sense of disparagement, of course. All of us had the greatest admiration for his scholarship. We had read his essays, and we agreed that very few, if any, could write so beautifully. When we heard that he was having constant difficulties with his staff, we naturally drew the conclusion that the fault could not be with this scholar but with the staff. How could it be otherwise, knowing as we do so well the quality of these minor officials? My own family has been in official life for many generations: I knew that if you had a good, honest, upright superior on the one hand and a group of mean and corrupt underlings on the other, friction was inevitable. That, we presumed, was what took place in our embassy in Berlin.'

'In a sense, then, Father was doomed to fail. Isn't that so?'

'If he had had support from the Tsungli Yamen, things would have been different. But we were told that he had political enemies there. His position was thus untenable.'

Ting-lo thought he had been too frank; he said: 'Forgive me for being so outspoken. But you understand that I speak only with respect for your father. He should have left diplomacy alone.'

'He realized it afterwards. But it was too late. Well, thank you, Ting-lo, for this valuable information.'

'Perhaps it is best that things happened as they did. At least your father didn't have to go through all the pain and tragedy which you and I are going through at this very moment.'

They stood up and took a few steps to inhale the fragrance of the oleanders and lilacs. They then turned into another patio separated from the one they had just left by an exquisite moon gate.

As they went farther on, Ping-mo noticed a peculiar kind of smell. It was a sickening smell, and there in front of them were two open wells, like large cisterns, full of mutilated and decaying corpses.

Ping-mo didn't want to see them, yet there was an urge, for both of them, to have a glimpse of that scene of horror. They saw a thigh with deep gashes on it, then a hand, apparently of a woman, still wearing a ring, and then finally, horror of horrors, they saw the intimate part of the body cut off by a bayonet and stuck in her own mouth.

Whether it was the Boxers or the foreign troops who had inflicted these atrocities, the two young men were not interested in finding out. They left the scene in a hurry and went on. Ping-mo was beginning to have grave doubts. The corpses he saw seemed mostly to be those of women. There was also the body of a girl child cut up, still pressing a doll to her bosom. And he imagined seeing even Golden Orchid herself among the piles and piles of corpses which they passed. What if he should see her head, severed from her body, being feasted upon by a pack of wild dogs!

It was then three o'clock in the afternoon, and by chance the two young men, thanks to the passes they carried, found their way without much trouble to the camp guarded by the Japanese. They had difficulty in making themselves understood. Ping-mo hit upon the happy thought of writing out the purpose of their visit in Chinese characters, for he knew that all Japanese who had been to school must understand Chinese. Sure enough, the soldiers nodded their heads and took the young men into the camp in a friendly manner, but there was not a sign of Golden Orchid or of Yang Mah. When they found out, from talking to the refugees, that many of them were well-born, they questioned them about Golden Orchid, describing

o

her. A girl of about their own age said: 'Yes, there was such a person, accompanied by an older woman, perhaps her maidservant. They were here for a few days, but suddenly this morning they disappeared.'

Ping-mo became excited. 'Where do you think they went?'

'I don't know. But I understand it was her own choice to leave. Wait a minute — that old man over there may know something.'

So the girl took Ping-mo and Ting-lo to the old man, and he confirmed the girl's story.

'Yes,' said the old man, 'there were an old and a young woman this morning who said they could not stand this life any longer and went over to that small house over there. They said they would come back. We all advised them not to leave, as there might be danger. But they went, and we have not seen them since.'

'Could anything have happened to them, do you think?'

'I don't want to frighten you, but we did hear that a few soldiers went into the house soon afterwards. What happened after that, who can tell? You know how these foreign soldiers behave. We are thankful to be here. As long as we stay together in the camp, there is much less danger.'

Ping-mo became excited. Although there was no reason to believe that the girl in question was Golden Orchid or the woman accompanying her was Yang Mah, they might be the very people whom he was looking for.

What had happened was this: After a long period of confinement in the camp Golden Orchid became terribly dejected. One day she blurted out: 'How long, Yang Mah, will this terrible life last?'

Yang Mah as usual was patient and answered her mistress that it could not last long. 'When it is all over, Tai-tai, we shall leave at once, and life will be sweet and full of smiles again down in the south, in Soochow.'

Yang Mah whispered quietly into Golden Orchid's ear, as if afraid someone might overhear her, that she would recover all the gold and silver and jewels which she had buried in the coffin of Golden Orchid's mother. She knew exactly in which corner of the coffin the treasures were hidden, under a thick layer of lime put there to absorb the moisture that might seep in.

It was good for Golden Orchid to hear the reassuring words of

Yang Mah. As she listened, she indulged in the luxury of polishing her fingernails, which was another of the habits she had acquired in Europe. The small bottle of alcohol which she had used against head lice was now practically empty. It had also saved her from other kinds of skin trouble which had become almost epidemic in the camp. The thought that before long she might be exposed to the same affliction was disconcerting. It was then she began to toy with the idea that she might not run into any special danger if she lived apart for short stretches of time in a nearby house where life could be slightly more comfortable.

'Yang Mah,' said Golden Orchid, 'if we could only stay in that small house during the daytime and come back here at night, I should be much happier.'

Yang Mah was willing to do anything to please her mistress, but in this instance she had misgivings. She knew the house Golden Orchid had in mind — it was barely a hundred yards from the camp. Quietly she found out that they could rest there and be provided with food and water on payment of a small sum of money, to which Golden Orchid readily agreed. The house was poorly furnished, but the prospect of being away from the stench, the dirt and squalor of the camp, made doubly worse by the intensely hot weather, was irresistible. Yang Mah's doubt and hesitancy gradually melted, until finally one afternoon the two women visited the house. At dusk they were back in the camp.

Having tasted this new life, they resolved to return to the house every day as soon as morning came. But on the third day something happened which shocked them. For, after all, life was still far from normal. The chaos which immediately followed the occupation had subsided, but foreign soldiers were still prowling around, looking for treasures, which they dumped together and auctioned for ready cash and for *kuniang*, which, the local population told them, meant pretty girls. On the morning of the third day, shortly after the two women returned to the house, four young European soldiers appeared. They were happy to find two utterly defenceless women.

Both Yang Mah and Golden Orchid still wore ragged clothes but, the weather being warm, the clothes were thin, and the shapely young body of Golden Orchid looked inviting to the young soldiers. For a while they could not believe what they saw in front of them.

One of the soldiers gave a faint smile. After looking at his comrades he slowly advanced towards Golden Orchid, who stood tremulously in the corner of the small room with Yang Mah by her side. He stopped and commented: 'She is a pretty girl. She is young — quite young.'

'Look at her hands', said one of the others. 'They are so soft — and white.'

'Why, she is very sweet and lovely,' was another comment.

The young soldier stepped forward and grasped Golden Orchid's arms.

In a fit of desperation she cried out: '*Halt! Es tut mir weh!* [Stop! You are hurting me.]'

These five little words appeared to have magical power. The four young soldiers, completely stunned, were speechless and gazed at each other in bewilderment. They had been sent ten thousand miles to conquer a strange land with strange people of even stranger manners and language; and here was a young woman, a dirty, ragged woman, speaking their own German language with almost flawless precision. It was unbelievable! They continued to stare at each other, their faces drawn, and then somehow their better nature began to reassert itself. The young soldier loosened his grip on Golden Orchid's arms, and one behind him said to her: 'So you speak German, young lady.'

'Yes, I have lived in your country. I was in Berlin for three years. I was also received in audience by your Kaiserin — in the Schloss Charlottenburg.'

The soldiers felt so stupid that they didn't know what to do with themselves.

By this time Golden Orchid had regained her poise, and she quickly asked: 'Where is your General von Scheidermann now? I used to know him.'

At the mention of the name of their supreme commander, who was also the commander-in-chief of the allied forces of occupation in Peking, the four young soldiers automatically clicked their heels and stood at attention. In unison they replied, '*Der General ist jetzt in Peking.*'

'He is in Peking? Is that possible? Then I must visit him.'

The soldiers held a brief conference, and offered to escort her to the palace where the General had his headquarters.

Yang Mah was not yet out of her fright. She did not understand a word of what was said, and asked her mistress: 'But what are they going to do to us? I am terribly afraid.'

Golden Orchid assured her that everything was all right and, tidying herself as much as she could, went with the soldiers. Yang Mah followed. As they walked, the soldiers agreed that they should report the matter to their own officers first, and thus they came to the Taoist temple. Ping-mo, Ting-lo, and the other two young men were at their work. There was some commotion in the temple when Golden Orchid arrived, but they had no knowledge of what was going on. A soldier led away one of the horses and harnessed it to a carriage. All the young men learned later was that two women had been in the temple and had then driven away.

5

For seven weeks — seven long and agonizing weeks — Peking had now been under occupation. Still Ping-mo found no trace of Golden Orchid; he went on doggedly, persistently, scouring the city with Ting-lo, but it was always the same futile and fruitless search.

In the meantime, Golden Orchid was comfortably settled at the Phoenix Palace and had become accustomed to her new surroundings. She was given a small apartment, with Yang Mah continuing to minister to her needs. The apartment was at one end of the palace, to every part of which, of course, she had access. In fact, General von Scheidermann insisted that she consider as her own anything in the palace that might strike her fancy. He spread in front of her every morning the richest jewels, precious stones, silks, furs, antique bronzes and porcelains that came pouring into the palace. Whether out of discretion or patriotism, Golden Orchid refused to take anything. Yang Mah was less particular. Her eyes popping at the sight of these valuable things, she urged her mistress to choose at least a few of them, which she would then hide in the coffin of Golden Orchid's mother. But Golden Orchid firmly refused.

The apartment, with its high ceiling, was cool even in the daytime in the hot weather. It had once been the private apartment of one of the eunuchs who attended on the Emperor Dowager. It was simply furnished, and in the little courtyard were night-blooming jasmines which filled the room with unearthly fragrance. The eunuch had had unusual poetic and artistic inclinations, in contrast to the chief eunuch, who was as vulgar as he was cruel, but none the less the Empress Dowager's great favourite.

One morning General von Scheidermann found himself in an exceptionally cheerful mood and, taking Golden Orchid's hand, said: 'My sweet little Orchid, you know you are a godsend to me. I don't know where I would be without you. You have made my life here so much easier and more pleasant.'

Tall, good-looking and with striking manners, the General was in the prime of life. In the first few days of Golden Orchid's stay at the palace, he was stiff and formal, even addressing her with the honorific '*Excellenz*'. Though he had now become the commander-in-chief of the occupation forces in Peking, it had been as the favourite aide-de-camp of Their German Majesties that he had first come to know Golden Orchid in Berlin. She had matured in the meantime and he was the same handsome man with a touch of grey round the temples. Much had taken place during the interval, but the sudden meeting revived past memories.

'I knew, my dear little Orchid,' continued General von Scheidermann, 'that I was going to meet you again somewhere. Didn't I say so during the ball in the Schloss? You were dressed in that beautiful blue gown, I remember — oh, no, it was purple. And that exquisite embroidery which contrasted so wonderfully with the delicate ivory of your face . . .'

Golden Orchid smiled a gentle smile, showing the same small pearly white teeth she had had in Berlin. 'I had no idea, General,' she said, 'that you had such a memory.'

She asked him if everything in Peking was going as well as he expected.

'I can imagine that life for a foreign soldier, in a strange land, is not what it should be. I don't speak of yourself, of course.'

'I know exactly what you mean, my dear little Orchid. It's good of you to think of us in this way. As a matter of fact, that was why I regarded you as my godsend. I have problems, pressing problems, and without you I wouldn't attempt to solve them.'

'Well, if I can be of any service to you, I shall be most happy.'

General von Scheidermann began to pace up and down the spacious room which had been the audience hall of the Empress Dowager. He looked at the high ceiling and admired the intricate beauty of its coloured designs. The floor was covered with a huge rug of imperial yellow, with here and there a few symbolic Chinese decorations in blue. When he stopped pacing he found his feet resting squarely on the design of a bat. Not a very good omen, the General thought, and he turned to Golden Orchid and asked her what the design meant.

'A bat,' replied Golden Orchid, '*Viel Glück!* Why, this is wonderful. Do you know, General, that for thousands of years the bat in China has meant good fortune? Let me tell you why. The Chinese word for the bat is *fu*. Another word with the identical sound means good luck. Therefore the bat and good luck are one and the same thing.'

'*Wunderbar!* And how interesting!' ejaculated the General. 'That's what I like to hear. Let me tell you what I have in mind. You see, I have two problems, and you must help me to solve them. The first is that I am afraid many of the foreign troops are being overcome by illness. The second is that they do not have enough food.'

'Well, General,' replied Golden Orchid, 'if you allow me to say so, these two questions really amount to the same thing. However, you have a third problem, and that is, when you take care of the foreign troops, are you also going to take care of the people in the city? The troops and the people have now merged. Their destiny is tied together.'

'Interesting! I had not considered that. Please go on.'

'They have never been enemies. So you really cannot do anything for the one without doing as much for the other. The population has already suffered and continues to suffer for lack of food, even though things have quietened down considerably since you assumed command. That is why I propose helping the people at the same time as the troops.'

The General was much impressed by Golden Orchid's sense of loyalty to her own people. He thought her words well advised and full of wisdom. 'Yes, yes, I see what you mean,' he said. 'After all, the people in the city have been victimized just as much as we.'

'Even worse, General. First they were victimized by the Boxers who are their own people, and now by the foreign troops. They haven't done anything to deserve this. You can see that they are a gentle people trying to carry on their normal work and to live as peaceful a life as they can find.'

'You are right. But all the same my first duty is to look after the welfare of the troops. However, I am glad I spoke to you. Frankly, I was going to issue orders to force the people to sacrifice all they have for my troops.'

'But that would not succeed, General,' continued Golden Orchid. 'I would suggest that you work with the people and not against them. If you let them know that you are working for their interests, they will work for you in return, and that will mean a great deal to the troops under your command.'

'You are wonderful, my dear little Orchid.'

'That is a simple Confucian principle which I learned from my husband. He used to say that when a Chinese Government in the past failed it was only because it worked against the interests of the people. As long as they know that you are working for them, they will do everything to work for you.'

'Why, if Confucius said that, we must listen to him, mustn't we? It all sounds very sensible. But how are you going to set about it? Remember that we are the conquerors and the Chinese people are the conquered.'

General von Scheidermann had other words in his vocabulary, but he thought it best to restrain himself in the presence of his 'dear little Orchid'. Indeed, he could very well have said that, as the representative of the most highly developed 'white' race, it was his mission to squash 'the yellow peril'. Didn't the Kaiser say as much?

All this would have been beyond the comprehension of Golden Orchid. She had no idea what the General was thinking; but when he spoke of the relationship between the conqueror and the conquered, she said: 'If I were you, I shouldn't think in those terms. The problem now is how to feed the hungry and heal the sick, and I know they are everywhere.'

'That is so, and I know that I can't solve the problem unless I have the co-operation of some responsible Chinese. That's why I say you are a godsend to me, my dear little Orchid. All your officials seem to have disappeared like rats. I can't find them. But, really, there is nothing they need be afraid of. . . . I am going to decorate

those young soldiers who discovered you and brought you here.'
And then the General repeated: 'Oh, it is such joy meeting you
again!'

Golden Orchid thought that this was too good an opportunity to
miss, and her mind immediately flashed to Ping-mo and Hai-ming,
the two persons whom she wanted to save most of all. Wherever they
were, she thought — and she hoped they were still alive — they
must be having a very miserable time indeed. The order to search
for them was at once issued from the headquarters of the commander-in-chief. The relationship between herself and the General
had become so intimate that she was sure he would agree to anything
she wanted.

6

To find Ping-mo was the easiest thing in the world. He was traced
only a few hours after the order was issued.

The order came to the headquarters of the German officers in the
Taoist temple where, as usual, Ping-mo and his friend Ting-lo and
the other two young men were cleaning the stables and caring for the
horses. The officer in charge on that day was Oberst Ulrich, a man
who was singularly punctilious and, as befitting an officer, very strict
and inflexible in the execution of his duties. His immediate reaction,
on receiving the order, was to summon Ting-lo and Ping-mo, who
had proved themselves to be more capable than Cheng and Li-san.
The manner in which they were called bespoke something urgent
and serious.

'I should like the two of you to find out,' began Oberst Ulrich,
'within the next twenty-four hours, a young man by the name of —'
He then spelled out SHEN PING-MO. 'His father was at one time
Chinese ambassador in Berlin.' To the Colonel the two young men
standing in front of him were merely X and Y. None of the officers
ever took the trouble to learn their names. They were not important enough, and anyway Chinese names, they thought, were much
too difficult.

Ting-lo and Ping-mo stood there completely aghast. They were
speechless. Ping-mo's face turned as pale as a ghost's. He started to

tremble, thinking, not unnaturally, that he was wanted for his anti-foreign activities and that he might even be executed with other anti-foreign elements and the Boxers who were still being rounded up. Ping-mo thought it best to announce that he was the very person the Colonel was looking for. Then he said to himself, Why should I give myself up? I can disappear into the crowd again as I did before.

'Ting-lo, I hope to meet you again — when the troubles are over. I must leave you before they get hold of me,' said Ping-mo when they left Oberst Ulrich.

'No, no, Ping-mo,' protested Ting-lo, 'you are not to leave. Don't be silly. No harm is coming to you. That doesn't mean danger — an order from the headquarters of the commander-in-chief. Can't you see? — Well, anyhow, where would I be and what would they do to me if they found out that you had disappeared?'

Ting-lo urged that Colonel Ulrich be informed at once. It was early afternoon. The Colonel, somewhat drowsy, was irritated when he saw the two young men coming back to his office.

'Well, what do you want?' the Colonel yelled. 'Aren't my instructions clear enough? Why don't you get busy and find the fellow for me?'

'We have found him, Herr Oberst,' replied Ting-lo.

'You have? How *wunderbar*! And so quickly? Where is he? And why don't you bring him in?'

'He stands in front of you, Herr Oberst!'

'Where? Are you *verrückt*? What do you mean by this?'

'Herr Oberst,' slowly explained Ting-lo, 'this is Shen Ping-mo, the son of the former Chinese ambassador in Berlin.'

Ping-mo nodded to confirm the announcement, but he said nothing.

Oberst Ulrich was perplexed. He had been in China only a few months and had not become sophisticated, like one of those 'old China hands' who knew exactly how to handle all situations affecting the Chinese by assuming an attitude of superiority. The Colonel had come to China as a conqueror, but even so he was now face to face with the son of an ambassador, and his German instinct prompted him to stand up, stretch out his hand to Ping-mo and congratulate him — a thing no 'old China hand' would have done.

Ping-mo was completely in the dark. He had no idea what it all

meant. But he was slowly reconciling himself to the fact that
Ting-lo was probably correct in his supposition. Two orderlies were
summoned by Oberst Ulrich to accompany him to the Phoenix
Palace; and when he said goodbye to Ting-lo, his friend replied:
'Good luck to you, Ping-mo! If something good turns up, don't
forget that you still have a friend cleaning the stables at the Taoist
temple.'

The first person Ping-mo met at the palace was Yang Mah, who
came running out and greeted him noisily. 'Young master, young
master,' she said with tears in her eyes, 'I knew you were safe and
sound somewhere. Oh! I am so happy to see you again. Protected
by these foreign soldiers! Why, that is as it should be. Now let me
go and convey the good news to Tai-tai.

'Tai-tai,' she said in excitement, 'the young master Ping-mo is
here. He looks as well as ever. The old master and the ancestors
must have given him protection and blessing during this horrible
period. Now we are all together again.'

When Ping-mo was conducted into the presence of Golden
Orchid, he just looked at her. He could not believe that such a
thing had happened. And then for a long time he held her hands,
still without uttering a word. Ping-mo felt that it was like a dream,
that at long last he should see again the girl whom he thought he had
lost — perhaps for ever — his father's concubine, within the inner-
most and sacrosanct walls of the Forbidden Palace itself. Golden
Orchid led him to an empty chair while she herself sat on the side of
her bed.

'But how did you come here, Golden Orchid?' Ping-mo asked.
'Into the palace of the Empress Dowager!'

'By a stroke of sheer luck. But never mind, I'll tell you later.
However, the commander-in-chief, General von Scheidermann,
was one of my friends when I was in Berlin with your father.'

'Really? That is unbelievable!'

'We have now something very important to do, and I want your
help. I asked the General to issue orders to find you wherever you
might be in Peking, and I knew that you would be found.'

Ping-mo was still dumbfounded and speechless.

That night he was brought into the presence of General von
Scheidermann, who he thought was a very agreeable person. He
did not appear as overbearing to Ping-mo as those foreigners who

had lived long in the treaty ports like Shanghai. All the foreigners Ping-mo had ever known were of that type, and he had learned to loathe them from the very bottom of his heart. In fact, it was because of his bitter and unpleasant experiences with such foreigners that he had taken on the role of a revolutionary and joined the secret society. Albeit a military man, Von Scheidermann proved to be a refreshing exception.

After a good night's rest Golden Orchid was ready to tell Ping-mo what she proposed to do. 'The General and I, as you can see,' she began, 'are on very friendly terms. He is meeting difficulties which he cannot overcome without the co-operation and assistance of some of us Chinese. I have decided to give him that help, because by helping him we shall be helping ourselves.'

'But surely he can find other Chinese?' queried Ping-mo.

'Unfortunately he can't. You know what our officials are like. They have all disappeared, as the General said to me, like rats. I am terribly ashamed. There may still be a few in Peking, but they are in hiding. In any case, they would be unfamiliar to him even if they were brought to him. But he has known me for a long time. We have even danced together in the presence of the Kaiserin,'

'But what are the difficulties that you referred to?'

'There is a shortage of food among the foreign troops. Also a good many of them are ill with diarrhœa, dysentery and typhoid. Since your father died, I have learned much about these diseases of the intestines. These troops are new here, and they are careless about eating and drinking.'

'But what can you do?'

'As I said, Ping-mo, by being of service to them, we shall be helping our own people. I know how the poor people are suffering, by the little that I have gone through. I want to recommend to General von Scheidermann certain measures that will make it possible for food to come into the city and reduce the number of sick people. I want you to be a part of my plans so that he will consider you as important as myself.'

Ping-mo was surprised that Golden Orchid had such easy access to the most powerful person now living in Peking. General von Scheidermann had become much more powerful than the Empress Dowager, for both the Chinese and foreign populations had to obey his every word. Ping-mo realized that his father's concubine and the German commander-in-chief were on the most intimate terms. He was disturbed, but then the circumstances were most unusual.

'My dear General,' said Golden Orchid, as she stepped into the audience hall with Ping-mo and their feet sank into the thick, soft rug, 'I wish you would do one thing for me. I want Ping-mo to go down to Tientsin and bring back as much foreign medicine as he can to Peking. To save time he will need to go by a special train, and carry a special pass from the headquarters of the commander-in-chief.'

'That can be arranged,' said General von Scheidermann. 'But my dear little Orchid, do we need more medicine? There is enough to go round for my troops, but it's no use. They continue to fall sick, and only this morning a ship left Tientsin bound for Japan with a hundred and fifty new cases of dysentery. The hospitals there are already full of our soldiers. The important thing is to stop the spread of the disease.'

'That's exactly it, General. The merchant in Tientsin whom I know quite well has a large collection of Chinese and foreign medicine which, I am sure, is hidden somewhere but will be made available to us. My husband, the ambassador, Ping-mo's father, died of the disease. And when I came back here from the south, I was taken ill with the same disease. It was that merchant's Chinese herbs that cured me. There will be no harm in trying these herbs on the troops.'

General von Scheidermann had serious doubts about their efficacy, but when Golden Orchid insisted, he knew that she had some definite purpose in mind. He did not wish to thwart her.

'I will myself visit the hospitals and dispensaries while Ping-mo is gone,' continued Golden Orchid.

She could not explain to the General what the herbs were, but it was true that she had taken the dried seeds of the plantain or *plantago major*, which very efficiently cured her of dysentery. She did not know, however, that plantain could not cure typhoid, the only remedy for which, the Chinese learned, was to allow the fever to run its natural course while the patient lay almost motionless without any food.

As soon as Golden Orchid left the General, she had another talk with Ping-mo and disclosed her plans. 'What I want you to do,' she said, 'is to see and to learn at first hand the conditions of the people and to tell them that from now on they will not be molested. They must know that it will be all right to resume normal work and carry their produce into the city to be sold, so that everybody can have some food. The pass you carry will give you the necessary authority, and the people will believe you as they would not believe any other Chinese.'

While he was away, Golden Orchid visited the hospitals in which the foreign troops were being treated, and by her pleasant and gracious manner, and especially by the beauty of her face and body and by her radiant smiles, she succeeded in reducing considerably the acerbity between the conquering troops and the conquered people. It wasn't long before everyone began to ask who this charming and attractive young lady was.

When Ping-mo reached Tientsin, he found, as he had expected, that the tension among the people had not relaxed. They were morbid with fear, having been victimized for so long. Those that had left Peking were not thinking of returning, and the fields immediately outside the Peking gates were virtually abandoned. October had come, and the wheat and corn looked yellow and ripe. It appeared to him that, when the time arrived to harvest them, there would be no one to do the work. It was then that his thoughts went back to the branches of the secret society which were scattered in the villages. Through these branches he could give assurances that normal conditions were being restored, and the farmers would begin to have the courage to step out into the open again.

Ping-mo was gone for about five days, and when he came back to see Golden Orchid again, he felt as if they had been the most useful days of his life.

'Golden Orchid,' he said with satisfaction, 'I feel there is any amount of food lying about. But the people are still panic-stricken. It is a question of restoring their confidence. We want all the help we can get. There is one person who was with me in the officers' quarters in the Taoist temple. How about asking him to help us? He understands German and you will find him useful.'

But Golden Orchid was not responsive and made no comment.

'His name is Ting-lo,' continued Ping-mo. 'He comes from a Manchu family. What's more, he says that he saw you in Berlin.

He admires you. He was a student in Germany when you were there.'

The idea of introducing an unfamiliar person into the situation at this juncture did not appeal to Golden Orchid. Especially she did not want to meet any Chinese from Berlin and be reminded of the nightmare she had known there. So she merely asked Ping-mo what they should do to encourage the people to carry food into the capital.

'We need to issue orders at once that the farmers must come out to harvest the ripening fields. They said they would, but they must have the guarantee that foreign troops and riff-raff will not disturb them. Also we should issue licences to the farmers and merchants giving them permission to carry their foodstuffs and merchandise into the city.'

'These are good suggestions, Ping-mo, and I am happy that your journey has brought such good results.'

By the second part of October Peking was almost a normal city again. Eggs and produce from the countryside had started to pour in. The hawkers on the streets had begun to sing their songs, and with the exception of a few isolated cases in which the Cossacks and the Senegalese were involved, the behaviour of the foreign troops was as good as could be expected.

It is unbelievable how far a small light can go in a dark night. What Golden Orchid had accomplished, with the help of Ping-mo, was not much. But the night had been a long one, and it was a relief that it was beginning to end. When the soldiers and sailors from eight different nations in the hospitals once more set their eyes on fresh eggs, which they had thought were non-existent in China, their spirits lifted. One boy from Ohio who had been ill with dysentery for a month wept with joy one morning when he was given a boiled egg for his breakfast.

'You've got to thank that smart Chinese girl,' explained his friend, 'They say all good things come from her.'

'You mean also that nasty liquid which I had to drink yesterday?'

'Well, don't you feel better today? Diarrhœa ten, fifteen, twenty times a day. Weren't you sick of that? No energy, no vitality! And today I feel chipper again. That nasty liquid did it.'

'All the same it was awful stuff. I felt as if I were swallowing a lot of dirty tadpoles. That was what it looked like.'

Ping-mo had brought back stalks of the dried plantain seeds and Golden Orchid tried them on some of the patients. She cooked the stalks and took out the leaves. The seeds now became black little balls with a coating of something gelatinous, and they floated on the water like so many tiny tadpoles. For some chemical reason these seeds have the power of checking diarrhœa. The result was that Golden Orchid became an angel of mercy to all the foreign troops no less than to her own people.

None of the Peking population ever saw her, but the legend grew that Kuan-yin, the Goddess of Mercy, had descended from the heavens into the body of this young woman Golden Orchid, and her name began to hang on the lips of everybody. Most of the temples had been destroyed, but the people in Peking made pilgrimages to their ruined shrines and prostrated themselves before the image of Kuan-yin. In fact, a new trade grew up in Peking; porcelain figures of that goddess sold by the hundreds of thousands. People even began to swear by Golden Orchid, and when there were quarrels and differences of opinion they would say: 'Let's bring them before the judgement of Golden Orchid!'

But the greatest of all questions remained unanswered. With the coming of peace, people also began to wonder when the Empress Dowager and the young Emperor would move back to the capital. Opinion on the matter was widely divided. Some strongly urged that it was time for the throne to come back. Others were just as insistent that Golden Orchid had now become the Empress, having done more good for the people than the Old Buddha or the Emperor had ever done. But that was treason, and no one had the courage to express such sentiments in public. The people did not know, however, that it was no longer possible for the throne to come and go as it pleased. The commander-in-chief of the foreign troops was now in control of the imperial city; and until the treaty, concerning which the eight governments were in constant consultation, was presented to the Chinese Government and signed by it, the throne could not return nor the foreign troops be withdrawn.

7

PING-MO continued to be busy with liaison work between Golden Orchid and the outside world. From early morning till late in the afternoon streams of people came and wanted to see Golden Orchid. Except when he was asked to go on short missions for a day or two, Ping-mo tried as much as possible to be near and available to Golden Orchid, who for her part was happy that she had someone to rely upon.

'Well, Ping-mo, we at least have the satisfaction that we are doing something.'

'Something? As yet it is nothing when compared with what will come to us quite soon. I have a feeling that you will have to play an important part in the peace negotiations,' asserted Ping-mo.

'No, no, I am not interested in the peace negotiations. What we are doing is already too much for me. Besides, my only interest is to see the people happy again. I am glad that things are quieter and the city is resuming its normal activities. We must thank our stars that events are turning out so well. When the proper time comes, we shall leave for the south. I want my mother to be properly buried, and that is all that I now care for.'

But Ping-mo's mind was still on the peace negotiations. He said they might take place at any moment, and he had heard that there was one thing in which her services would be indispensable. 'You remember that the Boxers, a few months ago, killed a member of the Japanese Embassy and also the German ambassador. The Japanese can perhaps be pacified, as the man was only a minor official, but the Germans would be most difficult to appease. As Von Scheider-mann is German, and as you are known to be on good terms with him, I am sure our Government would want you to mediate.'

'I'll do what I can of course, but that may be little.'

But Ping-mo continued. 'Look at the number of presents that are constantly being sent to you. Have you ever noticed that when the ordinary people wish to see you, it is out of curiosity — they wish to have a glimpse of the Phoenix Palace where you live — or they merely want to express their thanks to you? You are their Kuan-yin, their Goddess of Mercy. But when officials wish to see you, they are usually preceded by all kinds of expensive gifts.'

'I am leaving all these gifts behind — for charity.'

As Golden Orchid spoke, Yang Mah rushed in with a teakwood box. Ping-mo raised the lid and on the top of a neat package enclosed in rich imperial yellow silk was a large red visiting-card measuring some seven inches wide and ten inches long, and on it were inscribed three large black characters, the name of the most important dignitary in the entire Chinese Empire.

All three of them stood gazing at the package with amazement. Then Ping-mo exclaimed, 'From Li Hung-chang himself!' *

Yang Mah's eyes almost jumped out of their sockets as she heard that name mentioned. 'Ah-ya,' she exclaimed. 'Is that possible?'

Ping-mo gradually untied the silk cover and removed a few layers of cotton. There lay the most magnificent pieces of jade they had ever seen. Golden Orchid was stunned, but gave a deep sigh. Yang Mah could not understand her mistress. She felt a strong urge to touch the jewels but dared not. 'Look at them, look at them, Tai-tai,' she screamed with joy. 'How beautiful they are, and how precious and valuable they must be!'

Ping-mo took the central piece in his hand. It was a string of thirty-six stones of perfect jade, each as large as a robin's egg, uniformly green and translucent, and between them were smaller beads of red jade. Evidently they were audience beads such as only the highest officials of the land could wear during the most exalted functions. It had now been restrung to grace the soft neck of the most privileged woman in the land. Yet all that Golden Orchid could say was: 'Hm! I didn't know that in a period of such deep sorrow, when everyone is suffering so much, there were still such things available in the city.'

Golden Orchid asked Ping-mo to close the box and then ordered Yang Mah, in a casual fashion, to take it away to her bedroom.

'Ping-mo,' she said after Yang Mah had left, 'I don't know what all this means. But I have no interest in these gifts, nor in the people who swarm to shower gifts on me or smother me with favours and compliments. How sordid, how mean is the human heart! I have seen too much of official life. What have I done to deserve all this? There was a time when these favours would have meant something, and I would have appreciated them. When I was with

---

* Li Hung-chang (1823–1901) was China's most prominent statesman and diplomat of that period.

your father in Berlin, we accomplished something for the good of the country. But what was our reward? Your father died of a broken heart. The fever which was the cause of his death was merely incidental. After his experiences as an ambassador, he had no desire for anything, no will to live. And now — now they praise me to the skies. Why? Simply because a sing-song girl happens to be living in the Phoenix Palace with the commander-in-chief of the foreign troops!' And Golden Orchid gave a sardonic, bitter smile of which she was not thought capable.

'Listen, Golden Orchid,' responded Ping-mo, 'all that you have said is true. I understand and appreciate it. But after all, both you and I are young —'

Before Ping-mo could finish his sentence, Golden Orchid's thoughts went back to Yung-kai, to the delightful days she had with him, and she began to sob. She thought how wonderful her life could have been if she had come back to Peking with Wen-ching, under happier circumstances, to find Yung-kai still her most devoted friend and lover. But that was all over. Fate had been cruel, or was it the cruelty of the human heart that had brought on such a fate? It was a blur in her mind, but she knew she was not happy, even in her privileged position, and with the love and devotion which Ping-mo had been giving to her, but which she could not reciprocate.

'Do please console yourself, Golden Orchid,' said Ping-mo. 'As I tried to say, we are both young, and there is much that we can still do and accomplish. I don't see why you shouldn't make use of your present influence and do something memorable.'

'But these officials may be laying a trap for me. I have no confidence in them.'

'Exactly what do you mean?'

'I don't know. I don't know anything — perhaps you are right.'

'But one thing I do know. The German Kaiser is going to make it very difficult for us because the Boxers murdered his ambassador in the streets of Peking. I have heard so many people talk about it. It looks to me as if this gift of the jade necklace will be followed by an attempt to solicit your help on this very matter.'

8

PING-MO'S guess was correct. Two days later it was announced that Lord Li Hung-chang would pay his respects to Golden Orchid. But His Lordship had his scruples. Even though the Empress Dowager and the Emperor were away in Sianfu, he could not, out of respect, entertain the idea of being physically present in the Phoenix Palace. He approached the brother of Lee Pan-king, the former President of the Board of Rites who had committed suicide with his family, and asked him to invite Golden Orchid and Ping-mo to dinner. If Lee had been alive, he would certainly have been chosen to approach Golden Orchid; but it was thought that his brother might touch her heart.

Ping-mo urged strongly that the dinner invitation be accepted. When he accompanied Golden Orchid to Lee's residence, which had been restored to its former elegance and beauty, there were at least six or seven dignitaries already in the spacious reception room. Li Hung-chang greeted them with unusual graciousness. There was no talk of any official business — only reminiscences of the achievements of Wen-ching both as a man and as a scholar. There was no reference even to the tragic way in which Lee's brother had died.

The dinner was for a specific purpose, and both Golden Orchid and Ping-mo were touched by the lavish and unstinted encomiums which everyone at the table bestowed upon the deceased ambassador. More than once Golden Orchid felt a lump in her throat, even though at heart she was cursing everyone, including Li Hung-chang, as a hypocrite and liar.

Then, towards the end of the dinner, the host brought up the subject of the murder of the German ambassador. That led, naturally, to the way in which the matter could be satisfactorily settled. Li Hung-chang himself made no comment. The task of explaining the difficulty was left to the host.

'The attitude of the German ambassador's wife is extravagant and unreasonable,' the host explained. 'She doesn't know herself what she wants. I was told that she even wants Her Imperial Majesty's own life. There is no sense of proportion in these ocean devils.'

'What can you expect?' commented one official. 'The foreigners have treated us as inferiors all along, and they will continue to do so

now that we are under their military occupation. Cut China up —
that's what they have been saying, and that's what they will do.
What is there to prevent them from doing it?'

'Well,' said the host, 'this is a very critical situation, but the matter
is fortunately in capable hands.' He looked at Li Hung-chang as he
spoke. 'But on this matter of the German ambassador's wife, Mistress
Golden Orchid, we look to you for help.'

A note of sincerity was lacking in these last words, and Golden
Orchid felt it at once. She thought of replying: 'But I am merely a
sing-song girl. Isn't it too much to expect that I can do anything of
such importance when there are so many capable high dignitaries?'

Ping-mo saw the expression on Golden Orchid's face and knew
exactly what was in her mind. Fortunately he was seated next to
her and, dropping his hand under the table, he gently tugged her
dress and said on her behalf: 'I am sure Mistress Golden Orchid is as
deeply patriotic as any of us and will do the best she can.'

Soon afterwards the dinner ended.

Upon their return to the Phoenix Palace Ping-mo suggested to
Golden Orchid that she must do as the officials expected her to do.
'This is not the time for the satisfaction of personal feeling,' he said.
'Can't you see, Golden Orchid, that heaven has placed you where
you are? Call it destiny, call it accident, call it what you will. But
it is the will of heaven that you and the commander-in-chief should
have this very special relationship. You will have to use it for the
good of the country and of the people. That is what you have always
wanted to do, and here is your chance.'

It was not often that Ping-mo spoke in this way to Golden Orchid.
She was surprised, and he continued: 'We don't want those good-
for-nothing officials to ask the German ambassador's wife to come to
see you tomorrow. They will spoil everything. We have better and
more effective ways. Why don't you ask von Scheidermann to invite
her to tea tomorrow here in the palace and then casually bring the
matter up?'

In the present friendly mood of von Scheidermann, Ping-mo was
convinced that his plan would work. And so it did. Baroness von
Ditmar, the murdered ambassador's wife, considered it an honour
to be invited by the commander-in-chief and arrived at the palace.
She had heard of Golden Orchid and was delighted to meet her.
Golden Orchid described her pleasant memories of Berlin, and the

Baroness was gracious. And then Golden Orchid very tactfully offered profuse apologies for the discomforts of the Baroness's life in Peking and said that with the approach of Christmas she must be eager to return to Germany.

'Yes,' replied the Baroness. 'I would have gone back long ago if it weren't for this matter of my husband, who was murdered, as you may know, by these horrible Boxers.'

'As for me,' Von Scheidermann interrupted, 'I am looking forward to Christmas in Peking. It will be an interesting experience. Snow on the roofs of the Chinese palaces, and everywhere the flags of the German Reich. Wonderful experience!'

'But then, General,' said Golden Orchid, 'the Baroness has children whom she is anxious to see. I understand that, as at our Chinese New Year, you like to meet your family during Christmas.'

Von Scheidermann stood up and excused himself, leaving the two ladies to discuss the matter of the murdered diplomat. Time and time again the Baroness had spoken with the commander-in-chief on the matter of compensation, but always there was no result. Von Scheidermann was prepared to be firm and resolute on a matter affecting the prestige and dignity of his country, but he insisted that the Baroness's demands were too extravagant. It was just as well to let the two ladies talk it over.

'I have been wanting to see you, Madam,' said the Baroness as soon as the commander-in-chief had left the room. 'I have heard so much about you, but I thought I would never have the opportunity of meeting you. . . . As you know, I am now a widow. My husband has been dead about five months now, and I shall not rest until adequate compensation is paid.'

'What strange fate has brought us together?' said Golden Orchid slowly. 'I too am a widow. And it so happens that my husband was China's ambassador in your country. You and I have much in common, and I know how you suffer. But let us try to take matters calmly. These are unusual times, and we are all victims in one way or another.'

Baroness von Ditmar had strange feelings when she heard this. All she had known was that Golden Orchid was a beautiful sing-song girl to whom Von Scheidermann had taken a fancy. But even so she saw no reason why she should modify her original demands.

'But, Madam, my husband was brutally murdered by the Boxers, and the Empress Dowager was the instigator of the whole movement. The case cannot be settled until she pays with her life.'

So, at long last, Golden Orchid heard with her own ears the extraordinary demand of the Baroness. It was the demand that had held up all negotiations. Delegation after delegation of Chinese officials had been frightened and paralysed the moment the subject was brought up. Von Scheidermann asked for extensive concessions from the Chinese Government to give the Baroness personal satisfaction, and the Chinese delegations agreed to consider those concessions. But always the Baroness insisted upon having the life of the Empress Dowager herself.

Golden Orchid was not perturbed. In the same quiet way she said 'I completely sympathize with you, Frau Baronin. If I may say so, my situation is similar to yours. My husband also was murdered: it was worse than murder. And here I am a young widow. I am only twenty-three years old, and I am trying to reconcile myself to the new conditions which fate has created for me.'

'But I am a Christian and you are a fatalist,' pursued the Baroness. 'I cannot so easily give up.'

'Let us not speak about religion,' replied Golden Orchid, smiling apologetically. 'You see, I do not belong to any particular religion. All I try to do is to be sensible and rational. Baroness, this new situation in which I find myself is something over which I have no control. I cannot change it. I feel sorry for myself. But I feel there is no sense in making myself more wretched. Besides, as I see it, you are much, much better off than I am.'

'In what way?'

'Well, for one thing, the Boxers who murdered your husband — have they not been defeated? Killed, shot and executed by the thousand? And thousands upon thousands more of our people and our officials have all paid for the life of your dear husband.'

'But that is another question.'

'I think he has been amply vindicated. Isn't that in a sense true? You said you are a Christian a moment ago. I understand the Christian does not look for revenge. He is supposed to show mercy and charity.'

The Baroness regretted having brought up the subject of Christianity, but she did not show it. She wanted to convince Golden Orchid that, even so, her firm stand was completely justified. On second thoughts, she believed it wiser not to express her feelings, for after all she was not negotiating with a delegation of Chinese officials. She was paying a social visit to someone who was only a sing-song girl, though she might be a unique one.

But Golden Orchid was quick and, as it were, drew the thoughts from the Baroness's mind. 'You see, Baroness, we have treated you Germans well, and we mean to be good friends again. I have many friends in Berlin. General von Scheidermann happens to be one of them. On every occasion when there has been the slightest trouble between China and Germany, we have always given concessions. You remember a couple of years ago when a German missionary was killed? We gave an entire bay in Shantung, our sacred province, as compensation to settle the matter. That is why I feel quite sure that there will be adequate compensation for the murder of your husband.'

The Baroness remained silent; similar thoughts had been simmering in her mind. If a missionary's life was compensated for with an important territorial concession, surely the life of the Kaiser's diplomatic envoy should be compensated for with the life of the Empress Dowager.

But again Golden Orchid took the thought out of the Baroness's mind. 'You have talked,' she continued, 'about the Empress Dowager giving her life for that of your husband. Well, supposing that my husband for some reason had been murdered in Berlin, and I began asking for the life of your Kaiserin, what would you and the entire German nation think of me? You would think that I was out of my mind, and I wouldn't blame you for thinking so. Besides, I love your Kaiserin. She is an adorable woman, and charming, too, and she made me feel so happy and at home when I was introduced to her at the Schloss Charlottenburg.'

The Baroness was visibly surprised — and impressed. Golden Orchid had been received in audience by the Kaiserin when she herself had not been anywhere near Her Majesty! She began to wonder what kind of person she was having the honour of taking tea with.

At this point Von Scheidermann returned. 'I can see that you are enjoying each other's company,' he said.

'Indeed we are,' replied the Baroness. 'Madam has so many interesting things to tell me. She has had such a rich life.' Looking round the magnificent room she commented on how beautiful the Peking palaces were, and indeed the entire architectural plan of the imperial city.

'On some other day, Frau Baronin,' pursued Golden Orchid, 'I hope to have the pleasure of your company on a visit to the Summer Palace just outside the city. It will be superbly beautiful under a blanket of snow. But have you also noticed, as you go about the streets, the gorgeous arches, in all their lovely colours, spanning them?'

'Yes, what are they, Madam? They are strikingly beautiful. It's not only the colours which are so exquisite, but also the dignity and restraint of the lines. And then to think that thousands and thousands of people pass under them every day, as if to show their respect and homage.'

Golden Orchid began to pull the most effective arrow from her armoury of weapons. If these arches appealed to the Baroness, that was the very subject on which she wanted to say a few words.

'I admire your wonderful power of understanding, Frau Baronin,' said Golden Orchid slowly. 'These arches are indeed monuments for people to show their respect. They have indeed a meaning . . .'

'I myself would like to know what they are for,' said Von Scheidermann.

'Well, when I was in Berlin, I saw a number of statues of your eminent persons. Your warriors, Herr General, have more statues than anyone else.'

'And what's wrong with that?' asked the General.

'I am afraid it won't please you to be a General in China, for we do not admire military people.'

'You don't, eh?' The General laughed heartily. 'That is the trouble with China. You see, my dear young lady, you pay heavily for ignoring these warriors. You wouldn't be where you are now if you showed greater respect to them.'

'Perhaps you are right, General, and I am not going to argue with you on this point. But there is an old proverb which says: "The success of one General is derived from the corpses of ten thousand people." We don't respect those who kill. However, that is not the point. What I was going to tell you is that we do admire an act of loyalty on the part of a great prime minister for noble deeds performed for the good of his people. We also admire a great poet, a great artist, and most of all women who live a life of chastity, or children who show filial devotion to their parents. All these we commemorate not with statues but with arches.'

'What strange ideas you people seem to have!' said the commander-in-chief.

'But it's interesting,' added the Baroness. 'Please go on.'

'These arches, as you can see, are more magnificent than your statues. And what's more, they are erected only through imperial edict. They are there to be looked up to and to be walked under by countless people for countless generations.'

'In other words, something like the Brandenburger Tor in Berlin or the Arc de Triomphe in Paris,' commented the Baroness.

'Exactly,' said Golden Orchid, 'except that with you those monuments embody an idea. With us the arches are erected in honour of individual people.'

There was a short pause, and then the Baroness took the commander-in-chief aside and spoke to him for some time. Von Scheidermann then turned to Golden Orchid and said: 'If the arches are what you have described them to be, then we shall insist that such an arch be erected to the memory of Baron von Ditmar. If you think that the Chinese Government can agree to this, then the Baroness will drop her original demand of asking for the life of your Empress Dowager.'

There was silence. The Baroness sat waiting.

'Very well,' said Golden Orchid. 'I shall convey the idea to Lord Li Hung-chang. I shall persuade him to ask the throne to agree to the construction of the most magnificent arch in all Peking on the very spot where the Baron met his death. I would even suggest something further.'

'What is it?' the Baroness asked.

'I would suggest that the significant events in the Baron's life be inscribed on the arch so that everyone will know what a great man he was. Also the Empress Dowager and the Emperor will express their personal regret for his tragic end. That will amount to an eternal apology to Germany by the Chinese imperial house.'

When the Baroness left, Von Scheidermann was so happy that he kissed Golden Orchid on the mouth.

'How marvellous, how incredibly clever you are, my dear young lady!' he exclaimed. 'Oh, you have done so much for everybody.

This question has been a thorn in my side ever since I came, and now you have neatly pulled it out with your dainty little hand. You don't know how much you have done for Germany. And if your Government is in its proper senses, it should realize and appreciate how much you have done for your own country.'

'Thank you, General, for saying so. I don't expect any good deed ever to be appreciated by my own Government. I shall be lucky if I am not maligned or even punished for what I have suggested. I have had too much experience for that. But I am glad you are happy. I am sure the people in the city know what I have done for them. That is all I care for.'

'What a country! What a country! But, in any case, with this issue on the way to being settled, I can attend to other matters.'

'For instance?'

'For instance, I have the most reliable information that the Russian Government is pressing, independently of all of us, for special rights and privileges in Manchuria. We are not going to allow any such thing. . . . And now, my dear young lady, *auf Wiedersehen* till dinner-time. It is only when I dine with you alone that I find any relaxation.'

Later, Yang Mah came in with some tea, and she said to Golden Orchid: 'Tai-tai, where do you think this tea comes from?'

Golden Orchid took the lid from her cup and gently inhaled the aroma. 'Why, Yang Mah, this is green tea from the Dragon Well in Hangchow. Times have indeed become normal again if we can have such tea in Peking.'

'This is a little gift from a rice merchant who has just returned from the south. He says he is thankful for what you have done for him, and he tells me that everyone in Shanghai, Hangchow, Soochow and Nanking talks about the wonderful things you are doing.'

After a short pause Yang Mah pressed her favourite idea. 'Don't you think, Tai-tai, that we should be leaving for the south? That's where you and I belong. Let's be back in Soochow before the New Year. What do you think? Do you remember how, when you were younger, you were fond of eating those *chuang yuan* cakes and the good luck they brought you? Don't you want to eat them again?'

Golden Orchid thought for a while and then lifted the lid of her teacup again. The water was crystal clear, delicately yellow but with a suggestion of green, and the leaves by now had unfolded themselves and were resting gently on the bottom. In the middle were two halves of a raw green olive, which enhanced the quiet fragrance of the tea.

'Where did you get that olive, Yang Mah?'

'Never mind where. But this is another reminder that we should return to the south.'

'You are right, Yang Mah. The south is where we belong. But I have no one to return to now. Master Wen-ching is no more. Mother is no more. Besides, I still have work to do here. We will leave when spring comes round again. Travel will then be more pleasant, and with the approach of the *ching-ming* festival it will be time to have Mother properly buried in the family graveyard.'

'Perhaps I shouldn't say it, but I feel we should leave as soon as possible, because I had a dream only the other night.'

'A bad one, I presume.'

'Well, not good. I dreamed that this entire palace was in flames, and you cried out for me, and I came and took you out into the open courtyard.'

Golden Orchid was silent.

9

Now that Golden Orchid was playing so important a part in the life of Peking, she clearly could not leave, even though Yang Mah continued to press for it. The suggestion that an arch should be erected to the memory of the murdered German ambassador was received with satisfaction from all quarters: it had reduced diplomatic tension, and peace negotiations began proceeding smoothly. The finest marble had been found, and the labourers worked on it day and night. No one would think of allowing Golden Orchid to leave Peking. Von Scheidermann would not hear of it. The Chinese officials, even though they did not relish the idea of a mere sing-song girl being given all the credit, must at least feign enthusiasm for her to remain: for the time being at least she was serving their purposes. But most of all, the people in the city would not allow their angel of

mercy to leave them under any circumstances. They implored her
to remain with them, even though few of them had ever succeeded in
catching a glimpse of her.

And so almost another year passed. By September the final peace
negotiations were brought to a successful end, and the arch was
nearly complete. It promised to be an imposing structure, in
unadorned marble with here and there a touch of colour, most of it
blue.

Exactly two months after the conclusion of the peace treaty which
he had signed, Lord Li Hung-chang, now in his seventy-seventh year,
was on his deathbed. He struggled hard, but in vain, to see the Empress Dowager back in Peking and to place at her disposal all the
rich experience which he had garnered in a lifetime of diplomacy and
contact with the 'ocean people'. It was not, however, until two
months later that the Empress Dowager and the Emperor could
return from their exile in Sianfu.

But on that November day Li Hung-chang had the premonition
that he was taking his last look at the world. It was a dark and
sombre day. The winds howled, and they carried as usual small
particles of yellow sand from Mongolia and Siberia. Inside the death
chamber were the great man's relatives and closest friends and
colleagues. He had also summoned a few of the high officials to
whom he was to reveal some of his closely guarded secrets, with
instructions that they be made known to the Empress Dowager upon
her return. But none of them dared to disturb him. They kept
themselves away from the inner chamber and gathered in knots in
the spacious drawing-room and in the study.

Li's eyes were closed. Whether he was in a coma or just resting,
not even those near the bed knew. Suddenly he opened his eyes and
looked round as if to note who was in the room. He saw one of his
adopted sons, who immediately went up to him at the indication that
his father wanted to speak to him.

'Is the sky clearing outside, son?' asked Li feebly and almost
inaudibly.

'Somewhat, but not much, Father.'

The old man gave a faint flicker of a smile. 'Troubles always
come from the north, even as I lie dying. The sands from the north
have covered us like a blanket.' Li paused, and then in a sudden

upsurge of energy he said to his adopted son: 'Beware of Russia. In all these years my wits were pitted against those of the Russians. Five years ago I went to St Petersburg ostensibly for the coronation of their Emperor. Do you remember? They sent their representative to the Suez Canal to welcome me. Actually they wanted to prevent me from coming in contact with other countries. Their mind was on Manchuria, which they coveted and wanted to annex. It is the same now. It will be the same fifty years from now. Don't ever forget —'

'Don't you think, Father, you should rest now?' said the son.

'I am all right. But I want you to know that they have put all kinds of pressure on me to agree to their terms. They even wanted to bribe me with half a million roubles. One of these days they are going to seize Dairen and Port Arthur. China will in no way be able to resist foreign aggression after these Boxer troubles, and the future is dark for us — as dark as it is today. All the foreign countries are robbers, but Russia is the worst of all. The English, the French, the Germans, will want their spheres of influence in the south. The Americans talk about the open door. It's a different version of the same thing. They all want their share. But the Russians — the Russians, now that they have the concession to build the railway across Manchuria, will annex that large and rich territory. In those days, when I was in Russia, our ambassador Shen Wen-ching was a great help to me. But he, poor man, died of a broken heart. There were so many who were jealous of his ability and wanted to damage him. They succeeded.'

'Father, I really think that you should rest now. Talk to me tomorrow when you are better.'

'All of a sudden, curiously enough, I feel I have a fresh supply of energy. There is one great lesson that I have learned in more than half a century of public life, and I want you to know it — now.'

'All right, I am listening. But promise me that, after this, you are going to rest.'

'The trouble is that our official life stifles and kills off any person with talent and ability and honesty. It thrives on jealousy, suspicion, and flattery. Flattery, yes' — the old man smiled a little again, and then he continued — 'No one is ever weary of flattery. It is the deadliest and most effective weapon. I should know, because I've had a goodly share of it myself. I am afraid a good man has little chance of survival. Sometimes it is a wonder that I myself have survived for so long. Shen Wen-ching was too good, too honest, too much of a scholar to know the wickedness of our official life. It is the evil man who triumphs and forges ahead. The good — well, they are often trampled upon. I have known case after case where this is true. Isn't it sad? I tried to help Shen, but it was too late. The country is where she is for very sound reasons. I say this because I want you to avoid official life.'

'But, Father, what else can I do? That is the only channel through which I hope to become rich and powerful. If others have done it, why not I?'

Having said this, the young man regretted it. Hoping that his father had not heard, he asked him whether there was anything else on his mind.

'My mind has been dwelling on Shen Wen-ching. I helped to have him acquitted by the special session of the Grand Council, but the damage had been done. . . . I understand that this Golden Orchid who was so helpful in the great national crisis we have just passed through was Wen-ching's concubine. How strange! How strange! . . .'

The old diplomat looked better as he spoke. There was a spark in his eyes. 'Do you know, Golden Orchid did more for the country and for the people than even I myself?'

'How can you say that, Father, when everyone knows that nobody can ever do any better than you have?'

'You say this because you are my son. But I know exactly what happened. If Golden Orchid had not won over the wife of the German ambassador, there would have been hardly any peace negotiations. And during the peace negotiations, if she had not exerted some subtle influence over the allied commander-in-chief, the terms would have been much worse, and we would have had to accept them. There was no alternative for us.'

'Well, then, Father, what would you want me to do?'

'Ah, I feel sorry. I feel very sorry,' said the dying man with a sigh.

'What is there to be sorry about?'

'Because what Golden Orchid has done and accomplished will destroy her.'

'Destroy her? I don't understand.'

'When the foreign troops are gone and times are normal again,

official life will go back to its ancient jealousies, suspicions and the
murder of good people. Everyone will claim the honour of having
brought about the peace, and those who did the real work will be
smothered and destroyed. Golden Orchid will be the first victim. I
see the future all too clearly. Mark my words.'

'You mean this applies even to those officials who are now under
this very roof?'

'Yes, even they. Those who struggle to flatter Golden Orchid now
will be the first to destroy her. So take care of her.'

So saying, the old man closed his eyes. He looked tired. His son
gently pulled up his blanket a little and left him. He went into the
drawing-room, and the groups of officials rushed up to him, each
vying to show deeper concern than the other. 'How's the Prime
Minister? How is he? Is he better? And what has he to say?'

No one was really interested in his health. They all knew the inevitable hour was rapidly approaching. What each one thought, in
his own way, was how to step into the Prime Minister's place when
at last it was empty.

'He sleeps, gentlemen,' replied the adopted son, 'and wants me to
convey to all of you his deep appreciation of your concern and
solicitude.'

Late in the evening there was a change for the worse in Li Hung-
chang's condition. Before midnight China's great official and
diplomat had breathed his last. The storm outside had subsided,
and there was quietness. It was as if the city mourned the passing of
a man who had played so significant a role. And indeed he had.
For had he not, exactly two months before, placed his seal on a
document which started the twentieth century for his country on a
note of tragic defeat and humiliation? But it could have been worse.

10

THE Empress Dowager and the Emperor came back to Peking from
the wilderness in the early days of 1902. The Dowager had been
transformed into a different person. The enforced simplicity of her
life at Sianfu had allayed the turbulence of her soul. Formerly proud,
haughty and bitter towards the 'foreign devils' for their treatment of

her and her country, she was now, after the futile Boxer episode had blown over, full of sweetness and light.

Her face was bathed in smiles, and she was ready to treat the same devils with meekness and humility. She remained abysmally ignorant — unfortunately ignorance is not something that can be removed by a change of milieu — and she could still be cruel and wicked, reserving her cruelty and wickedness for those who were helpless, as, for instance, the Emperor, who continued to be virtually a prisoner. Towards the world of the erstwhile barbarians, however, she was now prepared to be conciliatory. And there was good reason for it. For the very first thing she did upon arrival at Peking was to dig in an obscure corner of her palace, and she found to her very great joy and satisfaction that all the gold and jewels which she had buried on the eve of her escape from Peking were intact.

From that day of discovery she decided to be generous to all foreigners. As if to express her gratitude, she gave a huge reception, scarcely a week after her return to Peking, in the very same Palace of Peaceful Longevity where she had recovered her hoarded gold, and received in person the wives of all the diplomatic representatives.

A British General who was about to retire and who happened to be a guest was so overwhelmed with the Old Buddha's sudden munificence that he wondered whether what was happening to him was true. The one great passion of his life was the acquisition of Chinese porcelain, which he loved as dearly as his wife, now dead. During the reception he expressed the casual wish that, before he left Peking to spend his retirement in his own dear Devonshire, he might take with him two specimens of the Chinese potter's supreme art. The wish found its way to the Empress Dowager's ears. Whereupon she issued orders that the General should visit the storehouse of the imperial museum and make his choice on the spot.

On the appointed day the General appeared at the treasure-house — alone. He was taken by a guide from one room to another, each more beautiful than the last. There were large and small vases, amphorae, plum jars, brush jars, gorgeous plates and platters in blue and white, blanc-de-chine statues of Buddhas and bodhisattvas, and other delicate wares of the subtlest hues, belonging to the Tang, Sung, Ming and early Ching periods. The General stood in the midst of this fabulous collection utterly speechless. He tried to choose the two pieces he had asked for. Damn it, why didn't I ask for

P

more? Why did I ask for only two? It's impossible to choose! Impossible! he said to himself, holding his head in complete bewilderment. He first took one small jar of apple green, then another as 'blue as the heaven after rainfall'. But there were thousands of others, equally beautiful, and he stretched out a greedy hand for more.

'But my instructions are,' reminded the guide, 'that you select only two.'

'Oh, is that it? Only two?'

Whereupon the General piled one piece on top of another and said, 'This is one complete piece, and I am entitled to another.' Tenderly he touched and caressed every piece, and began putting them into his pockets until they bulged in every direction.

The guide looked at him with amused anxiety and muttered to himself, This is the way with all foreigners. You give them one and they want two. You yield one inch and they want a foot. Finally he burst out: 'I was told that you love porcelain as dearly as you love your wife. But according to your custom, as I understand it, one husband can have only one wife. How is it that you want so many of these porcelains?'

The General paid no attention and thought that this was no time for such cruel humour. He went on taking all his hands and pockets could carry and thanked the guide profusely for the generosity he had shown him. 'You see, sir,' he said before saying goodbye, 'since I came to reside in your country, I have contracted your habit of taking concubines. A single piece of porcelain does not satisfy me any more.'

When the report was given to the Empress Dowager that the General had taken all he could carry instead of the two pieces he had been promised, she was most happy and said that so small a matter must not affect friendly international relations!

More parties and receptions followed in which the Old Buddha sat in amused silence on the throne dais while her nephew, whom she herself had chosen as the Emperor, occupied an insignificant seat at her feet. The palace swarmed with the ladies of the diplomatic corps while the Chinese dignitaries, who were once again in their element, mingled with the diplomats and vied with one another in showing their knowledge of foreign manners. Food was no longer eaten with chopsticks but with knives and forks, which until now had been considered fit only for the barbarians. But the Chinese officials began to use them with alacrity, and in their eagerness to show off, many mouths were cut, though none was willing to admit that anything had gone wrong.

Two years passed, and, as Li Hung-chang had predicted on his deathbed, official Peking had gone back to its normal life of intrigue, bickering and conspiracy. The chief eunuch, as ugly as any living creature on two legs and unbelievably wicked, cruel and grasping, had now become the most powerful person. Without his help nothing could be done, and that meant he was always stretching out his itching palm for gold and more gold. It was a wonder that, with the country reduced to dire poverty, its financial life having been placed under the rigid control of the foreigners to ensure that the heavy indemnity of nearly five hundred million dollars was paid, there was still so much wealth to go round. But sooner or later it found its way into the pockets of the chief eunuch and his henchmen, and the officials who knew how to lay their hands on it.

Golden Orchid was no longer in the public eye. Until the signing of the peace treaty in the autumn of 1901 she was the idol of Peking. Not that now, three years later, she had been forgotten. The memory of her and of what she had done was treasured and hidden in the inmost recesses of the people's heart. They could never forget how much she had helped them. They wondered what had become of her. Had she gone away and left Peking altogether now that the foreign troops had been withdrawn and her work completed? The people were curious to know, but all they could do was cherish a dear and fond memory.

When Von Scheidermann took leave of Peking and of Golden Orchid, he made a last futile attempt to persuade her to accept jewels, furs, antiques and above all gold and silver. But she firmly declined. Yang Mah was in complete agreement with the departing General. She seemed to have a clear view of her mistress's future. She had a deeply practical mind, and wanted her mistress to take what was offered to her and then live in reasonable ease and comfort in retirement in Soochow.

But Golden Orchid disliked the idea of taking advantage of a favoured position. She disliked even more the idea of retirement and of living merely on the memory of the past. She shunned the thought of being in close proximity to Madam Wen-ching, much as she admired her, and so she continued to live in Peking — in obscurity. Ping-mo too, as fervent as ever in his revolutionary ideals, preferred to remain in Peking, to be at hand if fresh developments should take place. In the meantime, Hai-ming had found her way back to Golden Orchid. She was anxious to take up again the only profession which could provide her with a living by establishing a house of entertainment with the help of Golden Orchid.

So for the second time Golden Orchid became the mistress of a sing-song house. For over two years all went well, and she again became affluent. But she was not to be left in peace. Officials, high and low, were again struggling for recognition and political advantages, and they found to their dismay that Golden Orchid was a serious obstacle to their advancement, for the simple reason that, though not openly acknowledged, she still had the credit of being the benefactress of her people and the saviour of her country. The officials wanted this credit for themselves, and so there began an extensive campaign to suppress all the good she had ever done and undermine her reputation. In the time of Wen-ching it had been Hu-mou alone who decided to destroy him in order that his ambitions might be realized. Now all the high officials combined to seek her destruction, not three years from the time Li Hung-chang had made his prediction.

'A sing-song girl saved the country? What nonsense! Whoever heard of such a thing?' . . . 'A shameless prostitute who lived with a foreign commander-in-chief — in the very palace of Her Majesty! What sacrilege!' . . . 'Oh, what harm she has brought to her people!' . . . 'When a country is on the verge of collapse, monsters appear. Such a monster is this shameless Golden Orchid!' These and other sentiments were freely and openly circulated by officials as they drank tea and partook of wine during the dinners which again became a very noisy part of the social life of Peking.

The result of all this was inevitable.

It happened in the spring of 1904, thirty months after the treaty which Golden Orchid had made possible, even as a new war was being fought between Russia and Japan on Chinese soil for the possession of Chinese territory and the acquisition of China's own rights and privileges. But the Chinese officials as usual were supremely indifferent. Their minds were still on how they could rid themselves of the woman who had won such nation-wide acclaim. At long last they found an excuse — 'to incriminate a person there is always no lack of excuses,' says a Chinese proverb — and without any hesitation they plunged her into the deepest misery imaginable.

In the western part of Peking, in a small vermin-infested dungeon and its attached court, a drama of great excitement and sorrow was being enacted. Golden Orchid had been confined there for some time. On a fine spring morning when the air was full of the fragrance of flowers and life was burgeoning with a new vitality and promise, Golden Orchid was taken out of the dungeon, with manacles on hands and feet, to face trial for murder. It was a bare one hundred feet from the dungeon to the courtroom, but to be out in the open, even for one brief moment, was enough to give her a peculiar sense of joy. She was led across a small patio.

At first she had difficulty in adapting herself to the glare of the sun when for a long time she had not seen any light. But she thought of the cicada, the sign of longevity with which she had become familiar on most of the lovely old Chinese bronzes and porcelains that were her toys at the Phoenix Palace. The insect burrows its way into the soil with the approach of cold weather, is transformed into a grub, and lies dormant until summer comes again, when it emerges in its full regalia. 'That is what I have become, I hope — a cicada,' Golden Orchid said to herself as she walked slowly into the courtroom.

The courtroom was dirty and shabby. Golden Orchid was literally thrown into the middle of its earthen floor like any common criminal. In the middle of the room was a raised platform on which was a table covered with a cloth. Golden Orchid lay on the floor, and from the corner of her eye she could see four vicious-looking men, two on each side of her, carrying murderous-looking knives on staffs which were at least six feet high. It was fully half an hour before a small, unimpressive nincompoop stepped into the room. His face was ashen grey, his thin moustache drooped round the corners of his mouth, and it was clear that he had been an opium addict for many years. But at this moment he was for Golden Orchid the most important man in the world. For he was the judge, and his words might well determine whether she was to be a cicada or a mere common insect to be crushed and seen no more.

When the opium addict took his seat, he struck the table once with a long block of wood, which was the symbol of his authority. The trial began. There was no counsel for the defence. The matter was entirely between the miserable man seated on the platform and the woman slumped on the floor.

The judge began reading a long indictment. When he had finished, he looked at the prisoner without saying a word. There was an awful silence. There were only six people in the room, perhaps a few others outside eavesdropping. The public was rigidly excluded, as was the custom. There was not the least doubt in the minds of all six as to what the judgement was going to be.

The little man with the ashen face then spoke: 'You have heard the indictment. You have been charged with the murder of an innocent woman. Your penalty is death by decapitation. Have you anything to say to defend yourself?'

The words had been spoken, and Golden Orchid had heard them. Curiously, she was not frightened, for she had known all along that such would be the verdict. From the crouching position she had been in since the time she was thrown into the room, she now raised the upper part of her body. Gently she spoke, but the words were clearly audible. 'Yes, Great One,' said Golden Orchid, 'I have heard your judgement. But I am innocent. I did not murder the woman. She committed suicide. She killed herself with her own hands.'

The judge was taken aback. It was not his habit to listen to what his prisoner had to say. But today he was patient, unusually patient. He looked at Golden Orchid with kind and even friendly eyes. 'So you think you are innocent. I'd like to know what evidence you have. You can present that to me later.'

Even in her confused state of mind, Golden Orchid knew what this meant. The little man knew who his prisoner was and believed that she must be fabulously wealthy after her long residence at the palace, where she wielded so much power and had access to every-thing. Golden Orchid correctly suspected that what he wanted was a large portion of that imaginary wealth. Keeping a sing-song house had given her a comfortable living, but the long period of incarcera-tion had taken every penny from her. The jailer had to be satisfied at all times, and he had an enormous appetite. Every time Hai-ming or Yang Mah brought her some food, it meant paying the jailer an adequate sum of money or else she would have had to feed on mere offal.

The winter had been long and rigorous. Fortunately the dungeon was not damp, thanks to the dry weather in Peking. But all the same it was cold, and with no heating of any kind it meant that the cold cut to the very marrow of her bones. Yang Mah always came with warm clothing, but the itching palm of the jailer had to be scratched first before that clothing could reach Golden Orchid. Ping-mo and Hai-ming, without letting her know, had already resorted to borrowing. But she knew where she stood, and the little man's broad hints were more than her present means could ever satisfy.

Golden Orchid thought over the little man's proposition for some time and could not suppress a bitter smile. How incredible! she said to herself. They all want the riches from the palace which they think I must possess.

Then, deciding that she could not meet the proposition, she determined to make a vigorous defence, no matter what the consequences might be.

'Great One,' Golden Orchid exclaimed in a firm voice, 'I have said it and I say it again. I am innocent. I had nothing whatever to do with the death of that girl Phoenix Bell. She committed suicide.'

The judge had not expected such a reply. He had to go on. 'The evidence shows,' he said, 'that two days after the Moon Festival last autumn, Phoenix Bell decided to leave your house of entertainment. She was not being well treated by you. Is it not true that you gave no remuneration for her services while all the other girls got paid? How do you explain that?'

'There was a difference in the remuneration. That is true. But as you know perfectly well, Great One, the circumstances under which the girls came to my house differed widely. I paid one thousand dollars to the woman who previously owned Phoenix Bell, and according to our agreement, that sum had to be paid back before she was entitled to any remuneration.'

'On the evening in question did you not, after a violent quarrel, shut her in a room all by herself?'

'That is positively not true. There was no quarrel, and everyone in the house can testify to that.'

'Did you not also afterwards enter the room with a bowl of raw opium, which you compelled her to swallow? Was that not murder pure and simple?'

'That again is absolutely untrue. Phoenix Bell did die of opium, but she swallowed it herself — of her own will.'

'What evidence have you to show that she swallowed the opium herself and that it was not you who forced her to take it? Where did she get the opium in the first place?'

'I can answer these questions easily, Great One. Phoenix Bell was an opium smoker of long standing. Everyone knew that. And then, as you know perfectly well, we always keep opium in the house. It is part of our trade. We keep opium as we keep rice and other kinds of food. We keep it for our guests, and everyone has free access to it whenever there is need for it.'

The judge could not very well contradict these statements, as he was an opium smoker himself and knew how essential opium was to such people. Besides, he had visited such houses of entertainment and the facility with which he had access to opium substantiated the prisoner's remarks.

But he insisted on asking: 'What proof is there that Phoenix Bell was not forced by you to take the raw opium in sufficient quantities to kill her?'

It was apparent to Golden Orchid that the judge was determined to find her guilty and that the only way to overcome this would be to meet him in private and hand him a lot of gold. Golden Orchid again thought hard, but saw no way in which she could meet the wishes of the little man. She could only give her version of the entire story and see what would happen.

'I think, Great One, that you have been hearing a lot of rumours. And I think also that I am entitled to tell you exactly what happened. Whether you believe me or not, I leave entirely to you, Great One.'

The judge was placed in a peculiar position, and for reasons best known to himself he agreed to hear what Golden Orchid had to say. 'Well, then, go on. I am prepared to hear your story.'

'To begin at the beginning, Great One, when I established the sing-song house over two years ago, I was given to understand that I could employ one very attractive girl for a consideration of a thousand dollars. She was described to me as a pure, clean girl from the country. So I agreed to have a look at her. That was how Phoenix Bell was first brought to me. I thought she was a pleasant-looking girl and agreed on the payment of the amount in addition to two hundred dollars as remuneration for the man who acted as go-between. The papers were then signed.'

At this point Golden Orchid took from her pocket a dirty and badly crumpled document, which she handed over to the judge. She then continued the story: 'Subsequently I found out that Phoenix Bell was not a peasant girl from a poor family: she had come from a cheap house of entertainment where she had become very friendly with a man who had agreed to marry her. But the man could afford to pay only seven hundred dollars to the owner of the house, and so nothing came of it. The man was very unhappy and was heard to say that one of these days he was going to abduct the girl and save himself the seven hundred dollars. When the owner learned of this, she became terribly worried. She knew there was nothing she could do if the man should carry out his threat. It was then that she heard about my wanting some girls for my house and so brought Phoenix Bell to see me. What she told me about the girl was a lie from beginning to end, but she succeeded in getting from me the amount she wanted, which was a thousand dollars.'

'I can see,' interrupted the judge, 'that you are rather free with your money. You must be a rather wealthy woman.'

The crude hint was not lost on Golden Orchid. The judge went on: 'Am I to believe that you would throw away all this money without making a careful investigation of the girl in the first place?'

'Great One, we all make mistakes. I admit I was somewhat careless. Anyhow, it did not take me long to find out the real facts, but it was too late. The deal had been concluded and there was nothing I could do. That, however, was not so important. The really important thing was my finding out that she had been addicted to opium smoking for a long time, and you know what opium smokers are. They are lazy, sloppy, and have no ambition to do well.'

As an opium smoker himself, the judge regarded this as a slap in the face. He coughed a few times and showed intense displeasure.

But Golden Orchid went on with her story: 'Well, anyway, I found out that Phoenix Bell was not performing her duties as an entertainer but was consuming a good deal of my opium, which was, as I have said, reserved for my guests. I was not happy about it, and I asked my partner, Mistress Hai-ming, to do what she could to persuade Phoenix Bell to improve herself. That brought no result. Her heart was with the man she wanted to marry. Then I had to take matters into my own hands. I admit that the relations between Phoenix Bell and myself were not of the best.'

'I am glad that you now admit that.'

'My guests began to find Phoenix Bell positively objectionable. She could sing but would not. That of course made my guests very unhappy. Also she would often, in the midst of her duties, creep away and lie down for a few puffs of opium before going back to her guests. In time Phoenix Bell became more of a liability than an asset to me, and our relations grew steadily worse. Of course Phoenix Bell was not happy herself, for she continued, as I have said, to think how she could be married to the man she loved. I was prepared to release her after I had regained the amount I had paid for her. That was part of the agreement. It's all written in the document.'

The judge glanced through the document, which clearly gave that stipulation, but said nothing.

'As time went on, the conflict in Phoenix Bell's mind became more violent,' continued Golden Orchid. 'On the one hand, there was this desire to be married, for which she had to wait. On the other, she was unhappy to remain where she was. It was this situation which ultimately led her to end her life. All she needed to do was to swallow a large quantity of raw opium.'

'I am glad that you have made the confession. When you say that you were responsible for her unhappiness which ultimately led her to death, isn't that a confession that you were the cause of her death?'

This was an unexpected twist, and for a moment Golden Orchid thought she had been caught by her own words. She was stupefied.

'But I insist on saying,' she continued, 'that I had no part whatever in the final step which Phoenix Bell decided upon. If she chose to kill herself, it was her own resolution, her own responsibility, and no one could be held accountable but Phoenix Bell herself. One night there was a large number of guests in the house. There was music, many of the girls were singing, and the guests were in a happy frame of mind. There was much drinking of my best Shaoshing wine, but no one could find Phoenix Bell. Mistress Hai-ming asked the housemaid to look for her. She went up to her room and found her in bed with her clothes on. Her face was flushed and her eyes seemed to emit fire. The maid shook her, called her, but there was no response. It was then that many of us went in, found a bowl of raw opium empty by her side, and came to the obvious conclusion that she had committed suicide. We pumped a large amount of soapy water into her — which is the usual way of reviving people who have swallowed opium. But the effects of the opium had gone too far, and Phoenix Bell never recovered consciousness. So that is the entire story, Great One, and I want to swear that every word I have said is the truth and nothing but the truth.'

'If what you have told me is the truth,' replied the judge, 'why did the family of the deceased Phoenix Bell bring the case before the court and say that there had been foul play?'

'I am glad you have brought up this matter. If you look into it carefully, you will learn that the so-called family consists of no more than that woman who is the owner of that cheap house of entertainment which kept Phoenix Bell before she was sold to me. The name of that woman is recorded in the document in your hands, Great One. She is the same woman who brought the case before the court. Her motive is blackmail and extortion. She came to me shortly after the death of Phoenix Bell and said that she would drop the matter for a consideration. I gave her a piece of my mind and told her that I would not be led into any trap by admitting that the girl was murdered when it was a clear case of suicide. The approach reminded me so poignantly of what happened to my husband not many years ago. The woman didn't think that I would have kept the document to establish her identity, and that was why she was bold enough to try to injure me.'

Golden Orchid was correct in saying that the owner of the cheap house of entertainment wanted to blackmail her, and that, having failed, she wanted to harm her. But she did not know that behind her accuser was the hand of some official.

As Golden Orchid finished presenting her case, a man came in with a message for the judge. He read it, then read it again; and as he did so, his pallid face was seen to go through many expressions. Placing the message under the long wooden block with which he had begun the session, he assumed a much firmer tone.

'Golden Orchid,' said the little man, 'there is nothing in all you have said to show that you have not committed the murder of an innocent person. I repeat: your penalty is death by decapitation.'

Golden Orchid collapsed and curled herself up on the dirty floor waiting to be dragged away — perhaps back to the dingy cell where she had been confined and then later to the execution ground. Her distraught mind became feverishly active. She imagined herself on that execution ground outside the Gate of Heavenly Peace, with her hands tied behind her. She saw herself on her knees, and on her back was a long wooden plaque on which her 'crime' was inscribed for everyone to see. She saw a huge crowd of spectators — men, women and even children for whom she had done so much good, but who now no longer recognized her. They howled, they yelled, they began throwing stones at her. She imagined vividly those last moments of her life on earth, and she decided that before the axe of the executioner fell on her neck, she would think only of those supremely happy moments — the days she spent in Berlin with Yung-kai and the days she spent here in Peking itself with him.

And then she thought she heard the noise of a crowd in the distance. It grew louder and louder. Before very long it seemed to be immediately outside the miserable courtroom in which she still lay crouching. Before she knew what it was all about, the four men with the long knives hurriedly covered her with a hood, took her out, and dumped her on a waiting mule-cart, which carried her away to she knew not where. In the meantime, the little man who had pronounced her sentence had also disappeared — through the back door.

No, the people had not forgotten Golden Orchid. In all those years they had been wondering what had become of her. Golden Orchid did not want them to know that she had gone back to the entertainment profession after those exciting days of foreign occupation when she did so much for them. That was understandable. Not that she was ashamed. But why let the people know it when it served no purpose?

But Golden Orchid had come in close contact with the people on one occasion. It was six months after her sing-song house had opened. Money was rolling in; there was wide patronage by the officials, as she had expected. Now and then she could have a few moments to herself, and she thought it would be fun to learn to ride a horse. How nobly did Yung-kai sit on the white charger as he left

Berlin! That was the last time she saw him. And then, only a few months back, she had seen Von Scheidermann — also a picture of great impressiveness — on his white horse as he went about inspecting the allied troops. He had presented her with a number of good horses when he left. One, of a steel-grey colour, was an especially handsome animal. Golden Orchid had a groom employed to take care of it, and it gave her pleasure to ride on its back below the magnificent walls of Peking.

But one day she was foolish enough to venture into the city. She came on a funeral procession. There was a cacophony of noises to which the horse was not accustomed, and it became irritated. All of a sudden a large gong clanged. The horse was badly frightened, reared and began dashing through the narrow streets as if it were possessed by the devil. Golden Orchid was thrown on the stone pavement but luckily suffered only a mild concussion, with minor cuts and bruises over her body. She was taken to a near-by house to await the arrival of the doctor. But when it was discovered that she was the same goddess of mercy who had done so much for the people, expressions of sorrow were deep and sincere. Crowds of people went to the temples to pray for her early recovery, and kept vigil over her. And when she regained consciousness, it was a source of enormous satisfaction to her that she was still so warmly and affectionately remembered.

That episode had a secure and fond place in her memory. But it was beyond her wildest dream to think that, on this day when her life hung in the balance, when she was about to die from the executioner's axe because a pallid and sickly-looking opium addict had so decided, she was to be saved by the same simple, common people.

What had happened was the work of Ping-mo. His contacts with the secret societies which had been so active before the Boxer uprising were still intimate. For weeks and months he pleaded for some action which would take Golden Orchid away from the horrors of the dungeon. When he heard that the day of the trial was drawing near, which meant certain death for Golden Orchid, Ping-mo became frantic. But at long last he succeeded in persuading some of his fellow members to bring the matter to the attention of the people, and their response was immediate, spontaneous and overwhelming.

There was not one man or woman who was unwilling to carry

some weapon to storm the dungeon in which Golden Orchid was confined. Some carried bamboo poles, others long knives, and still others the horrid-looking daggers with which they slit the throats of their hogs. In a matter of an hour Ping-mo and Hai-ming were leading a mob of some five hundred people who were bent on demolishing the prison and releasing their erstwhile benefactress. They arrived about the time when the verdict was being given by the judge. They tore down the prison and set free all the prisoners. But there was no trace of Golden Orchid.

Ping-mo became desperate and tried to obtain some information from the prisoners, but they had practically all disappeared. Only one was left behind, a woman. Ping-mo asked her whether she knew Golden Orchid.

'Yes, I do,' was the answer.

'Well, where is she?'

'I don't know. They took her away about three hours ago. She and I were confined in the same room.'

'What is your name?'

'They call me Little Tigress.'

'Little Tigress? You look like one. Why are you in prison?'

'For killing my uncle.'

'Killing your uncle? What a wicked girl you are!'

'Wicked? Then must your Golden Orchid be wicked also.'

'How dare you say that?'

'I know what she did and what she did not do.'

'Then you should not have said what you said.'

'Both she and I have been falsely accused. You want to know what happened to me?'

'I am not interested. I want to find Golden Orchid. Where is she?'

'I'll help you to find her. I know you are a good man who has come to save us, and I want you to know that you are not helping a criminal.'

'Well, be quick about it and say what you wish to say.'

'I am one of three sisters. My father was an official. He died at the hands of the Boxers, and after that the three of us went to live with his younger brother. He began to have designs on us. So I killed him. Don't you think I should have? Now! . . .'

'So you did kill your uncle. But Golden Orchid didn't kill anybody.'

'I don't deny that I killed my uncle. But can't you see that I killed him in self-defence? My uncle deserved to die.'

'All right, let's not argue about it. Perhaps you are right. But help me to find Golden Orchid. Where is she?'

'As I said, they took her away some three hours ago. Perhaps they took her to the courtroom. It's over there — See?'

Ping-mo yelled to the crowd to follow him to the courtroom, but when they got there, all they found was a dirty, deserted little room. There was a table in the middle with the trimmings of authority. Ping-mo went up to the table and saw a document lying underneath the oblong wooden block. He read it, and to his horror and dismay he found this message: 'There is to be no leniency with this girl Golden Orchid. It is the wish of many high officials that she be charged with murder. She deserves to receive the extreme penalty. Fan-lin.'

Fan-lin was no less than the President of the Board of Military Affairs who had been in collusion with Hu-mou in trying to incriminate Wen-ching. He had found out all he could about Golden Orchid since the end of the Boxer uprising and was working hand in glove with Lord Li Hung-chang's adopted son in extorting money from her. They simply could not believe that she did not possess a huge fortune stored away somewhere. Having had no success, they began doing everything they could to hurt her.

I I

FROM disappointment Ping-mo sank into a delirious frenzy. If only he had gone straight to the courtroom instead of to the dungeon, he thought, he could have rescued Golden Orchid. Those few minutes delay were costly. Why did I talk to that Little Tigress? he cursed himself. But he consoled himself with the thought that, in any case, he was now on the right track; and with the power which he enjoyed over the crowd, whose numbers continued to grow, he could rescue Golden Orchid wherever she might have been taken.

He gave orders that the table, before which only a bare half hour ago the miserable-looking judge had sat, be taken into the patio. He had it placed on a platform, and then, gathering his followers in front of him, he spoke to them in a simple and straightforward language which they understood.

'Friends, this noble and selfless woman whom you all know and love is in danger of her life.'

'Let's go and find her,' responded the crowd. 'Let's not lose any time. Let's save her!'

'Yes, we must save her,' continued Ping-mo. 'But the people who are torturing her are full of tricks. It is possible that she is so well hidden that we shall have to use very strong means. I want to know whether we are prepared to do out utmost.'

Without one single dissenting voice the crowd shouted: 'You only have to tell us. We will do anything you want to us do. Golden Orchid is our Goddess of Mercy, and we must save her.'

'Thank you! Now let me tell you something which you perhaps don't know.'

Ping-mo went on to speak of the officials' plot against Golden Orchid, and read them the document he had found on the judge's table. Enraged, they set off on the search for her, cursing their corrupt government and brandishing their knives and spears.

But Golden Orchid was nowhere to be found. When she was put on the waiting mule-cart with a hood over her head, she was taken far away to the north-western part of the city and placed in solitary confinement. For the first few days she was not treated much better than she had been in prison. But the news of the angry mob quickly came to the ears of the officials. Some of them felt it was an outrage that such a thing could happen and urged prompt action against the people, but they soon came to their senses when reports arrived that some officials had been molested and their houses burned.

Then they agreed that times had indeed changed and that the situation might become worse if any repressive measures were taken. They held a meeting to decide what they should do. The President of the Board of Military Affairs, Fan-lin, still took the view that Golden Orchid should be disposed of as quietly and expeditiously as possible. While this view would have received overwhelming support if the popular demonstrations had not taken place, now, however, everyone was afraid of the people. For it was characteristic of such officials that they were not only greedy and avaricious and much given to petty jealousies and all manner of underhand means of getting what they wanted, but also faint-hearted.

And the demonstrations under the leadership of Ping-mo struck terror into their hearts, so much so that they now wanted no part in any harsh treatment of Golden Orchid. When someone made the proposal, therefore, to banish Golden Orchid to Soochow, it was so overwhelmingly supported that two days later Golden Orchid was on her way back to the south. It was good riddance, everybody thought, and they all seemed happy about it. The final instructions to the local magistrate of Soochow were that Golden Orchid should be allowed to live a normal life in Soochow but that she was not to leave the city without permission.

It was the last thing in the world that Golden Orchid had expected. When the information was conveyed to her, she could not believe it. She was asked whether she would agree to the conditions of her return. She smiled faintly and then said: 'Can you add two more conditions? One is that I may take my mother's coffin, which is still here in Peking, with me to Soochow. The other is that I want my Yang Mah to accompany me. She knows where the coffin is. So let her attend to the matter.'

Golden Orchid's requests were complied with. And so she travelled back to Soochow with her mother's coffin, attended by the ever-faithful Yang Mah, by the same route over which she had accompanied Wen-ching some five years before. Ping-mo heard nothing of this. He was still trying to find her when she left.

There was one consolation. It was spring, and the slow journey through the Grand Canal was pleasant and cheerful, with balmy weather following her wherever she went. The life of a cicada. True, indeed! 'The spring winds blow, and life is born anew,' so says the poet. She recalled that her journey with Wen-ching had been cold and unpleasant.

'Tell me, Yang Mah,' Golden Orchid asked, 'why is it that my life has been so full of bitterness? Look at those stars for me, Yang Mah. Do you understand them? And what do they say about my life?'

Yang Mah looked up. The boat was anchored, and the surrounding darkness was indescribably peaceful and quiet. There above her was the Milky Way, and on all sides were millions and millions of stars.

'Yes,' replied Yang Mah, 'our lives are indeed determined by the stars. But sometimes we can control our destiny. We could have left Peking long, long ago. I always said so.'

'You are right, Yang Mah.'

'But cheer up, Tai-tai. As the years go round, so do our lives. Already it is spring, and high in the heavens do you see the weaving maid? Before long the cowherd will cross the Silvery Stream and meet her. It is a long time they have to wait, but the important thing is that they continue to meet every year.'

'But my heart is loaded with ashes, Yang Mah. I have had my share of life, and what I see ahead is dark indeed.'

'I should say not,' Yang Mah said with a tone of authority. 'There are men who are in love with you. I know who they are, and there will be others who will fall in love with you when you go back to Soochow.'

'How can you talk about such things, Yang Mah? What will people say of me?'

'It is not what people say that counts, but what you yourself feel.'

Without knowing it, Yang Mah had voiced a truth deeper and wiser than she would ever discover. She had a tremendous zest for life, and she did not feel that social conventions or the accepted ethical codes should dampen it. 'The stars tell me that you will have another proposal of marriage from a high and distinguished person. Your life is only just beginning.'

Golden Orchid gave no reply. She was too deeply absorbed in remembering what had passed.

Not until Golden Orchid arrived at Soochow did Ping-mo find out what had happened. He soon hurried back, taking the quicker route by steamer from Tientsin to Shanghai, forgetting even that these steamers were operated by the hated foreigner, and then by houseboat to Soochow. He was happy to see his mother, who looked as calm and as unruffled as ever. She did not, in fact, look a day older. It was as if time had stood completely still for her. She was engaged in the same kind of work that she had been doing when he left her more than three years before.

'My son,' said Madam Wen-ching, putting down her painting brush, 'you have been away for so long. When are you going to resume your studies and sit for the examinations as you promised your father?'

'Mother, I am going to Father's tomb tomorrow morning to pray for his soul. I shall also report to him what has happened so that he will continue to rest in peace. But I feel I have more important work to do than to sit for examinations. Times have changed, and I know what I should be doing.'

'That sounds interesting.'

'What I want to tell you, in the first place, is that I have been spending a lot of time with Golden Orchid.'

'Is that a proper thing to do?'

'You don't know what a wonderful woman she is. Oh, the things she has done! I must tell you all about them.'

'But I don't care what you tell me. She was your father's concubine. And for you to tell me that you have been seeing her a great deal, away from home — why, times have indeed changed. Where is she now?'

'She came back to Soochow only half a month ago. What I want to tell you is that not only have I been seeing her a great deal, but also she and I have been doing a number of great things together.'

'Now whatever may that mean?'

'Oh, Mother, you don't understand. Can't you see that our country has gone through a great crisis? And, believe it or not, Golden Orchid has done more than any other person to save the country. The things she did for the people are unbelievable.'

'Well, yes, but how can I believe what you say? What can a mere girl of her age and accomplishments do? I suppose she went back to the life that your father took her from — in spite of my objections? What can a sing-song girl do during a national crisis?'

But Ping-mo could only say: 'She is the most wonderful girl I have ever known. She is already a historic person. She may be only a concubine, but what a fabulous concubine! Oh, I wish I could —'

'Stop, Son, I know you are beginning to say things that will put a blemish on this house.'

'Mother, if you care to know, the money you promised to give Golden Orchid was never received by her. Uncle was supposed to have handed over the money. He still has it or, rather, I presume, he has spent it.'

'What blasphemous words! I can't believe them.'

'Like many other things which you don't know, this is the absolute truth. I wish you would find out for yourself.'

'Indeed I will.'

'And, what's more, Golden Orchid has not said a word about it. She has not bothered even to tell you about it. Where else can you find so large-hearted a person?'

Three days later, Madam Wen-ching asked to be taken to see Golden Orchid, who was living in the same small house that she used to occupy with her mother and grandmother. She was not lonely, as Yang Mah was always with her, and the pock-faced sister was also a frequent visitor.

'I owe you a deep apology, Golden Orchid,' said Madam Wen-ching the moment she saw her husband's former concubine.

'Oh, Madam, it is such joy seeing you again after all these years. Why speak about apologies? You owe me nothing.'

'No, no, I have found out that the money which I had promised you was never given to you. I am looking into the matter, but first I must ask for your forgiveness.'

'Please don't ever mention the matter again. It is such a small thing. And how have you been these many years, Madam? I am so happy to see you in such excellent health.'

'Golden Orchid, Ping-mo has been telling me all that has happened to you since you left here. I feel that at least you should come and live with me. It will be more comfortable than here. After all, you are alone.'

'That is very kind of you, Madam. I will think it over. Yes, I am alone, but I think I have all that I need in this small house. Thank you so much for your kind offer.'

'I want you to feel that you are always welcome whenever you wish to move into my house.'

'Thank you again. Life is full of mystery. Here you are, Madam, so full of poise and quiet dignity. How wonderful that you have been able to develop such a sense of detachment from the whirlwind into which I have drifted!'

Madam Wen-ching was surprised; Golden Orchid was speaking to her as one woman to another, and not as a concubine should to the 'big wife'. Also, Golden Orchid seemed to know her own mind: she spoke with assurance and self-confidence.

Golden Orchid had some inkling of what Madam Wen-ching was thinking. 'Excuse me, Madam, that I do not speak as the former concubine of your husband should speak. But that is just the point.

You, Madam, and my humble self had the same man, and yet our lives are so widely different. Here you are a lady over fifty, and yet you look so young and beautiful. I don't know how you manage it. It is the beauty of inner calm and serenity.'

Much to her own surprise, Madam Wen-ching enjoyed being spoken to in this manner. 'There is no secret, Sister,' — it was the first time Golden Orchid had been addressed by her with such affection — 'I know nothing about the larger world around me. I have no interest in politics. I yearn and struggle for nothing. All these years I have confined myself in my study, looking at the eternal beauty of the surrounding hills and trying to capture their essential spirit in my paintings and poems.'

'Is it possible that I might learn these secrets from you?'

'When I want some diversion, I turned to my orchids, which this year are the most perfect I have ever seen. Then there are the ethereal goldfish with their absurd fins and tails spreading out like gossamer. They always amuse me with their various shapes and colours. I am happy and contented as I am. It is true, as you said, that I am not easily disturbed.'

'I must from now on take your life as an example.'

'That is why I want you to stay with me,' Madam Wen-ching said. 'I think you can acquire that spirit and mood very quickly.'

'Yes, I must learn to control my emotions. They have been running in all directions like a herd of wild horses. The result is that all my energy has been consumed and wasted. Young as I am in years, I feel exhausted and worn out. I must look for a haven of safety where my tired soul can have some much-needed rest.'

'All the more reason why you should accept my invitation to stay with me. Let me teach you how to paint and write. Practising calligraphy has the most soothing effect on one's inner life. The principal thing is to learn to find enjoyment in the simple things of life which are eternally beautiful.'

The conversation was longer and more fascinating than Madam Wen-ching had expected. She was glad, and Ping-mo was happy that he had succeeded in bringing about an understanding and reconciliation between his mother and the girl whom he so much admired and loved.

12

A MONTH passed and Golden Orchid continued to live an uneventful life. Then one day Yang Mah rushed in to announce the arrival of an unexpected guest.

'Tai-tai, Tai-tai, guess who is here to see you? That foreign lady who went with you from Tungchow to Peking. How does she know that we are here?'

'It is unbelievable,' said Golden Orchid. 'I have been thinking of her only recently.'

She went into the small and unpretentious living-room, and there was Nancy Kendrick.

'Nancy!' cried Golden Orchid with great joy. 'How is it that you are in Soochow? I have been wondering where you had gone and how your family has been all these years. Oh, I am so very happy to see you again.'

'And I am so very happy to see *you* again.' Nancy gave Golden Orchid a long look, and the two women warmly embraced each other.

'I have been in Soochow for two years now. As soon as the troubles were over in Peking, our mission thought that we had had enough of a hectic life in the north and asked us if we cared to be stationed in the south. We promptly agreed, and then we were asked to choose a city. Of course we chose Soochow, knowing that some day we should see you here. So here we are!'

'That is wonderful. Tell me, how is Peter and how is little Margaret?'

'Oh, they are fine. And how they have grown! Peter is quite a young man now, and Margaret is a beautiful girl.'

'Do you think they still remember me?'

'Of course they do. Only the other day they were talking about you and said that they would be so happy to see you again. John has gone to Shanghai and will be back in a few days.'

'How glad I am to know that you have all survived those horrible days! Can I ever forget that journey from Tungchow to Peking? Such danger, and yet there was excitement.'

'Golden Orchid, we have been following the events of your life since last we met in our embassy. What a brave girl you have been! We heard of your return to Soochow. Everyone is proud of you, proud of the wonderful work you have done.'

Golden Orchid smiled, and in deep modesty said that she had not done anything worthy of such praise.

'Oh, yes, you have — the things you have done for the people in Peking and for your country. And can we ever forget the things you did for us? You have been a courageous and selfless girl. Look, Golden Orchid, there is something I want to talk to you about.'

'What is it, Nancy?'

'You see, it's like this. We've been talking about you. That is, we among the missionaries. You have been our greatest friend, and we feel that you are really one of us.'

Golden Orchid could not understand what Nancy was driving at. She wore a look of bland surprise, and Nancy went on hesitantly: 'I am glad, Golden Orchid, that we shall be here for a few years, and so we shall see a good deal of you. We feel that you have gone through so much and need some spiritual consolation.'

'Thank you for your sympathy, Nancy. I am in a sense tired of it all. I do need quiet and rest. And I need also to think over all that has happened to me. But it was the will of heaven, and I gladly accept what has been given to me.'

'But all suffering has a deep spiritual meaning. If you allow me, as an older woman, to say so, you have grown much richer, fuller and more mature. Since I met you on the steamer going to Europe, you have become an entirely different person. It is almost eight years since I first met you, or is it nine? Well, anyway, you are still young, very young, and we feel that there is a glorious future ahead of you.'

Golden Orchid was greatly moved by these words, spoken, she was convinced, with sincerity and by one whom she had reason to consider a friend. She felt her eyes beginning to be a little moist.

Then Nancy quietly made the point which was the primary object of her visit. 'Why don't you come to church with us one of these days? There we shall pray together, pray to Our Lord Jesus Christ, and you will find real consolation and joy. It will give new courage to a life which has always been courageous. What do you say, Golden Orchid?'

There was a long silence. No one could bring up the subject of conversion so ably as Nancy Kendrick. All the circumstances conspired to favour her and to bring her to success. Nancy made no further remark, but in her mind she was thinking that to lead Golden

Orchid into the Christian fold would not be merely to make an additional convert; she might bring in hundreds or even thousands of other converts. She waited eagerly for Golden Orchid's answer.

Golden Orchid thought over many things. Then, very quietly, she replied: 'Thank you, Nancy. Thank you for your kind offer. But I think I choose to remain where I am. I visited a Christian church once when I was in Berlin. It was a beautiful experience. But you don't mind my being perfectly frank with you, do you?'

'No, Golden Orchid, of course not. Be absolutely frank with me.'

'You want me to be a Christian. Isn't that true?'

'Well, yes . . .''

'I understand. That is what you are in China for. But, you know, I have wondered why you people are so anxious to convert the Chinese to your religion.' Golden Orchid smiled as if to soften the words she had spoken.

'That's very simple, Golden Orchid. We feel that we worship the only true God, and that it is our duty, as our Bible teaches us, to spread the gospel to the four corners of the world.'

'That is all very well. But, excuse me for saying so, why don't you leave other people to their own religions? Now, please, Nancy, don't misunderstand me.' And then, taking Nancy's hand into her own, Golden Orchid said: 'Let's not talk about these things today.'

Nancy agreed, thought she was reluctant to leave the subject that was the main purpose of her visit.

'Tell me, Nancy,' Golden Orchid continued, 'have you found life here as agreeable as in the north?'

'Oh, yes. John is to have a new hospital here, and we expect to do so much for the poor people.'

'I am very glad to hear that, Nancy. Isn't it true there is no greater satisfaction than to be doing something for the people? They are always so deeply appreciative.' The memory of what she had done in Peking and the grateful expressions of the people came crowding into her mind.

'That is true, Golden Orchid. But we are doing all this for the glory of Our Lord Jesus Christ.'

'I see. To me the difference is not important — so long as we do perform good deeds. But for the present I need a long, long rest.'

'And what do you plan to do afterwards?' pressed the ever-anxious Nancy.

'I don't know. But I have met my husband's first wife. She is such a beautiful woman, and I admire her. Such calm and serenity. That is what I envy most in my present mood.'

'And that is why I am so anxious that you go to church with me. You will have all that and much more.'

Golden Orchid smiled again. 'Thank you, Nancy, for saying so. There is another person I am anxious for you and John to meet one of these days. He is the son of my husband and Madam Wen-ching. He is a young man of remarkable accomplishments and intelligence. And he seems to know so much. If you want to be informed about recent Chinese history, he is the man you should meet. I have learned so much from him myself.'

There was no particular reason why Golden Orchid should want the Kendricks to meet Ping-mo. But Golden Orchid felt that the Christian nations, as she had learned from Ping-mo, had done things to China which were the very opposite of the Christian principles. The Boxer uprising itself would not have taken place if they had only practised one small fraction of what they preached. But she was determined not to hurt Nancy's feelings. In fact, she thought she had already said things which were too pointed. She would rather leave it to Ping-mo, at some uncertain date in the future, to explain the whole matter to Nancy and John.

Nancy, on her part, was interested only in seeing Golden Orchid won over to her views, and she came back to her central theme.

'Golden Orchid, if you would only believe what I believe, and go to church with me regularly, you would grow in strength and power.'

Golden Orchid did not know what to do or say to so assertive and positive a woman. She said reluctantly: 'Let me think it over carefully. But, Nancy, leave me for the present to the faith of my own people. I believe that, like trees, human beings have roots. If you take trees up by the roots, they wither. So no one who has been taken out of the faith of his own people can live and remain true to himself. This applies to me as much as it does to you.'

Nancy thought for a while and admitted: 'You may have a point there, Golden Orchid. But still I say that no other religion teaches the divine truth. Only in Christianity do you find the highest truth.'

Once more Golden Orchid cast about for an evasive answer.

'Nancy, do you still remember the story I told you about the jar of vinegar?'

'I think so. But I should be glad to hear it again.'

'It was a story which my husband used to tell me over and over again. It was about an event which was supposed to have taken place in a great monastery in the Diamond Mountains in Korea. Three remarkable persons were standing one fine morning in the courtyard of that monastery, and in front of them was a tall glazed jar of vinegar. The central figure was dark and swarthy. His head was partly shaven, and over it was a halo. He was deeply wrapped in thought, and his face wore an expression of sorrow and pity, but there was also calm and serenity. He was the first to be asked to dip his finger into the jar, and he said that the vinegar tasted bitter. The next one was a venerable sage with a flowing beard. His was a kind and benevolent face, and when he tasted the vinegar, he found it sour. Then the third was called. He had an even longer beard, all white and floating in the air. As he looked into the heavens, his face seemed to be lighted with spontaneous joy. There was also something roguish in his eyes. He had a sense of humour and seemed at peace with the universe. When he tasted the vinegar, he at once pronounced it sweet and delicious. These three people were respectively Buddha, Confucius, and Lao-tse.'

Nancy smiled and said that this was really an interesting story. 'I wonder what Christ would have said if He had been asked to dip his finger into the jar. It's a pity that He was not there. But, Golden Orchid, of the three, whom would you yourself agree with?'

'It is hard to say. I wish I could be like Lao-tse. But having gone through life as I have, I think I have tasted a good deal of bitterness.'

Yang Mah came in and brought tea. It was getting late, and Nancy stood up and said to Golden Orchid: 'I shall talk it over with John and ask him what he thinks Christ would say of the vinegar. I'll let you know the answer the next time I see you. But remember what I told you about going to church with me.'

Golden Orchid smiled once more as Nancy left.

13

IT was summer again, and the lotus as usual could be seen every-where. It was barely six o'clock in the morning, but the summer heat was already beginning to be oppressive. It promised to be a hot day, and Ping-mo arrived very punctually. During the previous night Yang Mah had been sent to tell him that her mistress wanted to make a voyage up-river and that she hoped he would accompany her.

Golden Orchid had put on the simplest dress Ping-mo had ever seen. It was a plain light-blue linen tunic, and her black hair was done in a neat little knot behind her head. Not one hair was out of place. She looked like a new and different person, for Ping-mo had never seen her in this fashion. But the total effect was very attractive. There was a kind of inner composure, and her eyes seemed to look at the world with unusual tranquillity. The face was devoid of wrinkles, and it shone with its own lustre. It had its usual tinge of rosiness, and the warm morning weather had covered it with a thin layer of moisture. Golden Orchid did not tell Ping-mo exactly where they were going, but she said they were going to spend a few days in a large houseboat which she had hired.

There was no one else on the boat, and there was no physical barrier between Golden Orchid and Ping-mo. But each knew, deep down in their hearts, that, drawn as they were to each other, there was a wide chasm which they could not bridge. Yang Mah saw the situation differently. She was overjoyed that the houseboat carried only the three of them, and that what she had predicted was coming true. For her barriers could only mean physical barriers, and what was more natural than that she should serve as a link for the grand harmony of these two souls, which was for her the only logical end? Ping-mo was now twenty-nine, the unmarried son of a distinguished father. Golden Orchid was two years younger, and for a long time had been attracted to him. Could there be a more perfect union? Yang Mah thought she would be the happiest woman if she could bring the two together as her pock-faced sister had brought together Golden Orchid and Ping-mo's father.

But as time passed, there were no indications that what appeared so logical to Yang Mah was developing. She wondered, she even eavesdropped, but learned nothing. Her mind had never penetrated that crust of social reality and convention which was as obstinate as it was irresistible. For a son to be joined in matrimony to a deceased father's concubine would bring a wrathful heaven to vengeance and calamity, and no one had the strength to thwart the will of heaven.

As the houseboat placidly passed through Chinkiang on its way to Nanking, its destination, the mighty river became even wider. Hundreds of junks with their tall, brown, tattered sails danced on the waves like little toys, and the peasants with their wide-brimmed bamboo hats and grey cotton shirts were busy with a thousand toils.

'Isn't this a pleasant sight?' said Ping-mo. 'This is as it should be. I have seen it many times. Every time I see it I have a new sense of exhilaration. But Nanking is unfortunately a city of unhappy memories. That was where we had to sign the first sad treaty with a foreign power — with England: it was the beginning of our national woes. Since then there has not been one day of peace. It is for me and for young people like me to work hard so that these peasants may continue to enjoy their lives without being intimidated or struck with fear either by foreigners or their own corrupt officials.'

When the houseboat finally lay tied to the shore, Ping-mo was anxious to see the old monk, the same bronze-faced man who was the recognized revolutionary leader in the south, and had given Ping-mo the fifty bastinadoes.

'Come and see me three days from now,' Golden Orchid said to him.

'But where shall I find you?'

'At the Temple of the Singing Rooster.'

'At the Temple of the Singing Rooster? Why, I know that temple well.'

'But there is one part which perhaps you do not know. Ask for me when you visit the chief abbot.'

Three days later Ping-mo went to the temple with the old monk. They walked on the ancient wall, and in front of them there were patches of the inevitable lotus. Instinctively Ping-mo turned over some of the broken bricks, as he had done nine years before. But there were no crickets yet, as the summer was not over. The old monk looked as sturdy as ever, and, going over the landmarks which they both knew so well, they became deeply absorbed in their conversation, making plans for the future.

The old monk then took Ping-mo to visit the chief abbot. He was dressed in the saffron toga of sackcloth and made the visitors sit down and feel at home. The windows of the spacious room were all wide open, giving a magnificent view of the lake. There was more lotus in all the fullness of its beauty. A few moments later a nun in coarse grey garments entered accompanied by a woman attendant. The nun's hair had been cut short, but not shaven. Ping-mo at first did not recognize her. . . .

I suspected that she would go as far as this, Ping-mo said to himself when he realized who she was. He could not bear the thought of Golden Orchid renouncing the world, and as he left he said quietly to Yang Mah: 'Take good care of your mistress.'

'She is no longer my Tai-tai,' replied Yang Mah. 'I am merely in the service of the nunnery. But I understand.'

When Ping-mo left, he felt a lump in his throat.

Two months passed. The lotus had withered, leaving behind a wide expanse of jagged stalks that looked like ten thousand spears of a defeated army. The air had become cold and sharp. A visitor came to the temple and asked that he might see the new acolyte of the nunnery. Accompanied by the same attendant, she entered the abbot's room. A distinguished-looking gentleman stood up.

'Golden Orchid,' said Lord Yu Kung, 'how happy I am to see you at long last! Let me tell you what happened. The Empress Dowager, before her return to Peking, made me governor of the province where she lived during the crisis. I had to remain there. When I came back to the capital, I was told you had left for Soochow. When I arrived in Soochow, I was told you had moved to Nanking. And when finally I find you here —'

'I am in a nunnery,' Golden Orchid finished for him.

'Yes, always too late. I must accept what heaven commands.'

'But it need not be too late,' replied Golden Orchid quietly and gently. 'I have only been taking a much-needed rest.'

Lord Yu Kung's face became animated. He knew it was possible for a woman to stay in a nunnery for some time before she decided to become a nun.

'What do you mean?' he asked excitedly. 'Do you mean that you have not yet taken your vows?'

'No, not yet. I have been here two months — two blessed months of peace and prayer. Kuan-yin, the Goddess of Mercy, has been my constant companion. I had a dream the other night, and she told me that those who live on in the world are the people in whom she has confidence. I was going to take my vows. But my prayers have now been answered, and I have decided not to take them.'

'Then do you mean that I —' Lord Yu Kung held both her hands. They looked at each other and smiled. Then he turned to the young man who was with him and said: 'This is Ting-lo, a distant nephew. He saw you in Berlin, Golden Orchid. He admires you and was anxious to see you again.'

'Why, Ping-mo has talked about you so often. He told me that the two of you have done so much together. You will do much greater things . . . in the days ahead. You will have much to work for.'

The valet Lao Chuang, in the meantime, had been edging himself to Yang Mah's side. 'I went back to my village,' he said, 'only to find my wife killed. My two sons have disappeared.' He looked at her as if imploring her, and then said, 'May I also . . .'

'I will think it over,' replied Yang Mah. 'My hunchback husband is nowhere to be found. No one knows where he is. It makes matters easier for me.'

ABOUT THE AUTHOR

CHANG HSIN-HAI was born in Shanghai. After schooling there and in Peking, he went to the United States to study, first at Johns Hopkins and later at Harvard, where he received his Ph.D. After touring western Europe, Dr Chang returned to China, where he taught in the major universities and became one of the most prominent interpreters of Western ideals.

Joining the Chinese foreign service, Dr Chang was envoy to many European countries, including Portugal, Czechoslovakia and Poland. In 1941, during China's desperate struggle against Japan, he went to the United States to interpret the Chinese war effort to the American people. After the war he left the diplomatic service to resume his original career of academic work, lecturing and writing. Dr Chang and his wife, who is on the staff of the United Nations, now live in Great Neck, Long Island.

Dr Chang has contributed articles to *Atlantic Monthly*, *Foreign Affairs* and other periodicals both in America and in England on subjects ranging from Confucianism and Chinese poetry to politics and international affairs. *The Fabulous Concubine*, for which he has drawn freely from his wide knowledge of official and diplomatic life, is his first novel.

*Some other Oxford Paperbacks for readers
interested in Central Asia,
China and South-east Asia, past and present*

Titles marked with an asterisk have restricted rights